The Works

OF

Alphonse Daudet

One Volume Edition

BLACK'S READERS SERVICE COMPANY

ROSLYN, NEW YORK

PRINTED IN THE UNITED STATES OF AMERICA

Contents

VOLUME I
TALES

STUDIO LOVE

CHAPTER   PAGE

   I. Cousin 1
  II. Olga 11
 III. To Our Bed-Room 16
 IV. The Culprit 17
  V. Ophelia 22
 VI. The Ball 26

A BOHEMIAN NIGHT 28
THE GIRL FROM ARLES 36
COME, PARISIANS! 38
THE PALE DUKE 41
THE SIEGE OF BERLIN 44
ADVANCE GUARD 49
A TRANSITORY TOMB 52

THE COLORS

CHAPTER

   I. A Target 54
  II. War-Dog 54
 III. September 55
 IV. Take My Flag! 56
  V. Soiled 56

MY NEIGHBOR 57

VOLUME II
TALES

MAN WITH THE GOLDEN BRAIN 61
THE POET MISTRAL 63
THE FRIEND OF MAURICE 67

CONTENTS

VOLUME II—*Continued*

	PAGE
THE WRECK	71
LOSS OF THE SEMILLANTE	74
THE COAST GUARDS	77
AN ESCAPE	80
WHAT THE ABBE SAW	83
MY FIRST DRESS COAT	86
LAST CLASS	92
GAME OF BILLIARDS	95
M. SEGUIN'S GOAT	98
THE BEAUCAIRE DILIGENCE	102
THE POPE'S MULE	105

VOLUME III
TALES

SANGUINAIRES LIGHTHOUSE	111
PROTECTED BY STARS	114
DEATH OF THE DAUPHIN	118
MASTER CORNILLE'S SECRET	120
THE DRUMMER	123
THREE HUNDRED THOUSAND FRANCS	131
HORTENSE	133
A PRINCE OF THE BLOOD	137
AH! PARIS, PARIS!	144

VOLUME IV
NOVELS

SAPHO

CHAPTER

		PAGE
I.	The Staircase	147
II.	Known Distress	152
III.	Trapped	160
IV.	Into the Fire	169
V.	Libertine and Gambler!	176
VI.	Scarlet	185
VII.	Hold Your Tongue!	196
VIII.	The Child	206
IX.	Low Divans	216
X.	A Cause for Escape	223

CONTENTS

CHAPTER   VOLUME IV—*Continued*   PAGE

XI.   Senility 228
XII.   He Is Leaving Me! 233
XIII. Weakness 240
XIV.   The Mire 246
XV.   One Kiss, the Last! 253

VOLUME V

NOVELS

KINGS IN EXILE

I.   The First Day 259
II.   The General Duc 263
III.   A Royalist 272
IV.   Shameful Celebrity 280
V.   The Court 287
VI.   The Queen's Nook 293
VII.   The King Takes His Pleasure 298
VIII.   Nervous Colette 307
IX.   Levis' Agency 316
X.   A Long, Soft Glance 323
XI.   Bohemian Exile 330
XII.   The Worm! 337
XIII.   At the Fair 343
XIV.   Nothing 347
XV.   The Grand Stroke 352
XVI.   Séphora 361
XVII.   The Academie 366
XVIII.   To Recognise Her 373
XIX.   Wrath of a Queen! 378
XX.   Moulded by the Jesuits 382
XXI.   The Vigil 385
XXII.   The Fête 392
XXIII.   The Night Train 399
XXIV.   A Divine Intervention 407
XXV.   The Condemned Cell! 413
XXVI.   Abdication 416
XXVII.   Candid Eyes 420
XXVIII. Little King 424
XXIX.   Dark Room 429
XXX.   A Stifled Sob 434

CONTENTS

CHAPTER   VOLUME V—*Continued*   PAGE

XXXI.	Fides, Spes	436
XXXII.	Elysee's Room	441
XXXIII.	Last of a Race	445
XXXIV.	Oh! My Darling!	450

VOLUME VI

NOVELS

A PASSION OF THE SOUTH

I.	The Arena	455
II.	Love	462
III.	Roumestan!	468
IV.	Portal House	475
V.	The Reds	479
VI.	Transfigured	484
VII.	The Passage	490
VIII.	Equal to Beauty	495
IX.	A Soiree	505
X.	Felinities	513
XI.	Arvillard	521
XII.	Her Eyelids	527
XIII.	Numa's Speech	535
XIV.	Victims	541
XV.	Hortense's Romance	548
XVI.	Audiberte's Revenge	552
XVII.	Rosalie's Trial	559
XVIII.	Sins of Youth	564
XIX.	A Pretty Voice	572
XX.	A Baptism	578

VOLUME VII

TALES

LA BELLE NIVERNAISE

I.	A Rash Act	585
II.	Yes or No?	591
III.	Under Way	594
IV.	Life Is Hard	600
V.	Maugendre Has a Son!	607

CONTENTS

VOLUME VII—*Continued*

THE THIRD LOW MASS

CHAPTER   PAGE

I. Two Turkeys 615

II. Midnight 617

III. The Vision 619

A VIOLET! 621

THE TWO INNS 623

THE ELIXIR 625

THE CAMARGUE

CHAPTER

I. The Departure 631

II. The Cabin 633

III. The Espere 634

IV. Red and White 635

V. Lake Vaccares 636

Studio Love

CHAPTER I

COUSIN

"WOMEN certainly are a horrid invention!

"How I wish that a Black Plague or a second Deluge would carry you all off! What an abode of peace, what an oasis this world would then be!"

This chivalrous amiable sentiment is uttered by my cousin, a fine young man of five-and-twenty, about six-foot-two in height, and with an eyeglass always stuck in his eye, which seems to expand when he gives vent to ferocious invectives against my sex. The above philippic is provoked by my determination to go and spend a few months in Paris in order to study painting at Madame Latour's *atelier*. I had been meditating some time upon this move, when a letter received that morning from my friend Olga Soultikoff, a young Russian, then in Paris, chiefly for painting purposes, decided me. This is the letter, which unfortunately, I had read to my cousin:

"Chez Madame Dupont,
"Quai des Grands Augustine, Paris.

"My Dear Louisa,—You must keep the promise you made me to come and spend some time in

'Ce cher pays de France
Berceau de ton enfance.'

Come at once, to brightness and sunshine. How can you remain so long in dreary, dirty, dismal, damp, depressing London? where the sun only shines through a thick yellow flannel dressing-gown, as if that luminary suffered from a cold in his head and gets up late, well muffled in blankets.

"The London climate has upon me the effect of a pall, and the dismal grandeur, contrasted with the hideous poverty, makes me shudder. There is no lightness, no *abandon*, no grace; nobody seems to care for anybody else, and everybody tries to outshine his neighbor. Still there is much goodness in old England: roast beef, porter, and plum-pudding are the emblems of Great Britain; solid, heavy, respectable, wholesome. Perhaps champagne may be typical of France: light, airy, intoxicating; but my artistic temperament prefers this to the respectable heaviness of England.

"However, I must not speak too harshly about that mighty country, as I have only spent a few months there. Italy and France are the Promised Lands of the artist nature. This is a delightful *pension*, not far from the Louvre—that sanctuary consecrated to the *chefs-d'œuvre* of the great old masters! Madame Dupont is a nice little woman; never interferes with anybody, never asks indiscreet questions; *enfin*, this is Liberty Hall. There is a live Genius flourishing here, or rather, like most geniuses, on the brink of ruin. He wears his hair long, dresses very shabbily, has holes in his wide-awake— for the sake of ventilation, he declares;

1

he is stuffed with queer, strong, artistic ideas, and he and I are great friends.

"There are about forty boarders, most of them odd, but come and judge for yourself. I go to Madame Latour's studio; she is a great artist, coloring gorgeous, worthy of Rubens or Correggio; she is also a musician and a mathematician, is *originale* and eccentric, and is separated from her husband, simply because Monsieur Latour bored her and was always prowling about her studio; so she told him that her apartment was too small and he had better go off.

"The meek husband obeyed, and he is now in Belgium, quite happy, for he fears his artist wife. They had one child, but Madame Latour one day, in a fit of absence of mind, sat upon her baby, and, as she is a very stout woman, the baby never recovered being sat upon, and died a few days after. She did not feel the loss much, and now lives but for art; her enthusiasm, her love, are concentrated in that. In her early youth she loved passionately, was deceived, and so she threw her mind, her soul, her very body, into her painting. If I were a man, I should be devoted to such a woman.

"She has so much soul, so much power; her great black eyes shine like seas of light, with that sacred fire which seems to consume her. Such women are rare because genius is rare. Madame Latour, though a genius, is fond of the pomps and vanities of this wicked world; she intends giving a grand fancy ball in six weeks from this, and I want you particularly to be there. Write at once to let me know what day I am to expect you, and do not be persuaded into not coming by that cousin of yours. Is he still a woman-hater? *Au fond,* I think he loves us all too much, and that to conceal his tender heart he puts on an armor of cynicism and indifference.

"Your affectionate friend,
"OLGA SOULTIKOFF.

"P. S.—Tell your cousin that I heard that he is already much in love. I am glad to hear it, for when he is married he will think better of all women, and will espouse our cause, stand up for and discuss our rights and our wrongs, perhaps vote for our having the franchise."

My cousin Horace scowls atrociously over this *post scriptum.* "Fall in love indeed! No one will ever find me suffering from that complaint."

"But you are certain to be in that condition some day or other, and the attack will be bad; for love is like the measles; if you get it early in life you recover easily, but once on the shady side of thirty you will suffer terribly."

"There might have been some danger for me if I had lived a century ago, when there were a few charming women on the earth—quiet, innocent beings, satisfied with the sphere of home duties; but now they are merely amphibious creatures struggling to the front, wanting to take our place, to govern the world, to vote, to become doctors, clergymen—I hate them all!

"There is an open antagonism between the sexes, an uncivil war. And you, instead of keeping in your orbit, which means happiness, want to join that horrid faction of strong-minded females—a third sex, a social excrescence. Do not be a blooming idiot. Remain at home; you are more likely to marry than if you scamper about the Continent and become an artist. Men do not like independent women; we do not want to be ruled by our wives. Women ought to have the qualities which are generally wanting in men; to complete us, as it were."

"Ah! you are getting afraid of us. You lords of the creation, you do not like to look up to, but down upon us; but surely, Horace, you could not respect me if I remained at home forever, tatting and tatting, with a kind of label all over me, 'Waiting to be married. Fragile.' I know a woman who hates her sex; her advice is, matrimony, *coûte que coûte.*"

"Burn them alive," growls Horace, his eyeglass getting to look wicked and large, "and I think that I should begin with Mademoiselle Olga.

"She is a dangerous young person, very *exaltée,* enthusiastic, wild—an undetected young lunatic; but I am sorry, though, for her; she is young, alone, and extremely pretty," adds my cousin, relenting, and the eyeglass slips off. "She is an orphan too, poor girl! no one to look after her. But you have no excuse, so I advise you to remain and take plenty of exercise, for you seem to me to be expanding fearfully, and that may spoil your chances in life."

Now this is a stab, a Parthian shot. The skeleton in my closet is the dread of growing like Falstaff, or a more recent hero. I had tried Banting, but to no effect. However, I do not betray my mortification, only shrug my shoulders, leave the room in order not to hear any more unpleasant truths, and write off to Olga; for if a thing has to be done let it be done quickly.

Then I go out and post the letter, for I never believe that my letters reach their destination unless I drop them with my own hands into the letterbox.

* * * *

It is with a mixed sensation of pleasure and regret that later on I find myself at the station alone!

A sense of loneliness creeps over me, I almost wish to be back in the snug drawing-room, listening to Horace's invectives and sermons. Here all is turmoil, life, bustle, glare, glitter, restlessness, noise of cabs, porters rushing about with big trunks, everybody and everything hurrying to and fro. Suddenly I hear my name called out, two arms are round my neck, and there stands bright, pretty little Olga, accompanied by two gentlemen.

"So delighted to see you, *chérie!* Welcome to la belle France! Let me introduce you to two of my friends who are staying at the boarding-house —both Englishmen—Mr. Morris and Mr. Blake."

We all shake hands.

"Mr. Morris is evidently the Genius," I mentally ejaculate; he looks helpless, bewildered, and inspired; he wears a velveteen coat quite clean, and his wideawake is guiltless of holes; he is rather handsome, very dark, just a dash of the demon about him.

Mr. Blake is a contrast—a short, spruce, dapper little figure, dressed most carefully, quite *un petit maître;* he has a lovely white flower in his buttonhole, and looks as if he had just stepped out of a bandbox.

I confide my keys to him, and he politely goes off and looks after my luggage, which has to undergo the process of being examined.

"Now, Mr. Morris, won't you go and get us a *voiture?*" says Olga, in her sweet, foreign accent. "I do wonder if he will be able to do that; for of course you have guessed that he is the Genius, always up in the heights—a great deal of power about him, but not much practicality."

But Olga's remarks are cut short by the reappearance of Mr. Blake, followed by a porter carrying my trunk. "The *fiacre* is waiting. What a wonder that it is not a hearse!" exclaims Mr. Blake, with a shrug of compassion. "I did not think that Morris could discern one vehicle from another."

The trunk is placed on the roof, my innumerable parcels fill up nearly the cab, Olga and I squeeze into a corner, and the two men bid us good-evening.

Off we rattle through the brilliant streets. It is a lovely evening in May, the trees are clothed in delicate young green, the stars are just beginning to shine, the shops are beautifully lit, the streets are crowded. How poetical Paris looks from the Place de la Concorde on to the bridge!

The towers of Notre Dame and of St. Jacques la Boucherie, standing there like guardian angels protecting the beloved city. The dismal prison of the Conciergerie, the ruins of the Tuileries, lend a solemnity to the scene. The Seine is twinkling with many lights, the bathing-houses are slightly lit up, giving it a weird appearance. A few dark barges are gliding warily by, like dreary, troubled spirits. The equestrian statue of Henri Quatre looks well in the evening light—the gay monarch there in effigy watching over his dear Paris. At last the cab stops.

Olga rings a bell; the door is opened by a neat *bonne* in a very white cap and apron, holding a brass candlestick. The *bonne* ushers us into a large sitting-room furnished with crimson curtains, chairs, etc., gilt clock and ornaments on the mantelpiece; and the floor is so highly waxed that it is almost impossible to walk without slipping. A tiny lady in black silk comes forward.

"This is my friend, Miss Louisa Larcom," says Olga in French.

Madame Dupont makes a graceful *révérence,* is enchanted to see me, inquires after my journey, and says that she will send me up *du thé* in my room. Olga says that I shall have tea with her in her own sitting-room. So, bidding the little lady good-night, we go upstairs to Olga's apartment.

"What a lovely *sanctum sanctorum!*" I exclaim; and certainly it is a charming room worth describing. The furniture is of bright blue damask silk, white lace curtains, and the *fond* of the carpet is white, with wreaths of roses entwined with blue ribbon. A bookcase of carved oak filled with beautifully-bound books.

On all sides are statuettes of Dresden china. A Venus de Milo and a Venus de' Medici in bronze, mount guard on each side of the bookcase. A fine Erard piano stands in the middle of the room. On a rosewood easel is a study of a head in black and white just begun. Out of this is a small bedroom with a pretty bed and toilette all white. Engravings of Ary Scheffer's famous pictures—of "Les deux Mignons," "Ste.-Monique," and "St.-Augustin," decorate the walls, besides photographs of nearly all the great masterpieces in art.

"This is your room, leading out of mine," says Olga opening a door. "Of course yours is not so beautiful as mine, for mine is furnished out of my own pocket, and yours is Madame Dupont's taste. Still it is pretty and cosy, furnished in pink *perse*. You have everything *couleur de rose,* and I am all in the blues. Still I am not going to exchange. Now take off your things, and let us make ourselves comfortable. I love luxury, ease, comfort."

So saying, she takes off her walking-dress and puts on a delicious gray soft cashmere dressing-gown, puts her tiny feet into lovely velvet slippers, and throws herself into a large arm-chair, forces me down into another, and rings the bell for tea.

How pretty she looks now, as she indolently reclines back. She is small; her figure is round, supple, graceful; her skin is clear and white; her hair, golden and wavy, is plaited round her small well-shaped head; her eyes are very dark and soft, but there is often a twinkle of mischief in them; her mouth is lovely and surrounded by dimples.

"What a luxurious creature! what an epicure you are, Olga!" I exclaim, half enviously, thinking of all the gifts and good things she had. "How thoroughly happy you ought to be! You have everything you want—beauty, wealth, talent, liberty, youth. You have indeed too much of the good things of this world, you spoilt child of fortune!"

"Yes, I ought to be very happy," she slowly answers, with rather a sad smile; "and it may seem strange and ungrateful on my part to say that I am not so. Happiness is within ourselves, and not derived entirely from outward circumstances. At times I feel quite happy; at others I am low and depressed. I am lonely, for I have no one belonging to me alive. When I feel very low I rush off to Madame Latour, and her influence, the feeling of her genius, seems to put new life into me; but there is a *void* within me. I do not care for people generally, so that I now live but for myself."

A knock at the door: the *bonne* comes in with a tray full of good things, which she deposits on a table close by, inquires if we require her services, and then retires.

"But, Olga, you are sure to be loved by some one worthy of you; you are so young—only two-and-twenty."

"Yes, that is my age; still, at times I feel middle-aged, for I have had great experience of life. Of course I have inspired love, and have tasted the bitterness of it, with little of its sweets!"

"You amaze me!" I exclaim. "You, so admired, so *recherchée,* to talk like this!—you, who seem, such a sunbeam, such a butterfly, is it possible that you have cause for talking so? The bitterness of love!—you almost make me laugh. It seems so incongruous for such *un enfant gâté* to talk thus."

"Well, then, I shall give you a few details about my past life; and then you will see if all is gold that glitters, and if I have not reason at times to be a little *triste.* But before I tell you my unfortunate love affair, 'let us eat, drink, and be merry,' This is Russian tea—a treat for you."

How charming she looks, as she gracefully pours out the delicious beverage from a small silver teapot into our two cups! I cannot imagine how so fascinating a girl can ever have had a love disappointment. Her movements, as she rushes about the room, remind me of those of a pet kitten— soft, purring, graceful; the small head is well placed on the sloping shoulders, the eyes are so luminous, the light hair looks like an *auréole* of glory, shedding light around it. Olga has a wonderful inner smile—a smile that Leonardo da Vinci alone could have rendered, and which he has so inimitably painted in that famous portrait, "La Joconde," or "Mona Lisa."

"We shall get on together," suddenly exclaims Olga, while she is cutting me a large slice of plum cake. "I require a certain kind of sympathy, not pity. As a rule I hate sympathy, for though surrounded by society I live in my own thoughts. I have such a horror of being bored. Liberty is my cry—liberty of ideas, of life; no shackles of any sort. I am a Republican at heart, and the conventionalities of society and the lies of the world sicken me."

As she utters these words her eyes flash, her cheeks flush, and she looks like a young goddess of revolt.

Suddenly she rushes to the piano, and sings a wild Russian air, and evidently forgetting me, the tea, and everything else, pours her soul into her music. And then, in a low, tragic voice, with an intensity that appals me, she intones the "Marseillaise." It is almost terrible to hear her, her eyes

seem to see beyond, and, as she utters these words,

"Amour sacré de la patrie!"

there are tears in her very voice; then, not to give further vent to her emotion, she rattles off "Le Sabre de mon père." Schneider's famous song, from Offenbach's "Grande Duchesse." I look at Olga with astonishment.

"You are an enigma, a sphinx, an imp, a creature from another world, are you not?"

"Indeed I am not. I belong very much to this earth; only at times I feel so lonely, so dissatisfied with myself, with everybody and everything, that I should like to get away from myself and my thoughts, to rush off to some wild spot, be blown about by the winds of heaven, and have new thoughts and ideas driven into me. Why is there not a Lethe—a wonderful stream where one could take a plunge and forget what one wishes to forget?

"Music is an intense resource to me, for I can pour out my wrongs and give way to my many moods in music. Sometimes, when painting, I take my brush and create a grotesque demon torturing some wretched soul, and you may laugh, but it does relieve me; or I tease my cat. I often wish that I could hire a slave, that I might bully him when those dreadful fits of revolt come over me. Of course you must be horrified, and no wonder; but how can I help it, if I have a *diavolina* within me?—perhaps seven devils, and they all kicking inside me. I feel the wretches are there, and some days they are so powerful, that if I did not take a ride on horseback, or some very violent exercise, I should do something wicked."

"What an undisciplined young rebel you are, Olga!"

"It is inherited," she answers. "My mother was an Italian prima donna, with a voice like Malibran. I have been told she had an unhappy home life; her step-mother tortured her by her despotism; her artist nature could not stand the petty worries of a small narrow-minded household; she ran away, went on the stage, loved, was deceived. Disappointed, she married my father, who was a Russian merchant, for his wealth. He was (you know he died when I was quite a child) tyrannical, but generous; so my parents were not happy in their short married life.

"I am the offspring of these two widely different natures: the warm, genial, artistic, imaginative, rebellious Italian on one side: the cruelty, perhaps, from my father's side. So I am an odd mixture, and am not entirely accountable for my moods. I would gladly be different—glad to have no aspiration, no dreams of happiness, no longing for ideal love, no wish for something beyond—to be quiet, unemotional, unimaginative, and satisfied with that state of life to which I have been called. But I am talking of nothing but my horrid self. The fact is, it does me good to give vent to my inner feelings: it is a great sign of friendship, my boring you thus."

"You are not boring me; on the contrary, dear Olga, I am deeply interested, and sympathize with your nature and understand it. You are capable of feeling great unhappiness and great happiness; but you must try and discipline yourself, and not let yourself be run away with. Put a bridle on your wild feelings."

"Yes, you are very wise, Miss Minerva; and I am an ungrateful wretch. Some days, when the sun is bright, I feel so happy that I should like to live on forever and do some good; but to-day I am *agacée*, mischievous. I should like to scratch some one."

"I shall run away," I exclaim laughing. "But now be sensible, Olga, and tell me all about these little love-affairs that seem in a measure to have altered your nature; for when I knew you five years ago you had no bitterness, no cynicism."

"Well, perhaps I had better confide this tale of woe, though, as a rule, I hate talking about myself."

So, leaving the piano, she threw herself upon the soft rug, and placing her pretty perfumed head on my lap, related what follows:

"Don't you remember, four years ago, meeting at mamma's apartments on the Boulevard des Italiens a young Pole, Stanislas Marilski?"

"Oh, yes, very well, for I was much struck with his appearance; he was *distingué* looking, handsome, and artistic; but I only saw him that one evening. Is he the hero?"

"Yes; he was the first man who inspired a new feeling. Before I met him I was a joyous, light, merry, thoughtless girl, *insouciante*. Sufficient for the day is the evil or the good thereof, was certainly my motto. But Stanislas Marilski's advent changed the course of my thoughts, and I was no longer as joyous as a bird. I felt that life was a mystery; nature was different, and art was different, from what they had been to me before. I felt a capacity for greater happiness and for greater pain. He was certainly good-looking; but it was not his handsome features that attracted me, so much as the peculiarity of his disposition and the originality of his mind. He was an orphan, a rebel, a revolutionist: he believed in nothing that was past; history was a lie to him, he cared but for the future.

"Melancholy, cynical, passionate, we were both strongly attracted towards each other the minute we met. I met him for the first time at a *bal* at the Hôtel de Ville. I had been dancing merrily about with a very insipid polite Frenchman. I was resting, enjoying thoroughly the bright scene, the music, the lights, the wonderful dresses, the diamonds; when, looking around, I was suddenly attracted by that very pale face and those large, dark, melancholy eyes, gazing at me so keenly.

"I looked at him, and from that moment I really did feel a different being; a new interest had come into my life. He got introduced to my mother, called at our house; we had long talks together—curious to say, chiefly on political topics. But that ceased. We used to meet out of doors, and have long walks together in unfrequented parts of Paris. He told me that he loved me, but that for a few months he could not make a regular offer of marriage. I did not mind that; to be cared for by such a man was sufficient happiness. And as my mother, who was then in extremely delicate health, allowed me entire liberty, I saw Stanislas every day for

five months. One day, calling at a friend's house, she informed me that several people had seen me walking with Mr. Marilski—that remarks were passed; so that my friend had made inquiries; and did I know that Mr. Marilski was engaged to be married to a Polish young lady?—and she mentioned the name.

"I shall never forget what I felt when she told me this horrible piece of news. The room seemed to whirl round and round; the blood rushed to my throat and head. I tried to conceal my emotion. My friend was shocked at having told me this so abruptly. To cut a long, sad story short, I wrote to Stanislas, telling him what I had just heard. I received a miserable letter from him, confessing that there was an engagement, but that he had ceased to care for the girl, and only loved me, begging me to run away with him, and that he would gladly give up everything for my sake.

"I was considering what I had better do, when I received a letter from the mother of the girl, saying that if I married Mr. Marilski it would certainly cause her daughter's death, she was so desperately attached to him; and that Stanislas' late behavior had made her seriously ill. This piece of news decided me. I broke off entirely from him, and my poor mother took me to Dresden for change of air, scene and people.

"Strange to say, that instead of dreading love, I longed for it.

"Life seemed to me so stale, dull, and unprofitable, so uninteresting without it. I did everything to forget Stanislas, to drive away his image. I did my best even to think ill of him.

to picture him in a ludicrous light. I really felt as if my soul had left me, for my body simply vegetated; but I resolved to fight against my misfortune, and not allow this dull oppression to warp my existence. Always fond of art, I resolved to devote myself to painting. I went to the Dresden Gallery, that ideal of a picture gallery, a perfect little temple; where every picture is a gem. It was at the Dresden Gallery that I met my fate number two, in the shape of an artist who was copying the same picture (curious coincidence) that I had begun—'Kinder' von C. L. Vogel.

"My easel was close to his, and from the very first he became most attentive, prepared my pallet, gave me valuable hints about the mixing of colors, how effects were produced—impossible to be kinder. He was a great contrast to Stanislas, but there was something about him which attracted me. I shall repeat to you some of his remarks, and you will judge what sort of man number two was.

"After having looked at several of the *chefs-d'œuvre* in the Gallery, I remarked rather petulantly to him that he was too fond of analyzing the different manners in which the pictures were painted; that he was completely absorbed by the technical process and missed the spiritual idea, the soul, the genius of the conception. A picture to him was a kind of plum-pudding. Why not chiefly admire the thought, and not merely how an effect is produced?"

"'You are an *exaltée* enthusiastic young girl,' he said to me after a few hours' talk. You must calm yourself. You have a dash of genius, but you require a rudder I shall be your rudder.'

"Cool, *n'est-ce pas?*" said Olga, looking up at me with an arch smile. He went on:

"'Those high-flown ideas are very youthful. You must not allow your imagination to run away with you.' And, fixing his cold gray eyes upon me: 'I can read your character in your face, for you are very transparent. I can read the inner workings of your mind. You have suffered, young lady; you are disappointed; you are not now in your normal condition. You have been taken out of your small orbit, and you are in a feverish state, and are trying to fling yourself into another sphere. I know the sensation well, for I have been in that condition. I have loved and lost.'

"His impudence took me by storm. 'What right have you to form such a conclusion?' I said to him.

"'Do not be offended with me; I understand your nature, and see it all in your face; do not contradict me, but take my fatherly advice, for I am over forty and know life. Fly from love; never let a man know how much you care for him. Devote yourself to Art; that will never deceive or disenchant you, and the labor you bestow upon it will be recompensed in this world. You will have hours of real joy over your own creations—that is my experience. I looked for love, and while under the fatal spell I felt intoxicated, and like the sunflower basked in sunshine; but I have never met with a being that satisfied my heart and my soul; whilst the beauties of Nature and of Art are unfailing sources of happiness.'

"Do you mean to say, Olga, that this man spoke to you thus, on so short an acquaintance?"

"Yes, exactly," she replied, slightly coloring, and tossing back her wavy hair.

"What is his name, and who is he?"

"His name is Crawford, and he is half Irish, half English; a very clever artist, musician and poet, with just a dash of mystery to make him interesting. We met every day for several months at the Dresden Gallery. I felt myself alive again. Mr. Crawford made it a point to copy the same picture I copied, and the hours spent in his society were hours of happiness. At times he would recite to me ballads of his own composition, weird, strange, grotesque, and full of fancy. His voice was deep, strong and yet soft. This man puzzled and fascinated me.

"Outwardly he seemed calm, conceited, vain, obstinate; at other times he was full of tenderness, flavored with cynicism. He had a dramatic, powerful way of expressing himself, and an utter absence of ideality. We grew confidential, and I told him about Stanislas. I do not know if he was actuated by a feeling of jealousy or if he really wished to cure me entirely, but he turned the whole affair into ridicule. 'Fancy Mr. Marilski with a bad cold in his head, red nose, eyes swimming, no pocket-handkerchief, sneezing, etc.; or, in a dozen years, with a big stomach like an alderman, gouty, with a dozen children! No: analyze the feeling, and you will find that love is built on a very slight foundation. You excite an interest; there is some objection in the way, your imagination is at work, and that object

becomes a dire necessity as long as you cannot possess him or her; but when you do possess, illusion vanishes, love often flies, and you find yourself tied down for life to a log.' Though Mr. Crawford talked to me thus, he did everything to excite my interest in himself; he spoke to me of his plans, his aspirations, his doubts, fears,—and ended by confessing that he loved me.

"Now comes wound number two.

"One evening at an artistic party where I went with a lady friend, somebody mentioned Mr. Crawford's name, speaking in great praise of his artistic merit and general fascination. Then somebody else remarked, and I still hear the words as if they were words of fire—

"'Yes, poor fellow, what a miserable thing for him, that wife of his being such a confirmed drunkard! and though separated, he cannot marry again. There ought to be a divorce in such cases. Married and not married! What a sad position for a man still in the bloom of his life.'

"'I never knew that Crawford was a married man,' said a fat, elderly gentleman. 'He has dined several times at my house in London, and I have often asked him why he did not enter the blessed state of matrimony; and he simply said he could not, and I thought perhaps it was because his means did not allow him.'

"'He is very well off,' answered speaker number one. 'I met him yesterday, and he told me that he felt restless and unhappy. He is getting on splendidly as an artist, but I hear that he has fallen in love with a pretty girl who is studying Art and copying at the Gallery here.'

"I could stand it no longer. Rushing off to my *chaperone*, I complained of a sick headache; once home, I burst into tears, felt the world again to be a wide desert, and did not return to the Gallery. My mother soon after this died; so that month was indeed a black epoch in my life, and made lovely Dresden a perfect nightmare.

"A few days after my mother's funeral, when I was trying to pack up my things in order to get away from the now hateful place, and come to Paris, where I had, at all events, a few friends, I received a long, touching letter from Mr. Crawford, telling me all about his unfortunate marriage, his love and sympathy for me.

"I wrote back to bid him adieu, and telling him that my wish was that we should never meet or correspond any more. This is the end of my love stories, so you see that I have not been lucky in that department."

"Poor little Olga!" I said, taking her soft white hand in mine, "you have indeed suffered; but you are still very young, and will be more fortunate another time."

"Oh, no, no more love-affairs! *C'est fini.* I have made a firm resolve to work hard to become a great artist if possible. Adieu to romance, it is a waste of time—

"'I slept and dreamt that life was beauty:
I woke, and found that life was duty.'"

We part for the night, both of us vowing and declaring that we should throw ourselves heart and soul into the Art career, and give up all idea of marriage. "Yes," says Olga, "all men are deceivers; false, vain, conceited, jealous, wicked, etc., etc., etc. I shall be a nice, clever, artistic old maid. That is my final decision."

CHAPTER II
OLGA

NEXT morning Olga comes into my room, looking so sweet and fresh in the pretty lavender muslin, and passing her arm through mine we go down the staircase together.

On our way to the dining-room we meet several boarders, issuing from their respective bedrooms. No need to inquire after the nationality of these beings. Alas! Englishwomen cannot be mistaken on the Continent; their want of taste and tact in dress is an unmistakable badge. This thought shot across my brain as I perceive a large family preceding us downstairs; the mother, tremendously stout and beefy-looking, is in ill-fitting many-colored garments; with such feet! encased in immense boots. She wears two large brooches, evidently family portraits— one pinning a collar, the other doing nothing, just for show. Four pretty daughters follow her closely, guiltless of any attempt at style. Perhaps this want of taste in dress is made more conspicuous by the presence of two young American girls, elegantly attired in the very last new fashion.

"How are you, Mademoiselle Soultikoff?" they both exclaim, in strong nasal accent. "I guess this is the friend you have been expecting all along?" and on receiving from Olga an affirmative nod they shake hands cordially with me. "So glad to see you. Are you come to

Paris alone? I reckon that you are one of our sort; you find your family an inconvenience?

"I told my people," said the elder of the two, "all very well to stay under the maternal and paternal wing when one is a chicken, but once that period over we want our liberty. How well you have fixed your hair, Mademoiselle Soultikoff. That's the style, I guess, that Mr. Morris likes. Now do not blush, no harm having a genius for an admirer, though he ought to fix himself better, cut his hair short; but he is a lovely fellow, and you need not be ashamed of your conquest; he never takes any notice of any one but of you. You are both kindred spirits."

I could not help laughing, but Olga seemed rather annoyed and confused.

At the bottom of the staircase we were greeted by a very fat *bonne* in a very white frilled cap; her round face beams with good nature. She stands at the door of the *salle à manger*, and as I am the last new arrival she indicates my place, which is quite at the end of the long table. Olga is near the top, and sits close to the genius, Mr. Morris. About fifty people sit on each side of a very long table. At a sideboard the fat *bonne*, whose name is Uranie, pours out tea and coffee, with wonderful celerity, serves everybody right and left; she darts from one to another with a quickness of step that is delightful to witness; while serving she has a funny, witty repartee always ready. At my right sits an Irish girl, as I instantly discover by her rich musical brogue. She is pretty; large gray eyes and auburn hair. Her mother sits next to her: they are on their way home from Italy. Opposite to me is a large tribe of

Americans. "Well! do they call that breakfast on this side of the pond?" exclaims the man of the party, putting up his eyeglass. "I really see nothing. In our country, madam," addressing the Irish girl, "we have for breakfast stewed beefsteaks, chops, tongue, ham, eggs, potatoes dressed in a dozen different ways, oatmeal cakes, pumpkin pie, jams, jellies, creams, and hot bread of different kinds; but here I just spy a few unhappy-looking sardines and some eggs. Call this breakfast? Well, I suppose we must make the best of it, but I pronounce this starvation.

"In the States we breakfast at seven o'clock, for every man goes to business at eight; but Europe is a slow place, and the French have nothing to do but smoke and go to *cafés*, I guess. In England we always get the same food; no variety, and everything so greasy."

The two American young ladies are flirting desperately with a fair young Englishman.

"I guess," says the prettier of the two, "that you like better travelling without your mother."

This speech is accompanied by a look that cannot be described. The young man blushes, and says that his mother is old, and naturally prefers the quiet of her country home in England.

A little higher up the table sits the funny little man of the boarding-house. His name is Mr. Smiles. He is a fine, tall, good-looking man, with splendid teeth, loud voice, and such a ringing laugh! It shakes the room, and is so infectious that everybody joins in it. He is sitting by the side of a very ugly old lady with a brown wig on one side, and we hear him all over the room saying:

"Now, dear Mrs. Kingsley, you have not done your hair properly this morning; you know that it hurts my feelings to think that you no longer care to appear charming in my eyes. Are you beginning to care less for Theophilus Smiles?" And he puts his hand on his heart, and turns his eyes up in a sentimental comical way, which is diverting.

Mrs. Kingsley titters and seems pleased.

Not far from Olga sits a pretty English girl, with brown eyes and brown hair. This young lady is having a hot altercation with a gentleman opposite, who is evidently more amused than excited. This young lady is a red-hot republican. She is declaring that the only thing worth living for is the republic; that is her chief thought, her first principle. She would give up life readily for that glorious cause. She has come over to Paris on purpose to see the Gambetta. She takes in all the American and Spanish papers, so that she may be well *au fait* with passing events in republican countries. She argues that England is republican at heart; that the Queen is merely an ornament, but that the masses are democrats. Of course this speech is a bomb-shell. Miss Hutchinson is called to order.

The Americans scream out nasally that royalty is mere fancy-work, and everything and everybody appertaining to it a mistake, a nuisance. Yes, democracy is making rapid strides. In less than twenty years the republic will be established everywhere.

Miss Hutchinson is so pleased at finding herself thus supported that she gets up from her chair, rushes to the American camp, and they all shake hands. Then Mr. Smiles solemnly rises,

stretches out his long fingers, and says, "Bless you, my children."

This causes general laughter, and for the present the discussion is at an end.

Mr. Blake is sitting next to a nice ladylike widow, who my pretty neighbor tells me is on the lookout for a third husband.

Breakfast is over; the boarders disappear. I join Olga, who is still talking to Mr. Morris. This man is evidently under her spell: his look, his manner, denote that profound admiration which cannot be acted. Mr. Morris advances towards me, and asks me if I will honor his small studio with a visit, and accompany Mdlle. Soultikoff. I gladly consent, and we both follow him upstairs to the top of this very big house.

"It is an honor that he is paying you," whispers Olga. "He has never, with the exception of myself, invited any one to his studio, and nearly all the people entreat him to let them have a peep; but no use. So he is not a favorite in this house; people generally think him conceited. But really he is not so: he is conscious of his power, and is sensitive and refined."

Mounting a queer little back staircase we enter a kind of garret in the roof of the house. What a delightful view! The Seine is twinkling at our feet; steamers are rushing by; we can just see the towers of Notre Dame and the Sainte Chapelle, the quays, and old book stalls, and curiosity shops. The room is hung all round with sketches in oils and water colors.

One of the first things that attracts my attention is the picture of a girl in white standing in an autumnal landscape; the tints of the foliage are of a golden brown, at her feet are crisp brown leaves, while she holds some dead leaves in her white hands. There is a listless, lonely look in the face, but the likeness to Olga is striking: the same graceful figure, the same light, untidy, wavy masses of fair hair, the same concentrated thought, and just a tinge of sadness in the large dark gray eyes. Same sweetness in the mouth, but a little more determination in the chin, and slightly knitted eyebrows. The painting of the face is beautiful; there is a tenderness of treatment which is remarkable, and the coloring in full of harmony. The background is a sunset, the clouds are purple and gold.

"This picture is the only production of mine which gives me any sort of pleasure," says Mr. Morris; "and I shall never part with it." And he gives Olga a tender look, but she does not respond to it, and calls my attention to some of the sketches which are sufficient to show that Mr. Morris is a man of genius. Some striking landscapes are lying about—a dark pool of water, illuminated by one streak of strong, rippling light, long tall willows, and a stork sleeping and standing on one leg; a sea-piece, gray sky, gloomy shore, a white bird fluttering sadly over the white-crested waves; studies of rocks by moonlight, in deep purple shadows and strong silvery lights.

The charm in these various productions is the intense feeling, the pathetic striving after a something beyond—unattainable. They are the productions of a man that has evidently suffered acutely. He has, I suspect, loved deeply and has been disappointed. These are my thoughts as I see on all sides heads full of sadness, wistfulness, and even despair.

"I suppose you do not care to make money by your art?"

"No. In my opinion art is a religion, a creed, a faith. The creation of the beautiful ought to be the highest ambition of an artist. Our notions of the beautiful vary according to our temperament and education. Perfection of form, harmony of color, depth of expression, is what I strive to render. When I shall be satisfied, then perhaps I shall send to the different exhibitions."

"And now, before we leave this delightful studio, play something on the piano for my friend," says Olga, opening the instrument.

"You know that I must obey my queen," he answers, bowing; "but as a rule I do not play for any one. The music I enjoy is not popular, for it is generally found incomprehensible by the masses, but I firmly believe that it will be the music of the future. Gounod is my favorite master."

He sits down, and after a few strange, wild preludes, plays portions of that ideal masterpiece, "Faust." I feel transported into a world of strange fancies, inhabited by mystical visionary beings. It is all vague, striking, original.

I am roused by Olga, who taps me on the shoulder and tells me it is time to leave. Mr. Morris makes us promise to return soon again, and we bid him *au revoir*.

"It is curious how much genius, power, and passion are contained in this small room, and how much *ennui*, stupidity, nonsense, shallowness, and gossip, inhabit the remainder of this large house," remarks Olga, as we descend the staircase and enter our room. "Lunch with me in my sitting room; I find it such a tremendous bore to assist at the general luncheon; one gets so tired of seeing always the same people, hearing the same jokes, and eating the same food."

"Well, Yankee is right," I remark, "when he said that money is power, and gives liberty; if you had not plenty of filthy lucre you could not afford to have your own way, and eat *pâté de foie gras* in your own room instead of joining at the common table and partaking of more homely fare. I like money, though I admire Mr. Morris's views—he is so full of imagination, that he must be quite happy."

"No," answers Olga, "Mr. Morris is not really a happy man. Of course he must have moments of intense gratification, but his ideal of beauty is so elevated that he is miserable when he cannot attain it."

"There is no doubt, Olga, that Mr. Morris is in love with you: his manner, his look show that you occupy his thoughts, and that beautiful picture is an expression of his feelings."

"Yes, I think Mr. Morris admires me very much. Why should he not do so?

"I am pretty, artistic, and with all my faults, I am attractive; but his nature is rather like mine, so I simply feel sympathy and admire his lofty views; but I have not a bit of love for him; my heart does not beat any quicker, my pulse is just the same when he approaches me. I think quite calmly of him, and would not be at all jealous if he fell in love with any other girl.

He is very odd; his mother was a German, and I fancy that she was rather queer—in fact, I imagine that she was slightly insane; he has inherited from her unhealthy, odd notions. He has often told me that he would rather not marry a woman he was in love with; love is such a strange feeling that he would like to feel eternally the pleasure and pain it occasions, and to enjoy the torture of not possessing what he longs for. It is a curious idea, but I daresay he is right; marriage must, in a way, destroy the poetry of love.

"A sincere attachment and quiet happiness follows, but many illusions vanish. He told me, that as a young fellow, he fell in love with a beautiful girl, who sang and danced like an angel, and whose face was a vision of beauty—well, she loved him; they met often at a country house and she promised to marry him. Strange, the idea frightened and disenchanted him so much, for fear his love should vanish, he went away engaged to her. In his absence, she caught a fearful cold, and three weeks after his departure she was lying in her grave. He was travelling about, and did not know of her death till he returned. His grief was intense, and still he confesses that to him there is a melancholy pleasure in the idea that she died loving him entirely, without having belonged to him. He is an eccentric creature, and as he has frankly spoken to me about his odd notions, he cannot expect me to wish to marry him. He is a poet, an artist, and a musician, utterly unfitted for the prose of married life."

CHAPTER III

TO OUR BED-ROOM

WHAT a clamor, clatter, and babel
of tongues!

The musical English of America, the
rich brogue of Ireland, some nasal English voices—all talking and laughing
at once, so loudly.

Miss Magee is laughing musically,
and making fun of Mr. Smiles, who
had been flirting vigorously in the
vaults underneath the Pantheon, and
had proposed to a wrong lady in the
dark.

Mr. Blake sits this evening at my
right hand, and Mrs. Merriman, the
widow, at Mr. Blake's left.

A deaf elderly gentleman sits opposite to me, and is talking out loud
to himself. I hear him muttering,
"Why will that silly old woman, Mrs.
Kingsley, wear a brown wig instead
of her own white hair, and why will
she bob her foolish head up and down,
while that idiot Smiles makes an ass
of himself? If that fellow could only
see himself as others see him he would
stop. I hate to see a man grimacing,
gesticulating, and behaving altogether
like his ancestors, the monkeys." I
laugh; but the uproar at dinner is so
great that nobody listens to anybody
else.

"I like that old boy," remarks Mr.
Blake. "I often go and smoke in his
room. Old Douglas is a chip of the
old block; he is a great reader, a traveller; but, he is as cynical as Diogenes,
and generally rude to his equals; but
he is fond of animals, children; but
curiously enough, despises women."

"I suppose Mr. Douglas has had a
disappointment in his youth, poor man!

I am sorry for him," lisps Mrs. Merriman with a gentle sigh.

"The devil take her," mutters out
loud Mr. Douglas. "There! she has
just carried off my favorite bit of
chicken, just the slice I have had my
eye upon. What a greedy woman she
is, to be sure!"

This ebullition of deaf Mr. Douglas is intended for Mrs. Melligrew, a
fat, ruddy faced Englishwoman, in military mourning, scarlet and black, who
is just depositing upon her plate the
wing of a chicken, some stuffing, etc.,
unconscious of Mr. Douglas's remarks.

The dinner is over, and we all go
up to the drawing-room.

Olga, Mrs. Blake and I go and
sit in the balcony, and from that ob-
servatory watch the different boarders.
Mr. Morris disappears to his den. All
the old ladies sit together at one end
of the room. The girls cluster round
Mr. Smiles and a Mr. Chambers, a
mild disciple of Mr. Smiles, who laughs
at all his jokes, and is his shadow. Mr.
Smiles is now in his element, he stalks
off to the piano, and with great *entrain*
sings the famous couplet "L'amour est
un enfant de bohême." All the young
ladies join in this chorus, even Olga
and Mr. Blake chime in from the balcony. Mr. Smiles sings this very comi-
cally, and with all the appropriate gestures of an artist.

"Do you see that nice-looking old
lady sitting there?" says Olga, pointing out an old lady with soft brown
eyes and white hair, "that is Miss
Peleg. If anybody feels at all poorly—
it does not matter about the symptoms, those are of no consequence—
we go to Miss Peleg, and she gives
everybody the same medicine: two tea-

spoonfuls of Birch's Salts. A cold in the head, indigestion, neuralgia, rheumatism, etc., etc., treated in the same way; for Miss Peleg believes implicitly in this unfailing remedy and when any of the boarders feel queer, they go up to Miss Peleg to be *Birched;* and if anybody dies, it is because they have not taken those wonderful salts in time. Since I am at Madame Dupont's, I have had Birch's Salts, at least forty times, and I live!"

Mr. Blake is now called upon to play. He is very obliging—does not make a fuss. He plays the "Coulin," that grand, pathetic, old Irish air, and he plays it so exquisitely that he is made to play it a second, and even a third time. He then accompanies Miss Magee, who sings "Kate Kearney," "My Love is like a red, red Rose," and "The Wearing of the Green." Olga and I remark that Mrs. Merriman's smile is no longer child-like and bland, as she watches the pretty Irish girl sing those wild pathetic airs as only an Irish girl can sing them. Perhaps the widow feels a little jealous as she perceives the admiration that Mr. Blake evidently has for this charming Hibernian, with her sunny smile, her ringing laugh, and musical brogue.

"I am sure that Mr. Blake is a little bit in love with Miss Magee," whispers Olga to me on the balcony; "and I fancy that the widow does not like it. I should like Mr. Blake to marry Mary Magee; they would be so well suited. They are both musical, very Irish, and she is such a bright, unaffected girl. Now Mrs. Merriman is a kind of female Blue Beard—a wolf in sheep's clothing. I should not like her to kill Mr. Blake, for he is a nice little fellow."

"You and Miss Magee are hard upon this unfortunate widow. I think her rather attractive; she has a low sweet voice; her manners are good. I confess that this eternal sweet smile provokes me."

"Now let us retire to our bedroom," says Olga. "We have had a good dose of gossip and scandal, let us go before we either of us have said something that we shall regret profoundly the next morning. I do envy those quiet people, who never do, say or write an impulsive thing; who never get into scrapes. They may be a little dull, perhaps, but how safe they are—how respectable!"

CHAPTER IV

THE CULPRIT

OLGA and I now go regularly to Madame Latour's studio. An old man with a long white beard, furrowed face, attired in the costume of a monk, is our model. I feel that I make great strides in art, Madame Latour is such a good teacher. She comes into our studio once a day for about an hour; but her advice is so good, her correctness so conscientious, that the progress we make is remarkable. My study of the monk is the second best; Olga's is the best. She signs those two works, as a proof of her approbation.

Madame Latour allows us now and then to come into her studio and watch her process of working. She is painting a Bacchante: the head thrown back, vine leaves encircling the red-brown hair, and eyes full of voluptuousness and fire; the throat and neck are beautifully modelled, and over the bosom is a gorgeous leopard skin. One hand presses a bunch of grapes, the other hangs listlessly at her side.

At four o'clock the pupils leave the studio. Olga and I usually saunter through the streets of Paris, look into the shops, and often drop into some of the beautiful old Roman Catholic churches. The quiet, the subdued light pouring in through the colored windows, the paintings, the incense, the solemn peals of the organ, the fresh voices of *les enfants du chœur* in their white and colored garments, the harmony of the architecture, is an attraction to the artistic temperament.

One afternoon we had a sort of religious discussion. I said that I found the so-called Low Church cold, unsympathetic, and even very dull; and going to pray at stated hours and days formal and unnatural.

Now, in Catholic communities the churches are always opened; and when you need prayer, and would desire repose, it is a comfort to drop into one of those old churches; and even if no service is going on, it is soothing to listen to the silence, to be in an atmosphere of subdued light. There is more poetry in the Roman Catholic faith, with all its grievous errors.

"I am a pagan," says Olga. "Nature is my god; the sun, the stars, and the yellow moon are my deities. On Sundays I generally take long rambles in the country with Fido, my dog, and my little maid Nina. Sometimes, when the spirit moves me, which is seldom, I go to hear the celebrated *pasteur*, Monsieur Bonchemin, *le pasteur à la mode*. All the ladies run after him, and that is one of the reasons I go so seldom to his chapel, for it makes me ill to see

how women turn the heads of those servants of God! Monsieur Bonchemin is a man of great eloquence.

"His sermons are great intellectual treats: he never reads his sermons, and that is such an advantage! His utterance is delightful, voice beautiful; he never hesitates for a word. He is very handsome, like a St. John, with a slightly melancholy *rêveur* expression, which is fascinating. His hands are beautiful, and he knows it, for one of these appendages he lets hang gracefully down the pulpit cushion. He is the woman's *pasteur*—a kind of Protestant Pope: his power is great, his appeals to the conscience are searching and keen, and he certainly makes me feel horribly uncomfortable; but when I see all those elegant toilettes, those wonderful Paris bonnets, I do not feel at all as if I was worshipping an unseen God—merely listening to a handsome, eloquent preacher.

"So I prefer nature: I feel more elevated looking at a fine sunset, or at the sea, than kneeling upon a hard footstool, surrounded by silks, satins, and prosperity. *Vanitas vanitatum, omnia vanitas!* Do you know Mr. Morris is a Positivist, a follower of Comte? He worships humanity. He tells me he does his duty, and tries to love his neighbor. As far as I know, his notion of duty is to paint pictures, and I do not think he cares for his neighbors. He is often much depressed; and really I do not wonder at it, for it is hard to have little in this world, and to think he will have nothing at all in the next."

At this point of the conversation, who should we see but Mr. Morris, in an old battered wide-awake, a very shabby coat, and a portfolio under his arm. Olga taps him on the back with her parasol. He starts, and looks uncomfortable. We tell him that we were just talking about him, and saying that it was a pity he did not believe in a future state.

"The boulevards are scarcely a fit place for a discussion upon the immortality of the soul," answers Mr. Morris smiling; "but if you are anxious to know my belief, all I can say is, that my mind is not made up. I feel that I have a soul, and do not think it will perish."

"Let us leave the soul alone," exclaims Olga, looking into a cake shop. "I shall perish if I do not eat. Let us enter this *pâtisserie*, and fill our inner beings!"

Mr. Morris tries to escape. He declares that he is not in a fit state to be seen walking in ladies' society; he has been sketching all day at the Jardin des Plantes.

"You know, Mr. Morris, that I am also a Bohemian, and do not mind how shabby you look."

We insist so much that he consents to remain with us, and so we enter the shop, devour a number of cream *éclairs*, and Olga orders a parcel of cakes, biscuits, and *bonbons* to be made up for a small *protégé* of hers, a cripple boy, whom she is going to visit the following day.

We walk through the Tuileries Gardens. How imposing the ruins of this once mighty palace look in this twilight!

There is something very grand about the old Château now, as it stands there mutilated. What pages of history have been enacted there!—a whole past

swept away! The Gardens are at this hour deserted. The statues seem quite mournful, and look like ghosts in this dim gray light. A solitary white swan is gliding warily in a dismal pond; the trees make a dark background; the clouds are purple; there is a thin mist over everything, and just over the ruined helpless palace peeps a young crescent moon. The sentinel looks like an uneasy spirit, as he stands at the gate of the Garden.

We cross the bridge, down the Quai Voltaire, and peep leisurely into all the bric-a-brac shops, and lastly we enter an old curiosity shop, full of quaint odd pieces of furniture, old china, old plate, etc. It is a queer little den. The shopman is a Jew, named Solomon—a thin, wiry old fellow, with a few scanty white hairs brushed carefully over his narrow head, spectacles falling down his long thin nose. In his wrinkled hand he holds a lamp, which casts mysterious shadows here and there in the small shop. "A picture for Rembrandt," I think, as I watch the old Jew ferreting out his antique wares, beautiful bronzes, laces, old books, prints, etc.

"What a splendid bit of old tapestry! It would look well in my little studio," exclaims Mr. Morris, "but I must not be tempted to buy it."

Olga goes up to the shopman, whispers something mysteriously, and the piece of tapestry is folded up and presented to Mr. Morris. "A souvenir from me," says Olga to him, "in remembrance of this charming walk."

Mr. Morris changes color, looks bewildered, refuses, but Olga insists, so he naturally ends by gratefully accepting it.

I am presented with a pair of antique gold earrings, which in the innocence of my heart I had admired.

"You see what it is to go out with this Lady Bountiful; one dare not express a wish," says Mr. Morris.

"The pleasure is greater in giving than in receiving, so say nothing more about it."

We meet Uranie at the door of the *pension,* who tells me, to my great amazement, that my cousin, Mr. Horace Dashwood, "a varie prettie boy," is upstairs, waiting to see me.

"How very absurd!" Olga and I both exclaim, and before we can make any further remark my cousin stands before us.

"Glad to see you both," Horace shouts, shaking hands with us heartily; "what wild Bohemians you are to be sure!—meandering about Paris, not coming in to dinner, and not telling anybody where you go."

"I am the culprit," says Mr. Morris, "I really thought it a pity to go indoors such a lovely evening, so I begged the young ladies to dine at a restaurant."

Mr. Morris looks much confused, bids us good-night, and Horace follows us upstairs.

"Who on earth is that fellow? in such a shabby old coat and battered wide-awake? An artist, of course. I cannot understand how two fashionably dressed girls could walk out with a man in such a beggarly costume. You consider him a genius, innocent young creatures, simply because he looks dirty."

"Now, Mr. Dashwood, I will not allow you to call Mr. Morris dirty; he is a great artist, and no doubt a man

of genius too. You think, evidently, that the coat makes the man. Some men do depend entirely upon their tailor for success in the world; Mr. Morris is above such a consideration. He has a soul above buttons."

"Well, I wish he had some more buttons to his coat. I am sorry, Mademoiselle Olga, if I have hurt your feelings. All I can say is, that if artists are all like Mr. Morris then I would rather not know any. But let us drop this very unpleasant topic. You look very cross, Mademoiselle Olga."

Olga pouts, and disappears from the room.

"I suppose I have annoyed her. Is she engaged to that wild Bohemian in the old wide-awake?"

"No, she is not; but he is a very great admirer of hers—in fact, I am sure the man is in love with her. So you ought to be more careful, and not give vent to all your notions about artists. Mr. Morris will one day make his mark in the world."

Horace gives a long contemptuous whistle: "I do not pretend to understand artists; they are a race apart."

After a little talk about family affairs Olga returns. To my amusement she has changed her dress, and put on a most becoming lilac silk dress, and placed a coquettish lilac ribbon in her wavy hair. I, of course, make no outward and visible sign of my astonishment; but evidently this inconsistent little maiden is a flirt, and consequently, bent upon making a conquest of my cousin, the famous woman-hater!

"Won't you and Mr. Horace come into my parlor and have some supper? —but you must not abuse Mr. Morris. or we shall quarrel dreadfully."

An exquisite little supper is laid out on the table. A couple of lamps shed a soft light. The water is hissing in the urn. Comfort, luxury, and artistic objects make the room a little Paradise. The windows are open, and in the balcony stand masses of roses, heliotropes, and lilies of the valley.

"What a lovely room!" exclaims Horace. "Paris taste, good English comfort: what more can a mortal require?"

"Yes, Mr. Dashwood, though I am an artist and a Bohemian, I do like pretty things, and no end of luxury. I hope that you admire my dress? it is made by a very fashionable dressmaker." And she makes him a profound courtesy.

"I have been admiring you; such a toilette could only come out of the hands of a Parisian dressmaker, and those dear little shoes that I spy are works of art."

Olga takes off her slipper, and hands it to Horace for nearer inspection. It is very small, of lilac satin, embroidered with silver braid.

"Cinderella's slipper; and you, Horace, are the Prince," I remark.

"Oh no, Mr. Dashwood is not gallant enough for that: his chief failing is not to admire us poor women, alas! But I think we can do without his admiration. Have some sparkling moselle or champagne, or both, and eat come of the *pâté de lièvre*, Mr. Horace, and tell me what you have been doing with your great self since I had the pleasure of seeing you, more than a year ago."

"Well. I have been doing what most of us Englishmen spend the greater part of our lives in doing, that is, kill-ing beasts, birds, and fishes, viz., hunting, shooting, and fishing. You foreigners can hardly understand or appreciate this mode of life."

"Well, I do think," answers Olga, "that hunting and shooting is very cruel sport: to see a number of big, burly men, spending their energies running after a poor fox, or a little hare, it seems wicked; and as for deer-stalking, I simply think it is a crime. I cannot understand how any man can wound a beautiful deer, with its splendid horns and lovely piteous eyes, looking so pleading; no, I think it cowardly. I do not think fishing so bad," says Olga. "It is rather nice sport; one sits in a boat, with a pretty landscape all about, for the scenery is generally lovely, the water delicious, and one has merely to wait for the fish; and when it is caught the poor thing does not seem to dislike it so very much, he does not scream or bleed No, fishing is rather a poetical pastime."

Horace laughs heartily. "You know little about fishing if you imagine that one has merely to wait quietly for the fish to be hooked; but it is no use my trying to initiate you into the mysteries of fishing in your drawing-room. When you come over to England we shall have some fishing together, I hope."

"Oh, that will be so jolly! I shall be mad with delight if I can just fish up a salmon." And Olga claps her hands at the mere anticipation of such a triumph.

"We shall not begin by salmon-fishing, I assure you; but I must retire, Mademoiselle Olga. I have much enjoyed my evening here. We shall meet to-morrow at breakfast, for I am staying in this house. So *bon soir.*"

The next morning, at breakfast, Horace sits between Olga and me, to the evident disgust of poor Mr. Morris, who watches us gloomily from his side of the table. Mr. Blake is sitting near Mary Magee, in close confabulation, to the dismay of the widow. Mr. Smiles is between the two young American girls, flirting cleverly with the two. Miss Hutchinson is smiling radiantly upon a red-hot Radical. We can overhear a little of their conversation.

"Why should not women be in Parliament? they are more eloquent, more tenacious than men."

"Did you ever hear such rubbish?" says Horace. "If that fellow goes on talking such arrant bosh I shall surely have an indigestion. I hate Radicals; they never look gentlemanly. Now look at this man, his coat does not fit him properly, his nails are black. Now a Conservative always looks a gentleman."

Immediately after breakfast we all three decide upon going to Asnières to see Olga's little *protégé,* the cripple boy.

CHAPTER V

OPHELIA

It is a glorious morning. We got out of the train at Asnières. The river looks so tempting, that we get into a little boat and Horace rows us.

He decidedly looks to great advantage in the boat. He is attired in a well-made suit of light gray cloth; his bright, deep blue eyes are full of fun and honesty; his chest is broad and well-developed; he is the best type of the "muscular" school. We get out

of the boat and walk across a field full of wild flowers. We all pick some daisies and buttercups to give to poor little Victor.

"I am afraid that he is not long for this world," says Olga. "I fear he is slowly pining away. His mother died during the siege of Paris, literally of starvation, for she could not swallow either horseflesh, rats, or cats; so little Victor is living with his old *grand'-mère.* The little boy is a cripple, and in a consumption; but his father, a most intelligent, honest workman, will not believe that his child is seriously ill. There is the house, that little white place amongst the trees; it is a kind of modest inn, where one can have fish, or rather *friture,* bread and butter, and cheap wine."

"All right," shouts Horace; "I am hungry. I shall order all the fish in the house to be fried; besides, it will put some money into those poor people's pockets."

The old *grand'mere* is standing at the door of the small inn; a fine type of old age. Her hair is snowy white, a colored *fichu* is pinned across her broad chest; by her side totters a pale, thin, emaciated little boy, so transparent looking, that one could almost fancy a strong breath of wind would waft him away, holding to his *grand'-mère's* skirts. On seeing Olga a bright sunny smile illuminates his wan, white face.

"He has been inquiring after you, mademoiselle," says the *grand'mère,* "*n'est-ce pas,* Victor? You are glad to see Mademoiselle Olga?"

The child creeps to her, and Olga gives him some toys, cakes, and *bonbons.*

Horace takes him on his knees, and gives him a box of soldiers; the child at first seems a little frightened, but my cousin soon makes friends with him, and they chatter quite gayly together. *La mère* Gigun looks sadly at her delicate grandchild, and tells us with a big sigh that he is getting weaker and weaker.

"What a lovely face he has!—such long, soft brown, curly hair, large hazel eyes, with such a wistful expression in them. How I should like to have a good picture of him!" mutters *mère* Gigun, "for no photograph can do justice to him."

"That is an idea! Let us come and paint him," says Olga.

"I will do his portrait and give it to you and his father; but you must allow my friend, Miss Larcom, to paint you and the child also. She wants a *sujet* for a picture."

"Only too happy to think that my old face can be of use. I am quite at your *disposition,* mademoiselle."

I thank the old woman. We arrange to come the following day with our easels, canvases, and paint-boxes. Before leaving we order some fried *goujons* for our lunch. Horace compliments the old woman upon her cookery, and insists upon her accepting a twenty-franc piece, in order that she may get a few delicacies for the child.

Before leaving, Olga takes Victor upon her knee and tells him a story. That is his greatest treat; for he is an imaginative child, and likes to hear about fairies, imps, elves, etc. Victor exists in a kind of Wonderland, and firmly believes that he is always surrounded by fairies. His *grand'mère*

tells us that he often says he will be glad to go and live among the fairies: that is his notion of death; a change from what he is now to a beautiful being who lives among flowers, feeds upon honey and fruits, has wings, and visits the stars.

* * * *

Upon returning to the boarding-house that evening we find our invitations from Madame Latour; it is for the promised fancy ball to take place that day fortnight.

No one can make up their minds as to who or what he or she will personate.

Olga first thinks of going as a star, next as a dryad, or as a sea-nymph.

"Do go as an Ophelia," suggests Mr. Morris.

"Oh, I should have to look melancholy all the evening! A lively Ophelia would be so absurd."

"You would be an ideal Ophelia," continues Mr. Morris. "You have just the right hair, the eyes, the figure, and the expression."

"The crazy look in the eyes," barks out Horace. "Do take my advice, Mademoiselle Olga, and go in a costume that suits your general mood and disposition."

"Happy thought!" exclaims Olga. "I shall go as a *diavolina*—an imp from the regions downstairs."

"That's right. Hurrah!" shouts Horace; "and I shall attend the ball as his infernal majesty himself, with a long tail, horns, and a pitchfork."

"*Convenus,*" laughs Olga.

Mr. Morris looks pale and very cross, and scowls furiously at my cousin, who screams out:

"Louisa, you might as well dress as an Ophelia; only your fat, red cheeks and tendency to *embonpoint* might be a little incongruous."

"You are very rude! I mean to go as a *vivandière des zouaves*. In a blue vest, scarlet knickerbockers, white waistcoat, a gold *képi* on my head, and a little barrel filled with cognac at my side."

"Delightful idea. We shall all have a drop now and then to revive our drooping spirits."

"Now, Mr. Morris, how will you dress? I particularly wish you to look to advantage," says Olga, going up to him. Let me think what would suit your character as an artist, a poet, a philosopher." (Olga darts a saucy look at Horace, who is studying pertinaciously the pattern of the carpet.) "I have it. You must go as Hamlet in the 'Inky cloak.' I order you, Mr. Morris. Now, will you? won't you obey me?"

"I should have gladly gone as Hamlet if you had consented to be Ophelia," whispers Mr. Morris.

"Oh, that would have been too remarkable! Besides which, I should very likely be in wild spirits, and that would not do for Ophelia. No, go as Hamlet, and I shall dance the first dance with you."

Mr. Morris promises, and bidding us good-night, disappears to his den upstairs.

"I do not like that man," growls out my cousin, the moment the door closes upon Mr. Morris; "he is so unhealthy in all his views and notions of life. That artist nature seems unnatural to me. It would do Mr. Morris a vast deal of good to hunt, shoot, and fish.

It would make him manly; his notions of everything are sickly, false, and absurd."

"Well, Mr. Dashwood, I am surprised at your disobedience!" exclaims Olga, standing up and flushing with excitement. "I did tell you several times that nothing can annoy me more than to hear Mr. Morris abused. Your idea of life is sport. All right. Mr. Morris loves art; he is a great artist and musician. He might dress better, but it is not affectation on his part; simply he does not care about the cut of his coat nor about the particular shade of his necktie, etc. Mr. Morris will, I am sure, be a great man one of these days. Meanwhile, let him alone or we shall quarrel seriously. You are a naughty boy; the more you abuse Mr. Morris the more I shall like him."

"Well, I shall not mention Mr. Morris's name again."

When Horace is gone, I ask Olga if she thinks that my cousin is improved.

"I have not thought much about him, one way or the other." ('What a story!' I inwardly ejaculate.) "He has good qualities, but he is fearfully prejudiced. He is a type of the modern young man; no feeling for Art, but fond of sport. He is generous and manly."

"I wonder if he will ever fall in love?"—saying this I peep slyly at Olga through the corners of my eyes. She colors up. "I do not think that it is in him to care much for any one."

"Well, I think you are mistaken, and I sometimes think that he does actually care for some young lady."

"Really? Oh! do tell me all about it: he is your cousin, so it is natural that I should take some interest in him."

"Ask no questions and I shall tell you no stories. I cannot say anything for certain, it is a supposition on my part. I should like Horace to marry; he would make a first-rate husband."

"Have you seen the girl you think he is in love with?"

"I have seen her, she is a great friend of mine." And I look hard at Olga, who pretends not to understand, gets very red, rushes off to the piano and plays deliciously a valse of Chopin.

The next morning Olga and I go to Asnières. We have our easels, canvases and painting materials. When we reach the quiet inn, we perceive *mère* Gigun at the door, looking very dismal; the child is sleeping.

"I am afraid that before next month he will be lying by his poor mother's grave, in the little *cimetière* over there, he is ebbing away."

We both go up to the bedroom. In a small white bed lies the child, a feverish spot on each cheek: he opens his big eyes and smiles a welcome.

"We are come to paint your picture," Olga says, kissing him. "Here are some flowers for you."

Victor brightens up, he is propped by pillows. The old *grand'mère* sits close to him, the window is open, and an acacia tree in full bloom casts a delicious fragrance; a cage with two canaries stands on the sill.

I sketch the room as it is; the sick child sitting up playing with the flowers, the *grand'mère* with her wrinkled face and sweet, sad gray eyes and snowy hair, making such a contrast to the spiritual, unearthly face of the wee

grandson. The old woman knits a brown woollen stocking, and a tear now and then drops on her hands as she looks at the child.

Olga, while painting, tells Victor a story of a little boy who was carried away by the fairies, and is still living with them in a beautiful blue palace up in the clouds; he is the only little boy there, the fairies are very fond of him, pet him much, so he is quite happy.

Victor's expression gets more and more ideal and Olga's portrait is growing wonderfully like.

"What a treasure it will be to us!" exclaims the old woman. "We shall prize it, oh so much, mademoiselle!"

"Why do you look so *triste, grand'-mère?* Suppose the fairies take me away up in their blue palace, you, papa, and mademoiselle must come also."

A tap at the door; a fine stalwart *ouvrier* in a blue blouse comes in; his face is sunburnt, but very handsome. He bows respectfully to us, hopes that he does not disturb us, and going up to Victor kisses him.

"How are you, *mon fils?*"

"Better, *petit père.* Look at the pictures the ladies are painting of me."

"With your permission, mademoiselle," and he looks at Olga's work. "It is a very good likeness; the expression is perhaps a little more sad, *mais c'est bien lui!* The eyes are perfect, just the color and the expression."

Then he comes round to look at mine.

"Ah, that will make a capital picture, old age and childhood. I compliment you upon your artistic talent."

"Is he not a type of the best kind of

French workman? so intelligent, refined, and so artistic?" whispers Olga to me. "Well, how are you getting on, Monsieur Lenoir?" she continues, addressing the *ouvrier*.

"Pretty well, mademoiselle, the *commerce* is just beginning to get on, and we must work hard."

"I do admire the French workman so much!" says Olga. "Lenoir is not an exception; no, as a rule, the *ouvriers* are honest, intelligent, and refined; such a contrast, so superior to those horrid little men one meets on the boulevards, sipping *café*, absinthe, and *eau de vie*."

But it is now getting too dark to work, so kissing Victor, we go down stairs and have a quiet little dinner in the garden.

CHAPTER VI

THE BALL

A FEW evenings after this sad visit Horace comes into my room, looking rather meek, and, indeed, sheepish.

"I know," he says, "that you are going to laugh at me. Can you guess what I have done?" and he stares uncomfortably out of the window.

"Well, I think I can guess," I reply laughing.

"Oh yes! you can laugh. Go on. Well, what is it?"

"Why, you silly old boy, you have of course fallen head over ears in love with that little sprite, Olga, though she is a Bohemian, a Radical, an artist, independent; in fact, the very contrary of what you pretend to admire."

"Well, you have found me out!" and he colors up very much; "but the wonder of wonders is, that she cares a little for me, also, and has consented to become my wife!"

"Nothing surprises me, she is such an inconsistent little damsel. She declared to me not many weeks ago that she would never marry; but I am so glad that she has so soon changed her mind. You are to be congratulated, for she is a charming girl, though she is fond of art, and a Radical."

"It was at the funeral of poor little Victor that I decided upon proposing to her. A look she gave me, a general something in her demeanor that morning, made me feel that I was not indifferent to her; and Olga tells me that my kindness to the child made her care for me against her will."

So the poor little fellow was the unconscious means of making up a match.

I rush off to Olga's room. I find her lying full length upon the hearthrug; her cheeks are very flushed and her eyes sparkling.

On seeing me she throws a handkerchief over her face, saying, "What will you think of me, Louise? I am really ashamed, and cry peccavi; but I really feel so happy. I did not think it possible for me ever to care for any one again, and I now find that I never really loved either number one or number two. I have told your cousin all about those previous affairs; he is such a good fellow, he does not mind at all. Don't laugh at me too much, I am sure you must think me a very odd girl."

"Indeed I do; that is your charm— so unlike everybody else. But I congratulate you, you and Horace will be very happy together."

"I shall leave the boarding-house as soon as I have packed up all my pretty things, and have them all sent to London."

"You will come and stay at our house till the wedding?"

"Just what I should like. I have no home, no relatives, no one in the world. Horace will now be everything to me."

* * *

THE fancy ball at Madame Latour's studio is a great success. It is a picnic ball; the ladies send the eatables, the men the wines. Olga and I sent a tremendous *pâté de foie gras* and a boar's head.

The *atelier* looks quite grand, brilliantly illuminated and festooned with flowers and evergreens, and a long table laden with all the delicacies of the season. Olga is the belle of the ball, as a *diavolina* in scarlet, gold, and black skirts; little gold horns in her hair, a pitchfork in her hand, and black and red flames worked into the patterns of her dress.

Horace changed his mind, and disguised himself as a wolf. His tail was constantly trodden upon, and then he would roar lustily, to the great amusement of everybody. He and Olga were in high spirits. Naturally, poor Mr. Morris, having heard of their engagement (such secrets always get known), did not appear at the ball; a sure sign that he really cared for Olga.

Mr. Blake is disguised as an orange-tree, Miss Magee as a shepherdess. It is noticed by many that she rests continually under that particular tree, and that the tree hovers continually over her.

My costume of *vivandière* is a great

success. One particular gentleman, whose name I shall not divulge, drank more cognac out of my barrel than was good for him.

Madame Latour looks very fine as Queen of the Night, all in black tulle, with silver stars, a crescent moon in her dark hair, and a stuffed owl perched upon her shoulder.

"Well, Olga, so you are going to give up art for matrimony? I am grieved to hear this piece of news; you cannot serve two masters. You will fail."

"Yes, madame, I shall paint more than ever. I do not see why a woman should become a nonentity when she marries. I shall have a studio in our town-house; besides we shall be six months every year on the Continent."

"We shall see," growls Madame Latour. "Do not believe the promises made before marriage. Tell me what Mr. Dashwood says after the ceremony is over. No, I am disappointed; you ought not to have promised me to give yourself entirely to art, and then, when a handsome young fellow comes over here, you give up everything for him. *Violà les femmes!*—no tenacity, no decision of character, no strong will."

"I am catching it," whispers Olga to me; "but it is no use my trying to persuade Madame that I shall paint pictures after my marriage; but I *will*, and very likely I shall make Horace study art."

A few days after the ball, Horace departs, Uranie calling him a "varrie naughtie boy." He feels he deserves the reproach; he gives Uraine twenty francs to pacify her, and tells her that she must not abuse him when he is gone.

Mr. Morris leaves the *pension* without bidding Olga or me good-bye. There is a report that he is engaged to be married to the wily widow, who has been making herself strong in Art, and copying at the Louvre.

Mr. Blake goes to Cork to visit his family; it is rather a curious coincidence that Miss Magee and her mother should be going over to Erin at that particular time. Miss Hutchinson has gone to New York to study the institutions of the mighty republic. Olga and I, with great regret, bid adieu to Madame Dupont, and all the inmates of the *pension*.

We leave on a sultry morning at the end of June. Uranie has tears in her eyes as she bids us adieu, and declares that we really are "varrie naughtie" to leave. When we reach the station we do not find either Mr. Morris or Mr. Blake awaiting us; and it is with mixed feelings of pleasure and pain that Olga and I leave bright, beautiful Paris for dreary London; but Olga declares, with a blush, that it will no longer be dismal, but delightful.

A Bohemian Night

WHEN I was about eighteen, I made the acquaintance of a somewhat singular individual, who now seems to me, after a certain lapse of time, to be the very personification of a world to itself, with special language and peculiar manners, a world that has disappeared and is now almost forgotten; but which at one time held a prominent place in the Paris of the Empire. I allude to that gipsy band, guerillas of art, rebels against conventional philosophy and literature, fantastic to the very uttermost, which had insolently ensconced itself before the Louvre and the Institute, and which Henri Murger—not without embellishing and poetizing the remembrance of it—has celebrated under the title of *Bohemia*. We will call my personage Desroches. I had met him at a ball of the Quartier Latin, with some friends, one summer evening. I had returned home very late to my little room in the Rue de Tournon, and was sleeping as soundly as a dormouse the next morning, when suddenly there appeared, at the foot of my bed, a man in a black coat, a scanty, threadbare coat, of that peculiar black only seen on policemen and undertakers.

"I come from M. Desroches."

"M. Desroches? What M. Desroches?" said I, rubbing my eyes, for my recollections that morning obstinately refused to be aroused as quickly as my body.

"M. Desroches of the *Figaro*. You spent the evening together last night; he is in the lock-up, and he refers to you."

"M. Desroches—ah, to be sure—exactly—he refers to me—well, tell them to let him out!"

"Beg pardon, there is fifteen-pence to pay!"

"Fifteen-pence! Why?"

"It is the custom."

I gave the fifteen-pence. The black-coated man disappeared, and I remained sitting on my bed, half dreaming, and not clearly understanding in consequence of what eccentric adventures I found myself brought to the point of ransoming, like a new brother of mercy—for fifteen-pence—a contributor to the *Figaro* from the clutches not of the Turks, but of the police.

I had no long time for reflection. Five minutes later, Desroches, freed from his fetters, came smiling into my room.

"A thousand pardons, my dear colleague; all this is the fault of the *Raisins muscats*. Yes! the *Raisins muscats*, my first article, which appeared yesterday in the *Figaro*. Confounded *Raisins muscats!* You see, I had got the payment—my first payment—and it flew to my head. We patrolled the whole quarter after we left you, indeed towards the end my recollections are somewhat mixed; still I have a sensation as if I had received a kick somewhere or another. Then I found myself in the station-house—a charming night indeed! First of all they poked me into the furthest den—the black hole, you know. How it smelt! But I made the gentlemen laugh—they were good enough to take me into their guard-room—we talked, played cards. They insisted on my reading them *les Raisins muscats*, such a success! . . . It is really astonishing the taste these policemen have!"

Imagine my stupefaction, and the effect produced on my simple and provincial boyish mind by the revelation of these eccentric literary habits and customs! And the colleague who thus related his adventures was a little round fellow, well brushed and shaved, affecting polite manners, and whose white

gaiters and frock coat of *bourgeois* cut made the most marked contrast with his extravagant gestures and the grimaces of his buffoon-like features. He astonished me, half frightened me, saw that he did so, and evidently took pleasure in exaggerating, in honour of me, the cynicism of his paradoxes.

"I like you," he said, as he took his leave; "come and see me next Sunday afternoon. I live in a delightful spot, near the Castle of Fogs, on the hillside looking over Saint-Ouen, you know it well—the vineyard of Gérard de Nerval! I will introduce you to my wife; she's worth taking a journey to see. Happily, too, I have just received a barrel of new wine; we will drink it in mugs, as one does at the wholesale dealers at Bercy, and we will sleep in the cellar. Then, too, a friend of mine, a Dominican monk, unfrocked only a day or two ago, is coming to read me a drama in five acts. You will hear it; superb subject! full of rape and ravishment! Now you understand. Gérard de Nerval's vineyard; don't forget the address!"

All came to pass exactly as Desroches had promised. We drank out of the cask the new wine, and in the evening the pretended Dominican read us his drama. Dominican or not, he was a fine handsome Breton, with large shoulders, well fitted for the frock, and with something of the preacher in the rounding of his sentences and gestures. He has since made himself a name in literature. His drama did not much astonish me, but it must be owned that, after an afternoon spent in Gérard de Nerval's vineyard—in what Desroches called his home—astonishment was no longer easy to attain.

Before climbing the slopes I had be-thought me of re-reading the exquisite pages that Gérard, the lover of *Sylvie*, in his *Promenades et Souvenirs*, has consecrated to the description of this northern declivity of Montmartre, a scrap of country inclosed in the midst of Paris, and therefore so much the more cherished and precious: "There still remain to us a certain number of gently sloping hillsides, girdled with thick green hedges, which the barberry decorates alternately with its violet flowers and purple berries. There are there windmills, rustic inns and sum-mer-houses, elysian fields and deep-cut silent lanes; there may even be found a vineyard, the last of the celebrated vintage of Montmartre, which in the time of the Romans rivalled those of Argenteuil and Suresnes. Year by year this humble hillside loses a row of its stunted vine-stocks, swallowed up by the stone quarry. Ten years ago I could have bought it for four hundred pounds. I should have built in this vineyard so dainty an edifice! a little villa in the Pompeiian style, with an *impluvium* and a *cella*."

In this poet's dream of antiquity lived my friend Desroches. There! horrible antithesis! did he present to me, under a blue summer sky, in the shade of an arbour of flowering elder, all musical with the hum of bees, an androgynous monster in the dress of a carter, blue smock, short velveteen skirt, cap striped with red perched over the ear, a whip drawn round her neck:

"M. Alphonse Daudet, Mme. Des-roches!"

For this monster was really his wife, his legitimate wife, always arrayed in this costume, which pleased her fancy, and than which, certainly, nothing could have been found to suit better with her masculine voice and face. Smok-ing, spitting, swearing, with all the vices of a man, she kept the whole household in awe; her husband in the first place, who was much henpecked, and, besides, two thin daughters—her daughters!—of strange and boylike as-pect, and who, too early matured and run to seed, promised at thirteen and fifteen to become some day all that their mother was at forty. It certainly was worth the trouble, as he had said, to have a sight of such a household.

Desroches was nevertheless the son of a rich and orderly Parisian manu-facturer; a jeweller, I believe. His father had disowned him more than once, and now made him a small allow-ance. It is not rare to find in France instances of these lunatics, positive scourges of Heaven, appearing sud-denly in the midst of peaceful families, troubling their calm repose, putting in circulation their accumulated gold, smiting the *bourgeosie* in short, in its tenderest spot. And I have known several of these ducklings set under hens, which, when once out of the shell, rush to the water. The water, to them, is art, literature, that trade open to all, without patent or diploma. Desroches, when he left college, had dabbled in art—in all the arts. He had begun with painting, and the career through the studios of this cool, orderly and re-served cynic, who preserved in the midst of the wildest fancies, the in-delible stigma of his *bourgeois* origin, has become a standing legend. The at-tempt at painting proving a failure, Desroches attacked literature. Inspired perhaps by his vineyard, he managed to accomplish the *Raisins muscats*—a hundred lines — a complete article! Vainly afterwards, did he try to write another; he could never again find the right inspiration, and reached the age of forty, having as the work of a lifetime, written the *Raisins muscats.*

The conversation and sallies of friend Desroches amused me; but his household did not suit me at all. I never returned to Montmartre, but I crossed the river sometimes in order to visit him at the tavern in the rue des Martyrs. The Brasserie (tavern) of les Martyrs, nowadays the quiet resort of the worthy linendrapers of the neighbourhood for their evening game of draughts, represented then a power in literature. The Brasserie sat in judgment; and made famous whom it would; and in the overpowering silence of the Empire, Paris was aroused by the noise made there every evening, by eighty or a hundred choice spirits, while smoking their pipes and drinking their beer. They were called Bohemians, and the name did not displease them. The *Figaro* of that day, non-political, and appearing only once a week, was generally their rostrum.

The tavern was a sight worth seeing—we used to call it "THE BRASSE-RIE," simply, as the Romans spoke of Rome as "THE CITY,"—it was worth seeing about eleven o'clock at night, with all its cheerful hubbub of voices, and clouded by the smoke of all those pipes!

Murger reigned absolute, at the middle table; Murger, who was at once the Homer and Columbus of this little world, and to which his exquisite fancy lent a rose-coloured tinge. Decorated with the Legion of Honour, and hence-forth famous, publishing his stories in the *Revue des deux Mondes*, he nevertheless continued to frequent *the Brasserie*, "to keep alive," he said, "his impressions of the worthy folk he had described, and also to receive their homage and applause." He was pointed out to me—a large, melancholy head, the eyes reddened, the beard scanty, sure signs of very indifferent Parisian blood. He lived at Marlotte, in the forest of Fontainebleau; constantly to be seen with a gun on his shoulder, he pretended to shoot, but it was more a search after health than after partridges or hares. The fact of his abode in the village had drawn thither quite a Parisian colony of men and women, natives of the asphalt and the tavern, producing a strange contrast under the great oaks; there are traces of it in Marlotte to this day. Ten years after the death of Murger, who died, as all know, in the Hospital Dubois—I was there with some friends at the famous inn kept by Mother Antony. An old peasant sat drinking near us, such a peasant as Balzac describes, soil-stained and weather-beaten. An old hag, arrayed in tatters, and a red handkerchief round her head, came to fetch him away. She called him drunkard, spendthrift, good-for-nothing; while he tried to make her drink with him.

"Your wife is none too gentle!" said some one when she was gone.

"She is not my wife; she is my mistress!" replied the old peasant.

You should have heard the tone in which this was uttered. Evidently the good man had known Murger and his friends, and sought to lead a Bohemian life according to his lights.

To return to the Brasserie. As my

eyes became accustomed to the smarting caused by the smoke, I could see to the right and left, and in every corner, well-known faces.

Each great man had his table, which became the nucleus, the centre of a whole clique of admirers.

Pierre Dupont, old already at forty-five, fat and stooping, his mild bovine eye scarcely visible beneath the drooping eyelids, sat, elbows on table, trying to sing some of the political or rustic songs with swinging rhythm, vibrating still with the fair dreams of '48; or re-echoing the many sounds of work and labour of the Croix-Rousse, and scented with the thousand perfumes of the Lyonnaise valley. But there was no longer any voice; burnt away by alcohol, it was but a hoarse rattle.

"You require the fresh air of the fields, my poor Pierre," said Gustave Mathieu, the bard of *les Bons Vins*, of *le Coq Gaulois*, and of *les Hirondelles*. This last, who came of good *bourgeois* blood in Nevers, had travelled much in his younger days, and retained from his travels, a passion for fresh air and wide horizons. He found all this round his little house at Bois-le-Roi, and when he came to the Brasserie, it was only to walk through it smiling, erect, with a Henri IV. air, and at all times of the year with a wild flower in his button-hole.

Dupont died sadly enough in the black manufacturing town of Lyons. Mathieu, tough and healthy as a vine-stock, long survived him. It is only a few years ago, that after a short illness his friends laid him to rest in the little cemetery of Bois-le-Roi—a cemetery only separated by a simple hedge from the neighbouring fields—a true poet's resting-place, where he sleeps beneath roses in the shadow of the oak-trees.

The evening on which I first saw Gustave Mathieu, there sat near him a great spare red-headed fellow with the braggart airs of a corsair, who imitated his voice and copied his movements; this was Fernand Desnoyers, an original, who wrote *Bras-Noir*, a pantomime in verse! On the other side of the table some one was arguing with Dupont; it was Reyer, who, nervous and excitable, jotted down the airs which occurred with so much facility to the poet—Reyer, the future author of *la Statue*, of *Sigurd*, and many other fine works.

What memories rise before me at the mere sound of the name of the Brasserie! How many faces did I there behold for the first time amidst the reflections and gleams of the beer-glasses and the canopy of thick smoke!

Let us choose at hazard among the numbers of the departed and the lesser band which yet survives. Here is Monselet, delicate prose writer, yet more dainty poet, smiling, curled, plump. M. Cupid might be taken for a gallant abbé of the olden time; one looks at his back for the short mantle fluttering like a pair of wings. Champfleury, then leader of a school, father of realism, and confounding in one and the same passion the music of Wagner, old pottery, and pantomime. Pottery, in the end, won the day, and Champfleury, transported to the height of his ambition, is now curator of the ceramic museum at Sèvres.

Here too is Castagnary in double-breasted waistcoat, *à la Robespierre*, cut out of the velvet of some old arm-chair. Chief clerk in a lawyer's office he used to escape from his work to come and recite the *Châtiments* of Victor Hugo, with all their delightful flavour of forbidden fruit. He is surrounded, applauded; but he rushes away in search of Courbet, he must see Courbet, he wishes to consult with Courbet upon his *Philosophy of Art exemplified in the* Salon *of* 1857. Without altogether neglecting art, and while still contributing with lively pen more than one remarkable page to our annual Salon, the shrewd native of Saintonge, always smiling a mocking smile beneath his long drooping moustache, has little by little become absorbed in politics. He was first a municipal councillor, then editor of the *Siècle,* now a member of the Council of State, and no longer recites verses nor wears a red velvet waistcoat.

Here also is Charles Baudelaire, tormented in art by a thirst for the undiscoverable, in philosophy by the alluring terror of the unknown. Victor Hugo said of him that he had invented a perfectly new shudder; and indeed by no one has the heart of humanity been so well persuaded to speak aloud its secrets; no one has searched more deeply for those flowers of evil, startling and strange as tropical blossoms, with poison lurking in their very core, which lie in the mysterious depths of the human soul. Patient and delicate artist, weighing carefully the turn of every phase, the choice of every word, Baudelaire, by a cruel irony of fate, died paralyzed, his intelligence remaining intact, as the mute complaint of his black eye sorrowfully testified, but incapable of expressing his thoughts save by a confusedly murmured oath mechanically repeated. Correct and

cold, of paradoxical politeness, his wit as keen as English steel, he astonished the frequenters of the Brasserie by drinking foreign liqueurs in company with Constantin Guys the designer, or Malassis the publisher.

This last was a publisher of a kind unknown nowadays. Witty and well-read in curious by-ways of literature, he squandered royally a fine provincial fortune in publishing the writings of men who pleased his fancy. He too is dead; died smiling, with scanty fortune left, but without a complaint. And it is not without emotion that I recall that pale mocking face, lengthened by the points of a red beard—a Mephistopheles of the time of the Valois.

Alphonse Duchesne and Delvau appear also in a corner of the tavern—two more who have joined the majority. It was a singular fate which pursued this generation, so early laid low, not one having passed the age of forty! Delvau, a Parisian, connoisseur of his Paris, admiring its beauties, loving its defects, offspring of Mercier and of Rétif de la Bretonne, whose choice little volumes, full of small insignificant facts and picturesque observations, have become the delight of the literary epicure and the joy of the bibliophile. Alphonse Duchesne still hot over his great quarrel with Francisque Sarcey, who, opposing the standard of the Normal School to that of the Bohemians, had just launched forth into literature with a warlike article entitled *Les Mélancoliques de Brasserie* (the melanc nly haunters of the tavern).

It was at the Brasserie that Alphonse Duchesne and Delvau wrote those "Junius' Letters" which were brought every week to the *Figaro* by a mysterious messenger, and which convulsed the whole of Paris. Villemessant swore by that mysterious Junius. He was clearly a great personage—everything pointed to it—the style of the letters, their curt yet well-bred tone, a faint perfume of nobility and the old faubourg clinging tenderly to them. What then was his rage when the mask was dropped, and he learned that these aristocratic pages were written day by day by two needy Bohemians at a beer-shop table! Poor Delvau! poor Duchesne! Villemessant never forgave them.

I leave out many, for it would take a whole volume to describe the frequenters of the Brasserie table by table. Here is the table of the thinkers; they say nothing, neither do they write; they only think. They are admired on the faith of their own word; it is said they are deep as a well. It is possible to believe this when one watches them filling themselves with beer. Bald heads, flowing beards, with an odour of strong tobacco, cabbage soup, and philosophy.

A little further on are pilot coats, Spanish birettas, cries of animals, rough jokes, puns, in a glorious confusion; there crowded together are artists, sculptors, painters. In the midst of all this appears a refined and gentle head —that of Alexandre Leclerc—whose fantastic frescoes, destroyed by the Prussians, once adorned the walls of the Moulin-de-Pierre inn at Châtillon. One day the poor fellow was discovered hanged; he had strangled himself sitting down, and pulling the rope tight, among a crowd of tombstones at the top of the cemetery of Père-Lachaise, just at the spot where Balzac

points out the immensity of Paris to Rastignac. In my recollections of the Brasserie, Alexandre Leclerc always appears in the best of spirits, singing songs of Picardy; and these rural airs, airs of his native province, seemed to spread around his table in the tobacco-laden atmosphere, a penetrating and poetical aroma of cornfields and green plains.

I had nearly forgotten the women, for there were women too; former models, fine creatures, but somewhat faded in appearance. Queer physiognomies and strange names, nicknames that spoke of low haunts and aristocratic affectations: *Titine de Barancy* and *Louise Coup-de-Couteau*. Curious specimens of a singular refinement, having passed from hand to hand, and caught from their thousand and one *liaisons* a veneer of artistic erudition. They express their opinions on every subject, and according to the lover of the moment, declare themselves materialists or idealists, catholics or atheists. Touching, and at the same time somewhat ridiculous.

Amongst them were a few new recruits, quite young, admitted by the dreaded areopagus; but the majority were composed of those who had grown old in the service, thereby acquiring a kind of undisputed authority. Then there were the pseudo-widows of well-known authors and artists, who were busily engaged in educating some raw provincial fellow just arrived from his province. All these people were rolling and smoking cigarettes, sending up their little spiral clouds of thin blue smoke amongst the thick gray fog of the pipes and breaths.

The beer flows, the waiters rush

about, the discussions become more animated, and in the midst of the shouting and upraised arms, the tossing of many shaggy and mane-like locks, Desroches screaming louder, gesticulating more violently than any, stands on a table, looking as if he were swimming over an ocean of heads, leading and dominating with his clown's voice, the noisy uproar of the thronged room. He looks well thus, with an inspired air, his shirt unbuttoned, his cravat floating half untied, true descendant of Rameau's nephew.

Every night he comes there to forget his worries, to intoxicate himself with words and beer, to secure collaborators, to relate his literary projects, to lie to himself, and to forget that his home has become unbearable, that he is incapable of settling to any work, that it would even be impossible for him to re-write the *Raisins muscats*. No doubt amongst the medley at the tavern there were some noble minds, some serious thinkers, and at times a fine verse or an eloquent paradox would lighten the atmosphere, like a current of fresh, pure air, dispelling the smoke of the pipes. But with the exception of a few men of talent, were not most of them Desroches! For a few moments of fine inspiration how many dull and wasted hours!

Then also what a sad feeling the next day. What cruel awakenings! what sickening discouragement! What disgust for such a life, without having courage enough to change it. Look at Desroches; he no longer laughs; his grin subsides. He is thinking of his children, who are growing up; of his wife, who is ageing and sinking lower and lower, with her whip, her cap her smock, her carter's costume, thought so original the first time it was worn for a masqued ball, and now become so repulsive.

When his fits of depression were upon him, Desroches used to disappear and go off into the provinces, dragging his strange family after him.

Now selling watches; then actor at Odessa, bailiff at Brussels; or companion of a mountebank. What extraordinary callings had he not tried? But he soon returned, tired and disgusted even with that.

One day, in the Bois de Boulogne, he tried to hang himself, but the keepers found him and took him down. He was even chaffed about it at the *brasserie,* and himself spoke of his adventure with a little forced laugh. Shortly after, determined to put an end to his life, he threw himself into one of those terrible quarries—an abyss of chalk and clay—which abound round the Paris fortifications. There he lay all night, his ribs crushed, his wrists and thighs broken. He was still alive when he was taken out.

"Ah, well!" he said, "they will call me the man who always misses his mark."

These were his last words. After an agony which lasted sixty days, he died. I shall never forget him.

The Girl from Arles

On the way to the village, one passes before a *mas* built close to the road, at the bottom of a great courtyard planted with nettle-trees. It is a true dwelling of the Provençal farmer, with its red tiles, its broad brown façade with irregular windows, and high above, the weathercock of the hayloft, the pulley for hoisting grain, and a few bunches of brown hay protruding.

Why had this house struck me? Why did this closed gate cause my heart to beat? I could not have told, and yet this house gave me a chill. There was too much silence about it. When one passed, the dogs did not bark, the Guinea fowl ran away without screaming. Within, not a voice,—nothing, not even a mule's bell. Had it not been for the white curtains at the windows and the smoke rising above the roofs, one would have thought the place uninhabited.

Yesterday, on the stroke of noon, I was coming back from the village, and, in order to avoid the sun, I was walking close to the walls of the farm, in the shade of the nettle-trees. On the road, before the *mas*, silent labourers were loading a cart with hay. The gate had remained open. I cast a glance as I passed, and saw, at the end of the courtyard, with his elbows on a large stone table, and his head in his hands, a tall old man with white hair, wearing a waistcoat too short for him. and trousers in rags. I stopped. One of the men said to me in a low voice,—

"Hush! It is the master. He has always been like that since his son's misfortune."

At that moment a woman and a little boy, clad in black, passed near us, carrying large gilded prayer-books, and went into the farm.

The man added:—

"The mistress and Cadet coming back from Mass. They go there every day, since the child killed himself. Ah, sir, what desolation! The father still wears the dead boy's clothes; they cannot make him leave them off. *Dia! hue!* get up!"

The cart shook as it was about to start. I who wished to know more about the matter, asked leave of the driver to mount beside him; and it was up there, in the hay, that I learned all this heart-rending story.

His name was Jan. He was an admirable peasant, twenty years old, as virtuous as a young girl, strongly built, and with an open face. As he was very handsome, the women looked at him; but he had but one in his mind,—a little Arlésienne, dressed all in velvet and lace, whom he had once met on the Lice at Arles. At the farm they did not at first look upon this intimacy with pleasure. The girl was said to be a coquette, and her parents did not belong to the neighbourhood. But Jan wanted his Arlésienne at any cost. He said,—

"I shall die if they do not give her to me."

They had to yield. It was decided that they should be married after the harvest.

Well. one Sunday morning the family was finishing dinner in the courtyard of the farm. It was almost a wedding-feast. The betrothed was not there, but they had drunk her health throughout the meal. A man appeared at the gate, and in a trembling voice asked to speak to Master Stephen, to him alone. Stephen rose, and went out upon the road.

"Master," said the man, "you are about to marry your child to a vile jade who has been my mistress for two years. I can prove what I assert; here are the letters. Her parents know everything, and had promised her to me; but now that your son wants her, neither they nor the girl will have anything more to do with me. Yet I should have thought that after this she could not be the wife of another."

"Very good!" said Master Stephen, when he had looked at the letters; "come in and drink a glass of Muscat."

The man replied: "Thank you! I am more unhappy than thirsty."

And he went away.

The father walked in, impassible; he resumed his place at the table, and the meal was finished gayly.

That evening Master Stephen and his son went off together into the fields. They remained out a long while; when they returned, the mother was still waiting for them.

"Wife," said the farmer, leading his son to her, "kiss him! He is unhappy."

Jan spoke no more of the Arlésienne. He still loved her, however, and more than ever since she had been shown to him in the arms of another. Only, he was too proud to say anything; it was that which killed him, poor child! Sometimes he would spend whole days alone in a corner without moving. On other days he would attack the ground with fury, and accomplish by himself the work of ten day-labourers. When evening came, he would take the road to Arles, and walk until he saw rising before him in the sunset the slender belfries of the town. Then he would return. He never went farther.

Seeing him thus, always sad and alone, the people at the *mas* did not know what to do. They dreaded a misfortune. Once, at table, his mother said as she looked at him with eyes full of tears,—

"Well, listen to me, Jan; if you wish her in spite of everything, we will give her to you."

The father, scarlet with shame, hung his head.

Jan made a gesture of refusal and went out.

From that day he changed his manner of life, always pretending to be gay in order to reassure his parents. He was seen again at balls, at the tavern, and at the *ferrades*. It was he who led the farandole at the fête at Fonvieille.

His father said, "He is cured." His mother was still afraid, and watched her child more than ever. Jan slept with Cadet, close to the silkworm nursery; the poor old woman had a bed placed for herself next to their room. The silkworms might need her in the night.

Then came the fête of Saint Eloi, patron saint of farmers.

There was great joy at the *mas*. There was Château-Neuf for everybody, and mulled wine as though it rained it. Then there were fireworks and firecrackers, and the nettle-trees were full of coloured lanterns. *Vive Saint Eloi!* They danced the farandole till they were nearly dead. Cadet burned his new blouse. Jan himself appeared pleased; he insisted on dancing with his mother, and the poor woman cried for happiness.

At midnight they went to bed. Everybody needed sleep. But Jan did not sleep. Cadet told afterward how he sobbed all night. Ah! he was badly bitten, I tell you!

The next morning at dawn the mother heard some one run through her room. She had something like a presentiment.

"Jan, is it you?"

Jan did not reply; he was already on the stairs.

The mother rose quickly, so quickly—

"Jan, where are you going?"

He went up into the garret; she went after him:—

"My son, in the name of Heaven!"

He closed the door and bolted it.

"Jan, my Janet, what are you going to do?"

With her old, trembling hands she felt for the latch. A window opening, the sound of a body falling upon the pavement of the courtyard, and that was all.

The poor child had said to himself: "I love her too much. I will go." Ah, the miserable hearts that we have! Yet it is a little hard that contempt cannot kill love!

That morning the people in the village wondered who could be screaming so down there in the direction of Stephen's *mas*.

It was the mother, all naked, in the courtyard, before the stone table, covered with dew and with blood,—the mother, lamenting, with her dead child in her arms.

Come, Parisians!

ONE morning in the month of October, a few days before leaving Paris, there came into my room while I was breakfasting an old man in a threadbare coat, dirty, knock-kneed, bent, shaking on his long legs like a plucked crane. It was Bixiou. Yes, Parisians, your Bixiou, the savage and charming Bixiou, that mad mocker who has so delighted you these fifteen years with his pamphlets and his caricatures. Ah, poor fellow, what wretchedness! But for a grimace which he made as he came in, I should never have known him.

With his head on his shoulder and his cane between his teeth like a clarinet, the illustrious but bitter jester advanced to the middle of the room, and ran against my table as he said in a whining voice,—

"Pity a poor blind man!"

It was so well imitated that I could not help laughing. But he said very coldly,—

"You think that I am joking; look at my eyes!"

And he turned toward me two great white sightless eyeballs.

"I am blind, my dear fellow, blind for life. That is what comes of writing with vitriol. I have burned up my eyes at this pretty trade; yes, down to the very *bobèches!*" he added, pointing to his charred eyelids, upon which there did not remain the ghost of a lash.

I was so much moved that I could think of nothing to say to him. My silence made him uneasy.

"Are you at work?"

"No, Bixiou, I am breakfasting. Will you join me?"

He did not reply, but by the quivering of his nostrils 1 saw that he was dying to accept. I took him by the hand, and made him sit down beside me. While they were serving him, the poor devil sniffed the table with a quiet laugh.

"How good it all smells! I shall have a feast; it is so long since I have breakfasted! A sou's worth of bread every morning, as I go about the ministries,—for, you know, I haunt the ministries now; it is my only profession. I am trying to obtain a government tobacco-shop. What can I do? The people at home must eat. I can no longer draw or write. Dictate? What? I have nothing in my head; I invent nothing. My trade was to see the grimaces of Paris and to depict them. I can no longer do it. Then I thought of the tobacco-shop; not on the boulevards, of course. I have no right to such a favour, being neither the mother of a ballet-dancer nor the widow of an officer of high rank. No! only a little shop in the provinces, somewhere very far away, in a corner of the Vosges. I will have a big porcelain pipe; I will call myself Hans or Zébédé, as in Erckmann-Chatrian, and I will console myself for no longer writing by making packages of tobacco with the works of my contemporaries.

"That is all that I ask. Not much, is it? Well, it is the devil's own work to get it. And yet I ought not to lack protection. I used to be very popular. I dined with the marshal, the prince, the ministers; they all wished to have me because I amused them or because they were afraid of me. Now I no longer frighten anybody. Oh, my eyes, my poor eyes! And they do not invite me anywhere. The face of a blind man at table is so sad.—Give me the bread, please.—Ah, the villains! they will have made me pay dear for this wretched tobacco-shop! For six months I have been going from ministry to ministry with my petition. I arrive in the morning at the hour when they are lighting the stoves and exercising his Excellency's horses in the courtyard; I do not go away till night, when they are bringing the big lamps, and the kitchens are beginning to smell good.

"My whole life is passed upon the wooden benches in the antechambers. How well the ushers know me! At the Interior, they call me 'that good gentleman.' And I, to gain their protection, make puns, or draw with a stroke or two on the corner of their blotters big mustaches which made them laugh. That is what I have come to after twenty years of wild success; that is the end of an artist's life! And to think that there are in France forty thousand hobbledehoys whose mouths water at the idea of our profession! To think that there are every day, in the departments, locomotives getting up steam to bring us carloads of imbeciles who hunger for literature and printers' ink! Ah! romantic provinces, if Bixiou's misery could only serve you as a lesson!"

With that he turned to his plate, and began to eat ravenously, without saying a word. It was pitiful to see him. At every turn he would lose his bread or his fork, and would feel about to find his glass. Poor man! he was not yet accustomed to it.

After a moment he resumed:—

"Do you know what is the most horrible thing for me? It is to be unable to read my newspapers. One has to belong to the trade in order to comprehend that. Sometimes on my way home in the evening, I buy one only to smell that odour of damp paper and fresh news. It is so good! but there is nobody to read them to me. My wife might, but she will not; she says that among the paragraphs there are things which are not proper. Ah! these old mistresses, once married there are no such prudes as they. Since I made one Madame Bixiou, she has been obliged to be a bigot, and an extreme one at that. She actually wanted me to rub my eyes with holy water. And then her sacrament, her charity collections, her worship of the Infant Jesus, her little heathen, and I know not what else. We are in good works up to our necks. All the same it would be a good work to read the papers to me. If my daughter were at home, she would read them to me; but since I have become blind I have gotten her into Notre-Dames-des-Arts, in order to have one mouth the less to feed.

"And she is another one who has led me a pretty life. She has not been in the world nine years, and she has already had every possible disease. And melancholy! And ugly! Uglier than I, if possible,—a monster! But how could I help it? I have never been able to make anything but caricatures. But come! I am kind to be entertaining you with my family affairs. What can you care about them? There, give me a little more of that brandy, I must get up my spirits. When I leave here, I am going to the Public Instruction, and the ushers there are not easy to put in a good humour. They were all professors once."

I poured him out his brandy. He began to sip it with a softened expression. Suddenly, I know not what fancy moving him, he rose, glass in hand, turned his head two or three times—the head of a blind viper—with the amiable smile of a gentleman who is about to speak, and then cried in a strident voice, as if to harangue a banquet of two hundred guests,—

"To the arts, to letters, to the press!"

And off he set on a toast ten minutes long, the wildest and the most marvellous improvisation which ever came from this mountebank brain.

Fancy a New Year's Review entitled "The Highway of Letters in 186–:" our so-called literary assemblages, our pamphleteering, our quarrels, all the absurdities of an eccentric society, a dungheap of ink, a hell without grandeur, where they throttle and stab and rob one another, where the talk is of personal interests and sordid gains far more than among the bourgeois, which does not prevent them from dying of hunger more than elsewhere; all our basenesses, all our meannesses; the old Baron T—— of the Tombola going about the Tuileries saying, "Gna—gna—gna—" with his wooden bowl and his blue coat; then our deaths for the year, the advertising burials, the delegate's funeral oration, always the same: "Dear and regretted, —poor fellow!" about a man for whose tomb he refuses to subscribe; and those who committed suicide, and those who have become mad,—fancy all that, narrated, detailed, acted by a mimic of genius, and then you will have an idea of what Bixiou's improvisation was.

When he had finished his toast and drunk off his glass, he asked me the time, and went away with a savage air, without bidding me good-by. I do not know how M. Duruy's ushers enjoyed his visit that morning, but I know that I never felt so sad or so little in the humour for work as after the departure of this terrible blind man. My inkstand made me sick, I loathed my pen. I should have liked to go far away, to move about, to see the trees, to smell something fragrant. Good heavens! what hatred, what bile, what a desire to spit on and sully everything! Ah, the wretch!

And I walked up and down my room furiously, still fancying that I heard the sneer of disgust with which he spoke to me of his daughter.

Suddenly I felt something move beneath my foot, beside the chair in which the blind man had been sitting. As I stooped down I recognized his pocket-book,—a large, shining pocket-book, with broken corners, which never leaves him, and which he calls, laughing, his venom-pouch. This pouch was as famous among us as M. de Girardin's scrap-books. It was said that there were terrible things in it. It was a capital occasion to inform myself. The old pocket-book had been stuffed too full, and had burst when it fell; all the papers were on the carpet, and I had to pick them up one by one.

A bundle of letters written on flowered paper, all beginning "My dear Papa," and signed "Céline Bixiou, of the children of Mary."

Old prescriptions for children's diseases,—croup, convulsions, scarlatina, measles (the poor child had not missed one of them).

Finally, a large sealed envelope, from which escaped, as from a little girl's bonnet, two or three curly yellow hairs, and on the envelope, in a large trembling hand, the hand of a blind man:

"Céline's hair, cut May 13th, the day she entered school."

That was what was in Bixiou's pocket-book.

Come, Parisians, you are all the same Disgust, irony, diabolical laughter, ferocious jests, and then, to end with,—

"Céline's hair, cut May 13th."

The Pale Duke

AFTER dinner the worthy natives of the Cevennes insisted upon showing me their club. It was the usual club of a little country town, four rooms in a line, on the first floor of an old house which overlooked the parade, with great tarnished mirrors, tiled floors without carpets, and here and there, upon the mantel-pieces,—where the Paris papers, dated the day before yesterday were strewn about,—were bronze lamps, the only lamps in the town which were not blown out as nine o'clock struck.

When I arrived, there were as yet, very few people present. Some old fogies were snoring with their noses buried in their papers, or playing whist in solemn silence; and beneath the green-tinted light of the lamp-shades, these bald heads nodding towards each other and the counters heaped in the little plush basket, all alike, had the even, yellow, polished tone of old ivory. Outside on the parade was heard the evening bugle, and the footsteps of pedestrians turning homewards. dispersing along the sloping streets and many steps connecting the different inclines of this mountain town. After a few last knocks inflicted upon the doors, and re-echoing through the perfect silence, the youth of the town, freed from the family meals and evening walk, sprang noisily up the stairs of the club. I beheld an invasion of some twenty solidly built mountaineers, in new gloves, vast shirt fronts, open collars and some faint attempts at hair-curling à la Russe, which made them all look like great over-coloured dolls. You could imagine nothing more ludicrous. It seemed to me that I was assisting at a purely Parisian piece by Meilhac, or Dumas fils, played by amateurs from Tarascon, or from even some still more remote spot. All the soft speech, the ennui, the used-up, tired-out airs which are the height of good form among the Parisian mashers, I found before me, two hundred miles away from Paris, and exaggerated still more by the awkwardness of the actors. It was worth while to see these lusty fellows greeting each other with a languid: "How are you, old man?" sink down on the divans in attitudes of the utmost dejection, stretch themselves in front of the mirrors, and say with the strong accent of the country: "Life's a swindle! Everything's a bore." It was touching to hear them call their club the *clob*, which word, as good meridionals, they pronounced *clab*. One heard nothing else—"The *clab* waiter, the *clab* rules."

I was in the act of asking myself how all these Parisian absurdities could have got there, and have taken root in the keen and healthy mountain air, when there appeared before me the pretty little pale and curled head of the young Duke de M——, member of the Jockey Club, the Rowing Club, the Delamarre stable, and of several other learned societies. This young gentleman, whose extravagances have made him famous on the boulevard, had just managed to get through the last million but one of the paternal fortune, and his guardians, seriously alarmed, had sent him to rusticate in this forgotten corner of the Cevennes. I understood at once all the languishing airs of these provincial youths, the display of shirt fronts, the pretentious pronunciation: the model was before my eyes.

Scarcely had he entered the room, than the member of the Jockey Club was surrounded and made much of. His witticisms were repeated, his gestures and attitudes were copied, so much so that this pale shadow of a dandy, fagged, unhealthy, yet distinguished looking in spite of all, seemed to be reflected in every direction, in coarse countrified mirrors which grossly exaggerated his features. That evening, no doubt in my honour, the Duke talked a great deal of literature, and of the theatre. But, good heavens, with what contempt! what ignorance! It was enough to hear him call Emile Augier "that gentleman," and Dumas fils "little Dumas." The vaguest ideas about everything floated amongst unfinished phrases, wherein *what's his name, and what d' you call 'em* stood in place of words he could not find, and held the same position as those lines of dots so much in favour with dramatic authors, who do not know how to write. In short, this young gentleman had never given himself the trouble of thinking; but he had mixed much in the world, and from the wild circle of his acquaintance had carried away an expression here, a judgment there, superficially preserved and forming a part of himself, as much as the curls that shaded his delicate forehead. What, however, he did most thoroughly understand, was heraldry, liveries, light women and race-horses; and on these points, the young provincials whose education he had undertaken, were becoming almost as learned as himself.

The evening wore heavily away amid the prattlings of this melancholy stable man. Towards ten o'clock, the old men having left, and the whist tables being deserted, the younger men seated themselves for a little *baccarat*. It had become the correct thing since the Duke had been among them. I had taken up a position in the shade, on a corner of the divan, and from thence I had a good view of all the players, under the shaded and concentrated light of the lamps. The member of the Jockey Club was enthroned in the centre of the group around the table, superbly indifferent, holding his cards with perfect grace and caring little whether he won or lost. This Parisian with pockets cleared out was yet the wealthiest of the party. But they, poor fledgelings, what an effort of courage it cost them to affect impassibility! As the excitement of the game increased, I followed with curiosity the expressions of the various faces. I saw lips tremble, eyes fill with tears, fingers close with feverish agitation upon the cards. To conceal their emotion, the losers uttered an occasional ejaculation amid their bad luck, "I've lost my head, I'm dreadfully bored;" but uttered in the terrible meridional accent, always so emphatic and so hard, these Parisian exclamations had no longer the air of

aristocratic indifference which they wore on the lips of the little Duke.

Among the players was one in particular who interested me. He was a tall youth, very young, who had grown too quickly, the big good-natured face of a bearded child, simple, unpolished and primitive, notwithstanding all his *Demidoff* curls, and on whose open countenance every passing impression was easy to read. This lad lost continually. Two or three times I had noticed him rise from the table and leave the room quickly; then after a few minutes, he would return to his place, red and perspiring, and I said to myself: "You have been to your mother, or sisters with some pitiful tale, to get money from them." The fact is, that each time, the poor devil returned with full pockets, and resumed play with redoubled fury. But luck was persistently against him. He lost, he lost incessantly. I felt him to be trembling, every nerve tingling, no longer having even the power to put a good face upon misfortune. As each card fell, he dug his nails into the woollen cloth: it was heart-rending.

Gradually hypnotised, however, by the atmosphere of provincial ennui and idleness, very tired too by my journey, I only beheld the card-table as a very faint and vague luminous vision, and I ended by falling asleep to the murmur of voices and shuffled cards. I was awakened suddenly by a noise of angry words, sounding loud in the empty rooms. Everyone was gone. There remained only the member of the Jockey Club and the great boy in whom I had been interested, both seated at the table and playing. The game was serious, *écarté* at ten louis (eight pounds), **and** it was enough to see the despair depicted on the great good-natured bull-dog face, to understand that the mountaineer was still losing.

"My revenge," he cried with rage, from time to time. The other held his own; and at each fresh stroke of luck, it seemed to me that an evil smile, disdainful and almost imperceptible, curled his aristocratic lip. I heard him announce "the conqueror!" then there was a violent blow of the fist upon the table; it was all over, the unfortunate wretch had lost everything.

He remained for a moment stunned, looking at his cards without a word, his frockcoat hunched up, his shirt front rumpled and damp as if he had been fighting. Then, all at once, seeing the Duke picking up the gold pieces scattered on the cloth, he rose with a terrible cry: "My money! Good God! Give me back my money!" and then like the child he still was, he began to sob: "Give it back to me, give it back to me!" Ah! I can assure you he lisped no longer, his natural voice had returned to him; affecting as that of all strong beings to whom tears come rarely and are a true suffering. Still cold, still ironical his adversary watched him without moving a muscle. Then the poor fellow went down upon his knees, and said quite low, in a voice that trembled: "That money was not mine. I stole it. My father left it with me to meet a bill." Suffocated by shame, he could say no more.

At the first mention of stolen money, the Duke had risen. A faint animation glowed in his cheeks. The head assumed an expression of pride which became him well. He emptied his pockets on the table, and himself dropping for a moment his dandy's mask he said, in a kind and natural voice: "Take it back, you idiot. Did you suppose we were playing seriously?"

I could have hugged that true gentleman!

The Siege of Berlin

WE ascended the Avenue des Champs Elysées with Doctor V——, reading, upon those walls pierced with shells and sidewalks dug up with grapeshot, the story of the Siege of Paris. Just before we reached the Rondpoint de l'Etoile, the Doctor paused, and pointing out to me one of those great corner-houses which face the Arc de Triomphe with such a pompous air, he said,——

"Do you see those four closed windows up there over the balcony? In the early part of the month of August of last year, that awful month full of storm and disaster, I was summoned to that apartment to attend a severe case of apoplexy. My patient was Colonel Jouve, an old cuirassier of the First Empire. Love of country was his ruling passion, and his mistress was Glory. At the beginning of the war he had taken up quarters in the Champs Elysées in that apartment with the balcony. Do you guess why? That he might witness the triumphal re-entry of our troops. Poor old man! The news of Wissembourg reached his ears just as he was rising from table. He saw the name of Napoleon at the end of that bulletin of defeat, and the sudden shock prostrated him.

"When I reached the old cuirassier, he was stretched at full length upon the carpet of his room. His face gave no signs of life, but it was bleeding as if he had received a tremendous blow upon the head. Standing, he must have presented an imposing figure. As he lay there, he looked like a giant. His features were so noble, his silvery locks curled so thickly, he had such splendid teeth, that this octogenarian looked scarcely more than sixty years of age. Near him knelt his granddaughter in tears. She resembled him strongly. The sight of both together suggested two beautiful Greek medals struck from the same impression; but one was old and dull, its outlines somewhat worn, while the other was bright and clear-cut, having all the smoothness and brilliancy of a first impression.

"The child's grief touched me. Her grandfather had been a soldier. Her father, too, was a soldier, an officer of MacMahon's staff; and at sight of this stately old hero prostrate, my imagination pictured a scene not less terrible. I did my best to reassure her, but at heart I felt no hope. We had to deal with a severe case of hemiplegia, and at eighty recovery is extremely doubtful. And, in fact, for three days the sick man never rallied from the stupour in which I had found him. Meanwhile news of the battle of Reichshoffen had just reached Paris. You will remember how strangely we were deceived. Until evening we all believed a great victory had been gained, twenty thousand Prussians

slain, the prince royal a prisoner. Through some agency scarcely less than miraculous, some echo of the nation's joy must have reached the patient, deaf and dumb though he was, some magnetic current must have penetrated even that paralyzed frame, for that evening, when I approached his bedside, I saw that he was a new man. His eye was clear almost, his tongue no longer thick. He was able to smile, and twice he stammered 'Vic-to-ry!'

" 'Yes, colonel, a great victory!'

"And as I acquainted him with the details of MacMahon's glorious success, his features relaxed, his face brightened.

"As I was about to leave the apartment, I found the young girl waiting for me. She was weeping. 'But he is out of danger!' I said, taking her hands in mine.

"The unhappy child scarcely ventured a reply. The bulletins had just announced the true story of Reichshoffen. MacMahon was retreating, the army cut to pieces. Our eyes could not conceal the consternation both felt. The child was heartbroken. She was thinking of her father. But I trembled at thought of the old man. Surely he could not survive this fresh shock. But what should we do? Leave him to enjoy that happiness, those illusions which had breathed new life into him? But in that case we must feed him upon lies. 'Very well, I will lie to him!' said the young heroine, quickly drying her eyes, and her face was wreathed in smiles when she returned to her grandfather's chamber.

"She had undertaken no light task. During the first days it was not so difficult a matter, for the good man's head was very weak, and he was as easily deceived as a child. But as health returned, his ideas grew clearer. It was necessary to keep him informed of the movement of the various armies, and to manufacture military bulletins for him. And it was truly pitiable to see that lovely child buried night and day in a map of Germany, pinning tiny flags upon it, endeavouring to invent the details of a glorious campaign. Bazaine had advanced upon Berlin, Froissart was in Bavaria, MacMahon on the Baltic! Sometimes she consulted me, and I aided her as far as I could, but in carrying out this imaginary invasion no one rendered us greater assistance than the grandfather himself. He had conquered Germany so many times during the First Empire! He knew every move in advance. 'This is where they will go next!' 'This will be their next move,' he would say; and his anticipations never failing to prove themselves correct, he took not a little pride in them.

"But, alas! to no avail did we take cities, win battles. We did not move rapidly enough to suit him. That old man was simply insatiable. Every day I visited him I heard news of some fresh exploit.

"'Doctor, we have taken Mayence,' said the young girl, advancing towards me with a heartrending smile, and through the door I heard a joyous voice exclaiming, 'We move! we move! in a week more we shall enter Berlin.'

"As a matter of fact, the Prussians would reach Paris in another week. We asked ourselves at first whether it would not be better to remove our patient from the city, but, once outside of Paris, the condition of France would have told him all; moreover, he was too weak, too much benumbed from the effect of the first shock, to learn the truth then. It was decided to remain.

"The first day of the investment of the city, I climbed up to my patient's apartment. Well I remember that day! My heart was heavy, full of anguish. For the gates of Paris were closed the enemy under her very walls, and even her outskirts converted into frontiers I found the ingenuous old man sitting up in bed, proud and jubilant.

"'Well,' he said, 'at last the *siege* has begun!'

"I looked at him; I was stunned. 'Why, colonel,' I asked, 'how do you know that?'

"His grand-daughter glanced in my direction.

"'Oh, yes, doctor; this is great news! The siege of Berlin has begun.'

"And as she spoke, she plied her needle with a little affectation of composure. How should he suspect anything? Though the cannons were firing from the forts, he could not hear them. And although unhappy Paris was turned upside down, and filled with gloom and forebodings, he saw nothing of it all. But where he lay, he could get a glimpse of the Arc de Triomphe, and his chamber was filled with bric-à-brac of the First Empire, admirably fitted to nourish his illusions. Portraits of marshals were there, engravings of battles; there was a picture of the *King of Rome* in baby robes. There were tall, stiff consoles ornamented with trophied brass, and loaded with imperial relics, medallions, bronzes; there was a bit of the rock of St. Helena under a glass globe; there were numerous miniatures always representing the same lady, in ballroom costume, in a yellow robe with leg-of-mutton sleeves, a pair of bright eyes glancing from beneath her carefully curled locks.

"All these ornaments, the King of Rome, the marshals, the yellow ladies, those short-waisted, high-girdled figures whose stiff and artificial lines were considered the very embodiment of grace in 1806—gallant colonel!—it was such things as those, it was that atmosphere of victory and conquest, which, far more than any words of ours, made him accept the story of the siege of Berlin with such childlike simplicity.

"From that day, our military operations were far less complex. To take Berlin was simply a question of patience. From time to time, when the old man grew weary of waiting, we would read him a letter from his son; of course, an imaginary letter, for Paris was cut off from the outer world then, and, besides, since the battle of Sedan, MacMahon's aide-de-camp was confined in a German fortress. You may imagine that poor child's despair, living from day to day with no news of her father, but knowing that he was a prisoner, deprived of everything, sick, perhaps,—imagine her agony knowing all this, but compelled to speak for him, to invent such joyous epistles in his behalf, a trifle brief, perhaps, but the brevity of a soldier in the field, who answers his country's cry, 'Forward!' and sees her arms everywhere victorious. Sometimes she had not the heart for these letters. and then weeks passed without news. But the old man would grow restless and could not sleep. Then a letter would at once

arrive from Germany, and she would read it gayly at his bedside, repressing her tears. The colonel always listened religiously, with a very wise air; he approved, criticized, explained to us here and there a passage which seemed slightly obscure. But his finest efforts were replies he sent his son. 'Never forget that you are a Frenchman,' he would say. 'Be generous to these poor people. Invade their country, but not as an oppressor.' Then followed suggestions without end, delightful twaddle concerning a right observance of propriety, and what constituted courtesy towards women,—in short, a whole military code for the guidance of these *conquerors;* he added some reflections upon politics in general, and outlined the conditions of peace which must be imposed upon the vanquished. I must add that, as regards the last subject, his demands were not severe.

"'A war indemnity, only that; what good would it do to seize their provinces? A France could never be made out of Germany!'

"He dictated these words with a steady voice, with such candour, and such noble faith in his country, that it was impossible to listen to him unmoved.

"And all the while the siege was progressing, not, alas! that of Berlin. There were days of severe cold, of bombardment, of epidemics and famine. But, thanks to our cares, our efforts, and all those proofs of indefatigable tenderness which were multiplied about him, the old man never felt a moment's anxiety. To the very end I was able to obtain white bread and fresh meat for him. Of course, there was none for anyone else, and you can

not imagine anything more touching
than this grandfather's breakfasts, of
which he partook with such innocent
egotism, the old man sitting up in bed,
fresh and smiling, his napkin under his
chin, the grand-daughter ever at his
side, her pale face revealing the privation she had suffered; she guided his
hands, compelled him to drink, aided
him as he ate all the good things saved
specially for him.   Enlivened by his
repast, enjoying the comfort of his
warm chamber while the cold winter
wind blew without, and the snow
whirled about his windows, the aged
cuirassier would recall his campaigns in
the North and related to us for the
hundredth time the tale of that mournful retreat from Moscow, when there
was no other food than frozen biscuit
and horse-flesh.

"'Do you know what that means,
child? We ate horse-flesh!' I think
she understood perfectly. She had been
eating no other meat for two months.
From day to day, as convalescence approached, the patient began to make
our task a more difficult one.   That
lethargy of all his senses, of all his
limbs, had aided us up to this time,
but was beginning to leave him.   Several times those terrible volleys from
the Porte Maillot made him start suddenly, his ear as alert as a hound's:
we were obliged to invent a final victory for Bazaine before Berlin, and to
explain that the salutes in front of Les
Invalides were in honour of the event.
Another day, when we had pushed his
bed close to the window, I think it was
the Thursday the battle of Buzenval
occurred, he saw the National Guard
quite distinctly as it formed in front
of the Avenue de la Grande Armée.

"'What troops are those?' asked our
colonel, and we heard him mutter to
himself,——

"'Badly drilled! badly drilled!'

"Nothing came of this incident, but
we realized that it now behooved us to
take greater precautions than before.
Unfortunately we were not cautious
enough.

"One evening on my arrival, the child
came to me, her face full of anxiety.

"'Tomorrow they enter,' she said.

"Was the door of the grandfather's
room ajar? I do remember, and have
often thought in recalling that evening,
that his features wore an unusual expression. It is very likely that he had
heard what we were saying. But we
were speaking of the Prussians, and he
was thinking of the French army, and
of that triumphal entry he had been
expecting for many a day,—MacMahon
descending the avenue to martial music,
along a path strewn with flowers, his
son at the Marshal's side, and there
upon the balcony, the old warrior himself in full uniform, as upon the field
of Lutzen, saluting the flags that had
many a rent in them, and our eagles
blackened with powder.

"Poor Father Jouve!   Doubtless he
fancied we would not permit him to
assist at that entry of our troops, anxious to spare him the excitement of
so great an event. For he said nothing to anyone, but the following day,
just at the hour when the Prussians
advanced somewhat timidly upon the
long avenue leading from the Porte
Maillot to the Tuileries, an upper window opened softly, and the colonel
himself appeared upon the balcony,
wearing his helmet, his long cavalry
sword, and all the antiquated but glo-

rious toggery of an old cuirassier of Milhaud. I still ask myself what tremendous effort of his will, what sudden start of life, had put him on his feet again, and in all his war trappings. But one fact is certain. There he stood upon the balcony, amazed to find the avenue so wide and still, the blinds of the houses closed, and Paris itself as gloomy as a vast lazaretto, flags everywhere, but strangely enough, only white flags with red crosses, and no one to meet our soldiers.

"For a moment he must have believed he had made a mistake,—but, no! yonder behind the Arc de Triomphe, issued an indistinct rattle, a black line advanced steadily into the morning light. Then by degrees the tops of helmets could be seen flashing in the sunlight, and the drums of Jena began to beat. And then beneath the Arc de l'Etoile, accented by the rhythmic tramp of the regiments and the clashing of sabres, resounded the strains of Schubert's triumphal march.

"Then through the dismal silence of the place was heard an awful cry, 'To arms! to arms! the Prussians!' and the four uhlans of the advance-guard, looking towards the balcony above, could see the majestic figure of an old man reeling, his arms outstretched. He fell heavily. This time the shock had indeed proved fatal. Colonel Jouve was dead."

Advance Guard

WE were drinking tea the other evening, at the house of the *tabellion* of Nanterre. I take a certain delight in using the old word *tabellion,* because it is in keeping with the Pompadour style of the pretty village, where *rosières* flourish, and of the antiquated salon where we were seated round a fire of logs, blazing up brightly in a large chimney, decorated with *fleurs de lis.* . . . The master of the house was absent, but his good-natured, shrewd face, hanging in a corner of the room, presided over the festive scene, and peacefully smiled down from the depths of an oval frame, on the strange guests occupying his drawing-room.

A curious medley indeed, for an evening party at a notary's. Braided overcoats, beards eight days old, forage caps, hooded capes, and military boots; and all around, on the piano, on the little tables, pell-mell with the lace-covered cushions, the boxes of Spa wood, and the work-baskets, were lying sabres and revolvers. All this made a strange contrast with the patriarchal dwelling, in which still seemed to linger an odour of the famous Nanterre cakes, offered by some handsome *notaresse* to the rosières in muslin. Alas! there are no longer any rosières in Nanterre. They have been replaced by a battalion of *Francs-Tireurs* from Paris, and it was the staff of this battalion—billeted in the notary's house—that had invited us to tea, that evening.

Never did chimney-corner seem to me more delightful. Outside, the wind blew over the snow, and brought us with the sound of the shivering hours, the challenge call of the sentinels, and from time to time the dull report of a chassepot. In the drawing-room, we talked but little. Outpost duty is rough work, and we were very tired by nightfall. And then, the perfume of familiar comfort, rising from the teapot in pale clouds of steam, had taken possession of us all, and as it were hypnotised us, in the notary's large arm-chairs.

Suddenly, there was a sound of hurried steps, and a breathless telegraph messenger with flashing eyes made his appearance:

"To arms! to arms! The outpost at Rueil is attacked."

It was an advance guard, established by the *francs-tireurs* at about ten minutes' distance from Nanterre, in the railway station at Rueil, one might almost say in Pomerania, it seemed so far off! In the twinkling of an eye, all the officers of the staff were on their legs, armed and buckled, and were scurrying into the streets to muster the companies. There was no need of bugle-call for that. The *first* was quartered at the parish priest's; a couple of kicks at the door quickly roused them.

"To arms! Get up!"

And then they ran off to the registrar's office, where the *second* was lodged.

Oh! that little dark village, with its pointed steeple covered with snow, its tiny stiffly planted gardens, where the little gate bells sounded like shop doors, as you opened them; those mysterious houses, those wooden staircases up which I climbed, groping my way behind the big sabre of the adjutant-major; the warm breath of the sleeping-rooms, in which we shouted the alarm call, the guns that resounded in the darkness, the men heavy with sleep,

stumbling as they rejoined their post, while at the corner of a street, five or six stupefied peasants with lanterns in their hands, said in low tones: "The attack has begun, the attack has begun;" all this seemed to me at the time a mere dream, but the impression it has left upon me is distinct and ineffaceable.

Here is the square, with the town-hall all black, the lighted-up windows of the telegraph office, the ante-room where the bearers of despatches are waiting, lantern in hand; in a corner, the Irish surgeon of the battalion phlegmatically preparing his case of surgical instruments, and, charming silhouette amidst all the confusion of a skirmishing party, a little *vivandière*—dressed in blue, like the children in an orphanage—sleeping before the fire, a gun between her legs; and, quite at the back of the room, the telegraphic bureau, the camp beds, the large table, white under a flood of light, the two clerks bent over their instruments, and leaning over from behind them, the major, following with anxious gaze the long strips which unroll and bring, minute by minute, fresh news from the attacked post. Decidedly, it appears that it is getting hot over there. Despatch follows despatch. The telegraph wildly shakes its electric bells, and hurries the tic-tac of its sewing-machine sounds till you suppose it will break.

"Come quick," says Rueil.

"We are coming," replies Nanterre.

And the companies start off in haste.

Certainly, I must admit that war is the saddest and stupidest thing in the world. I know nothing, for instance, so lugubrious as a January night spent shivering like an old soldier in the trench of an outpost; nothing more absurd than to receive on the head half an iron pot from a distance of five miles; but to start off to battle on a fine frosty night with a full stomach and a warm heart, to dash at full speed into darkness and adventure, shoulder to shoulder with a company of good fellows, is a delightful pleasure, and resembles a delicious intoxication, a peculiar intoxication, however, which sobers any drunkard, and sharpens the dullest sight.

For my part, my sight was excellent that night. Nevertheless, there was little moonlight, and it was the earth white with snow that lighted the sky,—a theatrical light, cold and raw, spreading to the furthest end of the plain, and on which the smallest details of the landscape, a bit of wall, a sign-post, a line of willows, stood out sharp and black, as though divested of their shadows. In the little road by the side of the railway the *francs-tireurs* sped at double-quick time. Nothing could be heard but the vibration of the telegraph wires, the panting breath of the men, the whistle-call thrown to the sentinels, and, from time to time, a shell from Mont Valérien passing over our heads, like a night bird with a formidable flapping of wings. As we advanced, we saw in front of us, on a level with the ground, distant shots starring the darkness. Then on the left, at the end of the plain, the great flames of some conflagration rose silently upwards.

"In front of the manufactory, in skirmishing order!" commanded our Captain.

"Some one is going to pay for it to-night!" said my left-hand neighbour, with an accent of the faubourg.

In one bound the officer was upon us:

"Who spoke? Was it you?"

"Yes, Captain, I."

"All right; go away; return to Nanterre."

"But, Captain——"

"No, no; be off with you. I don't want you. Ah! you're afraid of having to pay for it to-night. Come, make yourself scarce, go away!"

And the poor devil was obliged to leave the ranks; but in five minutes he had stealthily returned to his place, and in future only asked to be allowed to pay for it.

After all, fate willed that no one should pay for it that night. When we reached the barricade the fray had ended. The Prussians, who had hoped to surprise our small post, finding it on the alert and safe from a *coup de main*, had prudently retired; and we were just in time to see them disappear at the end of the plain, silent and black as cockroaches. However, for fear of another attack, we had orders to remain at Rueil station, and we finished the night on the alert, with our arms ready, some on the platform and others in the waiting-room.

Poor Rueil station, I had known it so cheerful and so bright; aristocratic station of the Bougival boating parties, where the Parisian summer seemed to flaunt its muslin flounces and its feathered bonnets! It is hard, indeed, to recognize it in this lugubrious cellar, this iron-case, padded tomb, smelling of powder, petroleum, and mouldy straw, where we talk in low tones, closely pressed against one another, and have for sole light the spark of our pipes and the streak of light from the officers' corner. From hour to hour, to keep us alive, we are sent in detachments to skirmish along the Seine, or to patrol the village of Rueil, whose empty streets and almost abandoned houses are lighted up by the cold gleam of a conflagration, set alight by the Prussians at Bois-Préau.

The night was thus spent without accident, and in the morning we were sent back.

When I reached Nanterre it was still dark. On the square of the town-hall the telegraphic window shone like a light-house, and in the drawing-room occupied by the staff, in front of his hearth, where the smouldering embers were dying out, M. the *tabellion* was still smiling peacefully.

A Transitory Tomb

PUT not your trust in the names of streets, nor in the peaceful appearance thereof! When, after having clambered over barricades and mitrailleuses, I reached the top of Montmartre, and from behind the windmills looked down and saw the little Rue des Rosiers, with its pebbled roadway, its gardens, and small houses, I could have fancied myself far away in the provinces, in one of those quiet suburbs where the town as it becomes more scattered, finally dwindles down and disappears in the surrounding fields. In front of me, nothing was to be seen but a flight of pigeons and two sisters of mercy in their large caps, timidly skirting the wall. In the distance, rose the Solferino tower, a vulgar and heavy fortress, Sunday resort of the neighbourhood that the siege has almost rendered picturesque, by reducing it to a ruin.

By degrees, as I advanced, the street widened out, and wore a more animated appearance. There were tents laid out in a line, cannon and stacks of guns, and on the left-hand side a large gateway, in front of which national guards were smoking their pipes. The house

was at the back and could not be seen from the street. After some parley, the sentinel allowed me to enter. It was a two-storied house, situated between a court-yard and garden, and had nothing tragic about it. It belongs to the heirs of M. Scribe.

The rooms on the ground floor, light, airy, and hung with flowery papers, opened into the passage leading from the little paved court-yard to the garden. It was here that the former *Comité Central* held its meetings. It was hither, that on the afternoon of the 18th, the two generals were conveyed and that they endured the anguish of their last hour; while the mob yelled in the garden outside, and the deserters came and stuck their hideous faces against the windows, scenting blood like wolves; here, at last, that the two corpses were brought back, and remained exposed for two days to the public gaze.

With heavy heart, I went down the three steps leading to the garden, a true suburban garden, where each tenant has his corner of currant bushes and clematis, separated by green trelliswork with belled gates. The fury of a mob had passed over all. The enclosures were knocked down, the flowerbeds torn up. Nothing was left standing but certain quincunxes of limes, some twenty trees, freshly trimmed, with their hard grey branches uprising in the air, like a vulture's talons. An iron railing went round the back by way of wall, showing in the distance the immense, melancholy valley, and the tall smoking factory chimneys.

The calm brought by time, steals over things as well as over human beings. Here I am on the very scene of the drama, and yet I experience a certain difficulty in recalling an impression of it. The weather is mild, the sky clear. These Montmartre soldiers who surround me seem good-natured fellows. They sing, and play at pitch and toss. The officers laugh as they saunter to and fro! The great wall alone, riddled with bullets, and with crumbled coping, stands up like a witness and relates the crime. It was against this wall they were shot.

It appears that at the last moment General Lecomte, who till then had been firm and resolute, felt his courage fail him. He struggled and tried to escape, ran a few steps in the garden, was seized again immediately, shaken, dragged, jostled, fell on his knees and spoke of his children.

"I have five," he said sobbing.

The heart of the father had burst the tunic of the soldier. There were fathers also in that mad crowd, and some pitying voices answered his despairing appeal; but the inexorable deserters would not listen.

"If we do not shoot him to-day, he will have us shot to-morrow."

He was thrust against the wall. Immediately after, the sergeant of an infantry regiment approached him.

"General," he said, "you must promise us——"

Then suddenly changing his mind, he took a couple of steps backwards, and discharged his chassepot full in his chest. The others had only to finish him off.

Clément Thomas, however, did not give way for one instant.

Placed against the same wall as Lecomte, at two paces from his body, he faced death to the end, and spoke in a dignified manner. When the guns were lowered, he instinctively raised his left arm before his face, and the old Republican died in the attitude of Cæsar. At the spot where they fell, against the cold wall, bare like the target of a shooting gallery, a few branches of a peach-tree are still spread out, and at the top blooms an early flower, all white, spared by the bullets and unsullied by the powder.

On quitting the Rue des Rosiers, through the silent roads rising one above the other, along the sides of the hill, full of gardens and terraces, I came to the former cemetery of Montmartre, that had been reopened a few days before, to receive the bodies of the two generals. It is a village cemetery, bare, without trees, adorned by nothing but grave-stones. Like those rapacious peasants, who in ploughing their land encroach each day on the pathway that crosses their fields, making it finally disappear altogether; so here, death has invaded everything, even the alleys. The tombs crowd one above the other. Every place is filled. One is at a loss to know where to step.

I know nothing sadder than these old cemeteries. One feels oneself to be in presence of a vast assemblage, and yet no one is visible. Those who lie there, seemed indeed twice dead.

"What are you looking for?" inquired a kind of half gardener, half gravedigger, in a national guard's forage cap, who was mending a railing.

My answer astonished him. For a moment he hesitated, looked around him, and lowering his voice:

"Over there," he said, "near the cowl."

What he called the cowl, was a sentry-box in japanned sheet-iron, sheltering a few tarnished glass-beaded wreaths, and old filigree flowers. By its side was a wide slab, which had been recently raised. Not a railing, not an inscription. Nothing but two bunches of violets, wrapped in white paper, with a stone placed on their stalks that the strong wind of the hill-side may not blow them away. It is here they sleep side by side. It is in this transitory tomb, awaiting restoration to their families, that a billet has been given to these two soldiers.

The Colors

CHAPTER I

A TARGET

THE regiment was engaged on the banks of a railway, and served as a target to the whole Prussian army massed in an opposite wood. They were firing on each other at a distance of eighty yards. The officers shouted, "Lie down!" but no one would obey, and the proud regiment remained standing, gathered round their colors.

In the great horizon of the setting sun, of cornfields, of pasture land, this confused group of men, enveloped in smoke, were like a flock of sheep surprised in the open country by the first whirlwind of a terrific storm.

It rained iron on that slope! nothing was heard but the crackle of the volleys and the prolonged vibration of the balls which flew from one end of the battle-field to the other. From time to time the flag, which waved overhead in the wind of the mitrailleuse, disappeared in the smoke, then a voice grave and steady, dominating the firing, the struggles of the dying, the oaths of the wounded, would cry: *"Au drapeau, mes enfants, au drapeau!"* Instantly an officer, vague as a shadow in the red mist, would spring forward, and the standard, once more alive as it were, showed again above the battle.

Twenty-two times it fell. Twenty-two times its staff, still warm, slipping from a dying hand, was seized and upheld, and when, at sunset, what remained of the regiment—scarce a handful of men—retreated slowly, firing as they went, the colors were mere rags in the hands of Sergeant Hornus, the twenty-third ensign of the day.

CHAPTER II

WAR-DOG

SERGEANT HORNUS was a crusty old war-dog, who could hardly write his own name, and who had taken twenty years to gain his sergeant's stripes. All the miseries of a foundling, all the brutalizing effects of barrack-life, could be traced in the low projecting forehead, the back bent beneath the knapsack, that air of careless self-neglect acquired in the ranks.

Besides all this he stammered, but then eloquence is not essential to an ensign. On the evening of the battle his colonel said to him, "You have the colors, my brave fellow; keep them." And on his coarse hood, frayed by war and weather, the *vivandière* stitched the gold band of a sub-lieutenant.

This had been the one ambition of his humble life. From that moment he drew himself up; he who was wont to walk with bent head and eyes fixed on the ground, henceforth looked proudly upwards to the bit of stuff which he held very straight, high above death, treachery and defeat. Never was there a happier man than Hornus on days of battle, holding his staff firmly in its leather socket with both hands.

He neither spoke nor moved, and was as serious as a priest guarding some sacred thing. All his life, all his strength, were concentrated in the fingers grasping that gilded rag upon which the balls beat so persistently, and in his defiant eyes looking the Prussians full in the face, as if saying, "Try, if you dare, to take it from me!"

No one did try, not even death.

After Borny, after Gravelotte, those murderous battles, the colors came out, tattered, in holes, transparent with wounds, but it was still old Hornus who carried them.

CHAPTER III

SEPTEMBER

THEN came September with the army around Metz, the investment, and that long pause when the cannon rusted in the mud, and the finest troops in the world, demoralized by inaction, want of food and want of news, died of fever and *ennui* beside their piled arms. No one, neither chiefs nor soldiers, had faith in the future; Hornus alone was still confident. His ragged *tricolor* was all in all to him, and as long as he could see that, nothing seemed lost.

Unfortunately, as there was no more fighting, the colonel kept the colors at his house in one of the suburbs of Metz, and poor Hornus was much like a mother whose child is out to nurse. He thought of it constantly. Then when the yearning was too much for him, he went off to Metz, and, having seen it still in the same place, leaning against the wall, he returned full of courage and patience, bringing back to his dripping tent dreams of battle and of advanceing marches, with flying colors floating over the Prussian trenches.

An order of the day from Marshal Bazaine put an end to these illusions. One morning Hornus on awakening found the whole camp clamorous, groups of soldiers in great excitement, uttering cries of rage, all shaking their fists towards one side of the town as though their anger were roused against some criminal. There were shouts of "Away with him!" "Let him be shot!" And the officers did nothing to prevent them. They kept apart with bent heads as if ashamed of being seen by their men. It was indeed shameful

The Marshal's order had just been read
to 150,000 fighting men, well armed
and still efficient—an order which sur-
rendered them to the enemy without
a struggle!

"And the colors?" asked Hornus,
growing pale. The colors were to be
given up with the rest, with the arms,
with what was left of the munitions of
war—everything.

"*To-To-Tonnerre de Dieu!*" stuttered
the poor man. "They shan't have
mine." And he started at a run towards the town.

CHAPTER IV

TAKE MY FLAG!

HERE also there was great disturbance: National Guards, civilians, *gardes
mobiles* shouting and excited, deputations on their way to the Marshal; but
of this Hornus saw and heard nothing.
All the way up the Rue du Faubourg
he kept saying to himself:

"Take my flag from me indeed! It
is not possible. They have no right to
it! Let him give the Prussians what
is his own, his gilded carriages, his fine
plate brought from Mexico! But that,
it is mine. It is my honor. I defy any
one to touch it."

These fragments of speech were
broken by his rapid pace and by his
stammer, but the old fellow had his
idea notwithstanding; a very clear and
defined idea—to get the standard, carry
it to the regiment, and cut his way
through the Prussians with all who
would follow him.

When he reached his destination he
was not even allowed to enter the
house. The colonel, furious himself,

would see no one; but Hornus was not
to be put off thus.

He swore, shouted, hustled the orderly!

"My flag, I want my flag." At last
a window opened.

"Is it you, Hornus?"

"Yes, Colonel; I——"

"The colors are all at the arsenal—
you have only to go there and you will
get an acknowledgment."

"An acknowledgment! What for?"

"It is the Marshal's order."

"But Colonel——"

"Leave me alone," and the window
was shut.

Old Hornus staggered like a drunken
man.

"An acknowledgment, an acknowledgment," he repeated mechanically, moving slowly away, comprehending only
one thing, that the flag was at the
arsenal and that he must get it again, no
matter at what price.

CHAPTER V

SOILED

THE gates of the arsenal were wide
open, to allow the passage of the Prussian wagons which were drawn up in
the yard. Hornus shuddered. All the
other ensigns were there, fifty or sixty
officers silent and sorrowful; those
sombre carts in the rain, with the men
grouped bare-headed behind them, had
all the aspect of a funeral.

In a corner the colors of Bazaine's
army lay in a confused heap on the
muddy pavement. Nothing could be
sadder than these bits of gay-colored
silks, these ends of gold fringe and of
ornamented hafts, all this glorious paraphernalia thrown on the ground, soiled

Ly rain and mud. An officer took them one by one, and as each regiment was named, its ensign advanced to receive an acknowledgment. Two Prussian officers, stiff and unmoved, superintended the ceremony.

And must you go thus, oh sacred and glorious flags!—displaying your brave rents, sweeping the ground sadly like broken-winged birds, with the shame of beautiful things sullied? With each of you goes a part of France. The sun of long marches hid in your faded folds. In each mark of a ball you kept the memory of the unknown dead falling at random around the standard, the enemy's mark!

"Hornus, it is your turn, they are calling you; go for your receipt."

What did he care about a receipt! The flag was there before him. It was his, the most beautiful, the most mutilated of all. And seeing it again, he fancied himself once more on that railway bank. He heard the whistling balls and the colonel's voice. *"Au drapeau, mes enfants!"* He saw his twenty-two comrades lying dead; himself, the twenty-third, rushing forward in his turn to support the poor flag which sank for want of an arm. Ah! that day he had sworn to defend it to the death—and now!

Thinking of all this made his heart's blood rush to his head. Distracted, mad, he sprang on the Prussian officer, tore from him his beloved standard, tried to raise it once more straight and high, crying *"Au dra——"* But the words stuck in his throat—he felt the staff tremble, slip through his hands. In that paralyzing atmosphere, that atmosphere of death which weighs so heavily on capitulated towns, the standard could no longer float, nothing glorious could live. And old Hornus too, choked with shame and rage, fell dead.

My Neighbor

SOME years ago I was living near the Champs Élysées, in one of the small apartments in the back court of the Douze-Maisons. Imagine if you can such an out-of-the-way human hive in the suburbs, nestling in the midst of those big aritsocratic avenues that are so cold and quiet that it seems as if one could pass them complacently only in a carriage. I do not know what whim of a proprietor, what mania of an old miser it was thus to leave in the midst of these beautiful surroundings those empty lots and small uncultivated gardens; those low houses, all lop-sided with creaky staircases on the outside, and their wooden verandas full of clothes-lines, rabbit-cages, and dozing, emaciated cats. Here lived several households of work-people, retired small shop-keepers, and a few artists—the latter one finds in every place where there are trees. There were also here one or two boarding-houses of sordid aspect, covered with a crust of generations of misery. Amid the splendor and noise of the Champs Élysées could be seen and heard a continuous rolling of carriage wheels, a clanking of harness-chains, and the tramp of horses' feet, filling the whole avenue; while the slamming of front doors and half-smothered sounds of pianos and violins came from a long string of grand houses with rounded architectural curves; their windows shaded by light silk curtains, through which one could perceive the gilded candelabra and the rare flowers in the jardinières.

This dark little street of the Douze-Maisons, lighted only by a single gas-lamp at the end, was like the stage wing of some grand theatre compared with its beautiful surroundings. All the refuse of this luxurious quarter sought shelter here; clowns in tights, English stablemen, circus-riders, two little postilions of the Hippodrome, with their twin ponies, bill-posters, goat-carriage attendants, Punch and Judy men, sweet-meat-vendors, and, last but not least, a whole tribe of professional blind men, who came back at night bearing their chairs, accordeons, and little tin money-cups. One of these "blinds" was married while I lived there. That meant for us a whole night of "music"; a medley of discordant sounds of clarionettes, flutes, hand-organs, and accordeons, in which one could easily recognize every bridge of Paris by the different melodies. Generally, however, the passage was as quiet as the majority of its residents, who, as I have said, came back after night-fall and were too tired to be noisy.

But late Saturday night there was always sure to be a great racket in the street, for it was then that Arthur received his week's pay.

Arthur was my neighbor.

A low wall, covered by a clinging vine, was the only separation between my apartment and the furnished rooms in which he lived with his wife and children. Therefore, in spite of myself, his life was to a certain extent mixed with mine, and every Saturday night I heard without a chance of missing the least item, the horrible Parisian drama enacted in that household of work-people.

It would always begin in the same manner; the wife making ready the dinner while the children stood around, she talking to them while busy preparing the evening meal. The clock would strike seven and then eight o'clock and still no Arthur had come. As the time passed, her voice would change in tone and become pathetic and full of tears. The children would get hungry and sleepy and begin to cry, and as the father had not yet come they would eat without him and then go to bed and sleep like a lot of little chickens.

The mother would come out on the piazza and mutter between sobs, "Oh, the scoundrel, the scoundrel!" Neighbors coming home would see her there and say, sometimes pityingly:

"Why don't you go to bed, Mrs. Arthur? You know he will not come home, as it is his pay-night."

Sometimes, they would linger awhile, mixing a little advice with much gossip.

"If I were you, I would do so and so."

"Why don't you tell his employer?"

"Your father ought not to allow it," etc., etc., till they had exhausted their stock of remedies for such cases as hers.

But all this pity and advice would only make her cry and lament the more. She would still persist in her hope, in her waiting, until completely unnerved.

At last the street would become quiet.

and all doors would close, but she still remained there with but the one idea, relating to herself, and alone, all her sorrows, with that abandon of the lower classes which always lives half its life in the street. She would speak of rent behind, of creditors tormenting her, the baker refusing bread.

What would she do if he again came home without his money?

At last, overcome with fatigue, exhausted by watching belated passers-by, she would go in. Long after, when I thought everything was quiet, I would hear her cough. She was again on the stoop, brought back by anxiety, straining her eyes to look down the black street and seeing nothing there but misery and distress.

Towards one or two o'clock, and often later, some one would ring at the end of the passage. It was Arthur coming home. Usually he had a companion, dragging him to the very door and urging him to enter. Then he would loiter around, undecided whether to enter as yet, well knowing the reception that awaited him.

In climbing the stairs to his rooms, the silent house, sending back the sounds of his heavy footsteps, like so many remorses, seemed to embarrass him. He would stop before every one of those misery-hovels, on his way up, and shout: "Good-evening, Madame Weber;" or "Good-night, Madame Mathieu." Then if he received no answer he would fling at them an assortment of vile epithets and oaths until every one in the neighborhood had been aroused, and the doors and windows open to answer him with insults and curses. That was exactly what he was waiting for. The wine he had drunk seemed to provoke quarrels and fights. When he had once worked himself into a rage then he had no fear in going home.

That home-coming was the climax of the affair. Approaching his door, he would find it locked and then he would shout: "Open! It is I!" Then I would hear the bare feet of the wife on the cold tiles; the scratching of matches; and, at last, the opening of the door. The man on entering would begin stammering out his story, always the same. He had met comrade so and so, who worked on the railroad, or at the wharf, and they had spent the evening together. The woman would not even listen, but would interrupt him repeatedly with inquiries for money. At last he would answer:

"The money? Oh, I haven't any left, you know I——"

"You lie!"

He was indeed lying. Even in the excitement of his debauch he would always reserve a few sous, thinking of the great thirst which would torment him on the following Monday. It was that small remainder of his pay which his wife was now trying to get from him.

She would hang on him, shake him, search him, and turn all his pockets inside out. After a few moments I would hear the money rolling over the tiles and the woman throwing herself on it in triumphant glee.

Then I would hear swearing and smothered blows. The drunkard was revenging himself. Once beginning to beat her, he would not stop. The terrible suburban wines which he had imbibed, by this time mounted to his brain, had now crazed him. The woman would howl, the furniture would be smashed, the children would begin screaming, and then in the street the windows and doors would fly open again and I would hear:

"It's only Arthur." "He's making a bigger row though than ever," and such-like remarks.

Sometimes the father-in-law, an old rag-picker living in the next room, would come to his daughter's assistance. Arthur would lock the door so as not to be disturbed in his operations, and then a most sickening and horrible dialogue would take place through the key-hole.

"Haven't you had enough, with your two years in jail?" the old man would cry. Then the drunkard would reply in bantering tones:

"Well, yes, I have been in prison two years, but what of that? I've paid my debt to society; when will you pay yours?"

But if the old man would again speak of the prison-episode and dwell too long on that fact, Arthur would angrily open the door and fall heavily over his father-in-law, mother-in-law, and neighbors who had collected on the landing outside. Then would ensue a general *mêlée*, after which Arthur would be carefully picked up and put to bed, to sleep off his debauch.

Yet, with all this, he was not a bad man. Often on Sunday, the day following those awful scenes, the drunkard, now appeased, without a cent with which to buy drink, would spend the day at home. They would bring the chairs out of their rooms and spend the day on the balcony.

Madame Weber, Madame Mathieu, and the whole house would congregate there, and they would talk and gossip; Arthur of course being their leader.

You would have thought him one of those model working-men who patronize night-schools. He would speak in a low soft voice, eloquently putting forth fragments of ideas, which he had caught here and there, upon the rights of the working classes and the tyranny of capitalists. His poor wife, subdued by the beating of the previous night, would look at him with new admiration, forgetting the wrongs he had inflicted on her.

The neighbors would ask him to sing, and he would render in his throaty voice full of false tears, "Les Hirondelles" by Belanger. Oh! that voice, and the stupid sentimentalism of the lower classes. It was enough to drive all but his devoted listeners indoors.

The neighbors looked tearfully out at the pale blue sky as Arthur finished, and wondered if he would now become the ideal man of their kind.

But no; this little scene of softness did not prevent him from coming home drunk the next Saturday night to beat his wife anew and arouse the neighborhood.

There, in the midst of that misery, was a small army of other Arthurs, waiting but for the years to pass that they might be old enough to drink their pay and beat their wives too.

And it is such a race that wishes to govern the world. "Ah, the evil of it!" as my neighbors of the passage would say.

Man with the Golden Brain

THERE was once a man who had a golden brain; yes, madam, a brain all of gold. When he came into the world, the physicians did not think that the child would live, his head was so heavy and his skull so huge. He did live, however, and grew in the sunlight like a fair olive-tree; only his large head always dragged him down, and it was pitiful to see him knocking against the furniture when he walked. He often fell. One day he rolled from the top of a flight of steps and struck his head against a marble stair, when his skull rang like an ingot. They thought him dead; but when they picked him up, they found only two or three drops of clotted gold in his blond hair. It was in this way that his parents learned that the child had a golden brain.

The matter was kept secret; the poor little fellow himself suspected nothing. Once in a while he would ask why they no longer allowed him to play in the street with the other boys.

"They would steal you, my beautiful treasure!" his mother would reply.

Then the child would be terribly afraid of being stolen; he would return to his solitary play without saying anything, and drag himself heavily about from room to room.

Only when he was eighteen years old did his parents reveal to him the monstrous gift which he had received from fate; and as they had thus far brought him up and supported him, they asked in return for a little of his gold. The boy did not hesitate; on the spot—how and by what means the legend does not tell—he tore from his brain a lump of virgin gold, as large as a nut, which he threw proudly upon his mother's knees. Then, dazzled by the wealth which he bore in his brain, mad with passions, intoxicated by his power, he left his father's home and went through the world squandering his treasure.

From the manner in which he lived, —royally, and sowing his money broadcast,—one would have thought that his treasure was limitless. Nevertheless, his brain began to be exhausted, and proportionately his eyes could be seen to grow dim and his cheek hollow. One day, finally, on the morrow of a mad debauch, the poor wretch. left alone amidst the paling lights and the fragments of the feast, was appalled by the enormous breach which he had made in his ingot; it was time to stop.

From then on he led a new life. The man with the golden brain went off to live alone by the labour of his hands, timid and suspicious as a miser, flying from temptation, striving to forget the fatal wealth which he would not touch. Unhappily, a friend had followed him into his solitude; and this friend knew his secret.

One night the poor man was suddenly awakened by a pain in his head, a frightful pain; he sat up, terrified, and by a beam of moonlight saw his friend hurrying away with something concealed beneath his cloak.

Another bit of his brain stolen from him!

A little later the man with the golden brain fell in love, and this time it was all over with him. He loved with his whole soul a little blond woman, who also loved him well enough, but who loved still better pompons, white feathers, and pretty reddish tassels tapping the tops of her boots.

In the hands of this dainty creature —half bird and half doll—the bits of gold melted away like snow. She had a fancy for everything, and he could never say her nay; he even, for fear of paining her, concealed from her to the end the sad secret of his fortune.

"So we are very rich?" she would say.

"Oh, yes, very rich!" the poor man would reply.

And he would smile lovingly at the little bluebird which was unconsciously devouring his brain. Yet sometimes he would become frightened, and would long to be miserly; but then the little woman would come dancing to him and say,—

"My husband, you who are so rich, buy me something which costs a great deal."

And he would buy her something which cost a great deal.

This lasted for two years; then, one morning, the little woman died without their knowing why, like a bird. The treasure was nearing its end, but with what remained the widower gave his dear dead a splendid funeral. Bells pealing, heavy black-draped carriages, plumed horses, silver tears upon the velvet,—nothing seemed to him too fine. What did he care now for his gold? He gave of it to the church, to the bearers, to the sellers of immortelles; he gave everywhere, unquestioningly. And so, when he left the cemetery, almost nothing of this marvellous brain remained, hardly a few grains on the walls of his skull.

Then he was seen wandering through the streets with a dazed look, with hands outstretched, and staggering like a drunken man. At night, at the hour when the bazaars were lighted, he stopped before a large show-window in which a mass of stuffs and jewelry glittered in the light, and remained a long while looking at a pair of blue satin boots trimmed with swan's-down. "I know somebody who would like those boots," he said to himself with a smile; and, already forgetting that his little wife was dead, he went in to buy them.

From her back room the shopkeeper heard a great cry; she hastened in, and recoiled with terror on seeing a man leaning against the counter and looking stupidly at her with an expression of pain. He had the blue boots with swan's-down trimming in one hand, and held out the other, all bloody, with scrapings of gold under his nails.

This, madam, is the legend of the man with the golden brain.

In spite of its likeness to a fantastic tale, this story is true from end to end. There are in the world poor folk who are condemned to live on their brains, and pay in pure gold, with their marrow and their substance, the smallest things in life. It is a daily pain to them; and then, when they are weary of suffering—

The Poet Mistral

Last Sunday, when I rose, I thought that I had waked in the Rue du Faubourg-Montmartre. It was raining; the sky was gray, and the place dreary. I was afraid to spend this cold, rainy day at home; and suddenly the desire seized me to go and warm myself a bit with Frédéric Mistral, that great poet who lives three leagues from my pines, in his little village, Maillane.

No sooner said than done; a myrtlewood stick, my Montaigne, a waterproof, and I was off.

There was no one in the fields. Our fair Catholic Provence allows the earth to rest on Sunday. The farms were shut up, with no one at home but the dogs. At long intervals I would meet a wagoner's cart with its dripping tilt, an old woman wrapped in her brown cloak. or a team of mules in their gala trappings,—saddle-cloths of blue and white esparto. red pompons, and silver bells.—drawing at a slow trot a wagonful of farm-people going to Mass; then, in the distance. through the mist, a boat on the *roubine* and a fisherman casting his net.

It was impossible to read on the way that day. The rain fell in torrents, and the Tramontana dashed it in one's face in bucketfuls. I made the journey without stopping, and finally, after walking three hours, I saw the little cypress groves amid which Maillane shelters itself for fear of the wind.

Not a cat in the streets of the village; everybody was at High Mass. When I passed before the church, the trombone was snoring, and I saw the candles shining through the stained glass.

The poet's dwelling is at the extreme end of the village; it is the last house on the left-hand side of the road to Saint-Remy, — a one-storied cottage with a garden in front. I enter quietly. Nobody! The door of the drawing-room is closed; but I hear some one behind it, walking, and speaking aloud. How well I know this step and this voice! I stop a moment in the little whitewashed passage with my hand on the knob, deeply moved. My heart beats fast. He is there, at work. Must I wait till the verse is finished? After all, never mind; let us go in.

Ah! Parisians, when the poet of Maillane came to visit you, to show Paris to his Mireille, and you saw him in your drawing-rooms,—this Chactas in a black coat, with a tall collar and a high hat which embarrassed him as much as did his glory. you thought that that was Mistral. No, it was not he. There is only one Mistral in the world, —him whom I surprised last Sunday in his village. with a felt hat on the side of his head, without a waistcoat, in a jacket, with his red Catalan sash about his waist, his eye alight, the fire of inspiration on his cheeks, superb with his kindly smile. elegant as a Greek shepherd. and walking rapidly to and fro, with his hands in his pockets, composing verses.

"What! is it you?" cried Mistral, throwing his arms about my neck; "what a lucky idea of yours to come! It just happens that this is the fête-day of Maillane. We have the band from

Avignon, the bulls, the procession, the farandole,—it will be magnificent. My mother will soon be back from Mass; we will have breakfast, and then, zou! we will go and see the pretty girls dance."

While he spoke I was looking with emotion at this little room with the light paper, which I had not seen for so long, and where I had already passed such happy hours. Nothing was changed. There were still the sofa with its yellow plaid covering, the two straw chairs, the armless Venus and the Venus of Arles on the mantelpiece, the poet's portrait by Hébert, his photograph by Etienne Carjat, and, in a corner, by the window, the desk,—such a poor little desk as a clerk of registry might have,—loaded with old books and dictionaries. In the middle of this desk I saw a large open blank-book. It was "Calendal," the new poem by Frédéric Mistral, which is to appear at the end of this year, on New Year's Day. Mistral has worked at this poem for seven years, and he wrote the last line of it nearly six months ago; still, he dares not part with it yet. There is always a verse to polish, you see, a more sonorous rhyme to be found. It makes no difference that Mistral writes in Provençal; he works over his verses as though all the world were to read them in the original and hold him to account for his good workmanship. Ah, the fine poet! It might well have been of Mistral that Montaigne wrote: "Remember him who, when they asked him why he took so much trouble in an art which could come to the knowledge of but few people, replied: 'A few people are enough for me. One is enough. Not one is enough.'"

I was holding the manuscript of "Calendal" in my hand and turning over the leaves, full of emotion. Suddenly a sound of fifes and tambourines arose in the street, before the window; and my Mistral ran to the closet, took out bottles and glasses, dragged the table into the middle of the room, and opened the door for the musicians, saying to me,—

"Do not laugh. They have come to serenade me. I am a municipal councilman."

The little room fills with people. They place the tambourines on chairs, the old banner in a corner; and the mulled wine goes around. Then, when they have emptied a few bottles to the health of M. Frédéric, when they have conversed gravely about the fête,—whether the farandole will be as fine as last year, and whether the bulls will behave well,—the musicians withdraw and go to serenade the other councilmen.

In a twinkling the table is laid with a white cloth and two plates. I know the custom of the house; when Mistral has visitors, his mother never comes to dinner. The poor old woman knows only Provençal, and would feel ill at ease in conversing with Frenchmen. Besides, she is needed in the kitchen.

Dieu! what a good breakfast I had that morning,—a piece of roast kid, some mountain cheese, must preserves, figs, and Muscat grapes, with the whole washed down by that good Château-Neuf des Papes, which has such a fine red colour in one's glass.

At dessert I go for the manuscript of the poem, and place it on the table before Mistral.

"We said that we would go out," said the poet, with a smile.

"No, no! 'Calendal! Calendal!'"

Mistral gave way, and with his soft and musical voice, beating the time of his lines with his hand, he begins the first verse:—

"Of a girl mad for love—now that I have told the sad story—I will sing, God willing, a child of Cassis,—a poor little fisher of anchovies—"

Without, the bells were calling to vespers, fire-crackers were exploding on the Place, the fifes passed and repassed in the streets with the tambourines. The Camargue bulls, which they were bringing for the bull-fight, bellowed.

I, with my elbows on the table and tears in my eyes, listened to the story of the little Provençal fisherman.

Calendal was only a fisherman; love made him a hero. To win the heart of his love, the beautiful Estérelle, he attempted miracles; and the twelve labours of Hercules were nothing beside his.

Once, when he had taken it into his head to become rich, he invented wonderful fishing-machines, and brought into port all the fish of the sea. Another time it was a terrible bandit of the gorges of Cllioules, Count Sévéran, whom he pursued to his very den, among his cut-throats and concubines. A terrible fellow was this little Calendal! One day, on Sainte Baume, he met two parties of lads who had come there to settle their quarrel with the knife at the tomb of Master Jacques, a Provençal who made the carpenter-work of the Temple of Solomon, if you please! Calendal threw himself into the midst of the slaughter, and pacified the lads by talking to them.

His undertakings were superhuman. There was, away up among the rocks of Lure, an inaccessible forest of cedars where no woodman had ever ventured. But Calendal went. He remained there alone for thirty days. For thirty days they heard the noise of his axe which rang and sank into the tree-trunks. The forest cried aloud: one after another, the giant old trees fell and rolled to the bottom of the chasms; and when Calendal went down again, there was not left a cedar on the mountain.

Finally, as the recompense for so many exploits, the fisher obtains the love of Estérelle, and is elected consul by the inhabitants of Cassis. That is the story of Calendal. But what matters Calendal? What there is in the poem, before everything else, is Provence,—the Provence of the sea and the Provence of the mountain,—with its history, its customs, its legends, its scenery,—a whole people, simple and free, which has found its great poet before dying. And now mark out railroads, plant telegraph-poles, drive out the Provençal language from the schools! Provence will live eternally in "Mireille" and in "Calendal."

"Enough of poetry!" said Mistral, closing his book. "We must go and see the fête."

We went out. The whole village was in the streets. A strong breeze had swept the heavens, and the sky shone joyfully upon the red roofs, wet with rain. We arrived in time to see the return of the procession. For an hour there was an interminable tramp of penitents in hoods,—white penitents, blue penitents, gray penitents, sisterhoods of veiled girls, red banners with golden flowers, large saints of ungilded wood borne upon four shoulders, saints of coloured faience like idols with great bouquets in their hands, copes, monstrances, canopies of green velvet, crucifixes framed in white silk,—all this undulating in the wind to the light of candles and the sun, amidst psalms, litanies, and pealing bells.

The procession being ended and the saints returned to their chapels, we went to see the bulls, then the sports on the threshing-floor, the wrestling, the three leaps, the *étrangle-chat* and *jeu de t'outre*, and all the pretty round of a Provençal fête. Night was falling when we returned to Maillane. On the Place, before the café where Mistral goes to play his game in the evenings with his friend Zidore, they had lighted a bonfire. The farandole was forming. Lanterns cut out of paper were lighted everywhere in the dusk; the young people took their places, and soon, upon a call from the tambourines, there began about the flame a mad, uproarious round which was to last all night.

After supper, too weary to go out again, we went up to Mistral's room. It was the modest bedroom of a peasant, with two large beds. The walls have no paper, and the beams of the ceiling are uncovered. Four years ago, when the Academy awarded the author of "Mireille" the three-thousand-franc prize, Madame Mistral had an idea.

"Suppose we have your room papered and ceiled," she said to her son.

"No, no!" replied Mistral. "That is the poets' money; we must not touch it."

And the room remained bare; but so long as the poets' money lasted, those who knocked at Mistral's door always found his purse open.

I had brought the manuscript of "Calendal" up to the bedroom, and I wished Mistral to read me another passage before I went to sleep. He chose the faience episode. This is it, in a few words:—

It was at a great feast, I do not know where. They place on the table a magnificent service of Moustiers faience. On the bottom of each plate, painted in blue in the enamel, is a Provençal subject; the whole history of the country is contained in them. And so you should see how lovingly these beautiful faiences are described; there is a verse for each plate,—so many little poems of simple but skillful workmanship, as finished as a picture by Theocritus.

While Mistral was reading me his verses in that beautiful Provençal tongue, which queens once spoke and which now our shepherds alone understand, I admired this man within myself, and, thinking of the state of ruin in which he found his mother tongue, and what he had made of it, I pictured to myself one of those old palaces of the Princes of Baux, such as one sees in the Alpilles; no roofs, no balustrades on the staircases, no glass in the windows, the trefoils of the arches broken, the scutcheon over the doors eaten away by moss, chickens pecking in the court of honour, swine wallowing beneath the delicate colonnades of the galleries, the ass nibbling in the grass-grown chapel, pigeons coming to drink from the great holy-water basins, filled with rain, and finally, amid these ruins, two or three families of peasants who have built their huts in the bowels of the old palace.

Then, some fine day, the son of one of these peasants falls in love with these great ruins, and is indignant at seeing them thus profaned. He quickly drives the cattle from the court of honour, and, the fairies helping him, he all alone repairs the grand staircase, restores woodwork to the walls and glass to the windows, rebuilds the towers, regilds the throne-room, and re-establishes the vast palace of the olden time, in which lodged popes and empresses.

This restored palace is the Provençal language.

This peasant's son is Mistral.

The Friend of Maurice

A LETTER, Père Azan?"

"Yes, sir. It is from Paris."

He was quite proud that it came from Paris, that good Père Azan. But not I. Something told me that this Parisian from the Rue Jean-Jacques, falling upon my table unexpectedly and so early, was going to make me lose my whole day. I was not mistaken, as you will see.

"You must do me a service, my dear friend. You must go at once to Eyguières. Eyguières is a large town, three or four leagues from you,—a mere walk. When you arrive, you will ask for the Convent of the Orphans. The first building beyond the convent is a low house with gray shutters and a little garden in the rear. You will go in without knocking,—the door is always open,—and when you enter, you will call out in a loud voice, 'Good-day, good people! I am the friend of Maurice.' Then you will see two little old people—oh! but old, old, so old!—hold out their arms to you from their great easy-chairs, and you will embrace them for me, as though they belonged to you. Then you will talk. They will talk to you of me, of nothing but me;

they will tell you a thousand absurdities to which you will listen without laughing. You will not laugh, will you? They are my grandparents,—two beings whose whole life I am, and who have not seen me for ten years. Ten years is a long while; but what would you have! Paris holds me fast, while with them it is their great age. They are so old that if they were to come to see me they would break on the way. Happily, you are there, my dear miller; and when they embrace you, the poor things will think that they are almost embracing me. I have so often spoken to them about you and of that good friendship which—"

The devil take friendship! That morning it happened to be superb weather, but by no means good for a long walk; there was too much Mistral and too much sun,—a real Provençal day. When that confounded letter arrived, I had already chosen my *cagnard* (shelter) between two rocks, and I was dreaming of remaining there all day, like a lizard, drinking in the light and listening to the song of the pines. But what could I do? I locked up the mill grumbling, and placed the key under the step, took my stick and my pipe, and set out.

I arrived at Eyguières about two o'clock. The village was deserted, for every one was in the fields. In the elms on the parade, white with dust, crickets were singing lustily. There were, indeed, in the Place before the *mairie* an ass sunning itself, and a flock of pigeons on the church fountain; but no one was there to point out the Orphanage to me. Happily an old fairy appeared suddenly, crouching and spinning in her doorway. I told her what I wanted; and as she was a very powerful fairy, she had only to raise her distaff, and immediately the Orphanage rose before me as if by magic. It was a large building, dark and gloomy, proud of showing above its arched gateway an old cross of red sandstone with a little Latin around it. Beside this building I saw another, smaller, with gray shutters and a little garden behind it. I recognized it at once, and went in without knocking.

All my life I shall recollect this long corridor, cool and calm, with its walls painted pink, the little garden which quivered at its farther end across some light-coloured blinds, and on all its panels flowers and violins fast fading. It seemed to me that I was arriving at the house of some old magistrate of the time of Sédaine. At the end of the corridor, to the left, I could hear through the open door the tick-tack of a tall clock, and the voice of a child, but a child at school, who was reading and stopping at every syllable. "Then — Saint — I — ré — née — cried — I — am — the — wheat — of — the — Lord — I — must — be — ground — by — the — teeth — of — these —

an—i—mals—" I went quietly up to the door, and looked in.

In the calm and half light of a little room, a good old man with red cheeks, wrinkled to the ends of his fingers, was asleep in an armchair, with his mouth open and his hands on his knees. At his feet a little girl clad in blue—a large cape and small hood—was reading the "Life of Saint Irénée" from a book larger than herself. This miraculous reading had affected the whole house. The old man was asleep in his chair; the flies upon the ceiling, and the canaries in their cage beyond, by the window, were also asleep. The tall clock was snoring, tick-tack, tick-tack. In the whole room nothing was awake but a great ray of light, which fell straight and white between the closed shutters, full of living sparks and microscopic waltzes. Amid this universal doze the child continued her reading in a grave voice: "And — straight — way — two — li — ons — fell — up — on — him — and — de — voured — him —" It was at that moment that I entered. Saint Irénée's lions bounding into the room could not have produced more amazement than I. The child uttered a cry; the big book dropped, the flies and the canaries awoke, the tall clock struck; the old man sat up suddenly, startled; and I myself, a little embarrassed, stopped upon the threshold, and cried very loud,—

"Good-day, good people! I am the friend of Maurice."

Oh! then if you could have seen the poor old man come toward me with outstretched arms, embrace me, press my hands, and run bewildered about the room, saying,—

"Mon Dieu! Mon Dieu!"

Every wrinkle in his face smiled. He was very red, and stammered,—

"Ah, Monsieur! Ah, Monsieur!"

Then he went to the end of the room and called out,—

"Mamette!"

A door opened, and there was the footstep of a mouse in the passage; it was Mamette. Nothing could be prettier than this little old woman with her sheli-shaped cap, her Carmelite gown, and the embroidered kerchief which she held in her hand, to do me honour, after the old fashion. Most touching of all, they looked alike! With the same cap and Carmelite he too might have been called Mamette. Only the true Mamette must have wept a great deal in her life, for she was still more wrinkled than the other. Like the other, too, she had with her a child from the Orphanage,—a little attendant in a blue cape, who never left her; and to see these old people protected by these orphans was the most touching thing imaginable.

Mamette had begun by making me a low courtesy when she came in; but the old man cut her courtesy short with a word.—

"He is Maurice's friend."

And instantly she began to tremble and weep, drop her handkerchief, and become red,—very red, still redder than he. These old people have only a drop of blood in their veins, and at the slightest emotion it flies to their faces.

"Quick, quick, a chair!" said the old woman to her child.

"Open the shutters!" cried the old man to his.

And each taking me by a hand, they led me to the window, which had been opened wide, in order to see me the better. Chairs are drawn up; I sit down between them on a campstool, with the little blue girls behind us; and the interrogatory begins.

"How is he? What is he doing? Why does he not come? Is he happy?"

And *patati!* and *patata!* It was like that for hours.

I replied as well as I could to their questions, giving all the details about my friend that I knew, brazenly inventing those that I did not know, and above all taking care not to confess that I had never observed whether his windows closed well, or what was the colour of the paper in his room.

"The paper in his room? It is blue, madame, bright blue, with flowers on it."

"Really?" said the poor old woman, quite moved. Then she added, turning to her husband: "He is such a dear child!"

"Oh, yes, he is a dear child!" replied the other, with enthusiasm.

And all the time that I was talking there passed between them little nods, and winks, and laughs of intelligence; or the old man would lean toward me to say,—

"Speak a bit louder. She is a little hard of hearing."

And she, on her side,—

"A trifle more distinctly, please. His ears are not so good as they used to be."

Then I would raise my voice, and both would thank me with a smile; and in these faded smiles, which leaned toward me striving to read in my eyes the picture of their dear Maurice, I was deeply touched to find that likeness,—vague, veiled, almost intangible, as though I saw my friend smiling at me from afar through a fog.

Suddenly the old man sat up in his chair,—

"But, Mamette, perhaps he has not breakfasted."

And Mamette, frightened, with up-lifted arms, cried,—

"Not breakfasted? Good heavens!"

I thought that they were still speaking of Maurice, and was about to reply that that dear child never waited later than twelve o'clock for his breakfast. But no, they meant me; and you should have seen what an excitement there was when I confessed that I was still fasting.

"Set tne table quickly, children! Put it in the middle of the room, and bring the Sunday cloth and the flowered plates. And do not laugh so much, if you please, and make haste!"

And indeed they did make haste. Breakfast was ready in the breaking of only three plates!

"A nice little breakfast," said Mamette, conducting me to the table. "Only, you will be alone. We have already breakfasted."

These poor old people! No matter at what hour one finds them, they have always already breakfasted.

Mamette's nice little breakfast consisted of a glass of milk, some dates, and a barquette,—a kind of small tart, enough to feed her and her canaries for a week. And to think that I alone made an end of all these provisions! And consequently, what indignation there was about the table! The little blue girls whispered, nudging each other; and how the canaries seemed to say in their cages, "Oh, look at that gentleman who eats up all the bar quette!"

I ate it all, indeed, and almost with out being conscious of it, busy as I was in looking about me in this bright and peaceful room, where there floated in the air something like the odour of ancient things. Above all, there were two little beds, from which I could not remove my eyes. These beds were almost two cradles, and I could fancy them early in the morning when they are still enclosed by their great curtains. Three o'clock strikes. It is the hour when all old people awake.

"Are you asleep, Mamette?"

"No, my love."

"Is not Maurice a dear child?"

"Oh, yes, a dear child."

And I could fancy a whole conversation like this, simply from seeing the two little beds standing side by side.

During this time a terrible drama was being enacted at the other end of the room, before the wardrobe. The question was to get, up at the top, on the highest shelf, a certain jar of brandied cherries which had been awaiting Maurice for ten years, and which was to be opened for me. In spite of Mamette's entreaties, the old man had insisted on going for them himself, and, standing on a chair to the great terror of his wife, was striving to reach them. You can imagine the scene,—the old man, trembling and a-tiptoe, the little blue girls clinging to his chair, Mamette behind him panting, with arms outstretched, and over it all a faint perfume of bergamot exhaling from the open wardrobe and the great piles of russet linen. It was charming.

Finally, after many efforts, they succeeded in getting this wonderful jar out of the wardrobe, and with it an old silver cup, embossed,—Maurice's cup when he had been a child. They filled it to the brim with cherries for me; Maurice was so fond of cherries! And as the old man waited on me, he whispered to me in the tone of a gourmand,—

"You are very lucky to be able to eat them! My wife made them. You will taste something good."

Alas! his wife had made them, but she had forgotten to put any sugar in them. It could not be helped; we become careless as we grow old. Your cherries were atrocious, my poor Mamette, but I ate them to the last one without making a wry face.

Breakfast over, I rose to take leave of my hosts. They would have liked to keep me longer to talk more about the dear child; but day was declining, the mill was a long way off, and I was obliged to set out.

The old man had risen when I did.

"Mamette, my coat! I will go with him as far as the Place."

No doubt in her heart Mamette thought that it was already somewhat cool for him to accompany me to the Place; but she did not let it appear. Only, while she was helping him to put on his coat,—a fine snuff-coloured coat with mother-of-pearl buttons,—I heard the dear creature say to him softly,—

"You will not stay out too late, will you?"

And he, with a mischievous air, replied,—

"Eh! eh! I don't know—perhaps."

Thereupon they looked at each other laughing, and the little blue girls laughed at seeing them laugh. and in the corner the canaries too laughed after their fashion. Between ourselves. I think that the odour of the cherries had intoxicated them all a little.

Night was falling when the grandfather and I set out. The little blue girl followed us at a distance to bring him back; but he did not see her, and was proud of walking on my arm like a man. Mamette, radiant, watched from her doorstep; and as she looked at us, shook her head prettily, as much as to say,—

"Nevertheless, my poor old husband can still walk!"

The Wreck

ALAS! this year the garden is still full of roses, but the house is also full of Prussians. I have carried my table to the further end of the garden, and there I write, under the delicate and scented shade of a large bush of Spanish broom full of the buzzing of bees, which prevents my seeing the Pomeranian knitted jerseys hanging out to dry on my poor grey shutters.

And yet I had sworn I would not return here till long after *they* had left; it was, however, absolutely necessary in order to avoid Cluseret's horrible conscription, and I had no other asylum. And thus, I have not been spared, any more than so many other Parisians, one of the miseries of these sad times: the anguish of the siege, the civil war, the emigration, and, to complete our wretchedness, the foreign occupation. However philosophic, however much above and beyond every-day affairs, the impression is singular, when, after six hours trampling along the magnificent roads of France, all white with the dust of the Prussian battalions, you find on reaching your door, a German signboard hanging under the falling clusters of laburnum and acacia, with the following inscription in Gothic letters:—

5TH COMPANY.
BOEHM,
SERGEANT-MAJOR,
AND THREE MEN.

This M. Boehm is a tall, queer, silent fellow, who keeps the shutters of his room always closed, and sleeps and eats without light. Withal, rather too free and easy manners, a cigar ever in his mouth, and most exacting! His lordship requires a room for himself, a room for his secretary, and one for his servant. You are forbidden to go in by this door, to leave by that other. Did he not want to prevent our going into the garden? At last the mayor came, and the Captain and we were once more at home. It is not cheerful at home this year. No matter how you look at it, this proximity disturbs and galls. Their hideous jargon heard all around you, and in your very home, mingles with all you eat, withers the trees, throws a mist over the leaves of your book, dims your sight, and brings tears to your eyes. Even the child, without understanding the wherefore, is under the influence of this strange oppression. He plays quietly in a corner of the garden, checks his childish laughter, hums in an undertone; and in the morning, instead of his joyous awakenings, full of delight and life, he lies quite still with his eyes wide open behind the curtains, and from time to time asks in a low voice:

"May I awake now?"

Would it were only the sadness of the foreign occupation that spoilt our springtide; but the hardest and most cruel thing, is to hear the constant roll of the cannon and mitrailleuse, which reaches our ears, when the wind blows from Paris, shaking the horizon, pitilessly tearing the rosy haze of the mornings, and filling with a sound of thunder those lovely clear nights of the month of May, those nights full of the song of the nightingales and the chirp of the crickets.

Last night was terrible. Loud reports followed one another rapidly, furiously, desperately, accompanied by perpetual flashes like lightning I had opened my window looking towards the Seine, and I listened—with beating heart—to the dull sounds that reached me, borne by the deserted waters through the silence. At times, it seemed to me as though over there, in the distant horizon, some large vessel in distress were wildly firing off its alarm guns, and I remembered how ten years ago, on a night such as this, I was on the terrace of an hotel at Bastia, listening to an ominous boom, sent to us by the raging sea, like a despairing cry of agony and fury. It lasted all through the night, and in the morning they found on the beach, amid a confusion of broken masts and torn sails, shoes with bright-coloured bows, a harlequin's wand, and a heap of tatters and ribbons spangled with gold, drenched by sea-water, and daubed with blood and mud. This was, as I heard later on, all that remained of the wreck of the

Louise, a large steamer coming from Leghorn to Bastia with a company of Italian mummers on board.

To anyone who can realise how dreadful is a night's battling with the sea, the groping and sterile struggle against an irresistible force; to anyone who can picture to himself the last moments of a ship, the rising abyss, the slow and inglorious death, the watery grave; to anyone who knows the rage, the mad hope followed by a brutish prostration, the drunken agony and delirium, blind hands beating the air, clenched fingers clutching the empty space; that harlequin's wand lying in the midst of bloodstained wreckage would have presented a burlesque and terrifying object. Imagination would conjure up a tempest falling like a clap of thunder during a representation on board, the audience invaded by the sea, the orchestra drowned, desks, violins, violoncellos, rolling pell-mell, the Columbine wringing her bare arms, running from one end of the scene to the other, half dead with fright and still pink under her paint; the Clown, even in his terror, not more ghastly than before, climbing up side scenes, watching the rising waters, and already in his great eyes, grotesquely circled for the farce, the terrible horror of death; Isabelle, hampered with her gala attire, crowned with flowers, and dissolved in tears, ridiculous in her very gracefulness, rolling about on the deck like a bundle, clinging to each bench, and lisping childish prayers; Scaramouche, a barrel of brandy between his legs, laughing with an idiotic laugh, and singing at the top of his voice; while Harlequin, seized with madness, solemnly continues the play, jumps about and switches his white wand; and old Pantaloon, carried off by a wave, floats away on the billows, with his brown velvet coat and his toothless mouth wide open.

Well, this wreck of mountebanks, this funereal masquerade, this farce *in extremis,* all these convulsions, all these grimaces, rose up again before me at each shock of last night's cannonade. I felt that the Commune, on the eve of foundering, was firing off its alarm guns. At each instant I saw the tide rising, the breach widening, and all the while the men of the Hôtel de Ville clinging to their stage, continuing to issue decree after decree, amidst the turmoil of wind and storm; till at last, one big wave swept over them, and the great vessel was swallowed up with its red flags, its golden scarfs, its delegates dressed up as judges or generals, its battalions of gaitered and plumed amazons, its circus-like soldiers, decked out with Spanish caps and Garibaldian hats, its Polish lancers, its fantastic Turcos, drunken and furious, singing and whirling. All this confused mass was vanishing helter skelter, and of all the noise, folly, crime, pasquinade, sometimes even heroism, nothing would be left, but a red sash, a military cap with eight galoons, and a braided frock-coat, found one morning on the bank of the river, all besmeared with dirt and blood.

Loss of the Sémillante

ALLOW me to relate to you a terrible story of the sea of which the pearl-fishers thereabout often speak in the night-watches, and concerning which chance has furnished me with some very curious particulars.

It was some two or three years ago.

I was sailing the Sea of Sardinia with seven or eight coast-guards. It was a hard trip for a novice. During the whole month of March we had not one fair day. The wind beat furiously upon us, and the sea never went down.

One evening, as we were running before the gale, our boat took refuge at the entrance to the Strait of Bonifacio, amidst a group of small islands. Their appearance was in no way attractive. They were great bare rocks covered with birds, a few bunches of wormwood, thickets of lentiscus, and here and there, in the slime, pieces of wood rotting. But as a place to pass the night, these rocks were far more comfortable than the cabin of an old, half-decked boat, in which the sea made itself quite at home; and we were satisfied with them.

Hardly had we disembarked, and the sailors lighted a fire for the *bouillabaisse*, when the skipper called me, and, pointing to a little enclosure of white masonry, half lost in the mist at the end of the island, said,—

"Will you come to the cemetery?"

"A cemetery, Captain Lionetti! Why, where are we?"

"In the Lavezzi Islands, sir. This is the burial-place of the six hundred men of the 'Sémillante,' the very place where their frigate was lost ten years ago. Poor fellows! they do not receive many

visitors; it is the least that we can do to go and say good-day to them, since we are here."

"With all my heart, skipper."

How sad it was, that cemetery of the "Sémillante"! I can still see it, with its little low wall, its rusty iron gate so hard to open, its silent chapel, and its hundreds of black crosses hidden by the grass. Not a wreath of immortelles, not a memento, nothing! Ah, poor abandoned dead! how cold they must be in the tombs which have fallen to their lot!

We remained there a moment, kneeling. The captain prayed aloud. Enormous gulls, the only guardians of the cemetery, circled above our heads, and mingled their harsh cries with the lamentations of the sea.

When the prayer was finished, we came sadly back to the quarter of the island where the boat was moored. The sailors had not been idle during our absence. We found a large fire blazing under the lee of a rock, and the pot steaming. We sat down in a circle with our feet to the fire, and soon each had upon his knees in a red earthen bowl two slices of black bread with a liberal supply of broth. The meal was a silent one; we were wet and hungry, and then there was the cemetery close by. Still, when our bowls were empty, we lighted our pipes and began to talk a little. Naturally we spoke of the "Sémillante."

"But how did it happen?" I asked the skipper, who, with his head in his hands, was looking at the fire with a thoughtful air.

"How did it happen?" replied the

good Lionetti, with a deep sigh. "Alas! sir, no one in the world can tell. All that we know is that the 'Sémillante,' laden with troops for the Crimea, had sailed from Toulon the evening before, in bad weather. That night it grew worse. There were wind and rain, and such a sea as never was known before. In the morning the wind fell a little, but the sea was still as high as ever, and with it was such a devil's fog that one could not have seen a lighthouse four paces off. No one has any idea, sir, how treacherous those fogs are. Still, that is no matter; my idea is that the 'Sémillante' must have lost her rudder during the morning. For no fog would account for it; but for an accident the captain would never have run ashore here. He was a fine sailor, whom we all knew. He had commanded the Corsican station for three years, and he knew the coast as well as do I, who know nothing else."

"At what time do they suppose the 'Sémillante' was lost?"

"It was at mid-day,—yes, sir, at mid-day. But with the fog at the time, that mid-day was little better than a night black as a wolf's mouth. A coast-guard of the neighbourhood told me that that day, about half-past eleven o'clock, having gone out of his house to fasten his shutters, his cap had been blown off by a gust of wind, and at the risk of being carried away by the surf he was chasing it along the shore on his hands and knees. Coast-guards are not rich, you know, sir, and a cap costs dear. Well, it seems that at a certain moment our man, raising his head, saw in the fog quite close to him a large ship driving under bare poles toward the Lavezzi Islands. This ship was moving so fast

that the coast-guard had scarcely time to see it. Still, everything leads us to believe that it was the 'Sémillante,' for half an hour later the shepherd on these islands heard— But here is the shepherd of whom I was speaking, sir; he will tell you the story himself. Good-day, Palombo! come and warm yourself a little. Do not fear."

A man in a hood whom I had seen for a few moments prowling about our fire, and whom I had taken for one of the crew,—for I did not know that there was a shepherd on the island,—drew near us timidly.

He was an old cripple, three fourths idiotic, afflicted with some scorbutic disease which gave him great swollen lips, horrible to behold. They explained to him with much difficulty what was wanted of him. Then, raising his diseased lip with his finger, the old man told us that on the day in question, about noon, he heard in his cabin a frightful crash upon the rocks. As the island was covered with water, he could not go out, and it was only on the next day that, upon opening his door, he had seen the shore strewn with wreckage and with corpses thrown up there by the sea. Horrified, he had fled at full speed to his boat, and had gone to Bonifacio to fetch some one.

Fatigued by having said so much, the shepherd sat down, and the skipper resumed:—

"Yes, sir, it was this poor old man who came to bring us the news. He was half mad with fright, and his brain has always remained disordered by the occurrence. Indeed, there was good reason for it. Fancy six hundred corpses piled upon the shore, mingled with splinters of wood and fragments of sail.

Poor 'Sémillante'! The sea had crushed her at a blow, and shivered her so thoroughly that it was with great difficulty that Palombo found, amid all her wreckage, sufficient to make a fence about his hut. As for the men, they were almost all disfigured.—frightfully mutilated; it was pitiful to see them clinging to one another in clusters. We found the captain in full uniform, and the chaplain with his stole about his neck; and in a corner, between two rocks, was a little ship's boy with his eyes open. One would have thought that he was alive, but, no! it was decreed that not one should escape."

Here the skipper interrupted himself. "Take care, Nardi. the fire is going out."

Nardi threw upon the embers two or three pieces of tarred wood, which blazed up; and Lionetti went on:—

"The saddest thing about the story is this: three weeks before the wreck a little corvette which was bound for the Crimea, like the 'Sémillante,' had been wrecked in the same way, almost in the same spot; only, on that occasion we had succeeded in saving the crew and twenty artillerymen who were on board. These poor *tringlos* were out of their element, as you can fancy. We took them to Bonifacio, and kept them with us for two days at the barracks. When once they were well dried and recovered, it was 'Good-by! Good luck!' They returned to Toulon, where they were shortly afterward again embarked for the Crimea. Guess upon what ship? Upon the 'Sémillante,' sir! We found them all, the whole twenty, lying among the dead where we now are. I myself picked up a handsome sergeant with a beautiful mustache, a youngster from

Paris, whom I had taken to my house, and who had kept us laughing all the time with his stories. It broke my heart to see him there! *Ah, Santa Madre!"*

With that the good Lionetti, deeply moved, shook the ashes from his pipe, and rolling himself up in his cloak, wished me good-night. For some time longer the sailors talked in a low tone. Then, one after another, the pipes went out. No one spoke again. The old shepherd went away, and I remained alone, dreaming in the midst of the sleeping crew.

Still under the impression of the gloomy narrative which I had just heard, I endeavoured to reconstruct in my mind the poor lost ship, and the story of that wreck which the gulls alone had witnessed. Some details which had struck me—the captain in full uniform, the chaplain's stole, the twenty artillerymen,—helped me to divine all the occurrences of the drama. I saw the frigate leaving Toulon at night. She comes out of the harbour. The sea is high, the wind terrible; but their captain is a brave sailor, and every one on board is unconcerned.

In the morning comes the fog. They commence to be uneasy. The whole crew is on deck. The captain never leaves the quarterdeck. Between decks, where the soldiers are shut up, it is dark, and the atmosphere is warm. Some of them are sick, and are lying on their knapsacks. The ship rolls horribly; it is impossible to stand. They talk seated on the deck in groups, clinging to the benches; they have to shout to make themselves heard. There are some who are beginning to be afraid. Just listen! Shipwrecks are common in these waters; the *tringlos* are here to tell us that, and what they relate is not reassuring. Their sergeant especially, a Parisian, who is always chaffing, gives one gooseflesh with his jokes.

"A shipwreck? Why, a shipwreck is very amusing. It will cost us only an ice-bath, and then they will take us to Bonifacio to eat blackbirds with Skipper Lionetti."

And the *tringlos* roar.

Suddenly there is a crash. What is it? What has happened?

"The rudder has been carried away," replies a dripping sailor, who runs through between-decks.

"A pleasant journey to it!" cries this devil of a sergeant; but nobody laughs at him now.

There is a great tumult on deck. The fog prevents every one from seeing. The sailors come and go, frightened, feeling their way. The rudder is gone. Steering is impossible. The "Sémillante," uncontrollable, drifts like the wind. It is at this moment that the coast-guard sees her pass; it is half-past eleven o'clock. They hear ahead of the frigate something like a cannon-shot. "The breakers! the breakers!" It is all over, there is no more hope; they are driving straight ashore. The captain goes down into his cabin. After a moment he returns to take his place on the quarter-deck in full uniform. He wishes to make himself fine to meet death.

Between decks the soldiers look at each other anxiously, without speaking. The sick strive to rise; the little sergeant laughs no longer. It is then that the door opens and the chaplain appears upon the threshold, wearing his stole.

"To your knees, children!"

Every one obeys. In a ringing voice the priest begins the prayers for the dying.

Suddenly there is a terrible shock, a cry,—a single, immense cry,—outstretched arms, clinging hands, frightened looks into which the vision of death passes like a lightning-flash.

God pity them!

It was thus that I passed the whole night in dreaming, calling up, after ten years, the soul of the poor ship whose fragments lay about me. Off in the strait the tempest was raging; the flame of our camp-fire flickering in the blast, and I could hear our boat tossing at the foot of the rocks and tugging at the rope which moored it.

The Coast Guards

THE "Emily," of Porto-Vecchio, on board which I made a gloomy journey to the Lavezzi Islands, was an old coast-guard vessel, half-decked, where there was no place in which one could take refuge from the wind, the sea, and the rain, but a little tarred half-cabin, hardly large enough to hold a table and two bunks. And so our sailors, in rough weather, were a sight! Their faces streamed, their soaked jerseys smoked like linen in a boiler, and in winter the poor wretches spent whole days crouching on their wet benches shivering in this unhealthy moisture; for they could not light a fire on board, and it was often difficult to land. Well, not one of these men complained. In the roughest weather I have always seen them show the same placidity, the same good-humour. And yet what a miserable life was that of these poor coast-guardsmen!

Almost all married, having wives and children at home, they remain at sea for months, coasting along these dangerous shores. Their food is scarcely anything but mouldy bread and wild onions. Never do they taste meat or wine,—for meat and wine are dear, and they earn only five hundred francs a year! You can fancy whether the hut on the seashore must be black and the children go barefoot! But no matter. All these people seem contented. In the stern, just forward of the little cabin, there was a large tub of rain-water, from which the crew came to drink; and I recollect that when he had finished the last swallow, each of these poor devils would shake his cup with an "Ah!" of satisfaction, and an air of enjoyment which were at once comic and touching.

The gayest, the best satisfied of all, was a bronzed and sturdy little Bonifacian named Palombo. He did nothing but sing, even in the worst weather. When the sea became rough, and the dark and lowering sky became filled with sleet, and they were all there, face to the wind and hand to the ear, watching for the coming squall, then amid the great silence and anxiety, the tranquil voice of Palombo would begin:—

Non, monseigneur,
C'est trop d'honneur.
Lisette est sa . . . age,
Reste au villa . . . age . . .

And no matter how the tempest might blow, making the rigging moan, and tossing and filling the boat, the song of the coast-guardsman would still go on, poised like a sea-mew on the crests of the waves. Sometimes the wind accompanied it too loudly, and the words could no longer be heard; but between each wave, amid the rippling of the water as it ran off, the little refrain would always return:—

Lisette est sa . . . age,
Reste au villa . . . age.

But one day, when it rained and blew very heavily, I did not hear it. It was so extraordinary that I put my head out of the cabin:—

"What! Palombo, have you stopped singing?"

Palombo did not reply. He was motionless, lying on a bench. I went up to him; his teeth were chattering, and his whole body shaking with fever.

"He has a *pountoura*," said his comrades, sadly.

What they call a *pountoura* is a pain in the side, a pleurisy. I have never seen anything more dismal than that leaden sky, the dripping boat, and the poor sick man wrapped in an old rubber cloak which glistened in the rain like the skin of a seal. Soon the cold, the wind, and the tossing of the boat increased his illness; he grew delirious, and it became necessary to get him ashore.

After much time and labour we entered toward evening a barren and silent little port, which was enlivened only by the circular flight of some gulls. All about the beach rose high, steep rocks, and tangled thickets of dark, evergreen shrubbery. Below, at the water-side, was a little white house with gray shutters; it was the coast-guard station.

In the midst of this desert, this building belonging to the State, numbered like a uniform cap, was singularly forbidding. It was there that they took the unfortunate Palombo. Gloomy refuge for a sick man! We found the coast-guard eating at the fireside with his wife and children. All of these people had haggard yellow faces, with enlarged eyes surrounded by circles caused by the fever. The mother, still young, with a child at her breast, shivered as she spoke to us.

"It is a terrible post," said the inspector to me in an undertone. "We are obliged to replace our coast-guardsmen every two years. The swamp fever kills them off."

It was necessary, however, to obtain a physician. There was none nearer than Sartène,—that is to say, six or eight miles from there. What should we do? Our sailors were exhausted; it was too far to send one of the children. Then the woman, leaning out, called,—

"Cecco! Cecco!"

And there entered a tall, well-built fellow, a typical poacher or bandit, with his red woollen cap and his goatskin *pelone*. I had already noticed him when we landed, seated before the door with his red pipe between his teeth, and a gun between his legs; but he had fled at our approach, I know not why. Perhaps he thought that we had gendarmes with us. When he came in, the coast-guard's wife blushed a little, and said to us,—

"It is my cousin."

There was no danger that this fellow would get lost in the thickets.

Then she spoke to him in an undertone, pointing to the sick man. The cousin bowed without replying, went out, whistled to his dog, and set off with his gun upon his shoulder, springing from rock to rock with his long legs.

During this time the children, who seemed terrified by the presence of the inspector, hastily finished their dinner of chestnuts and *brucio* (white cheese). And again there was water, nothing but water, on the table. Still, a drop of wine would have been very good for these little ones. Ah, poverty! Finally the mother went upstairs to put them to bed; the father, lighting his lantern, went to inspect the coast, and we remained before the fire, tending our sick man, who kept tossing upon his pallet as though he had been still at sea, shaken by the waves. To alleviate his *pountoura* somewhat, we heated stones and bricks, which we placed upon his side. Once or twice, when I approached his bed, the poor wretch recognized me, and to thank me held out his hand to me with an effort,—a large hand, rough and burning as the bricks fresh from the fire.

It was a gloomy watch. Without, the bad weather had returned with nightfall, and there was a roar, a surge, a tossing of spray, the battle between rocks and waves. From time to time the wind from the sea would succeed in entering the bay and sweep about the house. We could tell it by the abrupt rising of the flames which would suddenly light up the mournful faces of the sailors grouped about the fireplace, and looking at the fire with that placidity of expression given by familiarity with great distances and similar horizons. Now and again, too, Palombo would moan feebly. Then all eyes would be turned toward the dark corner where our poor comrade was dying, far from his family and without help; breasts would heave and heavy sighs be heard. This was all that was wrung from these gentle and patient toilers of the sea by the consciousness of their misery. No revolts, no outbursts,—a sigh and noth-ing more! But, yes, I am mistaken. As one of them passed me to throw a stick on the fire, he said to me in a heart-broken voice,—

"You see, sir, we sometimes have a hard time in our business!"

An Escape

ON one of the last days of the month of March five or six of us were seated at a table, in front of the Café Riche, watching the battalions of the Commune march past. There had been as yet no fighting, but assassinations had already taken place in the Rue des Rosiers, Place Vendôme, and at the Préfecture de Police. The farce was rapidly turning into a tragedy, and the boulevard laughed no longer.

In serried ranks round the red flag, with their canvas bags slung across the shoulder, the *communeux* tramped along with resolute step, covering the whole roadway; and when one looked at all these people under arms, so far from their working districts, with cartridge-pouches tightly buckled over their fustian jackets, the workmen's hands clutching the butt end of their guns, it was impossible not to think of the empty workshops and the abandoned factories.

This march past was in itself a menace. We all understood it, and the same sad, undefinable presentiment chilled our hearts.

At this moment, a tall, indolent and bloated swell, known to all the boulevard, from Tortoni to the Madeleine, approached our table. He was one of the most contemptible specimens of the fast man of the late Empire, a second-hand exquisite, who had never done anything but pick up on the boulevard all the eccentricities of the upper ten; baring his throat like Lutteroth, wearing ladies' dressing-gowns like Mouchy, bracelets like Narishkine, keeping for five years a card of Grammont-Caderousse stuck in his looking-glass; and withal painted like any old actor, dropping all his r's, in the affected style of the Directoire, saying: *"Pa' ole d'honneu'. Bonjou' Ma'ame,"* bringing the smell of Tattersall's stables everywhere on his boots, and with just enough education to be able to scratch his name on the mirrors of the Café Anglais, which, however, did not prevent him from posing as a thorough theologian, and from exhibiting from one restaurant to another his disdainful, used-up, blasé manner, which at that time constituted the height of "form."

During the siege, my fine fellow had had himself attached to some kind of staff—merely to save his riding horses—and from time to time, his ungainly figure might be seen, parading the neighbourhood of the Place Vendôme, amongst all the other grand gold-laced gentlemen; since then, I had lost sight of him. Therefore, to find him again suddenly in the midst of the insurrection, ever the same, in this convulsed Paris, produced on me the lugubrious and comical impression of an old veteran of the first empire, carrying out his pilgrimage of the 5th of May in the midst of the modern boulevard. The race of wretched Dundrearies was not ended then? There were still some left! In reality, I think that had I been given a choice, I would have preferred those infuriated *communards* who gathered on the ramparts, with a dry crust at the bottom of their rough canvas wallets. These at least had something in their heads, some vague, wild ideal which floated above them, and took some fierce colouring from the folds of that red rag, for which they were going to die. But he, empty rattle, with his vacant, breadcrumb brain!

That day precisely, our friend was more insipid, more indolent, more full of fine airs than usual. He wore a little straw hat with blue ribbons, his moustache was well waxed, his hair cropped Russian fashion; a short coat displayed all his figure, and to be thoroughly complete, at the end of a silken cord, used as a leash, he led a lady's lap-dog, a little Havanese dog the size of a rat, which, buried in its long hair, looked as bored and fatigued as his master. Thus got up, he planted himself in a languid attitude in front of our table, and watched the *communeux* defiling past, made some foolish remark, then with a slouch and a swing that were positively inimitable, declared to us that these fellows were beginning to make his blood boil, and that he was going off at once to "place his sword at the service of the Admiral!" The fiat had gone forth, the declaration was launched! Lasouche or Priston have never found anything more comic. Thereupon he turned away, and strolled off languidly, followed by his little sulky dog.

I know not whether in reality he did place his sword at the Admiral's disposal; but in any case, M. Saisset did not make much use of it, for eight days later, the flag of the Commune floated over all the mayors' offices, the drawbridges were raised, fighting had begun everywhere, and from hour to hour the side walks grew emptier and the streets more deserted. Everyone tried to escape as best he might—in the market-gardeners' carts, in the luggage vans of the embassies. Some disguised themselves as bargemen, stokers, or navvies. The most romantic crossed the ramparts at night with rope-ladders. The boldest went thirty at a time, and passed through a gate by storm; others, more practical, simply offered a bribe of five francs. Many followed hearses, and went wandering about the fields of the surrounding suburbs, with umbrellas and chimney-pot hats, black from head to foot, like village tipstaffs. Once outside, all these Parisians looked at each other laughingly, breathed freely, capered about, made fun of Paris; but soon the nostalgia of the asphalt regained possession of them, and the emigration, begun as truant schoolboys, became sad and burdensome as an exile.

My mind full of these ideas of escape, I was one morning strolling down the Rue de Rivoli, in pouring rain, when I was stopped by seeing a familiar face. At that early hour, there was scarcely anything in sight but the sweeping-machines, gathering up the mud in little gleaming heaps along the side of the pavement, and the row of tumbrels filled one after the other by the scavengers. Horror! it was under the bespattered smock of one of these men, that I recognized my masher, well disguised indeed!—a battered felt hat, a neck-handkerchief tied like a wisp round the throat, and the wide trousers called by the Parisian workman (pardon me the word) a *salopette;* all this was wet, shabby, threadbare, covered with a thick coating of mire, that the wretched creature did not even then consider thick enough, for I detected him trampling in the puddles, and kicking the mud up to the very roots of his hair. It was this peculiar manœuvre that attracted my attention.

"Good morning, Vicomte," I said to him in an undertone as I passed. The Vicomte grew pale under his mud stains, threw a terrified glance around him, then seeing everyone busy, he regained a little assurance, and told me that he had not chosen to place his sword (always his sword) at the service of the Commune, and that his butler's brother, mud contractor at Montreuil, had fortunately contrived for him this possibility of leaving Paris. He could not add more. The carts were full, and the procession was beginning to move on. My fellow had but time to run to his team, take up his position in the file, crack his whip and, hoi! go on! he was off. The adventure interested me. In order to see the end of it, I followed the tumbrels at a distance, as far as the Porte de Vincennes.

Each man walked at the side of his horses, whip in hand, leading his team by a leathern rein. To make his task easier they had put the Vicomte the last, and it was pitiful to see the poor devil striving to do like the others, to imitate their voice, their gait, that heavy bent, drowsy gait, swinging along with the rolling of the wheels, regulated by the step of the overladen animals. At times they stopped to allow some battalion to pass on its way to the ramparts. Then he would assume a bustling air, swear, use his whip, and make himself as much of a carter as possible; but, from time to time, the man of fashion re-appeared. This scavenger looked at women. In front of a cartridge manufactory, Rue de Charonne, he paused for a moment to watch the factory girls entering. The aspect of the great faubourg, all the swarms of people seemed to astonish him very much, and the startled glances he threw right and left showed his surprise, as though he fancied himself in an unknown country.

And yet Vicomte, you have travelled over these long streets leading to Vincennes often enough, on fine spring and autumn Sundays, when you were returning from the races, with a green card stuck in your hat, and a leather bag slung over your shoulder, cracking your whip in delicate and masterly style. But then you were perched up so high in your phaeton, you were surrounded with such a mass of flowers, ribbons, ringlets, and gauze veils, the wheels that almost touched your own, enveloped you in such a luminous and aristocratic dust, that you never saw the dark windows opening at your approach, nor the workmen's homes, where, at that very hour, they were sitting down to dinner; and when you had passed by, when all that long train of luxurious existence, the bright silks and startling golden locks of the women, all had disappeared towards Paris, bearing away with it its gilded atmosphere, you did not know how much more gloomy the Faubourg became, how much more bitter seemed the bread, how much heavier the tool appeared, nor what you left there of accumulated hatred and anger. A volley of oaths and cracks of the whip cut short my soliloquy. We had reached the Porte de Vincennes. The drawbridge had been lowered, and in the twilight, in the downpour of rain, in the midst of the obstruction caused by the crowding carts, the national guards examining the permits, I perceived the poor Vicomte struggling with his three large horses, which he was trying to turn round. The unfortunate fellow had lost his place. He swore, tugged at the rein; large drops of sweat rolled down his face. I can assure you his languid look had vanished. Already the *communeux* were beginning to notice him. A circle was formed round him, laughing at him;

his position became dangerous. Luckily the head carter came to his assistance, tore the bridle from his hands with a rough push, then, with a lash of his large whip, started the team, which rushed over the bridge at a gallop, with the Vicomte running and splashing behind. The gate passed, he resumed his place, and the long file was lost in the waste land outside the fortifications.

It was, indeed, a piteous egress. I watched it from the top of an embankment, the fields full of rubbish in which the wheels stuck; the scarce and muddy grass, the men bending low under the downpour, the long line of tumbrels rolling heavily, like hearses. It might have been some shameful burial, as it were all the Paris of the *Bas Empire* disappearing, drowned in the mud of its own creation.

What the Abbé Saw

EVERY year at Candlemas-tide the Provençal poets publish at Avignon a joyous little book, overflowing with beautiful poems and charming stories. That for this year has just reached me, and I find in it a delightful tale in verse, which I will try to translate for you, abridging it somewhat. Stretch forth your baskets, Parisians! It is the fine flower of the Provençal harvest which is to be served to you this time.

The Abbé Martin was curé of Cucugnan.

Good as wheat, true as gold, he loved his Cucugnanais like a father. His Cucugnan would have been an earthly paradise for him if only the Cucugnanais had given him a little better

satisfaction. But, alas! the spiders spun their webs in his confessional, and on the holy day of Easter the host remained in the ciborium. The good priest's heart was broken, and he was ever praying God to grant him not to die before he should lead his scattered flock back to the fold.

Now you will see that God heard him.

One Sunday, after the Gospel, M. Martin mounted the pulpit.

"My brothers," said he, "you may believe me if you will: the other night I found myself—I. a miserable sinner—at the gate of Paradise.

"I knocked; Saint Peter opened the door to me.

"'Ah! it is you, my good Monsieur

Martin,' said he. 'What good wind?—and what can I do to serve you?'

" 'Good Saint Peter, you who keep the great book and the key, can you tell me, if I am not too curious, how many Cucugnanais you have in Paradise?'

" 'I can refuse you nothing, Monsieur Martin. Sit down, and we will look over the matter together.'

"And Saint Peter took his great book, opened it, put on his spectacles:—

" 'Let us see a bit; Cucugnan, we were saying. Cu—Cu—Cucugnan. Here we are, Cucugnan. My dear Monsieur Martin, the page is perfectly white. Not a single soul! No more Cucugnanais than there are fishbones in a turkey!'

" 'What! No one here from Cucugnan? Not one? It is impossible. Look again!'

" 'Not one, holy man. Look yourself, if you think that I am joking.'

"I, *pécaïre*, I stamped my feet, and with clasped hands cried *'Miséricorde.'* Then said Saint Peter,—

" 'Come, Monsieur Martin, you must not be so put out about it, for you might bring on an apoplexy. It is not your fault, after all. Your Cucugnanais must certainly be spending their little quarantine in Purgatory.'

" 'Ah! *par charité*, great Saint Peter, let me at least see and console them.'

" 'Certainly, my friend. Here, put on quickly these sandals, because the roads thither are not of the best. There, that is right. Now go straight ahead. Do you see down there at the turn? You will find on the right hand a silver door studded with black crosses. You will knock, and they will open. *Adessias!* Keep well and hearty!'

"And I walked—I walked. What a trip! I am gooseflesh at the very thought of it. A little footpath, full of briers and carbuncles which glowed and serpents which hissed, led me to the silver door.

"Pan-pan!

" 'Who knocks?' said a hoarse and mournful voice.

" 'The Curé of Cucugnan.'

" 'Of—'

" 'Of Cucugnan.'

" 'Ah! Come in!'

"I went in. A great, beautiful angel with wings as black as night, and a robe as resplendent as day, with a diamond key hanging at his girdle, was writing, *cra-cra cra,* in a great book larger than Saint Peter's.

" 'To be brief, what do you wish?' said the angel.

" 'Beautiful angel of God, I wish to know—I am very curious, perhaps—if you have here the Cucugnanais?'

" 'The—'

" 'The Cucugnanais, the people of Cucugnan; I am their curé.'

" 'Ah! the Abbé Martin, is it not?'

" 'At your service, Monsieur Angel.'

" 'You say, then, Cucugnan—'

"And the angel opened his great book, and turned the leaves, wetting his finger with saliva to make the pages slip the better.

" 'Cucugnan,' said he, heaving a deep sigh. 'Monsieur Martin, we have nobody in purgatory from Cucugnan.'

" *'Jésu! Marie! Joseph!* You have no one from Cucugnan in Purgatory? *O grand Dieu!* where are they, then?'

" 'Eh! holy man, they are in Paradise. Where the deuce would you wish them to be?'

" 'But I have just come from Paradise.'

" 'You have come from there? Well?'

" 'Well, they are not there. *Ah, bonne mère des anges!*'

" 'What would you have, Monsieur le Curé? If they are neither in Paradise nor in Purgatory, there is no other choice; they are—'

" '*Sainte croix! Jésu, fils de David! Aï, aï, aï!* is it possible? Could great Saint Peter have lied to me? But I did not hear the cock crow! Ah, poor me! How shall I go to Paradise if my Cucugnanais are not there?'

" 'Listen, my poor Monsieur Martin. since you wish to be certain about all this, cost what it may, and to see the truth of it with your own eyes, take this path, and run if you know how to run. You will find a large gateway on the left. There you will make sure of everything. Good-by!'

"And the angel closed the door.

"It was a long road, all paved with red embers. I staggered as if I had been drinking. At every step I stumbled; I was fairly streaming, every hair on my body had its separate drop of sweat, and I was panting with thirst. But, *ma foi,* thanks to the sandals which the good Saint Peter had lent me, I did not burn my feet.

"When I had made enough missteps as I went *clopin clopant* along, I saw on my left a door—no, a gateway, an enormous gateway, yawning like the door of a gigantic oven. Oh, my children, what a spectacle! There they did not ask my name; there they kept no register. They go in there in batches, and freely, as you go into the tavern on Sundays.

"I was streaming with perspiration, and yet I was freezing, shivering. My hair stood on end. I could smell burning and roast flesh, something like the odour which spreads through Cucugnan when Eloy, the blacksmith, burns the hoof of an old ass before shoeing it. I could not breathe in this evil-smelling, stifling atmosphere, I heard a horrible outcry, groans, roars, and cursing.

" 'Well, are you coming in or not coming in,—you?' said a horned devil, prodding me with his pitchfork.

" 'I? I am not coming in. I am a friend of God.'

" 'You are a friend of God? Then what the devil are you doing here?'

" 'I have come—ah! do not speak to me, I can hardly stand—I have come —come a long way to ask you humbly if—if by chance—you have here any one—any one from Cucugnan?'

" 'Ah, *feu de Dieu!* You are playing the fool, you, as if you did not know that all Cucugnan is here. Here. ugly crow, look, and you will see how we arrange them here,—your famous Cucugnanais.'

"And I saw, in the midst of a frightful whirlwind of flame, the tall Coq-Galine,—you all knew him, my brethren, —Coq-Galine, who got drunk so often, and who so often beat his poor Clairon.

"I saw Catarinet, that little hussy, with her head in the air, who used to sleep alone in the barn. You recollect her, you knaves! But we will go on; I have said too much already.

"I saw Pascal Doigt-de-Poix, who used to make his oil with M. Julien's olives.

"I saw Babet the gleaner, who in order the sooner to make up her sheaf would snatch handfuls from the reapers.

"I saw Master Grapasi, who oiled the wheel of his barrow so carefully.

"And Dauphine, who sold the water of her well so dear.

"And Tortillard, who when he met me carrying the host, would walk on with his cap on his head and his pipe in his mouth, and proud as Artaban,—as if he had met a dog.

"And Coulau with her Zette, and Jacques, and Pierre, and Toni—"

Horrified, white with fear, the congregation groaned at seeing in this hell, opened before them, one his father, another his mother, this his grandmother, that his sister.

"You must see, my brethren," continued the good Abbé Martin,—"you must see that this cannot go on. I have charge of your souls, and I wish—I wish to save you from the abyss into which you are all about to fall head-foremost. To-morrow I shall set to work, not later than to-morrow. And I shall have no lack of work! This is how I shall arrange it. For all to go well, all must be done in order. We will go row by row, as they do at Jonquières when they dance.

"To-morrow, Monday, I will confess the old men and the old women. That is nothing.

"On Tuesday, the children. That will be quickly over.

"On Wednesday, the lads and lasses. That will take a good deal of time.

"On Thursday, the men. We will cut it short.

"On Friday, the women. I shall say —No Gossip!

"On Saturday, the miller! A whole day alone for him will not be too much.

"And if we have finished on Sunday, we shall be very lucky.

"You see, my children, when the grain is ripe, it must be cut; when the wine is drawn, it must be drunk. We have enough dirty linen; we must wash it."

C'est la grâce que je vous souhaite. Amen.

It was done as he said; the linen was washed.

Since that memorable Sunday the perfume of the virtues of Cucugnan is breathed for ten leagues around.

And the good pastor, M. Martin, happy and joyful, dreamed the other night that, followed by his whole flock, he was ascending in a brilliant procession, amid lighted candles, a cloud of fragrant incense, and choir children chanting the Te Deum, the dazzling road to the city of God.

And that is the story of the Curé of Cucugnan as I have been charged to tell it to you by that great rascal Roumanille, who had it himself from another jolly companion.

My First Dress Coat

How did I come by it, that first dress coat? What primitive tailor, what confiding tradesman was it, trustful as Don Juan's famous Monsieur Dimanche, who upon the faith of my fantastic promises, decided one fine morning on bringing it to me, brand new, and artistically pinned up in a square of shiny green calico? It would be difficult for me to tell. Of the honest tailor, I can indeed recall nothing—so many tailors have since then crossed my path—save perüaps a vision as in a luminous mist, of a thoughtful brow and a large moustache. The coat indeed is there, before my eyes. Its image after twenty years still remains indelibly graven on my memory, as on imperishable brass. What a collar, my young friends! What lappels! And, above all, what skirts, shaped as the slimmest tail of the swallow! My brother, a man of experience, had said: "One must have a dress coat if one wishes to make one's way in the world." And the dear fellow counted much upon this piece of frippery for the advancement of my fame and fortune.

This, my first dress coat, made its *début* at Augustine Brohan's, and under what circumstances worthy of being transmitted to posterity, you shall now hear.

My little volume had just made its appearance, fresh and virginal, in rose-tinted cover. A few critics had noticed my rhymes. Even *l'Official* had printed my name. I was a poet; no longer hidden in a garret, but printed, published and exposed for sale in the shop windows. I was astonished that the busy folk in the streets did not turn round to look at me, as my eighteen years wandered along the pavement. I positively felt upon my forehead the pleasant pressure of a paper crown, made up of flattering paragraphs culled from the papers.

One day some one proposed to get me an invitation to Augustine Brohan's soireés. Who? some one. Some one, egad! You know him already: that eternal some one, who is like every one else, that amiable institution of Providence, who, of no personal value in himself and a mere acquaintance in the

houses he frequents, yet goes everywhere, introduces you everywhere, is the friend of a day, of an hour, of whose name even you are ignorant, that essentially Parisian type.

You may imagine with what enthusiasm I accepted the proposal! To be invited to Augustine's house! Augustine, the famous actress, Augustine, the laughing representative of Molière's comic muse, softened somewhat by the more modern poetic smile of Musset's genius;—for while she acted the waiting maids at the Theatre Français, Musset had written his comedy *Louison* at her house; Augustine Brohan in short, in whom all Paris delighted, vaunting her wit, quoting her repartees; and who might already be said to have adorned herself with that swallow's plume, unsullied yet by ink, but already well sharpened, with which she was hereafter to sign those charming *Lettres de Suzanne!*

"Lucky dog!" said my brother, helping me on with the coat; "your fortune is made."

Nine o'clock was striking as I sallied forth.

At that time Augustine Brohan was living in the rue Lord Byron, at the top of the Champs Elysées, in one of those pretty coquettish little houses which seem to ignorant provincials the realization of the poetical dreams which they weave for themselves from the pages of the novelist. A railing, a tiny garden, four steps covered by an awning, an entrance hall filled with flowers, and then opening immediately from it, the drawing-room, a brilliantly lighted room in green, which I can see now vividly before me.

How I managed to get up those steps,

how I made my entry, and how I presented myself, I cannot now remember. A footman announced my name, but this name. which he mumbled, produced no effect on the brilliant assembly. I can only recollect hearing a woman's voice say: "So much the better, here is another dancer." It appears they were short of dancers; but what an entry for a poet!

Startled and humiliated, I tried to lose myself among the crowd. How can I describe my dismay, when, a moment later, another mistake arose? My long hair, my dark and sombre looks excited general curiosity. I heard them whispering near me: "Who is it? Do look," and they laughed. At last some one said,

"It is the Wallachian Prince!"

"The Wallachian Prince? Oh yes, very likely."

I suppose that a Wallachian Prince had been expected that evening. My rank being thus settled for me, I was left in peace. But for all that, you cannot imagine how heavily my usurped crown weighed upon me all that evening. First a dancing man! then a Wallachian Prince! Could not these good people see my lyre?

Fortunately for me, a startling piece of news, flying from mouth to mouth, spread rapidly through the ballroom, casting into oblivion both the dancer and the Wallachian Prince. Marriage was at that time much the fashion among the feminine portion of the Comédie Company, and it was generally at Augustine Brohan's Wednesday receptions, where all the choicest talents of journalism, together with bankers and high government officials gathered round the lovely members or associates of the

Français, that the foundations were laid of most of these romantic unions.

Mdlle. Fix, the witty actress, with her long Hebrew eyes, was soon to marry a great financier and die in childbirth. Mdlle. Figeac, Catholic and romantic, was already dreaming of the future day when a priest would solemnly bless her immense shop on the Boulevard Haussmann, just as if it were a vessel about to be launched. Emilie Dubois, the fair Emilie herself, although destined by the delicate style of her beauty to the perpetual representation of artless maidens, had visions of orange blossoms from behind the protecting shelter of her mother's shawl. As for Madeleine Brohan, the handsome and majestic sister of Augustine, she was not marrying, but was unmarrying just then; thereby giving Mario Uchard time and money to devote himself to the four acts of his *Fiammina*. What an explosion was therefore caused in that circle so highly charged with matrimonial electricity, when this news spread: "Gustave Fould has married Valérie." Gustave Fould, the minister's son! Valérie the charming actress! Now, all this seems very far off. After a flight to England, after letters in the papers and pamphlets written, after waging a war in Mirabeau's style against a father as inexorable as the "people's friend;" after the most romantic of romances, ending up in the most prosaic fashion, Gustave Fould, following, in that, Mario Uchard's example, wrote the *Comtesse Romani*, and eloquently displayed the history of his misfortunes on the stage. Mdlle. Valérie laid aside her married name, and signed, under the pseudonym of Gustave Haller, volumes entitled *Vertu*. with a lovely picture on the palest of blue covers. So the passionate language of love calmed down in an ocean of literature! But what endless gossip, what emotion it created that evening in Augustine's green drawing-room! The men, the officials, shook their heads, and with mouths round with astonishment, said, "Oh! This is very serious, very serious!" One overheard the following broken sentences. "Everything is going to the dogs." "Respect has died out." "The Emperor ought to interfere." "Sacred rights." "Paternal authority." The women on their side openly and gaily stood up in defence of the two lovers who had fled to London. "Well, if they are fond of each other!" "Why should not the father consent?" "He is a minister, but what of that?" "Since the Revolution, thank God, there is no longer a Bastille or a Fort-i'Evêque!" Picture to yourself all these people talking at the same time, and rising brilliant above the noisy hubbub, like a thread of gold on a piece of embroidery, the clear ringing laugh of Augustine, her full prominent eyes (those pretty short-sighted eyes) gleaming with fun, and the whole of her little plump figure the very embodiment of mirth.

At last comparative calm was restored and the quadrilles began. I danced. I was obliged to do so! I danced moreover somewhat badly for a Wallachian Prince. The quadrille once ended, I became stationary; foolishly held back by my short sight—too shy to sport an eyeglass, too much of a poet to wear spectacles, and dreading lest, at the slightest movement, I should bruise my knee against the corner of some piece of furniture, or plunge my nose into the trimming of a bodice. Soon hunger and thirst interfered in the matter; but for a kingdom I should never have dared to approach the buffet with all the rest of the world. I anxiously watched for the moment when it should be deserted; and while waiting, I joined the groups of political talkers, assuming a serious air, and feigning to scorn the charms of the smaller salon, whence came to me, with the pleasant sound of laughter and the tinkling of teaspoons against the porcelain, a delicate aroma of scented tea, of Spanish wines and cakes. At last they came back to dance, and I gathered up my courage I entered, I was alone.

What a dazzling sight was that buffet! A crystal pyramid under the blaze of the candles, brilliant with glasses and decanters, white and glittering as snow in sunshine! I took up a glass as fragile as a flower, careful not to hold it too tightly lest I should break the stem. What should I pour into it? Come now, courage, I say to myself, since no one can see me. I stretched out my hand, and took at haphazard a decanter. It must be kirsch, I thought, from its diamond clearness. Well, I'll try a glass of kirsch; I like its perfume, its bitter and wild perfume that reminds me of the forest! And so, like an epicure, I slowly poured out, drop by drop, the beautiful clear liquid. I raised the glass to my lips. Oh, horror! it was only water. What a grimace I made! Suddenly a duet of laughter resounded from a black coat and a pink dress that I had not perceived flirting in a corner, and who were amused at my mistake.

I endeavoured to replace my glass.

but I was nervous, my hand shook, and my sleeve caught I know not what. One glass, two glasses, three glasses fell! I turned round, my wretched coat tails swept a wild circle, and the white pyramid crashed to the ground, with all the sparkling, splintering, flashing uproar of an iceberg breaking to pieces.

At the noise of the catastrophe the mistress of the house rushes up. Luckily, she is as short-sighted as the Wallachian Prince, and he is able to escape from the buffet without being recognized. All the same, my evening is spoilt. The massacre of small glasses and decanters weighs on my mind like a crime. My one idea is to get away. But the Dubois mamma, dazzled by my principality, catches hold of me, and will not allow me to leave till I have danced with her daughter, or indeed with both her daughters. I excuse myself as best I can; I escape from her, and am stealing away, when a tall old man, with a shrewd smile, stopped my egress. It is Doctor Ricord, with whom I had exchanged a few words previously and who like the others, takes me for the Wallachian. "But, Prince, as you are inhabiting the Hôtel du Sénat, and as we are near neighbours, pray wait for me, I can offer you a seat in my carriage." How willingly would I accept, but I have no overcoat. What would Ricord think of a Wallachian Prince without furs, and shivering in his dress coat? Let me escape quickly, and hurry home on foot, through the snow and fog, sooner than allow my poverty to be seen. Always half blind and more confused than ever, I reach the door and slip out, not however without getting somehow entangled in the tapestries. "Won't Monsieur take his coat?" a footman calls after me.

There I was, at two o'clock in the morning, far from my home, alone in the streets, hungry and frozen, with the devil's own self, a badly lined purse, in my pocket. But hunger inspired me with a brilliant idea: "Suppose I go to the markets!" I had often heard of the markets, and of a certain Gaidras, whose establishment remained open all night, and where for the sum of three sous they provided a plateful of succulent cabbage soup. By Jove, yes, to the markets I would go. I would sit down at those tables like the veriest prowling vagabond. All my pride had vanished. The wind is icy cold; hunger makes me desperate. "My kingdom for a horse," said another prince, and I say to myself as I trot along: "My principality, my Wallachian principality, for a basin of good soup in a warm corner."

Gaidras' establishment looks a mere filthy hovel, all slimy and badly lighted, thrust back beneath the colonnades of the old market place. Often and often since then, when noctambulism was the fashion, have we future great men spent whole nights there, elbows on table, amidst tobacco smoke and literary talk. But at first I must own, notwithstanding my hunger, I almost drew back at the sight of those blackened dingy walls, that dense smoke, those late sitters, snoring with their backs against the wall or lapping up their soup like dogs; the amazing caps of the Don Juans of the gutter, the enormous drab felt hats of the market porters, and the healthy rough blouse of the market gardener side by side with the greasy tatters of the prowler of he night. Nevertheless I entered, and I may at once add that my black coat found its fellows. Black coats that own no great coat are not rare in Paris after midnight in the winter, and they are hungry enough to eat three sous' worth of cabbage soup! The cabbage soup was however exquisite; full of perfume as a garden, and smoking like a crater. I had two helpings, although a custom peculiar to the establishment —inspired by a wholesome distrust— of fastening the forks and spoons with a chain to the table, hindered me a little. I paid, and fortified by the substantial mess, resumed my way to the Quartier Latin.

What a picture that return home! The return of the poet, trotting up the rue de Tournon, with his coat collar turned up, while dancing before his sleepy eyes are the elegant shadows of a fashionable evening party mingling with the famished spectres of the market-place. He stands knocking his boots against the kerbstone of the Hôtel du Sénat, to shake off the snow, while opposite, the bright lamps of a brougham light up the front of an old mansion, and Doctor Ricord's coachman cries out: "Gate, if you please." Life in Paris is made up of these contrasts.

"A wasted evening!" said my brother, the next morning. "You have been taken for a Wallachian Prince, and have not succeeded in launching your book. But all is not yet lost; you must make up for it when you make your 'digestion call!' as we say in Paris."

The digestion of a glass of water, what irony! It was quite two months before I made up my mind to pay that call. However one day I summoned up courage. Besides her official receptions on Wednesdays, Augustine Brohan received more unceremoniously on Sunday afternoon. I resolutely started off.

In Paris a *matinée* that respects itself cannot decently begin till three or even four o'clock in the afternoon. I, poor unsophisticated mortal, taking the word *matinée* literally, arrived there at one o'clock, and thought myself already late.

"How early you come, sir!" said a fair-haired little boy of five or six years of age, who, dressed in an embroidered velvet suit, was riding a mechanical toy horse through the fresh spring greenery of the garden. The young man impressed me! I bowed to the fair curls, the horse, the velvet, the embroideries, and too bashful to retrace my steps, I went in. Madame was not yet dressed, and I waited all alone for half an hour. At last Madame made her appearance; screwing up her eyes she recognized her Wallachian Prince; then by way of beginning the conversation, she said: "You are not at *La Marche*, Prince?" At *La Marche*, I, who had never seen a race nor a jockey!

Really I felt too much ashamed! a sudden throb rose from my heart to my brain; and then the bright sun, the sweet perfume of spring wafted from the garden through the open casement, the absence of all ceremony, the smiling and kind-hearted little woman, all combined to encourage me, and I poured forth my whole heart. I told her all—confessing everything: how I was neither a Wallachian, nor a Prince, but a simple poet; and the adventure of my glass of kirsch, and my supper at the markets, and my wretched return home, and my provincial timidity, and my short sight, and my aspirations—all seasoned by the accent of my southern province. Augustine Brohan laughed heartily. Suddenly a bell rang.

"Ah! my dragoons," she exclaimed.

"What dragoons?"

"Two dragoons they are sending me from the camp at Châlons, and who, it appears, have a wonderful taste for acting."

I wished to take leave.

"No, no. stay; we are going to rehearse *Lait d'ânesse*, and you shall help me with your criticisms. Sit down by me on the sofa!"

Two huge fellows came in, shy, awkward, tightly belted, purple in the face (one of them acts somewhere at the present day). A folding screen is arranged, I settle myself, and the representation begins.

"They do not act so badly," said Augustine Brohan in a low tone, "but what boots! My dear critic, do you smell those boots?"

To be on these intimate terms with the wittiest actress in Paris raised me to the seventh heaven. I threw myself back on the sofa, nodding my head and smiling in a capable manner. I was positively intoxicated with delight.

Even now I can recall the smallest details of that interview. But see how all depends upon our point of view. I had told Sarcey the comical story of my first appearance in society, and one day Sarcey repeated it to Augustine Brohan. Well the ungrateful Augustine —whom, it is true, I have not seen for thirty years—swore most sincerely that she knew nothing of me but my books. She had forgotten everything! Everything—all that had played such an important part in my life—the broken glasses, the Wallachian Prince, the rehearsal of *Lait d'ânesse*, and the boots of the heavy dragoons.

Last Class

I was very late for school that morning, and I was terribly afraid of being scolded, especially as Monsieur Hamel had told us that he should examine us on participles, and I did not know the first thing about them. For a moment I thought of staying away from school and wandering about the fields. It was such a warm, lovely day. I could hear the blackbirds whistling on the edge of the wood, and in the Rippert field, behind the sawmill, the Prussians going through their drill. All that was much more tempting to me than the rules concerning participles; but I had the strength to resist, and I ran as fast as I could to school.

As I passed the mayor's office, I saw that there were people gathered about the little board on which notices were posted. For two years all our bad news had come from that board—battles lost, conscriptions, orders from headquarters; and I thought without stopping:

"What can it be now?"

Then, as I ran across the square, Wachter the blacksmith, who stood there with his apprentice, reading the placard, called out to me:

"Don't hurry so, my boy; you'll get to your school soon enough!"

I thought that he was making fun of me, and I ran into Monsieur Hamel's little yard all out of breath.

Usually, at the beginning of school, there was a great uproar which could be heard in the street, desks opening and closing, lessons repeated aloud in unison, with our ears stuffed in order to learn quicker, and the teacher's stout ruler beating on the desk:

"A little more quiet!"

I counted on all this noise to reach my bench unnoticed; but as it happened, that day everything was quiet, like a Sunday morning. Through the open window I saw my comrades already in their places, and Monsieur Hamel walking back and forth with the terrible iron ruler under his arm. I had to open the door and enter, in the midst of that perfect silence. You can imagine whether I blushed and whether I was afraid!

But no! Monsieur Hamel looked at me with no sign of anger and said very gently:

"Go at once to your seat, my little Frantz; we were going to begin without you."

I stepped over the bench and sat down at once at my desk. Not until then, when I had partly recovered from my fright, did I notice that our teacher had on his handsome blue coat, his plaited ruff, and the black silk embroidered breeches, which he wore only on days of inspection or of distribution of prizes. Moreover, there was something extraordinary, something solemn about the whole class. But what surprised me most was to see at the back of the room, on the benches which were usually empty, some people from the village sitting, as silent as we were: old Hauser with his three-cornered hat, the ex-mayor, the ex-postman, and others besides. They all seemed depressed; and Hauser had brought an old spelling-book with gnawed edges, which he held wide-open on his knee, with his great spectacles askew.

While I was wondering at all this, Monsieur Hamel had mounted his platform, and in the gentle and serious voice with which he had welcomed me, he said to us:

"My children, this is the last time that I shall teach you. Orders have come from Berlin to teach nothing but German in the schools of Alsace and Lorraine. The new teacher arrives to-morrow. This is the last class in French, so I beg you to be very attentive."

Those few words overwhelmed me. Ah! the villains! that was what they had posted at the mayor's office.

My last class in French!

And I barely knew how to write! So I should never learn! I must stop short where I was! How angry I was with myself because of the time I had wasted, the lessons I had missed, running about after nests, or sliding on the Saar! My books, which only a moment before I thought so tiresome, so heavy to carry—my grammar, my sacred history—seemed to me now like old friends, from whom I should be terribly grieved to part. And it was the same about Monsieur Hamel. The thought that he was going away, that I should never see him again, made me forget the punishments, the blows with the ruler.

Poor man! It was in honor of that

last lesson that he had put on his fine Sunday clothes; and I understood now why those old fellows from the village were sitting at the end of the room. It seemed to mean that they regretted not having come oftener to the school. It was also a way of thanking our teacher for his forty years of faithful service, and of paying their respects to the fatherland which was vanishing.

I was at that point in my reflections, when I heard my name called. It was my turn to recite. What would I not have given to be able to say from beginning to end that famous rule about participles, in a loud, distinct voice, without a slip! But I got mixed up at the first words, and I stood there swaying against my bench, with a full heart, afraid to raise my head. I heard Monsieur Hamel speaking to me:

"I will not scold you, my little Frantz; you must be punished enough; that is the way it goes; every day we say to ourselves: 'Pshaw! I have time enough. I will learn tomorrow.' And then you see what happens. Ah! it has been the great misfortune of our Alsace always to postpone its lessons until tomorrow. Now those people are entitled to say to us: 'What! you claim to be French, and you can neither speak nor write your language!' In all this, my poor Frantz, you are not the guiltiest one. We all have our fair share of reproaches to address to ourselves.

"Your parents have not been careful enough to see that you were educated. They preferred to send you to work in the fields or in the factories, in order to have a few more sous. And have I nothing to reproach myself for? Have I not often made you water my garden instead of studying? And when I wanted to go fishing for trout, have I ever hesitated to dismiss you?"

Then, passing from one thing to another, Monsieur Hamel began to talk to us about the French language, saying that it was the most beautiful language in the world, the most clear, the most substantial; that we must always retain it among ourselves, and never forget it, because when a people falls into servitude, "so long as it clings to its language, it is as if it held the key to its prison." Then he took the grammar and read us our lesson. I was amazed to see how readily I understood. Everything that he said seemed so easy to me, so easy. I believed, too, that I had never listened so closely, and that he, for his part, had never been so patient with his explanations. One would have said that, before going away, the poor man desired to give us all his knowledge, to force it all into our heads at a single blow.

When the lesson was at an end, we passed to writing. For that day Monsieur Hamel had prepared some entirely new examples, on which was written in a fine, round hand: "France, Alsace, France, Alsace." They were like little flags, waving all about the class, hanging from the rods of our desks. You should have seen how hard we all worked and how silent it was! Nothing could be heard save the grinding of the pens over the paper. At one time some cockchafers flew in; but no one paid any attention to them, not even the little fellows, who were struggling with their straight lines, with a will and conscientious application, as if even the lines were French. On the roof of the schoolhouse, pigeons cooed in low tones, and I said to myself as I listened to them:

"I wonder if they are going to compel them to sing in German, too!"

From time to time, when I raised my eyes from my paper, I saw Monsieur Hamel sitting motionless in his chair and staring at the objects about him, as if he wished to carry away in his glance the whole of his little schoolhouse. Think of it! For forty years he had been there in the same place, with his yard in front of him and his class just as it was! But the benches and desks were polished and rubbed by use; the walnuts in the yard had grown, and the hopvine which he himself had planted now festooned the windows even to the roof. What a heartrending thing it must have been for that poor man to leave all those things, and to hear his sister walking back and forth in the room overhead, packing their trunks! For they were to go away the next day—to leave the province forever.

However, he had the courage to keep the class to the end. After the writing, we had the lesson in history; then the little ones sang all together, the *ba, be, bi, bo, bu.* Yonder, at the back of the room, old Hauser had put on his spectacles, and, holding his spelling-book in both hands, he spelled out the letters with them. I could see that he, too, was applying himself. His voice shook with emotion, and it was so funny to hear him, that we all longed to laugh and to cry. Ah! I shall remember that last class.

Suddenly the church clock struck twelve, then the Angelus rang. At the same moment, the bugles of the Prussians returning from drill blared under our windows. Monsieur Hamel rose, pale as death, from his chair. Never had he seemed to me so tall.

"My friends," he said, "my friends, I—I——"

But something suffocated him. He could not finish the sentence.

Thereupon he turned to the blackboard, took a piece of chalk, and, bearing on with all his might, wrote in the largest letters he could:

"Vive la France!"

Then he stood there, with his head resting against the wall, and without speaking, he motioned to us with his hand:

"That is all; go."

Game of Billiards

As they have been fighting two days, and have passed the night with their knapsacks on, beneath a flood of rain, the soldiers are completely exhausted. And yet for three mortal hours they have been left waiting, with grounded arms, in the puddles of the highroads and the mud of the saturated fields.

Benumbed by fatigue, by sleepless nights, and with their uniforms drenched with rain, they crowd together to warm and comfort one another. There are some who sleep standing, leaning against a neighbor's knapsack, and weariness and privations can be read distinctly upon those relaxed faces, overcome with sleep. Rain, mud, no fire, nothing to eat, a low, black sky, and the enemy in the air about. It is funereal.

What are they doing there? What is going on? The guns, with their muzzles pointed towards the wood, have the appearance of watching something. The mitrailleurs in ambush stare fixedly at the horizon. Everything seems ready for an attack. Why do they not attack? What are they waiting for?

They are awaiting orders, and headquarters sends none.

And yet the headquarters are not far away. They are at yonder stately Louis-Treize château, whose red bricks, scoured by the rain, glisten among the trees half-way up the hill. Truly a princely dwelling quite worthy to bear the banner of a marshal of France. Behind a broad moat and a stone wall which separate them from the road, smooth green lawns, lined with vases of flowers, extend to the porch. On the other side, the private side of the house, the hornbeam hedges show luminous gaps; the pond in which swans are swimming lies like a mirror, and beneath the pagoda-like roof of an enormous aviary, peacocks and golden pheasants flash their wings and display their plumage, uttering shrill cries amid the foliage. Although the owners have gone away, one does not feel the abandonment, the desolation of war. The oriflamme of the leader of the army has safeguarded even the tiniest flowers in the lawns, and it is an impressive thing to find so near the battlefield that opulent tranquillity that is born of perfect order, of the accurate alignment of the shrubbery, of the silent depths of the avenues.

The rain, which fills the roads yonder with such disgusting mud, and digs such deep ruts, here is nothing more than an elegant, aristocratic shower reviving the red of the bricks and the green of the lawns, polishing the leaves of the orange-trees and the white feathers of the swans. Everything glistens, everything is peaceful. Really, but for the flag floating on the roof, but for the two soldiers on sentry-go before the gate, one would never suspect that it is the headquarters of an army. The horses are resting in the stables. Here and there one sees a groom, or an orderly in undress uniform, loitering about the kitchen, or a gardener in red trousers placidly drawing his rake over the gravel in the great courtyards.

The dining-room, the windows of which look upon the porch, discloses a half-cleared table; uncorked bottles, soiled and empty glasses on the rumpled cloth; the end of a banquet, after the guests have gone. In the adjoining room one may hear loud voices, laughter, the clicking of balls, and the clinking of glasses. The marshal is playing his game of billiards, and that is why the army is waiting for orders. When the marshal had begun his game, the heavens might fall, but nothing in the world could prevent him from finishing it.

Billiards! that is the weakness of that great warrior. He stands there, as grave as in battle, in full uniform, his breast covered with medals, with kindled eyes, flushed cheeks, excited by feasting, grog, and the game. His aides-de-camp surround him, zealous and respectful, uttering admiring exclamations at each of his strokes. When the marshal makes a point, they all hasten to mark it; when the marshal is thirsty, they all rush to prepare his grog. There is a constant rustling of epaulettes and plumes, a jingling of medals; and to see all those sweet smiles, those artful courtier-like reverences, all those new uniforms and embroidery in that lofty apartment, with its oaken wainscoting, looking upon parks and courts of honor, recalls the autumn days at Compiegne, and affords the eyes a little rest from the stained cloaks that shiver yonder along the roads, forming such sombre groups in the rain.

The marshal's opponent is a young captain of the staff, belted and curled and light-gloved, who is in the first rank of billiard-players and capable of beating all the marshals on earth; but he has the tact to keep a respectful distance behind his chief, and devotes his energies to the task of not winning, and at the same time not losing too easily. He is what is called an officer with a future.

Attention, young man, let us be on our guard! The marshal has fifteen, and you ten. The point is to keep the game in that condition to the end; then you will have done more for your promotion than if you were outside with the others, beneath those torrents of water which drown the horizon, soiling your natty uniform, tarnishing the gold of your aiguillettes, awaiting orders which do not come.

It is really an interesting game. The balls roll and clash and mingle their colors. The cushions send them merrily back; the cloth waxes hot. Suddenly the flash of a cannon-shot passes across the sky. A dull sound rattles the windows. Everybody starts, and they look at each other anxiously. The marshal alone has neither seen nor heard anything; leaning over the table, he is busily engaged in planning a magnificent draw-shot; draw-shots are his strong point.

But there comes another flash, then another. The cannon-shots succeed each other in hot haste. The aides-decamp run to the windows. Can it be that the Prussians are attacking?

"Very well, let them attack!" says the marshal, chalking his cue. "It's your turn, captain."

The staff quivers with admiration. Turenne asleep upon a gun-carriage was nothing compared to this marshal, who plays billiards so tranquilly at the moment of going into action. Meanwhile the uproar redoubles. With the roar of the cannon is mingled the tearing sound of the mitrailleuses, the rattle of musketry. A red steam, black at the edges, rises around the lawns. The whole park is on fire. The terrified peacocks and pheasants shriek in the aviary; the Arabian horses, smelling the powder, rear in the stables. The headquarters begins to be excited. Despatch after despatch. Couriers arrive at full speed. They ask for the marshal.

The marshal cannot be seen. Did I not tell you that nothing could prevent him from finishing his game?

"It is your turn, captain."

But the captain is distraught. That is what it is to be young. Behold he loses his head, forgets his tactics, and makes two runs in succession, which almost give him the game. Thereupon the marshal becomes furious. Surprise and indignation animate his manly face. Just at this moment a horse ridden at a hard gallop rushes into the courtyard. An aide-de-camp covered with mud forces his way past the sentries and ascends the steps at one bound. "Marshal, marshal!" You should see how he is greeted. Puffing with anger and red as a rooster, the marshal appears at the window, his billiard-cue in his hand:

"What is the matter? What's all this? Isn't there any sentry there?"

"But, marshal——"

"All right, in a moment; wait for my orders, in God's name!"

And the window is violently closed.

Wait for his orders! That is just what they are doing, the poor fellows. The wind drives the rain and the grape-shot full in their faces. Whole battalions are wiped out, while others stand useless, with their arms in readiness, utterly unable to understand their inaction. Nothing to do. They are awaiting orders. However, as one needs no orders to die, the men fall by hundreds behind the shrubs, in the moats, in front of the great silent château. Even after they have fallen, the grape tears them still, and from the open wounds the generous blood of France flows noiselessly. Above, in the billiard-room it is getting terribly warm too; the marshal has recovered his lead, but the little captain is defending himself like a lion.

They hardly have time to mark the points. The roar of the battle draws nearer. The marshal has but one more to go. Already shells are falling in the park. Suddenly one bursts over the pond. The mirror is shattered; a swan in deadly alarm swims wildly about amid an eddy of bloody feathers. That is the last stroke.

Then, a profound silence. Only the rain falling on the hedges, a confused rumbling at the foot of the hill, and, along the muddy roads, a sound like the trampling of a hurrying flock. The army is in full retreat. The marshal has won his game.

M. Seguin's Goat

You will always be the same, my poor Gringoire!

What! they offer you a place on a good Paris newspaper, and you have the coolness to refuse? But look at yourself, poor fellow! Look at that threadbare coat, those ragged trousers, that thin face which cries hunger! Yet that is where your passion for fine rhymes has brought you! That is what you have earned by ten years of loyal service among Apollo's pages. Are you not ashamed of yourself?

Go and be a journalist, imbecile! be a journalist! You will earn fair rose nobles, you will have a plate at Brébant's, and you will be able to show yourself on first-nights with a new feather in your cap.

No? You will not? You are determined to remain free, after your own fashion, till the end? Very well; just listen to the story of M. Seguin's goat. You will see what people gain by wishing to live free.

M. Seguin had never been fortunate with his goats.

He lost them all in the same way; some fine morning they would break their rope, go off upon the mountain, and up there the wolf would devour them. Neither their master's caresses nor fear of the wolf could restrain them. They were, it appears, independent goats, wanting open air and liberty at any cost.

The good M. Seguin, who could not at all understand the character of his animals, was appalled. He would say,—

"It is of no use; goats are bored at my house. I shall never keep one."

Still he was not discouraged, and after having lost six goats in the same fashion, bought a seventh; only this time he was careful to choose a very young one, in order that she might the better become accustomed to live with him.

Ah, Gringoire, how pretty M. Seguin's little goat was! How pretty she was, with her soft eyes, her beard like a non-commissioned officer, her black and shining hoofs, her striped horns, and her long white hair which made a great-coat for her! She was almost as charming as Esmeralda's kid,—you recollect, Gringoire?—and then, docile and caressing, allowing herself to be milked without moving or putting her foot in the bowl. A love of a little goat!

M. Seguin had behind his house an enclosure surrounded by hawthorns. It was there that he placed his new tenant. He fastened her to a post in the finest part of the lawn, taking care to leave her plenty of rope; and he would come from time to time to see whether she was comfortable. The goat was very happy, and cropped the grass so heartily that M. Seguin was delighted.

"At last," thought the poor man, "here is one that will not be bored with me!"

M. Seguin was mistaken; the goat did become bored.

One day she said to herself, looking at the mountain,—

"How nice it must be up there! What a pleasure it would be to gambol in the heather without this wretched tether which galls one's neck! It is all very well for the ass or the ox to graze in an enclosure; goats need freedom."

From that moment the grass in the enclosure appeared insipid to her. She became bored. She grew thin, and her milk began to fail. It was pitiful to see her pulling all day upon her tether, with her head turned toward the mountain and her nostrils open, crying *Mê!* sadly.

M. Seguin perceived that something was wrong with his goat, but did not know what it was. One morning, as he was finishing milking her, the goat turned around and said to him in her patois,—

"Listen, Monsieur Seguin! I am pining here; let me go away upon the mountain."

"Ah! Good heavens! She too!" cried M. Seguin, appalled; and with that he dropped his bowl. Then, sitting down upon the grass beside his goat,—

"What, Blanquette, you wish to leave me?"

And Blanquette replied.—

"Yes, Monsieur Seguin."

"Have you not enough grass here?"

"Oh. yes, Monsieur Seguin."

"Perhaps you are tied too short; would you like me to lengthen the rope?"

"It is not worth while, Monsieur Seguin."

"Then, what do you need, what do you want?"

"I want to go upon the mountain, Monsieur Seguin."

"But, unhappy child, you do not know that the wolf is on the mountain. What will you do when he comes?"

"I will butt him with my horns, Monsieur Seguin."

"Much the wolf cares for your horns! He has eaten up other goats of mine with far better horns than yours. You know poor old Renaude, who was here last winter? She was a terrible goat, as strong and cross as a he-goat. She fought with the wolf all night; then, in the morning, the wolf ate her."

"*Pécaïre!* Poor Renaude! That makes no difference, Monsieur Seguin; let me go upon the mountain."

"Good gracious!" said M. Seguin; "but what is the matter with my goats? Here is another which the wolf will eat for me! Well, no, I will save you in spite of yourself, hussy! And for fear that you may break your rope, I will shut you up in the stable, and you shall remain there always."

Thereupon M. Seguin took the goat into a dark stable, the door of which he locked. Unfortunately, he had forgotten the window; and he hardly had his back turned when the little one went off.

You laugh, Gringoire? Naturally; you take the part of the goats against that good M. Seguin. We shall see whether you laugh after a little.

When the white goat arrived upon the mountain, there was general rapture. Never had the old pines seen anything so pretty. They received her like a little queen. The chestnuts bowed to the earth to caress her with the ends of their branches. The golden furze opened before her as she passed, and smelt as sweet as it could. The whole mountain fêted her.

You can fancy, Gringoire, how happy our goat was! No more cord, no more post,—nothing to prevent her from gamboling and grazing at her will. And how much grass there was there,— higher than her horns, my dear fellow! And what grass,—succulent, fine, serrated, made up of a thousand plants! It was a very different thing from the turf of the enclosure. And the flowers! Great blue campanulas, purple digitalis with long chalices,—a whole forest of wild flowers overflowing with intoxicating juices!

The white goat, half drunk, wallowed in it with her legs in the air, and rolled along the slopes, helter-skelter, with the fallen leaves and the chestnuts. Then suddenly she sprang upon her feet with a bound. Hop! Off she went, head-foremost, through the maquis and the thorns, sometimes on a peak, sometimes at the bottom of a ravine, up, down, everywhere. One would have said that there were ten M. Seguin's goats upon the mountain.

For Blanquette was afraid of nothing. She would cross with a bound great torrents which spattered her with spray and foam as she passed. Then she would go and stretch herself out streaming upon some flat rock, and have the sun dry her. Once, advancing to the edge of a plateau with a wild flower between her teeth, she saw below, away down upon the plain, M. Seguin's house, with the enclosure behind it. This made her laugh till the tears came.

"How little it is!" she said. "How could it contain me?"

Poor little thing! Seeing herself perched so high, she believed herself at least as big as the world.

In short, it was a pleasant day for M. Seguin's goat. Toward noon, as she ran from right to left, she fell into the midst of a herd of chamois which were nibbling away at a wild vine. Our little wanderer in the white gown created a sensation. They gave her the best place at the vine, and all the gentlemen were very gallant. It even appears—this should be between ourselves, Gringoire —that a young chamois with a black coat had the good fortune to please Blanquette. The two lovers strayed in the wood for an hour or two; and if you wish to know what they said, go and ask of the babbling springs which run invisible through the moss.

Suddenly the wind grew chill. The mountain became violet; it was evening.

"Already!" said the little goat; and she stopped, much surprised.

Down below the fields were drowned in mist. M. Seguin's enclosure disappeared in the fog, and nothing could be seen of the cottage but the roof and a little smoke. She listened to the bells of a flock which was being driven home, and her heart felt quite sad. A gerfalcon returning to its eyrie brushed her with its wings as it passed. She shuddered; then there was a howl upon the mountain.—

"Hou! hou!"

She remembered the wolf; the madcap had not thought of him all day long. At the same moment a horn sounded afar off in the valley. It was that good M. Seguin, who was making a last effort.

"Hou! hou!" said the wolf.

"Come back! Come back!" said the horn.

Blanquette wished to go back; but when she thought of the post, the rope, and the hedge of the enclosure, she thought that now she could never endure this life, and that it was better to remain.

The horn sounded no longer.

The goat heard behind her a rustling of leaves. She turned about quickly, and saw in the dusk two short ears, straight upright, with two eyes which shone. It was the wolf.

Enormous, motionless, seated upon his haunches, he was there, looking at the little white goat and tasting her in advance. As he knew very well that he would eat her, the wolf did not hurry; only, when she turned about, he began to laugh wickedly.

"Ha! ha! Monsieur Seguin's little goat!" and he passed his big red tongue over his leathery chops.

Blanquette felt that she was lost. For a moment, when she recollected the story of old Renaude, who had fought all night only to be eaten in the morning, she said to herself that it would be just as well, perhaps, to allow herself to be eaten at once; then, having thought better of it, she placed herself on guard, with her head low and her horns thrown forward, like the brave goat of M. Seguin that she was. Not that she had any hope of killing the wolf,—goats do not kill wolves,—

but only to see if she could hold out as long as Renaude.

Then the monster advanced, and the little horns began to dance.

Ah! the brave little goat, with what good-will she went at it! More than a dozen times—I am not exaggerating, Gringoire—she forced the wolf to draw back to recover his breath. During these minute-long truces the gourmand would hastily pluck another tuft of her dear grass; then she would return to the combat with her mouth full. This lasted all night. From time to time M. Seguin's goat would look at the stars dancing in the clear sky and say to herself,—

"Oh, if only I can hold out till dawn!"

One after another the stars went out. Blanquette redoubled her efforts, and the wolf his. A pale light appeared upon the horizon. The crow of a hoarse cock floated up from a farm.

"At last!" said the poor thing, who had been waiting to die only till day should come; and she lay down upon the ground in her pretty white hide, all spotted with blood.

Then the wolf fell upon the little goat and ate her up.

Farewell, Gringoire!

The story which you have heard is not a tale which I have invented. If ever you come to Provence, our peasants will often talk to you of the *cabro de moussu Seguin, que se bat-tégue touto la neui emé lou loup, e ļieï lou matin lou loup la mangé.*

You hear what I say, Gringoire,—

E piei lou matin lou loup la mangé.

The Beaucaire Diligence

IT was the day of my arrival here. I had taken the Beaucaire diligence, a respectable old vehicle which had not far to go before reaching home again, but which sauntered all along the way, in order to have the appearance at night of arriving from a long distance. There were five of us on the imperial, without counting the driver.

First, a rover from Camargue, a short, thick-set, hairy man, with an odor of herds, and with large blood-shot eyes, and silver rings in his ears; next, two natives of Beaucaire, a baker and his son-in-law, both very red-faced and short-breathed, but with magnificent profiles, like two Roman medals with the image of Vitellius. Lastly, on the box-seat with the driver, a man—no, a cap, an enormous rabbit skin cap, which did not say much and gazed at the road with a distressed expression.

All these people knew one another and talked aloud of their affairs very freely. The man from Camargue said that he had come from Nimes, summoned by the examining magistrates because of a blow with a pitchfork that he had dealt a shepherd. Tempers are quick in Camargue. And what about Beaucaire! Would you believe that our two Beaucairians actually threatened to cut each other's throats on the subject of the Blessed Virgin? It seems that the baker was from a parish devoted from time immemorial to the Madonna to her whom the Provençals call the Good Mother, and who carries the little Jesus in her arms; the son-in-law, on the contrary, sang in the choir of a brand new church, consecrated to the Immaculate Conception, that lovely smiling image which is represented with her arms hanging at her sides and her hands full of rays of light. The quarrel arose from that fact. You should have seen how those two good Catholics abused each other and their Madonnas:

"A pretty creature your Immaculate One is!"

"Get out with your Good Mother!"

"She saw some fine doings in Palestine that hussy of yours!"

"And what about yours, hey? The ugly witch! Who knows what she didn't do? Ask St. Joseph."

Nothing save the gleaming of knives was lacking to make us fancy that we were on the wharfs at Naples; and in faith, I believe that that edifying theological contest would have ended in that way if the driver had not interfered.

"Let us alone with the Madonnas," he said laughingly to the Beaucairians; "that's all women's nonsense; men ought not to bother with it."

Thereupon he cracked his whip, with a skeptical expression which brought everybody over to his opinion.

The discussion came to an end, but the baker, having got started, felt that he must spend the rest of his ammunition, and, turning to the unfortunate cap, which sat silent and melancholy in its corner, he said with a bantering expression:

"And how about your wife, knife-grinder—which parish does she favor?"

Evidently there was some very comical allusion to that question, for the whole imperial roared with laughter. The knife-grinder did not laugh. He did not seem to have heard. Observing that, the baker turned to me:

"You don't know his wife, do you, monsieur? She's a queer kind of a churchwoman! There aren't two like her in Beaucaire."

The laughter redoubled. The knife-grinder did not budge; he simply said in a low tone, without raising his head:

"Hold your tongue, baker."

But that devil of a baker did not propose to hold his tongue, and he continued with greater zest:

"Bless my soul! the fellow isn't to be pitied for having a wife such as she. No man can be bored for an instant with her. Think of it! a beauty who has herself abducted every six months, she always has something to tell you when she comes home. It's a curious little household, I tell you. Just imagine, monsieur, that they hadn't been married a year, when paff! the wife goes off to Spain with a chocolate-peddler. The husband was left alone in the house, to weep and drink. He was like a mad-man. After some time, the charmer came back to the province dressed as a Spanish woman, with a little tambourine. We all said to her: 'Keep out of his way, or he will kill you.' Kill her! not much! they went to living together again as quietly as you please, and she taught him to play the tambourine."

There was a fresh outburst of laughter. The knife-grinder in his corner muttered again, without raising his head:

"Hold your tongue, baker."

The baker paid no heed, but continued:

"Perhaps you think, monsieur, that after her return from Spain the charmer kept still. Not a bit of it; her husband had taken the thing so well that it made her inclined to try it again. After the Spaniard, it was a military officer, then a boatman on the Rhone, then a musician, then a—I don't know whom. The amusing part of it is that the same comedy is acted every time. The wife goes off, the husband weeps; she returns and he is consoled. And they keep on abducting her, and he keeps on taking her back. Don't you think that the fellow has patience? I must say, however, that the little woman's mighty pretty—a genuine morsel for a cardinal: dainty, and lively, and well-built; and a white skin, too, and nut-brown eyes that always laugh when she looks at a man. Faith, my Parisian, if you ever pass through Beaucaire——"

"Oh! hold your tongue, baker, I beg you!" said the poor knife-grinder once more, in a heartrending tone.

At that moment the diligence stopped. We were at the farm of Des Anglores. The two men from Beaucaire alighted, and I promise you that I did not try to detain them. That wag of a baker! we could hear him laugh after he was in the farmyard.

When they had gone the imperial seemed empty. We had left the man from Camargue at Arles; the driver was walking beside the horses. The knife-grinder and I were alone, each in his corner, saying not a word. It was hot, and the leather of the hood was scorching. At intervals I felt my eyes close and my head become heavy; but it was impossible to sleep. I had always in my ears that "hold your tongue, I beg you," so gentle, yet so heartrending. He did not sleep, either, the poor man; from behind I could see his broad shoulders quivering, and his hands, a long, colorless, stupid hand, tremble on the back of his seat, like the hand of an old man. He was weeping.

"Here you are at home, Parisian," the driver suddenly called to me; and with the end of his whip he pointed to my green hill with the mill perched upon it like a great butterfly.

I made haste to alight. As I passed the knife-grinder I tried to look under his cap; I was anxious to see his face before leaving him. As if he had understood my thought, the wretched man abruptly raised his head and, fastening his eyes upon mine, he said in a hollow voice:

"Look well at me, my friend, and if you hear one of these days that there has been trouble at Beaucaire, you will be able to say that you know the man who did it."

His face was sad and lifeless, with little faded eyes. There were tears in those eyes, but in the voice there was hatred. Hatred is the wrath of the weak! If I were the knive-grinder's wife, I should be on my guard.

The Pope's Mule

OF all the shrewd sayings, proverbs, or adages with which our Provençal peasants embroider their talk, I know none more picturesque or more singular than this. For fifteen leagues around my mill, when they speak of a rancorous, vindictive man, they say: "Beware of that man! He is like the Pope's mule, which saved his kick for seven years."

I sought for a long while whence this proverb could come, what were this papal mule and this kick saved for seven years. No one here could enlighten me not even Francet Mamai, my fife-player, who nevertheless has the Provençal legends at his fingers' ends. Francet thinks, as I do, that there exists thereanent some ancient chronicle of Avignon; but he has never heard of it, save as the proverb.

"You will never find it anywhere but in the crickets' library," said the old fifer, laughing.

The idea appeared good to me; and as the crickets' library is at my very door, I went and shut myself up there for a week.

It is a marvellous library, admirably arranged, open to poets day and night, and served by librarians with cymbais who play all the time. I spent several delightful days there: and after a week's research on my back, I at last discovered what I wanted,—that is to say, the story of my mule and his famous kick saved for seven years. The story about it is pretty, although somewhat simple, and I will try to tell it to you just as I read it yesterday morning in a manuscript the colour of the weather, fragrant of dried lavendar, and having large threads of gossamer for markers.

He who did not see Avignon in the time of the Popes has seen nothing. There never was such a town for gayety, life, animation, and the spirit of its fêtes. From morning till night there was nothing but processions, pilgrimages, the streets strewn with flowers and hung with tapestry, the arrivals of cardinals by the Rhone with banners flying and galleys adorned with flags, the Pope's soldiers singing Latin upon the public places, the baskets of the begging brothers; then, from top to bottom of the houses which pressed humming about the great papal palace, there were the tick-tack of the lace-makers, the to-and-fro of the shuttles weaving the gold of the chasubles, the little hammers of the carvers of vases, the sounding-boards which were being adjusted by the lute-makers, the songs of the weavers; above all this, the sound of the bells, and always certain tambourines whose clatter could be heard down toward the bridge. For with us, when the populace is happy, it must dance; and as in those days the streets of the town were too narrow for the farandole, fifes and tambourines took their stand on the bridge of Avignon, and there, in the cool breeze from the Rhone, they danced day and night. Ah, the happy times, the happy times! Halberds which did not cut; state-prisons where they put wine to cool! Never want or famine! That is how the Popes of Avignon knew how to govern their people; that is why their people so regretted them.

There was one, above all, a good old man named Boniface. Oh, as for him, what tears were shed in Avignon when he died! He was so amiable, so affable a prince! He laughed so heartily from the back of his mule! And when you passed near him, were you a poor little madder-dyer or the grand provost of the town, he would give you his blessing so politely! A real Pope of Yvetot, but of a Provençal Yvetot, with a trace of shrewdness in his laugh, a sprig of marjoram in his baretta, and not a bit of a Jeanneton. The only Jeanneton whom this good father was ever known to possess was his vineyard,—a little vineyard which he had planted himself, three leagues from Avignon, among the myrtles of Château-Neuf.

Every Sunday, on coming from vespers, the worthy man would go and make love to it; and when he was up there, seated in the pleasant sunlight, with his mule near him and his cardinals all about him, lying at the foot of the trees, then he would have them uncork a flask of the wine of the vineyard,—that b e a u t i f u l ruby-coloured wine which has since been called the Château-Neuf des Papes,—and would sip it, looking tenderly at his vineyard. Then, when the flask was empty and the night beginning to fall, he would return joyfully to the city, followed by his whole chapter; and when he passed over the bridge into Avignon, amidst the tambourines and the farandoles, his mule, excited by the music, would fall into a little skipping amble, while he himself would mark the measure of the dance with his baretta,—a thing which greatly scandalized his cardinals, but caused all the people to say: "Ah, the kind prince! Ah, the good Pope!"

Next to his vineyard at Château-Neuf, what the Pope loved the most in the world was his mule. The good man doted upon the creature. Every evening before going to bed he would go to see whether its stable was well closed, whether nothing was lacking from its manger; and never would he rise from table until he had caused to be prepared before his own eyes a great bowl of spiced wine, with plenty of sugar and aromatic herbs, which he would himself carry to it, in spite of the comments of his cardinals. It must be confessed that the animal was worthy of the trouble. It was a fine black mule with red spots, sure foot, a glistening coat, a broad and well-rounded croup; and proudly did it carry its small, shapely head, bedecked with pompons, bows, and silver bells. Besides this, it was as gentle as an angel, with an innocent eye, and two long ears which were always wagging and gave it an air of good-nature. All Avignon respected it, and when it passed through the streets, people would show it all sorts of politeness; for everybody knew that this was the best way to stand well at court, and that for all its innocent expression, the Pope's mule had helped more than one man to fortune,—witness Tistet Védène and his marvellous adventure.

This Tistet Védène was, by nature, a brazen young rascal whom his father, Guy Védène, the gold-worker, had been obliged to drive from home because he would do nothing and debauched the apprentices. For six months he was seen loafing about Avignon, but chiefly in the neighbourhood of the papal palace; for the scamp had for a long time had an idea concerning the Pope's mule, and you will see that it was a clever one. One day, as his Holiness was riding alone upon the ramparts on his pet, Tistet came up to him and said, clasping his hands with an expression of admiration,—

"Ah! good heavens, Holy Father! what a splendid mule you have! Stop a moment, that I may look at him! Ah, your Holiness, what a beautiful mule! The Emperor of Germany has not its like!"

And he caressed it and spoke tenderly to it, as if to a young girl,—

"Come here, my jewel, my treasure, my pearl—"

And the good Pope, quite touched, said to himself,—

"What a nice little fellow! How good he is to my mule!"

And then, do you know what happened the next day? Tistet Védène exchanged his old yellow jacket for a fine lace alb, a camail of violet silk, and buckled shoes, and entered the Pope's choir-school, into which no one but the sons of nobles and cardinals' nephews had ever before been received. Such is intrigue! But Tistet did not stop there.

Once in the Pope's service, the rascal continued in the course which had served him so well. Insolent to every one, he showed attention and kindness to nobody but the mule; and people were always meeting him in the courtyard of the palace with a handful of oats or a bunch of *sainfoin*, whose pink clusters he would shake playfully as he looked up at the Holy Father's balcony, as much as to say, "Aha! for whom is this?" So that after a while the good Pope, who felt himself growing old, allowed him to take care of the stable, and to carry to the mule his bowl of

spiced wine,—at which the cardinals made a wry face.

And neither did it please the mule. Now, when the hour came for its wine, it would see the arrival of five or six little clerks belonging to the choir-school, who would quickly hide in the straw with their camails and their lace; then, a moment later, a good, warm fragrance of caramel and spices would fill the stable, and Tistet Védène would appear, carefully carrying the bowl of mulled wine. Then the poor brute's martyrdom would begin.

This perfumed wine, which it loved so much, which kept it warm and lent it wings, they had the cruelty to bring there, in the stable, and to make it sniff; then, when its nostrils were full of it, presto, change! Every drop of the rosy liquor went down the throats of these young rascals. And then, if they had done nothing worse than steal its wine! But these little clerks were like devils when they had been drinking. One would pull its ears, another its tail; Quiquet would mount on its back, Béluguet would put his baretta on its head; and not one of these little scamps remembered that with a single kick the honest brute could have sent them to the pole-star, or even farther. But no! To be the Pope's mule, the mule of benedictions and indulgence, does not count for nothing. No matter what the children might do, it would not get angry; and it was only against Tistet Védène that it had a grudge. As for him, when it felt him behind it, its shoe fairly itched; and really there was good reason for it. That good-for-nothing Tistet played it such brutal tricks, and devised such cruel machinations when he had been drinking!

Did he not one day make it go up with him into the bell-tower of the choir-school, away up in the highest point of the palace? And what I tell you is not a fiction; two hundred thousand Provençaux saw it. You can imagine the terror of this unhappy mule when, after turning blindly in a circular staircase for an hour, and climbing I don't know how many steps, it found itself suddenly upon a platform dazzling with light, and saw a thousand feet below it a fantastic Avignon, with the sheds in the market-place smaller than nutshells, the Pope's soldiers before their barracks looking like red ants, and away over there, across a thread of silver, a microscopic bridge where they danced and danced! Ah, poor brute! what a panic seized it! Every window in the palace shook with the cry which it uttered.

"What is it? What are they doing to him?" cried the good Pope, rushing out upon his balcony.

Tistet Védène was already in the court, pretending to weep and to tear his hair.

"Ah, Holy Father, what is it? Your mule—good heavens! what are we to do?—your mule has climbed up into the bell-tower."

"All by itself?"

"Yes, Holy Father, all by itself. See! —look up there, away up! Do you see the end of its ears showing? One would fancy them two swallows."

"Horrors!" said the poor Pope, raising his eyes. "Has it become mad? It will kill itself! Come down, wretched creature!"

Ah! it would have liked nothing better than to come down; but how? The staircase was not to be thought of; those things could be mounted, but to go down would be enough to break its legs a hundred times over. The poor mule was in despair; and as it wandered about the platform with its great eyes rolling from vertigo, it thought of Tistet Védène.

"Ah, scoundrel, if I get out of this, what a kick I will give you to-morrow morning!"

The idea of this kick put a little more courage into the mule, for without it it could not have stood erect. They finally succeeded in getting it down, but it was a serious matter. It was necessary to lower it with a derrick, ropes, and a sling. And you can fancy what a humiliation it was for the Pope's mule to see itself hanging from that height, paddling with its feet in the empty air, like a cockchafer at the end of a string. And all Avignon looking at it!

The unhappy creature never slept that night on account of it. It always imagined itself wandering about that accursed platform, with the laughter of the city beneath it. Then it would think of that infamous Tistet Védène, and the fine kick that it was going to give him in the morning. Ah, my friends, what a kick! They should see the smoke of it from Pampérigouste. But while this reception was being prepared for him in the stable, do you know what Tistet Védène was doing? He was singing as he went down the Rhone in a papal galley, on his way to Naples with the troop of young nobles who were sent by the city every year to the court of Queen Jeanne to learn diplomacy and good manners. Tistet was not noble; but the Pope wished to recompense him for the care which he had taken of the mule, and especially for the activity which he had shown upon the day of the rescue.

How disappointed the mule was the next day!

"Ah! the villain! he suspected something!" it thought, as it shook its bells furiously; "but never mind! Go rascal! you will find your kick upon your return; I will save it for you."

And it did save it.

After Tistet's departure, the Pope's mule resumed its quiet life and its former bearing. There were no more Quiquets or Béluguets in the stable. The happy days of the mulled wine had returned; and with them good humour, the long naps, and the little gavotte steps as it passed over the bridge of Avignon. Still, ever since its adventure, people showed it a little coldness in the city. There were whisperings as it passed; the old folk shook their heads, and the children laughed as they pointed to the bell-tower. The good Pope himself had not the same confidence in his friend; and when he would abandon himself to a little nap upon his back as they returned from the vineyard of a Sunday, it was always with this doubt: "Suppose I were to awake upon the platform up there?" The mule saw this, and suffered from it without saying anything; only, when they pronounced before it the name of Tistet Védène, its long ears would tremble, and it would sharpen its shoes upon the stones with a quiet laugh.

Seven years passed in this way; then, at the end of these seven years, Tistet Védène returned from the court of Naples. He had not yet finished his time there; but he had learned that the first mustard-bearer to the Pope had died suddenly at Avignon, and as the

position seemed to him a good one, he had arrived in great haste to compete for it.

When this intriguing Védène entered the hall of the palace, the Holy Father had difficulty in recognizing him, so much had he grown. It must also be confessed that the good Pope had likewise become old, and that he did not see well without spectacles.

Tistet was not abashed.

"What! Holy Father, do you not know me? It is I, Tistet Védène."

"Védène?"

"Yes, you know very well,—he who used to carry the wine to your mule."

"Ah! yes, yes, I recollect. A good little fellow, that Tistet Védène. And now what does he ask of us?"

"Oh, a trifle, Holy Father! I came to ask you— By the way, have you still your mule? And it is well? Ah, so much the better! I came to ask you for the place of your first mustard-bearer, who has just died."

"You my first mustard-bearer! But you are too young. How old are you, pray?"

"Twenty years and two months, Illustrious Pontiff,—just five years older than your mule. Ah, what a fine creature it was! If you only knew how I loved that mule, how I pined for it in Italy! Will you not allow me to see it?"

"Yes, my child, you shall see it," said the good Pope, deeply moved. "And since you love it so dearly, I do not wish you to live so far from it. From this day I attach you to my person as first mustard-bearer. My cardinals will remonstrate; but so much the worse for them! I am accustomed to it. Come to us to-morrow after vespers; we will bestow upon you the insignia of your grade in the presence of our chapter, and then—I will take you to see the mule, and you shall go to the vineyard with us. Ha, ha! Come, you may go now."

I need not tell you that Tistet Védène was pleased as he went out of the great hall, or with what impatience he awaited the morrow's ceremony. Still, there was some one in the palace who was happier and more impatient than he; it was the mule. From the moment of Védène's return until after vespers on the following day, the terrible creature never ceased to cram itself with oats, and to lunge at the wall with its hind feet. It also was preparing for the ceremony.

And so the next day, when vespers were over, Tistet Védène made his entrance into the court of the papal palace. All the higher clergy were there, —the cardinals in red robes, the advocate of the devil in black velvet, the abbots of convents with their little mitres, the wardens of Saint-Agrico, the violet camails of the choir-boys, the lower clergy also, the Pope's soldiers in gala uniform, the three brotherhoods of penitents, the hermits from Mount Ventoux with their wild looks, and the little clerk who goes behind bearing the bell; the flagellant brothers, naked to the waist; the ruddy sacristans in judge's gowns,—everybody, down to those who give holy water and those who light and extinguish the candles.— not one was missing. Ah! it was a fine ordination, with bells, petards, sunlight, music, and even those mad tambourines which beat time for the dancing over there upon the bridge of Avignon.

When Védène appeared in the midst of the assembly, his bearing and his handsome looks aroused in it a murmur of admiration. He was a magnificent Provençal, but of the blond kind, with a mass of hair curling at the ends, and a little downy beard which seemed made from the shavings fallen from the burin of his father, the gold-worker. That day, to do honour to his own nation, he had replaced his Neapolitan dress by a jacket with rose-coloured embroidery, and on his cap trembled a long feather from a Camargue ibis.

As soon as he entered, the first mustard-bearer bowed courteously, and went toward the high flight of steps where the Pope was waiting to confer upon him the insignia of his rank,—the spoon of yellow boxwood and the saffron-coloured robe. The mule was at the foot of the steps, fully harnessed and ready to set out for the vineyard. When he passed near it, Tistet Védène smiled kindly, and stopped to give it two or three friendly little taps upon its back, looking out of the corner of his eye to see whether the Pope noticed it. The position was a good one. The mule collected all his strength.

"There! take that, scoundrel! I have been saving it for you for seven years."

And it gave so terrible a kick that the smoke of it was seen even in Pamperigouste,—a whirlwind of blond dust, in which fluttered an ibis feather; it was all that remained of the unfortunate Tistet Védène.

The kick of a mule is not ordinarily so annihilating, but then this was a Pope's mule; and besides, just think, it had been saving it up for him for seven years! No finer example of ecclesiastical rancour exists.

Sanguinaires Lighthouse

I WAS not able to sleep last night. The Mistral was raging, and the noise of its mighty voice kept me awake until morning. Heavily flapping its mutilated arms, which whistled in the wind like the yards of a ship, the whole mill creaked. Tiles fell from its half-ruined roof. In the distance the thick-set pines with which the hill is covered waved and murmured in the darkness. One might have fancied oneself far out at sea.

It recalled to me distinctly my fine, sleepless nights three years ago when I lived in the Sanguinaires lighthouse, down on the coast of Corsica, at the entrance to the Gulf of Ajaccio.

That was another charming corner which I had discovered, wherein to dream and be alone.

Fancy a red, wild-looking island, with the lighthouse on one end and on the other an old Genoese tower in which, in my time, an eagle lived. Low down, at the water's edge, was a ruined lazaretto, everywhere overrun with weeds; then there were ravines, thickets of maquis, great rocks, a few wild goats, and little Corsican horses prancing about, with their manes waving in the wind. Finally, above, at the very top, in a cloud of sea-birds, was the lighthouse, with its platform of white masonry, where the keepers walk to and fro, its green arched door, the short tower, and above it the great many-sided lantern, which blazes in the sun and gives out light even in the daytime. That is the Sanguinaires Island as I

saw it again last night, when I heard the roaring of my pines. It was in this enchanted isle that before I possessed a mill I used to go and shut myself up sometimes, when I needed fresh air and solitude.

What did I do there?

What I do here,—even less. When the Mistral or the Tramontana did not blow too hard, I would come and take my place between two rocks at the level of the sea, amid the gulls, the blackbirds, and the swallows, and remain there almost all day in that sort of stupor and delicious torpor which comes from watching the sea. You know, do you not, this delightful intoxication of the soul? One does not think, nor does one dream. One's whole being escapes from one, is wafted away and dissipated. One is the seamew which dives, the foam which floats in the sunlight between two waves, the white smoke of that vanishing steamer, that little coral-fisher with its red sail, that drop of water, that whiff of spray,—everything, except oneself. Oh, how many of these delightful hours of half sleep and abstraction have I spent on my island!

On days when there was a high wind, as the water-side was untenable, I would shut myself up in the court of the Lazaretto,—a melancholy court, fragrant of rosemary and wild wormwood,—and there, leaning against a fragment of the old wall, I would allow myself to be gently overcome by the vague perfume of sadness and neglect which floated with the sunlight in these stone cells which stood open all about me like ancient tombs. From time to time I would hear the slamming of a door or a light step in the grass; it was a goat which had come to graze where it would be sheltered from the wind. When it saw me it would stop amazed, and remain motionless before me, with an alert air and head erect, gazing at me with the look of a child.

Toward five o'clock the keeper's speaking trumpet would call me to dinner. Then I would take a little path through the maquis which climbed perpendicularly above the sea and return slowly to the lighthouse, turning at every step toward this immense horizon of light and water which seemed to grow larger as I ascended.

Up above it was charming. I can still see that fine dining-room with its large flag-stones and oak wainscot, with the *bouillabaisse* smoking in the middle, the door open on the white terrace, and the whole sunset streaming in. The keepers were there, waiting for me before sitting down. There were three of them,—a Marseillais and two Corsicans,—all three small and bearded, with the same tanned and seamed faces, the same goat-skin *pelone* (cloak), but wholly dissimilar in manner and disposition.

From the mode of life of these men, one could feel at once the difference between the two races. The Marseillais, industrious and active, always busy and in motion, would trot about the island from morning till night, gardening, fishing, picking up gull's eggs, or hiding in the bushes to milk some passing goat, and be always concocting an *aïoli* or a *bouillabaisse*.

The two Corsicans, on the other hand, did absolutely nothing but their official duties. They considered themselves as public functionaries, and spent all their days in the kitchen playing endless games of *scopa*, pausing only to light their pipes gravely or to chop up with scissors large leaves of green tobacco in the palms of their hands.

For the rest, all three, Marseillais and Corsicans, were kindly, simple fellows, full of attentions for their guest, although he must, after all, have seemed to them a very extraordinary gentleman.

Just fancy! To come and shut oneself up in a lighthouse for pleasure! And they thought the days so long, and were so happy when it was their turn to go ashore! In the fine season this happiness comes to them every month. The regulation is ten days ashore for twenty in the lighthouse; but in winter and bad weather no rules hold. The wind blows, the sea rises, the Sanguinaires are white with foam, and the keepers on duty remain besieged for two or three months at a time, and sometimes in terrible circumstances.

"This is what happened to me, sir," old Bartoli said to me one day as we were dining; "this is what happened to me five years ago, at this very table where we are seated, one winter night, like this. There were only two of us in the lighthouse that night,—I and a comrade named Tchéco. The others were ashore,—ill or on leave, I don't remember which. We were finishing dinner very quietly. Suddenly my comrade stopped eating, looked at me a moment with a strange expression in his eyes, and pouf! fell upon the table with outstretched arms. I went to him, and shook and called him,—

" 'Oh, Tché! Oh, Tché!'

"It was useless; he was dead. Just fancy what a shock it was! I remained for more than an hour stupid and trembling before this corpse; and then suddenly this idea came to me,—'But the lighthouse!' I had only time to go up to the lantern and light the lamp. It was already dark. What a night it was, sir! The wind and the sea no longer had their natural voices. Every moment I fancied that some one was calling me from the staircase. And such a fever and thirst! But you could not have made me go down; I was too much afraid of the dead man. Still, at dawn my courage returned to me in a measure. I laid my comrade upon his bed, placed a covering over him, said a bit of a prayer, and then hurried to the alarm signal.

"Unfortunately the sea was too high; it was in vain that I called and called. Nobody came. There I was alone in the lighthouse with my poor Tchéco, and Heaven only knew for how long! I hoped to keep him with me until the arrival of the boat, but it was not possible after the third day. What should I do? Take him outside? Bury him? The rock was too hard, and there are so many crows on the island! It would be a pity to give up this Christian to them. Then it occurred to me to put him in one of the cells of the lazaretto. The painful task took me nearly a whole afternoon, and I can tell you that it needed all my courage. Why, sir, even now, when I go to that side of the island of an afternoon when it blows hard, it seems to me that I have that corpse upon my shoulders!"

Poor old Bartoli! The sweat streamed from his brow at the mere thought of it.

Our meals passed in long conversations about the lighthouse and the sea, stories of shipwrecks, or tales of Corsican bandits. Then, at nightfall, the keeper who had the first watch would light his little lamp, take his flask, his pipe, and a large Plutarch with red edges,—the entire library of the Sanguinaires,—and disappear in the darkness. After a moment there would sound through the whole lighthouse a noise of pulleys and chains, and heavy clock-weights being wound up.

During that time I would go and sit down outside. The sun, already very low, would descend faster and faster, drawing the whole horizon after it. The wind would grow colder, the island become violet. In the sky, quite close to me, a great bird would fly heavily; it was the eagle of the Genoese tower returning home. Little by little the fog would rise, and soon one could see only the white border of foam about the island. Suddenly there would burst over my head a great wave of soft light; it was the lighthouse lamp which had been lighted. Leaving the whole island in shadow, the bright ray would fall afar upon the sea, and I was lost in the darkness under these vast luminous billows which scarcely bespattered me as they passed. But the wind would grow still colder; it was time to go in. Feeling my way, I would close the great door and put the iron bars in position; then, still groping, I would mount a little cast-iron staircase which shook and sounded beneath my feet, and I would reach the top of the lighthouse. There, at my rate, there was plenty of light.

Imagine an immense Carcel lamp, with six rows of wicks, about which circled slowly the walls of the light, some filled with an enormous lens of crystal, others open upon an immense motionless lantern, which sheltered the flame from the wind. When I came in, I was always dazzled. This brass and tin, these white metal reflectors, these curved walls of crystal which turned with great bluish circles,—all this flashing and clashing of lights would make me dizzy for a moment.

By degrees, however, my eyes would become accustomed to it, and I would sit down at the very foot of the lamp beside the keeper, who was reading his Plutarch aloud for fear of going to sleep.

Without was darkness, an abyss. The wind runs like a madman, howling, upon the little balcony which surrounds the lantern. The lighthouse groans; the sea roars. At the end of the island, in the breakers, the waves sound like cannon-shots. Occasionally an invisible finger knocks upon the lantern; it is some night-bird which, attracted by the light, has broken its neck against the glass. In the warm, dazzling lantern there is nothing but the crackling of the flame, the noise of the dripping oil, the sound of the chain as it runs out, and a monotonous voice drawling forth Plutarch's Demetrius.

At midnight the keeper rises, casts a last glance at his machines, and we go down. On the staircase we meet the comrade who has the second watch, rubbing his eyes as he goes up; the gourd and the Plutarch are turned over to him. Then, before retiring to our beds, we go into the lowest room, all littered up with chains and heavy weights, tin cans and ropes; and there by the light of his little lamp, the keeper writes in the diary of the lighthouse, which stands always open,—

"Midnight. Heavy sea. Gale. A sail in sight."

Protected by Stars

In the days when I used to keep sheep on the Luberon, I would remain for whole weeks without seeing a living soul, alone in the pastures with my dog Labri and my flock. Now and again the hermit of Mont-de-l'Ure would pass my way in search of herbs, or I might catch a glimpse of the black face of some charcoal burner from Piedmont; but they were simple folk, silent from the habit of solitude, having lost the taste for talking, and knowing nothing of what was going on down below in the towns and villages. Therefore, when I would hear, every two weeks, on the road up the mountain, the bells of the mule of our farm, bringing me provisions for the next fortnight, and see gradually appearing above the hill the bright face of the little *miarro* (farm-boy) or the red headdress of old Aunt Norade, I was really very happy. I would make them tell me the news from below,—the baptisms and marriages; but what interested me most was to know the doings of the daughter of my masters, our Demoiselle Stéphanette, the prettiest girl for ten leagues around. Without having the appearance of taking too much interest, I inquired whether she went much to fêtes and parties, and whether she was always having new beaux; and to those who may ask me what difference these things could make to me, I will reply that I was twenty years old, and that this Stéphanette was the most beautiful thing that I had ever seen in my life.

Well, one Sunday when I was awaiting my fortnight's provisions, it happened that they did not arrive till very late. In the morning I said to myself, "It is on account of High Mass;" then, toward noon, there came a great storm, and I thought that the mule had not been able to start because of the bad state of the roads. Finally, about three o'clock, the sky having cleared and the mountain being bright with water and sunlight, I heard, through the murmur of the overflowing rivulets, the mule's bells, as gay and lively as the great chimes of a church on an Easter day. But it was not the little *miarro* nor old Aunt Norade who was riding it. It was—guess who—our y o u n g lady, children! our young lady in person, seated upright between the willow baskets, all rosy from the mountain air and the coolness of the storm.

The boy was ill, and Aunt Norade on a holiday visiting her children. The pretty Stéphanette told me all this as she dismounted from her mule, and also that she was late in arriving because she had lost her way; but to see her in such gala dress, with her flowered ribbon, her brilliant skirt, and her lace, she had rather the appearance of having lingered at some dance than of having sought her way among the thickets.

Oh the dainty creature! My eyes could not weary of looking at her. It is true that I had never seen her so near. Sometimes in the winter, when the flocks had gone down into the plain, and I would go to the farm in the evening to supper, she would pass through the room quickly, scarcely speaking to the servants, always finely dressed, and a little proud. And now I had her there before me, all to myself; was it not enough to make me lose my head?

When she had taken the provisions from the baskets, Stéphanette began to look about her curiously. Lifting her handsome Sunday skirt a little, for it might have become soiled, she entered the fold, wished to see the corner where I slept, the manger filled with straw and covered with a sheepskin, my great cloak hanging on the wall, my crook, my flint-lock gun. It all amused her.

"So it is here that you live, my poor shepherd? How it must weary you to be always alone! What do you do? What do you think about?"

I should have liked to reply, "Of you, mistress," and I should have told the truth; but my confusion was so great that I could not even find a word. I think that she perceived it, and that the teasing creature took pleasure in increasing my embarrassment by her mischievous questions.

"And your sweetheart, shepherd; does she sometimes come up to see you? It must be on the golden goat, or that fairy Estérelle, who runs only on the tops of mountains."

And she herself, as she talked to me, looked like the fairy Estérelle, with her pretty laugh, her head thrown back. and her haste to be gone, which made of her visit an apparition.

"Good-by, shepherd."

"My respects, mistress."

And off she went, taking her empty baskets.

When she disappeared down the path, it seemed to me that the pebbles, rolling beneath the hoofs of her mule, fell one by one upon my heart. I heard them for a long, long time; and until the end of the day I remained as if in a doze, not daring to move for fear of driving away my dream. Toward evening, as the bottom of the valleys began to become blue, and the sheep pressed against one another, bleating, anxious to return to the fold, I heard some one calling me on the slope, and I saw our young lady appear, not laughing as a little while ago, but trembling with cold, fear, and wet. It seems that at the bottom of the hill she had found the Sorgue swollen by the storm, and that wishing to cross at any risk, she had been in danger of drowning. The terrible part of it was that at that hour she could not think of returning to the farm; for she would never have been able to find her way alone by the cross road, and I could not leave the flock. This idea of spending the night upon the mountain disturbed her greatly, especially because of the anxiety of her family. I reassured her as well as I could.

"The nights are short in July, mistress. It is only an unpleasant moment."

And I quickly lighted a large fire to dry her feet and her gown, all wet with the water of the Sorgue. Then I set before her milk and cheese; but the poor child did not think of warming herself or of eating, and when I saw the great tears which rose to her eyes, I felt like crying too.

Meanwhile night had come on. There remained on the crests of the mountains only a sprinkling of sun-dust, a haze of light in the direction of the sunset. I wanted our young lady to go into the fold and rest. Having spread a new sheepskin on some fresh straw, I wished her a good-night, and went and sat down before the door. God is my witness that in spite of the fire of love which burned in my blood, no evil thought came to me; nothing but a vast pride that in a corner of the fold, close beside the curious flock which was watching her sleep, the daughter of my masters—like a sheep whiter and more precious than the rest—was reposing, intrusted to my care. Never had the heavens appeared to me so deep, the stars so brilliant. Suddenly the gate opened and Stéphanette appeared. She could not sleep. The sheep caused the straw to rustle, as they moved or bleated in their dreams. She preferred to come beside the fire. Seeing this, I threw my goatskin over her shoulders, stirred up the fire, and we remained seated close to each other without speaking. If you have ever spent the night in the open air, you know that at the hour when we are asleep a mysterious world awakens in the solitude and silence. Then the springs sing much clearer, and the pools send up little flames. All the spirits of the mountain come and go freely; and in the air there are rustlings, almost imperceptible noises, as if one could hear the branches growing and the grass springing. The day is the life of beings, but the night is the life of things. When one is not accustomed to it, it frightens one. And so our young lady fell a-trembling, and would press against me at the slightest noise. Once a long, melancholy cry, rising from the pool which glistened beneath us, ascended toward us, quavering. At that instant a beautiful falling star shot above our heads in the same direction, as though this wail which we had just heard bore a light with it.

"What is that?" Stéphanette asked me in a low voice.

"A soul entering Paradise, mistress;" and I made the sign of the cross.

She also crossed herself, and remained a moment with her head thrown back, deep in thought. Then she said to me,—

"Is it really true that you shepherds are magicians?"

"Not at all, mistress; but here we live nearer the stars, and we know what goes on among them better than the people of the lowlands."

She was still looking upward with her head leaning on her hand, wrapped in the sheepskin like a little heavenly shepherd.

"How many there are! How beautiful it is! I have never seen so many. Do you know their names, shepherd?"

"Oh, yes, mistress. See! Just above us is Saint James's Way (the Milky Way). It goes from France straight to Spain. It was Saint James of Gallicia who marked it out, to show the road to the brave Charlemagne, when he was making war against the Saracens. Farther on you have the Wain of Souls (the Great Bear), with its four shining wheels. The three stars which go before it are the Three Horses; and this very little one, opposite the third, is the Wagoner. Do you see all about it that

rain of falling stars? They are souls which the good Lord does not want in heaven. Here, a little lower, is the Rake, or the Three Kings (Orion). That is the one which serves as our clock. Simply by looking at it I know now that it is after midnight. A little lower, still toward the south, shines John of Milan, the torch of the stars (Sirius). This is what the shepherds tell about that star. It appears that one night John of Milan, the Three Kings, and the Hen-coop (the Pleiads), were invited to the wedding of a star, one of their friends. The Hen-coop, being in the most haste, set out first, it seems, and took the upper road. Look up there, in the very depths of the sky! The Three Kings cut across lower, and caught up with it; but this lazy John of Milan, who had slept too late, was left quite behind, and being furious at this, threw his staff at them to stop them. That is why the Three Kings are also called the Staff of John of Milan. But the most beautiful of all the stars, mistress, is ours,—the Shepherd's Star, which lights us at dawn, when we take out the flock, and again in the evening when we bring it back. We also call it Maguelonne, the beautiful Maguelonne, who runs after Peter of Provence (Saturn), and marries him every seven years."

"What! shepherd, are there marriages of stars?"

"Oh, yes, mistress."

And as I was trying to explain to her what these marriages were, I felt something cool and soft pressing lightly upon my shoulder. It was her head, heavy with sleep, which was leaning against me with a pretty rustling of ribbons.

lace, and wavy hair. She remained thus until the stars grew pale in the sky, blotted out by the rising day. I watched her sleep, somewhat agitated in the depths of my being, but protected by the holiness of this clear night, which never gave me any but beautiful thoughts. About us the stars continued their silent march, as docile as a great flock of sheep; and at times I fancied that one of these stars, the finest and most brilliant, having lost its way, had come and lighted upon my shoulder to sleep.

Death of the Dauphin

THE little Dauphin is sick; the little Dauphin is going to die. In all the churches of the realm the Blessed Sacrament is exposed night and day, and tall candles are burning for the recovery of the royal child. The streets in the old residence are sad and silent, the bells no longer ring, and carriages go at a foot-pace. About the palace the curious citizens watch through the iron grills the porters with gilt paunches talking in the court-yards with an air of importance.

The whole château is in commotion. Chamberlains, majordomos, run hastily up and down the marble staircases. The galleries are full of pages and of courtiers in silk garments, who go from group to group asking news in undertones. On the broad steps weeping maids of honor greet one another with low courtesies, wiping their eyes with pretty embroidered handkerchiefs.

In the orangery there is a great assemblage of long-robed doctors. Through the windows they can be seen flourishing their long black sleeves and bending majestically their hammer-like wigs. The little Dauphin's governor and equerry walk back and forth before the door, awaiting the decision of the faculty. Scullions pass them by without saluting them. The equerry swears like a heathen, the governor recites lines from Horace. And meanwhile, in the direction of the stables one hears a long, plaintive neigh. It is the little Dauphin's horse, calling sadly from his empty manger.

And the king? Where is monseigneur the king? The king is all alone in a room at the end of the château. Majesties do not like to be seen weeping. As for the queen, that is a different matter. Seated at the little Dauphin's pillow, her lovely face is bathed in tears, and she sobs aloud before them all, as a linen-draper's wife might do.

In his lace-bedecked crib the little Dauphin, whiter than the cushions upon which he lies, is resting now with closed eyes. They think that he sleeps; but no. The little Dauphin is not asleep. He turns to his mother, and seeing that she is weeping, he says to her:

"Madame queen, why do you weep? Is it because you really believe that I am going to die?"

The queen tries to reply. Sobs prevent her from speaking.

"Pray do not weep, madame queen; you forget that I am the Dauphin, and that dauphins cannot die like this."

The queen sobs more bitterly than

ever, and the little Dauphin begins to be alarmed.

"I say," he says, "I don't want Death to come and take me and I will find a way to prevent his coming here. Let them send at once forty very strong troopers to stand guard around our bed! Let a hundred big guns watch night and day with matches lighted, under our windows! And woe to Death if it dares approach us!"

To please the royal child the queen makes a sign. In a moment they hear the big guns rumbling through the courtyard; and forty tall troopers, halberds in hand, take their places about the room. They are all old soldiers with gray mustaches. The little Dauphin claps his hands when he sees them. He recognizes one of them and calls him:

"Lorrain! Lorrain!"

The soldier steps forward toward the bed.

"I love you dearly, my old Lorrain. Let me see your big sword. If Death tries to take me you must kill him, won't you?"

"Yes, monseigneur," Lorrain replies. And two great tears roll down his bronzed cheeks.

At that moment the chaplain approaches the little Dauphin and talks with him for a long time in a low voice, showing him a crucifix. The little Dauphin listens with an expression of great surprise, then, abruptly interrupting him, he says:

"I understand what you say, monsieur l'abbe; but tell me, couldn't my little friend Beppo die in my place, if I gave him a lot of money?"

The chaplain continues to speak in a low voice, and the little Dauphin's expression becomes more and more astonished.

When the chaplain has finished, the little Dauphin replies with a deep sigh:

"All this that you tell me is very sad, monsieur l'abbe; but one thing consoles me, and that is that up yonder, in the paradise of the stars, I shall still be the Dauphin. I know that the good Lord is my cousin, and that He cannot fail to treat me according to my rank."

Then he adds, turning to his mother:

"Let them bring me my richest clothes, my doublet of white ermine, and my velvet slippers! I wish to make myself handsome for the angels, and to enter paradise in the costume of a Dauphin."

A third time the chaplain leans towards the little Dauphin and talks to him for a long time in a low voice. In the midst of his harangue, the royal child angrily interrupts:

"Why, then, to be Dauphin is to be nothing at all!"

And, refusing to listen to anything more, the little Dauphin turns towards the wall and weeps bitterly.

Master Cornille's Secret

FRANCES MAMAI, an old fifer, who comes sometimes to pass the evening with me and drink mulled wine, told me the other evening of a little village drama which my mill witnessed some twenty years ago. The good man's story impressed me, and I propose to try to tell it to you as I heard it.

Imagine for a moment, dear readers, that you are seated before a jar of perfumed wine, and that it is an old fifer who is speaking.

Our province, my dear monsieur, has not always been a dead place, entirely unknown to fame, as i. is today. Long ago there was a big business done here in grinding grain, and the people from all the farms within a circuit of ten leagues brought us their grain to grind. The hills all around the village were covered with windmills. To right and left one could see nothing but the sails turning about in the mistral above the pines, long strings of little donkeys laden with bags climbing the hills and stretching out along the roads; and it was pleasant to hear all through the week the cracking of the whips on the hilltops, the creaking of the canvas, and the *Dia hue!* of the millers' men. On Sundays we went to the mills in groups. The millers treated to muscat. The millers' wives were as lovely as queens, with their lace neckerchiefs and their gold crosses. I used to carry my fife, and we danced farandoles till it was pitch-dark. Those mills, you see, were the pleasure and wealth of our province.

Unluckily, some Frenchmen from Paris conceived the idea of setting up a steam flour mill on the road to Tarascon. Very fine and new it was; the people fell into the habit of sending their grain there, and the poor windmills were left without work. For some time they tried to keep up the struggle, but steam was the stronger, and one after another, *pecaïré!* they were all obliged to close. We saw no more strings of little donkeys. The millers' pretty wives sold their gold crosses. No more muscat! no more farandoles! No matter how hard the mistral might blow, the sails did not move. Then, one fine day, the commune ordered all those shanties torn down, and vines and olive-trees were planted where they stood.

But, amid all the distraction, one little mill held out and continued to turn bravely on its hill, in despite of the steam-millers. That was Master Cornille's mill, the same one in which we are passing the evening at this moment.

Master Cornille was an old miller, who had lived for sixty years in flour and was crazy over his trade. The setting up of the steam mills made him act like a madman. For a week he ran about the village, collecting people round him and shouting at the top of his lungs that they intended to poison Provence with the flour from the steam-mills.

"Don't go there," he would say; "those villains use steam to make bread, steam, which is an invention of the devil, good Lord"; and he would spout a lot of fine words in praise of windmills, but no one listened to them.

120

Then, in a towering rage, the old
man shut himself up in his mill, and
lived alone like a wild beast. He
wouldn't even keep with him his grand-
daughter Vivette, a child of fifteen, who
since the death of her parents had no
one but her grandfather in the world.
The poor child was obliged to earn her
living and to hire herself out among
the farms for the harvest, the silkworm season, or the olive picking.
And yet her grandfather seemed to
love the child dearly. He often travelled four leagues on foot in the heat
of the sun to see her at the farm
where she was working, and when he
was with her, he would pass hours at
a time gazing at her and weeping.

In the province, people thought that
the old miller had been led by avarice
to send Vivette away; and it did not
do him credit to allow his grandchild
to travel about that way from one farm
to another, exposed to the brutality of
the laborers and to all the trials of
young women in service. People
thought it very wrong, too, that a man
of Master Cornille's reputation, who
up to that time had shown the greatest
self-respect, should go about through
the streets like a regular gypsy, bare-
footed, with a cap all holes and a
blouse all in rags. The fact is that
on Sunday, when we saw him come in
to mass, we were ashamed for him, we
old men; and Cornille felt it so keenly
that he didn't dare to come and sit in
the warden's pew; he always remained
at the back of the church, near the
holy-water vessel, with the poor.

There was something in Master
Cornille's life we couldn't understand.
For a long time no one in the village
had carried him any grain, and yet the
sails of his windmill were always in
motion as before. In the evening
people met the old miller on the roads
driving before him his donkey loaded
with fat bags of flour.

"Good evening, Master Cornille,"
the peasants would call out to him;
"is business still good?"

"Still good, my children," the old
man would reply, with a jovial air.
"Thank God, we have no lack of work."

Then, if anyone asked where in the
devil so much work could come from,
he would put a finger to his lips and
answer gravely:

"Hush! I am working for exporta-
tion."

No one could get anything more from
him.

As for putting one's nose inside his
mill, it wasn't to be thought of. Even
little Vivette herself never went in
there.

When people passed in front of it,
they always found the door closed, the
huge sails moving, the old ass brows-
ing on the platform, and a great thin
cat taking a sun-bath on the window-
sill, and glaring at them with a wicked
expression.

All this smelt of mystery, and made
people talk a great deal. Every one
had his own explanation of Master
Cornille's secret, but the general report was that there were even more
bags of silver in the mill than bags of
grain.

After a while, however, everything
came to light; this is how it happened:

One fine day, as I was playing on
my fife for the young people to dance,
I noticed that my eldest boy and little
Vivette had fallen in love with each

other. At heart I was not displeased, because after all the name of Cornille was held in honor among us, and then it would have pleased me to see that pretty little bird of a Vivette trotting about my house. But as our lovers had often had opportunities to be together, I determined, for fear of accidents, to settle the business at once, and I went up to the mill to say a word to the grandfather. Ah! the old sorcerer! you should have seen how he received me! It was impossible for me to induce him to open his door. I explained my reasons after a fashion, through the keyhole; and all the time I was talking, there was that lean villain of a cat snorting like a devil over my head.

The old man didn't give me time to finish, but shouted to me most impolitely to go back to my fife; that if I was in such a hurry to marry my boy, I could go and look for a girl at the steam-mill. As you can imagine, the blood went to my head when I heard such rough talk; but I was wise enough to restrain myself, and leaving the old fool in his mill, I returned to inform the children of my discomfiture. The poor lambs couldn't believe it; they asked me as a favor to allow them to go up together to the mill and speak to the grandfather. I hadn't the courage to refuse, and off my lovers went.

Just as they reached the mill, Master Cornille had gone out. The door was securely locked; but the old fellow, when he went away, had left his ladder outside, and suddenly it occurred to the children to go in by the window

and see what there might be insid that famous mill.

What a strange thing! the main roo of the mill was empty. Not a sac not a particle of grain; not the sligh est trace of flour on the walls or o the spider-webs. They couldn't eve smell that pleasant, warm odor o ground wheat that makes the air of mill so fragrant. The shaft was co ered with dust and the huge thin ca was sleeping on it.

The lower room had the same a pect of poverty and neglect; a wretche bed, a few rags, a crust of bread o one stair, and in a corner three or fou bursted sacks, with rubbish and plaste sticking out.

That was Master Cornille's secre It was that plaster that he paraded a night on the roads, to save the hono of the mill and to make people thin that he made flour there. Poor mil poor Cornille! Long ago the steam millers had robbed them of their la customer. The sails still turned, bu the mill ground nothing.

The children returned to me all i tears and told me what they had see It tore my heart to listen to them Without a moment's loss of time ran to the neighbors; I told them th story in two words, and we agreed in stantly that we must carry to Cornille mill all the wheat there was in th houses. No sooner said than don The whole village started off, and w arrived at the top of the hill with procession of donkeys loaded wit grain, and real grain, too!

The mill was wide-open. In from of the door Master Cornille sat on bag of plaster, weeping, with his fac in his hands. He had discovered on returning home that du ing his absence some one had entered his mill and discovered his sad secret.

"Poor me!" he said. "Now there's nothing left for me to do but to die. The mill is dishonored."

And he sobbed as if his heart would break, calling his mill by all sorts of names, speaking to it as if it was a living person.

At that moment the donkeys arrived on the platform and we all began to shout as we did in the palmy days of the millers:

"Holla! mill there! holla! Master Cornille!"

And the bags were piled up before the door and the fine red grain strewed the earth in all directions.

Master Cornille stared with all his eyes. He took up some grain in the hollow of his old hand, and said, laughing and weeping at once:

"It is grain! Lord God! real grain! Leave me; let me look at it."

Then, turning to us:

"Ah! I knew that you'd come back to me. All those steam-millers are thieves."

We proposed to carry him in triumph to the village.

"No, no, my children," he said; "first of all I must give my mill something to eat. Just think! it's so long since he has had anything between his teeth!"

And it brought the tears to the eyes of us all to see the poor old man rush about to right and left, emptying the sacks, looking after the millstones, while the grain was crushed and the fine wheaten dust rose to the ceiling.

I must do our people justice: from that day we never allowed the old miller to lack work. Then one morning Master Cornille died, and the sails of our last mill ceased to turn—this time forever. When Cornille was dead, no one followed in his footsteps. What can you expect, monsieur? Everything has an end in this world, and we must believe that the day of windmills has passed like that of barges on the Rhone, parliaments, and jackets with big flowers.

The Drummer

I WAS at home. and still in bed. one morning, when there was a knock at the door.

"Who's there?"

"A man with a large case!"

I naturally fancied that some parcel had arrived from the railway, but instead of the looked-for railway porter, a little man with the round hat and the short jacket of the Provençal shepherd greeted my eyes in the yellow light of the November day. I beheld two black eyes, anxious and gentle, an obstinate, and at the same time, ingenuous face, half lost behind thick moustaches, an accent flavoured with garlic, savouring outrageously of the sunny south. The man said,

"I am Buisson," and held out an envelope. on which I immediately recognized the pretty and regular handwriting of the poet, Frédéric Mistral.

His letter was brief. "I send you friend Buisson; he is a performer on the drum, and wishes to make himself known in Paris. Pilot him."

Pilot a drummer! These southerners have no conscience!

Having read the letter, I turned to Buisson.

"So you are a drummer?"

"Yes, M. Daudet, and the best of them all; you shall see!"

He went to fetch his instruments, which he had discreetly left on the landing, behind the door: a small, long, flat box, and a large cylinder covered with green baize, the same shape and size as the immense *tourniquets* that the sellers of sweet wafers drag about the streets. The small flat box contained the *galoubet,* the simple rustic flute or fife, which says "tu—tu," while the drum growls "pan—pan." The covered cylinder was the tabor (or drum) itself. What a drum it was! Tears came into my eyes when I saw it unwrapped: a real authentic tabor of Louis XIV.'s time, touching and comical at the same time in its hugeness, and growling like an old man if only the tip of a finger touched it. It was made of fine walnut wood, ornamented with light carvings, polished, slight, light, sonorous, and mellowed as it were by the touch of time. Solemn as a judge, Buisson hung his tabor over his left arm, took up the flute between three fingers of his left hand, (you have seen the attitude and the instrument in some antiquated engravings of the eighteenth century, or painted on a plate of old *Moustier*); and handling with the right hand the little stick tipped with ivory, he attacked the large drum, which, with its sonorous vibra-

tions, and its sharp whirr like that of a grasshopper, marked the rhythm, and formed a deep bass accompaniment to the sharp and shrill warbling of the flute. "Tu—tu—pan—pan! Lo! Paris was far off, and so was winter. I was transported to Provence, to the shores of a blue sea, under the shade of the poplars of the Rhone; serenades of the light and of the dawn resounded beneath the windows. I heard the singing of carols, saw the country dances of the *Olivettes,* of the *farandole* winding beneath the leafy plane-trees of the village greens, along the dusty whiteness of the high roads, amongst the lavender of the sunburnt hill sides; disappearing, reappearing, more and more impassioned and fantastic, while the drummer followed slowly, with even step, sure that the dance would not forsake the music by the way; solemn, grave, and hobbling a little. with the movement of the knee, which at every step pushes the drum on in front of him.

So many things in the beat of a drum!

Yes! and many more, that you, perhaps, could not have seen, but which to me were vividly present. Such is the Provençal imagination: made of tinder, and inflammable, even at seven o'clock in the morning; and Mistral did right in counting upon my enthusiasm.

Buisson also became excited. He told me of his struggles. his efforts, and how, midway on the downward path he had saved fife and drum from desecration.

Some barbarians. it appeared, wished to improve the fife by adding two holes to it—a fife with five holes! what a ᴛacrilege! He held religiously to the fife with three holes—the fife of his ancestors, without nevertheless fearing any rival in the suavity of his slurs, or the vivacity of his variations and shakes.

"It occurred to me," said he with a modest air of vague inspiration, and with that particular accent of the south which renders comical, even the most touching of funeral orations. "It occurred to me at night, one time when I was sitting under an olive tree, and listening to the nightingale; and I thought to myself: What! Buisson! can a wild bird of the good God's sing like that, and what it can do with one hole, art thou not man enough to manage with three?" Somewhat stupid in its pomposity, no doubt, this platitude, but that morning it struck me as charming.

A good southerner cannot thoroughly enjoy an emotion unless he can share it with others. I admired Buisson; others must admire him also. Behold me then, rushing all over Paris, showing off my drummer, presenting him everywhere as a phenomenon; hunting up friends, organizing a *soirée* at my own house. Buisson played and related his struggles, and again said, "It occurred to me." He was decidedly fond of that phrase, and my friends were kind enough, on hearing him, to appear marvellously struck by his talent.

But this was only the first step. At that time a play of mine, a Provençal play, was being rehearsed at the Ambigu. I recommended Buisson, his drum and his fife, to Hostein, the *impresario*, and you may fancy with what eloquence! During eight days, I ceaselessly extolled him. At last Hostein said,

"Suppose we put your drummer into the play? It wants a peg to catch the fancy of the public."

I am sure the Provençal lost his sleep from excitement. The next day, we all three got into a cab; he, the drum, and myself, and, at twelve for the quarter past, as the notices of rehearsal say, we were deposited amid a crowd of idlers, gathered together by the strange appearance of the machine, in front of that low, shamefaced little door-way, which in even the most luxurious theatres, serves as the unostentatious entrance alike for authors, actors, and underlings of all kinds.

"Good Heavens, how dark it is!" sighed the Provençal, as we followed the long passage;—damp and windy as all theatre passages—"how dark it is, and how cold!"

The drum seemed of the same opinion, knocking itself against all the windings of the passages, the steps of the corkscrew staircase, with many vibrations and much formidable rumbling. At last, limping and hobbling, we reached the stage. The rehearsal had begun. Thus seen, in all the barrenness of its undress, a theatre presents a most disenchanting appearance; devoid of movement and life, without the tinsel and brightness of the evening, full of busy folk stepping softly, and their low-voiced talk sounding as far off as if it came from shades on the banks of the Styx, or miners at the bottom of a mine. A smell of mouldy damp, and of escaping gas pervaded everything. Men and things. the moving crowd, all were fantastically mixed up with the scenery, and all wore the same dust-coloured hue, in the mean and paltry light of small hanging lamps, and gas jets protected with wire gauze, like Davy lamps. And, as if to make the darkness more heavy, the subterranean sensation more forcible, from time to time, far aloft, on the second or third tier of the darkened house, the door of a box would open, and, as if from the far away mouth of a well, let fall a ray of external light. This sight, new to my countryman, slightly unnerved him. But my fine fellow soon recovered himself, and pluckily took his place, alone in the shadow at the back of the stage, on a barrel that had been got ready for him. With his drum, it had the effect of two barrels, one on the top of another. In vain did I protest: in vain did I say: "In Provence the drummers play as they walk, and your barrel is impossible." Hostein assured me that my drummer was a strolling minstrel, and that a minstrel could only be represented on the stage on a barrel. Very well! then have the barrel! Moreover, Buisson, full of self-reliance, had already clambered up, and was stamping about to find a steady balance, saying to me: "It does not matter!" We left him therefore, his fife at his lips, his drumstick in his hand, behind a dense forest of scenery, side pieces, pulleys and ropes; and we all, director, author, and actors, settled ourselves in the front of the stage, as far off as possible, the better to judge the effect.

"It occurred to me—" sighed Buisson from out of the darkness, "it occurred to me at night, one time when I was sitting under an olive tree, listening to the nightingale—"

"That will do, that will do; play us

something!" I cried out, already exasperated by his phrase.

Tu—tu—! Pan –Pan—!

"Hush! he is beginning."

"We shall be able to judge of the effect!"

Great heavens! what an effect was produced upon this sceptical audience by this rustic music, bleating and shrill as the noise of an insect, buzzing over there in a corner! I saw the jeering actors, always professionally delighting in the failure of a comrade, ironically pucker up their smooth lips: the fireman under his gas jet, was laughing fit to split his sides; the prompter himself, drawn out of his usually somnolescent state by the strangeness of the occurrence, raised himself up on both hands, and peered out of his box looking like a gigantic tortoise. However, Buisson having finished playing again began his phrase, which he apparently thought very telling:

"What! can a wild bird of the good God's sing like that, and what it can do with one hole, art thou not man enough to manage with three!"

"What is this fellow of yours talking about, with his story of holes?" asked Hostein.

Then I tried to explain the point of the matter, the importance of the three holes instead of five; the originality there was in playing alone, the two instruments. "The fact is," observed Marie Laurent, "it would be infinitely more convenient if they were played by two persons."

I tried, in order to strengthen my argument, to sketch out a *farandole* step on the stage. It was of no avail. I began vaguely to understand the sad truth, that, to make others feel the impressions and poetical recollections evoked in my bosom by the drummer and his old-fashioned airs, the musician should have been able to bring at the same time to Paris, the top of a hill side, a space of blue sky, a whiff of the warm Provençal atmosphere: 'Come, my children, get on, get on!"

And without bestowing any further notice on the drummer, the rehearsal continued. Buisson never stirred, and remained at his post, feeling certain of success, and honestly believing that he was already acting a part in the play. After the first act, a feeling of remorse came over me, at leaving him over there on his barrel, where only his outline could vaguely be seen.

"Come, Buisson, get down, quick."

"Are we going to begin?"

The unfortunate fellow thought he had made a wonderful effect, and showed me a stamped paper, an agreement already prepared with the foresight characteristic of the peasant.

"No, not to-day; they will write to you; but take care! hang it! your drum knocks against everything, and makes a frightful row." I felt now quite ashamed of the drum, 1 trembled lest any one should hear it, and oh! what a joy and a relief it was, when I got it back into the cab! For a week I did not venture to return to the theatre.

Shortly afterwards, Buisson came again to see me.

"Well! how about that agreement?"

"That agreement? Ah yes! that agreement. Well, Hostein hesitates; he does not understand."

"He's a fool!"

On hearing the bitter and harsh tone in which the gentle musician pro-

nounced these words, I realized the extent of my crime. Intoxicated by my enthusiasm, and my praise; his equilibrium upset, and losing all sense of proportion, the Provençal drummer seriously believed himself a great genius, and expected—alas! had I not led him to expect it—that Paris held in store for him endless triumphs.

How could one stop a drum, uproariously careering through the rocks and thorny thickets of the slopes of imagination!

I did not even attempt it: it would have been madness, and labour lost.

Moreover, Buisson had now found some other admirers, and amongst the greatest celebrities,—Felicien David, and Théophile Gautier, to whom Mistral had written at the same time as to me. Poetic and dreamy spirits, easily charmed, prone to abstraction, the author of a *Journey in the East,* and the musician of the land of roses, had found no trouble in creating in their minds' eye a landscape around the rustic melodies of the drummer.

The one fancied, while the fife piped away, that he saw once more the shores of his native Durance, and the half ruined terraces on the slopes of Cadenet: while the dreams of the other carried him still further away, and he found in the dull and monotonous sound of the drum I know not what charming memories of nights at the Golden Horn and of Arab *derboukas.*

Both had been smitten with a sudden and violent caprice for Buisson's real talent, here however so out of harmony with all its surroundings.

For a whole fortnight there were incessant puffs in the newspapers about the drummer: the illustrated papers were full of his portraits, in an attitude of proud defiance, and a conquering look, the light flute between his fingers, the drum slung over his shoulder. Intoxicated with his success, Buisson bought the papers by the dozen, and despatched them to his own country.

From time to time, he came to see me and to relate his triumphs: smoking parties made up for him in some artists' studios, a few evenings spent in fashionable society in the Faubourg Saint Germain (he was full of the Faubourg de Séïnt Germéïn, as he called it), where the fellow brought back tender dreams to the old turbaned dowagers, as he repeated without the slightest bashfulness his famous phrase: "It occurred to me at night, one time, when I was sitting under an olive tree and listening to the nightingale." Meanwhile, as he was afraid of getting rusty, and wished, in spite of the thousand amusements of an artist's life, to keep up the mellowness of his touch and the delicacy of his mouthpiece, our ingenious Provençal conceived the idea of rehearsing his serenades and his *farandoles*, in the very heart of Paris on the fifth floor of the furnished lodgings he was occupying in the Quartier Breda. Tu—tu! Pan—pan! The whole Quartier protested wrathfully against this unwarrantable disturbance. The neighbours gathered together and made a formal complaint; but Buisson only continued the more, spreading around him a wide circle of harmony and sleeplessness; till one evening the door porter, utterly worn out, refused him the key of his room.

Draping himself in all the dignity of an artist, Buisson appealed to the magistrates, and gained his cause. French laws, so hard on musicians, relegating the performance on the horn to the depths of the cellars all the year round, with the exception of Shrove Tuesday, allowing them only one day out of three hundred and sixty-five on which to flourish their brass instruments in the open air; the French law it appears, had not foreseen the Provençal drum.

After this victory Buisson no longer doubted his own powers. One Sunday morning I received a card: that afternoon he was going to make his appearance at a large concert in the Salle du Châtelet. Duty and friendship compelled my attendance, I therefore went to hear him, not without a secret misgiving, and sad forebodings.

A capital house, full from the pit to the roof; decidedly our puffs and notices had borne fruit. Suddenly, amid the general excitement and breathless silence, the curtain drew up. I uttered a cry of amazement. Alone in the centre of the stage, on which six hundred supernumeraries can be manœuvred without crowding, stood Buisson and his drum, dressed up in a skimpy coat and wearing a pair of gloves which made him look like those long, yellow-legged insects that Granville (the famous caricaturist) portrays in his whimsical drawings, furiously playing on the most fantastical instruments. Buisson alone stood before us I could see him through the opera glass waving his long arms, fluttering his elytra; evidently the unhappy fellow was playing, drumming with all his might, blowing with all his strength but not the faintest note reached the audience. It was too far off, all th sound was swallowed up by the stage. It was like a baker's cricket chirping his serenade in the middle of the Champ de Mars! Impossible to count the flute holes at this distance, impossible to repeat the phrase: "It occurred to me," or to mention the "bird of the good God's!"

I blushed with mortification. Around me I saw nothing but amazement, and I heard the muttered words, "What poor joke is this?" The doors of the boxes slammed, the house, little by little, was emptying; however as it was a polite audience, they did not hiss him, but quietly left the drummer to end his tune in solitude.

I waited for him at the door to console him. Well! would you believe it! He fancied he had had an immense success, and more radiant than ever, exclaimed, "I am waiting for Colonne to sign!" at the same time showing me a large paper covered with official stamps. This time it was more than I could bear, I plucked up my courage and said roughly, all in a breath, what I thought.

"Buisson, we have all been mistaken in trying to make Paris understand the charm of your large drum; the melody of your fife. I have made a mistake, Gautier and David have made a mistake, and, as a natural consequence, you also have made a mistake. No, you are not the nightingale."

"It occurred to me," interrupted Buisson.

"Yes, I know it occurred to you, but you are not a nightingale. The nightingale sings everywhere, his songs are the songs of every country, and in every country his songs are understood. You are only a poor little

cicala, whose monotonous and dry note is in harmony with the pale olive trees, the pines weeping their rosin in tears of gold, the brilliant blue sky, the glorious sun, the stony hill-sides of Provence; but here, under this gray sky, midst rain and wind, you are nothing but a ridiculous, lamentable grasshopper with long damp wings. Return home, take back your drum, sing your love songs by daybreak and by twilight, play to the girls while they dance their *farandoles,* lead the triumphal march of the conquerors in the bull fights; down there you are a poet, an artist; here you are nothing but a misunderstood mountebank."

He did not answer, but in his mystic glance, in his gently obstinate eye, I read his thought: "My friend, you are jealous of me!"

A few days later, my fine fellow, proud as "Artaban," came to tell me that Colonne—another fool, like Hostein!—had refused to sign, but that another affair was offered to him, marvellous this time, an engagement in a *café* concert at a hundred and twenty francs a night, all settled and signed beforehand. He showed me the paper. Ah! what a capital paper! I learnt the truth later on.

I know not what puzzled director, borne away and blinded by the muddy current of bankruptcy, desperately seized upon that broken reed—Buisson's pitiful music. Certain that he would never pay, he signed all that was asked. But the Provençal did not see so far ahead; he had it down on stamped paper, and this stamped paper was sufficient for his happiness. Moreover, as it was a music hall, a costume was necessary.

"They have dressed me up as a Troubadour of the olden time," he said with a gracious smile, "but as I am very well made, it suits me, you will see." I did see!

It was one of those music halls near the Porte Saint Denis, so much in vogue during the last years of the Empire; with the tinsel of the barbarous ornamentation, half Chinese, half Persian; its daubs and gilding rendered more glaring by the exaggerated number of gas jets and lustres, and with closed and latticed boxes, in which, on certain evenings, duchesses and ambassadresses hid themselves to applaud the strange contortions or vulgar songs of some eccentric diva. A sea of heads and beer glasses all levelled like waves in foggy weather by the dense smoke of the pipes and the vapour of breath; the waiters running about, the consumers shouting their orders; and all dominated by the orchestra leader, white-tied, impassible and dignified, raising or calming with the gesture of a Neptune, the tempest of fifty brass instruments. Between the ridiculously sentimental song, bleated out by a somewhat pretty girl, with sheepish eyes; and an eclogue as hot as cayenne pepper, cynically bawled by a kind of Thérèsa with red arms, there appeared on the stage, in front of a semi-circle of some six simpering and yawning women in low white dresses, a personage whose appearance in all my life long I shall never forget. It was Buisson, the fife between his fingers, the drum on his left knee, in Troubadour costume, as he had threatened. But what a Troubadour! A jerkin (imagine such a thing!) half ap-

ple-green, half blue; one leg red, the other yellow, the whole attire so tight fitting that it made one shudder; a crenelated cap, shoes turned up like jester's; and with all this, moustaches his magnificent moustaches, too long and too black, which he could not bring himself to sacrifice, falling over his chin like a cascade of blacking!

Carried away apparently by the exquisite taste of this costume, the public greeted the musician with a long murmur of applause, and my Troubadour smirked with pleasure, and was happy at seeing before him this sympathetic audience, and feeling at his back a warm glow of inflammatory glances from the admiring and lovely creatures seated in a half-circle behind him. It was quite another affair however when the music began. The tu-tu, pan-pan failed to please the vitiated taste of ears surfeited by the vitriol-like repertoire of the place, as a palate loses its discrimination by the abuse of spirit. Then too it was not a distinguished and well-mannered company like that at the Châtelet. "Enough! Enough! Take him away! Shut up, squeaker!" Vainly did Buisson try to open his mouth and to say: "It occurred to me." The audience rose, the curtain had to be lowered, and the red, green, blue and yellow Troubadour, disappeared in a storm of hissing and hooting, like some poor draggled parrot, eddying round a tropical hurricane.

Would you believe it? Buisson persisted! An illusion springs up quick in a Provençal brain, and is difficult to uproot. Fifteen evenings running he reappeared, always hissed, never persisted, till the moment arrived when sheriff's officer came to fix a notice of bankruptcy upon the open iron work of the concert hall gates.

Then began the downfall of Buisson. From one low pothouse to another, lower and lower still, always believing in his success, always pursuing his chimera of an engagement made on stamped paper, the drummer trundled at last to the tea-gardens of the suburbs, where the players are only paid by the hour, have no other orchestra than a toothless piano, and form the delight of a public composed of tipsy and tired canoeists and counterjumpers out for their Sunday holiday.

One evening—the winter was scarcely over and the spring not yet begun—I was crossing the Champs Elysées. An open air concert, wishing to get the start of the others, had already hung its lanterns in the still leafless trees. There was a slight drizzle, an air of melancholy over all. Suddenly I heard Tu—Tu—Pan—Pan!— There he was again! I saw him through the opening, drumming away at a Provençal air, before some half dozen auditors, favoured no doubt with orders, and sheltering themselves under umbrellas. I dare not go in! "It was my fault," I thought, "after all! The fault of my imprudent enthusiasm." Poor Buisson! Poor half-drowned grasshopper!

Three Hundred Thousand Francs

HAS it ever happened to you to start out from home with light step and buoyant heart, and after a two-hours walk in the streets of Paris to return depressed and anxious, with a sudden and unaccountable sadness? On such an occasion you say to yourself: "What ails me? what is the matter?" but you find nothing, search as you may. Your walk has been pleasant, the sidewalks dry, the sun warm; and yet you experience such a painful anxiety, that weighs upon you like the impress of a newly-felt sorrow.

It is because in big Paris the crowd feels itself free and unobserved, so that one cannot walk a single step without encountering some fearful distress which, in coming in contact with, leaves its mark upon one. I do not speak solely of familiar misfortunes, the troubles of our friends, or the cares of people indifferent to us, to which we lend but a reluctant ear, but which nevertheless grieve us in spite of ourselves. I speak of afflictions, total strangers to us, of which we get but a glimpse, here and there, for one moment only perhaps, in the midst of our preoccupied walks and the bustle and confusion of the streets. They are either fragments of dialogues jerked out by passing carriages, deaf and blind preoccupations speaking to themselves and aloud, tired shoulders, wild gestures, feverish eyes, pallid faces swelled with tears, recent mournings clothed in black. And then, other slight details, scarcely noticeable! A frayed collar, brushed, oh how often! a velvet ribbon at the neck of a poor hunchback girl and cruelly and carelessly tied right between her deformed shoulders. All the visions of unknown misfortunes, passing quickly, which you forget almost immediately. But you have felt the swift touch of their sadness, your clothes have received the imprint of the misery they drag after themselves; and at the end of the day, you feel that everything emotional your heart contains has been unconsciously touched, for you have been caught either at a street-corner or on some threshold by the invisible thread which connects all misfortunes and sets them in motion at the least contact.

I was thinking of that the other morning (for it is especially in the morning that Paris shows its misery), watching a poor devil walking in front of me. His ill-fitting, shrunken trousers and thin overcoat seemed to exaggerate his gestures; while his big strides keeping pace with his big ideas, were all the more grotesque. Bent in two, his limbs crooked like those of an old tree during a heavy storm, the man was walking rapidly. Now and then his hand would dive into one of his coat-pockets and would take out a half-cent roll he was munching furtively, as if ashamed to be seen eating in the street.

Bricklayers and other working people generally give me an appetite when I see them, seated on the sidewalk, bite into their scant though fresh crust. The office-boys also make me envious, running from the bakery to their offices, with a pen behind their ears, their mouths full, and rejoicing in their open-air meal.

But here one could feel the shame of real hunger; and it was such a pity to watch the poor creature, daring to eat his bread by stealth and only a few crumbs at a time.

I had been following him for a good while, when suddenly, as it often happens in those uncertain lives, he seemed to change his mind with his direction, and, turning about, found himself face to face with me.

"Ha! here you are! It is you."

By chance I knew him a little. He was one of those business promoters of which there are so many in Paris, inventors, founders of impossible dailies, etc., about whom, for some time past, there has been much spoken, and written, and who, for three months previously, had disappeared entirely from view. A few days after he had taken himself off, nobody spoke of him or gave him a thought. Seeing me, he became confused, and so as to cut short all questions, and probably also to avert my attention from the sordid aspect of his clothes, as well as from the roll he was eating, he began to speak in a rapid and mock-joyous strain. . . . Business was getting along well, really splendidly now. . . . It was only for a few days he had been embarrassed. . . . But now, he had got hold of a magnificent thing. . . . A big industrial illustrated paper. . . . A great deal of money in it . . . famous advertising contracts! . . . And his face was full of animation as he spoke. He seemed to have grown taller. Little by little he assumed the air of a patron towards me, as if already in his editorial office, and he went even so far as to ask me for contributions: "And you know, it is such a sure thing," he added, with a triumphal air. "I am beginning with three hundred thousand francs Girardin promised me!"

Girardin!

It is always that name that comes first to those visionaries. When it is pronounced in my hearing it is as if I saw new cities, big unfinished buildings, freshly printed journals with long lists of stockholders and directors How often have I heard them say, speaking of impossible schemes: "We must speak to Girardin about this." And to him also, the poor creature, this idea of speaking to Girardin about it had come. All night long, probably, he had prepared his plans, made his estimates, then he had gone out, and thinking it over while eating his bread, the whole thing had become so beautiful, that when we met it appeared impossible to him that Girardin could refuse "the three hundred thousand francs." In saying that the money had been promised him, the unfortunate man was not lying; he was but continuing his idle dream.

While talking, we were pushed along by the crowd. It was on the sidewalk of one of the busy streets that run from the Exchange to the Bank of France, full of absent-minded people busy with their affairs; anxious shopkeepers hurrying to pay their notes, small brokers with ill-looking faces, whispering figures in each other's ear in passing. And to hear his beautiful plans in the midst of this crowd, in this place of speculators, where one feels the haste and fever of chance-games, it gave me the shivers, as if he had told me the story of a shipwreck out on the open sea. I could really see before me all the man was telling me—see his catastrophes upon other faces, and his radiant hopes in others' wild looks. He left me as abruptly as he had accosted me, thrown once more into the whirl and folly of dreams, of lies, which those people term with such serious faces "business."

Five minutes later, I had forgotten him. But, in the evening, when I reached home, as I was shaking off with its misery the street's dust, there rose before me a pale, painfully pinched face, with a small piece of bread in his hand, and I still could see his gesture when he emphasized those pompous words: "With the three hundred thousand francs Girardin promised me!"

Hortense

It is eight days since Lucien Bérard and Hortense Larivière were married. Madame veuve Larivière, the mother, has for thirty years past kept a toy-shop in the Rue de la Chaussée-d'Antin.

She is a stiff, sharp woman, with an overbearing temper, and not having been able to refuse her daughter to Lucien, the only son of a hardware-man of the quarter, she intends keeping a close watch over the young couple. Although by the contract she has relinquished the toy-shop to Hortense, reserving to herself a room only in the apartment, she still, in fact, manages the house, under pretence of showing the children the details of the business.

We are in August, the heat is intense and transactions are very dull. Madame Larivière is, of course, more sour than ever. She will not allow Lucien to forget himself even a moment when beside Hortense. Did she not find them one morning kissing each other in the shop! A proper thing to be sure, and likely to bring customers to the place. She had never allowed M. Larivière to touch her so much as with the tips of his fingers during business hours. He, it is true, never dreamt of such a thing. And that is how they had built up a business.

Lucien, not daring as yet to revolt, sends kisses to his wife when his stepmother's back is turned. One day, however, he plucked up courage enough to remind her that the families, previous to the wedding, had promised them a honeymoon trip. At this Madame Larivière puckered her thin lips.

"Well," she said, "take an afternoon walk in the Bois de Vincennes."

The newly-married pair looked at each other dumfounded.

Hortense now begins to find her mother really ridiculous. Even at night she can scarce be left alone with her husband. At the least noise, up comes Madame Larivière in her bare feet, who knocks at the door to ask if they are not ill. And when they answer that they enjoy the best of health, she exclaims:

"You had better go to sleep then. . . . I'll catch you again napping tomorrow behind the counter."

It is past endurance.

Lucien instances all the shopkeepers in the quarter who take short trips, while relations or trusty assistants are left behind to mind the shop. There is the dealer in gloves at the corner of the Rue Lafayette who is at Dieppe, the cutler of the Rue Saint-Nicolas

who has just left for Luchon, the jeweler near the Boulevard who has taken his wife to Switzerland. Nowadays anyone who is anything allows himself a month's holiday.

" 'Tis the end of all business, monsieur, do you hear?" exclaims Madame Larivière. "In the time of M. Larivière, we went once a year, on Easter Monday, to the Bois de Vincennes, and we were none the worse off for it! Shall I tell you what it is? You will be the ruin of the house with tastes for voyaging like this! Yes, the house is ruined."

"But it was well understood we should have a trip somewhere," put in Hortense. "Remember, mamma, you said so."

"Perhaps I did, but that was before the wedding. . . . One is apt to say all sorts of nonsense before the wedding. What? Come, now, let us be serious."

Lucien walks out to avoid a quarrel. He harbors a ferocious inclination to throttle his step-mother. When he returns, however, after two hours' absence, he is quite another man, speaks in a soft voice to Madame Larivière and has a queer smile at the corner of his mouth.

In the evening, he asks his wife:

"Have you ever been in Normandy?"

"Of course you know I haven't," says Hortense. "I have never been anywhere except to the Bois de Vincennes."

The following day, a thunderbolt burst in the toy-shop. Lucien's father, père Bérard, as he is called in the quarter, where he is known for a bon vivant with a sharp eye to business, calls round and invites himself to breakfast. When coffee comes on the table, he exclaims:

"I've brought our children a present," and triumphantly produces two railway tickets.

"What's that?" inquires the step-mother in a husky voice.

"Two first-class places for a circular tour in Normandy. . . . Well, my little ones, what do you say to that? A whole month of fresh air! You'll come back fresh as roses."

Madame Larivière is astounded. She has a mind to protest, but does not care to pick a quarrel with père Bérard, who has always had the last word. But when she hears the hardwareman speak of taking the travellers at once to the station, her amazement exceeds all bounds. He won't loosen his grip of them till he sees both off in the train.

"Very well," she mutters with inward rage, "take my daughter away from me. So much the better; they won't be kissing each other in the shop at least, and I can look after the honor of the house."

At last the married couple reach the Saint-Lazare station, accompanied by their step-father, who has barely given them time to throw some linen and clothing into a trunk. He bestows onorous kisses on their cheeks, advises them to see everything, and tell him all about it when they come back. Twill amuse him.

On the landing where the train takes its departure, Lucien and Hortense hurry along in quest of an empty carriage. They have the good luck to find one; they jump into it and are just preparing for a tête-à-tête, when to their mortification a spectacled gentleman gets into the same compartment,

who, as soon as seated, looks at them severely. The train starts; Hortense with a heavy heart turns her head and affects to scan the landscape; but tears well up into her eyes so that she cannot see even the trees outside. Lucien tries to hit on some ingenious plan whereby to get rid of the old gentleman, but his expedients are too high-handed.

A moment he hopes their fellow-traveller will get down at Melun or Verdun, but he soon finds out his mistake; the gentleman is bound all the way to Havre. Lucien, exasperated, decides to take his wife's hand in his; they are married, after all, and may openly avow their fondness. But the old gentleman's brow lowers more and more; it is evident he disapproves altogether any such outward mark of affection; so the young woman, blushing, withdraws her hand. The rest of the journey is got through with constraint and in silence.

Happily they are now at Rouen.

Lucien bought a guide-book on leaving Paris. They alight at an hotel which is recommended, and become a prey to the waiters. At the table d'hôte they scarce dare exchange a word before the crowd of people staring at them. So they retire early to rest; but the partition walls are so thin, that the neighbors to left and right cannot budge without their being made aware of it. They no longer dare to move or even cough in their beds.

"Let us go see the town," says Lucien on rising the next morning, "and start off quick for Havre."

They are on foot all day, visit the cathedral, where they are shown the

Tour-de-Beurre, a tower built from the proceeds of taxes imposed by the clergy on the butter of the country; go to the old palace of the Dukes of Normandy, enter the ancient churches now used as corn-lofts, see the Place Jeanne-d'Arc, the Museum, even the Monumental Cemetery. They seem to be accomplishing a duty, nor do they neglect to look at every historic house. Hortense is especially bored to death, and gets so tired that she falls sleep in the train the next day.

On reaching Havre, a fresh annoyance greets them. At the hotel where they get down, the beds are so narrow that they must needs take a room with double bedsteads. Hortense feels this almost as an insult, and sheds tears. Lucien consoles her as best he can, assuring her that they shall stay at Havre no longer than is just necessary to see the town. And their wild walks recommence.

Then they quit Havre, and stop for a few days at every important town set down in their itinerary. They visit Honfleur, Pont-l'Evêque, Caen, Bayeux, Cherbourg; their heads get crammed with such a rigmarole of streets and monuments and churches that they confuse the whole, and grow dizzy with the rapid succession of a set of horizons devoid of all interest to them.

They no longer look at anything, keeping the tenor of their way, strictly as it were a task they know not how to get rid of. Since they have set out, they must needs somehow find their way back. One evening, at Cherbourg, Lucien let fall this ominous expression of his views: "I think I like your mother's place better."

The next day they start for Granville. Lucien remains sombre and casts wild eyes over the country, where fields on each side the carriage expand to view like a fan. Suddenly, as the train comes to a stop at a small station, the name of which does not reach their ear, but where a lovely corner of verdure is seen among the trees, Lucien cries out: "Get down, my dear, get down quick!"

"But this is no station marked on the guide-book," expostulates Hortense.

"The guide-book, say you? Wait a bit, I'll show you what we'll do with the guide-book! Come, quick, get down."

"What about the luggage?"

"A fillip for the luggage!"

And Hortense did get down, the train started and left them both in the lovely corner of verdure. On leaving the station, they were in the open country. Not a sound. Birds were singing in the trees; a clear stream flowed at the bottom of the vale. Lucien's first care was to fling the guide-book into the middle of a pool of water as they went by. At last, it is over; they are free.

Three hundred steps off stands a secluded auberge or country-inn, where the housewife gives them a large room as cheerful to look at as sunshine in spring. The white-washed walls are a yard thick. Besides, there is not a traveller in the house, and the hens alone look at them with an inquisitive air.

"Our tickets are good for eight days yet," says Lucien. "We'll spend the eight days here."

What a delightful week! They go off in the morning by untrod paths, dive into the depths of a wood on the slope of a hill, and there spend the livelong day, lost among the tall grasses that hide their youthful love.

Anon they follow the stream; Hortense runs like an escaped schoolgirl, or pulls off her bottines and takes a footpath, while Lucien provokes her, so that she utters little screams when he comes up suddenly behind and smacks a kiss on the back of her neck. Their lack of linen, and dearth of everything generally, is highly amusing; they are, indeed, elated beyond measure to be thus left to themselves in a desert where none may think of looking for them.

Hortense has been obliged to loan some of the housewife's country underclothing, and the coarse stuff scratches her skin and makes her giggle. Their room is so gay! They lock themselves in at eight o'clock, when the dark, silent country no longer tempts them out. They give special directions not to be woke up too early. Lucien at times goes downstairs in his slippers and brings up the breakfast, eggs and cutlets, allowing no one to enter the room. And the breakfast is exquisite thus eaten on the bedside and endless from the kisses which outnumber the mouthfuls of bread. The seventh day they are surprised and desolate to find that they have lived through the week so rapidly. And so they take their departure as they came, without even wishing to be told the name of the country where they have loved.

Now at least they have had a quarter of their honeymoon. Not until they reach Paris do they come across their luggage. When, however, père Bérard questions them as to their trip, they get mixed up. They saw the sea at Caen, and locate the Tour-de-Beurre at Havre. "The deuce!" exclaims the hardwareman; "but you don't say a word about Cherbourg. What of the Arsenal?" "Oh! a wee bit of an arsenal," quietly responds Lucien: "it lacks trees."

At which Madame Larivière, still sulky, shrugs her shoulders, and mutters: "'Tis worth one's while to go voyaging! Why, they don't even know what monuments they've seen. . . . Come, Hortense, enough of this: go to the counter, please."

A Prince of the Blood

THIS time I will take you to spend the day in a little town in Algiers. It will give us a little change from tambourines and cicadæ.

It is going to rain; the sky is gray, the crests of Mount Zaccar are wrapped in mists,—a dreary Sunday. In my little hotel room, with my window open on the Arab ramparts, I am striving to distract myself by lighting cigarettes. The whole library of the hotel has been placed at my disposal; between a very detailed account of the registry and some novels by Paul de Kock, I find an odd volume of Montaigne. I open the book at random, reread the admirable letter on the death of Bœotia, and find myself more gloomy and thoughtful than ever. A few drops of rain are already falling. Every drop, as it strikes the window-sill, makes a large star in the dust which has collected there since the rains of last year. My book slips from my hands, and I spend a long time gazing at this melancholy star.

Two o'clock strikes from the clock-tower of the town,—an old marabout, the slender white walls of which I can see from here. Poor devil of a marabout! Who would have said, thirty years ago, that some day it would carry in the middle of its breast a large municipal clock-face, and that every Sunday on the stroke of two it would give to the churches of Milianah the signal to ring to vespers? Ding, dong! There the bells go! It will last a long while. Certainly, this room is gloomy. The big morning spiders which are called philosophic thoughts have woven their webs in every corner. Let us go out.

I arrive on the Grand Place. The band of the Third Regiment of the Line, which is not frightened by a little rain, comes to take its place about its leader. At one of the windows of the division headquarters the general appears, surrounded by his young ladies; on the Place the sous-préfet walks up and down on the arm of the juge-de-paix. Half-a-dozen little half-naked Arabs are playing ball in a corner with ferocious yells. Beyond, an old Jew in rags comes to seek a ray of sunshine which he left yesterday in the same spot, and which he is astonished not to find there now. "One, two, three, go!" The band begins an old mazurka by Talexy which the hand-organs played last winter under my windows. This mazurka used to bore me; to-day it moves me to tears.

Oh, how happy they are, these musicians of the Third! With their eyes fixed on their semi-quavers, drunk with rhythm and noise, they think only of counting the bars. Their souls, their whole souls, are contained in that square of paper, the size of one's hand, which trembles at the end of the instrument between two brazen teeth. "One, two, three, go!" All lies in that for these honest fellows; the national airs which they play have never made them homesick. Alas! I do not belong to this band, and its music pains me; so I move away.

Where in the world can I spend this dreary Sunday afternoon? Good! The door of Sid' Omar's shop is open; let us go in.

Although Sid' Omar has a shop, he is not a shop-keeper. He is a prince of the blood, the son of a former Dey of Algiers who was strangled by his Janissaries. On the death of his father, Sid' Omar escaped to Milianah with his mother, whom he adored, and lived there for some years like a philosopher-nobleman, with his greyhounds, his falcons, his horses, and his women, in pretty, cool palaces, full of orange-trees and fountains. Then came the French. Sid' Omar, who was our enemy at first and the friend of Abd-el-Kader, at last quarrelled with the emir, and made his submission. The emir, to revenge himself, entered Milianah in the absence of Sid' Omar, pillaged his palaces, cut down his orange-trees, carried off his horses and women, and had his mother's throat crushed by the cover of a large chest. The wrath of Sid' Omar was terrible; he placed himself on the spot at the service of France, and we had no better nor more savage soldier than he so long as our war against the emir lasted. When the war was over, Sid' Omar returned to Milianah; but even now, when Abd-el-Kader is mentioned in his presence, he becomes pale, and his eyes burn.

Sid' Omar is sixty years o'd. In spite of age and the smallpox, his face has remained handsome; he has long lashes, the glance of a woman, a charming smile, and the manner of a prince. Ruined by the war, nothing of his former wealth remains but a farm in the plain of Chélif and a house in Milianah, where he lives like a bourgeois with his three sons who have been brought up under his own eye. The native chiefs have a great veneration for him. When a dispute arises, they willingly make him arbitrator, and his word is almost always law. He goes out but little; he can be found every afternoon in a shop connecting with his house, and opening on the street. The furniture of this room is not rich,—whitewashed walls, a circular wooden bench, cushions, long pipes, two braziers. It is there that Sid' Omar gives audience, and administers justice,—a Solomon in a shop.

To-day, Sunday, the company is large. A dozen chiefs are squatting in their burnous around the room. Each of them has a long pipe beside him, and a little cup of coffee in a fine filigree holder. I enter. No one moves. From his place Sid' Omar sends his most charming smile to meet me, and invites me with a gesture to seat myself beside him on a large cushion of yellow silk; then, with one finger on his lips, he makes me a sign to listen.

This is the case: The Caïd of the Beni-Zougzougs having had some controversy with a Jew of Milianah about a piece of land, the two parties have agreed to submit their difference to Sid' Omar and to accept his judgment. They have agreed to meet this very day, and the witnesses are summoned, when suddenly our Jew changes his mind, and comes alone without witnesses, to declare that he prefers to refer the matter to the French juge-de-paix rather than to Sid' Omar. The affair has reached this point when I arrive.

The Jew, old, dirty-bearded, with a brown coat, blue stockings, and a velvet cap, raises his nose to heaven, rolls supplicating eyes, kisses Sid' Omar's slippers, bends his head, kneels, clasps his hands. I do not understand Arabic, but from the Jew's pantomime at the words, zouge-de-paix, zouge-de-paix, which recur at every moment, I can divine all this fine discourse:—

"We do not doubt Sid' Omar. Sid' Omar is wise, Sid' Omar is just. Nevertheless the zouge de-paix will settle our business much better."

The audience, indignant, remains impassible, like the Arabs that they are. Outstretched upon his cushion, with the amber mouthpiece between his lips, Sid' Omar—the god of irony—smiles as he listens. Suddenly, in the midst of his finest sentence, the Jew is interrupted by an energetic Caramba! which stops him short; at the same time a Spanish colonist, who has come there as a witness for the Caïd, leaves his seat, and approaching Iscariot, pours upon his head a whole basketful of imprecations in every language and of every colour,—among others a certain French expression too vigorous for repetition here. The son of Sid' Omar, who understands French, blushes at hearing such a word in his father's presence, and leaves the room. Note this trait of Arab education. The audience is still impassible, Sid' Omar still smiling. The Jew has risen, and is making toward the door backward, trembling with fear, but murmuring faster than ever his eternal *zouge-de-paix, zouge-de-paix.* He goes out. The Spaniard, furious, rushes forth after him, catches up with him in the street, and twice—vli! vlan!—strikes him in the face. Iscariot falls upon his knees, with his arms crossed before him. The Spaniard, somewhat ashamed, returns to the shop. As soon as he has gone in, the Jew rises, and casts a sneaking glance around the motley crowd which surrounds him. There are people of all sorts,—Maltese, Mahonais, Arabs,—all united in hatred of the Jews, and happy at seeing one of them maltreated. Iscariot hesitates an instant; then, taking an Arab by the corner of his burnous, says,—

"You saw it, Achmed, you saw it; you were there. The Christian struck me. You will be a witness,—good, good!—you will be a witness."

The Arab frees his burnous, and pushes the Jew from him. He knows nothing, he saw nothing; just at that moment his head was turned away.

"But you, Kaddour, you saw it,— you saw the Christian beat me," cries the unhappy Iscariot to a tall negro who is peeling a Barbary fig.

The negro spits in sign of contempt, and walks off; he has seen nothing. Neither has this little Maltese, whose fiery eyes shine viciously behind his cap, seen anything. And this Mahonais

girl with the brick-red complexion, who runs off laughing with her basket of pomegranates on her head, has seen nothing either.

It is in vain that the Jew cries, prays, takes on; he has no witness, no one has seen anything! Happily two of his co-religionists pass through the street at this moment, with hang-dog looks, hugging the walls. The Jew sees them.

"Quick, quick, brothers! Let us hasten to the agent! Quick, to the *zouge-de-paix!* You saw it, you saw the old man beaten."

Did they see it? I should think so! There was great excitement in the shop of Sid' Omar. The coffee-bearer refills the cups, and relights the pipes. They talk and laugh boisterously. It is so amusing to see a Jew beaten! Amidst the uproar and the smoke, I reach the door quietly; I have a fancy to go and walk a little in the neighbourhood of Israel, to see how Iscariot's co-religionists have taken the affront put upon their brother.

"Come and dine this evening, Moussiou," calls the good Sid' Omar.

I accept, thank him, and go out.

In the Jewish quarter every one is astir. The affair has already caused great excitement. There is no one in the shops. Emboiderers, tailors, harness-makers,—all Israel is in the street. The men, in velvet caps and blue woollen stockings, gesticulate noisily, in groups. The women, pale, bloated, stiff as wooden idols in their flat gowns with gold stomachers and with their faces surrounded by black fillets, go from group to group squalling. At the moment I arrive a great movement takes place in the throng. They press forward and crowd upon one another. Leaning upon his witnesses, the Jew—the hero of the adventure—passes between two hedges of caps, beneath a shower of exhortations:—

"Avenge yourself, brother, avenge us, avenge the Jewish people. Fear nothing; you have the law on your side."

A frightful dwarf, stinking of cobbler's wax and old leather, comes up to me with a piteous air and a heavy sigh.

"You see!" he says. "How are the poor Jews treated! He is an old man; look! They have almost killed him."

In truth, the poor Israelite looks more dead than alive. He passes before me, with dim eye and distorted countenance; he does not walk, he drags himself along. A heavy indemnity alone can cure him; and consequently they are not taking him to the doctor, but to the *agent d'affaires*.

There are many *agents d'affaires* in Algiers, almost as many as there are locusts. The trade seems to be a good one. In any case it has the advantage that one may take it up freely, without examination, security, or keeping terms. As we make ourselves men of letters in Paris, so in Algiers they make themselves *agents d'affaires*. For this it is enough to know a little French, Spanish, and Arabic, always to have a code in one's pocket, and above all to have a bent for the business.

The agent's functions are very varied; by turns barrister, attorney, broker, expert, interpreter, bookkeeper, commissionaire, and public writer, he is the Maître Jacques of the colony. But Harpagon had only one Maître Jacques, and the colony has more than it needs.

In Milianah alone there are dozens of them. Generally, in order to avoid the expense of an office, these gentry receive their clients in the café of the Grand Place, and give their consultations—do they give them?—between the absinthe and the *champoreau*.

It is toward the café of the Grand Place that the worthy Iscariot hies himself, flanked by his two witnesses. Let us not follow them.

On leaving the Jewish quarter I pass before the house of the Arab Bureau. From without, with its slate roof and the French flag floating over it, one would take it for a village mayor's office. I know the interpreter; so let us go in and smoke a cigarette with him. From cigarette to cigarette I shall certainly end by killing this sunless Sunday!

The court which precedes the bureau is crowded with ragged Arabs. There are some fifty of them there waiting, crouched along the wall, each in his burnous. This Bedouin antechamber exhales, although in the open air, a strong odour of human leather. Let us pass on quickly. In the bureau I find the interpreter struggling with two great fellows who are bawling at the tops of their voices, with wild gestures, the story of some stolen string of beads, themselves the while quite naked except for one long, greasy garment. I sit down upon a rug in the corner, and look on. A pretty costume, the interpreter's, and how well the interpreter of Milianah wears it! They look as if made one for the other. The costume is sky-blue, with black frogs and shining gold buttons. The interpreter is blond, pink, curled,—a pretty blue hussar, full of humour and fancy;

a little talkative, but he speaks so many languages! somewhat sceptical, but he knew Renan at the Oriental school! a great lover of sport, as much at home in an Arab bivouac as at the sous-préfet's parties, waltzing better than any one else, and without his equal for *cousscouss*. He is a Parisian, in short; there you have my man, and you need not be surprised that the women are wild about him. As a dandy he has but one rival, the sergeant of the Arab Bureau. The latter, in his tunic of fine cloth and his gaiters with mother-of-pearl buttons, is the envy and despair of the whole garrison. Detached to the Arab Bureau, he is free from fatigue duty, and is always showing himself in the streets, white-gloved and freshly curled, with huge registers under his arm. He is admired and dreaded. He is one in authority.

Evidently this story of the stolen beads threatens to be a long one. Good evening! I will not wait for the end.

As I go out, I find the antechamber in a hubbub. The crowd is pressing about a tall native, pale, proud, and wrapped in a black burnous. A week ago this man had a fight on Mount Zaccar with a panther. The panther is dead, but the man had half of his arm eaten off. Morning and night he comes to have it dressed at the Arab Bureau, and each time they stop him in the court to hear him tell his story. He speaks slowly, in a fine guttural voice. From time to time he opens his burnous, and shows fastened to his breast his left arm wrapped in bloody bandages.

Hardly have I reached the street when a violent storm bursts upon me,

—rain, thunder, lightning, sirocco. I hasten to shelter. I enter a gate at a venture, and find myself among a flock of gypsies lying beneath the arches of a Moorish court. This court belongs to the mosque of Milianah; it is the refuge of the lowest orders of Mussulmen, and is called the Court of the Poor.

Great, thin greyhounds, covered with vermin, come and prowl around me with ugly looks. Leaning against one of the pillars of the arcade, I try to look unconcerned, and, without speaking to any one, watch the rain splashing on the coloured pavement of the court. The gypsies are on the ground, lying in heaps. Near me a young woman, almost handsome, with neck and legs bare and heavy iron bracelets on her wrists and ankles, is singing a strange and melancholy air of three notes through her nose. As she sings, she suckles a naked bronze-ed baby, and, with her free arm, pounds barley in a stone mortar. The rain, driven by a cruel wind, occasionally drenches the nurse and her nurseling. The gypsy pays no attention to it, but continues to sing through the storm as she pounds barley and suckles her little one.

The storm diminishes. Profiting by a clear moment, I hasten to leave this Court of Miracles, and make my way to Sid' Omar's dinner; it is time. As I pass through the Grand Place, I meet my old jew. He is leaning on his agent, his witnesses walk joyfully behind him, and a band of filthy little jews gambol about them. All their faces are radiant. The agent will take charge of the affair; he will ask the tribunal for two thousand francs damages.

Sid' Omar's dinner is sumptuous. The dining-room opens on an elegant Moorish court, in which sing two or three fountains. There is an excellent Turkish repast. Among other dishes I remark a chicken with almonds, a *cousscouss à la vanille*, a *tortue à la viande*,—somewhat heavy, but of admirable flavour,—and biscuits made with honey, called *bouchées du kadi*. There is no wine but champagne. In spite of the Musselman law, Sid' Omar drinks a little of it—when the servants' backs are turned. After dinner we go into our host's room, where we are served with sweetmeats, pipes, and coffee. The furniture of this room is of the simplest,—a divan, some rugs, and at the back a large, very high bed on which are scattered little red cushions embroidered with gold. On the wall hangs an old Turkish picture representing the exploits of a certain Admiral Hamadi. It seems that in Turkey painters employ only one colour in a picture; this picture is consecrated to green. The sea, the sky, the ships, and Admiral Hamadi himself are all green, and what a green!

The Arab custom compels us to leave early. When our coffee is drunk and our pipes smoked, I say good-night to my host and leave him with his women.

Where shall I finish my evening? It is too soon to go to bed; the spahis' trumpets have not yet sounded the tattoo. Besides, Sid' Omar's golden cushions are dancing about me fantastic farandoles which would prevent me from sleeping. Here I am before the theatre; let us go in a moment.

The theatre of Milianah is an old forage storehouse, disguised, after a fashion, as a play-house. Large lamps, which they fill with oil during the intermissions, perform the office of chandeliers. The pit stands; the orchestra chairs are benches. The galleries are very proud because they have straw-seated chairs. All around the room is a long passage-way, dark and unfloored. Nothing is lacking to make one fancy himself in the street. The performance has already begun when I enter. To my great surprise the actors are not bad,—that is, the men; they have life and spirit. They are almost all amateurs, soldiers of the Third; the regiment is proud of them, and comes nightly to applaud them.

As for the women, alas! they are still the everlasting women of the little provincial theatres,—pretentious, exaggerated, and false. Yet there are two who interest me among these women,—two Jewesses of Milianah, quite young, who are making their début. Their parents are in the theater, and seem enchanted. They are convinced that their children are going to earn thousands of douros at this trade. The legend of Rachel—Israelite, millionaire, and actress—has already spread among the Jews of the East.

Nothing could be more comic or more touching than these two little Jewesses on the boards. They keep timidly in a corner of the stage, powdered, painted, low-necked, and stiff. They are cold, they are ashamed. Now and again they jabber a phrase without understanding it; and while they speak, their great Hebraic eyes look stupidly at the audience.

I leave the theater. Amidst the

darkness which surrounds me I hear cries from the corner of the Place. Some Maltese, no doubt, are having an explanation with the help of their knives.

I return slowly to the hotel, along the ramparts. Delicious odours of orange-blossoms and arbour-vitæ rise from the plain. At the end of the road stands an old ghost of a wall, the remains of some temple. This wall is sacred; every day Arab women come and hang upon it votive offerings, fragments of *haïcks* and *foutas*, long locks of red hair bound by silver threads, scraps of burnous. It all hangs fluttering beneath a slender ray of moonlight, in the warm night-breeze.

Ah! Paris, Paris!

THIS morning, at the first streak of dawn, the loud roll of a drum awoke me suddenly. Ran-plan-plan! Ran-plan-plan!

A drum among my pines at such an hour? That is singular!

I hastily leap out of bed and run to open the door.

Nobody there! The noise has ceased. Two or three curlews fly out from among the wild vines. A faint breeze sings beneath the trees. Toward the east, on top of the Alpilles, is a heap of gold dust from which the sun slowly emerges. A first ray already gilds the top of the mill. At the same moment the drum, invisible, begins to beat a march beneath the trees. Ran-plan-plan, plan, plan!

The devil take the ass's skin! I had forgotten it. But who can this savage be who comes into the woods to salute the dawn with a drum? I look in vain, but can see nothing,—nothing but clumps of lavender, and pines which extend all the way down the road. Perhaps some sprite is hidden down there in the underbrush, making sport of me. It is Ariel, no doubt, or Master Puck. The scamp must have said to himself as he paused before my mill,—

"That Parisian is too quiet in there; let us wake him up!"

Whereupon he must have taken a big drum and — ran-plan-plan! ran-plan-plan! Will you be quiet, you rascally Puck? You will awaken my cicadae!

It was not Puck.

It was Gouguet François, called Pistolet, drummer in the Thirty-first Regiment of the Line, and just now on furlough. Pistolet is bored in the country, he is homesick; and when they will consent to lend him the drum belonging to the Commune, he goes off in melancholy mood to beat it in the woods and to dream of the Prince Eugène barracks.

It is upon my hill that he has come to dream to-day. There he stands against a tree, with his drum between his legs, beating away to his heart's content. Coveys of terrified partridges fly up from beneath his feet without his perceiving them. The wild thyme sheds its perfume around him, but he does not smell it.

Neither does he see the delicate spider-webs which tremble in the sunlight between the branches, nor the pine-needles which dance upon his drum. Wholly absorbed by his dream and his music, he lovingly watches his drumsticks fly, and his broad, stupid face beams with pleasure at each roll.

Ran-plan-plan! Ran-plan-plan!

"How handsome the barrack is, with its paved courtyard, its straight rows of windows, its men in fatigue caps, and its low arcades full of the clatter of mess-bowls!"

Ran-plan-plan! Ran-plan-plan!

"Oh the ringing staircase, the white-washed corridors, the strong-smelling dormitory, the belts which they are cleaning, the bread-board, the pots of blacking, the iron beds with their gray blankets!"

Ran-plan-plan! Ran-plan-plan!

"Oh the pleasant days in the guard-house, the cards which stick to one's fingers, the hideous queen of spades with her feather headdress, the odd volume of Pigault-Lebrun lying on the camp bed!"

Ran-plan-plan! Ran-plan-plan!

"Oh the long nights of sentry duty at the gates of ministers, the old sentry-box into which the rain comes, the cold feet, the state carriages which bespatter you as they pass! Oh the extra fatigue duty, the days under arrest, the ill-smelling tubs, the board pillow, the cold réveille on rainy mornings, the retreat in the fog at the hour when they are lighting the gas the evening roll-call at which one arrives out of breath!"

Ran-plan-plan! Ran-plan-plan!

"Oh the Bois de Vincennes, the coarse white cotton gloves, the walks on the fortifications! Oh the Barrière de l'Ecole, the soldiers' girls, the cornet of the Salon de Mars, the absinthe in the bouisbouis, the confidences between two hiccoughs, the sabres which we draw, the sentimental romance sung with one hand upon the heart!"

Dream on, dream on, poor man! It is not I who would hinder you. Beat boldly on your drum, beat with all your might! I have not the right to think you ridiculous.

If you are homesick for your barrack, am not I too homesick for mine?

My Paris pursues me even hither, just as does yours. You play the drum under the pines while I produce copy. Ah, what good Provençaux we are! Up there, in the barracks of Paris, we longed for our blue Alpilles and the wild odour of lavender; now here, in the midst of Provence, we miss the barrack, and all that recalls it is dear to us!

Eight o'clock is striking in the village. Pistolet, without laying down his drumsticks, has set out for home. I can hear him going down through the woods, still playing. And I, lying in the grass, ill with homesickness, fancy that I see my Paris filing between the pines to the sound of the departing drum.

Ah, Paris, Paris! Always Paris!

Sapho

CHAPTER I

THE STAIRCASE

"LOOK at me!—so! I like the color of your eyes! What is your name?"

"Jean."

"Only Jean?"

"Jean Gaussin."

"From the South, I perceive. How old are you?"

"Twenty-one."

"Artist?"

"No, madam."

"Ah, so much the better."

These scraps of sentences, almost unintelligible amid the exclamations, the laughter, and the dance-music of a fancy ball, were exchanged—one night in June—between a *pifferaro* and a Fellah woman, in the conservatory, filled with palms and tree ferns, which formed the background of Dechelette's studio.

To the pressing questions of the Egyptian woman the *pifferaro* replied with the ingenuousness of youth, and with the freshness and vivacity of a Southerner who has long been silent. A stranger in that crowd of painters and sculptors, lost since his entrance to the ball-room by the friend who had brought him thither, he had been wandering listlessly around for two hours, displaying his handsome face browned by the sun, his hair in curls as close and short as his sheepskin costume, while a murmur of admiration, of which he scarcely seemed conscious, arose around him as he proceeded.

He was bumped by the dancers, ridiculed on account of the bagpipe which he was carrying so awry, and for his mountain costume, so heavy and uncomfortable on a summer night. A Japanese lady, with eyes of the faubourg, hummed teasingly, "Ah, how handsome he is, how handsome is this postillion;" while a Spanish novice attired in white silk lace thrust her bouquet of white jasmine beneath his nose as she was passing by on the arm of an Apache Chief.

He did not understand these advances; feeling extremely ridiculous he took shelter in the cool shade of a glazed gallery, bordered by a wide divan beneath the greenery. He was immediately joined by this woman, who came and sat down close to him.

Young? Pretty? He could not have told you. From the long, blue woolen costume which fell over her rounded form, two well-formed, rounded arms extended, bare to the shoulder; her small hands were laden with rings; her large gray eyes wide open, and gaining greater prominence by reason of the fantastic iron ornaments which hung upon her forehead, completed the harmonious whole.

An actress no doubt. Many of the profession came to Dechelette's house; and this reflection was not calculated to put him at his ease, for he had rather a fear of that class. She began to talk to him very familiarly, her elbow on her knee, her head supported by her hand, with a sad sweetness, a little senso of languor. "From the South, really? And with such fair hair, too! What an extraordinary thing!"

Then she wanted to know how long he had been in Paris, if the examination of the consular service for which he was preparing was very difficult; whether he knew many people, and how it had come to pass that he found himself at Dechelette's party in the Rue de Rome. So far from the Latin Quarter, too!

When he told her the name of the student who had brought him, "La Gournerie, a relative of the author—she knew him no doubt"—the expression of the woman's face changed, grew suddenly clouded; but he paid no attention to that, being at the time of life when the eyes sparkle without seeing anything. La Gournerie had assured him that his cousin would be there, and that he would introduce him. "I am so fond of poetry; I should be so glad to know him!"

She had a smile of pity, and a pretty shrug of the shoulders, for his ingenuousness, even while she held back the bamboos, and looked amid the dancers, to see whether she could find out the great man for him.

The dance was just then in full swing, it was like a fairy scene. The studio, or rather the hall, for scarcely ever was any work done in it, was raised to the full height of the mansion, and made one immense apartment of it. From the light gauzy hangings, the lacquered screens, the various colored glass, the clusters of the yellow roses which decked the high Renaissance fire-place, the varied and fantastic light of innumerable Chinese, Persian, Moorish and Japanese lanterns was reflected. Some

of these in iron open-work, with ogive apertures like the door of a mosque; some in paper resembling fruits, others displayed fan-wise cut into the shapes of flowers, ibis, and serpents. With startling suddenness great jets of electric light at times would pale the thousands of lanterns and blanch in their moonlike rays faces and bare shoulders, all the phantasmagoria of dresses, plumes, spangles, ribbons which were mingling with the ball, or seated on the Dutch staircase with wide balustrade which led to the first-floor corridors, above the necks of the double-basses, and the frantic time-beating of the conductor's baton.

From his place the young man could see all this through a lattice-work of green, and through creeping plants, which while mingling with the decorations framed them, and by an optical illusion cast here and there in the dance, garlands of wisteria upon the trailing white robe of a princess or crowned a Pompadour shepherdess with a dracæna leaf; and besides for the young man the interest of the spectacle was doubled by learning from his Egyptian acquaintance the names, all illustrious and well-known, which were concealed beneath costumes of such varied and whimsical character.

Yonder whipper-in carrying his whip slung over his shoulder was Jadin; while a little farther on that shabby cassock concealed the identity of the elderly Isabey, taller by a pack of cards in his buckled shoes. Père Corot smiled beneath the great pack of a Pensioner's cap. She also pointed out Thomas Couture as a bull-dog, Jundt as a convict-warden, and Cham as a bird of the West India Islands.

There were some serious and historic costumes; a plumed Marat, a prince Eugène, a Charles the First, worn by very young painters which indicated plainly the difference between the two generations of artists; the last arrivals serious, cold, with heads as one sees on the bourse, aged by those peculiar wrinkles which indicate money-cares; the others very *gamins*, boisterous, overflowing with high spirits.

Notwithstanding his fifty-five years and the palms of the Institute, the sculptor Caoudal as a hussar, his arms naked, showing his Herculean biceps, a painter's palette dangling about his long legs in lieu of a sabretache, was dancing *"cavalier seul"* of the time of the "Grande Chaumiere" opposite to a musician named de Potter who dressed as a muezzin out for a holiday, his turban awry, was imitating the "stomach dance" and squalling *Allah il Allah* at the top of his shrill voice.

A large circle of resting dancers surrounded these lively celebrities, and in the first rank was Dechelette, the master of the house, frowning beneath a high Persian head-dress, with his small eyes, Kalmuk nose, and grizzled beard, happy in the enjoyment of others, although he gave no evidence of it.

Dechelette, the engineer, a personage in the artist-society of Paris some ten or twelve years ago, a very good fellow, very rich, with a taste for art and that free-and-easy manner, the contempt for public opinion which travel and celibacy bestow, had then the superintendence of a railway between Tauris and Teheran; and every year, by way of refreshing himself after ten months of toil, of nights under canvas, of feverish gallops over sands and swamps, he came to spend the hot season in this mansion in the Rue de Rome, built after his own plan, furnished like a summer palace, where he assembled witty men and pretty women, only asking civilization to give him for a few weeks the essence of anything appetizing and exhilarating that it could bestow.

"Dechelette has arrived." That was the news in the studio as soon as the great canvas blind which shaded the glazed façade at the mansion was raised by his domestics. That meant that the fun was about to begin, and that for two months festivity and music, dancing and amusement would continue to intrude upon the dead silence of the Quartier de l'Europe at that season of country-visiting and sea-bathing.

Personally Dechelette counted for nothing in the bacchanalian feasts which were uproarious in his house night and day. That unwearied libertine regarded his pleasure with a coldness, a vague regard, smiling as if under the influence of hasheesh, but with coolness and imperturbable calmness. A faithful friend and open-handed, he nevertheless had for women all the contempt of an Eastern-born, with indulgence and politeness, and of those who came to his house attracted by his wealth or by the joyous life led there not one could boast of having been his mistress for more than one day.

"A good fellow, all the same," added the Egyptian woman, who had given Gaussin all these details. Then, suddenly interrupting herself, she exclaimed—

"There is your poet!"

"Where?"

"Before you—dressed as a village bridegroom."

The young man ejaculated an Oh! of disappointment. His poet! That fat, shiny, perspi ing man, exhibiting a clumsy grace in the shirt collar and the flowered waist-coat proper to Jeannut! The grand, despairing cries of the Book of Love came to Gaussin's mind, from that volume which he could never read without some feverish throbbings; and he mechanically murmured aloud—

"To animate the proud marble of thy body,
O Sapho, I have given my heart's blood!"

She turned quickly, her barbaric pendants jangling and cried—

"What are you muttering there?"

They were some of La Gournerie's verses; he was surprised that she did not know them.

"I don't like verse," she said shortly; then she stood up, her brows contracted, watching the dancers and nervously fingering the beautiful bunches of lilac-hued flowers which hung in front of her. Then with a decision which cost her an effort, she said, "Good-night," and disappeared.

The poor *pifferaro* sat quite motionless. "What is the matter with her? What have I said to her?" He considered, but could find no reason, and thought he would go to bed. He picked up his bagpipe mournfully and reentered the dancing-room, less troubled at the departure of the Egyptian than at the prospect of the crowd he had to thread before he could gain the door.

The sense of his own obscurity among so many illustrious people made him more bashful than ever.

Dancing had nearly ceased by this time; a few couples here and there were clinging to the dying strains of a waltz, and amongst them Caoudal, superb and majestic, was whirling about with his head high in the air with a little tricoteuse, whose head-gear was streaming in the wind as he lifted her in his brawny arms.

Through the large casement at the end of the rooms now thrown wide open, entered the gusts of the pallor-giving morning air, moving the palm leaves, and flaring the candles almost to the point of extinguishing them. A paper lantern caught fire, some sockets were cracked, and all round the room the servants were placing small round tables like those we see at cafés. The guests always supped in this fashion four or five together at Dechelette's; and sympathetic souls were seeking each other, and arranging themselves already.

Cries and shouts resounded. "The *'Pil-ouit'* of the faubourg answered the "you, you, you, you," in the rattling accents of the Eastern girls. There were remarks made in low tones, and the voluptuous laughter of women led to their places with a caress.

Gaussin was taking advantage of the confusion to make his way toward the door when his friend the student, in a great perspiration, his eyes almost starting from his head. a bottle under each arm, arrested him. "Where on earth are you going? I have been looking for you everywhere! I have secured a table, and some women are there—little Bachellery of the *Bouffes*, the Japanese girl, you know. She sent me to find you. Come quickly;" and he darted away.

The *pifferaro* was thirsty, and besides

the intoxication of the ball tempted him, as did the appearance of the actress who was beckoning to him from a distance. But a grave sweet voice murmured close to his ear:

"Do not go over there!"

She, his former acquaintance, was beside him, close to him drawing him away; and he followed her without hesitation. Why? It was not the attractiveness of the woman—he had scarcely looked at her; and the other yonder who was beckoning to him, arranging the steel knives in her hair, was much more to his taste. But he was obeying a will stronger than his own, the impetuous violence of a desire.

"Do not go over there!"

Suddenly they found themselves on the pavement of the Rue de Rome. Cabs were waiting in the pale morning light. Street-sweepers and working men going about their business looked at the noisy and crowded party, at the couple in fancy dress, a Shrove Tuesday masquerade in the height of summer.

"To your house or to mine?" she asked.

Without well knowing how to explain it to himself he thought that it would be better to go to his, and gave his distant address to the driver of the cab. During the long ride they spoke but little to each other. Only she continued to hold one of his hands between her own, which he felt were very small, and cold as ice; and had it not been for the chill of her nervous clasp he would have thought she was asleep, as she leaned back in the *fiacre* with the shadow of the blue blind upon her face.

They stopped at the Rue Jacob in front of a students' lodging. Four stories to mount; it was a high and steep climb. "Would you like me to carry you up?" he said laughingly, but in a low tone because of the sleeping inmates. She looked him over slowly, disdainfully, but tenderly; it was a glance of experience which gauged him and clearly said, "Poor little man!"

Then he, with a strong effort born of his youth and his southern blood, took her up in his arms and carried her like a child, for he was stout and lusty notwithstanding all his feminine fairness of feature; he ascended the first flight without pausing for breath, happy in the weight which two fresh, naked arms clasped around his neck.

The second flight was longer and less agreeable. The woman let herself go, and consequently the weight was greater in proportion. The iron of her pendants, which had at first only tickled him, began to indent his flesh cruelly.

At the third landing he was panting like a piano-carrier; his wind failed him, while she kept murmuring ravishingly, "O, my dear, how nice it is, how delicious it is!" and the last few steps which he scaled one by one seemed to him to pertain to a giant stairway, whose walls, banisters and narrow windows, kept turning round in an interminable spiral. He was no longer carrying a woman but something heavy, horrible, which suffocated him and which every moment he felt tempted to let go, to throw from him in rage at the risk of a brutal crash.

Arrived at the narrow landing, "So soon," she said, opening her eyes. He was thinking, "At last;" but he could not have said so, as he stood there deadly pale, his hands upon his chest which felt bursting.

Their whole history, this ascent of the staircase in the sad gray light of the morning!

CHAPTER II

KNOWN DISTRESS

HE kept her for two days, and then she left him, leaving behind her an impression of soft skin and fine linen. No other information about herself except her name and address and this: "When you wish for me call me, I shall always be ready."

The very small card, elegant and perfumed, bore these words:

FANNY LEGRAND,
6 *Rue de l'Arcade*.

He put it in his chimney-glass between an invitation to the last ball at the Foreign office, and the illuminated and quaint programme of Dechelette's party, his only two evening entertainments that year; and the memory of the woman, which remained some days about the mantelpiece in the delicate perfume, evaporated in the same time as it, without Gaussin, who had an aim in life, and who was a hard worker, distrusting above all things the allurements of Paris, ever having had the idea of renewing this *amourette* of a night.

The official examination was to take place in November. Only three months remained to him in which to prepare for it. Afterward would succeed a probation of three or four years in the Consular service; then he would be sent away to some distant land. This prospect of exile did not alarm him, for a tradition amongst the Gaussins of Armandy—an old Avignon family, decided that the eldest son of the house should follow what they called "the career" with the example, the encouragement, and the moral protection of those who had preceded him in it. For this provincial, Paris was only the first step upon a very long journey—a fact which prevented him from forming any close connections in love or in friendship.

A week or two after the ball at Dechelette's, one evening as Gaussin, his lamp alight, his books laid out on the table, was setting to work, a timid knock at the door was heard, and when he opened it a woman appeared dressed in becoming and elegant style. He only recognized her when she put back her veil.

"You see 'tis I. I have come back!"

Then interpreting the restless, bored glance which he cast upon the work on the table she said: "Oh, I shall not disturb you. I know what it is." Then she took off her bonnet, took up a number of the *Tour du Monde*, settled herself in a chair, and sat still, seemingly absorbed in her reading; but each time that he raised his eyes he met her gaze.

And indeed he needed all his strength to resist the impulse to take her then and there in his arms, for she was very tempting and charming, with her small head, low forehead, short nose, her pretty sensual lips, and the lithe maturity of her form displayed in her gown of most Parisian correctness, less alarming to him than the semi-costume of an Egyptian woman.

Though she left him the following morning she returned several times during the week, and always came back with the same pallor, the same cold clammy hands, the same voice broken with emotion.

"Oh, I know quite well I bore you," she would say to him—"I know I fatigue you; I ought to have more pride. If you will believe it—every morning as I leave your house I swear I will never enter it again; but I come back again in the evening as if I were possessed."

He looked at her, amused, surprised in his contempt for women by this amorous persistence.

Those he had known hitherto—girls whose acquaintance he had made at drinking places and skating rinks, sometimes young and pretty girls—always left him disgusted with their vacant laughter, their housemaids' hands, the grossness of their instincts and remarks which caused him to open the window when they had gone away. In his innocence he had fancied all "fast" women were alike. So he was very much surprised to perceive in Fanny a sweetness, a reserve truly feminine, with this advantage over the countrywomen he had met in the provinces at his mother's house; she possessed a smattering of art—of all things—which rendered her conversation interesting and varied.

Then she was a musician; she could sing, accompanying herself upon the piano, in a contralto voice, somewhat worn and unequal, but well-trained; some romance by Chopin or Schumann, country songs, airs of Berri, Burgundy or Picardy, of which she knew quite a large number.

Gaussin, who was passionately fond of music, that art of idleness and open air, in which his countrymen delight, was moved to ecstasy by the sound in his working hours, or while reposing in delicious rapture. And emanating from Fanny it was particularly ravishing. He

was surprised that she was not on the stage, and thus he learned that she had sung at the *Lyrique*. "But not for long —I found it much too tiresome," she said.

As a matter of fact there was nothing studied about her, nothing stagey; no shadow of vanity or deceit. Only a certain mystery concerning her life out of doors, a mystery even undivulged in moments of passion, and which her lover did not attempt to penetrate, feeling neither curious or jealous, permitting her to come at the time agreed upon without looking at the clock, ignorant so far of the feeling of expectation—those great throbs of the heart which are struck by desire and impatience.

Occasionally, the summer being very fine that year, they went about together in search of all those charming corners in the environs of Paris of which she knew every detail. They mixed in the noisy crowds of passengers at the suburban stations, breakfasted at some inn on the skirts of a wood or lake, only avoiding the too greatly frequented places. One day when he proposed to her to go to the Vaux de Cernay—she cried: "No, no, not there; there are too many artists there."

He remembered that this antipathy for artists had led to their first acquaintance. When he inquired the reason of it, "They are," she said, "such crazy, crack-brained fellows, who always tell more than ever has happened. They have done me a great deal of injury."

Then he would protest. "Nevertheless, art is beautiful. There is nothing to be compared with it for embellishing —for enlarging the sphere of life."

"Look you, dear, this is beautiful; to be simple and upright like you; to be twenty years old, and to love so well."

Twenty years old! One would not have said she was older, to see her so vivacious, always ready, laughing at anything, finding everything enjoyable.

One evening at Saint-Clair, in the valley of Chevreuse, they arrived the day before the fair, and could not find a room. It was late, and to reach the next village they must walk a league through the wood. At length they were offered a shake down at the end of a barn in which some masons were sleeping.

"Let us go there," she said laughing, "it will recall to me the time when I was in distress."

She had known distress then!

They groped their way between the occupied beds in the great whitewashed barn, where a night lamp was flaring in a niche in the wall; and all night lying close together, they smothered their kisses and laughter listening to the snoring of their wearied companions, whose working clothes and hobnailed shoes lay close by the silk dress and dainty boots of the Parisienne.

At daybreak a panel was opened at the bottom of the great door, a ray of light was admitted upon the sack beds and battered floor, while a hoarse voice called out: "Get up there, you people." Then in the again darkened barn a general movement arose, yawning, stretching, loud coughing, the sounds usual to an awakening of human beings; and then heavily and silently the Limousins departed one by one, without even imagining that they had been sleeping so close to such a pretty girl.

Behind them she arose, put on her dress by feeling only, and hastily arranged her hair.

"Stay there, I am coming back," she said. She returned in a moment with an enormous armful of wild flowers drenched with dew. "Now let us go to sleep," she said, as she cast on the bed the fresh and odorous blossoms which revivified the atmosphere around them. And in his eyes she never had appeared prettier than when she entered the barn, laughing, in the early dawn, her light hair flying about her, the wild flowers in her arms. On another occasion they were breakfasting at Ville d'Avray, by the lake. The mist of the autumnal morning rested on the calm water and the variegated forest in front of them, and alone in the little garden of the restaurant they were embracing each other while eating the white bait.

Suddenly from a rustic summer house in the plane-tree at the base of which their table was placed, a loud and mocking voice exclaimed: "I say, you two, when you have quite finished billing and cooing there!" And the leonine face and ruddy beard of the sculptor Caoudal peered through a loophole in the hut.

"I have a great mind to come down and breakfast with you. I am as melancholy as an owl up here."

Fanny did not reply, being evidently annoyed at the recognition; but he, on the contrary, accepted at once, being curious concerning this celebrated artist and pleased to have him at table.

Caoudal, very effectively got up in *negligee* costume, but every detail of which was studied, from the white tie of china crepe—to set off a complexion seamed with wrinkles and blotches—to the jacket which fitted closely to a still slim and muscular figure, Caoudal seemed older than at Dechelette's ball.

But what surprised, and even embarrassed him a little was the tone of intimacy which the sculptor adopted toward his mistress. He called her "Fanny" and "tutoyed" her. 'You know," he said, as he set his plate at their table, "that I have been a widower for the last fifteen days. Maria has bolted with Morateur. That made me feel rather quiet for a while. But this morning when I entered my studio I felt fearfully lazy; impossible to work, so I left my group, and came out to breakfast in the country. Ridiculous idea when one is alone, in a little while I should have been weeping into my rabbit-stew."

Then looking at the Provençal, whose soft beard and curly locks were the color of the Sauterne in the glasses, he said:

"How delicious is youth! No fear that this one will be let go; and what is better still, it is infectious. She looks almost as youthful as he."

"You wretch!" she exclaimed, laughing; her laugh rang out seductively, youthfully; the youth of a woman who loves and wishes to make herself beloved.

"Astonishing, astonishing," muttered Caoudal, who was scrutinizing her while he proceeded with his breakfast, a trace of sadness and envy hovering in the corners of his mouth. "I say, Fanny, do you remember a breakfast here—a long time ago indeed, Ezano—Dejoie and all the set were here—you fell into the pond! They dressed you up in man's clothes with the keeper's tunic on. It suited you to perfection!"

"I don't remember," she replied coldly, and truthfully, for these fickle casual beings never exist save in their love for the time. They have no recollection of what has preceded it and no fear for the future.

Caoudal, on the contrary, mindful of the past, recounted between his draughts of Sauterne the exploits of his lusty youth; love and drinking parties in the country, opera balls, horseplay in the studios, engagements and conquests. But when he turned toward the pair as the brightness returned to his eyes with the flames he stirred up, he perceived that they were scarcely paying any attention to him, and were engaged in plucking grapes from each other's lips.

"But all this is rather tame. I see I am boring you. Ah, the deuce! It is folly to be old." Then he rose and threw aside his table napkin, "I pay for the breakfast, Langlois," he called out in the direction of the restaurant.

He turned away sadly, trailing his feet as if he were suffering from some mortal disease. For a long while the lovers watched his tall figure as it stooped beneath the golden-tinted foliage.

"Poor Caoudal! it is true he's nearly played out," murmured Fanny in a tone of gentle commiseration, and when Gaussin betrayed his indignation that Maria, a girl, a model, could laugh at the sufferings of a Caoudal and choose in preference—whom? Morateur, a little painter without any talent, with nothing but his youth to recommend him, she began to laugh. "Ah, you innocent, you innocent," she said, and pulling his head down upon her knees she began to breathe on him, to fumble him, his eyes, his hair, all over like a bouquet.

That evening Jean for the first time slept at his mistress' house; she had been teasing him about this for the last three months.

"But now why do you not wish to?"

"I don't know—it worries me."

"When I tell you I am quite free, that I am alone—"

So the fatigue of the excursion assisting her she had seduced him to the Rue de l'Arcade, close to the railway station. On the first floor of a respectable looking and comfortable house, an old domestic in a peasant's cap and with a somewhat soured appearance, came to open the door.

"It is Machaume. Good-day Machaume," said Fanny, embracing her round the neck. "You see, here he is, my lover, my king, I have brought him. Quick, light all the candles, make the house look lovely."

Jean was left to himself in a very small drawing-room, with arched low windows draped with the same commonplace blue silk which covered the few pieces of lacquered furniture. On the walls some landscapes lighted up the drapery. and each bore a dedication to Fanny Legrand—to my dear Fanny—and so on.

On the chimney-piece was a half-size copy of Caoudal's "Sapho," in marble, the bronze counterpart of which may be met with anywhere, and which Gaussin had, as a child, seen in his father's study. By the gleam of the solitary candle he could perceive the resemblance, albeit refined and youthful, which this work of art bore to his mistress. The turn of the profile, the contour of the figure beneath the

drapery, the tapering roundness of the arms clasping the knees, were features all well and intimately known to him; his eyes feasted on them with the recollection of sensations more tender.

Fanny, finding him wrapped in contemplation before the figure, said in a free and easy tone, "That is something like me, is it not? Caoudal's model resembled me." And immediately she carried him off to her bedroom where Machaume, looking very cross, was laying supper for two on a round table. All the candles were alight, even to those fixed to the glass door of the wardrobe; a fine fire of logs, gay as the first of the season, was blazing behind the guard. It was the bed-room of a woman dressing for a ball.

"I preferred to have supper here," she said laughing, "we shall be in bed all the sooner."

Jean had never beheld a room more coquettishly furnished. The Louis Seize hangings, the clear muslin of his mother's and sister's rooms bore no resemblance to this padded nest, where wood was concealed beneath soft satin, where the bed was only a divan broader than the others, extended at the farther end of the room on white furs.

Delicious was this caress of light, of warmth, of elongated blue reflections from the beveled mirrors, after the journey across fields, the wetting they had had, the muddy roads in the fading daylight. But what prevented him from enjoying as a true provincial the full comfort of the occasion was the ill-humor of the servant, the suspicious look she fixed on him, until Fanny sharply dismissed her with, "Leave us, Machaume, we will wait upon ourselves," and as the woman banged the door as she retired, she continued, "Do not mind her, she is angry because I am so fond of you, she says I am throwing away my life. These country people are so rapacious, too. Her cooking is worth more than she is, just taste this jugged hare."

She helped him and uncorked the champagne, but quite forgot to help herself in her desire to see him eat; at every movement she threw back to the shoulder the sleeves of the Algerian gandoura of white soft wool which she always wore in the house. Thus she recalled to him her first meeting with him at Dechelette's and seated in the same easy-chair, eating from the same plate, they spoke of that evening.

"Oh, as for myself," she said, "as soon as ever I saw you come in I felt I should like you. I felt like carrying you away at once, so that none of the others should have you. And what did you think when you saw me?"

At first he had been rather afraid of her, then he felt quite confidential— quite at home with her. "By the by," he added, "I never asked you why you were so annoyed at those verses of La Gournerie's?"

She frowned as she had done at the ball, then with a toss of the head she answered, "Nonsense, do not say any more about it;" then embracing him she continued, "I was rather afraid myself. I tried to get away and pull myself together, but I could not,—I never shall do it."

"Oh! Never."

"You shall see."

He was satisfied to reply with the skeptical smile of his age, not noticing the passionate, the almost menacing accent which she placed on the words

"You shall see." This womanly action was so gentle, so submissive, that he believed he had only to make a movement to free himself from her.

But to what end? He was pleased in the abandonment of that voluptuous chamber, so deliciously stupefied by the caressing breath upon his eyelids, which heavy with sleep, were closed with fleeting visions of autumnal woods, meadows, water-mills, all details of their day of love in the country.

In the morning he was suddenly awakened by Machaume calling out at the foot of the bed, in the most unconventional manner, "He is there, he says he *will* speak to you."

"What! He *will?* Then I am not in my own house, you have admitted him?"

She sprang up in a rage, rushed from the room half naked, her night-dress open.

"Stay where you are, my own, I will return," she said. But he did not wait until she came back, and scarcely felt comfortable until he in his turn had risen, dressed, and felt firm in his boots.

While he was collecting his clothes in that hermetically sealed room in which the night-lamp was still disclosing the disorder of the supper table, he could hear the sound of a fierce quarrel subdued by the hangings of the sitting-room. A man's voice, irritable at first, then imploring, in which the outbursts were choked with emotion in pleading, alternated with another voice which he did not immediately recognize, hard and hoarse, full of hatred and coarse epithets, and assailed his ears like a brawl in a low tavern.

All this odorous luxuriousness was tainted by this; degraded like stains on silk; and the woman was as low; on the same level as those she had formerly contemned!

She came in again out of breath, twisting her flowing hair with a graceful movement. "What a fool a man is who cries!" she said. Then seeing Jean up and dressed she uttered a cry of rage—"You have got up! Go into bed again at once, I desire it." Then suddenly calming she continued, caressing him with voice and gesture, "No, no, don't go away, you can't leave me thus! I am sure you will never come back again if you do."

"Of course I shall, why shouldn't I?"

"Swear to me that you are not angry —that you will return. Oh, how well I know you!"

He swore what she desired, but he did not get into bed again notwithstanding her supplications, and the reiterated assurance that she was in her own house free to do as she pleased. At length she seemed resigned to his departure, and accompanied him to the door, having nothing of the angry nymph in her now; on the contrary, being very humble, and seeking pardon from him!

A long and close embrace detained them in the ante-room.

"Well, when?" she asked, as her eyes searched his to their depths. He was on the point of replying, or of lying, no doubt in his anxiety to get away, when a ring at the bell stopped him. Machaume came out of her kitchen, but Fanny made a sign to her not to open the door, and then they all three stood motionless and silent.

They heard a stifled complaint, then the rustling of a letter slipped under the door, and then slowly descending footsteps. "Didn't I tell you that I was free—look here!" She handed to her lover the letter which she had just opened, a poor love letter, very humble, very meek, penciled in haste upon the table of a café, in which the miserable individual begged pardon for his foolish behavior that morning, acknowledged that he had no claim upon her other than what she chose to grant of her own free will, begged humbly that she would not banish him for ever, promising to accept anything—resigned to everything—if only he did not lose her—O, God, not to lose her!

"Would you believe it?" she said, with an evil laugh, which was sufficient to complete the isolation of the heart that she wished to subdue. Jean thought her cruel. He had not yet learned that a woman who loves has no pity except for her love, all her feelings of charity, kindness, good nature and pity and devotion are concentrated in one individual and one only.

"You are very wrong to laugh. This letter is horribly beautiful and heart-rending." Then in a graver tone he added, seizing her hand, "Look here, why do you drive him from you?"

"I don't want him any more—I do not love him."

"Nevertheless he was your lover. He placed you amid all this luxury in which you have lived and which is necessary to you."

"My own," she replied with that frank tone of hers, "when I did not know you I found all that very nice. Now it is a trouble, a shame, my heart rejects it. Oh, I know you are about to say that you are not serious in this. That *you* do not love me, but that is

my business; whether you wish it or not
I will *make* you love me."

He made no answer; arranged a
meeting for the next day and left her;
giving a few louis to Machaume—all
his student's purse contained—in payment for the jugged hare. So far as he
was concerned the affair was all over.
What right had he to trouble this
woman's existence, and what could he
offer in exchange for what she had given
up on his account?

He wrote as much that very day,
putting the case as gently as he could,
but without confessing to her that of
their intimacy—of this light caprice—
he had felt a great disgust, when, after
his night of love, he had heard the sobs
of the deceived lover mingling with her
washerwoman's oaths.

In this big boy, brought up at a distance from Paris, in full Provençal
style, there was some of his father's
roughness and all the delicacy and nerv-
ousness of his mother whom he so
greatly resembled. And to protect him
against the allurements of pleasure he
had before him the example of his
father's brother whose dissipation and
folly had half ruined the family, and
imperiled the honor of its name.

Uncle Cæsar! With only these two
words, and the family scenes they called
up, one could obtain from Jean sacrifices much greater than the abandonment of a light love affair to which he
had never attached any great importance. But it was more difficult to
break off than he fancied it would be.

Formally turned away, she came again
undiscouraged by his refusals to see
her, by the closed door, by the inexorable orders. "I have no self-respect,"
she wrote. She watched for the time

of his meals at the restaurant, waited
in front of the café where he was reading the papers, and all this while no
weeping, no scenes. If he were with
a friend she simply followed him.
watching for the moment when he
would be again alone.

"Do you wish for me this evening?
No? Then it must be another time."
And she would go away with the quiet
resignation of the peddler who refas-
tens his pack, leaving him the feeling
of remorse at his own harshness and
the humiliation of the falsehoods which
he stammered out at every meeting.
The approaching examination—the little time before him. Afterward, later
on, if she still wished it—in fact he
had made up his mind that when he had
succeeded in passing he would take a
month's holiday in the south, and she
would forget him in that time.

Unfortunately when the examination
was passed Jean fell sick. A neglected
chill, caught in a passage at the ministerial offices, took a bad turn. He knew
no one in Paris except a few students
from his own neighborhood whom his
exigent *liaison* had estranged and kept
away. Besides, here was need for more
than common attention, and from the
very first it was Fanny Leg and who
took her place at his bedside, and did
not quit it for ten days, nursing him
untiringly without fear or disgust, as
adroitly as a hospital nurse, with the
tender blandishments which, sometimes,
in his paroxysms of fear carried him
back to a serious illness of his youthful
days, and made him address her as Aunt
Divonne, and say, "Thank you, Divonne," when he felt Fanny's hands
upon his clammy forehead.

"It is not Divonne, it is I; I am

tending you." She saved him from mercenary care, from the chances of extinguished fires, or drinks made up in the porter's lodge; and Jean could never reconcile to his mind the quickness and readiness of those hands of indolence and voluptuousness. At night she slept for two hours on the sofa—a lodging-house article of furniture—and as soft as the plank bed of the police cell.

"But my poor Fanny, don't you ever go home then?" he asked one day. "I am better now; you ought to reassure Machaume."

She laughed! There had been fine times at home. Machaume gone, and the whole house, too! They had sold everything, furniture, effects, even the bedding. There remained to her only the dress which she had on her back, and a little linen which the maid had saved. Now if he sent her away she must go into the street.

CHAPTER III

TRAPPED

"I THINK I have found it this time; Rue d'Amsterdam opposite the railway terminus. Three rooms and a large balcony. If you wish we will go there and see it after you have finished your official duties. It is high up—five flights, but you can carry me. That was delicious! Do you remember?"

And very pleased with the reminiscences she crept close to him, nestling in his neck, seeking the old place—her place.

In furnished lodgings, with the manners of the quarter, the "trapsing" up and down of slip-shod females, the paper partition behind which other lodgers swarmed; the promiscuous mingling of keys, of candles, and of boots, living together had become intolerable. Not to her though; with Jean, the roof, the cellar, even the sewer would have been acceptable to her. But the delicacy of the lover was offended by certain things which as a single man he would not have thought of. Those one-night lodgers annoyed him, dishonored his house, and gave rise to the same sadness and disgust which he experienced when watching the monkeys in the Jardin des Plantes grimacing and mimicking the gestures and expressions of human affection. The restaurant also bored him; the meals which he had to go and eat twice a day on the Boulevard Saint-Michel in a large room filled with students, art pupils, artists, architects. who without being on speaking terms with him had known him by sight for the last twelvemonth during which he had taken his meals there.

He would blush—when he opened the door—as all eyes were bent on Fanny, and entered with the aggressive shyness of all young men who are accompanied by a woman; and he also feared to meet one of his official chiefs, or some one from his native district. Then the question of economy arose.

"How dear it is," she would say every time as she came away, and commented on the bill for dinner. "If we had a home of our own, I could have kept house for three days for the same sum."

"Well, what prevents us?" So they set about looking for a domicile.

That is the trap. Every one is caught in it, the best, the most conscientious by this instinct of propriety, the taste for "home" which has been circulate i by family education and warmth of the domestic hearth.

The flat on the Rue d'Amsterdam was taken immediately and found delightful, notwithstanding that the rooms opened into each other and looked outward, the kitchen and the sitting-room on a damp back-yard where arose from a gin-shop the odor of slops and chlorine—the bed-room on the steep noisy thorough-fare shaken day and night by goods-vans, drays, cabs, omnibuses; pierced by the whistling of the arriving and departing trains, all the uproar of the Western Railway Terminus, with its glazed roof, the color of dirty water, opposite. The advantage was in knowing that the railway was at their door, and St. Cloud, Ville d'Avray, Saint Germain, the country stations on the banks of the Seine, almost under their balcony. For they had a balcony, large and roomy, which, thanks to the liberality of former proprietors, boasted a zinc awning painted like striped calico, dripping and depressing beneath wintry skies, but under which it would be very comfortable to dine in summer, in the open air as in a mountain chalet.

They occupied themselves in furnishing. Jean having told his relatives of his projects of housekeeping, Aunt Divonne, who was the steward of his father's house, sent the necessary funds; and her letter announced at the same time the early arrival of a chest of drawers, a wardrobe, and a large cane arm-chair taken from the "Windy Chamber" for the Parisian.

This chamber, which he could remember at the end of a passage at Castelet, never used, the shutters closely barred, the door locked—was open in consequence of its situation to the gusts of the mistral, which caused it to quiver like the lantern of a lighthouse. In it was accumulated the lumber which every succeeding generation of the family relegated to oblivion in the face of new acquisitions.

Ah, if Divonne had but known what singular siestas would be enjoyed in the cane arm-chair! What small petticoats and frilled underclothing would be stowed in the Empire chest of drawers. But Gaussin's remorse was stifled in the thousand little pleasures of furnishing and occupancy.

It was so delightful after office business to set off in the dusk on long journeys arm in arm to some by-street to choose the dining-room furniture, the sideboard, the table and six chairs; or curtains of flowered cretonne for the window and the bed. He would have taken everything on trust; but Fanny had eyes for both. She tried the chairs, and the sliding leaves of the table, and developed quite a bargaining spirit.

She was acquainted with houses where one could obtain at trade prices a kitchen range complete for a small family; four iron saucepans, the fifth lined with enamel for the matutinal chocolate; none of copper, it takes so long to clean! Six forks and spoons of metal with the soup ladle, and two dozen plates, English china, strong and of gay pattern; all these things packed up together like a doll's dinner service. For toilet and table linen she knew a shopkeeper, the representative of a large manufacturer at Roubaix, who might be paid at so much a month; and, always watching for sales, in search of those remains of shipwreck which Paris casts continually into the foam of her breakers, she discovered in the Boulevard de Clichy a splendid bed almost new, and big enough to accommodate in a row the seven daughters of the ogre.

After his return from his office he also attempted to make some purchases, but he did not understand it, not knowing how to say no, or how to leave without purchasing anything. One day he entered a second-hand shop to purchase a cruet stand which she had noted, and he brought back instead of the cruet stand, which had been already disposed of, a luster with pendants for the drawing-room, a very useless article to them as they had no drawing-room.

"We will hang it in the verandah," said Fanny to console him.

Then the enjoyment of taking measurement, the discussions respecting the position of a piece of furniture, and the cries, the foolish laughter; the uplifting of hands when they perceived that notwithstanding all precautions, notwithstanding the supposed complete list of necessary purchases, there had always been something forgotten.

It was thus with the sugar rasp. Fancy setting up house without a sugar grater!

Then—everything purchased and put in its place the curtains hung, a wick in the new lamp, how glorious it was when they installed themselves, the minute inspection of the three little rooms before they went to bed, and how she laughed as she held him a light to bolt the door by. "Another turn, another; shut it firmly. Let us be indeed at home."

Then this was such a new and delicious existence. After leaving his work he came home quickly, eager to arrive, and sit in slippers by the fire. And in the black sloppiness of the street he pictured their room warm and lighted, lighted up by the old provincial furniture which Fanny had thought would be only in the way, and which turned out to be very old and handsome pieces; particularly the wardrobe, which was a Louis XVI. gem, with painted panels representing Provençal fêtes, shepherds in flowered coats dancing to the music of the flute and tambourine. The presence of these old-fashioned things, familiar to his youthful eyes, recalled his paternal mansion, and consecrated his new residence of which he was to taste the enjoyment.

As soon as he rang the bell Fanny would come carefully, coquettishly dressed, "on the spot" as she used to say. Her dress of black woolen material, very plain, but cut after a good style—the simplicity of a woman who dressed properly, the sleeves turned back and the skirt protected by a white apron; for she did their cooking herself, and only had a charwoman for the dirty work which chaps, or spoils the shape of the hands.

She was quite an adept at cooking—knew a number of receipts, northern or southern dishes as varied as her collection of popular ditties which, when dinner was over and the white apron hung up behind the closed door of the kitchen, she chanted in her fascinating and passionate contralto.

Below was the murmur of the street, the torrent of traffic. The cold rain pattered upon the zinc verandah; and Gaussin, his feet to the fire, extended in his arm-chair, watched the windows of the station opposite, and the clerks bending over their writing beneath the white light of the large reflectors.

He was well, he permitted himself to be soothed. In love? No, but thankful for the love that surrounded him, for the never changing affection. How had he been able to deprive himself so long of this happiness in the fear—at which he now laughed—of some entanglement or some obstacle? Was not his life much more respectable than when he went from one flame to another, endangering his health?

No danger in the future. In three years, when he would go away, the breaking of the bond would come naturally and without any shock. Fanny was forewarned; they had talked it over together as they talked of death, of a distant, but certain, fatality. There remained the great grief that those at home would experience when they learned that he was not living alone, his father's indignation—so stern and so quick.

But how could they know it? Jean saw no one in Paris. His father, "the consul," as they called him in his own place, was detained at home all the year by the necessity for superintending the very considerable domain which he cultivated, and by his tough battles with the vines. His mother, helpless, unable to move a step unaided, had to leave Divonne the superintendence of the house, and the care of the little twin sisters Martha and Mary, whose unexpected birth had forever deprived their mother of her strength. As for Uncle Cesaire, Divonne's husband, he was a great baby, who was not permitted to travel alone.

And Fanny now knew all the family. When he received a letter from Caste-

let, to the end of which the twins had added a few lines in their large characters, she would read it over his shoulder and was affected by it as he was. Of her own life he knew nothing, did not make any inquiries. He had the beautiful unconscious egotism of his youth without any jealousy, without disquiet. Full of his own life he let it run over, thought aloud, let himself go, while she remained silent.

So the days and weeks passed on in a happy quietude, troubled for a moment by one circumstance which affected them both deeply but in a different manner. She believed herself *enciente*, and told him so with such delight that he could not but share it. In his heart he was afraid of it. A child—at his age? What could he do with it? Ought he recognize it? And what a tie it would be between this woman and himself; what a complication in the future!

Suddenly his fetters became visible to him, heavy, cold and riveted. At night he could not sleep any more than she, and side by side in their big bed they lay dreamily with their eyes open, a thousand leagues apart!

Fortunately this false alarm was not repeated, and they resumed their peaceful and deliciously close existence. Then winter passed away, the real sun came again. Their apartment was prettier still, enlarged by the balcony and awning.

In the evening they dined there under the green-tinted sky, which was flecked with the twittering swallows.

The street exhaled warm airs, and all the sounds from the neighboring houses; but the least sigh of the wind was for them, and they forgot the time as they sat close together, unconscious of everything but themselves. Jean recalled the evenings like those on the banks of the Rhône, dreamt of consular appointments in hot and distant lands, of the decks of vessels sailing away over which the wind would blow in those long breaths which shook the awning. And when she would murmur "Do you love me?" he would recall himself from afar to reply, "Oh, yes, I love you." That is what it is to take them so young, they have so many ideas in their heads at once.

On the same balcony, separated from them by the iron lattice-work, entwined with climbing plants, another couple were billing and cooing, Monsieur and Madame Hettema, married people, very stout, who kissed loudly. Most wonderfully mated in age, tastes, and in generally heavy appearance, it was touching to hear these lovers at the end of youthfulness, supporting each other by old sentimental songs.

"But I hear her sigh in the shade,
It is a sweet dream, ah, let me sleep."

These were agreeable people to Fanny and she would like to know them. Sometimes even she and her neighbor would exchange, beneath the iron barrier, the smiles of loving and happy women, but the men as usual were more stiff and did not address each other.

Jean was returning one afternoon from the Quai d'Orsay, when he heard himself called by name at the corner of the Rue Royale. It was a beautiful day—a warm light in which Paris was opening out at this corner of the boulevard, which toward eventide on a fine day, about the hour for the Bois, has no equal in the world.

"Sit down, beautiful youth, and drink; the sight of you is good for one's eyes."

Two great arms arrested him, extending from the awning of a café which encroached on the pavement with its three rows of tables. He made no resistance, being flattered to hear around him the crowd of provincials, strangers, striped suits and round hats, whispering Caoudal's name with curiosity.

The sculptor, seated at the table, with a glass of absinthe, which harmonized with his military appearance and his officer's rosette, had for a neighbor Dechelette, the engineer, who had reached Paris the day before. He was the same as ever, sun-burnt, yellow, his high cheek-bones making his small eyes more prominent, his greedy nose sniffing Paris again. As soon as the young man had seated himself, Caoudal, pointing at him in comic anger, exclaimed:

"Isn't he handsome—the creature? Fancy that I was once his age and as curly! Oh, youth, youth!"

"Still harping on the same string," exclaimed Dechelette, smiling at his friend's hobby.

"My dear fellow, don't laugh. I would give all I am worth, medals, decorations, the Institute, all for that hair and that color." Then turning abruptly to Gaussin he said:

"What have you done with Sapho? One never sees her now!"

Jean stared at him without comprehending him. "Are you not together still?" and perceiving his evident astonishment he added impatiently,

"Sapho—come now—Fanny Legrand—Ville d'Avray."

"Oh, that's done with—long ago."

How came he to tell such a lie? From a feeling of shame, of uneasiness at the name of Sapho applied to his mistress; from a distaste for discussing her with other men, perhaps also from the wish to learn something which otherwise they would not have mentioned to him.

"Eh! Sapho! She is in the swim still then?" said Dechelette absently, full of the delight of again seeing the steps of the Madeleine, the flower-market, the long vista of the boulevards edged with foliage.

"Don't you recollect she was at your party last year? She was superb as a Fellah woman, and one morning in the autumn when I found her breakfasting with this handsome fellow at Langlois' you would have fancied her a fifteen days' bride."

"How old is she then? Considering the years one has known her—"

Caoudal looked skyward to calculate. "How old? how old? Let me see. Seventeen in '53, when she sat as my model, and this is '73—so reckon it up." Then his eyes glistened. "Ah, if you had but seen her twenty years ago, tall, slender, the true Cupid's bow of her mouth, the bold forehead. Arms, shoulders—a little thin perhaps, but that was all the more suitable for the burning Sapho. And the woman! the mistress! what was there not in that delightful flesh! what fire could not be struck from that flint; from that keyboard in which not a note was wanting. 'The whole gamut,' as Gournerie used to say."

Jean, very pale, asked: "Was he her lover, too?"

"La Gournerie? I should think so—rather. I suffered enough on his account! For four years we lived together like man and wife—four years I took care of her, ruined myself to satisfy her caprices, singing masters, music masters, riding—and what not. And when I had her polished, fined down, like a precious stone cut to shape; cleansed from the gutter where I found her one night in front of the Bal Ragache—that rhymester came and took her from the table whereat he was welcomed ever Sunday!"

He breathed very hard, as if he thus would chase away the old tenderness which still vibrated in his voice; then he resumed more calmly:

"At any rate his dishonorable conduct availed him nothing. Their three years of housekeeping was an *inferno*. The poet, for all his taking ways, was mean, vicious, and a maniac. You should have seen them tearing each other's hair! When one called one found her with a bandage over her eye, and he with a torn, scratched face. But the beauty of it all was when he wished to separate from her. She stuck to him like a burr, followed him about, nearly knocking down his door to get in, and she would lie on his door-mat waiting for him. One night in midwinter she stayed for five hours outside the Farcy when the whole set of them had gone up. A pity! But the elegiac poet remained implacable; even going so far one day as to put the case into the hands of the police to rid himself of her. A nice gentleman he was! And as a final act—thank-offering to this beautiful young girl who had given him the best of her youth, her intelligence, and herself—he emptied upon her head a volume of driveling, spiteful verses and lamentations called the *Book of Love,* his best work!"

Gaussin sat motionless listening, sucking through a long straw the iced beverage which had been placed before him. Surely they had put in it some poison which was freezing his very heart and vitals!

He was shivering, notwithstanding the beautiful weather, and beholding in a blurred way, as shades that went and came, a watercart in front of the Madeleine, and the carriages passing and repassing upon the pavement as silently as if they were driven upon cotton wool. Paris was silent, there was no sound beyond the voices at table. Now Dechelette was speaking, he was pouring out the poison this time!

"What terrible things are these ruptures!" His quiet and mocking tone assumed an expression of softness and infinite pitifulness. "Two people live for years together in closest companionship. They have told each other everything, given each other everything. They have gained habits, modes of living, of speaking, from each other—they have even become alike in features. They are united hand and foot—cemented together. Then suddenly they part—are torn asunder. How do they do it—how have they the resolution? For my part I never could do such a thing. Yes, deceived, outraged, pelted with ridicule and abuse; if the woman were to weep and beg me to remain, I would not leave her. And that is why, when I do ally myself with one, it is only for a night. No to-morrow—as they used to say in old France—or else

marriage. It is definite and more correct."

"No to-morrow—no to-morrow! You are talking at random. There are women you cannot keep only for one night. *She,* for instance."

"I did not give her a moment's grace," said Dechelette, with a placid smile which the poor lover thought fiendish.

"Then you were not to her taste, for she is a girl who, when she loves, clings tightly. She has a taste for housekeeping, nevertheless she has no luck that way. She tried it with Dejoie the novelist—he died. She passed on to Ezano—he married; afterward came the handsome Flamant, the engraver, formerly a model—for she always had a bias for talent and good looks—and you know the terrible sequel."

"What?" asked Gaussin in a choking voice, as he addressed himself to his straw again, while listening to the drama of love which thrilled Paris a few years ago.

"The engraver was poor—mad upon the girl—and for fear of being dropped he forged bank notes to keep her in luxury. Discovered almost immediately, he was, with her, arrested; he got ten years' imprisonment, and she had six months at St. Lazare, her innocence having been proved."

And Caoudal reminded Dechelette who had been present at the trial how pretty she had looked in the prison headdress of St. Lazare, and brave, not cringing, faithful to her companion to the last. Her reply to the old owl of a judge, and the kiss which she threw to Flamant over the cocked hats of the gendarmes, crying to him in a voice sad enough to soften a heart of stone "Don't be downhearted, my own; the happy days will return and we shall love each other again." All the same she had been rather disgusted with her housekeeping, poor girl!

"Since that time launched into fast society, she has taken lovers by the month, the week, and never artists. She has a horror of them! I believed I was the only one whom she continued to see. At distant intervals she would come and smoke a cigarette in the studio. Then I did not hear of her again for months, until one day when I met her with this handsome lad at breakfast, eating grapes from his mouth. Then I said to myself, "There is my Sapho bitten again."

Jean could not listen to any more of this. He felt he was dying from the effects of the poison he had absorbed. After the cold he had felt, he had now a burning sensation in his chest, which ascended to his head that was buzzing, and felt as if it would split like an iron plate heated white hot. He crossed the street, staggering under the carriage wheels. Some drivers shouted—to whom were they calling, the fools?

Passing the market by the Madeleine he was irritated by the odor of heliotrope, the scent preferred by his mistress. He hurried on to escape it, and maddened, torn by his emotions, he thought aloud! My mistress? Yes, a nice thing. Sapho, Sapho! To think that I have lived a year with a creature like her! He repeated the name angrily, remembering that he had read it in the low-class papers among other women's nicknames in the grotesque Almanach de Gotha of fast society; Sapho, Cora, Caro, Phryne, Jeanne de Poitiers, le Phoque—!

And with the letters of her abominable name, all the life of this woman passed in a disgusting way before his eyes. The studio of Caoudal, the quarrels with La Gournerie, the watches of the night passed before the door, or on the mat, of the poet. Then the good looking engraver, the forgeries, the assize court, and the little prison headdress which so well became her; the kiss she had wafted to her forger, with the message, "Don't be downhearted, my own." The same name, the same caress which she bestowed on him! What a disgrace! Ah, he was going to sweep away all this dirt completely, and the smell of heliotrope continually pursued him in a twilight of the same pale lilac as the little flower.

Suddenly he discovered that he was still pacing the market like the deck of a ship. He resumed his way home, arrived in a flash at the Rue d'Amsterdam his mind made up to expel this woman from his rooms, to cast her out upon the staircase without any explanation, thrusting upon her the insult of her name.

At the door he hesitated, reflected, passed on a few paces. She would cry out, sob, and let loose upon the house all her vocabulary of the gutter, as she had already done yonder in the Rue de l'Arcade.

Write! yes, the very thing; it would be better to write, he would settle the business in four ferocious words. He entered an English beer shop, deserted and mournful, under the gaslight which was being turned on—seated himself at a smeared table near the only customer, who was a girl with a death's head, devouring smoked salmon without drinking anything. He called for a pint of ale, did not touch it, and commenced a letter. But too many words would come and he wanted to find expression all at once, which the thick clotted ink traced as slowly as possible.

He tore up two or three beginnings, was going out without having written, when in a low voice close to him a full and greedy mouth said timidly, "You are not drinking, may I have a sip?" He made a sign in the affirmative. The girl snatched at the pint measure and emptied it in one hasty draught, an action that revealed the distress of the unfortunate who had just money enough in her pocket to purchase some food without moistening it with a little beer. A feeling of pity came into his heart and softened him, suddenly revealed to him the miseries of a woman's life and he sat himself to judge more humanely, to reason with his trouble.

After all she had told him no falsehoods and—if he knew nothing of her life it was because he had never troubled himself about it. What should he reproach her with? Her time at St. Lazare? But as she had been acquitted—carried out almost in triumph, what then? With other men before him? Did not he know all about that? What reason had he to bear a greater grudge against her because the names of these lovers were known, celebrated; because he might meet with them, speak to them, see their portraits in the windows—? Ought he to think it a crime for her to have preferred such men?

And at the bottom of his heart there uprose an unspeakable, bad pride at the idea of sharing her with these great artists, saying to himself that they had found her beautiful! At his age one is never sure—one has not much experience. One loves the woman, and love; but the perception of things and the experience are wanting; and the young lover who shows you the portrait of his mistress seeks a look and some approbation to reassure him. The figure of Sapho seemed to him greater, encircled by a glory, since he knew that she had been sung by La Gournerie and modeled by Caoudal in marble or in bronze.

But quickly seized with anger, once more, he quitted the bench upon which he had thrown himself in an exterior boulevard amid the children, the gossiping wives of work-people in the dusty June evening, and resumed his way talking loudly, furiously. A pretty thing indeed that bronze of Sapho—bronze of commerce—which had been dragged everywhere, as common as the tunes in a street organ, as the word itself, Sapho, which by the force of rolling descent through ages is incrusted with unclean legends, and has degenerated from the name of a goddess to that of a malady. How disgusting is all this!

He proceeded thus, calm or furious by turns, in this whirligig of ideas and adverse sentiments. The boulevard became dark and deserted—a sickly odor hung in the hot air, and he recognized the gates of the large cemetery, whither he had come the year before with all the youth of Paris to see the inauguration of a bust by Caoudal on the tomb of Dejoie, the novelist of the Latin Quarter, the author of *Cinderinette*. Dejoie, Caoudal! What a strange sound the names of these two men had for him during the last two hours; and so, too, appeared false and mournful the history of the student and his housekeeping, now that he had become acquainted with the sad facts beneath the surface; since he had learned from Dechelette the horrible name bestowed upon these "marriages of the pavement."

The darkness, intensified now by the neighborhood of Death, frightened him. He returned the way he had come, rubbing against working people who were sauntering about silently as the wings of night; sordid dresses at the doors of hovels, the dirty windowpanes of which threw gleams as from magic lanterns on couples who were embracing each other as he passed. What time is it? He felt fagged out like the recruit after drill, and his smothered grief, fallen as it were into his limbs, he was only conscious of their stiffness. Oh, if he could only lie down and sleep. Then when he awoke coldly, his anger passed, he would say to the woman, "There, I know what you are. It is neither your fault nor mine, but we can no longer live together. Let us part!" And to put himself beyond her reach he would go and see his mother and sisters, and shake off in the breezes of the Rhône, in the free and stimulating mistral, the pollution and the fright of his bad dream.

She had gone to bed weary of waiting for him, and was sleeping full in the lamp light, an open book lying on the counterpane. His approach did not disturb her; and standing by the bed he gazed at her curiously as at a woman new to him—a stranger who had come thither.

Beautiful, oh, beautiful the arms, the neck, the shoulders like fine amber without spot or blemish. But beneath those eyelids, reddened perhaps by her reading, perhaps by her uneasiness of waiting—upon those features in repose and from which had passed away the strong desire of the woman who wished to be loved—what lassitude, what confessions! Her age, her history, her excesses, her caprices! St. Lazare, the blows, the tears, the terrors all were visible; and the deep markings of dissipation and sleeplessness, and the curl of distaste drooping the under lip, worn out, spent like a fountain at which the whole parish has been drinking, and the commencement of the bloated look which loosens the flesh for the wrinkles of age.

This treachery of sleep wrapped in the silence of death; it was grand, it was sinister—a field of battle by night, with all the horror which shows itself, and all that which is imagined in the vague moments of the shadows.

And suddenly there came upon the poor young man an irresistible, a suffocating desire to weep.

CHAPTER IV

INTO THE FIRE

THEY were finishing dinner, the window was open, the twittering swallows were saluting the dying day. Jean was not speaking, but he intended to do so, and always of that same cruel thing which haunted him, and with which he had tormented Fanny ever since the meeting with Caoudal. She, perceiving his eyes cast down and his simulated air of indifference, divined his thoughts and anticipated him.

"Listen; I know what you are going to tell me; spare us, I beg; one wears oneself out in the end. Since all that is dead and over and I love no one but you—since there is no one but you in the whole world—"

"If it were dead as you say—all this past!" and he gazed into the depths of her lovely gray eyes, which glistened and changed at every expression, "you would not cherish the things which recall it, yes, over there in your wardrobe."

The gray eyes looked black.

"You know that, then?"

So that collection of love-letters, photographs, those glorious love-archives of her past life, saved from so many breakings-up, must then be destroyed.

"At least you will credit me afterward!"

When she perceived his incredulous smile, she hurried away to seek the lacquered box, of which the picked out ironwork had so greatly puzzled her lover during the last few days when he beheld it amongst the delicate folds of her linen.

"Burn; tear; do what you please!"

But he was in no hurry to turn the little key; he was looking at the designs of cherry trees with mother of pearl fruit and the flying storks worked in on the lid. Then he opened it suddenly.

Every style and character of writing were there; tinted paper with illuminated headings, old yellow *billets* creased in the folding, scratches with pencil on the leaves of note books; *cartes de visite* in heaps without order as a drawer continually turned out might be, and into which he was now dipping his trembling hands.

"Pass them over to me, I will burn them before your eyes."

She spoke feverishly, kneeling down in front of the stove, a lighted candle was by her side on the floor.

"Give me—"

But he said: "No, wait!" Then in a lower tone and as if he were rather ashamed of himself, he added, "I wish to read them."

"Why? You will only worry yourself again."

She was thinking only of his pain, and not of the indelicacy of letting him see these secrets of passion, the bed confessions of all those men who had loved her; and coming nearer to him—still on her knees—she read with him, watching him closely from the corners of her eyes.

Ten pages signed La Gournerie, 1861, in a long feline hand; in which the poet, who had been despatched to Algeria to give a metrical and official account of the journey of the emperor and the empress, gave his mistress a stirring description of the festivities.

Algiers overflowing and crowded—a true Bagdad of the "Thousand and One Nights," all Africa assembled, encircling the town—rushing against the gates as if it would burst them with the force of a simoon. Caravans of negroes and camels laden with gum; tents of hides; a smell of human musk hanging over all this menagerie which had encamped by the seaside; dancing at night in the gleam of huge fires, dispersing every morning when the chiefs of the south arrived, like magi in oriental pomp; discordant music, reed instruments, little harsh drums, the Goum surrounding the tricolored standard of the prophet—and in the rear held in lassoes by negroes, the horses destined for the "emperour," with silk cloths, silver caparisons, and shaking at every pace their bells and trappings.

The genius of the poet put this all as a reality; the words sparkled on the page like diamonds exhibited by a merchant. Well might the woman at whose feet all these riches were cast feel proud. Must not she have been loved indeed, since notwithstanding the unique character of these *fêtes,* the poet thought only of her, and was dying to see her again?

"Oh, this very night I was with you in the grand divan in the Rue de l'Arcade. You were naked, maddened, and crying out with delight under my caresses, but when I awoke I was rolling in a rug on my terrace under the stars. The cry of the muezzin was ascending from a neighboring minaret, in clear and limpid tones, voluptuous rather than devotional, and it was you I heard as I awoke from my dream."

What evil spirit incited him to continue to read, notwithstanding the horrible jealousy that blanched his lips, and caused his hands to clench? Gently, in a coaxing way, Fanny endeavored to take away the letter, but he read it to the very end, and after it another, then another, letting them fall as soon as he had finished, one by one, in contempt and indifference, without paying any attention to the flames which roared up in the chimney from the lyrical and passionate effusions of the celebrated poet. And occasionally, when his passion boiled over at African heat, the lovers' communications would be infected with some gross indelicacy of the guardhouse, which would have much surprised and scandalized the

fashionable readers of the *Book of Love,* with its refined spiritualism, pure as the silvered peak of the Jungfrau.

Miseries of the heart! At these passages Jean paused chiefly, at these blots on the page, without dreaming of the nervous twitchings which puckered his face. He actually had the fortitude to sneer at the postscript, which succeeded a glowing description of the Feast Aïssaouas. "I have re-read my letter; there are really some rather good things in it—put it aside for me, I may make use of it perhaps."

"A gentleman who lets no chance slip," said Jean, as he passed on to another sheet of the same writing, in which in the cold tone of a man of business La Gournerie requested the return of a volume of Arab songs and a pair of rice straw slippers. This was the winding up of their love affairs. Ah, he had known when to retire; he was strong—that man!

And without stopping Jean continued to drain the cesspool whence arose such a noisome and unwholesome vapor. At nightfall he put the candle on the table and read some short notes almost illegibly traced, as with stilletto, by heavy fingers, which at every moment in the roughness of passion perforated and tore the paper. The first occasions of the meetings with Caoudal, assignations, suppers, picnics, then quarrels, suppliant returnings, appeals, insults coarse and common, interspersed all at once by drollery, jokes and piteous reproaches, all the weakness of the great artist laid out at the time of his dismissal and abandonment.

The fire seized that too; darting out great red jets of flame in which were smoking and frizzling the flesh, the blood, the tears of a man of genius; but what did it matter to Fanny, also devoted to her young lover, whose ardent fever burned through her clothing? He found a portrait there executed in pen and ink and signed Gavarni, with this inscription: "To my friend Fanny Legrand, in an inn at Dampierre one wet day." An intelligent and melancholy head, with hollow eyes, and something bitter and worn about it.

"Who is this?"

"André Dejoie. I have kept it because of the signature."

"Oh, you may keep it and welcome," he said, in so hard and unhappy a tone that she snatched the drawing and threw it, in pieces, on the fire, while he plunged into the correspondence of the novelist; a heartrending series of letters dated from winter resorts and watering places whither the writer had been sent for his health, and had grown desperate in his physical and moral distress, racking his brains to find ideas so far away from Paris and mixing up demands for potions, prescriptions, anxiety about his money or his work, the transmission of proofs, renewal of bills—always the same desire and adoration for the beautiful body of Sapho which the doctors forbade him.

Jean muttered, enraged, and rudely: "What on earth was the matter with all these men that they should come after you in this manner?"

That was for him the sole significance of these despairing letters, confessing the derangement of one of those glorious existences which young men envy, and of which young and romantic women dream. Yes, what was the matter with them? What had she given

them to drink? He experienced all the horrible suffering of a man who sees the woman he loves outraged, and nevertheless he could not make up his mind to empty at one stroke, with eyes shut, the papers which remained.

Now came the turn of the engraver, who miserable, unknown, with no reputation save through the *Police Gazette* only owed his place in the shrine in virtue of the great love which she had for him Very disgraceful were those letters dated from Mazas, and as stupid, awkward and sentimental as those of a recruit to his girl. But one felt that through all these romantic lugubrations there was a strain of sincerity in the passion, a respect for the woman, a forgetfulness of self which distinguished the convict from the others. Thus, when he begged Fanny's pardon for his crime in having loved her too well, or when from the Palais de Justice, just after condemnation, he wrote how pleased he was to hear that she was liberated. He made no complaint, he had had, thanks to her, in her company, two years of such deep and perfect bliss that the memory of them was sufficient to fill up the measure of his existence, to assuage the horrors of his fate—and he wound up by asking a favor of her:

"You know that I have a child in the country, whose mother died a long while ago. He lives with an old relative in such an out-of-the-way corner that they will never hear what has happened to me. I sent them the money I had left, saying that I was going out of the country far away, and I look to you, my dear Nini, to ascertain from time to time how this little fellow is and to send me news of him."

As a proof of Fanny's interest followed a letter of thanks, and another which was quite recent and dated only six months before. "Oh, how kind of you to have come! How pretty you looked, and how nice in comparison with my prison garb of which I am so greatly ashamed—" Then Jean burst out furiously, interrupting his reading by, "You have continued to see him then?"

"Now and then, just for charity's sake."

"Even since we have been living together?"

"Yes, once; only once in the visiting room where only they let you see the people."

"Ah, you are a nice girl!"

The idea that notwithstanding their connection, she continued to visit the forger, exasperated him more than all the rest. He was too proud to say so, but a packet of letters, the last, tied with blue ribbon across the fine sloping writing—a woman's hand—let loose all his anger.

"I change my tunic after the chariot race; come to my room."

"No, no; don't read that!"

She leaped upon him, snatched the packet from him and threw it on the fire before he could understand it at all, even when he beheld her on her knees, reddened by the reflection of the fire as well as by the shame of her avowal.

"I was young—it was Caoudal, the great fool. I did whatever he wished."

Only then he understood, and became very pale.

"Ah, yes; Sapho! the whole 'gamut,' " —and spurning her from him like an unclean animal, he said, "Leave me, do not touch me, you disgust me!"

Her cry of pain was lost in a terrible peal of thunder; very near and prolonged; at the same moment a vivid flame illuminated the apartment. Fire! She jumped up in terror, seized mechanically the water bottle on the table and emptied it upon the papers, the flame of which had set the soot of last winter's fires alight; then the water can and the jugs; but seeing her efforts were fruitless, she rushed out on the balcony screaming "Fire! Fire!"

The Hettemas came in first, then the concierge, and then the police. They cried out "Let the register down, get out on the roof. Water! Water! No, a blanket."

Quite confounded they continued to stare at the soiled and crowded room, then, when the alarm was over, the fire extinguished, the black crowd below under the gas in the street dispersed, and the neighbors reassured, gone back to their houses, the two lovers in the mingled mess of waters, soot, disarranged and ripping furniture, felt disheartened and exhausted, without energy to resume the quarrel, or to tidy the apartment. Something ominous and vile had come into their life, and that evening, forgetting their former repugnance, they went and slept at the lodging house.

The sacrifice Fanny had made did not have any good result. From the letters he had burned and otherwise destroyed, whole sentences kept recurring to his memory, mounted to his face in rushes of blood, as certain passages in bad books will do. And those former lovers of his mistress were almost all celebrated men. The dead ones arose again, the names and likenesses of those still living were everywhere; people spoke of them before him, and every time he experienced a feeling of uneasiness, as he might have felt in the sad rupture of some family tie.

This trouble sharpened his senses and his eyes. He soon began to notice in Fanny traces of former influences, and the words, ideas and habits, which she had retained. That habit she had of sticking out her thumb, as if to mold or fashion the thing of which she was speaking was a trick learned from the sculptor, with the expression, "You can see that!" From Dejoie she had contracted the habit of "clipping" her words, and the popular songs which he had made known in every corner of France. From La Gournerie she had learned that haughty and scornful intonation, and that severity of criticism upon modern literature.

She had assimilated all these, superposing the disparities by the same principles of stratification which enable us to learn the age, and the different systems of the earth, and the geological strata, and perhaps she was not so intellectual as she had at first seemed to him to be. But it was scarcely a question of intelligence; foolish and vulgar, ten years older, she would equally have held him by the strength of her past, by the low jealousy which was consuming him, and of which he could no longer restrain the irritation nor the upbraidings, which burst out on every occasion against one or the other.

Dejoie's novels sold no longer! the whole issue was going begging at twenty-five centimes a copy! And that old fool Caoudal—fancy his troubling himself about love at his age! "You know he has no teeth now. He eats like a goat with the front of his mouth.

His talent had deserted him. What a failure his Nymph at the *salon* was!" "It would not hold together"—this was an expression he had picked up from her, as she had learned it from the sculptor. When he was thus criticizing his former rivals, Fanny agreed with him to please him, and this lad, ignorant of art, of life, of everything; this girl, with the superficial polish of the talent of those famous artists, might have been heard criticizing them with an air of superior judgment, and condemning them oracularly.

But Gaussin's real enemy was Flamant, the forger. Of him he only knew that he was very handsome, as fair as himself, that he was addressed as "my own," that she went to see him in secret, and that when he attacked him in the same way as the rest, calling him the "sentimental convict" or the "handsome prisoner," Fanny turned away her head without replying. Then he began to accuse his mistress of preserving her regard for the forger, and she was obliged to explain gently, but with a certain firmness in her voice:

"You know quite well, Jean, that I love him no longer, because I love you. I no longer go to see him; I do not answer his letters; but you shall never make me speak ill of the man who loved me even to folly and crime." After this direct speaking—her best point—Jean did not insist any longer, but he suffered from horrible jealousy, sharpened by uneasiness, which carried him back to the Rue d'Amsterdam sometimes in the middle of the day to surprise her. "Suppose she has gone to see him!"

He always found her at home, domesticated, as inactive in this little house as an Eastern woman, or else at the piano, giving a singing lesson to their stout neighbor, Madame Hettema. They had become friendly since the evening of the fire with these good people, so pleased and plethoric, living in a perpetual draught, doors and windows all open.

Her husband, a draughtsman at the Artillery Museum, brought some work home, and every evening, and all day on Sunday, he might be seen bending over the large table on trestles, perspiring, puffing, in his shirt sleeves, shaking his wristbands to cool himself, and bearded to the eyes. Near him was his fat wife, in a dressing jacket, evaporating also, although she never did anything, and to refresh themselves they sung from time to time one of their favorite duets. Intimacy had been quickly established between these two households.

In the morning about ten o'clock Hettema would call out loudly, "Are you there, Gaussin?" and their offices being in the same direction they walked down together. Very dull, very vulgar, and some degrees lower in the social scale than his young companion, the draughtsman spoke little; he spluttered as if he had as much hair in his mouth as on his cheeks; but one felt he was a good sort of fellow, and that Jean's moral disorder had need of such contact. He continued it particularly on account of his mistress, who living in a solitude surrounded by memories and regrets, mo e dangerous perhaps than the life she had voluntarily renounced, found in Madame Hettema, ever occupied concerning her good man, and the tasty surprise which she was planning for his dinner, or the new song which

she would sing to him at dessert, a respectable and healthy associate.

Nevertheless when friendship proceeded so far as reciprocal invitations Jean had some scruples. These people believed him married; his conscience revolted at the deception, and he directed Fanny to give her neighbor an inkling of the true state of the case, so that no misunderstandings should exist. The idea made her laugh! Poor lady! No one but he had such simple notions! "They have never for one moment believed that we are married! They make a joke of the affair. If you only knew where he got his wife from! All that I have done, the 'Saint' John has equalled. He did not marry her except for the sake of having her all to himself—and you can see that the past does not worry him much."

This was too much for him! A former woman of the town! That motherly, bright-eyed woman, with a childish smile on her fat, soft face, with her drawling provincial accent, and for whom no ballads were sentimental enough, nor words too select; and he the man, so easy-going, so secure in his amorous well-being. He could see him walking at her side, pipe in mouth, emitting little sighs of content, while he himself was ever thinking and eating his heart out in his impotent anger.

"You will live it down, my own," Fanny would say to him gently at those times at which people tell everything to each other; and she would soothe him—tender and charming as on the very first day—but with a certain *abandon* about her which Jean scarcely knew how to define.

It was greater freedom of manner and expression, a consciousness of her power, strange confidences unsought by him concerning her past life, her old debaucheries and follies. She did not deprive herself of smoking now; she rolled, and in her fingers, put down on the furniture, the eternal cigarettes which help to pass the gay woman's day; and in her conversation she let fall her views of life, the infamy of men, the treachery of women, the most cynical theories on all subjects. Even her eyes assumed a different expression, dimmed by a film of moisture through which a libertine laugh flashed.

And the intimacy of their affection also changed. At first restrained by the youth of her lover, of which she respected the first illusions, the woman having seen the effect on the man, of her roughly disclosed, debauched past —did not now trouble herself to restrain the unwholesome fever with which she had infected him. So the wayward caresses long restrained, all the delirious words which her closed teeth had shut back—she let loose now, showed herself in her true colors, in all the nakedness of the amorous and practiced courtesan, in all the horrible glory of Sapho!

Modesty, reserve; what good were they? Men are all alike, hungry after vice, and corrupt practices—this youth like the others. To cram them with what they love is the only way to hold them. And all she knew, the depravities of pleasure with which she had been inoculated, she taught to Jean in turn to pass on to others. So the poison spreads, propagates itself, burning up body and soul like those torches of which the poet speaks which went from hand to hand through the stadium

CHAPTER V

LIBERTINE AND GAMBLER!

IN their room, beside a beautiful portrait of Fanny by James Tissot, a relic of her former splendor, there was a southern landscape all black and white, a badly executed picture by a country photographer.

A rocky eminence clothed with vines, buttressed in stone; and above, behind the rows of cypress trees sheltering it from the north wind, perched close to a small wood of pines and myrtle, stood the great white dwelling, half farmhouse, half château, with a wide flight of steps, Italian roof, escutcheoned doors in the ruddy walls of the Provençal *mas;* perches for peacocks; cattle pens; a black bay of open sheds with shining ploughs and harrows. The ruins of old ramparts, an immense tower, standing out boldly against the cloudless sky dominated all, with a few roofs and the Roman belfry of Châteauneuf-des Papes, where the Gaussin of Armandy had lived "for all time."

Castelet, farm and estate, rich in vineyards, as famous as those of La Nerte and the Hermitage, was transmitted from father to son, held jointly by all the children, but looked after by the younger son in virtue of the family tradition which destined the eldest to the Consular service. Unfortunately Nature often thwarts such projects, and if ever there were a being incapable of managing an estate, or of managing anything else, it was surely Cesaire Gaussin, on whom at four and twenty the responsibility devolved.

A libertine and a gambler, Cesaire—or rather Le Fenat—the good-for-nothing—the scamp—to give him his youth ful title—served to accentuate the contradiction in the type of individuals which appears at distant intervals in the most austere families, and to which they serve as safety valves.

After some years of neglect, of silly waste, of disastrous gambling at the clubs of Avignon and Orange, the farm was mortgaged, the stores of wine exhausted, the crops sold in advance; then one day on the eve of final seizure Le Fenat forged his brother's name and drew three bills on the Shanghai Consulate, assured that when they became due he would find the money to meet them; but they reached the elder brother in due course with a desperate letter announcing the ruin and the forgeries. The Consul hurried to Châteauneuf, repaired the mischief with his own savings and his wife's fortune, and perceiving the absolute incapacity of Le Fenat, he threw up his appointment, which promised him a brilliant career, and became a simple winegrower.

He was a true Gaussin, mad on tradition, violent and calm as the slumbering volcanoes which threaten eruption in future; hardworking withal and a clever agriculturist. Thanks to his efforts Castelet prospered, increased by all the land up to the Rhône, and as strokes of luck never come singly, little Jean made his appearance under the myrtles. All this time Le Fenat wandered about the house borne down by the burden of his sins, scarcely daring to look in the face of his brother who crushed him with his contemptuous silence; he only breathed freely in the fields, or when hunting or fishing, endeavoring to get rid of his grief in the performance of ridiculous tasks, pick-

ing up the snails, cutting splendid walking-sticks of myrtle or reeds, and breakfasting alone on a few little birds which he cooked over a fire of olive-stumps on the open common. In the evening when he came into dinner at his brother's table he never spoke, notwithstanding the indulgent smile of his sister-in-law, who felt for the poor creature, and kept him supplied with pocket-money unknown to her husband, who kept Le Fenat very close, less on account of his past follies than because of those he feared in the future; and, in fact, the great evil repaired, the pride of the elder Gaussin was destined to sustain a new trial.

Three days a week there came to do sewing at Castelet a pretty fisher girl, Divonne Abrieu, born amongst the osiers on the Rhône, a true water-plant, lithe and long. Beneath the "catalane," in three pieces, which encircled her small head, the strings thrown back so that one could admire the neck slightly sunburnt, like the face, as far as the delicate throat and shoulders, she reminded one of some *done* of the old courts of love formerly held all round Châteauneuf, at Courthezon, at Vacqueiras, in the ancient castles the ruins of which are dotted over the hills.

This historic memory had no weight in Cesaire's love affair, he, a simple soul without ideality or reading, but, of small stature himself, liked tall women, and was "caught" the first day. Le Fenat was quite at home in all village adventures, a quadrille in the Sunday dance, a present of game, then at the first meeting in the fields the quick attack in the lavender or in the hay. He found that Divonne did not dance, that she carried back the game to the kitchen, and firm as one of the white and flexible poplars by the river, she sent the would-be seducer rolling ten yards away. Since then she had kept him at a distance with her scissors suspended from her waist belt by a steel chain; made him madly in love, so much sc that he talked of marrying her, and confided in his sister-in-law. She knowing Divonne from her infancy, that she was serious and refined, fancied that this misalliance might be the saving of Cesaire; but the pride of the Consul revolted at the notion of a Gaussin d'Armandy marrying a peasant. "If Cesaire does this I will never see him again." And he meant to keep his word!

Cesaire married, and quitted Castelet to live on the banks of the Rhône in the home of his wife's parents, on a small allowance made to him by his brother, which his indulgent sister-in-law brought him every month. Little Jean accompanied his mother in these visits, and was delighted with the Abrieu's hut—a kind of smoky rotunda, shaken by the north winds or the mistral and sustained by a single upright beam like a mast. The open door gave a view of the little pier on which the nets were dried, on which shone and scintillated the bright and enameled silver scales; beneath it lay two or three heavy boats creaking and heaving at their moorings, and the great river, joyous, wide, and shimmering, tossed up by the wind against the islands which are tufted with pale green herbage. And there, when quite a child, Jean imbibed his taste for long voyages, and for the sea which he had never yet seen.

This banishment of uncle Cesaire was continued for two or three years, and perhaps would never have ended had not a family event—the birth of twins, Martha and Mary—brought it to a termination. The mother fell ill after the double birth; Cesaire and his wife went to see her. The reconciliation of the two brothers succeeded, unexpectedly, instinctively, by the all-powerful ties of blood. The couple came to live at Castelet, and as an incurable anæmia, complicated by rheumatic gout, rendered the poor mother a confirmed invalid, Divonne found herself established as housekeeper; to superintend the feeding of the infants, to rule the numerous domestics, to go twice a week to see Jean at school at Avignon, without reckoning the demands made upon her by the invalid at all hours.

A woman of orderly ideas and clever, she supplied her want of knowledge by her intelligence, her shrewdness, and the remains of learning which still lingered in the brain of Le Fenat, now subdued and disciplined. The Consul trusted her with all the expenses of the house, which were felt heavily in the face of diminishing revenue, in consequence of the failure of the vines through phylloxera. All the district was attacked, but the forlorn farm still held out, and the Consul was very much occupied in endeavoring to save it by means of experiments and investigations.

Divonne Abrieu, who remained faithful to her headdress and steel chain, and conducted herself so modestly in her position as housekeeper and companion, preserved the house in those hard times, procured the same costly things for the invalid, brought up the little girls like ladies, paid Jean's allowance, first at Avignon, then at Aix, where he studied law; and finally in Paris, whither he went to finish his education.

By what miracles of order and economy she arrived at such results no one knew any more than she did. But every time that Jean thought of Castelet, or raised his eyes to the faded photograph, the first name pronounced was that of Divonne, the great-hearted peasant woman, who he felt was keeping guard at the country house, and sustaining it by the exercise of her will. During the last few days, however, since he had become acquainted with the real character of his mistress, he had refrained from pronouncing the venerated name in her presence, as he avoided speaking of his mother and friends; even the sight of the photograph troubled him, out of place as it was on the wall above Sapho's bed.

One day when he came home to dinner he was surprised to see places laid for three instead of for two people; and still more astonished to find Fanny playing cards with a little man, whom he did not at first recognize, but, who, on turning round, revealed the bright "silly goat's" eyes, the large prominent nose, and the sunburnt and spruce face, the bald head, and the Convenanter's beard of uncle Cesaire. Hearing his nephew's exclamation he replied without stopping his game of cards:

"You see I am by no means dull. I am playing bezique with my niece."

His niece!

This to Jean, who had been carefully concealing his connection with everybody! This familiarity displeased him, as did the remarks which Cesaire made in an undertone while Fanny was getting dinner ready. "I congratulate you, my lad. What eyes! what arms! a dainty for a king." It was worse when at table Le Fenat began to chatter unreservedly concerning affairs at Castelet, and about what had brought him to Paris.

The pretext for the journey was money, some 8,000 francs which he had lent formerly to Courbebaisse, and which he had never expected to get, when a letter from a notary apprised him of the death of Courbebaisse—by Jove! and the payment of the 8,000 francs awaiting him. "But the real motive, is your poor mother's health, my poor lad. She has grown much weaker lately, and at times her memory fails her; she forgets everything, even the names of her children. The other evening your father was going out of her room when she asked Divonne who that kind gentleman was who came to see her so often! No one but your aunt has yet noticed this symptom, and she only told me so that I should decide to come and consult Bouchereau concerning the poor lady whom he formerly attended."

"Have you ever had madness in your family?" inquired Fanny in the professionally grave manner which she had picked up from La Gournerie.

"Never," replied Le Fenat, adding with a malicious smile, which puckered his temples, that he had been a little headstrong in his youth, "but my madness was not displeasing to the ladies, and they never shut one up for it."

Jean regarded them, heartsick. To the grief which the sad news caused him was added an oppressive sense of uneasiness at hearing this woman speak of his mother, of the infirmities of a critical time of life, with the freedom and experience of a matron, her elbows on the tablecloth as she rolled a cigarette; and the man, talkative, indiscreet, chattered away and let out all the private affairs of the family.

Ah, the vines. The vines were very bad, and the close itself would not last much longer; half the crop was already ravaged, and the rest could only be preserved by a miracle, by tending every bunch and grape like a sick child with drugs, which were expensive. The worst was that the Consul was bent upon planting new vines which were attacked by the worm, instead of cultivating olives and capers in all this good, but useless land, covered with dead and reddened leafy vine branches.

Fortunately he, Cesaire, had some acres on the banks of the Rhône which he was treating by immersion, a splendid discovery, applicable only to low-lying lands. A good crop already encouraged him. It was thin, not full, wine, a "Frog's Vintage" the Consul disdainfully said, but Le Fenat was obstinate also, and he was going to purchase La Piboulette with the 8,000 francs repaid by Courbebaisse's executors.

"You know it, my lad, the first island on the Rhône, below Abrieu's—but this is between ourselves, no one at Castelet must have an inkling of it yet."

"Not even Divonne, uncle?" said Fanny.

Hearing his wife's name, the eyes of Le Fenat grew moist.

"Oh, Divonne! I never do anything without her. She has faith in my idea, besides, and would be very happy if her poor Cesaire should rebuild the fortunes

of Castelet after having commenced their downfall."

Jean shivered; was the man going to confess; to tell the shameful history of the forgeries? But the Provençal, full of his love for Divonne, began to speak of her, of the happiness she gave him. And so pretty withal, so magnificently set up and put together.

"Ah, niece, you are a woman, you know, and should know something of the matter."

He handed her a carte photograph which he took from his pocketbook, and which he always carried with him.

Judging from the filial tone in which Jean always spoke of his aunt, from the motherly counsel of the peasant written in a large and rather shaky hand, Fanny had pictured in her mind one of the cottier women of Seine et-Oise, and was completely taken aback when she saw the beautiful face, with its pure lines set off by the white headdress, the elegant and lithe form of a woman of thirty-five.

"Well—yes; very pretty!" she said pressing her lips together—and speaking in a curious tone.

"And such a frame," said the uncle, who still held to his illustrations by carpentry.

Then they went on the balcony. After a hot day—of which the zinc of the verandah still retained the effects, a light rain was falling from a solitary cloud, and refreshing the air, dampening the roofs, and making the pavement glisten. Paris was smiling beneath the shower, and the movements of the crowd, of the carriages, and all the consequent murmur intoxicated the provincial, stored up in his empty and giddy head the memories of his youth, and of a three months' sojourn in Paris which he had made some thirty years before with his friend Courbebaisse.

What a time we had, young people! And their visit to the Prado one night in midlent! Courbebaisse as Chicard, and his mistress, the Mornas, as a ballad singer, a costume which brought her luck, as she had since become celebrated as a singer, at café concerts. He himself, the uncle, had under his care a little thing they called Pellicule. And quite rejuvenated he laughed all over his face, hummed dance tunes, and seized his niece around the waist to have a few steps. At midnight when he left them to go to the Hotel Cujas, the only one he knew in Paris, he sang at the top of his voice on the stairs, blew kisses to his niece who was lighting him down and called out to Jean:

"Mind you take care of yourself, you know!"

As soon as he had departed, Fanny, whose forehead was still thoughtful, passed rapidly into her dressing-room, and, through the open door of communication, while Jean was getting into bed, she said in a careless way:

"I say, that aunt of yours is very pretty, eh? I am not now surprised that you used to talk of her so much. I suppose you made poor Fenat jealous?"

He protested very angrily. Divonne! who had been a second mother to him, who when he was an infant took care of him, dressed him! She had pulled him through an illness—snatched him from death; no, never had he been tempted to commit such an infamous act as that!

"Go along with you," replied the strident voice of the woman as she held hairpins between her teeth, "you will never convince me, that, with such a figure of which that fool spoke, his Divonne has remained insensible to a good-looking, fair-skinned fellow like yourself. On the banks of the Rhône or elsewhere we are all alike."

She spoke with conviction, believing all her sex perfectly ready to yield, and overcome by the first desire. He defended himself in an awkward way, searching his memory and asking himself if ever the touch of an innocent caress had warned him of any danger whatever, and although he found nothing, the frankness of his affection remained sullied, the pure cameo was scratched.

"Wait, look here, the headdress of your country."

Upon her beautiful hair, arranged in two long plaits, she pinned a white handkerchief which bore a considerable resemblance to the *"catalane,"* the cap in three pieces worn by the girls at Châteauneuf, and standing before him in the milk-white drapery of her nightdress, her eyes glittering, she said:

"Am I like Divonne?"

Oh, no, not at all; she only was like herself in that little cap which reminded him of no other, that of Saint Lazare, which made her look so pretty, they said, while she blew her convict a farewell kiss in open court—saying, "Do not worry, my own; the happy days will come again!"

And this reflection made him so uncomfortable that, as soon as she was in bed, he quickly put out the light, so that he might not see her any longer.

Early next morning the uncle arrived in a noisy vein, with uplifted stick, crying out, "Ho, there, you children," with the airy and patronizing intonation which Courbelaisse formerly affected when he came to seek Cesaire in the arms of Pellicule. He appeared to be even more excited than he had been on the previous evening. The Hotel Cujas was responsible no doubt, and chiefly the 8,000 francs folded in his pocketbook. The money for La Piboulette of course; but surely he had the right to spend a few louis of it to give his piece a breakfast in the country!

"How about Bouchereau?" remarked his nephew, who could not remain away from the office two days in succession. It was arranged that they would breakfast in the Champs Elysées, and that the two men should go to the consultation afterward.

That was not what Le Fenat had anticipated, the arrival at Saint Cloud in style, a carriage stocked with champagne; but the repast was very pleasant all the same on the terrace of the restaurant, shaded as it was by acacias and Japanese importations, which was invaded by the sounds of a morning concert at a neighboring café. Cesaire, very communicative, very polite, put on all his graces to dazzle the Parisian lady. He "pulled up" the waiters, complimented the cook, and made Fanny laugh in a foolish, forced fashion, at a joke which pained Gaussin, so that an intimacy was established between uncle and niece "over his head."

One would have said that they were friends of twenty years' standing. Le Fenat, who became vinously sentimental about dessert time, talked of Castelet, of Divonne, and also of his little Jean; and was happy to see him with Fanny, who was a steady person, and would keep him straight; and concerning the somewhat desponding character of the young man, and the way to manage him, he also gave her some hints, as if she were a young bride; tapping her on the arm, his speech thick, his eyes "fishy" and watery.

He was sobered at Bouchereau's. Two hours waiting on the first floor, in the Place Vendôme, in those immense lofty cold rooms crowded with a silent and anxious assemblage, the *inferno* of grief, of which they traversed successively all the stages, passing from room to room, till they reached the study of the illustrious physician.

Bouchereau, having a wonderful memory, recollected Madame Gaussin very well, having gone to Castelet in consultation ten years before. when her illness commenced; he caused the details of the different phases of the malady to be related to him; re-read the old prescriptions, and immediately reassured the two men respecting the brain symptoms which had lately developed themselves, attributing them to the employment of certain drugs. And without moving, his bushy eyebrows knitted over his keen, observant eyes. he wrote a long letter to the Avignon doctor, while the uncle and nephew holding their breath, listened to the scratching of the pen upon the paper, which so far as they were concerned drowned all the murmur of luxurious Paris, and suddenly there appeared to them the power of the modern physician; the highest priest, supreme confidence, and invincible superstition.

Cesaire came away serious and cooled. "I am going back to the hotel to strap my portmanteau; the air of Paris does not agree with me. d'ye see, my lad?—if I remained here I would make a fool of myself. I will take the train at seven this evening. Make my excuses to my niece, will you?"

Jean was careful not to detain him. He was afraid of his puerilities and levity; and next day when he wrote he was congratulating himself upon his uncle's safe return to Divonne, when he saw the man appear, utterly cast down, and with his clothes very much disordered.

"Good God, uncle, what has happened to you?"

Sinking into a chair speechless, motionless at first, but recovering himself by degrees, the uncle confessed to a meeting as in Courbebaisse's time, a too-plentiful dinner, the 8,000 francs lost during the night in a gaming house. Not a *sou* left! Nothing! How could he go home and tell all this to Divonne; and the purchase of La Piboulette Suddenly seized by a sort of delirium, he covered his eyes with his hands, his thumbs thrust into his ears, and sobbing, screaming, quite unmanned, the Southerner gave way and in remorse made a full confession of his whole life. He was a disgrace and cause of shame to his relatives; people such as he should be killed off like wolves. Where would he be but for his brother's generosity? In the convict prison with forgers and such like.

"Uncle, uncle!" said the unfortunate Gaussin, trying to silence his relative.

But the other, wilfully blind and deaf, took a real pleasure in the public confession of his crime, relating even the smallest details of it, while Fanny listened to him with pity and admiration. A thorough-paced one, a scamp of the sort she liked; and sincerely moved, she was casting about in her mind for some

means to help him. But how could she? She had seen no one for a year. Jean had no other relative. Suddenly a name came into her mind—Dechelette! He must be in Paris, and he was such a good fellow!

"But I scarcely know him," said Jean.

"I will go myself," said she.

"What! you really would?"

"Why not?"

Their eyes met, and they both understood. Dechelette has also been her lover—the lover of a night whom she scarcely remembered. But he had not forgotten any of them; they were all ranged in order in his head like the saints in the calendar.

"If it will annoy you"—she began in an embarrassed way. Then Cesaire, who, while they were talking, had left off crying, turned to them, very anxiously, such a piteous look of despairing supplication that Jean resigned himself to fate and reluctantly consented.

How long the hour seemed to both the men, distracted by thoughts which they could not express, leaning over the balcony watching for the girl's return.

"Is it far from here—Dechelette's?"

"Why, no; Rue de Rome—close by," replied Jean furiously; he was also thinking that Fanny had been away a very long while. He attempted to console himself by recalling the engineer's words, "No to-morrow," and the contemptuous manner in which he had heard him talk about Sapho, as an old and "played out" member of the class; but his lover's pride revolted, and he would almost have wished that Dechelette would find her still pretty and winning. Ah, that old Cesaire had indeed re-opened all the old wounds.

At length Fanny turned the corner of the street. She came in beaming.

"It's all right; I've got the money!"

The 8,000 francs were before him; uncle Cesaire wept for very joy, and wished to give her a receipt; to fix the interest, and date of repayment.

"It is not necessary, I never mentioned you in the matter. He lent the money to me. You owe it to me, and you shall owe it as long as you like!"

"Such services as these, my dear, are repaid by a never ending friendship," said Cesaire, who was transported with gratitude. And at the railway station, whither Gaussin accompanied him, to be certain this time of his departure, he repeated, with tears in his eyes, "What a woman! What a treasure she is! You must do your very best to make her happy, mind!"

Jean was for a long while very much annoyed at this incident, feeling his chain, already so heavy, galling him, tightening more and more; and two things which his natural delicacy had always kept apart—his family and his intrigue, were becoming associated. After this Cesaire kept Fanny informed concerning his work, his plantations, giving her all the news of Castelet, and she would criticise the Consul's obstinacy, as regarded the vines, spoke of the health of Jean's mother, and irritated Jean by her solicitude or her misplaced advice. But she never made any allusion to the service she had rendered on the one hand; nor on the other, to the old escapade of Le Fenat, to that blemish upon the Armandy escutcheon which the uncle had confessed before her. Once only did she make use of it in repartee under the following circumstances.

They were coming back from the theatre, and were getting into a cab in the rain, at a cab stand in the boulevards.

The cab, one of those old four-wheeled abominations which only ply after midnight, was a long time getting under way; the driver was asleep and the horse was tossing up his nosebag While the pair were sheltered in the cab out of the rain, an old driver, who was fixing a lash on his whip, leisurely approached the window, the lash between his teeth, and said to Fanny in a cracked voice redolent of liquor:

"Good-night! How are you getting on?"

"Hello? Is that you?"

She started slightly, but quickly repressed the emotion; then in a whisper to her lover she said, "My father!"

Her father! This dirty wretch, in a long livery coat soiled with mud, the metal buttons torn off, his face blotched and soddened by alcohol; yet in the features Gaussin fancied he could trace a vulgar resemblance to Fanny's regular and sensual profile, and her large voluptuous eyes. Without troubling himself about the man who accompanied his daughter, and not even appearing to see him, père Legrand told her the family news. "The old woman has been at the Necker for the last fortnight, she's in a bad state; go and see her one of these Thursdays—it will give her some courage. I am fortunately all right, 'good whip, good lash.' Business is slack, though. If you want a good coachman by the month now it will just suit my book! No? Well so much the worse for me. Good-bye for the present."

They shook hands carelessly; the cab drove off.

"Well! Who would have believed it!" muttered Fanny—and then she began to relate to Jean a long story about her family, a topic she had always avoided—"it was so unpleasant—so vulgar!" But they knew each other better now, and need not hide anything from one another.

She had been born at the Moulin-aux-Anglais in the suburbs, of this father—an old cavalry soldier who drove the public conveyances between Paris and Chatillon—and an inn servant.

She had never known her mother, who died in childbed, but the owners of the establishment, good souls! compelled the father to recognize his child and to pay for the nurse. He did not dare to refuse, for he owed a great deal, and when Fanny was four years old, he used to take her in his carriage like a little dog, perched up under the hood, amused at being rolled along the roads, seeing the light of the lamps flitting by on each side, the backs of the horses steaming and panting, going to sleep in the dark, in the open air, and hearing the harness bells ringing.

But the father quickly tired of this pose of paternity; small as the expense was he had to clothe and feed the little waif. Besides, she rather interfered with his marriage with the widow of a wealthy market gardener, whose melon houses and cabbages he had noticed on his journeys. She had at that period the very clear idea that her father intended to lose her; it was the drunkard's fixed idea to disembarrass himself of the child at any hazard, and if the widow herself—kind mère Machaume had not taken the child under her protection—

"In fact you know Machaume," said Fanny.

"What? That servant I saw at your house?"

"That was my stepmother. She was so kind to me when I was little that I took her to get her away from her brute of a husband, who after squandering all her means, beat her, and compelled her to wait upon a low girl with whom he then was living. Ah, poor Machaume, she knows what a handsome man costs. Well, when she left me notwithstanding all I could say she would go back to him, and now she is in the hospital! How he has gone to seed without her, the old scoundrel! How dirty he is; what a rascal he looks! He has nothing but his whip; did you see how carefully he held it? Even when tipsy he carries it before him like a candle, locks it in his room; and it is the only thing about him ever taken care of. Good whip, good lash; that is his motto."

She spoke of him in a careless way as if of a stranger, without disgust or shame, and Jean was horrified as he listened. That father—that mother—compared with the stern features of the Consul and the angelic smile of Madame Gaussin. Fanny quickly perceiving all that was included in her lover's silence—all the repugnance against the social quagmire in which he was being plunged through her: "After all," she said philosophically, "there is something of this kind in every family; one is not responsible for it. . . . I have my father Legrand; you have your uncle Cesaire."

CHAPTER VI

SCARLET

"My dear child, I write to you still agitated in consequence of the great trouble which has come upon us. The twins disappeared from Castelet for the whole of one day, the night, and morning of the day after.

"It was on Sunday at breakfast time that we missed them. I had dressed them prettily for the eight o'clock Mass to which the Consul was to take them, then I did not think any more about them, being detained near your mother, who was more than usually nervous, as if she had a presentiment of some misfortune. You know that she has always had such a feeling since her illness, a prevision of what is about to happen, and the less she moves about, the more active is her brain.

"Your mother was fortunately in her room, and you can picture us in the dining-room waiting for the little ones. The people called them throughout the farm, the shepherd blew the great horn with which he summons the sheep, Cesaire went one way and I another. Rousseline, Tardive, and the rest of us went hurrying through Castelet and each time when we met each other we said, 'Well? We have seen nothing of them.' At last no one dared to ask the question; with beating hearts we searched the wells, and looked under the high windows of the granary. What a day it was; and I had to go every few moments to your mother, smile calmly, and explain the absence of the little ones by saying that I had sent them to pass the Sunday at their aunt's house at Villamuris. She seemed to believe that, but later in the evening while I was watching her, gazing through the window at the lights which were being carried about the plain and on the banks of the Rhône by those who were searching for the children, I could hear her weeping softly in her bed, and when I asked her the reason, 'I am crying because something is concealed from me, but which I have guessed all the same,' she replied in that childish voice which suffering has given her; and without either of us saying any more we resigned ourselves to our grief.

"Well, my dear child, not to dwell on this sad history, on Monday morning our little ones were brought back to us by the workmen whom your uncle employs on the island, and who had found them on a heap of vine cuttings pallid from cold and hunger after a night in the open air in the middle of the stream, and this is what they told us in the innocence of their little hearts. For a long time the idea had possessed them to do the same as their patron saints, Martha and Mary, whose history they had read, that is, to set out in a boat without sails, oars, or provisions of any kind, to preach the Gospel on the first land to which the winds of God would waft them.

"So on Sunday after Mass, loosing a fishing boat, and kneeling in it like the holy women while the current carried them down, they were gently stranded amongst the reeds of Piboulette, notwithstanding the floods of this season, the wind, the *revouluns*. Yes, the good God took care of them, and He had brought them back to us, the darlings with only their Sunday frocks disordered and their prayer-books spoilt. It was impossible to scold them, we could only embrace them with open arms, but we have all been ill in consequence of the anxiety they caused us.

"The most affected by it is your mother, who, though we told her nothing about it, felt, as she says, death pass over Castelet, and she, usually so quiet and cheerful, still retains the sadness which nothing can remove, notwithstanding that your father, myself and everybody else attend upon her most assiduously; and I tell you, my Jean, that it is for you above all that she languishes and distresses herself. She does not dare confess so much before your father, who wishes you to be left to your work, but you did not come home after your examination as you promised to do. Give us this pleasure at Christmas time, so that our invalid may assume a happy smile again. If you only knew, when you have these old people with you no longer, how you will regret not having devoted more time to them!"

Standing up by the window, through which the lazy, foggy, wintry daylight was filtering, Jean read this letter, inhaling the wild fragrance of it, and the dear remembrance of tenderness and sunshine.

"What is that? Let me see it."

Fanny had just woke up in the yellow light which the drawn curtain permitted to enter, and half stupefied with sleep, mechanically extended her hand towards the packet of Maryland tobacco, which was as usual by her bedside. He hesitated, knowing the jealousy which even the name of Divonne excited in his mistress, but how could he conceal the letter which she had already recognized?

At first the escapade of the little girls affected her slightly, as with arms and neck exposed she supported herself on the pillow, a cloud of brown hair about her, she read the letter and rolled a cigarette; but the end of it irritated her to fury, and tearing up the letter, she threw it on the floor. "All this about the holy women is a lie to make you leave me, the handsome nephew is wanted by that—"

He tried to stop her, to prevent her uttering the horrible word which she launched forth and many others after it. She had never before so demeaned herself in his presence, as in this breaking forth of disgusting rage, like a sewer launching forth its slime and stench. All the slang of the street women swelled her neck and distended her lip.

It is easy enough to see what they wanted down there. Cesaire had told them, and the family were combining to break the connection, to tempt him back to the country with that Divonne as a bait.

"In the first place I tell you plainly I will write to her cuckold of a husband and tell him all about it. Ah, but—!" As she was speaking she sat up in a spiteful manner in the bed, with pale and sunken cheeks, her features swelling like a wild beast, ready to spring upon him.

And Gaussin recollected having seen her in such a state in the Rue de l'Arcade, but now this wild hatred, which almost tempted him to fall upon and beat her, was directed against him, for in these merely passionate loves, in which esteem and respect for the person are wanting, brutality comes to the surface always, either in anger or caresses. He could not trust himself, so he rushed away to his office, and as he went he was indignant with himself for the life he was leading. This was teaching him what it was to put himself in the power of such a woman, what insults, what horrible expressions. His sisters, his mother, every one was spoken of alike. What, had he not the right to go and see his own relations? Was he shut up in prison then? And as all the past history of this connection came to his mind, he perceived how the beautiful naked arms of the Egyptian woman which had been clasped round his neck that evening at the ball, had tightened there despotically and strongly, isolating him from his friends and relatives. But now his resolution was taken; that very evening, come what might, he would start for Castelet.

Some business hurried through, his leave obtained, he returned home early, expecting a terrible scene, even a separation. But the gentle greeting which Fanny immediately bestowed on him, her swollen eyes, her cheeks bedewed with tears, scarcely left him courage to insist upon his determination.

"I leave here this evening," he said stiffly.

"You are right, my own, go and see your mother, and above all"—she approached caressingly—"forget how wicked I was this morning. I love you too much, that is my weakness."

All the rest of the day while packing his portmanteau with coquettish care, assuming all the sweetness of former days, she retained her repentant attitude, in the hope of retaining him perhaps. Nevertheless she never asked him to stay; and when, at the last moment, all hope lost in view of his final preparations, she sidled up and pressed against her lover, endeavoring to impregnate him with herself during his journey and during his absence, with her adieu and her kisses, only murmuring, "say, Jean, that you are not angry with me."

Oh, how delicious to wake up in the morning in his own little room, his heart still warmed by the affectionate embraces, the congratulations of his arrival; to find himself back in the same old place beneath the mosquito curtain of his little bed, the same bar of light which he sought there when waking, hearing the cries of the peacocks on their perches, the creaking of the well windlass, the pattering of the sheep's feet, and when he had fastened his shutters open against the wall he saw the beautiful warm light which came flooding in as through a sluice, and the marvellous prospectives of sloping vineyards, cypress and olive, and pine, losing themselves away to the Rhône, beneath a deep, clear sky, without a trace of mist notwithstanding the early hour—a green sky swept all night by the "Mistral," which still filled the wide valley with its strong and invigorating breath.

Jean compared this wakening with those in Paris under a sky as foul as his love, and he felt happy and *free*. He went downstairs. The white house was sleeping still, all the shutters were shut as closely as all eyes, and he felt happy at having a little time to himself to collect his ideas in the moral convalescence which he felt was commencing in him.

He advanced a few paces along the terrace, took a steep path through the park—what they called the park—a cluster of pines and myrtles growing at random on the rugged hillside of Castelet, intersected by rough footpaths, slippery with dead fir spikes. His dog, Miracle, now old and lame had come from his kennel and was following silently at his heels; they had so often taken this morning ramble together.

At the entrance to the vineyards when the great cypresses which inclose them were nodding their pointed heads the dog hung back; he was quite aware how the thick sand—a new preventive against the phylloxera which the consul was trying—would affect his old paws no less than the steep ascent. The pleasure of accompanying his master decided him, nevertheless, and there were at every obstacle painful efforts, whinings, stoppings, and sprawlings like the efforts of a crab on a rock. Jean did not take any notice of him, being so much occupied in the new Alicante plant which his father had told him all about the day before. The plants seemed to be doing well in the close and glittering sand. At length the poor man seemed in a fair way to be recompensed for his trouble; the vineyards of Castelet might revive, when those of La Nerte, the Hermitage and all the great "brands" of the south were destroyed.

A small white cap suddenly uprose before him.

Divonne! The earliest riser, she had a pruning knife in her hand and another thing which she threw away while her usually pale face flushed scarlet. "You, Jean! You did frighten me, I thought it was your father." Then recovering herself she kissed him. "Have you slept well?" she asked.

"Very well, aunt, but why were you afraid of my father being here?"

"Why?" She picked up the vine root she had thrown away, and said:

"The Consul told you, I believe, that this time he is sure to succeed—well, look here, there is the 'beast!'"

Jean looked at the little yellowish moss incrusted on the wood, the imperceptible moldiness which by degrees has spread through and devastated whole provinces. It was the irony of nature, on such a splendid morning under a vivifying sun, this infinitely small, this destroying and indestructible germ.

"This is the beginning of it. In three months the whole vineyard will be destroyed, and your father will have to begin again, for he has staked his reputation on it. There will be fresh plants, fresh remedies until—!"

A gesture of despair concluded and emphasized the sentence.

"Really? Have we come to that?"

"Oh, you know what the Consul is. He never says anything about it, gives me the monthly money as usual, but I can see he is preoccupied. He runs off to Avignon, to Orange. He goes to find money!"

"And Cesaire? The immersion principle?" asked the young man in consternation.

Thank God all was going well in that direction. They had had fifty butts of light wine at the last gathering, and this year they expected double the quantity.

In face of this success the Consul had given over to his brother all the vines in the plain which till lately had lain fallow in rows of dead wood like a country cemetery, and now they were under water three months.

And proud of her husband's—the Fenat's—work, the Provençale showed Jean from the high ground on which they were standing, the great ponds—*clairs*—banked up with chalk as at the salt-works.

"In two years that crop will bear; in two years also La Piboulette will also yield, and the isle of Lamotte, too, which your uncle purchased without telling any one. Thus we shall be rich, but we must hold on till then, and each one must help and sacrifice himself."

She spoke gaily of sacrifice as a

woman would who was not surprised by it; and in such an easy way that Jean was carried away and said, "sacrifice shall be made, Divonne."

That very day he wrote to Fanny to the effect that his parents could no longer continue his allowance, that he would be reduced to live on his official salary, and under such circumstances, their subsequent connection was out of the question. This was severing the tie sooner than he had anticipated—three or four years—but his mistress must accept the grave reasons he gave; she ought to pity him in his trouble, and might assist him in this painful accomplishment of a duty.

Was it such a sacrifice? Was he not rather relieved to finish an existence which seemed to him odious and unwholesome, especially since he had returned to nature, to his family, to simple and honest affections? His letter was written without struggle or pain, and he depended, to defend him from the reply—which he foresaw would be furious—on the honest tenderness and faithfulness of the good people who surrounded him; on the example of his father, upright and proud amid it all, on the frank smiles of the little "saints," and also upon the wide, peaceful horizon, on the healthy air of the mountains, the deep sky, the rapid river; for while thinking of his passion, of all the vile elements of which it was composed, it seemed to him as if he were getting over some dangerous fever such as one contracts from the exhalations of marshy ground.

Five or six days passed after his great decision. Morning and evening Jean went to the post and returned empty-handed, greatly troubled. What was

she about? What had she decided, and in any case why did not she reply? He could think of nothing else. And at night, when every one had been lulled to sleep by the sighing of the wind in the corridors, he and Uncle Cesaire talked the matter over in his little room.

"She is as likely to come as not," the uncle said; and his anxiety was doubled by this opinion, because he had to inclose in the letter breaking off the connection two bills, at six months and a year respectively, to settle his debt and interest.

How could he honor those bills? How explain matters to Divonne? He shivered at the bare idea, and gave his nephew pain when, as they had finished their chat, he said sadly, his long nose projecting, while he shook his pipe emphatically, "Well, good-night; at all events you have done the right thing."

At length the answer arrived, and at the very first lines, "My darling lad, I have not written sooner, because I wanted to prove to you otherwise than by words how well I understand and love you"—Jean stopped, surprised like a man who hears a symphony instead of the jig he expected. He turned quickly to the last page, where he read—"remain till death your dog who loves you whom you may beat, and who kisses you passionately."

So she had not received his letter. But reread carefully and with tears in his eyes, he could not doubt that it was an answer, telling him that Fanny had expected the bad news for a long while to the distress at Castelet was owing the inevitable separation. She had immediately set about seeking for a situation so as not to be a burden on him and she had found the post of manage of a boarding house in the Avenue du Bois de Boulogne on behalf of a rich lady. One hundred francs a month, board and lodging, and a holiday on Sundays.

"You understand, my dear; one whole day every week to love one another, for you still wish to, do you not? You will repay me for the great effort I am making to work for the first time in my life, for this drudgery by day and night, which I accept with humiliations which you cannot picture, and which weigh very heavily against my taste for independence. But I experience an extraordinary satisfaction in suffering for love of you. I owe you so much; you have made me understand so many good and honest things of which no one else has ever spoken to me! Ah, if we had only met sooner! But you were unable to walk when I was rolling in men's arms. Not one of them, at any rate, could boast of having inspired me with a resolution like this to retain him for ever so short a time. Now, return when you please, the rooms are ready. I have collected all my belongings; the hardest of all was to toss away the contents of drawers and souvenirs. You will only find my portrait, which will not cost you anything, only the kind looks which I would bespeak on its behalf. All, my own, my own! But if you will only keep Sunday for me, and my little place on your breast—my own place you know—" Then came affection, coaxing, voluptuous caressings, passionate words, which caused the lover to rub the satin paper against his face as if it could give him a warm human kiss.

"She does not say anything about my bills?" asked uncle Cesaire timidly.

"She sends them back to you—you may repay her when you get rich."

The uncle heaved a sigh of relief; his brows wrinkled with pleasure, and with a very wise gravity he exclaimed in his loud Southern accents:

"Look here, shall I tell you something? That woman is a saint."

Then passing to another train of ideas by that mobility—that want of logical sequence and of memory—one of the idiosyncrasies of his nature, he exclaimed:

"And what passion, too, my lad, what fire! My mouth is dry at the very thought of it, as when Courbebaisse read me Mornas' letters."

Once again Jean had to submit to the recital of the first journey to Paris, the Hotel Cujas, Pellicule, but he paid no attention to it, so he leaned out of the window in the silent night bathed in the light of the full moon, so bright that the clocks were deceived by it and welcomed it as the dawn of day.

So it was true; this redemption by affection of which the poets sing; and he experienced a feeling of pride in thinking that all those illustrious men whom Fanny had loved before him, far from reforming her had rather depraved her; while he by the simple force of his straightforwardness might draw her away from vice for ever.

He was grateful to her for having discovered this middle course, this half-rupture, by means of which she could assume new habits of work, so foreign to her indolent nature, and this old gentleman wrote next day in a paternal strain to encourage her in her reformation, expressing his uneasiness respecting the house she was managing, the people who frequented it, for he mistrusted her indulgence and the facility with which she said in resigning herself—"What do you wish? What must be, must!"

By return of post Fanny, with the docility of a little girl, gave him a picture of the boarding house, a regular family mansion inhabited by strangers. On the first floor were some Peruvians, father and mother with many children and servants; on the second floor Russians, and a wealthy Dutchman, a coral merchant. In the rooms above lodged two circus riders, "swells," Englishmen, very correct, and the most interesting little family party. Mademoiselle Minna Vogel, a zither player from Stuttgart, with her brother Leo, a poor little fellow in consumption, obliged to give up his study for the Conservatoire, whom his sister had come to take care of, without any other means than those gained by a few concerts to pay for board and lodging.

"Everything most correct and proper as you see, my dear man. As for me, I pass as a widow, and they pay me every attention. I could not admit any other conduct, your wife must be respected. When I say 'your wife' do not misunderstand my meaning. I am aware that you will go away some day, that I shall lose you, but after you none other. I shall remain yours forever, keeping the flavor of your caresses, and of the good instincts you have aroused in me. It is very curious, is it not? Sapho virtuous! Yes, virtuous when you will be with her no longer; but for you I remain as I was when you loved me, delirious, passionate—I adore you!"

Jean was suddenly seized with a deep, wearying sadness. These returns of the prodigal son after the delights of arrival, the supper of the fatted calf and the affectionate attentions suffer always from the pleasures of a nomad existence, the bitter husks and the lazy swine. It is a disenchantment which falls upon things and people suddenly, despoiled and discolored. The Provençal winter mornings no longer had for him their salubrious cheerfulness, neither was there any attraction in the otter hunting along the banks, nor in wild duck shooting in old Abrieu's decoy. Jean found the wind unpleasant, the water rough, and the strolls among the inundated vineyards, with the uncle to explain the system of sluices, dams and trenches, very monotonous.

The village which he had revisited at first, in his cheerful days, old houses, some abandoned, felt like the death and desolation of an Italian village. And when he went to the post-office he was obliged to submit on each doorstep to the rambling utterances of the old men bent double, their arms inserted in bits of knitted stockings, of the old women with chins yellow as boxwood beneath their tight caps, their little eyes glittering and sparkling like those of the lizards on the old walls.

Everywhere he heard the same lamentations concerning the death of the vines, the failure of the madder crop, the blight of the mulberry trees, the seven plagues of Egypt ruining this beautiful country of Provence, and to avoid all this he would sometimes return by the steep lanes which bordered the old walls of the *enceinte* of the Popes' château, lanes deserted and encumbered with briars, with those great "Herbes de Saint Roch," a cure for skin affections, in their proper place

In this corner of the middle-ages' character; shaded by the enormous battered ruin towering above the path.

Then he met the curé, Malassagne, coming from Mass, and descending the hill with long, hasty strides, his bands disordered, his cassock held up in both hands away from the briars and burrs. The priest halted, and held forth against the impiety of the peasantry, the infamy of the municipal council; he hurled his malediction upon the fields, the cattle, and the men; the evil-doers who would no longer go to chapel, who buried their dead without the offices of the Church, who tried to cure themselves by magnetism or spiritualism, so as to be independent of the priest or the doctor.

"Yes, Monsieur, spiritualism—that is what the peasants of Comtat have got to; and you cannot expect but that the vines should be destroyed."

Jean, who had Fanny's letter open and clasped in his pocket, listened with an absent air, and escaped as quickly as possible from the homily of the priest and returned to Castelet to shelter himself in a crevice of the rock in what in Provence is called a "cagnard," sheltered from the wind which blows in every direction, and concentrating the sun radiating from the stone.

He chose the most remote one, the wildest, protected by briars and kermes oaks, and threw himself down to read his letter; and little by little from the delicate scent which it exhaled, the caressing words, the images conjured up, there came over him a sensual intoxication which quickened his pulses, and gave rise to a hallucination which caused the river, the bushy islands, the villages in the hollows of the Alpilles—

the whole valley in which the wind swept up the dust in clouds, to disappear as useless accessories, and he was far away in their room in front of the railway station with its gray roof—a prey to those wild caresses, to the furious passions which made them clasp each other tightly with the grip of people who are drowning.

Suddenly there are footsteps on the path, clear laughter is heard, "Here he is!" His sisters appear, with little naked legs amid the lavender, led thither by old "Miracle," who was very proud at having tracked his master, and wagging his tail in a self-satisfied way; but Jean kicked him away and declined the offers to play hide-and-seek or run races, so timidly made by the children. Nevertheless he loved these twins, who loved their brother always so far away; he had made a child of himself for them since his arrival, amused himself in contrasting the pretty pair, born at the same time and yet so wonderfully unlike each other. One tall, dark, with curly hair, at once mystical and self-willed; she it was who, influenced by the reading of the curé Malassagne, had carried out her ideas of the boat; and this little Mary had carried off her fair-haired sister Martha, who was mild and gentle like her mother and her brother.

But what an odious contrast it was—while he was cherishing the past—this innocent coaxing of the children mingling with the perfume which rose from his mistress' letter—"No, leave me alone, I must work." And he was returning to the house, with the intention to shut himself up there, when his father's voice called him as he went along the passage.

"Is that you, Jean? Listen to me for a moment."

The post had brought fresh subjects of worry to this man, already gloomy by nature, still preserving the Eastern habit of silent gravity, broken by such reflections as "When I was Consul at Hong-Kong"—which burst out loudly as the crackling of a great fire.

While Jean was listening to his father reading and commenting on the morning papers, he looked toward the chimney-place, on which was Caoudal's Sapho, her hands clasping her knee, her lyre beside her—*all the lyre* (the whole gamut) bought twenty years before when Castelet was being furnished, and this common bronze, which turned him sick in the shop-windows in Paris gave him here in his isolation an amorous feeling, a desire to kiss those shoulders, to clasp those cold and polished arms, to cry out, "Sapho, for you, but only for you."

The tempting image rose when he quitted the room, it accompanied him, echoing the sound of his footsteps on the grand staircase. The name of Sapho was in the rhythm of the pendulum of the old clock, was sighed by the wind in the wide corridors—cold and paved in this estival mansion; her name he found in every volume in the library, old volumes with red edges which still held some crumbs of his infantine luncheons. And this oppressive recollection of his mistress pursued him even to his mother's bedroom, where Divonne was dressing the invalid's hair, brushing the lovely white locks from the face, still peaceful and rosy notwithstanding the perpetual pain.

"Ah, here is our Jean," said his mother.

But with her neck bare, with her little cap, her sleeves put back for the convenience of performing this toilette of which she had the sole charge—his aunt recalled to his mind other awakenings, again evoking his mistress, as she leaped out of bed in the fumes of her first cigarette. He was annoyed with himself for entertaining such thoughts —in that of all places. But how could he escape them?

"Our child is changed, sister," Madame Gaussin said sadly, "what ails him?" and they put their heads together. Divonne puzzled her brains over it; she longed to question the young man, but he seemed to avoid her now and to fear being left alone with her.

One one occasion after watching him she came to surprise him in his lair in the feverish excitement of his correspondence and his bad day-dreams. He rose with an ill-tempered air. She stopped him, and seating herself by him on the warm rock she said, "So you care for me no longer! I am not now your Divonne, to whom you used to tell all your troubles!"

"Oh, yes, yes," he stammered, confused by her affectionate manner of speaking, and turning away his eyes so that she should not see in them anything of what he had been reading, love appeals, lost entreaties, the delirium of passion at a distance.

"What is the matter, why are you so sad?" murmured Divonne, with all the tender coaxings of speech and hand which one employs with children. He was still in a way her "little one," he was for her only ten years old, when "little men" become independent.

As for him, still affected by his reading, he was stirred by the charms of the beautiful woman so close to him, by the luscious mouth, with lips heightened in color by the breeze which disarranged her hair and blew it down in Parisian fashion over her forehead. And Sapho's teaching, "All women are alike, with a man they have only one idea," tempted him to see a challenge in the peasant's happy smile, in her gestures a desire to detain him in tender confidences.

Suddenly he felt the rush of passion, and the effort he made to resist the temptation shook him convulsively. Divonne alarmed at seeing him so pale, with teeth chattering, exclaimed, "Ah, poor lad, he has got fever!" With a gesture of unreflecting tenderness she took off the large kerchief which covered her bust, to put it round his neck, when she felt herself roughly seized, embraced, madly kissed on bosom and shoulders, on all the dazzling skin thus bared. She had neither time to call out nor to defend herself; perhaps she had scarcely realized what had happened—as he fled away exclaiming "I am mad, mad!" and hurried off, the stones rattling with a sinister sound beneath his feet.

At the mid-day meal next day Jean announced his intention to depart, recalled by an order from the office. "Going already; you say. Why, you have only just come!" And so cries and supplications beset him. But he could no longer remain with them, because amid all their tenderness was insinuated the disturbing and corrupting influence of Sapho. Besides, had not he made the greatest sacrifice in his power by no longer living with her? The complete separation might come

later, and he would then return to love and kiss without shame or embarrassment those dear ones at home.

It was night: the inmates of Castelet were asleep, and the lights out, when Cesaire returned from seeing his nephew off by the train for Avignon.

When the horse had been fed, and Cesaire had scrutinized the sky after the manner of men who live by agriculture, he was going into the house, when he perceived a white figure resting on a seat in the terrace.

"Is that you, Divonne?"

"Yes, I am waiting for you."

Busy all day, separated from her Fenat, whom she adored, the pair would thus meet in the evening to talk or walk together. Was it because of the short scene between her and Jean, understood—and more than she cared for as she thought about it, or because she had witnessed the silent tears of the poor mother all day? But her voice was changed, and her mind exercised to a degree very unusual with her, the calm woman of duty! "Do you know anything? Why did he leave us so suddenly?" She did not believe the excuse about the "office," suspecting rather that some illegitimate attachment was enticing the lad from his family. So many dangers, so many fatal meetings in that dreadful Paris!

Cesaire, who could conceal nothing from her, confessed that as a matter of fact there was a woman in the case, but a kind creature incapable of estranging him from his relatives, and he spoke of her devotedness, the touching letters she wrote, praising above all else the courageous resolution which she had formed to work, which seemed only a matter of course to the peasant-woman. "For after all one must work to live!"

"Not that kind of woman," remarked Cesaire.

"It was then with a good-for-nothing woman that Jean was living. And you went to see him!"

"I swear to you, Divonne, that since she has known him no woman could have been more chaste and correct. Love has reformed her!"

But Divonne did not comprehend such hair-splitting. This girl in her view was one of those whom she called "bad women," and the thought that Jean had fallen a prey to such a creature made her very angry. If the Consul had only heard of it—!

Cesaire tried to calm her, and assured her that at the lad's age he could not do otherwise. "*Té, pardi;* let him marry then!" she said with determination.

"After all they are not together now—that is something."

Then she said, gravely, "Listen, Cesaire; you know that we have a saying, 'Evil lasts always longer than the author of it.' If all is true, and Jean has lifted this woman out of the gutter, he has most likely soiled himself in doing so. Possibly he may have made her better and more respectable, but who knows if the evil which was in her has not deeply corrupted our child?"

She returned toward the terrace. Night, clear and peaceful, lay upon the silent valley wherein naught stirred but the passing moonlight after the shadows, the rushing river, the rippling ponds like sheets of silver. One could breathe the calm, the isolation, the wonderful repose of sleep without

dreams. Suddenly the up-train, going at full speed, rattled along the bank of the Rhône with a loud noise.

"Oh, that Paris!" said Divonne, shaking her clenched hand toward the enemy on which the Provinces vent all their anger. "Oh, Paris, what do we give you—and what do you send us back!"

CHAPTER VII

HOLD YOUR TONGUE!

A COLD, foggy afternoon—dark at four o'clock, even in that wide avenue in the Champs Élysées through which the carriages were rolling with a muffled sound. It was with difficulty that Jean could read from the end of a small garden, the gate of which was open, the gilt letters above the entresol of a house which was luxurious and quiet-looking as a private villa. "Furnished Apartments, Family Boarding House." A small brougham was waiting at the gate.

Opening the door, Jean saw at once her of whom he was in search seated by the window, turning over the pages of a large account book, opposite another woman who was tall and elegantly dressed, holding her handkerchief and reticule.

"What is your pleasure, sir?" Fanny recognized him immediately, rose dumfounded, and passing in front of the lady, said in a low voice, "It is the young fellow!" The other woman scanned Gaussin from head to foot with the coolness of a connoisseur of experience, and then said aloud, "Embrace each other, young people, I am not looking." Then she took Fanny's place and continued to check the accounts.

They held each other's hands and muttered stupid phrases, such as "How are you?" "Pretty well, thank you." "Then you started last evening." But the reserved tone of their voices gave the words their true significance. And, seated on the sofa, Fanny, having recovered herself a little said: "You did not recognize my employer; but you have seen her before at Dechelette's ball—as a Spanish bride; somewhat faded!"

"Then she is—"

"Rosario Sanches, de Potter's woman."

This Rosario or Rosa, whose name was scratched upon all the looking glasses of the restaurants, and always in connection with something indecent, was formerly a character in the Hippodrome, well known for her cynical brazenfacedness and her "chaff," very celebrated among clubmen, whom she managed like her horses.

A Spaniard, from Oran, she had been more handsome than pretty, and she was still attractive by gaslight by reason of her coal-black eyes and straight eyebrows, but here in the fading light she had all her fifty years marked on her flat, hard face, and its yellow, wrinkled skin, like a lemon from her native land. She had been intimate with Fanny Legrand for years, had chaperoned her in her gay life, and her very name disgusted Jean.

Fanny, who understood the quivering of his arm, tried to excuse herself. To whom could she address herself to find a place? She had been in very straitened circumstances. Besides Rosa was quiet now, rich, very rich, she was living in her mansion in the Avenue Villiers or in her villa at Enghien, receiving a few old friends, but only one lover—always the same one—her musician.

"De Potter?" asked Jean, "I thought he had married."

"Yes, he is married, and has children, and his wife is a pretty woman, too, but that does not prevent him from seeing his former mistress; and if you could hear how she talks to him, and see how she treats him! Ah, he is bitten deeply!" She pressed his hand with tender reproachfulness. The "lady" at that moment interrupted her reading by addressing herself to the reticule which was wriggling about at the end of its cord, "Be quiet, can't you!" Then to Fanny in a tone of command she said: "Give me a piece of sugar for Bichito—quick!"

Fanny rose and brought the sugar, which she held near the opening of the reticule with a thousand endearing and infantine expressions. "Look at the pretty darling!" she said to her lover, and she exhibited to him a kind of large lizard reposing in cotton wool, unsightly, misshapen, a chameleon, in fact, sent from Algeria to Rosa, who kept it alive all the winter by dint of much care. She loved it more than she had ever loved any man and Jean discerned by Fanny's attention to it the position which the horrible beast held in the house.

The woman closed the ledger and prepared for her departure. "Not bad for the second fortnight. Only mind the candles."

She threw her glance of ownership round the little room, which was neat and tidy, the furniture covered with stamped velvet—blew the dust from the yucca of a round table, called attention to a hole in the lace curtains, and then in a knowing manner said: "Remember, young people; no nonsense; this house is most respectable," and entering her carriage at the gate she went off for her drive in the Bois.

"You can believe what a nuisance this is," said Fanny. "I have her or her mother down on me twice a week. The mother is more awful and more miserly still. I must indeed love you to put up with them! At length you have returned and I have you again. I was so afraid—" She stood up and clasped him in a long embrace, lips to lips, assured by the trembling of his kiss that she was still all in all to him. But people were passing to and fro in the corridor and they were obliged to be careful. When the lamp had been brought she sat down in her usual place, a little needlework in her hands, he sitting close to her as if he were paying a visit.

"Am I changed, eh? Is there a little of my old self left still?"

She smiled as she showed him her crochet, which she did as awkwardly as a child. She had always hated needlework; her book, her piano, her cigarette, or with her sleeves rolled up as she made some dainty dish—she never occupied herself in other ways than these. But here what was there to do? She could not play on the piano in the drawing-room, because she was in the office all day. Read novels? She knew better tales than books could tell her. Failing the prohibited cigarette, she had taken to lace-making which kept her hands busy and left her leisure to think; understanding now the taste which women have for these

trifling occupations, which she used formerly to despise.

And while she crocheted awkwardly with attention born of experience, Jean kept looking at her, very quiet as she was in her plain dress and stiff collar; her hair lying close to her antique-shaped head, her straightforward and rational demeanor. Outside in their luxurious "get up" the fashionable ladies drove by in the direction of the noisy boulevards, and Fanny did not appear to regret this glaring and successful phase of vice, which she might have shared, but which she disdained for his sake. If only he would consent to see her occasionally, she would accept her life of servitude willingly, and even find some interest in it.

All the boarders liked her. The ladies, foreigners, devoid of taste, consulted her concerning their dress purchases. She gave singing lessons in the morning to the eldest of the Peruvian children, and for the book to be read, the play to see, she was consulted by the men, who treated her with great respect and attention, one of them in particular, a Dutchman, who lived on the second floor. "He seats himself there, where you are, contemplating me, until I say to him, 'Kuyper, you bore me.' Then he replies 'pien,' and he goes away. He gave me this coral brooch; it is worth about a hundred sous. I took it for the sake of peace and quiet."

A waiter entered bringing a tray, which he put on a round table, moving back the green plant for the purpose. "I eat my dinner here alone—an hour before the *table d'hôte*." She pointed out two dishes in the long and full *menu*.

The manageress can have only two dishes and soup. "She is a beast, that Rosario! But I prefer dining here, I need not talk, and I reread your letters for company."

She stopped speaking as she sought for a tablecloth and table napkins; and at every moment she was interrupted; to give an order, to open a cupboard, a claim to arrange. Jean perceived that he would put her out if he remained, and besides her dinner was being sent up; so pitiful, too, the little tureen holding one portion of soup smoking on the table, which made them both regret their former *tête-à-tête*.

"Till Sunday, till Sunday," she murmured as she sent him away, and as they could not kiss because of the servants and the boarders who were about, she took his hand and pressed it against her heart, so that the caress might enter there.

All that evening — all night — he thought of her suffering in her servitude under that woman and her lizard; then the Dutchman troubled him, too, and until Sunday he scarcely existed. In reality this semi-separation, which was supposed to reduce the shock of their final separation, was for her the cut of the pruning-knife by which the worn-out tree is revived. Almost every day they sent each other tender *billets,* such as lovers indite, or else perhaps after office hours they chatted in the manager's room during the needlework hour.

She had said at the boarding-house that he was one of her relations, and under cover of this vague term he was enabled to pass the evening in the drawing-room a thousand leagues from Paris. He got to know the Peruvian family, with its innumerable girls dressed up gaudily, and arranged around the room like aras on perches— he listened to the zither of Mademoiselle Minna Vogel, who was wreathed like a hop-pole, and saw her brother, the consumptive invalid, nodding his head in time to the music, and running his fingers over the keys of an imaginary clarionette, the only one he had permission to play. He played whist with Fanny's Dutchman, a fat, bald, empty-headed man of sordid appearance, who had sailed all over the world, and when somebody asked him for some information about Australia, where he had lived several months, he replied rolling his eyes, "Guess, now, what potatoes cost in Melbourne!" having been struck by one fact only— the dearness of potatoes in every country which he had visited.

Fanny was the life and soul of their assemblies; she chatted, sang, played the Parisian woman of the world; and if anything remaining in her manner of the Bohemian of the studio escaped in the presence of these "exotics" it appeared to them the height of breeding! She dazzled them by her knowledge of the people famous in literature and art, gave the Russian lady information concerning the manner in which Dejoie, the novelist, worked, the number of cups of coffee he drank in a night, and the exact and ridiculous sum which the publishers of *Cenderinette* had paid him for his master-work that had made their fortune. The success of his mistress made Gaussin so proud that he forgot to be jealous, and would have passed his word on the subject if any-one had doubted the fact.

While he admired her in the quiet

drawing-room lighted by shaded lamps, pouring out tea, accompanying the singing of the younger girls, advising them as an elder sister, it was a curious experience to picture her to himself in very different circumstances, when she arrived at his house on Sunday morning wet and cold, and without even approaching the fire lighted in her honor, undressing rapidly.

They did not get up until the evening. There was no attraction elsewhere, no amusement, no one to call on, not even the Hettemas, who for economy's sake were living in the country. The little *déjeuner* prepared beside them, they listened in a languid kind of way to the murmur of the streets, the whistling of the trains, the rumbling of the laden cabs, and the pattering of the rain on the zinc of the balcony, without any notion of time until darkness set in.

The gas which was being lighted glanced in pale rays upon the curtains. It was time to get up; Fanny had to be home at seven o'clock. In the semi-obscurity of the room all her worries and disgust came upon her more heavily, more cruelly, as she put on her still damp boots and her garments, her black dress, the uniform of poor women.

And by way of augmenting her regrets there were all the loved and familiar objects around her; the furniture, the little dressing-room of the happier days. She had to tear herself away—"Let us go," she said; and in order to see as much of each other as they could Jean escorted her. Slowly and arm in arm they sauntered up the avenue of the Champs Elysées, in which the two lines of gas lamps with the

Arc de Triomphe above, distant in the darkness, and two or three stars peeping out from a strip of sky, composed the foundation of a diorama. At the corner of the Rue Pergolése, close to the pension, she put up her veil for a last kiss, and she left him lost, disgusted with his apartments which he re-entered as late as possible, cursing his lot, and almost blaming those at Castelet for the sacrifice which he was imposing on himself for them.

The pair dragged on this existence for two or three months, toward the end of which it became absolutely insupportable. Jean had been obliged to cease his visits at the boarding-house because the domestics chattered, and Fanny was more and more exasperated by the parsimony of the Sanches—mother and daughter. She thought of resuming her housekeeping again, and felt that his love also had outlived his patience, but she did not like to suggest a return to him.

One Sunday in April, Fanny arrived more smartly dressed than usual, in round hat, and a simple spring costume —she was not rich—which displayed her graceful figure to advantage.

"Get up quickly—we are going to breakfast in the country."

"In the country!"

"Yes, at Enghien—at Rosa's house; she has invited us; I said no at first, but she insisted—Rosa never forgives a refusal. You may as well consent for my sake; I have done enough, I think."

Rosa's dwelling was a large cottage on the margin of the lake of Enghien, to which a large lawn descends to a small bay in which some skiffs and gondolas were lying. The chalet was wonderfully decorated and furnished. The ceiling and the mirrors in the panels reflected the shimmering of the water, and the fine elms of the park were already pushing forth their early leaves, and the lilac was in bloom. The correct liveries of the servants, the walks carefully kept, did credit to the double supervision of Rosario and the old Pilar.

The company were seated at table when the pair arrived, a wrong direction having sent them astray round the lake along lanes between high garden walls. Jean was quite put out of countenance by the cold reception he experienced from the mistress of the house, who was furious at having been kept waiting, and by the appearance of the old hags to whom she introduced him in her "chariot-driver's" accents. Three *élégantes,* as these high-class women call themselves, three old frumps reckoned among the glories of the Second Empire, whose names were as famous as that of a great poet or a successful general—Wilkie Cob, Sombreuse, Clara Desfous.

"Élégantes," they certainly were, got up in the newest "mode," in spring hues, daintily clothed like dolls from neck to boots; but so faded, worn out, made up! Sombreuse without eyelashes, her eyes expressionless, her lip distended, feeling around for her plate, her fork, her glass! Desfous, very stout and pimpled, a hot-water bottle at her feet, extending on the tablecloth her poor gouty fingers all twisted, with sparkling rings on them, as difficult to get off or on as those in a catchpuzzle. And Cob, attenuated, with a youthful figure which made her sickclown's head more hideous still under its tangled yellow hair. She, ruined, sold up, had tried a last cast at Monte Carlo and had returned penniless, madly in love with a good-looking croupier, who would have nothing to say to her. Rosa having received her kept her, and took great credit for so doing.

All these females knew Fanny and welcomed her with a patronizing "How do you do, little one?" The fact was that with her dress at three francs a yard, without any other ornament than Kuyper's brooch, she looked quite a recruit amongst these veterans of sin, who, amid the luxurious surroundings, the reflected light from the lake and the sky, laden with fragrance, entering through the dining-room doors, looked more ghoulish than ever.

Old Mère Pilar, the "Chinge," as she called herself in her Franco-Spanish gibberish—a regular baboon with a shriveled pale skin, a ferocious and malicious look on her grinning face, was there; her hair cut like a boy's and gray; and over her old black satin dress she wore a great blue sailorcollar.

"And last Mr. Bichito," said Rosa, as she wound up the introduction of her guests by indicating to Gaussin a small heap of rose-colored wadding on the cloth on which the chameleon was shivering.

"Well, and won't you introduce me?" said a big fellow in tones of forced geniality; he wore grey moustaches and was well dressed, but rather stiff in the white waistcoat and stick-up collar.

"That's true; and Tatave?" said the woman laughing. The mistress of the house mentioned his name carelessly

Tatave was de Potter, the celebrated composer of *Claudia,* of *Savonarola;* and Jean, who had just had a glimpse of him at Dechelette's, was surprised to find him a man of so little geniality —a wooden mask with hard regular features; his colorless eyes confessing to a mad, incurable passion which for years had tied him hand and foot to that wretch of a woman, which caused him to neglect his wife and children, to remain as a dependant of the house in which he spent part of his large fortune, his gains from the theatre, and where he was treated worse than a servant. Rosa's bored look when he began to speak was something to see, and the contemptuous manner in which she imposed silence on him, while Pilar, following her daughter's lead, never failed to add in a most determined way—

"*Do* hold your tongue, my boy."

Jean sat beside her, and her old jaws groaned as she masticated her food like an animal chewing the cud, and her inquisitive looks at his plate further upset the young man, already worried by Rosa's patronizing air, as she joked Fanny about her musical evenings at the boarding-house, and on the silly greenhorns who believed she was some poor lady of fashion who had fallen on bad times. The old chariot-woman puffed up with unhealthy fat, uncut stones of the value of ten thousand francs in each ear, seemed to be envious of the return to youthfulness and good looks which Fanny's lover had communicated to her. But Fanny did not put herself out at all; on the contrary, she amused every one at the table by taking off the boarders, the Peruvian who had communicated to her—as he rolled his eyes—his wish to know a "*grande coucoute;*" the silent devotion, the puffing like a seal of the Dutchman, as he gasped behind her chair—"How much do you think potatoes cost in Batavia?"

Gaussin did not laugh; nor did Pilar, who was engaged in watching over the plate, or in seizing from a dish before her or from a neighbor's sleeves a fly or two, and presenting them with words of childish tenderness to the horrible little beast wrapped up on the cloth, as withered, shapeless, and as wrinkled as Desfous' fingers themselves.

Sometimes, all the flies having disappeared from her vicinity, she would jump up and capture one on the sideboard or on the glass door. This act, repeated, annoyed her daughter, who seemed very touchy that morning.

"Don't get up every moment like that; it is very trying."

In the same voice, a tone or two lower, the mother would retort:

"You are all stuffing yourselves; why shouldn't *he* eat, too?"

"Leave the table, or keep quiet. You annoy every one."

The old woman "gave it back," and then both of them began to "bullyrag" each other like devout Spaniards, mingling the devil and hell with gutter-language.

"Hija del demonio."

"Cuerno de Satanas."

"Puta!"

"Mi madre!"

Jean looked at them in supreme astonishment, while the others, accustomed to these family jars, proceeded quietly with their meal. De Potter only interfered for the sake of the stranger.

"Come now, don't go on fighting!"

But Rosa turning to him said: "What concern is it of yours? Are those your manners? Can't I speak if I like? Go home to your wife and see whether I come there. I've had quite enough of your fishy eyes and those three hairs of yours! Take them back to your simpleton at home! Isn't it time you did? Eh?"

De Potter smiled; he was rather white. "And one must live with *that!*" he muttered.

"That is as good as *that,*" she yelled at him, her body extended across the table, "and you know the door is open —you can go; hop!"

"Look here, Rosa,"—begged the poor spiritless eyes. But mother Pilar chimed in with her comical careless-ness, "*Do* hold your tongue, my boy," and every one shouted with laughter, even Rosa, and de Potter, who kissed his still grumbling mistress, and by way of currying favor with her he caught a fly and presented it tenderly by the wings to Bichito.

And this was de Potter, the cele-brated composer—the pride of the French School! How did this woman manage to retain her influence over him, by what magic, old in vice, coarse as she was, with her mother who was twice as infamous and who indicated what her daughter would come to twenty years later, as if seen in a re-flecting globe.

Coffee was served by the margin of the lake, in a small rustic grotto hung inside with light-colored silks which re-flected the ripples of the water—one of those delicious nooks for love-mak-ing invented by the counts of the eighteenth century with a glass on the ceiling which reflected the attitudes of the old hags who reclined on the wide divan while digestion proceeded; and Rosa, her cheeks flushed under her "make-up," held out her arms as she lay on her back crying out:

"Oh, my Tatave, my Tatave!"

But her warmth of affection evapo-rated with the chartreuse, and the idea of a pull on the lake having suggested itself to one of the women, she dis-patched de Potter to prepare the boat.

"The small boat, you understand, not the big one."

"Suppose I tell Désiré to—"

"Désiré is breakfasting."

"Well, the little boat is full of water and it will take a long while to bail it out."

"Jean will go with you, de Potter," said Fanny, who was afraid of another scene.

Seated opposite each other, their legs apart, each one seated on a thwart of the skiff, they bailed quickly with-out speaking and without looking at each other, as if hypnotized by the splashing of the water discharged by the two scoops. A large catalpa shaded with its odorous fragrance, was re-flected plainly in the glittering surface of the lake.

"Have you lived with Fanny long?" asked the musician, suddenly ceasing his efforts.

"Two years," replied Gaussin, rather surprised.

"Only two years! Then what you have seen here to-day may serve as a lesson to you. Look at me! I have lived with Rosa twenty years since my return from Italy; after my three years of the *Prix de Rome,* I went to the Hippodrome one evening and saw her standing driving her little chariot above me, her whip in the air, with her barrel helmet and her coat of mail which fitted her tightly to the hips. Ah, if any one had said—!"

He re-commenced bailing, and told how his relatives had at first laughed at this attachment; then, the affair becoming serious, prayers, sacrifices and all other means were employed to bring about its cessation. Two or three times the girl had yielded to bribes, but he had always rejoined her again. "Let us see what travel will do," his mother said. He traveled, came back, and went to her again. Then he permitted himself to be married; a pretty wife with money, the promise of the Institute as a wedding present. And in three months after he left his new home for the old one. "Ah, young man—young man!"

He set forth the events of his life in a dry way, without relaxing a muscle of his face, which was as rigid as his collar that held his head so stiff. And meanwhile boats full of students and girls, singing, laughing, full of fun, passed by; how many of these unconscious votaries of pleasure might have stopped and taken a hint from this terrible revelation! In the kiosk all this time, as if the word had been passed to separate Fanny and Jean, the old "*élégantes*" were preaching at her. "Good-looking your young man, but he has not a sou' To what can it lead?"

"But since I love him—"

Then Rosa shrugged her shoulders. "Let her do as she likes, she will let the Dutchman slip through her fingers, as I have seen her miss other good chances. After that business of Fla-

mant, she did try to become practical, but she's now sillier than ever."

"Ay vellaca!" groaned Madame Pilar.

The Englishwoman with the clown's head interposed with the horrible intonation which had made her so long successful.

"It is very nice to love for love, little one. Love is a very fine thing, you know, but you must love money also. If I were rich now, do you think my croupier would call me ugly?" She jumped with rage, and raised her voice to a shriek. "Oh, that was awful! To have been a celebrity, known all over the world like a monument of a boulevard. So well known that one had only to tell a wretched cabman to drive to Wilkie Cob's and there you were! To have had princes at my feet and kings, who if I expectorated said spitting was pretty—the right thing. And now that dirty wretch would have nothing to do with me because I was 'ugly,' and I had not money enough to pay him one evening."

So annoyed was she at the recollection that she had been considered plain, that she tore her dress open roughly.

"The face—yes, I have lost that; but here—the bust, the shoulders, isn't it white, isn't it firm?"

She impudently disclosed her flesh, which remained wonderfully young-looking, after thirty years in the furnace, surmounted by a head and neck, faded and death-like.

"Ladies, the skiff is ready," cried de Potter, and the Englishwoman fastening her dress over what remained of her youth, murmured with a comical despair—

"Well, after all, I couldn't go about naked to all those places."

In this setting of a picture by Lancret—in which the pretty whiteness of the villas dazzled the beholder amidst the young verdure, with the terraces, the grassy slopes, surrounding the little lake, what an embarkation was this of this old lame Cythera, the blind Sombreuse, the old clown, and Desfous the paralytic, leaving in the rippling water behind the boat the musk perfume of their "get up."

Jean took the sculls, his back bent, feeling shamefaced and disconsolate, fearful that any one should see him and attribute to him some low share in this shameful allegorical boat. Fortunately he had opposite to him Fanny, who was seated beside de Potter, who was steering — Fanny, whose smile had never seemed to him so young—no doubt by comparison.

"Sing us something, little one," said Desfous, who was somewhat softened by the influence of the spring day. In her deep and expressive voice, Fanny commenced the barcarolle from *Claudia*, which the composer, moved by the memory of his first great success, accompanied, imitating with his mouth the orchestra, that undulation which gives to melody the briskness of dancing water. At that hour amid such surroundings it was delicious! Some one on a terrace hard by cried out "bravo," and the Provençal, keeping time with his sculls, thirsted for this music from his mistress's lips, and experienced a desire to put his mouth to the source itself, and to drink in the sun, with head held back, forever.

Suddenly Rosa, who was furious, interrupted the song, in which this union of voices irritated her. "Here, when you have done singing in each other's faces! I suppose you think you are amusing us with your deadly chanting! We have had enough of it; besides it is late, and it is time Fanny returned to her desk."

And with a violent gesture she indicated the nearest landing-stage.

"Run the boat in there," she said to her lover, "they will be nearer the railway station."

This was brutal for a leave-taking, but the former chariot-rider had accustomed her people to this kind of thing and no one dared protest. The couple thrown out, as it were, on the bank, with a few words of frigid politeness addressed to the young man, and some orders given in a hissing tone to Fanny, the boat shoved off again, with cries, and disputes, which ended in an insulting burst of laughter that was carried to the ears of the lovers over the lake.

"You hear, you hear," said Fanny, pale with anger, "they are laughing at us."

And all her humiliation and troubles coming to the surface at this latest insult, she told him as they proceeded to the railway station of things which she had hitherto concealed. Rosa was only trying to separate her from him with a view to facilitate her deception of him. "She has said all she could to make me take the Dutchman. Just now, they all set at me about it. I love you too dearly, as you know, and that puts her out with her vices, and she has vices, the most monstrous, too! And all because I will not—"

She ceased; he became very pale, his lips trembled as they had trembled that evening when he was reading her letters.

"Oh, you need have no fear," she said, "your affection has cured me of all those horrors. And her dirty chameleon—they both disgust me!"

"I do not want you to remain with her any longer," said Jean, quite upset by his terrible jealousy. "There is too much dirt to eat there. You must come back and live with me, we shall manage to pull through somehow."

She had been waiting for this for a long while. Nevertheless she combated it, objecting that the housekeeping would be very hard to do on three hundred francs a month, and they would have to separate again. "And I suffered so much before, when I left our little home."

There were seats at intervals under the acacias which lined the road, and the telegraph wires overhead were covered with swallows; and to talk more at ease the pair seated themselves, very agitated, arm in arm.

"Three hundred francs a month," said Jean. "But how do the Hettemas manage on two hundred and fifty?"

"They live at Chaville, in the country, all the year round."

"Well, can't we do the same? I am not wedded to Paris."

"Really! You really will go! Ah, my own, my own!"

People were passing, a number of donkeys were carrying a wedding party homeward. So they could not embrace each other, but remained quiet, clinging close together, dreaming of the happiness to be renewed in the summer evenings which would possess this rustic sweetness, the warm stillness enlivened by the distant reports from the shooting galleries and the sound of the organs at a suburban *fête*.

CHAPTER VIII

THE CHILD

THEY settled at Chaville, between the higher and the lower ground, by the margin of the old forest road, which is called the Pave des Gardes, in an old hunting lodge at the entrance of the wood. They had three rooms scarcely larger than those in Paris, the same furniture, the cane chair, the painted wardrobe, and to embellish the frightful green paper in the bed-room only Fanny's portrait, for the photograph of Castelet had had its frame broken during the move, and was fading in an out-of-the-way corner.

They scarcely spoke now of poor Castelet, since uncle and niece had ceased corresponding. "A nice sort of humbug he is," she would say, as she recalled the anxiety of Le Fenat to encourage the first rupture. The children only supplied their brother with news, for Divonne no longer wrote to him. Perhaps she still cherished some anger towards her nephew, or guessed that the bad woman had come back to open and comment upon her poor maternal letters written in large rustic characters.

At times they could almost have believed themselves still in the Rue d'Amsterdam, when they were aroused by the singing of the Hettemas, who were again their neighbors, and the whistling of the trains which passed and repassed continually on the other side of the road, and were visible through the branches of the trees in a large park. But instead of the dirty dark roof of the Western railway station, of the curtainless windows showing the profiles of the working clerks and the uproar of the steep street, they enjoyed the silent and green space beyond their little plot surrounded by other gardens, and little houses amidst clumps of trees sloping to the bottom of the hill.

In the morning, before starting for Paris, Jean breakfasted in their little dining-room, the window of which opened on the wide, paved road, bordered with grass and perfumed hawthorn hedges. By this road he reached the station in ten minutes, skirting the rustling and cheerful park, and when he returned this noise became hushed as the shadows from the wood were thrown upon the verdure of the road empurpled by the setting sun, and as the cries of the cuckoos from every corner of the wood were interspersed with the trills of the nightingales from the ivy-clad trees.

But as soon as they settled down and the surprise at the quiet of their surroundings had passed away, the lover was again seized by the pangs of fruitless and morbid jealousy. The dispute between his mistress and Rosa, the departure from the boarding-house had given rise to an explanation between the two women, in which were such horrible insinuations on both sides that his suspicions and restlessness were aroused, and when he went away in the morning and saw from the train their low house and the round dormer window, his eyes would seem to pierce through the walls as he muttered, "Who knows?" and the suspicion would haunt him even amongst the official papers in his office.

On his return he would make her tell him all she had done during the day, even to the smallest events. Of her thoughts, seldom of any consequence, which he surprised her into telling by suddenly asking, "What are you thinking of?" always afraid that she was regretting something or somebody connected with that horrible past of hers, confessed to by her every time with the same unembarrassed frankness.

At any rate when they saw each other only on a Sunday, anxious for each other, he had not devoted himself to these outrageous and minute moral investigations. But now they were together with a continuity of life à deux, they were tortured even in their affectionate moments, agitated by a sort of dull anger by the sad consciousness of the irreparable; he endeavoring to impart to this blasée woman a feeling as yet unknown to her; she ready to make a martyr of herself to give him enjoyment such as ten others had never had, failing in so doing, and weeping in impotent rage.

Then a relaxation set in; perhaps in consequence of the satiety of sense, or more likely in the vicinity of the Hettemas. There is no doubt that of all the little households in the Parisian suburbs not one perhaps enjoyed like that one the liberty of the country, the joy of going about in old clothes, with hats of bark, the wife without corsets, the husband in sandals, of taking the crusts of bread from the table to the ducks, the potato skins to the rabbits, and then weeding, raking, grafting and watering.

Oh, that watering!

The Hettemas laid themselves out for it as soon as the husband came back, and had changed his office dress for a kind of Robinson Crusoe garment. After dinner they began again, and a long time after nightfall there arose from the little garden a smell of damp earth, the creaking of a pump, the clanking of great water-cans, and loud puffings amid the flower-beds could be hea.d, mingling with a dropping which seemed to fall from the foreheads of the workers into their watering pots. Then from time to time would be heard in triumphal tones:

"I have given thirty-two to those greedy peas!" "And I have given fourteen to the balsams."

These were the sort of people who were not content with being happy, but looked at their happiness and tasted it in a way to make your mouth water; the man particularly by the irresistible fashion in which he would recapitulate the delights of wintering together.

"It is nothing at all now, you'll see in December; then one comes home muddy and wet and worried, all the weight of Paris is on one's back, to find a good fire. a good lamp, a savory soup, and under the table a pair of wooden shoes stuffed with straw. Then do you see, when one has eaten well of cabbage and sausages and a piece of Gruyère, kept fresh under a cloth, when one has emptied a bottle of liquor, which has not passed by way of Bercy, free of baptism and duty, isn't it good to draw one's arm-chair to the chimney corner, to light a pipe, to drink one's coffee with a thimbleful of brandy in it, and then seated opposite each other to indulge in forty winks while the hoar frost is making patterns on the windows outside? Oh, no more than forty winks, just sufficient to enable one to get over the heaviness of digestion. Afterwards one can draw a little, the

wife clears away, completes her arrangements, turns down the bed, gets the hot bottle, and when she is between the sheets, and has warmed the place, one turns in, and feels as warm as if one had crept bodily into the straw in one's wooden shoes."

He became almost eloquent on this subject, this shaggy-haired giant with a heavy jaw, who was usually so timid that he could scarcely say two words without blushing and stammering.

This foolish timidity, a comical contrast with his black beard and colossal build, had made his marriage and the tranquillity of his life. At twenty-five years of age, overflowing as he was with strength and health, Hettema was ignorant of love and woman, when one day at Nevers, after a club dinner, his comrades dragged him, half tipsy, against his will, into a house of ill-fame. He returned again, paid the woman's debts, took her away with him, and for fear that some one would take her from him, and that he would have to begin a new conquest, finished by marrying her.

"A lawful household, my dear," Fanny said, with a smile of triumph at Jean, who listened in terror, "and of all those that I have known it is the most correct and respectable."

She made this statement in the sincerity of her ignorance. The married couples into whose home life she had been permitted to enter, no doubt deserved no other judgment, and all her notions of life were as false and as sincerely expressed as this one.

These Hettemas were quiet neighbors, of equable temperament, even capable of rendering services which did not put them out very much, having a particular horror of scenes, of quarrels in which they must take one side or the other, and in general of anything that tended to disturb digestion. The woman tried to initiate Fanny into the mysteries of rearing fowls and rabbits, and in the healthy enjoyment of watering, but in vain.

Fanny, a woman of the Faubourg, who had gone through the studios, only cared for the country, its freedom or its picnics, as a place in which one can shout, roll about, and lose one's self with one's lover. She detested effort or work, and her six months of boarding-house management having exhausted her energies for a long while to come, she sank into a dormouse state, a kind of stupor resulting from good living and open air, which almost deprived her of the strength to dress herself, to do her hair, or even to open her piano.

The interior management of the house was left entirely to a charwoman, and when in the evening she summed up the incidents of the day to relate them to Jean, she could not find anything to tell him except a visit to Olympe, talks across the palings, and cigarettes, a pile of cigarettes, the ends of which covered the hearth. Six o'clock already; there was hardly time to put on a dress, to fix a flower in her corsage, and to go and meet him on the green road.

But when the autumn fogs and rains and twilight fell she had more than one excuse for staying indoors, and he often surprised her on his return in one of her full white woolen dressing-gowns which she had put on in the morning, and her hair put up as when he had left home. He thought her charming thus with her young and well-cared for skin, nevertheless this slipshod fashion shocked him, and alarmed him like a danger.

He himself, after a great effort to work, in order to in some measure increase their means without having recourse to Castelet, long evenings passed poring over plans, drawings of artillery, caissons, rifles on a new model which he was designing for Hettema, felt himself overcome all at once by this enervating influence of the country and of solitude, to which the strongest and most active are liable, and of which his early infancy, passed in a remote corner of the earth, had implanted in him the deadening seed.

And the materialism of their stout neighbors assisting, communicating itself to both in the frequent comings and goings between them, with somewhat of their moral abasement and their enormous appetite, Gaussin and his mistress began also to discuss with much interest the questions of meals, and the time of going to bed. Cesaire having sent a small cask of his "frog's wine," they passed the whole of one Sunday in bottling it, the door of their little cellar open to the last sun of the year, a blue sky across which some rosy clouds, rosy with the tint of the heather, were floating. The day was not far distant from that of the wooden shoes filled with straw and the forty winks on each side of the fireplace. Fortunately there was a distraction in store for them.

One evening he found Fanny very much disturbed. Olympe had been telling her the history of a poor little lad who had been brought up by his grandmother at Morvan. The father and mother were wood merchants in Paris —they no longer wrote, nor had they paid any money for him for months. The grandmother had died suddenly, and some barge people had brought back the little brat by the Yonne Canal in order to restore it to its parents, but could not find them. The yard was closed, the mother had run away with a lover, the drunken father being bankrupt had disappeared. These lawful unions were so happy! There was the poor little fellow six years old, quite "a love" without bread or clothing, a castaway.

She was moved even to tears, and then said suddenly:

"Suppose we offer to take it, would you consent?"

"What nonsense!"

"Why?" Then coming close to him, coaxing him she continued: "You know how I wished to have a child, we could bring this one up and educate him. People love these little ones that they adopt quite as much as their own."

She pictured also the occupation which such a one would give her, left alone all day as she was, a prey to unpleasant thoughts. A child is such a safeguard. Then seeing him alarmed at the idea of the cost, she said: "Oh, the expense is nothing. Why, just think, at six years we can fit him out with your old things. Olympe, who understands all about it, assures me it would make no difference at all."

"Let her take him, then," said Jean, with the ill humor of a man who feels himself conquered by his own want of will. He endeavored nevertheless to resist, calling to his aid the decisive argument: "And when I am no longer here, what then?" He seldom spoke of their separation, so as not to distress Fanny, but he thought of it, by way of fortifying himself against the dangers of housekeeping and the melancholy confidence of de Potter.

"What a complication this child would make, and what a burden he will be to you in the future."

Fanny's eyes grew dim.

"You are quite mistaken, my own; the child would be something to talk to about you; a comfort, a responsibility, too, would give me strength to work and some pleasure in life again."

He reflected for a minute, picturing her all alone in the empty house.

"Where is this child?"

"At Bas-Meudon, at the house of a bargeman, who has kept him for some days. After that there is nothing but the workhouse."

"Well, then, you can go and fetch him, as you seem to be bent on it."

She clasped him around the neck, and was childishly happy all the evening; playing, singing, in high spirits, happy as if transfigured. Next day in the train Jean mentioned their determination to the stout Hettema, who seemed posted up in the business, but not desirous of interfering. Settled comfortably in his corner, and deeply engaged in the perusal of the *Petit Journal,* he stammered from beneath his beard:

"Yes, I know; this is the women's affair. It does not concern me." Then looking over his paper, he said: "Your wife seems to be very romantic."

Romantic or not, she was very much dismayed in the evening as she knelt, a plate of soup in her hand, endeavoring to bring to reason the little Morvandian lad, who, standing upright in a resentful attitude, hanging his head—an enormous head, with hair like hemp—obstinately refused to speak, to eat, or even to show his face, but kept repeating in a monotonous and choking voice:

"Want to see Ménine—see Ménine!"

"Ménine, that's his grandmother. I

think. I have not been able to get anything else out of him for two hours."

Jean also tried to make him swallow the soup, but unsuccessfully. And there they remained, both of them kneeling in front of him, one holding the plate and the other the spoon, as if he were a sick lamb, repeating encouraging and tender words, in the hope of reassuring him.

"Let us go to dinner; perhaps we frighten him. He will eat if we don't take any notice of him."

But he continued to stand there immovable, dumfounded; repeating his little plaint of "Want to see Ménine," which moved them to the heart, until he went to sleep, standing upright by the sideboard, and so soundly that they were enabled to undress him and put him to bed in a heavy country cot, which had been borrowed of a neighbor, without his opening his eyes for a second.

"Look how pretty he is," exclaimed Fanny, who was very proud of her new acquisition; and she forced Gaussin to admire the firm forehead, the refined and delicate features, notwithstanding the peasant tint, that perfection of shape, the stout arms, the legs of a little fawn, long and sinewy, already covered with downy hair. She quite forgot herself while contemplating this infantine beauty.

"Cover him now, or he will be cold," said Jean, whose voice made her start as if from a dream, and while she tucked him up tenderly, the lad heaved long, sobbing sighs, a murmur of despair, notwithstanding that he slept.

In the night he began to talk to himself, "Guerlaude me, Ménine."

"What does he say? Listen."

He wanted to be guerlaude, whatever that signified in his *patois*. Jean at this venture extended his arm, and began to rock the heavy cot. By degrees the lad became quieter, and went to sleep again, holding in his little fat and dimpled fist the hand which he fancied belonged to his Ménine, who had died a fortnight before.

He was like a wild-cat in the house, which scratched and bit, eating his meals alone, with growlings when any one came near his trencher. The few words which they could get him to speak were in the barbarous tongue of the Morvandian wood-cutters, which no one could have understood without the assistance of the Hettemas, who came from the same district. However, by dint of care and gentleness, they managed to tame him a little, "un pso," as he would have said. He consented to change his ragged garments for warm clean clothes, the sight of which made him first yell with rage, as if he were a jackal being clothed in a greyhound's coat. He learned to eat at table, to use his fork and spoon, and to reply when they asked his name, that in his own country, "i li dision Josaph."

As for giving him the least ideas of the most elementary education it was not to be thought of yet. Brought up in the depths of a wood, in a charcoal burner's hut, the murmur of a rustling and swarming nature surged through his brain like the noise of the sea in a shell, and there were no means of getting anything else into his head. Neither could they keep him in the house, even in the most severe weather.

In the rain and snow, when the leafless trees stood out like frosted coral branches, he would escape, range through the bushes, and explore the rabbit burrows with the clever cruelty of a ferret; and when he came home again, faint with hunger, he always carried with him in his ragged fustian vest, or in the pocket of his little trousers, begrimed with mud to the waist, some dead or stupefied animal—a bird, a mole, or a field-mouse—or, in default, some beet-root or potatoes, which he had dug up in the fields.

Nothing could overcome this poaching and plundering instinct, which was complicated by a stupid mania for hiding all kinds of glittering objects, such as brass buttons, jet beads, and tinfoil, which Josaph would seize and carry off to his magpie-like hiding-place. All this plunder he designated vaguely as food, and neither reasoning nor beating could prevent him from getting this food at the expense of everything and everybody.

Only the Hettemas could keep him in order, for the draughtsman kept within reach of his hand on the table around which the young savage would prowl, attracted by the compasses and colored pencils, a dog-whip, with which he flipped the lad's legs. But neither Jean nor Fanny would have used such means, although the lad showed himself toward them sullen and defiant, unappeasable even by tenderness, as if his Ménine when dying had deprived him of all demonstration of affection. Fanny, "because she smelt nice," succeeded now and then in keeping him on her knees for awhile, while toward Gaussin, who was nevertheless very gentle with him, he was always the same wild animal, with defiant look and extended claws, as he had been at first.

This invincible and almost instinctive repulsion of the child, the curious malice of his little blue eyes with white lashes, and above all the blind and sudden tenderness of Fanny for this strange lad who had tumbled so suddenly into their life, aroused anew the suspicions of her lover. It was perhaps a child of hers brought up by a nurse or at her stepmother's house, and the death of Machaume, which they heard of about this time, seemed a coincidence that justified his suspicions. Sometimes during the night when he was holding the little hand clasped in his own—for the child in his sleep believed always he was holding Ménine—he would ask, "Where do you come from? Who are you?" hoping to divine by the communication of heat with the little being, the mystery of his birth.

But his uneasiness disappeared at a word from Père Legrand, who came to ask them to help pay for his wife's funeral, and who called out to his daughter when he saw Josaph's cot:

"Hello! a young 'un! You ought to be happy now. You could never manage to get one."

Gaussin was so delighted, that he paid the expenses of the funeral, without asking to see the bill, and made old Legrand stay to breakfast.

Employed on the tramway between Paris and Versailles, full of wine and apoplexy but always lusty and looking respectable under his hat of polished leather, with his heavy band of crape, which made it a regular mute's hat, the old coachman appeared delighted with the reception accorded him by his daughter's young man, and from time to time he came to take a snack with him. His white pantaloons, hair falling over his shaven and blotched face, his tipsy haughtiness, the respect which he bore his whip, attitudinizing with it, placing it carefully in a corner as a nurse would a child, all this impressed the little lad very much, and they became great friends. One day when they were all finishing dinner the Hettemas came in unexpectedly.

"Ah! I beg your pardon," said madame, "a family party, I see," and the words struck Jean, in the face as it were, as humiliating as a blow.

His family! This foundling, who was rubbing his head on the tablecloth, that old ruffian, his pipe in the corner of his mouth, explaining in his hoarse voice for the hundredth time that two pennyworth of whip-cord lasted him six months, and he had not changed his whip-handle for twenty years. His family indeed! no more than his wife was that Fanny Legrand who was getting old and worn out, and now leaning on her elbows amid the smoke of her cigarettes. Before another year was out, all this would have disappeared from his life just as do the acquaintances one meets when travelling, and at the *table d'hôte.*

But at other times the idea of separation which he invoked as an excuse for his weakness when he felt himself drawn downwards and sinking, this idea instead of reassuring and solacing him, made him feel the numerous chains that were closing around him. What an uprooting this departure would be! Not one separation but ten; and what would it cost him to let fall the child's little hand which was at night inclosed in his own? Even to La Balue, the oriole, whistling and singing in his cage that was always going to be changed as it was too small or him, and in which his back was bent ike the old Cardinal in his iron prison—es, La Balue himself occupied a little

corner of his heart, and it would be painful to pluck him away from it.

This inevitable separation was approaching nevertheless, and the glorious month of June, when all nature was so gay, would probably be the last which they would ever pass together. Was it this that made her nervous and irritable, or was it the education of Josaph, undertaken with sudden ardor, to the great annoyance of the little Morvandian, who would remain for hours over his letters without looking at them or pronouncing them, his face as firmly set as the bars of a farmyard door? From day to day this woman's character developed itself in violence, and in tears, in scenes continually renewed, although Gaussin made every allowance for her; but she was so insulting, and there rose from her anger such spitefulness and hatred against the youth of her lover, against his education, his family, the separation which life would increase between them; she understood so well how to touch him on his tenderest points that he ended by losing control of himself and answering her in return.

Only in his anger he maintained a reserve; the compassion of a man well brought up; blows which he would not inflict as being too severe and to the point, while she launched forth in all the rage of a common girl without responsibility or modesty, making a weapon of everything, and spying out on the face of her victim with a cruel joy the suffering she inflicted; then all at once falling into his arms and imploring his pardon.

The countenances of the Hettemas, witnesses of these quarrels, which almost always broke forth at table at the moment they sat down, and when the soup was uncovered, or the meat being carved, was a picture. They exchanged a look of comic terror across the table. Would they be able to dine, or would the leg of mutton go flying into the garden, with the dish, the gravy, and the haricot stew?

"Now mind, no disturbance," they would say each time there was a question of taking a meal together; and it was with this understanding that they accepted an invitation to breakfast together in the forest, which Fanny had given them one Sunday over the wall. Oh, no! there would be no disputing that day, it was too fine. And she ran off to dress the child and to pack the basket.

They were all ready and about to start when the postman brought a registered letter, and kept Gaussin back to sign the receipt. He rejoined the party at the entrance of the wood, and said to Fanny in an undertone:

"It is from uncle; he is delighted. A splendid crop sold on the spot. He sends back the eight thousand francs you borrowed from Dechelette, with many compliments and thanks to his niece."

"Yes; his niece in the Gascon style. The old fool! Let him be," said Fanny, who did not preserve any feelings for uncles from the south; then in a joyful tone she added:

"We must invest this money."

He looked at her in astonishment, having always known her to be very scrupulous in money matters.

"Invest it; but it is not yours!"

"Well, the fact is, I never told you—" She blushed with that look that bore witness to the slightest deviation from the truth. That good fellow, Deche-

lette having learned what they were doing for Josaph, had written to her to say that the money would assist them to bring up the lad. "But if that annoys you, you know, you can send the eight thousand francs back to him. He is in Paris."

The voices of the Hettemas, who discreetly had gone on in front, resounded under the trees.

"To the right or the left?"

"To the right; to the right—toward the ponds," cried Fanny; then to her lover she said, "Look here, you are not going to give way to your absurd suspicions again; we have kept house too long for that."

She knew very well the significance of that trembling pallor of the lips, that glance at the child taking him in from head to foot; but this time there was a very small eruption of jealous violence. By this time he had become cowardly from habit, and made concessions for the sake of peace. "What is the use of torturing myself to get to the bottom of things? If this child is hers, what more natural than she should keep it, hiding the truth from me, after all the scenes and questions to which I have made her submit? Is it not better to accept the fact, and to pass the few months that remain to us in peace?"

And so he went along the undulating paths through the wood, carrying their breakfast in the heavy basket, covered with a white cloth, resigned, weary, his back bent like an old gardener; while before him walked the mother and the child, Josaph very awkward in a Sunday suit, purchased ready made at La Belle Jardinière—a suit which prevented him from running about; she attired in a bright-colored, loose-fitting gown, her head and neck bare, beneath a Japanese umbrella; her form somewhat stout, her walk languid, and in her beautiful wavy hair a large grey lock, which she no longer took the trouble to hide.

In front and below them the Hettemas had disappeared down the sloping path, wearing immense straw hats, like those of the Touareg horsemen, clothed in red flannel and laden with eatables, fishing tackle, nets, etc., and the wife, to save her husband, was bravely carrying across her chest the enormous hunting-horn, without which the draughtsman found it impossible to go into the forest. As they proceeded the pair sang:

"J'aime entendre la rame
Le soir battre les flots;
J'aime le cerf qui brame."

The repertory of Olympe was inexhaustible as regarded these common sentimental ditties, and when one pictures to oneself how she had collected them, in what shameful half lights, to how many men she had sung them, the serenity of the husband accompanying her seemed most extraordinary. The remark of the grenadier at Waterloo: "Ils sont trop—" must have been that of the philosophical indifference of this man.

While Gaussin, in an abstracted manner, was watching the stout couple plunging into the valley which he himself was entering in their tracks, the grinding of wheels ascending the walk with a peal of childish laughter of infantine voices were heard, and suddenly there appeared, a few paces from him, a number of young girls, their ribbons and hair waving in the breeze,

seated in a donkey chaise, which a young girl scarcely older than her companions was guiding along the rough road.

It was easy to see that Jean made one of the party whose curious appearance—particularly that of the stout woman girt with the hunting-horn—had awakened the undisguised merriment of the young people, so the young girl tried to silence them for a moment. But this new Touareg had let loose their merriment louder than ever, and when passing before the man who stood aside to let the chaise pass, a pretty and somewhat embarrassed smile begged pardon, and naïvely expressed itself astonished to find the old gardener had so pleasant and so young a face.

He raised his hat timidly and blushed with shame, he knew not why, and the chaise stopping at the top of the slope at the cross-roads, while a chorus of little voices read on the finger-post the half-obliterated names *Route des Etangs, Chêne du grand Veneur, Fausses Reposes, Chemin de Vélizy*, Jean turned round to see disappear in the green alley spangled with the sunlight, and carpeted with moss on which the wheels ran as upon velvet, this whirlwind of fair youth, this chaise-load of happiness in spring garb, in the midst of peals of laughter which echoed through the branches.

Hettema's horn furiously blown aroused him suddenly from his reverie. The party were seated on the border of the pond, and were busy unpacking the baskets, and from a distance the white cloth on the level grass, and the jackets of red flannel glaring amid the greenery like huntsmen's coats, could be seen reflected in the clear water.

"Now make haste, you have got the

lobster," cried the stout man; then came the sharp voice of Fanny.

"Was it the little Bouchereau who stopped you on the road?"

Jean started at the name of Bouchereau, which carried him back to Castelet, to the bedside of his sick mother.

"Yes, indeed," said the draughtsman, taking the basket out of his hands, "the tall girl who was leading the chaise is the Doctor's niece, his brother's daughter, whom they have taken to live with them. They stay at Vélizy during the summer—she is pretty?"

"Oh, pretty? Impudent-looking, rather," and Fanny, who was cutting the bread, looked sharply at her lover, feeling uneasy at his absent expression.

Madame Hettema, very grave, unpacking the ham, began to blame very much this fashion of allowing young ladies to roam through the woods at will. "You may tell me that it is the English custom, and that the girl was brought up in London, but all the same it is not conventional."

"No, but very convenient for adventures."

"Oh, Fanny!"

"I beg your pardon; I was forgetting. Monsieur believes in innocent girls."

"Well, let us have our lunch," said Hettema, who was getting alarmed. But Fanny found it necessary to state all that she knew about young ladies of fashion. She had some nice stories about them—the convents, the boarding schools, all so very proper! Girls left them *blasée* and exhausted, with a distaste for men's society, and so on. "And then they are given to you, you set of simpletons—an innocent girl! as if there were any innocent girls—as if, fashionable or not fashionable, all girls

did not know from their birth how certain things happen. As far as I am concerned, when I was twelve years old, I had nothing more to learn, nor you either, Olympe, eh?"

"Naturally," said Madame Hettema, with a shrug of her shoulders, but the fate of the breakfast made her anxious, especially when she heard Gaussin, who was losing his temper, declare that there were young girls and young girls, and that one could find still in families—

"Ah, ah, yes, in families," retorted his mistress in a contemptuous air, "let us talk of them, of yours, especially."

"Hold your tongue; I forbid you to—"

"Bumpkin!"

"Hussy! Fortunately this will soon end. I have not long to live with you."

"Go get out. I shall be delighted."

They were openly insulting each other thus before the child who was lying flat upon the grass, when a fearful trumpet blast, echoed a hundredfold by the pond in the sloping wood, suddenly overcame their quarrel.

"Have you had enough? Would you like some more?" And fat Hettema, with red face and swollen neck, having only this means of silencing the pair, waited with the mouthpiece to his lips and the bell of the horn threatening them.

CHAPTER IX

LOW DIVANS

As a rule their disputes did not last long, dispersed by a little music or by Fanny's coaxing, but on this occasion he was seriously annoyed with her, and for many days afterwards he preserved the same gloomy exterior, and the same offended silence, seating himself at his drawing immediately after meals, and refusing to go out with her at all.

A sudden feeling of shame came upon him at the degradation in which he was living, the fear of meeting again the little chaise coming up the path, and the pure youthful smile which constantly recurred to him. Then with the indistinctness of a departing dream, of a changing scene in a fairy extravaganza, the apparition became indistinct, lost itself in the wooded distance, and Jean saw it no more. Only the feeling of sadness remained, and of which Fanny, believing she knew the cause, resolved to ascertain the truth.

"It is done," she said to him joyfully one day. "I have seen Dechelette, and have paid him the money. He agrees with you that it is better thus, though I want to know why. However, it is done. Later on, when I am alone, he will consider the child. Are you satisfied? Are you still angry with me?"

And she told him of her visit to the Rue de Rome; her astonishment at finding there instead of the noisy house full of delirious acquaintances, a most respectable, peaceful mansion, most strictly guarded. No more galas, no more masked balls; and the explanation of the change was to be found in these words, chalked on the gate leading to the studio by some parasite, angry at being refused admission: "Fermé pour cause de collage."

"And this is the truth, my dear. Dechelette, on his arrival, was smitten by Alice Doré, a girl at the skating rink, and has been keeping her there for a month—a very nice, gentle little woman, a pretty lamb. They scarcely make a sound between them. I promised that we would go and see them; it will be a little change for us from the hunting horn and the ballads. Philosophy, with its theories, it's all one. No to-morrow, no entanglement. Ah, didn't I tease him!"

Jean allowed her to take him to Dechelette's house. He had not met the owner since their conversation by the Madeleine. He would have been very much surprised if any one had told him that he would come down to meet, without disgust, this cynical and disdainful lover of his mistress, and become almost his friend. At his very first visit he was astonished to find himself so much at his ease; charmed by the gentleness of this man with his childish laugh, in his Cossack's beard, and with a serenity of temperament which not even his bilious attacks, which turned his face and eyes to a leaden color, could alter.

And how well they understood the affection which he inspired in this Alice Doré—a girl with long, soft, white hands, of insignificant, fair beauty, which set off the brilliancy of her Flemish skin, as golden as her name. There was gold in her hair, in her eyes, in her eyelids, gilding the skin even under her nails. Picked up by Dechelette from the asphalt of the skating-rink, amidst the gross and brutal remarks and the clouds of smoke of the libertine crowd, his politeness had touched and surprised her. She felt herself a woman again, no longer the poor waif and stray she had been, and when he was about to dismiss her next day, she pleaded so sweetly, so humbly, "let me stay longer," that he did not have the courage to refuse her. Since then half from humanity, half from laziness, he kept his door closed on this accidental honeymoon, which he passed in the freshness and calm of his summer place, so well arranged for comfort; and they lived thus very happily— she the object of a tender care which she had never hitherto known, he in the happiness which he was conferring upon this poor creature, and in her naïve gratitude; also being influenced without understanding how, and for the first time, by the insinuating charm of a woman's intimate society, the mysterious magic of an existence together, in a union of goodness and sweetness.

For Gaussin the studio in the Rue de Rome was a diversion from the low, mean level in which his life was passing like that of a small clerk in similar circumstances. He liked the conversation of this clever man of artistic tastes, of this philosopher in the Persian robe as light and loose as his teaching, those recitals of his travels, which Dechelette sketched in the fewest possible words, were quite in keeping amongst the oriental hangings, the gilt Buddhas, the bronze monsters, the exotic luxury of that immense hall, to which the daylight entered through a lofty glazed roof, the true light of wooded depths, agitated by the graceful foliage of the bamboos, the serrated, palm-like leaves of the tree ferns, and the enormous leaves of the strilligias, mingled with phi!odendrons, as thin and flexible as water plants, seeking shade and humidity.

On Sunday particularly, in the large bay window looking upon the summer-deserted streets of Paris, the rustling of the leaves, the smell of the fresh earth around the plants, it seemed to be almost as much the country and the wood as at Chaville, less the promiscuousness and the horn of the Hettemas.

No people ever came there. On one occasion, however, Gaussin and his mistress coming to dinner, heard in the hall the sound of animated voices. Day was closing, people were drinking *raki* in the conservatory, and the discussion seemed to be lively.

"And I think that five years of Mazas, a lost name, life ruined, is paying dearly enough for one act of passion and folly. I will sign your petition Dechelette."

"It is Caoudal," said Fanny in a whisper, tremblingly.

Some one replied with the dry snappishness of a refusal. "For my part sign nothing, accepting no liability with the fellow."

"La Gournerie now." And Fanny pressing against her lover, murmured "Let us go if it will annoy you to see them."

"Why so? Not at all." In fact, he scarcely could realize what he would feel when he found himself face to face with these men, but he did not wish to shrink from the test, desirous perhaps to know the actual degree of the jealousy which had been the cause of his miserable love.

"Come along," he said, and they presented themselves in the rosy light of declining day which illuminated the bald heads and the grizzly beards of Dechelette's friends, reclining on low divans round an oriental table, on which was trembling in five or six glasses the aniseed-flavored and milky liquor which Alice was dispensing. The women embraced each other. "You know the gentlemen, Gaussin?" asked Dechelette with a lazy wave of his hand from his rocking-chair.

Did he know them? Two of them at least were familiar to him in consequence of his having studied their portraits for hours in the shop windows. How they had made him suffer! How he had hated them with a successor's hatred, a raging desire to spring upon them and to gnaw their faces when he met them in the street. But Fanny had truly said that the feeling would pass away; now they were to him as faces of acquaintances, almost of relatives, uncles from a distance whom he met again.

"Good-looking as ever, young fellow," said Caoudal, stretched at all his giant length and holding a screen above his eyes to shade them, "and Fanny, let me see," he raised himself on his elbow and examined her critically. "The face has lasted, but the figure! You must lace tighter; after all you may console yourself, my girl, La Gournerie is even fatter than you are."

The poet curled his thin lips disdainfully, seated cross-legged on a pile of cushions—since his journey to Algeria he pretended he could sit no other way—fat and pasty-looking, having no intelligence in his appearance, with the exception of his massive forehead beneath a forest of white hair, and his sharp overseer's glance; he affected a fashionable reserve, an exaggerated politeness towards Fanny, as if to read Caoudal a lesson.

Two landscape painters, with bronzed and rustic faces, completed the party. They also knew Jean's mistress, and the younger of the two as he shook her hand said:

"Dechelette has told us the history of the child, it is very nice of you to behave so, my dear."

"Yes," said Caoudal to Gaussin. "Yes; very smart indeed that adoption. Nothing at all provincial about it."

She seemed embarrassed by this praise, when some one knocked against a piece of furniture in the darkened studio and a voice asked, "Who's there?"

Dechelette said, "It is Ezano."

Jean had never seen him, but he knew what place this Bohemian, this fanciful fellow, now married, a leader in the *Beaux Arts*, had held in Fanny's existence, and he remembered a packet of passionate and charmingly written letters. A little sunken-faced, shriveled man came forward, stiffly giving his hand at arm's length, keeping people at a distance by his platform manner and administrative style. He appeared very much surprised to see Fanny, and particularly to find her looking so pretty after such a lapse of time.

"Why, Sapho!" and a faint blush tinged his cheeks.

This name of Sapho, which recalled the past and reminded her of all her old friends, caused a certain awkwardness.

"And M. d'Armandy, who has brought her here," said Dechelette quickly, to warn the new arrival. Ezano bowed and began to talk. Fanny reassured, when she saw how her lover was taking things, and proud of him, his good looks, his youth, before these artists and connoisseurs, became very gay and cheerful. Having relinquished herself entirely to her present passion, she scarcely remembered her former relations with these men, which for all that had imprinted on her habits and fancies, gained in contact with them, which survived in her even to the fashion she had of rolling cigarettes, as well as her preference for a certain cigarette paper and Maryland tobacco.

Jean perceived, without feeling the least trouble this small detail, which formerly would have enraged him, and felt, at finding himself so calm, the joy of a prisoner who has filed through his chain, and knows that the slightest effort will suffice to free him.

"Ah! my poor Fanny!" said Caoudal, in a quizzical tone, and pointing at the others, "see what a falling off is there. Are they not old? are they not worn out? You and I, you see, are the only good ones left."

Fanny laughed. "Ah, pardon, Colonel"—she called him that sometimes because of his moustaches—"it is not quite the same thing. I am of a later date."

"Caoudal always forgets that he is of a past age," said La Gournerie, and, noticing a movement of the sculptor, whom he knew he was touching to the quick, continued in his sharp voice, "Medallist in 1840. There's a date, my good fellow!"

There existed between these two old friends a tone of aggression, a sulky antipathy, which had never separated them, but which had been evident in their looks, in their slightest words, for the last twenty years, ever since the day on which the poet had carried off the sculptor's mistress. Fanny counted for nothing with them now. They had both sought other joys, felt other pain; but the antagonism still lived, growing deeper and deeper, as time rolled on.

"Now look at us both, and say frankly whether I am the more ancient." Tightly buttoned up in a jacket which displayed his muscles, Caoudal planted himself upright, thrusting out his chest

and shaking his flaming locks, in which was not one white hair.

"Medallist in 1840; fifty-eight years old in three months. Well, what does that prove? Is it age that makes a man old? It is only at the Comédie Française or at the Conservatoire that men are tottering at sixty, nodding their heads and pottering about with feeble limbs and shuffling gait. At sixty —sacré bleu!—one walks more upright than at thirty, because one is cautious, and the women take to one still if the heart is young, and warms and animates the body."

"Do you believe that?" said La Gournerie, with a sneer, and looking at Fanny. And Dechelette, with his cheerful smile, said:

"Nevertheless, you are always saying there is nothing like youth, you swear by it."

"It was my little Cousinard who made me alter my opinion. She is my new model. Eighteen years old; plump and dimpled all over—a Clodion. And she is such a good child, one of the people, and of the Paris markets, where her mother sells chickens. She says such silly things, you could almost embrace her for them. The other day in the studio she found a novel of Dejoie's; looking at the title—Thérèse—she threw it away with a little pout, saying, 'If that had been called Poor Thérèse I would have read it all night.' I am quite gone on her, I can tell you."

"So you are in for it again. In six months there will be another separation—tears, work distasteful, desperate rages, ready to kill everybody."

Caoudal's brow clouded.

"It is true that nothing lasts. One takes somebody and one separates."

"Why do you take any one then?"

"Well, and you yourself, do you think you are joined together for life with your Flemish woman?"

"Oh, we—we have not gone in for regular housekeeping. Eh, Alice?"

"Certainly not," replied, in a soft and gentle voice, the young girl, who, mounted on a chair, was gathering some wisteria and leaves for the table. Dechelette continued:

"There will be no rupture in our case, scarcely a leave-taking. We made an agreement for two months. On the last day of the term we shall part, without despair and without surprise. I shall return to Ispaham. I have just engaged my sleeping-car berth, and Alice will return to her little apartment in the Rue Labruyère, which she still retains."

"On the third floor above the entresol, which is the most convenient for throwing oneself out of the window."

The young girl smiled as she said this; her face was flushed, the light of the dying day was upon her, the heavy bunch of mauve flowers in her hand, but the tone of her voice was so sad and grave that nobody replied to it. The wind freshened, the houses opposite seemed to be higher.

"Let us go to dinner," cried the Colonel, "and let us talk nonsense."

"Yes, that's the thing. *Gaudeamus igitur.* Let us amuse ourselves while we are young. Isn't that right, Caoudal?" said La Gournerie with a laugh that had a false ring in it.

Jean some days afterward was passing down the Rue de Rome again, when he found the studio closed, the great canvas awning let down over the window, and a mournful silence reigning from the cellar to the terraced roof.

Dechelette had gone at the hour agreed upon. The agreement had come to an end, and Gaussin thought what a fine thing it is to do as one please in life—to rule one's reason and one's heart. "Shall I ever have the courage to do so?"

Just then a hand was placed upon his shoulder.

"Good-day, Gaussin."

Dechelette, looking fatigued, more yellow and more frowning than usual, explained to him that he had not yet departed, being detained in Paris by some business, that he was staying at the Grand Hotel, having a horror of the studio ever since that dreadful accident.

"What was that?"

"Don't you really know? Alice is dead—she committed suicide. Wait for me till I see whether there are any letters for me."

He returned almost immediately, and while he tore the newspaper wrappers asunder with nervous fingers, he spoke in a dreamy way like a somnambulist, without looking at Gaussin, who was walking beside him.

"Yes, she is dead—threw herself from the window, as she said she would that evening you were there. How could it have been prevented? I knew nothing about it. I had no idea of such a thing. On the day on which I intended to start she said to me, in a quiet way, 'Take me, Dechelette; do not leave me alone —I cannot live without you.' That made me laugh. Just fancy me with a woman over there amongst the Kurds— the desert, the fever, the nights of bivouac! At dinner she kept saying to me: 'I shall not worry you; you shall see how quiet I shall be.' Then, seeing that she only gave me pain, she desisted. Afterward we went together to a box at the Varieties, which had all been arranged beforehand. She appeared contented, held my hand all the time, and murmured, 'I am happy.' As I was going to leave at night I took her to her rooms in my carriage, but we were both sad and did not speak. She did not even thank me for the little packet which I slipped into her pocket that contained enough to enable her to live for a year or two When we reached the Rue Labruyère she asked me to go upstairs. I would not. 'I beg you to do so, if only to the door.' But I was firm, and would not enter. My place was taken, my luggage was packed, and then, I had said 'Good-bye' too often already. As I went down, feeling my heart somewhat bigger than usual, she called after me some words which sounded like 'Quicker than you,' but I did not understand them till I reached the street, when, oh! . . ."

He stopped, his eyes bent upon the ground before the horrible vision which the pavement now presented to him at every step—an inert, groaning black mass.

"She died two hours afterward without a word, without a complaint, her golden eyes fixed on me to the last. Did she suffer? Did she recognize me? We laid her on her bed just as she was, a large lace mantilla covering her head on one side to hide the wound on the skull. Very pale, with a little blood on her temple, she was still pretty—so sweet-looking. But as I bent over her to wipe away that drop of blood which always returned as if inexhaustible, her gaze seemed to me to assume an indignant and terrible expression—a mute male-diction which the poor girl hurled at me. Now what would it have mattered to me if I had remained a little longer, or had taken her with me, ready for anything, and so little in the way? No, it was pride, the obstinacy of my passed word. Well, I did not give way, and she is dead. Dead for me who loved her, too."

He was growing excited, speaking in a loud voice, and gazed at in astonishment by the people he pushed against as they went down the Rue d'Amsterdam; and Gaussin, passing before his former lodgings with its balcony and verandah, thought of Fanny and their own history, and shuddered while Dechelette continued:

"I followed her to Montparnasse, without any friends or relatives. I wished to be the only one to think about her, and here I have been since thinking of the same thing, not being able to make up my mind to go away with this ever-present idea, and avoiding my house in which I passed two months so happily with her. I live out of doors, I move about, I try to distract myself, to escape from that eye of death which accuses me under that blood-stained brow."

And stopping, struck by remorse—two great tears rolled down his little flat nose, so good-natured, so fond of life—he said, "Well, my friend, nevertheless I am not wicked, but it was a little too much for me to have done such a thing."

Jean tried to console him, attributing it all to chance and bad luck, but Dechelette repeated, shaking his head and with clenched teeth:

"No, no. I shall never forgive ny

self—I should like to punish myself for it."

This wish for expiation did not cease to haunt him; he talked of it to all his friends, to Gaussin, for whom he would call at his office when his work was done.

"You must go away somewhere, Dechelette; travel, work, that will distract your mind," Caoudal and the others would keep saying to him, for they became uneasy at his fixed idea, at his morbid wish to make them repeat that he was not wicked. At length one evening, either he wished to see his studio again before going away, or some idea to put an end to his trouble led him there, he entered his house again, and in the morning some workmen on their way through the street picked him up from the pavement before his door, his skull split, having killed himself in the same way as the woman; and with the same terrors, under the same crushing influence of despair, flung himself into the street!

In the dimly lighted studio a crowd thronged—artists, models, actresses, all the dancers, all the supper-eaters of his latest *fêtes*. There was a noise of shuffling feet, of whispering, murmurs as in a chapel under the flames of the tapers, people were looking through the creepers and the leaves, at the body, stretched at full length, wrapped in a flowered silk covering, crowned with a turban to conceal the wound on the head; the white hands in front spoke of abandonment, the final release, on the low divan shaded by wisteria, on which Gaussin and his mistress had first become acquainted with each other on the night of the ball.

CHAPTER X

A CAUSE FOR ESCAPE

PEOPLE do die, then, of such separations. So now when he and Fanny quarrelled he did not dare to speak of his departure; he no longer exclaimed angrily, "Fortunately there will soon be an end of this;" she had only to reply, "Very well then, go; I shall kill myself as the other girl did." And this menace, which he fancied he could perceive in the melancholy of her looks, in the songs she sang, and in her silent reveries, troubled him to the verge of apprehension.

Nevertheless he managed to pass the examination for consular *attachés*, the ministerial stage; well recommended, he was noted for one of the first vacant appointments, which was only a matter of a few weeks—of days. And around them, at this end of the sunny season, everything was hastening towards winter. One morning Fanny, opening the window to the first mist, exclaimed:

"Why, the swallows have gone!"

One after the other the tradespeople's country houses were closed. Along the Versailles road furniture vans followed each other in rapid succession, large omnibuses loaded with packages, with plumes of green plants on the "knife-board;" while the leaves on the ground were agitated by whirlwinds, tossed about like clouds under the leaden sky; and the stacks rose in the bared fields. Behind the orchard, now almost leafless, and looking smaller in consequence, the closed cottages, the drying grounds of the laundries with red-tiled roofs, stood out in clusters in the melancholy landscape, and on the other side of the house the railway, now fully visible, extended its dark lines through the gray-tinted woods.

How cruel it was to leave her alone all day in such a wretched place. He felt already relenting—he never would have courage to separate from her. It was no doubt on this that she was counting, waiting for the supreme moment, and till then quiet, not referring to it, faithful to her promise not to put obstacles in the way of his departure so long foreseen and agreed to. One day he came home with the news:

"I am nominated."

"Ah! to what place?"

She asked the question with an assumption of indifference, but with bloodless lips and vacant eyes, and with such a contraction of her features that he could not keep her in suspense. "No, no, I am not going yet. I have relinquished my turn to Hedouin; that will give us another six months at least."

Then succeeded an outburst of tears, of laughter, of foolish kisses, while she murmured, "Thank you, thank you; what a happy life I will make yours now! It was the idea of your departure that made me naughty, you know." She would now make up her mind to it, resign herself to it by degrees. And then in six months it would not be autumn, with all its miserable associations of decay.

She kept her word. No more attacks of "nerves," no more quarrels; and even to avoid the worry caused by the child, she decided to send him to school at Versailles. He only came home on Sunday, and if this new arrangement did not tame his rebellious, savage nature, it at least taught him hypocrisy. They lived peacefully, the dinners with the Hettemas were eaten without any disturbance, and the piano was once again opened for their favorite songs. But at heart Jean was more troubled, more perplexed than ever; questioning himself as to whither his weakness was leading him; thinking sometimes that he would relinquish his consulate and pass his service in the office. It meant Paris, and the housekeeping with Fanny indefinitely prolonged; but also the dream of his youth and the hope of his relatives shattered, his undoubted disinheritance by his father, who would never forgive him for throwing up his profession, especially when he became acquainted with the cause.

And for whom? For an elderly, faded woman, whom he no longer cared for! Of this he had had a proof in face of her lovers. What witchcraft confined him then, in this life à deux!

As he got into the train one morning in the last days of October the eyes of a young lady which met his recalled to him suddenly the meeting in the wood; the radiant grace of the girl-woman of whom the remembrance had haunted him for months. She was wearing the same bright-colored dress which the sun had touched so prettily through the branches of the trees, but now shrouded in a travelling cloak; and in the compartment, the books, the small bag, a bouquet of tall reeds and late autumn flowers, told of the return to Paris and the end of the sojourn in the country. She also recognized him with a half smile quivering in her limpid eyes, and there was for a second the unexpressed understanding of the same thought in both minds.

"How is your mother, Monsieur d'Armandy?" suddenly asked old Bouchereau, whom Jean, surprised, had not at first noticed as he reclined in the corner reading, his pale face bent down.

Jean told him the news very much touched by the remembrance of his relatives and of himself, and still more affected when the young lady inquired for the twins who had written such a pretty letter to her uncle, thanking him for the care of their mother. She knew them! the idea filled him with joy. Then, as it seemed, he was more than usually sentimental that morning, he immediately became sad on learning that his friends were returning to Paris, as Bouchereau was about to recommence his lectures at the School of Medicine. He would not have the chance to see her again; and the fields lying past him, so golden a moment before, now seemed dreary and in the semi-darkness of an eclipse.

There was a long whistling—they had reached Paris. He said "Good-bye" and left them, but at the exit from the station they met again, and Bouchereau in the crowd told him that after the following Thursday he would be at home in the Place Vendôme if he wished for a cup of tea. She took her uncle's arm, and it seemed to Jean that it was she who without speaking had invited him.

After having decided many times that he would go to Bouchereau's house, and having changed his mind—or why cause himself useless regrets?—he hinted nevertheless at home that there would soon be a grand evening party at the Ministry at which he was compelled to be present. Fanny looked over his dress, ironed his white ties, but suddenly on the Thursday evening she did not have the least wish to leave

home. But his mistress put before him the necessity of undergoing the infliction, reproached herself for having taken up so much of his time, and for being so selfish, so she decided him. She playfully helped him to dress, retouched the knot of his tie, the fashion of his hair, laughed because her fingers smelt of the cigarette which she took up and replaced upon the chimney every moment, and said it would cause his partners to make faces. Seeing her so gay and good-natured, he felt some remorse for the deception he was practicing, and would willingly have remained at home if Fanny had not insisted on his going, and pushed him out affectionately into the road.

It was late when he came back. She was asleep, and the lamp which revealed this tired slumber recalled to him a similar occasion three years before, after the terrible revelations which he had heard from her. What a coward he had shown himself then! By what want of sense had the fact which should have broken this chain riveted it more tightly? He felt absolutely sick and disgusted. The room, the bed, the woman, were all equally distasteful to him; he took the light and carried it into the next room softly. He wished so much to be alone, to think over what had happened to him. Oh! nothing; or almost nothing!

He was in love.

There is in certain words which we continually use a hidden spring which suddenly opens them down to the ground, as it were; explains them to us in all their exceptionable inner meaning, then the word folds itself up again, regains its everyday form and insignificant appearance worn out by habitual and mechanical use. Love is one of these words. Those for whom its depths have been for once entirely unfolded will understand the delicious agony in which Jean had lived for an hour without being able at first to give any account of his sensations.

Yonder in the Place Vendôme, in that corner of the room in which they sat talking for a long while, he was not conscious of anything except of a great happiness, of a soft charm which surrounded him.

It was only when he came away and the door was shut, that he had been seized with a foolish joyfulness, then with a weakness as if all his veins had been opened. "What is the matter with me?" And the portion of Paris which he traversed on his way home seemed to him quite new, fairy-like, more extensive, and altogether radiant.

Yes, at this hour, when the beasts of night are loosed and prowl around, when the filth from the sewers rises up and is apparent under the yellow gaslight, he, the lover of Sapho, an adept in all kinds of debauchery, saw Paris as the young girl returning from a ball with her head full of waltz tunes, which she repeats to the stars, beneath her white apparel may see it, the chaste Paris bathed in moonlight where blossom virgin souls—that was the Paris he saw. And suddenly, as he mounted the wide staircase at the railway terminus on his return to his miserable home, he surprised himself by saying aloud, "But I love her, I love her," and it was thus that he had learned it.

"Are you there, Jean? What are you about?"

Fanny had awakened with a start,

alarmed at not finding him beside her. He must kiss her, lie to her, tell her about the ball at the Ministry, of the pretty dresses, and with whom he had danced; but to escape from this cross questioning, above all from the caresses which he feared, all impregnated as he is with the memory of the other, he invents a press of work, some drawing for Hettema.

"There is no fire—you will catch cold."

"No, no."

"At least leave the door open, that I may see your lamp."

He was obliged to keep up the deception to the end, to set out his diagrams on the table; and then sitting down motionless, holding his breath, he began to think, to recall things; and to fix his dream he relates it to Cesaire in a long letter, while the night wind stirs the branches which creak without any rustling of leaves, while succeeding trains rumble on and La Balue, worried by the light, moves about restlessly in his little cage, leaping from perch to perch with half articulate cries.

He tells everything, the meeting in the wood, in the train, his curious feeling as he entered those rooms which had seemed so melancholy and so tragical on the day of the consultation, with the furtive whisperings in the doorways, the mournful glances exchanged from chair to chair, and which on this evening were thrown open, animated and noisy in one long illuminated suite.

Bouchereau himself no longer appeared so stern, nor had his eye that dark and disconcerting glance under his long and heavy eyebrows, but the quiet and paternal expression of the kind-hearted man who wished to see every-body happy in his house.

"Suddenly she came toward me and I beheld nothing more; her name is Irene; she is pretty, of pleasing appearance, her hair of the English golden brown, a childish mouth, always ready to laugh. Oh, not that joyless laugh which many women have, and which worries one so much, but the real expansion of youth and happiness. She was born in London, but her father was a Frenchman, and she has no accent at all, only a charming way of pronouncing certain words, of saying uncle, which every time makes the eyes of old Bouchereau beam affectionately. He adopted her to relieve his brother, who has a numerous family, in place of her sister who married his chief clinical assistant two years ago, but she, well, does not care about doctors. How she amused me with the folly of that young *savant,* who extracted from his *fiancée* a formal and solemn engagement to bequeath their bodies to the Anthropological Society. She is a bird of passage. She loves ships and the sea, and the sight of a barque going out quite stirs her heart. She told me all this in a very friendly way, quite an English miss in manner, notwithstanding her Parisian grace, and I listened to her, charmed with her voice, her laugh, and with the compatibility of our tastes, with the firm conviction that the happiness of my life was by my side, and that I had to grasp it, to carry it away, far away whithersoever my adventurous career would lead me."

"Won't you come to bed, my own?"

He started, stopped writing, and instinctively hid the letter.

"Directly; go to sleep, go to sleep."

He spoke to her rather angrily, and with back bent he listened for the return of sleep, for they were very near each other, and yet so far!

"Whatever happens, this meeting and this love will be my deliverance. You know what my life is; you understand, though we never talk of it, that it is just the same as it used to be, that I have not been able to release myself. But what you do not know is that I was ready to sacrifice fortune, future, everything to the fatal habits to which I was relinquishing myself every day. Now I have found the spring, the leverage which I wanted, and so as not to give my weakness another opportunity, I have sworn to myself not to present myself yonder except as a free man. To-morrow the escape will be made."

But it was neither the next day nor the following one, there must be a cause for escape, a pretext, the culminating point of a quarrel, when one cries, "I am going away, never to return;" and Fanny conducted herself as sweetly and pleasantly as in the first illusory days of their housekeeping.

Could he write "It is all over" without any further explanation? But this violent woman would never let herself be put away thus; she would seek him out, and beard him on the very door of his hotel, or at his office. No, it would be better to meet the question boldly, to convince her of the irrevocable nature of this separation, and without anger, as without pity, enumerate the reasons for it.

But with these reflections the fear of Alice Doré's suicide came over him. Opposite their house was a lane leading to the railway closed by a swing gate; the neighbors used to take that route when hurried and walk along the lane to the station. And the Southerner's imagination enabled him to see his mistress after the final scene of separation rush out across the road down the lane, and throw herself under the wheels of the train which was carrying him away. This fear oppressed him to such a degree that the mere sight of the swinging gate between the ivy-covered walls caused him to recoil from the explanation.

Still if he had only a friend, some one to look after her and to help her in the first crisis; but buried in their seclusion, like marmots, they knew nobody, and the unhappy woman would not have been able to call to her assistance the Hettemas, those monstrous egotists shining and wading in fat, and brutalized still more by the approach of their esquimaux-like hibernation.

Nevertheless the tie must be broken and broken quickly. In spite of his promise to himself Jean had returned two or three times to the Place Vendôme more and more smitten, and although he had as yet said nothing, the open-armed reception of old Bouchereau, the attitude of Irene, in which reserve was mingled with tenderness and indulgence, and as it seemed the fluttering expectation of a declaration, all warned him not to postpone his intention. Then there was the shamefulness of lying, of the excuses which he had to invent for Fanny, and the species of sacrilege in going from Sapho's kisses to a discreet and hesitating courtship.

CHAPTER XI

SENILITY

In the midst of these distractions he found on his office table a card left by a gentleman who had already called twice that morning as the messenger told him with a certain awe, inspired by the following description:

C. GAUSSIN D'ARMANDY,
President of the Submersionists of the Rhone Valley,
Member of the Central Investigation and Vigilance Committee,
Departmental Delegate, Etc., Etc.

Uncle Cesaire in Paris! Le Fenat a delegate, member of a Vigilance Committee. He had not recovered from his surprise when his uncle appeared, still brown as a pine cone, with his foolish eyes, his laugh in the corners of his temples, his Covenanter's beard; but instead of the Fustian jacket he wore a new cloth frock-coat buttoned over the chest, which gave the little man a truly presidential dignity.

What had brought him to Paris? The purchase of a force pump for the immersion of his new vineyards—he pronounced the word force pump with a conviction which made him seem greater in his own eyes—and also to order his own bust, which his colleague had requested to embellish the council hall.

"You have seen," he added modestly "that they have nominated me president. My idea of submersion has quite revolutionized the South, and t say that it is I, Le Fenat, who am i a fair way to save the vines of France There are no people like the crac brained, you see."

But the principal object of his journey was the separation of his nephew from Fanny. Understanding how the affair would drag on, he came to settle it at a blow. "I know what I am about, you may believe that. When Courbebaisse left his young woman to be married"—but before starting this story he stopped, unbuttoned his frock-coat and drew from it a bulky pocketbook.

"First of all relieve me of this. Why, certainly it is money—the liberation of the territory." He mistook his nephew's gesture, believing that he refused it from motives of delicacy. "Take it now, take it, I am proud to be able to repay to the son a little of what the father did for me—besides Divonne will have it so—she knows all about this business, and is very glad you think of marrying and shaking off your old fetters."

After a service which his mistress had rendered Cesaire, Jean thought this expression "old fetters" rather unjust, and it was with a touch of annoyance that he replied:

"Take back your pocketbook, uncle, you know better than anybody else how indifferent Fanny is to money."

"Yes, she was a good girl," said the uncle in a funeral oration tone. Then he added, winking his crow-footed eyes:

"Just keep the money all the same. With the temptations of Paris about me I would rather it was in your hands than in mine, and one must have it in cases of separation as in duels."

With that he rose, declaring that he was dying of hunger, and that this big question could better be discussed, fork in hand, at breakfast. Always the same frivolity of the Southerner when treating of matters connected with women.

"Between ourselves, my lad"—they were then sitting in a restaurant in the Rue de Bourgogne, and his uncle, a napkin tucked under his chin, was talking while Jean, too harassed to eat, was nibbling at his food—"I think that you take things too tragically. I know very well that the first step is a hard one, the explanation troublesome, but if it be too much for you, don't say anything, do as Courbebaisse did. Up to the morning of his marriage Mornas was in total ignorance of it. In the evening, after he had left the house of his intended, he went to meet the singer at the music hall and took her home. You will tell me this was very irregular and disloyal. But when one dislikes scenes, and has to do with such terrible women as Paola Mornas! For nearly ten years this great big fellow had trembled before this little dark-skinned creature; to rid himself of her he was obliged to be tricky and to manœuvre, and this was how he managed it.

"The day before the marriage, the 15th of August, the fête day, Cesaire proposed to the girl to go fishing with him on the Yvette. Courbebaisse was to join them at dinner, and they were all to return together the next evening, when the smell of dust, fireworks and lamp oil would have evaporated from Paris. All went well. There the two of them were lying on the grass on the bank of the little river, sparkling beneath its low banks, making the meadows so green and the willows so full of leaf. After the fishing came bathing. It was not the first time they had swam together like comrades, but on that day little Mornas, her arms and legs naked, her Maugrabin body molded in her costume as it were, perhaps the idea that Courbebaisse had given him *carte blanche*—Ah, the deceiver! She turned round, and looking at him very straight, said:

" 'Look here, Cesaire, don't try that again.'

"He did not persist for fear of spoiling his plan, and he said to himself, 'Wait until after dinner.'

"The dinner was very merry on the wooden balcony of the inn, between the two flags which the landlord had hoisted in honor of the 15th of August. It was a hot day, the hay smelt sweetly, and they could hear the drums, the crackers, and the music of the singers who were promenading the street.

" 'What a stupid that Courbebaisse is not to come till to-morrow' said La Mornas, who was stretching out her arms and looking as if the champagne had got into her eyes, 'I have a great mind to enjoy myself to-night.'

" 'And so have I.'

"He was leaning by her side over the railing of the balcony, which was still warm after the sunny day, and, slyly, to sound her, he put his arm around her waist: 'Oh! Paola, Paola,' he said. This time instead of getting angry the singer began to laugh, and so loudly and heartily that he could not help joining her. Another attempt, repulsed in the same fashion, in the evening, when they returned from the fair, where they had danced and shot for macaroons, and as their rooms adjoined she sang through the partition, 'You are too small, you are too small,' making all kinds of unkind comparisons between him and Courbebaisse. He had to put a restraint upon himself not to answer and to call her the widow Moras, but it was too soon for that yet. Next

morning he sat down to a good breakfast, but Paola got very impatient and restless at last because her lover did not arrive, and it was with a certain satisfaction that he pulled out his watch and said solemnly:

" 'Twelve o'clock; it is done.'

" 'What is done?'

" 'He is married.'

" 'Who?'

" 'Courbebaisse.'

"Smack!

"Ah, my friend, what a buffet that was! In all my love affairs I never received anything like it. And all of a sudden she was off. But there was no train before four o'clock, and by that time the faithless one was flying over the P. L. M. Railway towards Italy with his wife. Then in her rage she scratched me and rained blows upon me. My luck—I had locked the door; then she took the crockery and smashed it, and at last she fell into a fearful fit of hysterics. At five o'clock they carried her to bed where they kept her, while I, looking as if I had just come out of a bramble bush, ran to fetch the doctor from Orsay. In these affairs, as in a duel, one ought always to have a doctor with one. You can see me on the road, fasting, and that sun! It was night when I brought the doctor back. Suddenly as we approached the inn, we heard the murmur of a crowd which had assembled under the window. Ah, *mon Dieu*, had she committed suicide? She has killed some one perhaps. In her case the latter was the more likely. I rushed forward and what did I see? The balcony hung with Venetian lanterns, and the singer standing there, consoled and superb, wrapped in one of the flags, shouting out the

Marseillaise in the midst of the Imperial Fête above the head of the applauding multitude.

"There, my boy, that is how Courbenaisse's connection ended, but I do not say that it was all over at once. After ten years' penal servitude, one must always expect a little supervision, but I had the worst of it, and I would go through as much from your young woman if you wished."

"Ah! uncle, but she is not the same kind of a woman."

"Nonsense," said Cesaire, opening a box of cigars which he held up to his ear to assure himself that they were dry. "You will not be the first one who has left her."

Jean recovered his composure at this remark, which would have nearly broken his heart a few months previously; in fact, his uncle had somewhat reassured him by his amusing story; but what he could not bring himself to face was the double deceit for months, that hypocrisy, the division of his attention; he could never succeed in that, and had always waited too long.

"Then what do you wish to do?"

While the young man was in this state of uncertainty the member of the Vigilance Committee was stroking his beard, practicing smiles, effects, and poses of the head. Then in a careless way he asked:

"Does he live far from here?"

"Whom do you mean?"

"Why, that artist Caoudal, of whom you spoke to me concerning my bust. We might go and ascertain his price while we are together."

Caoudal, though celebrated and a spendthrift, still occupied the studio in which he had first made a success in the Rue d'Assas. Cesaire as they proceeded inquired concerning his artistic position; he would pay the price certainly, but the committee were determined to have a work of the best kind.

"Oh, you need not be afraid, Uncle, if Caoudal makes up his mind to do it," and he ran over the titles of the sculptor, Member of the Institute, Commander of the Legion of Honor, and a long list of foreign orders. Le Fenat opened his eyes widely.

"And you are friends?"

"Great friends."

"What a place this Paris is! What grand friends one makes here."

Gaussin would have nevertheless felt some shame in confessing that Caoudal was an old lover of Fanny's and that she had brought them together. But it seemed that Cesaire was thinking of this.

"He is the artist of that Sapho which we have at Castelet, isn't he? Then he knows your mistress, and can perhaps aid you to separate from her. The Institute, the Legion of Honor, all those things impress a woman."

Jean did not reply. He was also thinking how he could utilize the influence of the former lover.

And the uncle continued with a loud laugh:

"By the bye, you know the bronze is no longer in your father's room. When Divonne knew, when I had the misfortune to tell her that it represented your mistress, she would not have it there any longer. Considering the Consul's mania, the fuss he makes about the least change, it was not very easy, particularly without letting him suspect the motive. O the woman! she has managed so well that now M. Thiers presides upon your father's chimneypiece, and poor Sapho is seated covered with dust in the Windy Chamber, with the old fire-dogs and disused furniture. Even she suffered some injury in moving, for her chignon and her lyre are broken. The spite of Divonne no doubt brought these evils upon her."

They reached the Rue d'Assas. When he saw the modest and workmanlike appearance of this city of artists, the studios with numbered doors opening upon each side of a long court, bounded by the commonplace buildings of a communal school with its perpetual buzz of reading, the President of the Submersionists began to doubt once more respecting the talent of a man lodged in such an inferior way, but as soon as he had entered Caoudal's studio he knew what was in store for him.

"Not for a hundred thousand francs, not for a million," shouted the sculptor, almost as soon as Gaussin had opened his mouth, and raising by degrees his big body from the divan on which he was lying amid all the disorder and *abandon* of the studio, he said, "A bust —yes—well! but just look at that plaster cast broken into a thousand pieces. My statue for the approaching Exhibition, which I have just demolished with a mallet. That is what I do with sculpture, and however tempting may be the face of Monsieur—"

"Gaussin d'Armandy, President of—"

Uncle Cesaire was going through all his titles, but he had too many of them. Caoudal interrupted, and turning to the young man said:

"You are looking at me, Gaussin, you think me aged."

It is true that he looked all his age in the light which fell from above the scars, the hollows, and the wounds of this worn-out and dissipated face. His manelike hair, showing bald places like an old carpet, his pendent and flaccid cheeks, his moustache of the tone of worn-out gilding, which he no longer took the trouble to curl or to dye. What was the use? Cousinard, the little model, had left him, "Yes, my dear fellow, gone off with my molder—a savage, a brute, but twenty years old!"

With angry and ironical intonation he paced up and down the studio, knocking over a stool in his way. Suddenly he stopped before a mirror hung with flowers which was above the divan, and looked at himself with a frightful grimace: "Am I ugly enough, sufficiently knocked to pieces, as thin and wrinkled as an old cow!" He clasped his neck with his hands, and then in the lamentable and comic accents of an old beau who bewails himself, he said, "And to say that I shall be regretting even this next year?"

The uncle remained utterly astonished. This man, an academician, talking thus and relating his low amours! So there were insensate people everywhere, even in the Institute, and his admiration for the great man was diminished by the sympathy which he felt for his follies.

"How is Fanny going on? Are you still at Chaville?" asked Caoudal, suddenly growing calm, and seating himself beside Gaussin, whom he tapped familiarly on the shoulder.

"Ah, poor Fanny, we have not much longer to live together."

"You are going away?"

"Yes, soon, and I am to be married first. I must leave her."

The sculptor gave vent to a ferocious laugh.

"Bravo! I am glad. Avenge us, my lad. Avenge us on all these creatures, let them go—deceive them—let them weep—miserable jades—you will never do them as much harm as they have to other people."

Uncle Cesaire was intensely pleased. "You see, this gentleman does not look at matters in so tragical a light as you do. Can you understand that this innocent will not leave her for fear she should commit suicide?"

Jean frankly confessed to the impression which Alice Doré's suicide had made upon him.

"But that is not all the same thing," said Caoudal quickly. "She was a melancholy, spiritless girl, a poor doll who wanted sawdust. Dechelette was wrong in fancying that she killed herself on his account, it was a suicide because she was worn out and tired of life. While Sapho! ah! catch her killing herself— she is too fond of love, and will burn down to the end, to the very socket. She is like the race of young comedy actors who never change their class of character, who die without teeth, without eyebrows, but are young lovers to the last. Now look at me—am I likely to kill myself? It is no use to worry. I knew very well as this girl is gone I shall take another, and so on. Your mistress will do the same as she has done already. Only she is no longer young, and it will be more difficult now."

The uncle was more delighted—"Are you now reassured, eh?"

Jean made no reply, but his scruples were overruled and his resolution firmly taken. They were leaving the studio.

when the sculptor called them back to show them a photograph picked up from the dusty table, and which he was wiping with his sleeve. "Look, here she is! Isn't she pretty enough to worship? What legs, what a throat." And the contrast between the longing eyes, the impassioned voice and the senile trembling of the spatulate fingers was terrible, as the sculptor held this smiling portraiture of the dimpled charms of Cousinard, the little model.

CHAPTER XII

HE IS LEAVING ME!

"So it's you!! How early you are!"

She came up from the end of the garden, her dress full of windfall apples, and hurried up the steps, somewhat uneasy at the appearance—at once worried and stubborn—of her lover.

"What is the matter with you?"

"Nothing, nothing—it is the weather, the sun. I want you to take advantage of the last fine day to have a run in the forest, you and I together. Will you?"

She still retained an exclamation of the street boy, which occurred to her every time she was more than usually pleased.

"Oh, what a lark!" For more than a month they had not gone out together, having been prevented by the storms and rains of September. One cannot always amuse oneself in the country; as well live in the ark with Noah's animals. She had some orders to give in the kitchen because the Hettemas were coming to dinner, and while he was waiting outside on the Pavé des Gardes Jean kept looking at the little house glowing in the soft light of the late summer, at the country road and its wide moss-grown flags, with that farewell in his eyes, that clinging gaze of memory with which we regard places we are about to leave.

Through the open window of the dining-room he could hear the bird singing, and Fanny giving her orders to the servant. "Be sure you don't forget, half-past six. You will send up the guinea fowl first. Ah, I must give you the linen." Her voice rang out clear and happy amid the clattering of the kitchen and the warbling of the bird singing to the sun—but he himself, knowing that their housekeeping would only last two hours longer, was deeply affected by the sound of these tokens of festivity.

He had a great mind to go into the house and tell her everything straight out, but he was afraid of her cries, of the shocking scene of which the neighbors would all hear, of a scandal which would upset Chaville completely; he knew that if she once let herself go, no earthly consideration would restrain her, so he adhered to his former purpose of taking her into the forest.

"Here I am, quite ready."

She took his arm joyfully, telling him to speak in a low voice and to walk quickly, as they were passing the house of their neighbors, for fear that Olympe would want to accompany them and so spoil their excursion. She was not at ease until they had passed the railway bridge and had turned to the left into the wood.

It was a soft, mild day, the sun, tempered by a silvery vapor which pervaded the whole atmosphere, hung upon the copses in which some trees still bearing a few golden leaves, inclosing some magpies' nests, and some bunches of mistletoe high up, they could hear the cry of a bird like the noise of a file, and the tapping of beaks on the wood which answered to the strokes of the woodcutter.

They proceeded slowly, imprinting their footsteps on the ground softened by the autumnal rains. She was heated, having come so fast, her cheeks were glowing, her eyes brilliant, and she paused to take off her great white lace mantilla, a present from Rosa, which she had thrown over her head as they left the house—the delicate and costly relic of former grandeur. The dress she was wearing—a poor black silk frock split under the arms and in the gathers —he had known for three years, and when she held it up passing in front of him and crossing a puddle, he could see that the heels of her boots were worn down at the sides.

How cheerfully she had accepted this semi-poverty without regret or complaint, occupied with him and his well-being, never more happy than when she was close to him, her hands clasped over his arm. And Jean asked himself as he gazed at her, quite rejuvenated by the return of the sun and love, what a spring of sap there was in such a being; what a marvellous faculty of forgetting and of pardoning she possessed to enable her to retain so much gayety and carelessness of manner, after a life of passion, of troubles and tears, all imprinted on her features, but disappearing at the least expansion of gayety!

"It is a real one. I tell you it is a real mushroom."

She stooped under the brushwood and plunged up to her knees in the dead leaves, returning with her hair loose and tangled by the branches, and showed him the small network on the

stem of the mushroom which distinguishes the true from the false one.
"You see it has got the network." And
she was delighted.

He did not listen to her; he was
absent-minded, asking himself: Is this
the moment? Shall I? But his courage failed him, she was laughing so
merrily, or the place was not a favorable one, and he hurried her farther
away still, like an assassin who medi-
tates a crime.

He was about to bring matters to
the point when at the turn of the path
some one came upon them and disturbed them; it was Hochecorne, the
keeper, whom they met sometimes.
Poor fellow, he had lost successively in
the little hut which the State granted
him on the edge of the pond two children, then their mother, and all from
the same baneful fever. Immediately
after the first decease the doctor had
declared that the cottage was unhealthy,
being too close to the water and its
exhalations; but notwithstanding his
certificates and recommendations, the
Government had kept him there two—
three—years, time enough for him to
see all his loved ones die, with the exception of one little girl, with whom he
had gone to live in a new cottage at
the entrance of the wood.

Hochecorne, who looked an obstinate
Briton, with clear and bold eyes, a forehead receding beneath his uniform cap
—a true indication of fidelity, of superstitious obedience—had his gun slung
over one shoulder, while on the other
rested the head of a sleeping child
whom he was carrying.

"How is she?" asked Fanny, smiling
at the little girl, four years old, pale
and emaciated by fever, who woke and
opened her eyes surrounded by red circles. The keeper sighed as he replied:
"Not well, I must carry her with me
everywhere. She will eat hardly anything, she has no appetite. We must
have moved too late, and she must have
already caught the fever. She is so
light. Look, madame, she is like a leaf.
One of these days she will pass away
like the others. Good God!"

This expression, muttered through his
moustache, was the only protest he
made against officialism.

"She is trembling; one would think
she was cold."

" 'Tis the fever, madame."

"Wait, we will soon warm her."
Fanny took her lace mantilla which was
hanging on her arm, and wrapped it
round the little girl.

"Yes, yes, let me do it. It will serve
for her wedding veil later on."

The father smiled in a heartbroken
sort of way, and touching the little hand
of the child, who was going to sleep
again, looking as white as a little corpse,
he made her thank the lady, and then
left them with another "Good God!"
which was lost in the crackling of the
branches under his feet.

Fanny, no longer cheerful, clung to
Jean with all the timid affection of a
woman whom emotion, sadness, or joy,
brings closer to the one she loves. Jean
said to himself, "What a good girl she
is," but without faltering in his resolution; on the contrary, he felt more firm,
for upon the slope of the path which
they were entering arose the image of
Irene, the remembrance of whose radiant smile met him there and took
possession of him at once, even before
he recognized the profound charm of
it, the deep source of its intelligent

sweetness. He knew that he had waited till the last moment, that that day was Thursday. It must be done, and seeing a cleared space at a little distance he made up his mind that that should be the limit of his hesitation.

A clearing in the wood, some fallen trees surrounded by chips; pieces of bark; some fagots, and holes for charcoal burning. A little lower down the pond could be seen from which a white mist was ascending, and on its margin was the little deserted hut with dilapidated roof and open, broken windows, the pest house of the Hochecorne family. Beyond that the woods ascended towards Vélizy, a large slope of ruddy foliage, a thick and melancholy looking forest. He stopped suddenly and said: "Suppose we rest here for a little while."

They seated themselves upon a fallen tree, an old oak on which one could perceive where the branches had been by the marks of the axe. It was a pleasant spot, brightened by the pale reflection of the sun, and perfumed by the unseen violets.

"How nice this is," she said, as she leaned languidly upon his shoulder, and sought a place on his neck to kiss. He drew himself away a little, and took her hand. Then seeing the sternness of his face she became alarmed.

"Why, what is the matter with you?"

"Some bad news, my poor dear. Hedouin you know, the man who went away instead of me—" He spoke painfully, in a hoarse voice, the tones of which even astonished himself, but grew stronger as he proceeded with his story which he had prepared beforehand. Hedouin had fallen ill on reaching his post, and he had been directed to take his

place. He found that easier to say than to tell the truth. She listened to the end without interrupting him, her face of an ashy paleness, her eyes fixed. "When do you start?" she said, drawing her hand from his.

"Well, this evening—to-night." Then in a forced and mournful voice he added, "I hope to spend four and twenty hours at Castelet, then to embark at Marseilles."

"Enough. You need not tell any more lies," she said with a loud burst of passion as she started to her feet. "You need lie no longer, you don't know how to do it. The truth is that you are going to be married, for a long time your family have been working for this, they are so very much afraid that I shall prevent you from going out to catch typhus or yellow fever. I hope they are satisfied at last. The lady is to your taste I suppose—and when I think how I used to tie your evening ties on those Thursdays! Was I not a fool, eh?"

She laughed a sad, bitter laugh, which contorted her mouth and showed a space at the side caused by the breaking of one of her beautiful teeth of which she was so proud; it must have happened recently, for he had not observed it before, and this gap in the terrified, hollow, distorted face shocked Gaussin terribly.

"Listen to me," said he, taking hold of her, and pulling her toward him forcibly:

"Yes, I am going to be married, my father is bent on it, as you know very well, but it cannot matter to you since I must go in any case."

She released herself, but restrained her anger.

"And it was to tell me this that you made me come a league across the forest. You said to yourself, 'At any rate no one shall hear her if she screams out.' No, you see there is no screaming and not a tear. In the first place, I have had pretty well enough of you, handsome though you be. You can go your way, and I will never call you back. Off with you, then, abroad with your wife, your little one, as they say in your country. She ought to be a nice one, that same little girl, ugly as a gorilla, or else *enceinte,* for you are as stupid as those who have chosen her for you."

She restrained herself no longer, but launched out into a torrent of abuse and insult, until she could only stammer such words as coward, liar, coward, under his very nose as one thrusts a clenched fist.

It was now Jean's turn to listen without answering, without even an attempt to check her. He was glad she was thus insulting and low, the true daughter of Père Legrand, the separation would be less cruel. Was she conscious of this? At any rate she ceased suddenly, fell forward on her lover's knees with a great sob which seemed to shake her whole body, and in a broken voice she cried, "Forgive me; have mercy on me. I love you. I have no one but you. My love, my life, do not do this —do not leave me. What do you expect that I should become?"

Emotion overcame him. This is what he had been afraid of. Sympathetic tears rose in his eyes, and he had to throw his head back to keep them in, endeavoring to calm her by silly words and the reasonable argument, "But since I must go."

She raised herself up again with this cry which betrayed all her hope.

"Ah, you would not have gone, though. I would have said stay. Let me love you still. Do you believe that one can be loved twice as I love you? You have plenty of time to marry—you are so young. I shall soon be played out, and then we shall separate naturally."

He wished to rise, he had the courage to do so, and to tell her that all she was doing was useless, but clinging round him, dragging her knees in the mud which lay in the hollow, she forced him to resume his seat, and before him, between his knees, with her breath, the voluptuous glance in her eyes, and with childish caresses, her hands upon his fixed face, her fingers in his hair, in his mouth, she tried to rekindle the cold embers of their love, talked to him softly of their past joys, the happiness of their Sunday afternoons. All that was nothing to what she would do in the future, she would give him new pleasures, other delights and invent them for him.

And while she was whispering these words great tears ran down her face, on which rested an expression of agony and terror, as she writhed and cried in a dreamy voice, "Oh, it must not be! Say it is not true that you are going to leave me." And then came sobs, and groans, and cries for help as if she saw a knife in his hands.

The executioner was scarcely more brave than was the victim. He did not fear her anger more than her caresses, but he was defenceless against this despair, this clamor which filled the wood, and extended over the stagnant and fever laden water into which the sad red sun was setting. He had made up his mind to suffer, but not so acutely, and all the glamor of the new love was necessary to enable him to resist taking her by both hands and saying, "I will remain. Be quiet. I will stay."

How much time had they passed thus exhausting themselves? The sun was no more than a narrow bar of light in the west, the pond was of a leaden hue, and one would have said that its unhealthy exhalations were extending over the wastes, and the woods, and the hills opposite. In the gathering gloom he could see only the pale face uplifted to his, that open mouth ceaselessly moaning. Soon afterward as night fell the sound became hushed. Now there came floods of tears unending—one of those long rains which set in the climax of the storm—and from time to time an exclamation, an "Oh!" deep and hollow, as if some horrible thing was being pushed aside, and kept as constantly recurring.

Then it was all over. The horror is gone. A cold wind arises, shakes the branches, wafting toward them the echo of some distant chime.

"Come, let us go. Don't stop here."

He raised her gently, felt her unresisting in his hands, obedient as a child, and shaken with heavy sighs. She seems still to be afraid of something, to have a respect for the man who has shown himself so strong. She walks beside him step by step, but timidly, not arm in arm, and to see them thus walking unsteadily and dejected, making their way along the paths by the yellow reflection of the ground, one would have said that they were a couple of peasants going home, worn out by hard work in the open air.

At the edge of the wood a light appeared from Hochecorne's open door, revealing the forms of two men. "Is that you, Gaussin?" asked the voice of Hettema, who was coming with the keeper to meet them. They had begun to be uneasy at their absence, and in consequence of the groans which they had heard through the wood. Hochecorne was about to take his gun and set out in search of them.

"Good-evening, sir, and madame. The little girl is greatly pleased with her shawl. I was obliged to put her in bed in it."

Their last action in common, this act of charity so lately performed, their hands clasped for the last time around the little body of the dying child!

"Good-by, good-by, Hochecorne." And they all three hastened home, Hettema very much puzzled concerning the noise which had filled the wood. "It rose and fell as if some wild beast was being strangled. How was it you did not hear anything of it?"

Neither of the two made any reply.

At the corner of the Pavé des Gardes Jean hesitates.

"Stay to dinner," she said to him in a low, pleading voice. "Your train has gone, you can catch the nine o'clock train."

He goes in with them. What has he to fear? Such a scene could not be repeated, and it is the least he can do to give her this small comfort.

The room is warm, the lamp burns brightly, and the sound of their footsteps has already warned the servant, who was placing the soup on the table.

"Here you are at last," said Olympe, who was already seated, her napkin tucked under her short arms. She is uncovering the soup tureen, but stops suddenly, exclaiming, *"Mon Dieu,* my dear!"

Wan, ten years older, her eyes swollen and bloodshot, mud on her dress, even in her hair, having the startled disordered look of a street walker who has just escaped from the police, was Fanny. She breathes hard for a moment, her poor burning eyes winking at the light, and by degrees the warmth of the little house, the prettily laid table, arouse the memory of happy days. A new outburst of tears succeeds, through which one can distinguish these words:

"He is leaving me, he is going to be married."

Hettema, his wife, the peasant woman who waits on them, all look at each other and at Gaussin. "Well, let's have dinner, at any rate," said the fat man, who seemed to be very angry, and the noise of the spoons is mingled with the splashing of water in the next room where Fanny is sponging her face. When she returns all powdered, in a white woolen dressing-gown, the Hettemas watch her in agony, expecting some new outbreak, and are very much astonished to see her silently throw herself glut-tonously upon her food like a ship-wrecked person, filling the hollow of her grief and the gulf of her cries with anything she could lay her hands on— bread, cabbage, a guinea fowl's wing, potatoes. She ate and ate.

They talked at first in a constrained way, then more freely, and as with the Hettemas everything is flat and mate-rial, such as how pancakes would go with sweetmeats, or whether hair is bet-ter to sleep upon than feathers, they reach the coffee stage of dinner with-out any disturbance. The fat couple flavor their coffee with burnt sugar and sip it slowly with their elbows on the table.

It is a pleasure to see the confiding and tranquil glances which these heavy companions of stall and litter exchange. They have no wish to separate. Jean surprises these looks, and in the inti-macy of this room, full of memories and familiar objects, the torpor of fatigue, of digestion, of comfort, creeps over him. Fanny, who is watching him closely, brings her chair nearer to him, puts her hand on his knees, and passes her arm under his.

"Listen," he said, roughly, "there is nine o'clock, quick, good-bye, I will write to you."

He was up and across the road, feel-ing in the dark to open the gate. Two arms encircle him. "Kiss me at least."

He feels himself beneath the open dressing-gown against her flesh, pene-trated by the odor and warmth, upset by the parting kiss which leaves in his mouth the taste of fever and tears, and she says softly, feeling him yield, "Stay one more night, only one."

A signal on the line, the train is ap-proaching.

How had he the strength to disen-gage himself, to rush to the railway sta-tion, the lamps of which were glimmer-ing through the leafless branches? He was still wondering at himself, as seated breathless in the corner of the carriage, he watches through the win-dow for the lights of the little house for a white form at the gate. "Adieu, adieu!" And this cry relieved him from the silent fear which he had begun to entertain at the curve of the line of seeing his mistress in the place he had seen her in his dreadful dream. With his head out of the window he watched passing away and diminishing, becoming confused in the distance, their little house, the light in which was now but that of a wandering star. Suddenly he felt a joy, a great relief. How freely he could breathe, how beautiful was all that valley of Meudon, and those grand black hills, forming in the distance, a triangle twinkling with innumerable lights, trending toward the Seine in regular lines. Irene was waiting him there, and he was rushing to join her with all the speed of the train, with all the desire of a lover, with all his determination to lead an honest and new life.

Paris! he called a cab to drive to the Place Vendôme, but in the gaslight he perceived the condition in which his clothes were, covered with mud, as all his past life clung to him heavily and filthily. "Oh, no, not to-night." So he proceeded to his old lodgings in the Rue Jacob, where Le Fenat had bespoken a room for him next to his own.

CHAPTER XIII

WEAKNESS

NEXT day, Cesaire, who had undertaken the delicate commission of going to Chaville to bring away his nephew's effects and books, and clinch the separation by this removal, came back very late, so much so, that Gaussin had already begun to worry himself with all kinds of foolish and gloomy prognostications. At last a cab, heavy as a hearse, turned the corner of the street laden with corded boxes, and one enormous trunk which he recognized as his own; then his uncle entered, mysteriously and heartbroken.

"I have been a long time, but I wanted to make one journey of it, and not to be obliged to go there again." Then pointing to the boxes which the two servants were ranging round the room, he continued, "Here is the linen, the clothes; yonder are your papers and books. Nothing is wanting but your letters. She begged me to leave her those so that she might read them over again, and keep some thing of yours. I thought that would not matter, she is such a good girl."

He breathed hard for a long while, seated on the trunk mopping his face with an unbleached silk handkerchief as big as a napkin. Jean did not dare to ask particulars, or in what condition he had found her; his uncle told him nothing for fear of making him sad. And they filled up the awkward silence, full of unexpressed thoughts, with remarks about the weather, which had suddenly become cold the night before, the mournful aspect of that deserted suburb of Paris studded with factory chimneys and enormous metal cylinders, the reservoirs of market gardeners Then, after a while, Jean said:

"She did not give you anything for me, uncle?"

"No, you may be quite easy, she will not bother you any more. She has accepted the situation with great resolution and dignity."

Why did Jean see in these words an implication of blame, a reproach to him for his harshness?

"All the same," continued Uncle Cesaire, "I would rather have Mornas' nails than this unfortunate girl's despair."

"Did she weep much?"

"Ah, my friend, so much and so bitterly, that I myself sobbed at the sight of it without having the strength to" —he snorted and shook his emotion away with the movement of his head like an old goat. "After all, what could you do? It is not your fault; you cannot pass all your life there. Things have been very properly arranged. You have left her money and a furnished house, and now let your love go, let your marriage proceed. Such affairs are too serious for me, I declare; the Consul must interest himself in that. I am only useful in arranging left-handed settlements." Then, suddenly seized with a melancholy fit, his face against the window pane looking at the lowering sky and the rain on the roofs, "Ah, well, the world is becoming very sad; in my time people separated much more cheerfully than they do now," he said.

When Le Fenat had gone away with his pumping machine, Jean, deprived of his good-humored and chattering companion, had a long week to pass, an impression of vacancy and solitude, all the blankness of widowerhood to endure. In such a case as this, even without the regret of passion, one feels the want of the companion who is missing; for existence with another person, the cohabitation of table and bed creates a tissue of invisible and subtle bonds, the real strength of which only reveals itself in sorrow, or in the efforts to release oneself from them. The influence of contact and of habit is so wonderfully penetrating, that two people living the same life together come to resemble one another in time.

His five years with Sapho had not been sufficient to mold him to this form, but his frame preserved the marks of the chain, and he felt its weight. And even many times he involuntarily directed his steps toward Chaville on leaving his office. It often happened that he looked beside him on the pillow for the heavy black tresses, destitute of a comb, on which his first kiss used to fall.

The evenings seemed particularly wearisome in that room, which reminded him of the first days of his connection, the presence of another mistress, refined and silent, whose little card scented his glass with a subtle perfume, and with the mystery of her name—Fanny Legrand. At such times he would seek to fatigue himself with long walks, to daze himself with the popular ditties and the lights of some little theater, until old Bouchereau gave him permission to pass three evenings of the week with his *fiancée*.

All was at length arranged. Irene loved him. Uncle had no objection. The marriage was to take place in the beginning of April, at the end of the term. Three months of winter to see each other; to know and long for each other; to put a loving and delightful construction upon that first look which binds souls together, and on the first confession that troubles them.

On the evening on which the contract was signed, Jean returned home, and not feeling inclined to sleep, conceived the idea of putting his room into ship-shape and working order, in compliance with that natural instinct to put our life in accord with our ideas. He arranged his table and his books, which had hitherto remained unpacked, stowed away in the hastily made boxes, amid handkerchiefs and a garden jacket. From amid the leaves of a dictionary on commercial law, the most used book, there fell a letter, without envelope, in his mistress' handwriting.

Fanny had confided it to the chances of future work, distrusting Cesaire's too short-lived sentiment, believing that it would reach its destination more safely by these means. He was unwilling to peruse it at first, but yielding to the opening words, very tender, very sensible, and in which only the shaking hand and the irregular lines betrayed her agitation. She only asked one favor—only one—that he would go and see her now and then. She would complain of nothing, reproach him with nothing, not even with his marriage and the separation which she knew was absolute and definite. But only let her see him!

"Just reflect what a terrible blow this is for me; so sudden, so unexpected as it was. I feel as if there had been a death or a fire in the house—not knowing what to do. I weep, I wait! I contemplate the scene of my happiness. You alone could accustom me to the new condition of things. It would be a charity to come and see me, so that I may not feel quite so lonely. I am afraid of myself."

These complaints, this supplicating appeal, ran all through the letter, ending with the same words—"Come, come!" He could almost have believed that he was in the open space in the midst of the forest, with Fanny at his feet, and, in the violet hue of the evening light, that poor face, all tear-stained and swollen, uplifted to his, while the lips were parted in a cry. This vision haunted him all night, it troubled his sleep, and not the happy intoxication which he had enjoyed yonder with her.

It was the aged and seamed face which he saw, notwithstanding all his efforts to put between it and himself that pure countenance with the tint of a carnation in bloom, which the confession of affection tinted with little rosy flames under the eyes.

This letter was eight days old; eight days the unhappy woman had been expecting a line or a visit; the encouragement to resignation which she begged for. But how was it she had not written since? Perhaps she was ill, and all his old fears returned. He thought that Hettema might be able to give him some news, and confident of his punctuality and regularity, he went and waited for him outside the artillery department.

The last stroke of ten was booming from the church of St. Thomas Aquinas when the fat man turned the corner of the little square, his collar turned up, his pipe held in his mouth with both hands in order to warm his fingers. Jean watched him approaching from a distance, and felt greatly moved by the memories which his appearance conjured up, but Hettema accosted him with scarce concealed ill-temper. "You here! I think we have cursed you pretty well this last week—we who went into the country to be quiet!"

And, on the doorstep as he finished his pipe, Hettema told him how on the previous Sunday they had asked Fanny to dinner with them, and the child, too, whose day out it was, with the intention to divert her mind a little from distressing thoughts. As a matter of fact, she was cheerful enough at dinner, she even sang them a song during dessert; they separated about ten o'clock, and the Hettemas were about to turn deliciously into bed, when suddenly a knocking came at the shutters, and they heard little Josaph's terrified voice crying out:

"Come quickly; mamma is going to poison herself."

Hettema rushed out and arrived just in time to snatch forcibly from Fanny a phial of laudanum. There was a struggle; he had to pinion her in his arms, and defend himself from the blows which she showered on his head, and from the comb with which she scratched his face. In the struggle the phial was broken, the laudanum was spilt, and his clothes were saturated and tainted with the poison. "You may imagine what such scenes, with all the varied dramas, mean for quiet people. So I've done with it. I've given notice, and next month I move." He replaced his pipe in its case, and with a quiet *adieu* disappeared beneath the low arch of the little courtyard, leaving Gaussin quite upset by what he had heard.

He pictured to himself the scene in that room which had been their room. The fright of the child calling for help, the brutal struggle with the fat man; and he seemed to perceive the opium flavor, the somnolent bitterness of the spilled laudanum. This horror was present to him all day, aggravated by the thoughts of loneliness in which she would soon be left. When the Hettemas had gone, who would stay her hand from another attempt?

A letter arrived which reassured him somewhat. Fanny thanked him for not being as hard as he wished to appear, because he still took some interest in the poor abandoned creature! "You were told, were not you? I wished to die, because I felt so lonely. I have

tried—I could not succeed. They stopped me; my hand shook, perhaps, the fear of suffering—of becoming ugly! Oh! how had that little Doré the courage! After the first shame of failure it was a joy to think that I could write to you, love you at a distance, see you again—for I have not abandoned the hope that I may see you again once more; as people go to see an unhappy friend in a house of mourning from pity only—only pity!"

Thenceforth there came from Chaville every second or third day a capricious correspondence—long, short, a journal of sorrow—which he had not the strength of mind to send back, and which enlarged in his tender heart the sentiment of that pity without love, no longer for his mistress, but for the human being suffering on his account.

One day it was the account of her neighbors' departure: the witnesses of her past happiness who carried with them so many reminiscences. Now she had nothing to recall him but the furniture. The walls of the little house, and the servant—a poor, savage creature—as little interested in anything as the oriole, shaking with cold, sadly perched in a corner of his cage.

On another occasion a pale sunbeam brightening the window caused her to awake joyfully, with the impression that he would come that day. Why? It was merely an idea. Immediately she began to tidy up the house, and make herself neat in her Sunday dress and the headdress he liked; then toward evening till daylight died away she counted the trains from the window of his dining-room, listened for his footstep on the Pavé des Gardes. Must not she have been silly?

Sometimes there was only a line. It is raining—it is dark and gloomy—I am alone—weeping for you. Or, again, she would content herself with putting in an envelope a poor flower all damp and stiffened by the frost, the last in their little garden. Better than all complaints, this flower picked from under the snow spoke of winter, of solitude and abandonment. He could see the place at the end of the walk, and alongside the flower-beds a woman's dress, wet all round the hem, passing backwards and forwards in a solitary promenade.

The feeling of pity, which wrung his heart, caused him to live still with Fanny, notwithstanding the separation. He thought of her and pictured her to himself every hour, but by a singular failing of his memory, although scarcely more than five or six weeks had passed since their separation, and the smallest details of the interior of the house were still present to him—the cage of La Balue opposite the cuckoo clock won at a country fair, even to the branches of the nut-tree, which at the slightest movement of the air beat against the window of the dressing-room — the woman herself did not appear to him any longer distinct. He saw her as it was in a mist with one detail of her face, accentuated and distressful, the deformed mouth, the smile spoiled by the want of a tooth.

Aged to this extent, what would become of her, that poor creature with whom he had lived so long? When she had spent the money which he had left her, whither would she go? To what depth would she fall? And all of a sudden there came into his mind the remembrance of the unfortunate woman he had met in an English tavern that evening, dying of thirst before her plate of smoked salmon. Would she come to that? She whose care, whose passionate and faithful tenderness ne had so long experienced! This idea made him feel desperate; yet what was he to do? Because he had had the misfortune to meet with this woman and to live with her some time, was he to be condemned to keep her always, to sacrifice his happiness to her? Why should he, and not others, do so? Why, in the name of justice!

While preventing himself from seeing her, he wrote to her, and his letters, purposely decided and cold, betrayed his feelings under his practical advice. He suggested that she should take Josaph from school and keep him with her to amuse and occupy her, but Fanny refused. What was the use of bringing the child into the presence of her grief and dejection? It was enough on a Sunday, when he climbed from one chair to another, ran about from dining-room to garden, perceiving that some great misfortune had saddened the house, and no longer daring to ask for news of "Papa Jean," since he had been told with sobs that he had gone away, and would never come back again.

"All my papas go away, then!"

This remark of the little abandoned child, appearing in the heart-broken letter, lay heavy on Gaussin's heart. Very soon the thought of her remaining at Chaville became so oppressive that he suggested she should return to Paris, and see her friends again. With her sad experience of men, and her separations. Fanny in this offer saw only a terrible selfishness, the desire to be quit of her forever, by one of those sudden whims with which she was so familiar, and she expressed herself plainly on the subject.

"You know what I have told you before—I will remain your wife, in spite of everything, your loving and faithful wife. Our little house is so identified with you that I would not leave it for the world. What could I do in Paris? I am disgusted with my past, which drives you away, and then think to what you would expose us. You imagine then that you are very firm—well, come and see me once, you naughty fellow, only once." He did not go, but one Sunday afternoon, when he was working alone, he heard two gentle taps at his door—he trembled, knowing very well the manner in which she used to announce herself. Afraid of being stopped, she had come up direct without asking permission. He approached the door, his steps deadened by the carpet, hearing her breathing through the cracks of the paneling.

"Jean, are you there?"

Oh, what a humble and broken voice it was. Once more, and not loudly, "Jean," then a sad sigh, the rustle of a letter, and the kiss of farewell which she threw him.

Only when she had slowly descended the staircase, step by step, as if she expected to be called back, did Jean pick up and open the letter. They had that morning buried the little Hochecorne at the Hospital for sick children. She had come up with the father and some people from Chaville, and had not been able to resist mounting the stairs to see him, or to leave those lines written in anticipation. "Just as I told you —if I were to live in Paris I should always be on your staircase. Adieu, my own; I am going back to our house."

As he read this his eyes were suffused with tears; he recalled a similar scene in the Rue de l'Arcade, the sadness of the discarded lover—the letter slipped under the door, and Fanny's heartless laughter. So she loved him more than he loved Irene, or may it not be that the man, more mixed up in the business of life and its struggles, than the woman has not, like her, the exclusiveness of love, the forgetfulness and indifference toward everything which does not relate to her absorbing and single affection?

This torture, this access of pity from which he was suffering, was only appeased when he was with Irene—here alone his agony was alleviated and dispersed beneath the glance of her blue eyes. There only remained to him a great weariness, a wish to rest his head upon her shoulder, and remain without speaking, without moving, in the shelter of her presence.

"What is the matter with you?" she would say to him. "Are you not happy?"

"Yes, very happy." But why in his happiness was he so sad and tearful? There were moments when he felt inclined to tell her everything, as if she were an intelligent and good friend, never thinking, poor fool, of the troubles which such conferences give rise to in innocent hearts, of the incurable wounds which they inflict in trustful affection. Ah! if he could only have carried her off, eloped with her, he felt that that would put an end to his torture; but Bouchereau would not remit one hour of the time already fixed. "I am old, I am ailing, I shall see my child no more—do not deprive me of those last days."

Under his stern exterior he was the best of men; condemned unreservedly to die from the heart disease, whose progress he followed and noted; he spoke of it with wonderful coolness, continued his course of lectures, even half suffocating, and performed auscultation for patients less seriously attacked than himself. One single weakness in his mighty mind, and one indicating the peasant origin of the Tourangeau, was his respect for the nobility. So the remembrance of the little towers of Castelet and the ancient name of Armandy had not been altogether without their influence in causing him to accept their Jean so readily as his niece's husband.

The wedding was to take place at Jean's house, so that his mother would not have to be moved. Every week she dictated to Divonne, or to one of the twins, an affectionate letter to her future daughter-in-law, and it was a great pleasure to him to talk with Irene about his people, to find Castelet in the Place Vendôme, all his affections wrapped round his dear *fiancée*.

But he was rather alarmed at feeling so old, so worn out compared to her, to see her childish pleasure in things which no longer amused him, in joys of married life together, which he had already discounted. So the inventory of everything they would require to take out to the consulate, the furniture and materials to choose, had to be made, a list in the midst of which he suddenly stopped one evening, pen in hand, alarmed at the return which he was making toward his housekeeping in the Rue l'Amsterdam, and at the inevitable recommencement of so many happy joys, already done with, exhausted by those five years with one woman, in a travesty of marriage and its responsibilities.

CHAPTER XIV

THE MIRE

"YES, my dear fellow, he died last night in Rosa's arms. I have just left him to be stuffed."

De Potter, the composer, whom Jean had met coming out of a shop in the Rue du Bac, clung on to him with an effusion very foreign to his hard business-like appearance, and related the martyrdom of poor Bichito, killed by the Parisian winter; shriveled with cold, notwithstanding all the wadding, and the spirit lamp which had been kept burning for two months under his little nest, as one might do for prematurely born children. Nothing could prevent him from shivering, and the night before, when they were all standing round him, the last thrill shook him from head to tail, and he died a good Christian, thanks to the amount of holy water which mother Pilar sprinkled on his rough skin as his life ebbed away in changing colors and prismatic waves, while Pilar said, with eyes upraised to heaven, *"Dios loui pardonne!"*

"I laugh about it, but my heart is very heavy all the same, especially when I think of the grief of my poor Rosa, whom I have left in tears. Fortunately, Fanny was with her."

"Fanny!"

"Yes: it is some time since we saw her. She came this morning, in the midst of our drama, and the good girl remained to comfort her friend." Then he added, without noticing the impression his words made, "So it is all over? You are no longer together? You remember our conversation on the lake at Enghien. At any rate you profit by the lessons one teaches you." And it seemed as if envy were mixed with his approbation.

Gaussin, with knitted brows, experienced real uneasiness when he reflected that Fanny had gone back to Rosario's house, but he was annoyed with himself for this weakness, having, after all, no right to interfere with her existence.

Before a house in the Rue de Beaune, a very old street in that formerly aristocratic part of Paris, de Potter stopped. He lived, or was said to live, here for appearances' sake, for actually his time was spent either in the Avenue de Villiers or at Enghien, and he only appeared now and then under the conjugal roof, so that his wife and child should not appear altogether abandoned.

Jean was already about to continue his way, and was bidding de Potter good-by, but the latter held his fingers in his long hands, hard from continual playing on the piano, and without the least embarrassment, like a man whom his vice never worries, said:

"Do me a favor. Come upstairs with me. I ought to dine with my wife to-day, but I cannot leave my poor Rosa all alone in her despair. You will serve as a pretext for my going out, and will save me a worrying explanation."

The musician's study, in a splendid but cold suite of apartments on the second floor, made one feel the desolation of a room in which no work is done. It was too tidy. There was no disorder in it; none of that feverish activity which impresses itself on the furniture and other objects. Not a book, not a page on the table, which was occupied by an enormous bronze ink bottle as dry and as gleaming as it had been in a shop window, not the least piece of music score on the old piano, in the form of a spinette, which had inspired his first composition. And a bust in white marble, the bust of a young woman with delicate features and a sweet expression, quite pale in the fading light of day, made the draped and fireless grate look colder still, as it seemed to be gazing sadly at the walls charged with gilt and beribboned crowns, with medals and commemorative frames, the whole glorious and vain collection left generously to his wife as a compensation, and which she preserved as ornaments on the tomb of her happiness.

They had scarcely entered when the door of the study opened, and Madame de Potter appeared.

"Is that you, Gustave?"

She thought he was alone, but stopped at perceiving the stranger, visibly embarrassed. Elegant, pretty, and dressed in good style, she seemed even more refined than her bust indicated, the sweet features displaying a firm and courageous resolution. In society opinions were divided concerning the character of the wife. Some people blamed her for putting up with the plain disdain of her husband, that other connection being well known. Others, on the contrary, admired her silent resignation, but the general opinion held that she was an easy-going woman who preferred quiet to everything else, finding sufficient compensation for her "widowhood" in the caresses of a beautiful child, and her pleasure in bearing the name of an illustrious man.

But while the composer was introducing his companion, and concocting no matter what falsehood to get out of the embarrassment of a family dinner, by the uneasiness of the youthful feminine face, and the fixity of the regard which no longer saw anything, which heard nothing, like one absorbed in grief, Jean could pe ceive that some deep sorrow lay beneath this the story which she did not believe, and contented herself by saying softly:

"Raymond will cry; I promised him that we would dine at his bedside."

"How is he?" asked de Potter, absently and impatiently.

"Better, but he coughs incessantly. Will not you come and see him?"

He murmured something in his moustache, pretending to look around the room for something. "Not just now—in a hurry—an appointment at the club at six." He wanted to avoid being alone with her.

"Adieu, then," said the young wife, suddenly composing her features again, just as a sheet of pure water resumes its calmness after having been stirred to its depths by a stone. She bowed and disappeared.

"Let us be off!"

And de Potter, at liberty, dragged away Gaussin, who was looking at this deceptive personage, attired stiffly and correctly in his long English-cut overcoat, going downstairs before him. This person, who had been moved when he was carrying the chameleon to be stuffed, was going away without even kissing his sick child!

"All this, my dear fellow," said the composer, as if in reply to his friend's thoughts, "is the fault of those who compelled me to marry. What nonsense it was to try to make a husband and a father of me! I was Rosa's lover. I am so still, and so I shall remain until one of us is dead. A vice which lays hold of you at a favorable moment, which grasps you firmly, can you ever get rid of it? And you yourself, are you certain that if Fanny had wanted—!" He hailed an empty, passing cab, and as he got into it said:

"Ap opos of Fanny, you have heard the news? Flamant is pardoned—he has come out of Mazas. It was on Dechelette's petition. Poor Dechelette! He has benefited some one even after his death!"

Motionless, with an eager desire to run after and cling to those wheels, which were speeding along the dark street in which the gas was being lighted, Gaussin was astonished to feel himself so moved. "Flamant pardoned! Come out of Mazas!" he repeated these words to himself in a low voice, and in them perceived the cause of Fanny's silence for the last few days, her lamentations so suddenly interrupted, dying away amid the caresses of a consoler, for the first thought of the miserable man when he had been released would be for her—of course.

He recalled the amorous correspondence dated from the prison, the obstinacy of his mistress in defending him, while she now held the others so cheaply; and instead of feeling pleased at an incident which logically relieved him from all anxiety, all remorse, an undefinable anguish kept him awake and feverish a part of the night. Why? He no longer cared for her; he was only thinking of his letters, which remained in the hands of this woman, and which she would perhaps read to another man, and of which, for all one knew, she might make use of to trouble his repose and his happiness.

This anxiety about his letters, real or false, or hiding within it some care of another kind, decided him on visiting Chaville, which he had hitherto obstinately refused to do. But to whom could he have confided such a delicate mission? One morning in February he took the ten o'clock train, very composed both in heart and mind, only for fear that the house might be shut up, and that the woman might have gone away with her criminal lover.

When the curve in the line was reached, the open shutters, the curtained windows, reassured him; and recollecting his emotion, when he saw the small gleam of light twinkling behind him through the darkness, he smiled at himself, and at the vagueness of his impressions. He was no longer the same man who had lately passed that way, and assuredly he would not find the same woman. Yet only two months had elapsed. The wood beside which the train ran had put out no new leaves, it had retained the same brown look as on the day of their separation, of her echoing clamor.

He alone got out at the station, and in the chill and penetrating mist took the path, all slippery with frozen snow, beneath the railway arch, meeting no one before he reached the Pavé des Gardes, turning into which he encoun-

tered a man and a child, followed by a railway porter pushing a barrow laden with luggage.

The child, wrapped up in a comforter, his cap drawn down over his ears, suppressed a cry as he passed close to him. "Why, that is Joseph," said Jean to himself, somewhat surprised and sad at the lad's ingratitude, and turning round he met the gaze of the man who accompanied the child. That fine and intelligent face paled by imprisonment, those ready-made clothes only newly purchased, that fair beard which had not had time to grow long since he had been discharged from Mazas. Flamant, parbleu! And Joseph was his son.

In a flash the whole of the facts were revealed to him! He perceived understood everything, from the letter written in prison when the handsome engraver had confided to his mistress the child in the provinces, until the mysterious arrival of the lad, and the embarrassed manner in which the Hettemas had spoken of the adopted one; the glances exchanged between Fanny and Olympe, for they had all conspired to make him support the forger's son. Oh, what a fool he had been, and how they must have laughed! A feeling of disgust for all his hateful past came upon him, and a longing to run far away; but there were things troubling him which he was desirous to set at rest. The man and the child had gone, why not Fanny? And then his letters! He must have his letters, he could leave nothing behind him in this abode of uncleanliness and misery.

"Madame, here is monsieur."

"What monsieur?" asked a voice from the bed-room naïvely.

"I."

A cry was heard, a sudden bound out on to the floor, then, "Wait, I am getting up; I am coming."

Still in bed and past noon! Jean thought he very well knew why. He knew the reason for these broken, harassed mornings; and while he was waiting in the dining-room, in which the smallest objects were familiar to him, the whistle of the up-train, the bleating of a goat in the neighboring garden, the breakfast paraphernalia lying about the table, reminded him of former days, the hurried little meal before starting out.

Fanny entered, and came hurriedly toward him, then stopping short before his cold exterior, the pair stood for a second astonished, hesitating, as when one meets another after a broken friendship at either end of a broken bridge, some distance between the banks, and between them the wide space of the rolling, rushing waters.

"Good-day," she said, in a low tone, without moving.

She thought him altered and paler. He was surprised at finding her still so young, a little fatter, only less tall than he had pictured her, but bathed in that peculiar radiance, the brightness of complexion and eyes, the sweetness of a fresh grass plot, which was left to her even after long nights. She had remained in the wood then, in the depth of the ravine full of dead leaves the remembrance of which filled him with pity.

"One gets up very late in the country," he said ironically.

She excused herself—said she had a headache, and, like himself, she used the impersonal form of speech. not knowing quite whether to say thou or you; then at the silent questioning of his eyes, as he gazed at the breakfast table, she said, "It was for the child. He had his breakfast before going away."

"Going away, where to?"

He affected a supreme indifference, but the flashing of his eyes betrayed him, and Fanny said:

"The father has come back. He came to claim him again."

"After getting out of Mazas—is not that so?"

She shivered, but she did not attempt to tell a falsehood.

"Well, yes, I promised and I performed it. How many times have I been tempted to tell you, but I did not dare—I was afraid you would send him away, poor child, and," she added, "you were so jealous!"

He laughed loudly and disdainfully Jealous, he, of that convict! Nonsense. Then feeling his anger rising, he cut the matter short, saying quickly what his errand was—his letters. Why has she not given them to Cesaire? By so doing, an interview, painful to both would have been avoided.

"That is true," she replied, still very gently, "but I will give them to you. They are there."

He followed her into the bed-room saw how disarranged the bed was; the bedclothes thrown hurriedly over the two pillows. He breathed a smell of burnt cigarettes, mingled with the perfume of a woman's toilet, which he recognized, as well as the little mother of-pearl box placed on the table, and the same idea struck them both. "They are not voluminous," she said, as she opened the box. "We run no risk in burning them."

He made no answer, troubled, his mouth parched, he hesitated to approach the disordered bed, in front of which she was turning over the letters for the last time; her head bent down, a white and firm neck beneath the knot of her hair, and beneath the wavy woolen dressing-gown, her well-formed figure in an abandoned *pose*.

"There they are. They are all here."

When he had received the packet, and put it hastily in his pocket, for his thoughts had wandered, Jean asked:

"So he has taken away his child. Where are they gone to?"

"To Morvan, in his native district, to conceal himself—to do his engraving, which he will send to Paris, in an assumed name."

"And you—do you think of remaining here?"

She turned away her eyes to escape his glance, muttering that it would be very melancholy, so she thought she should perhaps soon take a little journey.

"To Morvan, no doubt; quite a family party." Then letting his jealous fury predominate, he said, "You may as well say at once that you are going to rejoin your convict, and live with him. You have had that idea for a long time. Go then, return to your den, bad woman and forger go well together. I was very good to take the trouble to try to lift you out of the gutter."

She preserved her motionless silence, but a gleam of triumph shot from her shaded eyes, and the more he scorned her with fierce and insulting irony the more proud she became, and the more

accentuated were the corners of her mouth. Now he spoke of his happiness, the young and honest love—the only love. Oh, what a sweet pillow to lie on is the heart of a pure woman! Then abruptly he lowered his voice, as if he were ashamed of himself.

"I have just met that Flamant of yours. He passed the night here?"

"Yes, it was late and snowing. I made him up a bed on the sofa."

"You are lying; he slept there. One has only to look at the bed and at you."

"Well, what of it?" She brought her face close to his, her great gray eyes lighted up with the flame of passion. "Did I know you would come? Having lost you, what did all the rest matter to me? I was sad, lonely, disgusted."

"And then the flavor of the convict prison. Considering the time you have been living with an honest man, that must have been particularly pleasing to you—eh? You must have had a nice time of it. You wretch. take that!"

She saw the blow coming. Without attempting to avoid it, she received it full in her face, then, with a murmur of pain, of joy, of victory, she leaped upon him, clasped him in her arms, exclaiming, "My own. my own, you love me still."

* * * * * *

The noise of a passing express awoke him with a start toward evening, and with eyes wide open he remained for some moments without knowing where he was, all alone in that great bed: his limbs stiff as after much walking seemed placed one against the other without joints and without strength.

During the afternoon a good deal of snow had fallen—in the dead silence one could hear it dripping, as it melted on the walls and along the windows, on the roof, and occasionally on the coke fire in the grate which it splashed.

Where was he? What was he doing there? By degrees, in the reflected light from the little garden, the room appeared to him to be all white, lighted up from underneath; the large portrait of Fanny rose opposite to him, and the recollection of his fall came upon him without the least astonishment. As soon as ever he had entered and faced that bed he had felt himself lost; and had said to himself, "If I fall here, I fall without reprieve and forever." He had fallen, and under the melancholy disgust for his cowardice, he felt some sort of relief in the idea that he would never emerge from his pit. He had the miserable comfort of the wounded man who, losing blood and dragging his wounded limb, stretched himself upon the dung-heap to die, and weary of suffering, of struggling, all his veins opened, sinks deliciously into the soft and fetid warmth.

What he had now to do was horrible, but very simple. To return to Irene after this treason, to risk an establishment à la Potter? Low as he had fallen, he had not got so low as that. He would write to Bouchereau, to the great physiologist who first studied and described the diseases of the will, and submit to him a terrible case, the history of his life since his first meeting with this woman, when she had placed her hand upon his arm, until the day when, believing himself saved in his great happiness, in the intoxication of love, she laid hold on him again by the magic of the past, that horrible past in which love occupied such a small space, only cowardly habit and vice in the bones.

The door opened. Fanny walked softly into the room so as not to awaken him.

Between his half-closed lids he watched her, alert and strong, rejuvenated, warming at the grate her feet which had been wet through in the snowy garden; and from time to time turning toward him with a slight smile which she had worn that morning while they disputed. She took the packet of Maryland from its usual place, rolled a cigarette, and was going away, but he stopped her.

"You are not asleep then?"

"No; sit you here and let us talk."

She sat down at the edge of the bed, somewhat surprised at his gravity.

"Fanny, we will go away together."

She believed at first that he was joking to test her. But the very minute details which he gave her soon undeceived her. There was an appointment vacant at Arica; he would ask for it. It would be a matter of a fortnight or so, just time enough to get ready.

"And your marriage?"

"Not a word on that subject. What I have done is irreparable. I see very well that all is over, and I cannot separate from you."

"Poor baby," she said, with sad sweetness, but with some disdain in her voice. Then after having taken two or three whiffs of her cigarette she asked:

"Is this place you speak of far away?"

"Arica? very far—in Peru." The

m a whisper, "Flamant will not be able to rejoin you there."

She remained thoughtful and impassive, surrounded by tobacco smoke. He, still holding her hand, or stroking her naked arm, and soothed by the dripping of the water all around the little house, closed his eyes and let himself sink gently into the mire.

CHAPTER XV

ONE KISS, THE LAST!

NERVOUS, shaking, on the move, like all those who are preparing for departure, Gaussin has been for two days in Marseilles, where Fanny is to join him and embark with him. All is prepared, places are taken, two first-class cabins for the vice-consul of Arica traveling with his sister-in-law; and he is here pacing up and down on the faded tiles of the bed-room in the hotel, in the doubly feverish waiting for his mistress and for the departure of the ship.

He must walk about and fidget, since he does not dare go out. He feels as uncomfortable in the street as a criminal, or as a deserter, in that crowded and busy Marseilles street, where it seems as if at every corner his father and old Bouchereau would come upon him, put their hands on his shoulders, recapture him, and take him back.

He shuts himself in his room, eats his meals there without even going down to the *table d'hôte*, reads without any attention, throws himself on his bed, relieving his vague *siestas* with the shipwreck of La Perouse, the death of Captain Cook, which hung on the walls fly-marked; and for whole hours he leans upon the worm-eaten wooden balcony which is shaded by a yellow piece of canvas patched like the sail of a fishing boat.

His hotel, the "Hotel de Jeune Anacharsis," a name taken at hazard from the Bottin, had tempted him when he had arranged a meeting-place with Fanny, is an old and not luxurious nor very clean inn, but which looks over the harbor on to the open sea, and on the voyage as it were. Beneath its windows are parrots, cockatoos and strange birds singing in a soft interminable warbling, all the stock of a bird fancier in the open air; and from the cages piled one above the other, they salute the break of day with a chorus one might hear in a virgin forest, overcome and dominated as the day advances by the strident noises of the port, regulated by the big bell of Notre Dame de la Garde.

There is a confusion of oaths in all tongues, cries of boatmen, of porters, of sellers of shells, mingling with the clang of hammers from the dock, the creaking of cranes, the sonorous noise of weighing machines falling on the pavement, ships' bells, steam whistles, the rhythmical beat of pumps, the clang of capstans, the splashing of bilge-water being pumped out, the noise of escaping steam and all this uproar redoubled and echoed from the neighboring sea from which arises occasionally the hoarse roar, the breathing of some marine monster of a great transatlantic steamer which is proceeding to sea.

And the odors also remind one of distant countries, of quays more sunny and hotter still than this, sandal wood and logwood, lemons, oranges, pistachio nuts, beans, ground nuts, the acrid smell from which ascends with whirlwinds of exotic dusts into the atmosphere saturated with brackish water, the cooking herbs and the greasy fumes of the cuddy.

As evening falls the noise is hushed, the thickened air falls and evaporates; and while Jean, reassured by the darkness, looks out from the awning over the sleeping port, dark amid the maze of masts, yards and bowsprits, when the silence is only broken by the rattling of an oar, or the distant bark of a dog on board ship, far away in the offing the Planier lighthouse throws a red and white revolving light into the gloom, and dispersing it, shows in a lightning flash, the outlines of the islands, forts and rocks. And this luminous eye, guiding thousands of lives out at sea, is still the voyage which invites him, makes signs to him, calls him in the voice of the wind, in the roaring of the open sea, and in the hoarse clamor of a steamboat, which is rattling and blowing off steam in some part of the roadstead.

Still four-and-twenty hours to wait. Fanny was not to join him till Sunday. The three days he had passed at the rendezvous he ought to have spent with his family, to have given to his best loved ones whom he might not see again for many years, perhaps never; but on the evening of his arrival at Castelet, when his father learned that his marriage had been broken off, and had divined the cause of it, a violent and terrible explanation had taken place.

What sort of people are we then? What are our tenderest affections, those nearest to our hearts, that when a feeling of anger comes between two beings of the same flesh and blood it tears and wrenches, sweeps away their tenderness, their natural feelings with all their deep and delicate ramifications, with the blind irresistible force of one of those typhoons of China seas which the most experienced sailors scarcely dare to remember, and turn pale as they say, "Do not let us talk about it."

He never will speak of it, but all his life he will remember that terrible scene upon the terrace at Castelet where his happy childhood had been spent, in face of that magnificent prospect—those pines, myrtles and cypress trees which stood motionless, shivering in the presence of the paternal malediction.

Forever in his mind's eye will that fine old man be present, his features convulsed and twitching, advancing upon him with that expression of detestation, giving vent to words that never can be forgiven, chasing him from the house, as from honorable connections. "Go; be off with your strumpet; you are dead to us!" The little twins weeping on their knees on the steps, begging for their big brother's pardon, and the pallor of Divonne, without one look, without one farewell; while above, behind the window-glass, the sweet and anxious face of the invalid was full of wonder as to the reasons for all the disturbance, and why Jean was going away so suddenly and without embracing her.

The thought that he had not embraced his mother came to his mind when he was half-way to Avignon; and he left Cesaire with the carriage, took a short cut and entered the grounds of Castelet through the close, like a thief. The night was dark, his feet got entangled in the dead branches of the vines, and he even lost his way seeking the house in the dark, a stranger already in his own house. The white plastered walls at length guided him by their pale reflected light, but the door at the top of the steps was locked, the windows dark. He did not dare to ring, or to call out, for fear of his father. Two or three times he made the circuit of the house, hoping to find some shutter carelessly shut. But Divonne had examined them all with her lantern as usual, and after a long look at his mother's room, a farewell with all his heart to his childhood's home, which also repulsed him, he fled away desperately, with a feeling of remorse which will never leave him.

Usually in view of long absences, these dangerous voyages, relatives and friends prolong their farewells until the actual embarkation; they pass the last day together, they visit the vessel, the cabin of the departing one, so as to picture him the better on the voyage. Many times a day did Jean see such affectionate groups pass by the hotel; parties sometimes numerous, sometimes noisy; but he was especially moved by a family party on the floor above him. An old man, an old woman, country people, in easy "turn out," with jackets of cloth and yellow cambric, have come to see their son off, to be with him until the vessel starts, and leaning out of their window in all the idleness of waiting, they could be seen all three, holding each other's arms, the sailor boy in the center, close together. They do not speak, but embrace.

Jean thought while he looked at them of the touching parting that might have been his. His father, his little sisters, and leaning on him with a soft

trembling hand, she, whose soul was entranced by the sight of ships putting out to sea! Vain regrets! The crime was committed, his "destiny" is on the railway, there is nothing for him but to go and to forget!

How long and cruel appeared the hours of that last night. He turned and tossed upon his bed at the hotel, watched for the daylight on the window panes in the slow change from black to gray; then to the white of the dawning day, which the lighthouse still pricked with a red point extinguished in view of the rising sun.

Only then does he sleep, but is awakened again suddenly by the flood of light in his chamber, by the confused cries from the cages of the bird fancier, the countless chimes of a Marseilles Sunday sounding over the restful quays, where all machinery is quiet, and where flags are floating at the mastheads. Ten o'clock already! And the Paris express is due at noon. Quickly he dresses to go out to meet his mistress; they will breakfast facing the sea, then they will have their baggage carried on board, and at five o'clock the signal for departure!

A magnificent day; a deep blue sky across which the gulls are flying like white specks. The sea is of a darker shade of blue, a mineral blue, upon which even to the horizon, sails, smoke, every object, is visible, everything glistening, dancing, and as the natural music of these sunny shores in the transparencies of atmosphere and water, some harps were being played beneath the windows of the hotel. The melody was Italian, and of a deliciously flowing nature, but whose sharp and prolonged notes jarred on his nerves cruelly. It was more than music, it was the winged interpolation of the enjoyments of the south, that plenitude of life and love overflowing even to tears. And the memory of Irene passes into the melody, vibrating and sorrowful. How far off it is! What a beautiful country lost; what a never-ending regret for things broken, irreparable!

Time to be off!

As he is leaving the hotel Jean meets a waiter. "A letter for M. le Consul. It had come that morning, but M. le Consul was so sound asleep." Travelers of distinction are rare at the "Hotel du Jeune Anacharsis," so the worthy Marseillais give out their guest's title at every opportunity. Who could have written to him? No one knew his address except Fanny. And looking more attentively at the envelope he is frightened; he understands!

*   *   *   *   *   *

"Well, no, I cannot go; it is too great a folly of which I do not feel the force. For such adventures, my poor friend, one should have youth, which I no longer possess, or the blindness of a headstrong passion, which neither of us have. Five years ago, in the happy days, a sign from you would have caused me to follow you to the other end of the world, for you cannot deny that I loved you passionately. I have given you all I had, and when it became necessary to part from you, I suffered as I never did for any man before. But such a love wears out, do you see? To know you are so handsome, so young, would make me tremble, always so many things to guard. Now I cannot, you have made me live too much, made me suffer too much. I am exhausted!

"Under such circumstances the prospect of the long voyage, the transplanting of one's life, alarms me. I who love so much to be quiet, I who have never been farther than St. Germain, just fancy! And besides, women age so rapidly in the tropics, and you would not have passed thirty before I would be as yellow and wrinkled as Mamma Pilar; then you would repent of your sacrifice and poor Fanny would have to pay for all. Mark you—there is a country in the east, I have read of it in one of your 'Tour de Mondes,' where, when a woman deceives her husband, they sew her up alive with a cat in a rawhide, and then cast the bundle struggling and howling on the seashore in the blazing sun. The woman shrieks, the cat claws—both fight for life, while the hide incloses and covers this horrible battle of the prisoners, until the last groan is heard and the movement of the sack ceases. That is the sort of fate which would await you and me!"

He ceased reading for a moment, crushed, stupefied. As far as the eye could reach sparkled the blue sea. Addio played the harps, with which was mingled another voice as warm and passionate as they. Addio! And the emptiness of his broken, wasted life, all wrecked and tearful, appeared to him: the field bare, the harvest reaped without any hope of return, and all for the woman who had escaped from him!

"I ought to have told you this earlier but I did not dare, seeing you so determined, so resolved. Your enthusiasm won me over then, the vanity of womankind, the very natural pride of having won you again after the separation. Only in my inmost heart I felt hat there was a void, something had one. How could you expect anything lse after such shocks? And do not magine it is because of that wretched 'lamant! For him, as for you and all he rest, it is all over; my heart is ead, but there is the boy without vhom I cannot exist, and who attracts ne to the father, poor man, who ruined imself for love, and who has come ack to me from Mazas as affectionate nd tender as at our first meeting. magine that when we met again he assed the whole night weeping on my houlder; you see there was nothing or you to worry yourself about.

"I have told you, my dear boy, I ave loved too much. I am exhausted. Now I want someone to love me in my turn—someone to pet me and admire me. He will always be at my knee, he will never see in my face a wrinkle, nor a gray hair in my head, and if he marry me, which he wishes to do, it will be a favor on my side. Compare! But above all no folly. My precautions are taken to prevent you ever finding me again. From the little railway *café* where I am writing this I can see amid the trees the houses in which we passed such happy and cruel hours, and the placard swinging on the door awaits new tenants. You are free, you will never hear me spoken of any more. Adieu! One kiss, the last, on the neck, my own!"

Kings in Exile

CHAPTER I

THE FIRST DAY

FREDERIQUE had been sleeping since the early morning,—a fevered and weary slumber, haunted by the grievous, mournful dreams of an exiled and dethroned queen, a slumber still agitated by the tumult and anguish of two months' siege, full of warlike and blood-stained visions, broken by sobs, shudders and nervous prostration, from which she started up with a feeling of terror.

"Zara? Where is Zara?" she exclaimed.

One of her women came forward, and gently reassured her, H. R. H. the Comte de Zara was quietly asleep in his room; Madame Eléonore was with him.

"And where is the king?"

He had gone out at noon in one of the carriages belonging to the hotel.

"What, alone?"

No. His Majesty was accompanied by the councillor Boscovich. By degrees, as she listened to the servant's Dalmatian dialect, clear and hard like the sound of shingle rolling on a beach, the queen felt her fears vanish, and little by little the peaceful hotel room she had vaguely caught sight of on arriving in the early dawn, revealed itself to her with all its reassuring and luxurious triviality, with its light hangings, tall mirrors, and soft-coloured carpets on which the silent and rapid flight of the swallows fell in shadows through the blinds, mingling together like the wings of huge night-moths.

"Already five o'clock! Come, Petscha, do my hair quickly, I am ashamed at having slept so long."

Five o'clock had struck; it was the finest summer's day of the year 1872 that had as yet brightened up Paris, and when the queen stepped on to the long balcony which stretched along the fifteen windows of the *Hotel des Pyramides,* shaded by pink canvas, situated in the very finest position of the Rue de Rivoli, she was lost in admiration.

Below, in the wide thoroughfare, the sounds of wheels mingled with the gentle sprinkle of the watering, as an uninterrupted line of carriages flowed onwards in the direction of the Bois de Boulogne, amid a glitter of harness and a profusion of light dresses, dashing by in a whirlwind of speed. Then from the throng pressing round the gilded gates of the Tuileries, the fascinated gaze of the queen wandered to the bright medley of white frocks, fair locks, gaudy coloured silks, and joyous games; towards all the childish bustle that on a sunny day pervades the terraces of the great Parisian garden; and from these she caught sight of the charming canopy of greenery, the immense round leafy dome of the chestnut trees which sheltered at that moment a military band, and quivered with the delighted screams of the children and the clang of the brass instruments. The bitter rancour of the exiled queen gradually subsided at the sight of the surrounding happiness, a sensation of warmth and comfort seemed to envelop her like a silken web; her cheeks, wan and paled by privation and night-watching, once more assumed a life-like hue, as she thought, "Ah! how charming and peaceful!"

The greatest misfortunes have such moments of sudden and unconscious relief, caused not by persons, but by the thousand-tongued eloquence of things. No human speech could have brought consolation to this despoiled queen thrown into exile with husband and child, by one of those upheavings of the people, which, like earthquakes, open yawning abysses and fiery volcanoes. Her low and haughty brow still seemed to bear the weight of one of Europe's noblest crowns; and now, it is Nature in the fresh joyousness of a marvellous Parisian summer that brings her soothing thoughts of hope and encouragement. As she greedily feasts her eyes on the green-clad horizon and a gentle calm steals over her, lulling her exhausted nerves, the exile suddenly starts and shudders. At her left, yonder, at the entrance of the garden rises a spectral monument with blackened walls, scorched columns, crumbled roof, gaping holes filled with blue space instead of windows, an open-worked façade on a perspective of ruins; and, at the furthest end—overlooking the Seine—one remaining pavilion, almost untouched, scorched only by the flames that have blackened the railings of its balconies. It is all that remains of the Palace of the Tuileries.

The sight filled her with deep emotion and stunned her as though she had fallen prostrate on those stones. Ten years ago, no, not even ten—by what unlucky and seemingly prophetic chance had she happened to lodge in front of these ruins—she had resided there with her husband. It was in the spring of 1864.

Only three months married, the Comtesse de Zara was then visiting the allied Courts, in all the pride of her new dignities of bride and hereditary princess. She was loved and courted by all, and at the Tuileries especially, fêtes and balls succeeded one another. Now from these crumbled walls brilliant visions arose before her; once more she saw the vast and magnificent halls, the dazzling glitter of lights and jewels, the long trains of the court dresses sweeping majestically up the broad stairs between the double rows of glittering breastplates; and the strains of music from the invisible band she heard at intervals floating upwards from the gardens, recalled to her the orchestra led by Waldteufel to which she had so often listened in the Salle des Maréchaux. Was it not to this lively and tripping measure that she had danced with their cousin Maximilian, a week before he started for Mexico? Yes, indeed it was the same! A quadrille made up of Emperors and Kings, of Queens and Empresses, whose movements and august countenances passed before her eyes in a mirage called up by the air of the *Belle Hélène* now being played. Max, full of gloomy presentiments, nervously gnawing his moustache, Charlotte opposite to him, by the side of Napoleon, radiant, transfigured in the triumph of her Imperial dignity. Where were they all now, these quondam dancers of the gay quadrille? Dead, exiled or mad! Death after death, disaster after disaster! Was God then no longer the God of kings?

Then she recalled all she had suffered since the death of old King Leopold had placed upon her brow the two-fold crown of Illyria and Dalmatia. Her first-born, a daughter, carried off in the midst of the festivities of the coronation by one of those mysterious diseases which betoken the end of a worn-out race, so that the tapers of the funereal vigil were mingled with the illuminations of the city, and the festive flags in the cathedral could not be removed before the funeral service took place. Then, besides this great sorrow, besides the continual torments of anxiety she endured from the sickly constitution of her son, other griefs were added, griefs known only to herself, hidden away in the most secret recesses of her womanly pride. Alas! the hearts of nations are not more faithful than those of kings. One day, without apparent reason, Illyria, who had shown so much enthusiasm, suddenly became indifferent to her princes. Then misunderstandings arose, feelings of distrust and stubborn opposition were awakened; hatred, the horrible hatred of a whole country, was felt in the air, in the silence of the streets, in the cold irony of the glances, in the quivering rebellion of the still bowed heads, making her dread to show herself at the windows of her palace, and shrink back in her coach during her short and rapid drives. Ah! as she gazed at the palace of the kings of France, she fancied she still heard the terrible outcries, the horrible threats of death under the terraces of her own palace of Leybach. She remembered the last cabinet council, the pallid faces of her terror-stricken ministers imploring the king to abdicate; then the flight at night, disguised as peasants, across

the mountains, the insurgent villages intoxicated with liberty as well as the towns, the bonfires crowning every hilltop, and the tears that had burst from her one evening in her joy at finding a little milk in a shepherd's cabin for the supper of her boy. Then finally the sudden decision she had induced the king to take, to make the still faithful Ragusa his stronghold, and the two months of privations and anguish endured there; the town besieged, bombarded, the royal child, her sickly boy, dying almost of hunger; and, to crown all, the shame of surrender, the lugubrious embarkation, in the midst of the silent and wearied spectators, on board the French ship which was to bear them to further trouble and misfortunes far away into the cold chill of exile, while behind them the flag of the Illyrian Republic floated new and victorious over the crumbling walls of the Royal Palace. The ruins of the Tuileries brought back all this to her mind.

Her musing was suddenly interrupted by a joyous exclamation uttered in a youthful but slightly nasal voice: "Is not Paris beautiful?"

The king had just appeared upon the balcony, holding the little prince in his arms, and was showing him the horizon of roofs, domes, and verdure, and the busy bustle of the street in the soft light of the closing day.

"Oh yes, very beautiful," said the child—a puny little creature five or six years old, with sharp-marked features and almost colourless fair hair cut close to the head, as after a long illness—he looked around him with a sweet, sickly smile, surprised at no longer hearing the roar of the cannon, and happy in the surrounding joyousness. For him, exile was a pleasant thing; neither did the king appear overcome with sadness; a couple of hours' stroll on the boulevards had imparted to him a certain exhilaration which contrasted with the depression of the queen. Moreover, these two presented types of a diametrically opposite character: the king, a slender man with pale complexion, curly black hair, and a thin moustache, which he constantly twirled between his white and supple fingers; soft uncertain eyes, with something irresolute and childish in their glance, giving him such an immature appearance, that notwithstanding he was over thirty years of age all who saw him could not help exclaiming: "How very young he is!"

The queen, on the contrary, was of the robust Dalmatian type, with an expression of seriousness and strength which made her the real male of the two, despite the exquisite transparency of her skin, and the magnificent auburn tints of her hair, which seemed to have borrowed its flashes of red from Oriental henna. Christian betrayed in her presence the shy attitude of a man who had accepted too much devotion, too many sacrifices from his wife. He timidly inquired after her health, asked whether she had slept off the fatigue of the journey. She answered him with a condescending gentleness, but was in reality solely occupied with her son, feeling his nose and cheeks, and watching every one of his movements with the anxious care of a most tender mother.

"He is better already," said Christian, in a low tone.

"Yes, the colour is returning to his cheeks," she answered in the same tone of familiarity which they only adopted when speaking of their child.

The boy smiled at both, drawing their heads together in a pretty caress, as though he knew his little arms formed the only true link between these two most dissimilar beings. Below, on the pavement, a group of bystanders who had heard of the prince's arrival stood gazing up at this King and Queen of Illyria, made famous by their heroic struggle at Ragusa, and whose portraits had figured in their illustrated papers. By degrees the numbers increased, gaping with open mouths, and noses in the air, as though they were idly watching some pigeon or escaped parrot on the roof. Soon a large crowd was gathered in front of the hotel, all eyes staring up at this young couple in travelling costumes, with the child's fair head upraised between them, their countenances beaming with the undying hope of the vanquished, and the joy of still possessing their treasure after the appalling tempest that had swept over them.

"Are you coming in, Frédérique?" asked the king, embarrassed by the attention of the crowd.

She, however, stood with head raised high as a Queen accustomed to brave the hostile looks of the rabble.

"Why? It is very pleasant here on the balcony."

"Yes; but I had forgotten to tell you —Rosen is here with his son and daughter-in-law. He wishes to see you."

At the name of Rosen, which reminded her of so many loyal services, the queen's eyes brightened.

"My brave duke! I was expecting him," she said, and as she threw a last haughty look on the assembled crowd before going in, a man opposite her sprang upon the stonework of the iron railing of the Tuileries, towering above the crowd for a moment, exactly as at Leybach when the windows of the palace had been fired at. Frédérique, vaguely dreading some similar attempt, instinctively drew back, but at the same moment, a hat upraised displayed a lofty forehead, with hair streaming back, lit up by the setting sun, and a calm powerful voice cried out, "Long live the king." Above the noises of the street, this was all she could catch of the unknown friend, who, in the heart of republican Paris, in face of the crumbling Tuileries, had thus dared to welcome the dethroned sovereigns. This sympathetic cheer, long grown unfamiliar, gave the queen the comforting sensation of a bright fire after a cold long march. It warmed her to the core, and the sight of old Rosen completed the genial and beneficent feeling of reaction.

CHAPTER II

THE GENERAL DUC

THE General Duc de Rosen, formerly at the head of the king's household troops, had left Illyria three years before, when the king had taken from him his post, which was one of trust, to bestow it on a liberal, thus favouring the new ideas to the prejudice of what was then called at Leybach the queen's party. He had certainly every right to resent this treatment at the hands of Christian, who had deliberately sacrificed him, let him go without an expression of regret or even a farewell, he, the victorious hero of Mostar, of Livno, of the Montenegrin wars. After having sold his houses and estates with an ostentation that was intended as a protest against injustice, the old general had settled in Paris, had established his son there, and after three years of anxious and vain expectation, had felt his anger at the royal ingratitude increase by the addition of the dreariness of absence, and of an unoccupied existence. And yet at the very first news of his princes' arrival he had hastened to them without a moment's hesitation; and now, he stood erect in their drawing-room, his immense stature towering up to the chandelier, waiting for the favour of a gracious welcome with such deep emotion, that his great legs trembled and his broad chest heaved under the wide ribbon of his order and the tight-fitting military looking frock-coat which he invariably wore. His head alone, the head of a bird of prey, with its steel glance, its scant, bristling white hair, and the thousand wrinkles of its parched fireproof skin, remained immovable. The king, who hated scenes and felt embarrassed by this first interview, tried to turn it off by affecting a sort of playful and off-hand cordiality.

"Well, general," he said, coming towards him with outstretched hands, "you were right after all. I kept too loose a rein. I have been roughly dealt with, and sharply too."

And, as he saw his old follower bend the knee, he raised him with a gesture full of nobility and clasped him in a long embrace. Nothing, however, could prevent the duke from kneeling before his Queen, and it was with a singular feeling of emotion, that she felt upon her hand the respectfully passionate touch of his old moustache.

"Ah, my poor Rosen! my poor Rosen!" she murmured.

She closed her eyes to hide her tears, but all those she had shed for years past had left their traces upon her soft fair lids, together with the anguish of night-watches and constant anxiety;—these leave scars that women fancy they can hide in the deepest recesses of their heart, but they will re-appear at the surface, just as the least motion of a lake furrows its surface in perceptible ripples. For the space of a moment the beautiful face assumed a tired, mournful expression which did not escape the attention of the old soldier: "How she has suffered," he thought, as he looked at her; then to conceal his own emotion, he raised himself abruptly, and turning towards his son and daughter-in-law, who had remained at the other end of the room, in the same stern voice in which he used to give the word of command in the streets of Leybach: "Draw swords. Charge the rascals!" he ordered: "Colette, Herbert, come and salute your queen."

Prince Herbert of Rosen, almost as tall as his father, with the jaw of a horse, and round babyish cheeks, came forward, followed by his young wife. He walked with difficulty, leaning on his stick. Eight months before he had broken his leg and a few ribs in a race at Chantilly; and the general was not sorry for the opportunity of saying that, had it not been for this accident which had put his son's life in danger, they would both have hurried to Ragusa to the aid of their sovereign.

"I should have followed you, father!" added the princess, in a heroic tone of voice, which contrasted oddly with her name of Colette, and her funny little catlike nose and frizzle of fair locks.

The queen could not help smiling, and held out her hand cordially. Christian, twirling his moustache, stared with an amateur's curiosity at this lively little Parisian, this pretty bird, with its long glittering plumage made up of flowers and skirts, whose dainty get-up was such a change from the majestic type and noble features to which he had been accustomed.

"Lucky dog! Where can Herbert have picked up such a little gem?" he said to himself, envying his old playfellow, that great booby with goggle eyes and hair parted and plastered down on a low narrow forehead; then it suddenly occurred to him that although in Illyria this type of woman might be rare, it was common in Paris; and at this thought exile appeared to him decidedly bearable. Moreover this exile could not possibly be a long one. The Illyrians must soon get tired of their Republic. It would be an affair of some two or three months, a sort of royal holiday, which he must try to spend as gaily as possible.

"Will you believe, General, that it has already been proposed to us that we should purchase a house? An Englishman came this morning and guaranteed he could procure one for me in forty-eight hours in whatever part of the city I should choose; a magnificent house, sumptuously furnished, with stables full of horses, coach-houses full of carriages, linen, plate, and servants—the whole thing complete."

"I know your Englishman, Monseigneur; his name is Tom Levis, a foreign commission agent."

"Yes, that was it, a name something like that. Have you had dealings with him?"

"Oh! all foreigners who come to Paris receive a visit from Tom. I trust for your Majesty's sake that the acquaintance may go no further."

The singular attention which Prince Herbert had devoted to his shoe-strings the moment Tom Levis was mentioned, and the furtive looks the princess cast at her husband, warned Christian that if he should stand in need of any information concerning the famous agent of the Rue Royale, he would know where to turn. But why should he ever stand in need of the services of the Levis agency? He required neither house nor carriages, and fully intended to spend the few months of his stay in Paris at the hotel.

"Is not that your opinion, Frédérique?"

"Oh yes, certainly it is the wisest plan," answered the Queen, although at the bottom of her heart she did not share her husband's illusions, nor his taste for temporary homes.

In his turn old Rosen ventured an observation. Life in an hotel hardly seemed to him compatible with the dignity of the royal house of Illyria. Paris was just then full of exiled sovereigns, and all lived in sumptuous style. The King of Westphalia occupied a magnificent residence in the Rue de Neubourg, with an annexe for the offices of his administration. The mansion of the Queen of Galicia in the Champs Elysées was a true palace, combining the luxury and pomp of royalty. The King of Palermo had a fine establishment at Saint-Mandé, with plenty of horses, and a whole troop of *aides-de-camp*. Even the Duke of Palma, in his small house at Passy, held a sort of court, and had always five or six generals dining at his table.

"No doubt," said Christian impati-

ently; "no doubt, but the case is not the same. They are all settled in Paris, it is an understood, definitive thing, whereas we——Besides, there is one very good reason, friend Rosen, why we should not purchase a palace. All we possessed has been taken from us. A few thousands at Rothschild's at Naples, and our poor crown which was rescued by Madame de Silvis and brought away in a bandbox, is all that remains. To think that the Marquise made the long journey into exile, on foot, by carriage or rail, even crossing the sea, always holding her precious bandbox in her hand! Really, it was too funny!"

And his childishness getting the better of him, he began to laugh over their poverty as if it were the most amusing thing in the world.

The duke, however, did not laugh.

"Sire," he said, so deeply moved that all his old wrinkles quivered, "you did me the honour just now of assuring me that you felt some regret at having kept me for so long a time absent from your heart and your council. Well, I now ask you a favour in return. As long as your exile lasts restore me to the post I filled at Leybach in the service of your Majesties—comptroller of the civil and military household."

"Eh! what ambition!" said the king gaily.

Then turning affectionately towards him, he added:

"My poor general, I have no household now, none, neither civil nor military. The queen has her chaplain and two women. Zara has his governess: as for me I have brought Boscovich to write my correspondence and Lebeau to shave my chin; and that is all."

"In that case, I shall still ask for

another favour. Will your Majesty consent to take my son Herbert as *aide-de-camp* and appoint the princess his wife to the post of reader and lady-in-waiting to the queen."

"Your request is granted, duke, as far as I am concerned," said the queen, smiling brightly to Colette, who stood bewildered by her new dignity.

As for the prince, he thanked his sovereign for the title of *aide-de-camp* he had just conferred upon him in the same gracious manner by a graceful neigh, a trick he had contracted at Tattersall's, where he spent most of his time.

"To-morrow morning I shall lay the three appointments before His Majesty for his signature," added the general in a respectful but curt tone, thereby intimating that he considered himself as already entered upon his new functions.

On hearing the voice and formula which had so long and so solemnly haunted him, the young king's face expressed a momentary ennui and discouragement; but he soon consoled himself as he looked at the princess, whose countenance was transfigured and improved by joy, as often happens to pretty insignificant faces whose beauty and piquancy lies in continual mobility of expression. Just fancy Colette Sauvadon, the niece of Sauvadon, wine merchant at Bercy, lady-in-waiting to the Queen Frédérique! What will the inhabitants of the Rue de Varennes and the Rue Saint-Dominique say, and all those select circles to which her marriage with Herbert had only admitted her on grand reception days, never on intimate terms. Her imagination was already conjuring up a fanciful court. She thought of the visiting cards she would order and of all the new dresses she would have made; for instance, she would certainly have one in the colour of Illyria, with rosettes to match on her horses' heads. Presently the king's voice recalled her from her dreams.

"This is our first meal in the land of exile," he said in a half-serious voice to Rosen; and, in a tone he purposely made emphatic, he added, "I wish the table to be cheerful and surrounded by all our friends."

But noticing the scared look of the general at this sudden invitation:

"Ah, I see, you are quite right. I forgot. We have dropped all habits of etiquette since the siege, and the comptroller of the household will have many reforms to make. Only I request that they shall not begin till to-morrow."

At this moment the doors were thrown open, and the butler announced their Majesties' dinner. The princess was already preparing to rise, full of importance, to take Christian's arm, but he offered his arm to the queen, and, quietly ignoring his guests, led her into the dining-room. All the ceremonial of the court had not, after all, remained buried in the casemates at Ragusa.

The sudden transition from the sunny room to the artificially lighted dining-room struck the guests as they entered. Notwithstanding a central chandelier, two side candelabras, and two large lamps placed on the sideboard, it seemed dim, as though the daylight revenged itself for having been thus brutally shut out before its time, by casting a dubious twilight on the scene. The length and disproportion of the table with the small number of guests also added to the appearance of gloom; it was a table that had been sought for all over the hotel to suit the demands of etiquette, and the king and queen took their places at one end of it, no one sitting opposite, or next to them. This filled the little Princess of Rosen with surprise and admiration. In the last years of the Empire, when she had dined at the Tuileries, she remembered having seen the Emperor and Empress seated opposite one another, just like any ordinary married couple at their wedding breakfast.

"Ah," thought the little *cocodette* as she shut her fan with a decided gesture, and placed it near her by the side of her gloves, "Legitimacy, that is the only real thing!"

And this thought transformed for her the sparsely attended kind of table d'hôte, which recalled the splendid dining-rooms along the Italian Corniche road, between Monaco and San Remo, at the beginning of the season before the tourists begin to pour in. The same medley of people and costumes; Chrisian in a shooting-jacket, the Queen in a travelling-dress, Herbert and his wife in fashionable costumes, fitted for the boulevards; the Franciscan cassock of Father Alphée, the queen's chaplain, side by side with the military-looking frock-coat of the general, covered with his many decorations. Nothing, in short, could be less imposing. One thing alone lent some grandeur to the scene,—the prayer of the chaplain, invoking a divine blessing on this, the first repast partaken of in exile.

"*Quæ sumus sumpturi prima die in xile,*" said the monk, with outstretched hands; and the words, slowly enunciated, seemed to lengthen out far into the future the short holiday contemplated by King Christian.

"*Amen!*" responded, in a grave voice,

the despoiled sovereign, as though in the Latin of the Church he had at last felt the thousand broken ties which cling with living and quivering hold, like the roots of an uptorn tree, to the banished of all times and places.

Nevertheless, the strongest impressions did not dwell long in this polished and caressing Slav nature. He was hardly seated, before his natural gaiety and heedlessness returned, and he began to talk in French, out of regard for the Parisian Colette, correctly, but with a slight Italian lisp that well suited his laugh. In a heroic-comic tone he related different episodes of the siege; the settling-down of the court in the casemates, and the singular figure cut by the Marquise Gouvernante Eléonore de Silvis, in her green feathered hat and her plaid. Fortunately, that innocent lady was dining in her pupil's room, and could not hear the laughter caused by the king's description. After her, Boscovich and his herbarium served the king as a butt. With boyish glee he seemed to wish to revenge himself for the gravity of the circumstances by turning them into ridicule. The aulic councillor Boscovich, a small middle-aged man, gentle and timorous, with rabbit's eyes looking always askance, was a learned jurisconsult, passionately fond of botany. The law courts being closed at Ragusa, he spent his time in botanising in the ditches of the fortifications, under fire of the shells, with the unconscious heroism natural to a mind utterly absorbed in one idea, and who, in the midst of the terrible disaster that had befallen his country, was solely preoccupied about the fate of a magnificent herbarium that had been left behind in the hands of the liberals.

"Fancy, my poor old Boscovich," said the king to frighten him; "fancy what a jolly bonfire they will have made of all that heap of dried flowers; unless, indeed, the Republic should have decided, out of economy, to cut new capes for its militia out of your great sheets of grey blotting-paper."

The councillor joined in the general laugh, with scared looks however, and abortive efforts to protest: *"Ma che! Ma che!"* which betrayed his childish apprehensions.

"How charming the king is! how witty! and what eyes!" thought the little princess towards whom Christian kept bending at every moment, as though he would fain lessen the distance made between them by the exigences of etiquette.

It was a pleasure to see her expand under the evident admiration of his august glance, toying with her fan, uttering little cries, and throwing back her supple figure, which shook with rippling and ringing laughter. The queen, by her attitude and her close conversation with her neighbour, the old duke, seemed to isolate herself from the overflow of gaiety. Once or twice when the siege was being spoken of, she had said a few words, speaking emphatically of the king's bravery, his knowledge of strategy, after which she had resumed her own conversation. The general, in a low voice, inquired about the persons of the court he had known, all companions in arms, who, more fortunate than himself, had followed their princes to Ragusa. Many had been left there, and as Rosen mentioned each name, the queen responded in her serious voice: "Dead, dead," the words sounding like the funereal knell of all those so recently departed.

However, after dinner, when they returned to the drawing-room, Frédérique was more cheerful. She made Colette de Rosen sit beside her on the sofa, and talked to her with the affectionate familiarity that attracted the sympathy of all around her; it was like the pressure of her beautiful hand with its tapered fingers and broad palm, which communicated by its firm grasp something of her own comforting energy. Suddenly she said:

"Come, princess, let us go and see Zara put to bed."

At the end of a long lobby, encumbered like the rest of the apartment with piled-up boxes, open trunks overflowing with linen and articles of clothing, all the disorder of a recent arrival, was the room of the little prince, lighted by a lamp, the lowered shade of which threw the light on to the blue bed-curtains at the level of the bed.

A waiting-woman was sleeping seated on a box, her head wrapped in the white coif and neck-handkerchief bordered with pink that forms the headgear of the Dalmatian women. Near the table, the governess, resting lightly on her elbow with an open book in her lap, was also undergoing the soporific influence of the story she had been reading, and retained even in her sleep the sentimental and romantic air which had caused the king's mirth and excited his mockery.

The queen's entrance failed to rouse her, but at the very first movement of the mosquito-net that veiled his bed the little prince stretched out his hand and made an effort to sit up, with wide open eyes and vacant gaze. For s-many months he had been accustomed to sudden wakings, hurried dressings, startings, and flights in the middle of the night, to find himself reawakening in new places with new faces around him, that he had lost the deep sleep of childhood—and his was no longer the ten hours' journeying in the land of dreams, which children accomplish to the accompaniment of the soft and almost imperceptible rhythm of their gentle breathing.

"Good night, mama," he said in a low voice: "are we going to start off again?"

By his resigned and touching exclamation all that the child had suffered was revealed, a suffering far beyond his years and strength.

"No, no, my darling; we are in safety at last. Sleep; you must try to sleep."

"Oh! very well. I shall go back to the mountain of glass with the giant Robistor; I was enjoying myself so much."

"Madame Eléonore's stories are muddling his brain," said the queen, softly. "Poor little one! Life is so dark and gloomy for him. Fairy tales are the only things that amuse him. We shall have, nevertheless, to make up our minds to put something else in his head before long."

As she spoke she arranged the child's pillow and settled him to rest with the caressing gesture of any other mother, which quite upset Colette de Rosen's grandiose ideas about royalty. Then, as she bent down to kiss her son, he asked in a whisper, what was the noise he heard rumbling in the distance, the cannon or the sea. The queen listened for a moment to the confused and constant rolling, which at times made the walls crack and the windows rattle, enveloping the house from top to bottom, then dying away and bursting out afresh, increasing and losing itself in an infinitude of similar noises.

"It is nothing, only Paris, my son. Go to sleep."

And the little fallen prince, who had heard of Paris as of a refuge, went off to sleep again, full of confidence, lulled by the sounds of the revolutionary city.

When the queen and the princess returned to the drawing-room they found the king standing by the side of a young and noble-looking woman, with whom he was talking. The familiar tone of their conversation, the respectful distance the rest of the company maintained, showed that she was a personage of some importance. The queen uttered a cry of emotion:

"Maria!"

"Frédérique!"

A mutual impulse threw them into each other's arms. In answer to an inquiring glance of his wife, Herbert de Rosen named the visitor. She was the Queen of Palermo. Somewhat taller and slighter than her cousin the Queen of Illyria, she seemed a few years older. Her black eyes, her dark hair brushed back off her forehead, and her pale complexion gave her the appearance of an Italian, although she was born at the Court of Bavaria. There was a certain Germanic look in her long flat figure, and the haughty expression of her smile; besides the unmistakable dowdiness and want of harmony in dress so peculiar to the other side of the Rhine. Frédérique, who had been left an orphan at an early age, had been brought up at Munich with this cousin, and they had retained a strong affection for one another.

"You see, I could not wait," said the Queen of Palermo, holding her hands. "Cecco did not return, so I came without him. I was longing to see you. You have been so constantly in my thoughts. Oh! that dreadful cannon of Ragusa, I fancied I heard it at night from Vincennes."

"It was but the echo of the cannon of Caserta," said Christian, alluding to the heroic conduct that a few years before had distinguished this poor queen, fallen and exiled like themselves.

She sighed:

"Oh, yes! Caserta. We were deserted by all, as you were. How pitiable; as if all monarchs should not stand by each other. But all that has come to an end. The world has gone mad!"

Then turning to Christian, she added: "Nevertheless, I must compliment you, cousin; you have fallen like a king."

"Oh!" he said, pointing to Frédérique, "the true king of us two——"

A sign from his wife stopped him. He bowed, smiled, and turning on his heel:

"Come and smoke, Herbert!" he said to his aide-de-camp. And they stepped out together on the balcony.

The evening was balmy and lovely, and the last glimmer of day was fading and disappearing in bluish tints round the brilliant gas-lamps. The dark mass of chestnut trees in the Tuileries maintained a fanlike breeze around them and quickened the flashing light of the stars. This background of verdure and space imparted to the Rue de Rivoli a less suffocating appearance than is usual to the streets of Paris in summer; but the constant drifting of the population in the direction of the Champs Elysées could be distinctly felt, wending its way to its open-air concerts under the flaring circles of gas-lights. All the amusements which in winter are confined within warmly-draped window-hangings, now filled the streets; pleasure sung and laughed freely, in flowering bonnets, fluttering mantillas, muslin dresses, revealing as they passed under a streetlamp a glimpse of a white neck and black velvet ribbon. The cafés and pastry-cook shops overflowed on to the pavement, with sounds of money, clinking of glasses and many calls.

"Paris is a wonderful place," said Christian of Illyria, puffing the smoke of his cigar out into the darkness. "The very air seems different from anywhere else; it has something exciting and heady about it. Fancy that at Leybach at this hour everything is closed, extinguished, asleep."

Then in a tone of delight he went on:

"I say, my dear aide-de-camp, I trust I am going to be initiated to the pleasures of Paris; you seem to know all about them, to be quite up in them."

"Yes indeed, monseigneur," replied Herbert, neighing with gratified vanity "At any club, at the opera, everywhere I am called the king of the *gomme!*"

While Christian made him explain the meaning of this new word. the two queens, who had gone into Frédérique's room to converse more freely, poured forth their sad confidences in low whispers that could be heard behind the half-closed shutters. In the drawing room Father Alphée and the old duke were also talking in a low tone.

"He is quite right," said the chap

lain; "it is she who is the king, the real king. If you could have seen her on horseback, at the outposts day and night! At the fort Saint-Angelo, when the balls were flying thick, in order to encourage the soldiers, she walked twice round the top of the trenches, proud and erect, her riding habit over her arm and her whip in her hand, as though she were quietly going round her own park. You should have seen our sailors when she came down! He, meanwhile, was gadding about, God only knows where! Brave he certainly is, as brave as she is, but without conviction or faith; and to save a throne as to gain Heaven, Monsieur le Duc, we must needs have faith."

The monk getting excited, seemed to grow taller in his long robe, and Rosen was obliged to calm him.

"Lower, Father Alphée. Speak lower, please." For he feared lest Colette should hear him.

Colette had been left to the tender mercies of the Councillor Boscovich, who was entertaining her with an account of his plants, mingling scientific terms with the minute details of his botanical expeditions. His conversation had an aroma of faded herbs and the musty atmosphere of an old provincial library. Nevertheless, such is the powerful attraction of greatness, so delightfully intoxicating is its atmosphere to certain little beings eager to breathe in, that the young princess, Princess Colette, the soul of Paris balls, of its laces, and its theatres, ever in the van of all its gaieties, this same Princess Colette bestowed her most fascinating smiles upon the councillor, as she listened to his arid nomenclature. It was enough for her to know that a king was talking at the window, that two

queens were exchanging confidences in the next room, to make the commonplace hotel room where even her own elegance seemed to be out of its element, assume the air of solemn grandeur and gloomy majesty which throws so melancholy an appearance over the wide halls at Versailles, and their polished floors that glisten as brightly as their mirrors. She could have remained there in an ecstasy until midnight, without stirring, or feeling the least ennui, slightly puzzled however by the lengthy conversation between the king and her husband. What serious subjects could they be discussing? What vast plans for the restoration of monarchy? Her curiosity increased when she saw them reappear with flushed faces, bright and resolute eyes.

"I am going out with Monseigneur," said Herbert, in a low tone; "my father will take you home."

The king approached her in his turn:

"You will not be angry with me, Princess, I hope; he is entering upon his functions."

"Every instant of our lives belongs to your Majesties," replied the princess, persuaded that they were bent on some important and mysterious business; perhaps indeed a first meeting of conspirators. Oh! if only she could follow them!

Christian had taken a step towards the queen's room, but when he reached the door, he paused.

"They are crying," he said to Herbert, turning back. "Good night, I shall not go in."

Once in the street he gave way to an explosion of joy and relief, and took his aide-de-camp's arm, after having lit a fresh cigar in the hall of the hotel

"You cannot understand how refreshing it is," he said, "to go alone into the crowd, to walk and mix with the rest of the world, to be master of one's words and actions, and if a pretty girl passes by, to be free to turn and look after her without any fear of upsetting the equilibrium of Europe. This is the advantage of exile. When I came to Paris some eight years ago, I saw it from the windows of the Tuileries, from the seats of the gala-coaches. This time I want to see it all, every corner, by Jove. But I forgot you were lame, my poor Herbert, and I am making you walk. Wait, let us hail a cab."

In vain did the prince strive to protest. His leg was not painful, and he felt quite able to walk. But Christian insisted.

"No, no, I will not have any guide knocked up on the very first evening."

He hailed a passing cab that was going in the direction of the Place de la Concorde with a rattle of strained springs and cracking of whip on the bony frame of the wretched horse; he jumped lightly in and settled himself on the faded blue cloth cushions, rubbing his hands with childish glee.

"Where are we going, *mon prince?*" asked the coachman. little aware of how exact was the appellation.

And Christian of Illyria answered in the triumphant voice of an emancipated school-boy:

"To Mabille."

CHAPTER III

A ROYALIST

CLOSE-SHAVEN and bare-headed under a fine sharp December drizzle, that rimmed like steel drops their brown woollen cassocks, two monks wearing the girdle and round cowl of the Franciscan order, walked with long strides rapidly down the rue Monsieur-le-Prince. In the midst of all the transformations of the Latin quarter, of those wide thoroughfares that have opened out and destroyed all the originality and memorials of ancient Paris, the rue Monsieur-le-Prince still preserves its original student aspect. The booksellers' shops, the office-houses, the cook-shops, the old clothes-dealers, "sale and purchase of gold and silver," succeed one another up to the heights of Sainte-Geneviève, and scholars still stalk up and down at all hours of the day, not indeed the students drawn by Gavarni, with long straggling locks and woollen Scotch caps; but lawyers of the future, tightly buttoned up in ulsters, carefully gloved, and carrying enormous leathern portfolios under their arms, assuming already the sharp, cold manners of men of business; or else doctors in perspective, more easy in their gait, retaining from the material, human side of their studies, an expansion of animal life as a compensation for their perpetual struggle with death.

At this early hour young women in loose wrappers and slippers, their eyes swollen from want of sleep, their hair rolled up in dangling nets, were already crossing the street to fetch milk for their breakfast from the dairy, some laughing and hastening through the sleet, others on the contrary, with prim dignity, swinging their milk cans, and trailing their slipshod feet and their faded finery with the majestic indifference of pantomime queens; and as notwithstanding ulsters and morocco portfolios, youthful hearts are always susceptible, passing students were smiling at the fair ones. "Hullo, Léa." "Good morning, Clémence." They hailed one another across the street, making appointments for the evening: "Be at the Medici's to-night," or else "I'll see you at the Louis XIII.'s." Then suddenly at a joke too coarse or misunderstood, one of the girls would break out in astounding indignation, with the invariable retort: "Get along with you, you saucy fellow!" Imagine how the two monks must have shuddered on coming in contact with all these gay young folk, constantly turning and laughing as they passed. The laugh, however, was speedily checked at the sight of one of the Franciscans, who, lean and lanky, possessed the grim countenance of a pirate under his dark bushy eyebrows, and whose cassock, tightened in coarse folds by a cord at the waist, revealed the sturdy loins and muscular form of an athlete. Neither he nor his companion appeared to notice anything in the street, but strode along hurriedly, gazing straight before them, absorbed in the object of their errand. Before reaching the flight of steps leading to the School of Medicine, the elder said to the other: "It is here."

He pointed to a lodging-house of poor aspect at the end of an alley, closed by a belled green gate, situated between a shop full of cheap newspapers, penny ballads, and coloured pictures in which the grotesque hat of Dom Basile figured in a multitude of attitudes, and a low beershop, bearing on its signboard the words: "*Brasserie du Rialto,*" so called no doubt because the waiting was done by young woman in Venetian headdresses.

"Is Monsieur Elysée gone out?" inquired one of the Fathers, as they passed the hotel office on the first storey.

A fat woman, who by her appearance must have roved through many a lodging-house before she became herself the mistress of one, lazily answered from her chair, without even taking the trouble of consulting the rows of keys hanking on the rack.

"Gone out, at this hour? You had better say, has he come home!"

Then changing her tone at the sight of the cassocks, she indicated Elysée Méraut's room.

"No. 36, on the fifth floor, at the end of the lobby."

The Franciscans went up, wandering through narrow passages, littered with muddy boots and high-heeled shoes of every description: grey, bronze, fantastic, luxurious, or miserable, that told many a tale of the occupier's existence; but they heeded nothing, sweeping the passage with their rough skirts and the crosses of their long rosaries, scarcely moved even when a handsome young woman in scarlet petticoat, and her bare arms and shoulders thrust into a man's overcoat, crossed the landing on the third floor and leant over the bannisters to scream out some order to the waiter, with a husky voice and laugh issuing from a peculiarly coarse mouth. They exchanged, however, a significative glance.

"If he is the man you describe," muttered the corsair in a foreign accent, "he has chosen singular company."

A smile full of malice and priestly indulgence crossed the face of the elder monk, an intelligent and shrewd-looking man.

"Saint Paul among the Gentiles!" he murmured.

When they reached the fifth storey, they had a moment's hesitation, the low ceiling of the dark staircase hardly allowing the numbers to be discerned, and several doors being ornamented by cards, such as "Mademoiselle Alice," without any mention of a business, a mention that would in truth have been superfluous, for there were several competitors in that line of trade in the house; but fancy if these excellent Fathers had by mistake knocked at one of their doors!

"We must call his name!" said the bushy-eyebrowed monk, and the hotel rang with a "Monsieur Méraut!" emphasized in a right martial manner.

Not a whit less vigorous, not a whit less vibrating was the response to his call, which issued from a room at the end of the passage. And when they opened the door, the voice continued cheerfully:

"Ah, it is you, Father Melchior! I'm out of luck! I hoped it was a registered letter. Come in all the same, Reverend Father, you are welcome, and, if you can, pray sit down."

Books, reviews, newspapers were indeed piled up on every article of furniture, hiding the sordid conventionality of a poverty-stricken lodging, the discoloured tiles, the broken-down divan, and the invariable *Empire* writing-table, and the three faded velvet chairs. On the bed lay scattered in a confused medley: printed papers, clothes, and a thin brown blanket, with files of proofs that the master of the locality, still in bed, slashed with great marks in coloured pencil. The wretched interior, the fireless chimney, the naked dustiness of

the walls were lighted up by the neighbouring roofs, the reflection of a rainy sky on glistening skies; and Méraut's wide brow, his powerful and passionate face was illumined by it, showing the sad but intelligent expression that distinguishes certain faces and is met with nowhere but in Paris.

"Still in my hovel, you see, Father Melchior! It cannot be helped. I alighted here on my arrival eighteen years ago. Since then, I have not budged. What dreams, what hopes have I not buried in every corner, how many conceits do I not find hidden away in the dust. I am sure that if I left this shabby little room, I should be leaving the best part of myself. I am so convinced of it, that I kept it on when I left to go yonder."

"Ah, to be sure, and what about your journey?" said Father Melchior, casting a glance at his companion. "I thought you had intended staying away for some time. What happened? Did not the situation suit you?"

"Oh! the situation was magnificent," replied Méraut, shaking his mane, "it would have been impossible to have a better berth. The pay of a minister plenipotentiary, lodged in the palace and horses, carriages, servants at my disposal. Everybody was most kind to me, the Emperor, Empress and Archdukes. Nevertheless I felt dull and bored. In spite of all, I longed for Paris, the Latin Quarter especially, the air we breathe here, so light and full of life. I missed the galleries under the Odéon, the new book turned over standing by the stalls, and the hunt for old books, those musty volumes piled up on the parapets of the quays, like a rampart sheltering studious Paris from the frivolity and selfishness of its other quarters. And then, that is not all—here his voice grew more serious—you know my ideas. Father Melchior. You know what was my ambition in accepting the position of a subaltern. I hoped to make a king of that little fellow, a king really kingly, such as we never see now-a-days. I intended to raise him, form him, prepare him for the grand part that overpowers and crushes them all, like the mediæval armour kept in old castles that shames our narrow chests and shoulders. Ah well, do you know what I found at the Court at X.? Liberals, my dear friend, radicals, men devoted to all the new ideas. Horrible plebeians who will not understand that if monarchy is condemned, it had better perish fighting, wrapped up in its flag, than die in an invalid's chair rolled towards the grave by some foolish Parliament. No later than my first lesson, there was an outcry through the whole palace. Where did this fellow come from? What designs had this barbarian? Then with many soft words I was requested to keep to my duties of pedagogue. An usher in fact! When I saw that, I took up my hat and said good-bye to their Majesties!"

He spoke in a strong full voice and a southern accent that had a metallic ring in every cord of it; and as he spoke his face was transfigured. His head, which at rest was large and ugly; a great bumpy forehead overshadowed by a shock of black hair streaked with one white tuft; a thick, broken nose; a powerful mouth devoid of any beard that might have concealed its appearance, for his skin had the wrinkles and cracks and hardness and sterility of a heated volcanic soil: this became mar-

vellously brightened and lightened by passion. Imagine a veil torn away, the black blower of a grate suddenly raised, displaying a joyous and reviving blaze, a revelation of inborn eloquence flashing from the eyes and mobile features, spread by the rush of heart's-blood over that face worn and marked by every kind of excess and every fatigue. The landscapes in Languedoc, Méraut's native land, bare, sterile, grey like the dusty olive trees, assume in the many-coloured settings of their relentless sun this gorgeous resplendence traversed by fairy-like shadows which seem the decomposition of a ray, the slow and gradual death of a rainbow.

"So you are disgusted with grandees?" said the old monk, in an insinuating and muffled voice, that was in a strong contrast with this explosion of eloquence.

"Certainly!" replied the other, energetically.

"Nevertheless, all kings are not alike. I know one whom your ideas——"

"No, no, Father Melchior. That is at an end. I do not wish to try such an experiment again. I should fear lest seeing sovereigns too closely, I might lose all respect for them."

After a moment's silence, the wily priest sought a subterfuge to carry back his thoughts to the same subject.

"This six months' absence must have been detrimental to you, Méraut."

"No, hardly. First, the uncle Sauvadon has remained faithful to me; you know Sauvadon, my rich Bercy fellow. As he meets a great many people at his niece's, the Princess of Rosen, and wishes to mix in the conversation, it is I whom he has appointed to give him three times a week what he calls 'ideas about things in general.' His confidence and simplicity are delightful, poor man! 'Monsieur Méraut, what am I to think about this book?' 'Execrable.' 'Indeed, yet it seemed to me; I heard some one say the other evening at the princess's——' 'If you have an opinion my presence here is useless.' 'No, no, my dear friend, you know very well I have no opinion of my own.' The fact is he really has none and blindly adopts any of my suggestions. I am his thinking matter. After I left, he no longer spoke, having no more ideas. And when I returned, you should have seen how he literally threw himself upon me. Then I have a couple of Wallachians whom I instruct in political law. And, besides, I have always some small job on hand. For instance, I am finishing just now a *Memorial of the Siege of Ragusa* drawn from authentic documents. There is not much of my scribbling in it, except the last chapter, which I am rather pleased with. I have the proofs here. Shall I read it to you? I have called it *Europe without Kings!*"

While he read his royalist memorial, with an animation that moved him to tears, the awakening of the inmates of the hotel surrounded them with the sounds of mirth and youth, mingled with the clinking of plates and glasses and the wooden clang of an old piano, on which was hammered the tune of a low music-hall ballad.—a strange contrast indeed, of which the Franciscans were hardly cognizant, absorbed and charmed as they were by the sounds of this forcible and brutal defence of royalty The taller one more especially quivered restlessly, striving to repress his enthusiastic exclamations with a gesture of his arms that seemed to crush his very chest. The chapter ended, he drew himself up erect, paced the room impatiently with mighty stride, overflowing with gestures and words:

"Yes, that is true; that is the real, legitimate, absolute, divine right"—only he pronounced it *lezitime* and *assolute*. "No more parliaments, no more talkers. Throw the whole gang into the fire!"

And his glance burnt and blazed like a faggot of the Inquisition. Father Melchior, however, was more calm and congratulated Méraut on his work.

"I trust you will put your name to this book," he said.

"Not any more than to the others. You know Father Melchior, that I am only ambitious for my ideas. The work will be well paid. It was through Uncle Sauvadon I got this windfall, but I would willingly have written it for nothing. It is such a grand thing to record the annals of that expiring royalty, to listen to the failing breath of the old world gasping and dying with the worn-out monarchies. Here, at least, a king fell in a way that gives a haughty lesson to all. Christian is a hero! Among those notes jotted down day by day, there is the account of a stroll he took while the shells were bursting around him at the fort Saint-Angelo. It is glorious!"

One of the Fathers bowed his head. He, alas, well knew the true story of that heroic manifestation, and that still more heroic lie. But a will more powerful than his had commanded silence; and he merely made a sign to his companion, who, rising from his chair said abruptly to Méraut:

"Well, it is for that hero's son, that accompanied by Father Alphée, almoner of the Court of Illyria, I have come to see you. Will you undertake the education of the royal child?"

"You will have neither palaces nor grand coaches with us," added Father Alphée, with a touch of melancholy, "nor the Imperial generosities of the Court of X. You will serve dethroned princes around whom an exile that has already lasted more than a year, and that is likely to be prolonged, has thrown a veil of gloomy solitude. Your ideas are ours. The king, it is true, at one time trifled with radicalism, but after his fall, he recognised its worthlessness. The queen is sublime, you will see her."

"When?" impetuously inquired the visionary, suddenly replunged into all his wildest dreams of creating a king by his genius, as a writer creates a drama.

An early interview was at once arranged.

Whenever Elysée Méraut thought of his childhood—and he often thought of it, for it was the starting point of his most powerful impressions—this is what his mind always conjured up. A large room with three windows bathed in light, each filled by a silk-weaving Jacquart loom, that stretched its tall frame and interwoven meshes like busy blinds through which was imperfectly seen the sunlight and the view; a medley of roofs, of houses above houses, every window of which was also furnished with a loom, at which sat two men in shirt-sleeves, alternately moving across the weft, like pianoforte players performing a piece for four hands. Between the houses, narrow little gardens wandered up the hill-side, tiny gardens of southern climes faded and burnt up,

arid and airless, full of cactus and aloes, of tall bottle-gourds and of great sunflowers turning their full-blown faces towards the west, with the bent attitude of corollas seeking the sun, and filling the atmosphere with the sickly odour of their ripening seed—an odour that Elysée after a lapse of thirty years still fancied he smelt whenever he thought of his native suburb. The view commanded by the stony hill on which this stirring hive-like working district was built, was crowned by a few old and deserted windmills, ancient purveyors of the town, left standing on account of their long services, the skeletons of their sails standing out against the sky like gigantic broken antennæ, their stones slowly loosened and scattered by the wind, the sun, and the stinging dust of the South. Under the protection of these ancestral windmills, the customs and traditions of former days had been safeguarded. The whole *bourgade*—this suburban quarter was also nicknamed *l'enclos de Rey*—had remained ardently royalist, and in every work-room there might be seen hanging on the walls, the fat, pink portrait—with long fair hair curled and pomatumed in the style usual in 1840—of him whom the inhabitants of this little borough familiarly termed *lou Goï* (the lame one). In Elysée's home under this frame hung a smaller one in which a great red seal with the two words *"Fides, Spes,"* as motto round a Saint Andrew's cross, stood out on a sheet of bluish writing-paper. From his seat, as he threw his shuttle, father Méraut could see the portrait and read the motto: *Faith, Hope.* And his wide massive features, outlined like some old medal struck under Antony, with also the aquiline nose and rounded contours of the Bourbons he loved so well, would swell and redden with emotion.

This fellow Méraut was indeed a terrible man, violent and despotic, whose voice had become full of the roar and thunder of the storm, in the attempt to drown the noise of the shuttle and loom. His wife, on the contrary, retiring and timid, imbued with the traditions of submissiveness which reduce the old-fashioned women of the South to the level of Eastern slaves, had resigned herself to silence

It was in this home that Elysée had grown up, rather less harshly treated than his two brothers, because he was the youngest and most delicate. Instead of setting him to the loom at eight years of age, he was allowed a breath of that freedom so necessary to childhood,—a freedom he employed in running all day about the *enclos,* and fighting in front of the windmills, white against red, Catholics against Huguenots; for in that part of Languedoc they still clung to the old hatreds! The children divided into two camps, chose a windmill whose crumbling masonry served as ammunition; and then insults were exchanged, stones flew from slings, and for hours they engaged in homeric struggles, always tragically ended by some bloody gash across a youthful forehead, or a deep cut through the silken locks—one of those childish wounds that leave a life-long mark on the tender skin, such as the one Elysée, when grown up, still showed on his temples and at the corner of his mouth.

Oh! those windmills, how the mother cursed them, when her little lad came home at dusk, covered with blood and tatters. As for the father, he merely scolded for appearance sake, and lest his thunder should become rusty; but once seated round the table, he would ask all the details of the battle and the names of the combatants.

"Tholozan! Tholozan! Are there still some of that lot? Ah! the rascal. I had his father at the end of my gun in 1815, I should have done well to have laid him low."

And then would follow a long story told in the Languedocian dialect, rough and full of metaphor, unsparing of phrase or words, of the time when he had enlisted under the Duke d'Angoulême's orders—a great general, a saint indeed.

This narrative, heard some hundreds of times, but varied each time by the paternal fervour, left as deep an impress on Elysée's heart, as the stones of the windmills on his face. He lived surrounded by a Royalist legend, in which St. Henri's day, and the 21st of January, were commemorative dates; imbued with veneration for martyr-princes who blessed the rabble with uplifted fingers like bishops, and of dauntless princesses springing on horseback to save the good cause, persecuted, betrayed, and surprised behind the black chimney-slab of some old Breton country house. Then in order to enliven the sad tale of death and exile which might have been too mournful for a child, the story of the *Poule au Pot,* and the ballad of the *Ver Galant* would be introduced, adding the mirth and glorious recollections of ancient France. It seemed to be the *Marseillaise* of the *Enclos de Rey,* this ballad about the *Vert Galant!*

When on Sundays, after vespers, the Mérauts dined on a laboriously propped up table in the sloping little garden, in the suffocating atmosphere engendered by a summer's day, when the accumulated heat emanating from the ground and walls poured forth more powerfully and more unhealthily than in the full glare of the noontide; when the old weaver struck up in a voice that had become celebrated among his neighbours, the ballad of *"Vive Henri Quatre, vive ce roi vaillant,"* all was hushed around them. Nothing broke the silence but the dry cracking of the reed-fence splitting from the heat, the shrill sound of some belated *cicala,* and the antiquated royalist song majestically rolling forth in all the rigidity of cadence suggestive of puffed hose and hooped skirts. The chorus: *A la santé de notre roi—c'est un Henri de bon aloi—qui fera le bien de toi, de moi,"* rhythmical and fugue-like, amused Elysée and his brothers, and they joined in, pushing and shoving one another, invariably calling down on their heads a cuff from their father; but this interlude would not interrupt the song, and it continued in the midst of blows, laughter, and sobs, like some demoniac's hymn, sung over the tomb of the deacon Paris.

Thus ever mingled with the family merry-makings, the name of king assumed in Elysée's mind, besides the natural prestige it still holds in fairy tales or in "history written for young people," a something more intimate and homelike. And what increased this feeling were the mysterious letters on thin foreign paper that came from Frohsdorff two or three times a year, addressed to all the inhabitants of the *Enclos,* autographs in the delicate writing penned by fat fingers, in which the king spoke to his people and enjoined

patience. On those days, father Méraut threw his shuttle more solemnly, and at night, with close-shut doors, he would read out loud the circular,—always the same mawkish proclamation, full of vague words of hope: "Frenchmen, you are deceived, and the country is deceived." And ever the same immutable seal: *"Fides, Spes!"* Ah, poor folk, it was neither faith nor hope that they lacked.

"When the king comes back," Méraut used to say, "I shall buy a comfortable armchair. When the king comes back, we will new paper the room."

Later on, after his journey to Frohsdorff, the formula was changed.

"When I had the honour of seeing the king," he would say on every occasion.

The good fellow had in truth accomplished this pilgrimage, a real sacrifice of time and money for a working man, and never did Hadji returning from Mecca bring back a more dazzling impression. The interview had, indeed, been short. To the faithful subjects introduced into his presence, the pretender had said: "Ah, here you are!" And not one of them had found a word in reply to this affable greeting; Méraut less than the others, for, suffocated by emotion and tears, he had not even been able to distinguish the features of the idol. However, as they were leaving, the Duc d'Athis, comptroller of the household, had interrogated him at some length on the state of feeling in France; and it is easy to imagine how the fanatical weaver, who had never quitted the *Enclos de Rey,* answered:

"Let him come, let him come quickly, our King Henri. We are all thirsting and pining for him!"

Whereupon, the Duc d'Athis, delighted at this valuable information, thanked him a great deal, and abruptly inquired:

"Have you any children, Master Méraut?"

"I have three, Monsieur le Duc."

"Boys?"

"Yes, three children," repeated the old burgher (for in those parts girls were not counted).

"Very well. I have put that down. His Royal Highness will remember them when the time comes."

Whereupon the duke had taken out his pocketbook, and *cra, cra*. This *cra, cra,* by which the worthy fellow described his patron's gesture in taking down the names of his three sons, invariably formed part of the narrative that had become one of the family annals, touching in its faithful repetition. Henceforth, whenever work was at a standstill, and his wife betrayed any anxiety at her husband's failing health, or diminution of their little savings, this *cra, cra,* was considered a sufficient answer to calm all her fears.

"Don't be uneasy! The Duc d'Athis has made a note of it."

CHAPTER IV

SHAMEFUL CELEBRITY

SUDDENLY grown ambitious for his sons, the old weaver, seeing that the two elder were already started in life on the old family lines, transferred all his hopes of grandeur to Elysée. He was sent to the Papel school, kept by one of those Spanish refugees who invaded the southern towns of France after the capitulation of Marotto. The establishment was situated in the quarter *des Boucheries,* in a tumble-down house, grown mouldy in the shadow of th cathedral, and revealing its state by th mildewed windows and crevices of it walls. It was reached through a net work of narrow, slimy, dirty streets between rows of shops bristling witl gratings and iron hooks, on which hun enormous quarters of meat, surrounde by an unwholesome buzzing of flies When, later on in life, Elysée recalle those days, it always seemed to him a though he had passed his childhood i the Middle Ages, under the rod an knotted rope of some terrible fanatic in a gloomy and sordid class-room where the Latin verbs were only inter rupted by the neighbouring bells ringin their blessings or curses over the aps of the old church, over its carved, foli ated scroll-work, and strange, weir gargoyles. Papel, a little man with a enormous greasy countenance, shade by a dingy-white cap rammed dow upon his eyes to hide a big, swoller blue vein that divided his forehead, re sembled a dwarf in one of Velasquez' pictures, minus the bright tunic and th bronzing of time. Withal, brutal an cruel, his large skull contained a prodig ous store of ideas, a living and luminou encyclopædia, locked, so to speak, by stubborn royalism laid like an iron ba across his brows, and which, indeec seemed physically revealed by the ab normal swelling of the curious vein o his forehead.

It was a common report in the towr that the name of Papel was assumed t hide another and more notorious on that of a *cabecilla* of Don Carlo famous for his mode of waging war, an for the ingenuity of his methods for ir flicting death. Living so near th Spanish frontier, his shameful celebrit inconvenienced him and necessitated his living under an assumed name. What truth was there in this story? Elysée, during the many years he spent at the school, and although he was Monsieur Papel's favourite pupil, never heard the terrible dwarf pronounce a single word, nor receive a single visit or letter that could confirm his suspicions. Only, when the child became a man, when he had finished his studies, and the *Enclos de Rey* had become too cramped a space for his laurels, diplomas, and the paternal ambition, when it was decided to send him to Paris, Monsieur Papel gave him several letters of introduction to the leaders of the Legitimist party, weighty letters indeed, sealed with mysterious coats of arms, which seemed to confirm the legend of the disguised *cabecilla*.

Master Méraut had insisted on this journey, for he began to think that the king was delaying his return too long. He made every sacrifice, sold his gold watch, his wife's silver chain, and his little vineyard, the patrimony of every burgher, and this he did simply, heroically, for his party.

"Just go and see what they are about," said he to his youngest son, "what they are waiting for? *L'enclos* is getting weary of waiting for ever."

Elysée Méraut arrived therefore in Paris at the age of twenty, brimful of ardent convictions, in which the blind devotion of his father was augmented by the militant fanaticism of his Spanish master.

He was received by the Legitimist party very much like a traveller who gets into a first-class carriage in the middle of the night, at some bye station, when all the previous occupiers are already comfortably settled for the night. The intruder, his blood warmed by the sharp air and rapid walking, longs to talk, move, and prolong his wakefulness; but he is greeted by the surly and somnoient bad humour of the other passengers, snugly ensconced in their furs, lulled by the motion of the train, who have even drawn the little blue curtain over the lamp, and who, heavy with sleep and drowsy warmth, dread both the draught and the intruder.

Such was the aspect presented by the Legitimist clan under the Empire; shunted travellers on an abandoned siding.

This black-eyed fanatic, with his thin leonine head, punching out each syllable he uttered, emphasizing each phrase by an energetic gesture, possessing within himself, ready for any occasion, all the dash of Suleau and daring of Cadoudal, struck the party with a mixed feeling of terror and astonishment. He was put down as a dangerous, restless fellow. Beneath the exaggerated politeness and hypocritical appearance of interest that good breeding can so easily assume, Elysée, with the clear-sightedness which a southern Frenchman ever retains, even in the midst of his most passionate excitement, Elysée quickly discerned all the selfish low cunning of these men. According to them there was nothing to be done for the present; nothing but to wait quietly, above all to cultivate calm, and avoid all excitement and juvenile enthusiasm. "Look at Monseigneur, what an example he sets us!" And these cautious and prudent words were in admirable keeping with the old mansions of the noble *Faubourg*, muffled up in ivy, deaf to the bustle of the streets, wadded with idleness and comfort behind the massive gates, heavy with the weight of time and traditions. Politely, they invited him to two or three political meetings held in great mystery, with all sorts of fears and precautions, in one of these retreats full of venomous spite. There he met the bearers of the great names illustrious in the Vendean wars, and the massacre of Quiberon; the whole list of those inscribed on the *champ des martyrs*, now borne by nice old clean-shaved gentlemen, sleek as prelates in their broadcloth, whose unctuous voices seemed heavy and sticky with luscious sweetmeats. They would arrive with the air of conspirators, all of them fancying they were followed by the police, who, in truth, made fun of these platonic appointments.

When they had settled down under the discreet shades of their tall waxcandles, bending their bald heads as shiny as ivory counters, some one would impart news of Frohsdorff, and they would admire the unalterable patience of the exile, and encourage one another to imitate it. In a low whisper, hush! They repeated Monsieur de Barentin's last pun on the Empress, or hummed in an undertone the song: *"Quand Napoléon—vous donnant les étrivières—aura tout de bon—endommagé vos derrières."* Then terrified at their own audacity, the conspirators would leave one by one, slipping along the walls of the wide and deserted rue de Varennes, which re-echoed with the alarming sound of their timorous steps.

Elysée soon discovered that he was too young and too active for these ghosts of former days. Moreover France was then basking in the full sunshine of the Imperial epopee; and the regiments returning from the Italian war were flying their victorious eagles under the decked-out windows of the boulevards.

The old burgher's son was not long in finding out that the opinion of *l'Enclos de Rey* was not that of all France, and that the King's return would not be so speedy as they fancied at his home. His royalism remained staunch, but now that action had become impossible, it expanded into an ideal that was broader and nobler even than the reality. He conceived the project of writing a book, a book in which his convictions and hopes, all that he wished to say and propagate, would stand revealed to that great Paris he longed to convince. His plan was at once made: he would gain his daily bread by giving lessons—he soon found as many pupils as he wished —and he would write his book in his leisure moments, and bestow on it all the time it would require.

Like all Southerners, Elysée Méraut was above all a man of speech and gesture. Ideas only came to him standing, at the sound of his own voice, as the peal of bells attracts lightning. Strengthened by reading, by facts, by constant meditation, his thoughts, which flowed from his lips in gushing streams, words following words in sonorous eloquence, from his pen fell slowly, drop by drop, as though coming from too vast a reservoir for such slow filtration and for the refinements of written composition.

It was a relief to him to give speech since he found no other means of communicating his convictions. He therefore seized every opportunity of speaking, in the cafés, at conferences, more especially however in the cafés of the

Quartier Latin, where alone in the crouching Paris of the second Empire, when books and newspapers were gagged, opposition was carried on. Every drinking shop had at that time its orator, its great man. It was then said: "Pesquidoux of the Café Voltaire is very powerful, but Larminat of the Procopse is even more so." In fact, these cafés were crowded with well-educated and eloquent youths, whose minds were filled with noble ideas, and who revived, with even more spirit, the glorious political and philosophical discussions carried on in the taverns at Bonn and Heidelberg.

In these creative centres of ideas, smoky and noisy, where, if shouting was great, drinking was still greater; the strange enthusiasm of this tall, ever-excited Gascon, who did not smoke, and was intoxicated without drink, his picturesque and brutal eloquence expressing opinions as old-fashioned as powder and panniers—as discordant with the surroundings in which they were exposed, as an antiquarian amid trumpery gewgaws;—soon procured Elysée both a reputation and an audience.

At the hour when the gas is flaring in the crammed and bustling cafés, when his thin lanky form was discerned crossing the threshold, his short-sighted and rather wild eyes seeming in an effort of vision to toss back his hair and hat, and a book or review with an enormous paper cutter ever under his arm, a shout of welcome would greet him: "Here comes Méraut!" And all crowded together to give him elbow room and space enough to gesticulate freely. These acclamations, this youthful enthusiasm, the heat and light, the heady intoxicating light of the gas, all contributed

to excite him. Every topic, whether culled from the day's paper or an open book, glanced at as he passed under the arcades of the Odéon, served as a theme; and he dashed off on his subject, seated or standing, holding his audience spellbound with his voice, grouping his public by a gesture. The domino players stopped, the billiard players upstairs hung over the banisters, pipe in mouth, ivory cue in hand. The window-panes, the glasses, the saucers rattled as if a post-chaise were dashing by, and the mistress of the establishment seated at her desk would say proudly to the new-comers: "Come in quick, we have Monsieur Méraut!" Ah! Pesquidoux and Larminat might be as powerful and eloquent as they could, he, Elysée, was more than a match for them. He became the orator of the Quartier Latin. This glory that he had not sought sufficed for him, and unfortunately arrested his steps towards fame. Such was the fate of many a Larminat of that period;—great powers were wasted—like a powerful machine uselessly and noisily lets off its steam through some defect in the regulator. With Elysée, there was yet another cause: devoid of intrigue or ambition, this Southerner, who had brought from his country nothing but the fervour of his convictions, considered himself the missionary of his own political faith, and he did in truth display the indefatigable proselytism, the strong independent nature of a missionary, the disinterestedness that disdains fees and fat livings and prefers the hard and dangerous life of mission-work.

Assuredly, during the eighteen years that he had been scattering broadcast his ideas among the youth of Paris, more than one who had made his way, and who now said with contempt: "Oh, yes! Méraut, an old student!" had derived the best part of his fame, from the crumbs that this singular fellow had carelessly dropped at many a table. Elysée knew it well, and when he found under the green coat of an academician one of his chimerical ideas toned down in a well-turned phrase, he was happy, with the unselfish affection of a father who sees the daughters of his love richly married, and yet lays no claim to their affection. It was the chivalrous abnegation of the old weaver of the *Enclos de Rey*, with something nobler added to it, since he lacked confidence in the success of the cause he served—a confidence which old Méraut retained unshaken to the very last. The day before his death —for he died almost suddenly from a sunstroke, after one of his open-air dinners—the old man still sang at the top of his voice: "Vive Henri IV." And at the last moment, when his eyes were already dim, and his speech dull, he still repeated to his wife: "Quite easy about children—Duc d'Athis—made a note." And with his dying hands he strove to write *"cra—cra"* on the sheet.

When Elysée, warned too late of this sudden blow reached his home, his father lay already stiff and cold, his hands folded across his breast, on the bed which stood against the wall of the room still waiting for its new paper. Through the door of the workshop, which had been left open for Death, who scatters, loosens and widens all around him, Elysée saw the silent looms; his father's, now forsaken, like a stranded vessel against which the wind was henceforth powerless; then the king's portrait and the red seal which had presided over

this laborious and faithful life; and overhead, high above the *Enclos de Rey,* rising up in bustling tiers on the hill, the old mills ever standing, uplifting their wings against the clear sky, like signals of despair. Never did Elysée forget the sight of that serene death, cutting off the humble workman at his post, and closing his eyes upon his familiar horizon. He was seized with a longing for death, he who was yet filled with dreams of adventure, he who was the living embodiment of the fantastic illusions of the fine old man sleeping there.

It was after his return from this sad journey, that he was offered the post of tutor at the Court of X——. His disappointment had been so great, the petty meannesses, jealousies, and envious slanders in the midst of which he had found himself; the painted pageantry of monarchy seen too close, from the side-scenes, had so saddened him, that, notwithstanding his admiration for the King of Illyria, after the first fever of enthusiasm had cooled and the monks had left, he regretted having accepted so quickly. The recollection of all the annoyances he had undergone in his previous post returned to him, with a feeling of the sacrifice he must make of his liberty and habits. Then his book, that famous book ever seething in his brain! In short, after a long self-debate, he resolved on refusing; and on Christmas Day, when the interview was at hand, he wrote to Father Melchoir to announce his decision. The monk did not remonstrate; he merely wrote the following lines:

"Come this evening to the rue de Fourneaux for the night service. I hope to convince you."

The Franciscan convent of the rue des Fourneaux, where Father Melchoir held the office of treasurer, is one of the most curious and unknown corners of Catholic Paris. This mother-house of a celebrated order, mysteriously hidden amid the wretched suburb that swarms and grovels behind the Montparnasse railway-station, is also called "the Commissariat of the Holy Sepulchre." Here it is that monks of strange and foreign appearance, their travelling-robes mingling with the profound poverty of the district, bring—for the trade in relics—bits of the true Cross, chaplets of olive stones from the Garden of Olives, roses of Jericho dry and fibrous, awaiting a drop of consecrated water, a whole cargo of miraculous goods which in the vast invisible pockets of the brethren changed into good sound coin, heavy and mute, that afterwards found its way to Jerusalem to keep in order the Holy Sepulchre. Elysée had been first brought to the rue des Fourneaux by a sculptor who was his friend, a poor artist struggling in a garret, named Dreux, who had just executed for the convent a Sainte Marguerite d'Ossuna, and who took as many people as possible to see his statue. The place was so curious and picturesque, harmonized so thoroughly with the convictions of the Southerner by linking them—thus saving them from modern clearness of thought—to the most remote centuries and countries endeared to him by tradition, that he often returned thither to the great joy of friend Dreux, proud, indeed, of the success of his Marguerite.

It was nearly midnight on the evening of the rendezvous when Elysée Méraut quitted the swarming streets of the Latin Quartier; from the general air of festivity of the Boulevard Saint Michel and the rue Racine, reeking with the odours of the cook shops and beribboned pork butchers, the provision stalls and taverns served by women, the students' lodgings, and the glaring liquor bars, he emerged into the melancholy of the deserted avenues where the passers-by, dwarfed by the reflections from the gas lamps, seemed to crawl rather than to walk. The feeble bells of the various religious communities tinkled behind their walls, above which peered the skeletons of trees; the noise and the warm odour of straw being stirred, of stables wrapped in sleep, came from the great closed yards of the cow-keepers; and while in the broad street a vague and trampled whiteness showed where the snow had fallen during the day, the burgher's son walked on in the deepest dream of ardent belief, fancying he recognized up above, among the stars sparkling in the cold, that which guided the kings to Bethlehem. As he gazed at this star he recalled the Christmases of former days: the white Christmas of his youth, celebrated at the Cathedral, and the return through the streets of the butchers' quarter—fantastic with the outlines of roofs against the moonlight—towards the family table in the *Enclos de Rey* where the Christmas supper awaited them; the traditional three candles set amid the scarlet dotted holly, the *estevenons* (little Christmas cakes), smelling deliciously of hot dough and the fried bacon. So well did he enwrap himself in these family recollections, that the lantern of a dustman passing along the pavement seemed to him that which was wont to swing from father Méraut's hand as he marched at the head of the party returning from these midnight masses.

Alas! poor father, he would never more see him! And while he held secret communion with these dear familiar shades, Elysée reached the rue des Fourneaux, a scarcely finished suburb, lighted by one lamp, made up of long factory buildings overtopped by tall chimneys, of wooden hoardings, of walls re-built of old materials. The wind blew violently over the great plains round the city.

From a neighbouring slaughter-house came mournful sounds, dull blows, a sickening smell of blood and fat; it is here they kill the pigs that are sacrificed to Christmas, as at the sacred feasts of some Teutates.

The gateway of the convent standing in the middle of the street was wide open, and in the court yard were two or three carriages with splendid harness that astonished Méraut. The service had begun; bursts of music from the organ and of chanting issued from the church, which was nevertheless deserted and in darkness; the only light being that from the little lamp on the altar and the pale reflection of the snow on the phantasmagoria of the painted windows. The nave was almost round, adorned with great banners from Jerusalem bearing the red cross which hung from the walls, and with somewhat barbaric coloured statues; in the midst of which Marguerite d'Ossuna in pure marble, pitilessly scourged her white shoulders, for—as the monks said with a certain coquetry—"Marguerite was a great sinner belonging to our order."

The ceiling of painted wood crossed by a network of small timbers, the high altar beneath a sort of canopy supported by columns; the semi-circle of the choir surrounded by the woodwork of the empty stalls with a ray of moonlight lying across the open page of the plainsong book, all this was indistinctly seen; but by a great staircase concealed beneath the choir, was the descent into the crypt, where—perhaps as a reminiscence of the catacombs—the service was being held.

Quite at the end of the vault, in the white masonry supported by great Roman columns was a reproduction of the tomb of Christ at Jerusalem, with its low doorway, the narrow interior lighted by a quantity of little funereal lamps, blinking—from the depths of their stony cells—on a Christ in coloured wax, the size of life, his bleeding wounds showing brightly scarlet where the shroud fell apart. At the other end of the crypt, as a singular antithesis, resuming in itself the whole Christian epopee, was displayed one of those childish reproductions of the Nativity, of which the manger, the animals, and the child begarlanded with bright colours and greenery in curled paper, are drawn each year from the stock of legends, just as they emerged of yore, more rudely shaped no doubt, but much larger, from the brain of some visionary.

Now as then, a group of children and old women, with an eager craving for love and the marvellous—the poor whom Christ loved—crowded round the manger. Among them, to Elysée's surprise, in the front row of these humble and faithful souls, two men in well-cut clothes, two elegant women in dark costumes, knelt lowly on the bare flags, one of them holding a little boy around whom she wrapped her two folded arms with a gesture of protection and prayer.

"They are queens!" an old woman

said to him in a whisper, breathless with admiration.

Elysée started. Then, drawing nearer, he recognised the delicate profile and aristocratic appearance of Christian of Illyria, and near him the brown, bony head, and still youthful but bald forehead, of the King of Pa'ermo. Of the two women nothing could be seen but the black and auburn hair and the attitude of passionately adoring motherhood. Ah! how well the wily priest, who had thus dramatically arranged the first interview between the young prince and his future tutor, how well he knew Méraut. These dethroned kings coming to offer their homage to God, who to receive it seemed to have concealed himself in this crypt, this assemblage of fallen royalty and religion in distress, the sad star of the exile guiding these impoverished Magi, without retinue and empty-handed towards a suburban Bethlehem, all this swelled his heart to suffocation. The child above all touched him, with his little head bent towards the animals of the manger, the curiosity natural to his age, tempered by a reserve born of suffering. And before this childish brow, wherein the future already lay hid like the butterfly in its golden chrysalis, Elysée fell to thinking how much science, how much tender care would be needed to make it bloom into splendour.

CHAPTER V

THE COURT

THE temporary arrangement at the *Hôtel des Pyramides* had lasted three months, then six months, with the half-unpacked trunks, the half-unstrapped bags, all the disorder and uncertainty of a camping out. Every day excellent news arrived from Illyria. In a new soil, deprived of roots, without a past or a hero, the Republic gained no ground. The people were tired of it, regretted their princes, and calculations of infallible certainty were brought to the exiles, saying: "Hold yourselves in readiness. To-morrow will be the day." Not a nail was put into the walls, not a piece of furniture was moved, without the hopeful exclamation: "It is scarcely worth while." Nevertheless, the exile became prolonged, and the Queen was not slow to understand that this sojourn in an hotel amid a host of strangers, a flight of birds of passage of all kinds, was gradually becoming derogatory to the dignity of their rank. The tent was therefore struck, a house was bought, and they settled down. From a nomad the exile became a settler.

It was at Saint-Mandé, on the Avenue Daumesnil, at the top of the rue Herbillon, in that part which skirts the wood and is bordered with elegant buildings, smart iron-work railings affording glimpses of well-kept gardens with gravel paths, rounded flights of steps, lawns of close turf that gave the spot the appearance of a corner of the avenue of the Bois de Boulogne. In one of these houses the King and Queen of Palermo, comparatively poor, had already sought refuge and seclusion from the turmoil of the luxurious quarters of the fashionable world. The Duchess of Malines, sister of the Queen of Palermo, had come to join her at Saint-Mandé, and the two easily induced their cousin to settle in the neighbourhood. Putting aside all question of friendship, Frédérique wished to stand aloof from the light-hearted merriment and festivity of

Paris, to protest against modern society and the prosperity of the Republic, and to avoid the curiosity attaching to well-known figures, which seemed to her an insult to their fallen fortunes. The king had at first raised an outcry at the distance of their habitation from the rest of the world, but soon he found it a convenient pretext for long absences and tardy returns. Finally, to crown all, living was cheaper there than elsewhere, and their usual comfort could be maintained at little expense.

The establishment was comfortable. The white house, three stories high, flanked by two turrets, overlooked the wood across the trees of its little park, while facing the rue Herbillon, between the offices and the conservatories opposite each other, was a great gravelled courtyard to which descended the doorsteps, surmounted by a marquee supported like a tent by two long lances. In the stable were ten horses, riding and carriage horses—the Queen rode every day—the liveried servants wore the Illyrian colours, powdered and bag-wigged; and a hall porter, whose halberd and golden shoulder belt were as legendary at Saint-Mandé and at Vincennes as the wooden leg of old Daumesnil; gave to all a suitable air of luxury and comfort. In truth it was scarcely more than a year since Tom Levis had improvised with all its decorations and accessories, the princely scenario whereon is to be played the historic drama we have to relate.

Yes, indeed! Tom Levis. Notwithstanding misgivings and repugnance, it had been necessary to have recourse to him. The little fat man was of surprising elasticity and tenacity. He had so many tricks, so many keys and jemmies to unlock or force all doors, however unwilling or resisting the lock, without counting the innumerable dodges peculiar to himself for gaining the goodwill of the tradesmen, the valets and the women-servants! "Above all, have nothing to do with Tom Levis." That was what everyone said to begin with. But then nothing got on. The tradesmen did not deliver their wares at the promised time, the servants rebelled, until the day when the man in the cab, with his gold-rimmed spectacles and his heavy watch-chain appeared, and then the hangings fell down of themselves from the ceilings and trailed upon the parquet floors, draped themselves into complicated arrangements of portières, curtains, or decorative carpets. The stoves lighted themselves, the camellias grew and blossomed in the conservatory, and the proprietors, quickly installed, had nothing further to do than to enjoy life and await on the comfortable seats in the drawing room, the bundle of bills which would arrive from all corners of Paris. In the rue Herbillon it was old Rosen, comptroller of the civil and military household, who received the accounts, paid the servants, managed the king's little fortune, and this so cleverly, that within this gilded frame allowed to their misfortune. Christian and Frédérique still lived handsomely. Kings both of them, children of kings, they knew nothing of the price of things, and were only used to see themselves in effigy on all the gold pieces, or to coin money according to their good pleasure. Far from being therefore astonished at their affluence, they felt on the contrary everything that was missing in their new existence, to say nothing of the chilly void that a fallen crown leaves around.

heads accustomed to wear it. The house at Saint-Mandé, so simple outside, had in vain adorned itself like a little palace in the interior; the queen's room exactly recalled that of the castle of Leybach, with its hangings of blue silk damask and old Bruges; while the prince's study was an exact copy of that he had left behind him; and on the staircase were reproductions of the statues in their royal residence, and in the conservatory a warm monkey-house, adorned with climbing creepers for the favourite marmosets. What were all these little details of delicate flattery to the possessors of four historic castles, and of those summer residences hanging between sky and sea, the lawns running down to meet the waves, in the green isles called "the gardens of the Adriatic."

At Saint-Mandé, the Adriatic was represented by the little pond in the wood that the queen overlooked from her windows, and gazed at as sadly as the exiled Andromache upon the false Simoïs. However restricted their mode of life, it occurred to Christian, more experienced than Frédérique, to wonder at this relative comfort.

"Rosen is a wonderful fellow. I really do not know how he manages to do everything with the very little money we have."

Then he would add laughing:

"We may be very sure, however, that not a penny comes out of his own pocket!"

The fact is, that in Illyria, Rosen was synonymous with *Harpagon*. Even in Paris, the fame for stinginess had followed the duke, and was confirmed by the marriage of his son, a marriage arranged by a matrimonial agency and that all the pretty charms of the little

Sauvadon could not prevent from being a sordid mésalliance. Rosen nevertheless was rich. The old Pandour who carried all his instincts of rapine and pillage written on his bird of prey face, had not made war against the Turks and Montenegrins solely for love of glory. After each campaign his waggons returned full, and the splendid mansion he occupied at the extremity of the Ile Saint-Louis, close to the Hotel Lambert, was overflowing with precious things, oriental hangings, furniture of the middle ages, triptydes of massive gold, sculptures, reliquaries, materials embroidered and spangled with gold, the spoil of convents or harems, piled up in a suite of immense reception-rooms opened only once, for the marriage of Herbert and the fairy-like fête then provided by old Uncle Sauvadon; but which since that day hoarded their wealth in the mournful locked-up rooms, behind drawn curtains and closed shutters, not even having to fear the indiscretion of a single sunbeam. Here the old man led the existence of an eccentric, confined to one floor of the vast hotel, restricting himself to two servants as his whole establishment and to the fare of a provincial miser; while the great kitchens in the basement with their motionless spits and unheated ovens remained as heremetically closed as the gala apartments above.

The arrival of his sovereigns, the nomination of all the Rosens to the appointments of the tiny court, had slightly modified the old duke's habits. In the first place the young people had come to live with him, their house in the Parc Monceaux—a real modern cage with gilt bars—being too far from Vincennes. Every morning at nine o'clock, no matter what the weather, the princess Colette was in readiness for the queen when she rose; and got into the carriage with the general in that riverside fog, that winter and summer mornings alike leave floating about the point of the island—like a veil upon the enchanted scenery of the Seine. At this hour, Prince Herbert tried to regain a little of the sleep foregone in the somewhat arduous night duty imposed by King Christian, who, having ten years of provincial life and conjugal curfew to make up for, found it so difficult to tear himself away from the charms of nocturnal Paris, that when the theatres and cafés were closed and he had left the club, he thought it delightful to wander along the deserted boulevards, dry and echoing, or shining with rain, between the line of the gas lamps, that like a guard of fire marked the edge of the long perspective.

The instant she arrived at Saint-Mandé, Colette went to the queen's apartments. The duke, on his side, settled himself in a small pavilion communicating with the offices, convenient alike for the tradespeople and the servants. It was called the steward's office; and it was touching to see the old giant seated in his leather chair, surrounded by files of papers of all kind and bill cases, receiving and settling petty accounts—he who formerly had under his orders a whole tribe of gold-braided underlings. Such was his avarice that, though he was not making payments on his own account, every feature of his face would contract with pain each time he must part with money —there was a nervous movement of every wrinkle as if they had been pulled together with the string of a money-bag

—his stiff and erect body seemed to protest, as did even the automatic gesture with which he opened the safe let into the wall. Notwithstanding everything, he managed to be always ready, and, with the modest resources of the Prince of Illyria, to provide for the waste inevitable in a large house, for the queen's charities, for the king's gifts, even for his pleasures, no light addition to the budget; for Christian II. had kept faith with himself and was spending his period of exile right merrily. An assiduous attendant of all Parisian festivities, welcomed in the best clubs, sought after in the drawing-rooms, his delicate and sarcastic profile, appearing in the animated confusion of a "first night," or the tumultuous crowd of a race course, had taken its place henceforward among the faces known to "all Paris," between the extravagant headdress of a fashionable actress, and the bleared features of that royal prince in disgrace, who haunts the cafés of the boulevards while waiting for the hour to strike that shall make him king. Christian led the idle and yet busy life of the gilded youth of the day. In the afternoon there was the tennis-court or the skating rink, then the Bois, later on a visit to a certain smart boudoir where the extreme luxury and the excessive liberty of speech pleased him. In the evening, the lighter theatres, the green room, the club, and, above all, the gambling table, the handling of the cards revealing all his Bohemian origin, with its passion for chance and all its wonderful presentiments. He scarcely ever went out with the queen, except on Sunday to accompany her to the church of Saint-Mandé, and only saw her at meal times. He felt in awe of this upright and reasonable nature, always ruled by a sense of duty, and whose contemptuous coldness embarrassed him like a visible conscience. It was a recall to the kingly responsibilities and ambitions that he would fain forget; and too weak to revolt openly against this silent dominion, he preferred to fly from it, to lie and so avoid it. On her side, Frédérique knew but too well this Slav temperament, ardent yet yielding, fragile and easily moved; she had so often had to pardon the escapades of this child-man, who retained all the characteristics of childhood: the grace, the laughter, even childhood's cruel caprice; she had so often seen him on his knees before her, after one of those follies in which he had risked his dignity and his happiness, that she was completely out of heart with him, both as husband and as man, though there did still remain to her some regard for him as king. This struggle had lasted nearly ten years, although outwardly they had seemed a most united couple. In these exalted circles, with vast suites of apartments, numerous servants, the ceremonial which makes distances greater and suppresses display of sentiment, this kind of deceit is possible. But exile was about to betray the truth.

Frédérique had at first hoped that this hard trial might ripen the king's mind, awake within him those noble feelings of revolt that make the hero and the conqueror. But on the contrary, she could see in his eyes a growing intoxication of festivities and excitement, created by the life in Paris, by its diabolic will-o'-the-wisp, by the incognito, the temptations and the facilities for pleasure. Ah! if she had been willing to follow him, to share his mad

career through the Parisian whirlwind, cause her beauty, her horses, her toilettes to be quoted, to lend all the coquetry of a woman to the frivolous vanity of the husband, a reconciliation might have been possible. But she remained more queen than ever, abdicating nothing of her ambitions, her hopes, and, from afar, still eagerly taking part in the struggle, sending letter upon letter to the royal adherents, protesting, conspiring, representing the iniquity of their misfortune to every court in Europe. The councillor Boscovich wrote from her dictation; and at noon, when the king came down, she herself presented the letters for his signature. He signed; he would sign anything she liked, but with an ironic twitch at the corner of his mouth. The scepticism of his jesting and chilly surroundings had infected him; to the illusions with which he had started had succeeded, by a reaction common to these extreme natures, a formal conviction that the exile would be indefinitely prolonged. Thus he imported an air of fatigue, of utter ennui, into the conversations in which Frédérique tried to raise him to the same fever height as herself, and vainly sought in the depths of his eye the attention she could not succeed in fixing. Absent, haunted by some foolish chorus, there ran for ever in his head a vision of the last night's amusement, the intoxicated and languid bewilderment of pleasure. And what an *"ouf"* of relief escaped him when he could at length get away, what a renewal of youth and life, that each time left the queen more lonely and more sad.

After this work of writing in the morning, the despatch of some of those short and eloquent notes, in which she revived the courage and the devotion of those about to waver, Frédérique's only amusements were readings chosen among the royal library of books, composed of memoirs, correspondences, chronicles of the past or works of high religious philosophy. Then she had the child's games in the garden, and some rides in the Bois de Vincennes, rides but rarely prolonged to that border of the forest where may be heard the last echoes of Parisian noise, where the vast misery of the suburb draws towards its verge; for Paris caused her an antipathy, and unconquerable alarm. Scarcely once a month, would she go in state, to make her round of visits among the exiled princes. She started without pleasure, and returned discouraged. Beneath these royal misfortunes, decently and nobly borne, she felt the underlying abandonment, complete renunciation, exile accepted, undergone with patience, grown into a habit, concealed and cheated by manias, childish fancies or worse.

The most dignified and proud of all these fallen majesties, the King of Westphalia, a poor, blind old man, who with his daughter, a fair-haired Antigone, was a touching sight, kept up the pomp and outward seeming of his rank, but no longer occupied himself with anything but the collection of snuff-boxes, and the setting up of glass-cases full of curiosities in his drawing-room; a singular jesting at the infirmity which prevented him from the full enjoyment of his treasures. In the King of Palermo was the same apathetic renunciation, complicated by mourning, melancholy, want of money, a disunited household, all ambition killed by the death of the only child. The king, nearly always absent, left his wife to her widowed and

exiled hearth; while the Queen of Galicia, extravagant, adoring pleasure, made no change in her turbulent habits of exotic sovereign; and the Duke of Palma from time to time unslung his carbine in an attempt to cross the frontier, which each time threw him back on the miserable idleness of his life. In reality, he was far more of a brigand than a pretender, waging war in order to obtain money and women, and making known to his unfortunate duchess all the emotions endured by the wretched girl married to one of those Pyrenean bandits, who, if they delay their return till daylight, are brought home upon a bier. All these dethroned beings had but one word on their lips, one device to replace the high-sounding mottoes of their royal houses: "Why do anything? Of what use?" To the active fervour of Frédérique. to her outbursts, the more polite replied by a smile; the women answered by talking of religion, the theatre, flirtation, or fashions; and, little by little, this tacit lowering of a principle, this disintegration of forces, gained upon the haughty Dalmatian herself. Between this king who no longer wished to be one, and the poor little, backward Zara, who grew so slowly towards manhood, she was overcome by the feeling of her own impotence. Old Rosen said nothing, and was shut up all day in his office. The princess was but a bird, occupied all day in smoothing its plumage; Boscovich a child; the marquise, a simpleton. There was Father Alphée, but this rough and stern monk could never have comprehended the doubts hinted in the queen's conversation, and the fears that began to steal upon her. The season had something to do with it too. The woods of Saint-Mandé, that in summer were all greenery and flowers, calm and deserted as a park during the week, on Sunday swarming with a joyous population; took, in the approaching winter, in the mournfulness of misty and wet horizons, in the fog ever floating over its lake, the desolate and piteous aspect peculiar to forsaken haunts of pleasure. Flocks of crows flew above the black bushes, above the great gnarled trees, to which magpies' nests and hoary bunches of mistletoe clung, swinging on their leafless summits. It was the second winter Frédérique had passed in Paris. Why did it seem to her so much longer, so much more gloomy than the other? Was it the bustle of the hotel that she missed? The busy movement of the rich and ever restless city? No. But in proportion as the queen diminished within her, the weaknesses of the woman overcame her, the troubles of the neglected wife, the nostalgia of the stranger torn from her native land.

CHAPTER VI

THE QUEEN'S NOOK

In the glass gallery forming an annex to the great reception-room, she had made a little winter garden, a comfortable nook removed from all domestic noises, decorated with bright hangings, and green foliaged plants in all the corners, and here she now often remained for whole days, doing nothing, gazing at the rain-soaked garden and the network of slender branches streaking the grey horizon, like an etching, with a mixture of the deep winter evergreen that the holly and yew preserve even beneath the snow, through the whiteness of which their sharp branches pierce a way.

On the three basins of the fountain, placed one above the other, the sheets of falling water assumed tones of frosted silver, and beyond the high ironwork running beside the Avenue Daumesnil, the silence and the solitude of the two leagues of wood was occasionally broken by the passage of the steam tramways, whistling as they went, their long line of smoke trailing far behind them, dispersing so slowly in the heavy yellow atmosphere that Frédérique could follow it for a long time and see it lose itself little by little, slow and aimless like her own life.

It was on a rainy winter morning that Elysée Méraut gave his first lesson to the royal child in this tiny nook, the home and shelter of the queen's sadness and her dreams, which on this day assumed the aspect of a school-room. Books, exercise books spread on the table, a shaded light like that of a work or class-room, the mother in a simple close-fitting dress of black cloth that set off her tall figure, a little lacquer worktable wheeled in front of her and the master and pupil, one as nervous and hesitating as the other, over this their first interview. The little prince vaguely recognized the great fiery head that had been pointed out to him on Christmas eve in the dim religious light of the chapel, which his imagination, crowded with the fairy tales of Madame de Silvis, had assimilated to some apparition of the giant Robistor or the enchanter Merlin. And the impression left upon Elysée was as chimeric and fantastic; for on his part, he imagined he saw in this delicate little boy, sickly and prematurely old, his forehead already lined as if it bore the whole six hundred years of his race—a predestined chief, a leader of men and of nations, and he said to him gravely, in a voice that trembled:— "Monseigneur, you will be a king some day. You must learn what a king is. Listen to me, look at me well, and what my lips may not explain clearly enough, the respect of my glance will teach you."

Then, bending over this diminutive intelligence, seeking words and figures of speech to suit its grasp, he explained to him the dogma of divine right, of a king's mission upon the earth, standing between God and the people, charged with responsibilities and duties that other men have not, and which are imposed upon him from infancy. That the little prince understood what was said to him is not altogether probable; perhaps he felt himself encircled by that vivifying warmth with which gardeners, tending a rare plant, surround the delicate fibre, the weakly shoot. As for the queen, bending over her embroidery. she listened with an exquisitely delighted surprise, as words reached her that she had been despairingly awaiting for many years, which answered to her most secret thoughts, calling them forth and rousing them from their torpor: for so long had she dreamed alone! How many things there were that she had not known how to say, and which Elysée now expressed for her! In his presence, from the very first day, she felt as an unrecognized musician, an artist who has not found expression, must do before the masterly executant of his work. Her vaguest sentiments upon this grand idea of royalty were so embodied, and so magnificently yet so simply expressed, that a child, quite a young child, could almost comprehend them. While she

looked at this man, his great rugged features animated with faith and eloquence; she saw in strong contrast the pretty indolent face, the undecided smile of her husband; she heard the eternal "Of what use?" of all these dethroned kings, the idle gossip of the princely boudoirs. And it was this plebeian, this weaver's son, with whose history she was acquainted, who had gathered up the lost traditions, preserved the relics and the shrine, the sacred fire, of which the flame was visible on his brow at this moment, communicating itself to others in the fervour of his discourse. Ah! if Christian could have been like this, they would still be upon the throne, or else both would have disappeared, buried beneath its ruins. It was singular that in the attention she could not prevent herself from bestowing upon him, Elysée's face brought to her an impression of returning recollection. From what shady place in her memory, from what secret recess of her heart arose this head of genius, these accents that stirred the profoundest depths of her being?

Now the master had set himself to question his pupil, not upon what he knew—nothing alas, or so little!—but to seek out what could be taught him. "Yes, sir; No, sir." The little prince had but these two words ready to his lips, and put all his strength into their pronunciation, with that pretty timidity common to boys brought up by women in a prolongation of their first early childhood. He strove nevertheless, poor little fellow, to unearth from beneath the heap of varied knowledge imparted to him by Madame de Silvis, some few notions of general history from among the adventures of dwarfs and fairies that bestarred his little imagination like stage prepared for a pantomime. From her place the queen encouraged and sustained him, bearing him aloft as it were on her own soul. When swallows take their flight, if the smallest one in the nest does not fly well, it is thus the mother aids it on her own wings. When the child hesitated in his answers, Frédérique's glance, a golden sparkle in sea-green eyes, dulled as the sea does beneath the passing squall; but, when his reply was correct, it was a beaming smile of triumph she turned upon the master!

For many a month she had not experienced such fulness of joy and comfort. The waxen hue of the little Zara, the depressed physiognomy of the sickly child seemed infused with new blood; even the landscape gained from the magic of this man's speech, the melancholy foregrounds seeming to fade away and leave in sight only what was grand and imposing in the vast barrenness of winter. And while the queen listened in rapt attention, leaning on her elbow, bending heart and soul towards that future where the child-king appeared to her in the triumph of the return to Leybach, Elysée wondering and trembling at a transfiguration of which he did not know himself to be the cause, beheld above the lovely forehead the sheen of the heavy coils of hair crossing and twisting and encircling the head like a kingly diadem.

Noon struck and the lesson was not yet ended. In the principal drawing-room where the little court assembled every morning at the hour of breakfast, a whispering began, and astonishment pervaded the group when neither king nor queen appeared. Hunger, and the idleness of the moment while waiting for the repast, caused a certain bad humour to mingle with the murmur of the conversations. Boscovich, pale with cold and hunger, who had been searching the copses for the last two hours in the hope of finding some late flowering plant, was thawing his fingers in front of the high white marble chimney, shaped like an altar, on which Father Alphée sometimes said a private mass on Sundays. The Marquise, majestic and stiff, on the edge of a divan, in a green velvet dress, shook her head with a tragic air, at the top of her long thin boa-entwined neck, while she imparted her confidences to the Princess Colette. The poor woman was in despair that her pupil should have been taken away from her and confided to a mere creature—positively a mere creature—she had seen him that morning crossing the courtyard.

"My dear, he would have frightened you; hair as long as this, the look of a madman. No one but Father Alphée could have made such a find."

"They say he is very learned," observed the princess, absently.

The other pounced on her words. Very learned. Very learned! Did a king's son require to be stuffed full of Greek and Latin like a dictionary? "No, no, my dear, these princely educations, you see, require special kinds of knowledge—I had them, I was ready. I had studied the treatise of the Abbé Diguet on the 'Education of a Prince.' I know by heart the different methods he indicates for knowing men, those for keeping mere flatterers at a distance. There are six of the first, and seven of the second. This is the order in which they come."

She began to repeat them to the

princess, who, wearied and sulky, did not listen, but sat on a cushioned ottoman, the long fashionable train of her pale-blue dress lying behind her, and her eyes fixed like loadstones on the door leading to the king's apartment, with the vexed air of a pretty woman who has composed her whole attitude for some one who does not come. Stiff and upright in his closely-buttoned coat, the old Duke de Rosen walked up and down with automatic step, regular as the pendulum of a clock, and occasionally stopping at one or other of the windows overlooking the garden or the courtyard, and standing there, his glance raised from under the lines of his forehead, looked like an officer of the watch in charge of the course and responsible for the safety of the ship. And certainly the aspect of the vessel did him honour. The red brick of the offices, the steward's pavilion, gleamed in the rain that splashed upon the great flight of steps at the door, and upon the fine gravel of the approach. In the murky daylight it seemed as if a light were reflected within from the mere orderliness of everything, extending even to the great drawing-room still further enlivened by the warmth spread from stoves and carpets, by the Louis XVI. furniture in white and gold, by the classic ornaments reproduced upon the woodwork of the panels and the mirrors, these being very large, on one of which a little gilt dial-piece hung, kept in place by garlands of gilt ribbons. In one corner of the great room, in a glass case, a bracket of the same date supported the diadem saved from the general wreck. Frédérique had wished it should be placed there; "that we may remember!" she said. And notwithstanding

Christian's mockery, for he thought it gave the room the air of a museum of royalty, the splendid jewel of the middle ages with its sparkling stones in the old pierced and chased gold-work, threw a note of antique chivalry in the midst of the coquetry of the eighteenth century, and the complex taste of our own.

The sound of familiar wheels on the gravel announced the arrival of the aide-de-camp. At last, here was someone.

"How late you are in coming for orders, Herbert," said the duke, gravely

The prince, for big fellow as he was, he always trembled before his father, reddened, stammered some excuses: "Awfully sorry—not his fault—on duty all night."

"Is that why the king is not down yet?" asked the princess, drawing near where the two men stood talking, and seeming to poke her dainty nose into their conversation.

A severe glance from the duke closed her mouth. The king's conduct was not to be criticized by anyone.

"Go to him at once, sir; His Majesty is probably awaiting you."

Herbert obeyed after having tried in vain to obtain a smile from his much-loved Colette, whose bad temper far from being calmed by his arrival, sent her pouting to her seat, her pretty curls disarranged, and the blue train crumpled by the grasp of her angry hand. Prince Herbert had, nevertheless, endeavoured to transform himself into a smart man during the last few months. His wife had ordained that, in his capacity of aide-de-camp, he must let his moustaches grow, and this gave a formidably martial air to his honest face, thinned and paled by the late hours and fatigue of his service with the king. Moreover

he still limped a little, and walked leaning on his cane like a veritable hero
from that siege of Ragusa, of which he
had written a memorial, famous even
before publication, and that being read
by the author one evening at the Queen
of Palermo's, had gained him a brilliant
social ovation and the formal promise
of a prize from the Academy. Imagine
what a position, what authority all this
gave to the husband of Colette! But
through it all he preserved his air of
simple, timid good-nature, above all before the princess, who continued to treat
him with the most graceful contempt,
which proves that no man is great in
the eyes of his wife.

"Well! What now?" she said in an
impertinent tone, when she saw him re-
appear with an astounded and agitated
countenance.

"The king had not yet come home!"

These few words of Herbert produced
the effect of an electric discharge in the
drawing-room. Colette, very pale, with
tears in her eyes, was the first to recover
speech:

"Is it possible?"

"Not come home! How is it I was
not told?"

Madame de Silvis' boa trembled and
twisted convulsively.

"I only hope nothing has happened to
him!" said the princess, in an extraordinary state of excitement.

Herbert was able to reassure her.
Lebeau, the king's valet, had been gone
an hour or more with a portmanteau.
He would certainly have news of him.

In the silence that followed, the same
disquieting thought hovered over all,
which the Duc de Rosen suddenly gave
utterance to.

"What will the Queen say?"

To which Boscovich tremblingly suggested:

"Her Majesty is probably aware of
it."

"I am sure she is not," affirmed Colette, "for the Queen said only a short
time ago that she would present the new
tutor to the king at breakfast."

And with a nervous tremour, she
added between her teeth but loud enough
to be heard by everyone:

"In her place I know what I should
do."

The duke turned indignantly, with
flashing eyes, to this little plebeian,
whom he had never been able to make
a lady of, and was probably about to
give her a sharp lesson on the respect
due to monarchy, when the queen appeared, followed by Elysée, who led
his royal pupil by the hand. All rose.
Frédérique, with a lovely smile of happiness that had long been banished from
her face, presented Monsieur Méraut.
Oh! what a bow the Marquise had ready
for him, distant, haughty and mocking;
she had been a whole week practising it.
The princess, on her part, could scarcely
find strength enough for a gesture.
From white she turned to crimson, as
she recognized in the new master the
tall ungainly young man who had breakfasted beside her at her uncle's and who
had written Herbert's book. Was he
there by chance, or by some diabolical
machination? What a disgrace for her
husband, what fresh ridicule if his
literary cheat were discovered! She was
a little reassured by Elysée's cold bow,
for he must certainly have recognized
her. "He is a clever man," she thought
to herself. Unluckily all was compromised by the naïveté of Herbert, his
stupefied amazement at the tutor's ap-

pearance, and the familiar handshake he gave him with a "Good morning, how are you?"

"You know Monsieur, then?" asked the Queen, who had heard through her chaplain of the history of the *Memorial* and smiled a little maliciously.

She was however too kindly to amuse herself long with a cruel sport.

"Decidedly the King has forgotten us," she added, "will you go and tell him, Monsieur de Rosen."

They were obliged to own the truth, that the King was not in the house, that he had passed the night out, and that his portmanteau had been sent for. It was the first time anything of the kind had happened; every one expected an outburst on the part of this proud and passionate nature, all the more that the presence of a stranger aggravated the offence. But no; she remained calm. Merely saying a few words to the aide-de-camp, inquiring the hour at which he had last seen Christian.

About three in the morning. His Majesty was walking down the boulevard with Monseigneur the Prince d'Axel.

"Ah! true, I forgot, they had some matters to talk over."

In these tranquil tones she completely recovered her self-possession. But no one was deceived. Everyone knew the Prince d'Axel and knew beforehand what kind of conversation there could be with this degraded prince and shady character.

"Let us go to breakfast," said Frédérique, rallying all her little court with a sovereign gesture to the calm she endeavoured herself to show.

The King not being present to offer his arm, she hesitated for a moment.

Then suddenly turning to the Comte de Zara, who with his great eyes and the intelligent look of a precocious and sickly child had been watching all this scene, she said with a deep, tender, almost respectful tone and a grave smile hitherto unknown to him:

"Come, Sire!"

CHAPTER VII

THE KING TAKES HIS PLEASURE

THREE o'clock in the morning strikes at the Church of Saint-Louis-en-l'Ile.

Enveloped in darkness and silence, the Rosen family mansion sleeps in all the heaviness of its massive old stones sunken down by the weight of years, of its ponderous, arched portals with their venerable knocker; and behind the closed shutters, the obscured mirrors reflect only the deep sleep of ages, a sleep of which the light paintings on the ceilings seem to be the dreams, and the murmur of the neighbouring river, the fleeting and uneven breath. But the deepest sleep of all in the house, is that of Prince Herbert, who has returned home from his club only a quarter of an hour ago. Exhausted, broken-down, cursing the harassing existence he is forced to lead, which deprives him of what he loves best on earth, his wife and his horses: horses because the king does not care for sport or any sort of out-door exercise: his wife, because the king and queen living apart and meeting only at the hours of meals, their aide-de-camp and lady-in-waiting must follow in the step of this conjugal separation, and live aloof from each other like confidant in a tragedy. The Princess goes off to Saint-Mandé long before her husban is awake; at night, when he returns home, she is fast asleep with her door closed and bolted. And if he complains, Colette majestically answers with a little smile which deepens all her dimples: "We surely owe this sacrifice to our Princess." A pretty evasion for the love-sick Herbert, who remains alone in his big room on the first story with a ceiling four yards high above his head, paintings by Boucher over his doors, and great mirrors fitted in the walls which send him back the reflection of his own figure in an interminable perspective.

Sometimes, however, when he is completely done up, as he is to-night, the husband of Colette experiences a certain comfort in stretching himself out in bed without having to furnish any conjugal explanations; resuming his comfortable bachelor habits, and to begin with enveloping his head in an enormous silk handkerchief; before the mocking eyes of his little Parisian wife he never would have dared to make such a figure of himself. Hardly is he in bed, his head upon the embroidered and emblazoned pillow, than the trap of restful oblivion opens, into which rolls the worn-out noctambulist aide-de-camp; but he is suddenly snatched from his beatitude by the disagreeable sensation of a light moving before his eyes, while a little shrill voice, pointed as a gimlet, whispers in his ear:

"Herbert. Herbert."

"Eh! What! Who is there?"

"Do be quiet. It is I, Colette."

Yes, it is Colette standing before his bed, her lace dressing-gown open at the throat, short sleeves displaying her arms, her hair turned up and twisted leaving bare the nape of her neck, a perfect little nest of fair curls; there she stands in the white glimmer of her little lantern, which makes her eyes look larger, widened as they are by a solemn expression, but now suddenly amused as she catches sight of the bewildered Herbert, looking stupid enough with his handkerchief ruffled into menacing points, while his head with its bristling moustaches rose out of his night-gear, voluminous as the raiment of an archangel, making him look like a bourgeois bully surprised out of a bad dream. But the hilarity of the Princess does not last long. Resuming her seriousness, she places her night lamp on the table with the resolute air of a woman who is determined to make a scene; and without any regard for the prince's continued drowsiness, she folds her arms, her little hands meeting the dimples of her elbows, and begins:

"Do you really think this sort of life can go on? Coming home every day at four o'clock in the morning! Do you think that a proper existence for a married man?"

"But, my dear, (he suddenly interrupted himself to snatch off his silk handkerchief and throw it aside) it is not my fault. I should be only too happy to be allowed to come home earlier to my little Colette, my darling wife whom I——."

He endeavours, on saying these words, to draw the tempting snow-white dressing-gown nearer to him, but he is harshly repulsed.

"Ah! I am not thinking of you, my poor fellow! I know you well enough, dear old simpleton quite incapable of committing the least—indeed, I should like to see it otherwise—but it is the king. Fancy, what a scandal, such a life, in his position! If even he were free, a bachelor. We all know young men must enjoy themselves, though in his case, his high rank and the dignity of exile." (Oh! how little Colette draws herself up on the high heels of her slippers to speak of the dignity of exile.) "But he is married, and I can't understand the queen. What in the world can she have in her veins?"

"Colette."

"Oh, yes! I know, you are like your father. The queen cannot do wrong! As for me, I think that she is as much to blame as he is; by her coldness, her indifference, she has driven him away from her."

"The queen is not indifferent. She is proud."

"Come, come! are we proud when we love? If she really loved him, the very first night he had spent away from her would have been the last. She would have spoken, threatened, asserted herself. She could not have kept this cowardly silence under the torture she would have endured from the unfaithfulness of a man she loved. The consequence is that the king spends all his nights at his club, in the low haunts of the boulevards, at the Prince d'Axel's, in company of Heaven knows whom!"

"Colette, Colette!"

But there was no stopping Colette when she was once started off on the rapid flow of speech natural to every little bourgeoise brought up in the exciting atmosphere of Paris, where the very dolls can talk.

"That woman cares for nothing, I tell you, not even for her son. If she did, would she have confided him to

that savage? They exhaust him with study, poor little creature! It seems that even at night he goes on repeating Latin and a lot of other trash in his sleep. The Marquise told me so. The queen does not miss a lesson. They are banded together against that poor child. And all, that he may be fit to reign; but they will have killed him first. Oh! that Méraut of yours! I hate him!"

"He is not such a bad fellow as all that. He might have been very disagreeable about that book you know, and he never said a word."

"Oh! really? Well, I can assure you the queen looks at you with a singular smile when you are congratulated upon it before her. But you are so simple, my poor Herbert!"

At the annoyed expression of her husband's face, who has flushed up, and pouts out his sulky lips like a child, the princess fears she has gone too far and may miss her aim. But how can he withstand the charm of the pretty woman seated on his bedside, her head half turned towards him with a coquettish grace that shows off the youthful supple figure under its flowing laces, the soft roundness of the neck, the malicious glance of the eyes between their lashes!

The prince's honest face soon resumes its amiable expression, and even becomes singularly animated as the soft, warm hand approaches his own, and he breathes in the well-known perfume of the beloved one. What in the world is little Colette after? What is it she wants to know? Nothing much, only this: Has the king a mistress or has he not? Is it the passion of gambling that carries him away, or only the love of pleasure, of wild amusement? The aide-de-camp hesitates before he answers. He feels it is a sort of disloyalty that he, the companion of all his adventures, should betray the king's secrets. But the little hand is so coaxing, so pressing, so full of curiosity, that the aide-de-camp of Christian II. can resist no longer.

"Well! yes, the king has a mistress at present."

Within his hand the little hand of Colette becomes cold and damp.

"And what is her name?" she asks, breathing hard and short.

"Amy Férat, an actress of the Bouffes Theatre."

Colette knows this Amy Férat; she always thought her atrociously ugly.

"Oh!" says Herbert by way of excuse, "His Majesty will soon be tired of her."

And Colette with evident satisfaction exclaims:

"Really!"

Upon which Herbert, enchanted with his success, ventures to play with a little knot of ribbon that flutters at her throat, and goes on in a light tone:

"Yes, I am afraid that before long poor Amy Férat will receive her marmoset."

"A marmoset? Why?"

"Only something I have noticed. All who live in the king's intimacy know as I do that when he begins to tire of a mistress he sends her one of his marmosets P.P.C.—a little way he has of saying good-bye to those he no longer cares for."

"Oh! how shocking!" cries the indignant princess.

"Quite true, though! At the Grand Club they no longer say 'drop a mistress,' but 'send her a marmoset.'"

He stops, surprised at seeing the princess abruptly rise up, take her lantern, and walk stiffly out of the alcove. "I say, Colette! Colette!"

But she turns upon him with disdain and disgust. "I have heard quite enough of your horrid stories; they sicken me."

And raising the door-curtain, she leaves the unfortunate king of *la Gomme* amazed and stupefied, with heart inflamed and arms outstretched, wondering why she came at this unearthly hour, and why she leaves him in this most startling manner. With the rapid step of an actress leaving the stage, the floating train of her dressing-gown caught up and crumpled over her arm, Colette returns to her room at the other extremity of the house. On the couch, lying on a cushion covered with oriental embroidery, sleeps the prettiest little animal in the world, its silky grey coat more like feathers than hair, its long tail wound around it, and a little silver bell tied with a pink ribbon round its throat. It is an exquisite little marmoset the king had sent her some days ago, in a basket of Leghorn straw, and which she had received with pleasure and gratitude. Ah! if she had only known the meaning of the present! Furiously she snatches up the little creature, a bundle of living and scratching silk in which shine out, now that it is so suddenly awakened, two human-looking eyes, and, opening the window on the quay, with a ferocious gesture, she flings it out.

"There, dirty beast!"

The little monkey falls headlong on the wharf, and not only does he disappear and perish that night, but also perishes the dream, frail and capricious as himself, of the poor little creature who throws herself upon her bed, and sobs bitterly with her face hidden in the pillows.

Their love had lasted a year, an eternity in the eyes of the incurably fickle and childish king. He had only had to make a sign. Fascinated and dazzled, Colette de Rosen had fallen into his arms, though, until then, her conduct had been irreproachable, not because she loved her husband or cared for virtue, but simply because, in this little linnet's brain, there lingered a certain concern for the neatness of its plumage, which had preserved her from the grosser faults; and also, because she was a Frenchwoman, of a race of women which Molière had declared long before the advent of our modern physiologists, to be devoid of temperament and open only to the temptations of their imagination and vanity.

It was not to Christian that the little Sauvadon had given herself, but to the King of Illyria. She had sacrificed herself to an ideal diadem conjured up from the romantic legends of her childhood's readings, and which she fondly believed she saw surrounding like a halo, the person of her selfish and sensual lover. She pleased him as long as he saw in her a new and brightly coloured plaything, a Parisian toy which was to lead him on to more exciting pleasures. But she had the bad taste to take her rôle as "mistress of the King" in earnest. The figures of the women who, through mere imitation, had shone more brilliantly in history than the real gems of the crown, glittered before her eyes in her ambitious dreams. She would not consent to be a Dubarry; she would fain be the Duchesse de Châteauroux of this stranded Louis XV.; and his restoration to the throne of Illyria, the conspiracies she would direct with a wave of her fan, the sudden strokes, the heroic landings on inhospitable shores, were the subjects of all her conversations with the King. She fancied herself stirring up the country, hiding in the corn-fields and farm-houses, like one of the famous women of the Vendean war, whose adventures she had read about in the convent of the Sacred Heart. She had even contrived in imagination a page's costume for herself (dress always played the principal part in her inventions), a sweet little Renaissance costume which should permit of her holding interviews at all hours, and constantly accompanying the King. Christian disliked these enthusiastic reveries, for he quickly saw their false and silly sentimentality. He had not taken a mistress to hear her talk politics; and when he held his little soft kitten, his pretty Colette on his knees in all the graceful unreserve of her love, to be told about the recent resolutions of the Diet of Leybach or the effect of the latest royal proclamation, cast upon his heart just such a chill as a sudden change of temperature, an April frost, casts upon the trees of a blossoming orchard.

Tardy scruples and remorse, the intricate remorse of a Slave and a Catholic, then began to assail him. Now that his caprice was satisfied, his conscience upbraided him with the odium of this intrigue carried on under the very eyes of the Queen; he saw the danger of the stealthy, brief repdezvous in hotels, where their incognito might so easily be betrayed; the cruelty of deceiving that poor good creature, Herbert, who always spoke of his wife with insatiable tenderness, and little thought, when the King joined him at the club with the beaming complexion and bright eyes of a successful lover, that he had just left the arms of Colette. But a still greater embarrassment was the Duc de Rosen, terribly suspicious of his young daughter-in-law, whose principles he mistrusted because she was not of his caste. He was uneasy for his son; he fancied he had all the air of a ——; he would say the word right out like an old trooper that he was, and he could not but feel a certain responsibility in the matter, for it was through his greed of money that this mésalliance had been made. He kept a watchful eye over Colette, accompanied her morning and evening, and would indeed have followed her everywhere if the supple creature had not slipped between his big clumsy fingers. It was a silent strife between these two.

From the windows of the steward's house, the duke, seated at his writing-table, could see, not without vexation, his pretty daughter-in-law ensconced in her carriage, exquisitely dressed in the beautiful costumes that she combined in such consummate taste with her fashionable tailor; in the cold weather, pink and white in the warm shelter of her brougham; or on bright days, shaded by her fringed parasol.

"You are going out?" he would enquire.

"On the queen's service," the little Sauvadon would triumphantly answer from behind her veil; and it was true.

Frédérique did not care for the noise of Paris, and readily confided her commissions to her lady-in-waiting; she had no pleasure in the vainglorious satisfaction of giving her name and title of queen in the fashionable shops, in the midst of the low-bowing clerks and the inquisitorial curiosity of the women. She was not popular in society. The colour of her hair and eyes, the somewhat stiff majesty of her figure, the ease with which she wore Parisian fashions, were not the subject of drawing-room discussion.

One morning the duke remarked in Colette such an expression of seriousness as she started from Saint-Mandé, such an air of over-excitement in all her little person, that instinctively—real sportsmen have these sudden inspirations—he determined to follow her. He gave chase for a long time, as far as a restaurant on the Quai d'Orsay. By dint of the greatest ruse and skill the princess had managed to elude the ceremonious repast at the queen's table, and was about to breakfast with her lover in a private room. They eat, seated before a low window which opened on a lovely view, the Seine golden in the sunlight; the Tuileries forming a mass of stones and trees, and near at hand the interlaced masts and cordage of the training-ship lying in the green shadow of the quay. The weather, well suited to a rendezvous, had the softness of a warm day, crossed every now and again by sharp fresh breezes. Never did Colette laugh more merrily; her laugh was the triumph of her grace, and Christian, who adored her as long as she consented to remain the joyous creature he loved in her, was thoroughly enjoying his breakfast in the society of his mistress. All of a sudden, Colette caught sight of her father-in-law walking up and down with measured step on the opposite pavement, determined, to all appearance, not to leave his post. The old man was mounting a regular guard before the door, which he knew to be the only exit from the restaurant, and kept a watch over the well-got-up officers from the neighbouring caval y barracks, as they entered one by one; for he imagined, being an old general of Pandours, that the uniform was irresistible, and he had not a doubt that spurs and sabretache were the moving spirit of his daughter-in-law's intrigue.

The perplexity of both Colette and the king was great; very much like that of the learned man perched up on a palm-tree, with a gaping crocodile at his feet. They were, however, sure enough of the discretion and incorruptibility of the restaurant people to be certain that the crocodile would not be allowed to come up. But how were they to get down? For the king it might yet be managed, for he had plenty of time, and must surely succeed in wearing out the patience of the animal. But Colette! the queen would soon be expecting her, and might join her suspicions to those of old Rosen. The master of the establishment who, at the request of Christian, had come up and had been informed of the state of affairs, after having ransacked his brain, found nothing better than to suggest piercing the wall of the neighbouring house—as in times of revolution. However, he suddenly struck upon a plan which was far more simple. The princess must disguise herself

as a pastry-cook's boy, and carry out on her head her own dress and petticoats in a flat wicker-basket; she could in this guise leave the restaurant, take refuge in the bar-maid's room, in a neighbouring street, and there resume her own clothes. At first Colette would not hear of such a thing. What! appear as a scullion before the king! She must perforce consent, under penalty of causing the most dreadful catastrophe; so she donned the freshly washed suit of a little lad some fourteen years of age, and the Princesse de Rosen, née Sauvadon, was transformed into the prettiest, the most coquettish little pastry-cook's boy that ever ran the streets of Paris at the hours when gourmands eat. But how far removed was this white linen cap, these boy's slippers, too large for her tiny feet, this jacket with its pockets full of jingling "tips," from the heroic page's costume, the pearl-hilted dagger, and the knee-boots in which she had longed to follow her Lara! Without a suspicion the duke saw two little boys pass out, their baskets on their heads exhaling such a pleasing odour of hot pastry, that he suddenly felt the first pangs of hunger—he was fasting, poor man! Upstairs the king, still a prisoner, but relieved of his anxiety, read the paper, drank his Roederer, peeping out every now and then through an uplifted corner of the curtain to ascertain whether the crocodile was still outside.

That evening, when he returned to Saint-Mandé, the duke was received by the princess with the most artless smiles. He understood that he had been outwitted and never breathed word of his adventure. It got about nevertheless. Who knows through what drawing-room keyhole, over what half-lowered brougham window, by what echo repeated and sent back from deaf walls to mute doors, a scandalous rumour will spread through all Paris, until it blazes forth in broad daylight, that is in the publicity of society papers; and from there is poured into thousands of ears and becomes a public disgrace, after having been only the subject of an amusing anecdote at a club. For a week Paris made merry over the story of the little pastry-cook's boy. The names, whispered low, as low as such great names could be, did not penetrate into the thick skull of Prince Herbert. But the queen had some suspicion of the adventure; for she, who since their terrible scene at Leybach had never made a reproach of any kind to the king, drew him aside shortly after this incident one day, as they were leaving the dinner-table:

"I hear much," she said gravely, without looking at him, "about a scandalous story in which your name is mixed. Oh! pray do not excuse yourself. I do not want to know more, only I beg of you to have some regard for the crown confided to your care (she pointed to the diadem in the veiled radiance of its crystal casket). Do not allow shame or ridicule to attain it. It must remain worthy of your son."

Did she really know the story? Did she guess the name of the woman whom public slander had only half revealed? Frédérique's nature was so strong, her self-possession so great, that not one of her immediate circle could have answered the question. Christian, however, took the warning to heart, and

his horror of scenes, the need his weak nature had of pleasant faces around him, smiling back to his own careless merriment, decided him to draw from its cage the prettiest, the tamest of his marmosets, and send it to Princess Colette. She wrote, but he never answered; he took no notice of her sighs or her doleful attitudes, but continued to address her in the tone of polite playfulness which attracted women to him; and no longer burdened by the remorse which he had felt growing heavier as his passion decreased, set free from the tyranny of an affection far more exacting than his wife's, he threw himself headlong into the pursuit of pleasure, thinking of nothing but what "swells" call in their loose and flabby slang: faire la fête, or, go it! It was the fashionable expression that year at the clubs; there is no doubt another now.

The words change, but the thing remains, immutable and monotonous; the great restaurants where it is carried on; the gilt, flower-decked rooms where the fashionable courtesans invite and receive each other; the enervating triviality of their pleasure sinking invariably into orgy, without the power of renewal. What never changes is the traditional, classical stupidity of this assembly of frail women and pleasure-worn men; the stereotyped form of their slang and laugh; the absence of all imagination or fancy in their commonplace, conventional society, quite as conventional as the other under its would-be appearance of mirth and folly;—it is regulated disorder, a programme of caprices to be followed out with yawning ennui by its broken-down victims.

The king, at least, went about amusing himself with all the ardour of a youth of twenty. He yielded to that craving for excitement and freedom which had carried him on the very first evening of his arrival to Mabille; he sought to satisfy the desires, sharpened long beforehand by the accounts he had read in certain Parisian newspapers, which give day by day the appetizing bill of fare of a life of gallantry, and by the plays and novels which relate and idealize such scenes for the delectation of the provinces and foreign countries. His intrigue with the Princesse de Rosen had arrested him for a while on his descent to this gross debauch, a descent resembling that of the narrow staircases of the night restaurants, flooded with light, and softly carpeted on the upper steps, down which come, step by step, the partially drunk, increasing their pace as the lights diminish and the sharp night air meets them, till at last the steep stairway seems to lead straight to the gutter, in those dark hours sacred to the burglar and the vagabond. Christian now abandoned himself to the rapid descent, to the inevitable end; and, in his fall, it was not so much the excitement of the heady Spanish wines that intoxicated him, as the little court, the clan of courtiers which surrounded him; ruined noblemen in search of royal dupes, Bohemian journalists, whose paid articles amused him, and who, proud of their intimacy with the illustrious exile, took him behind the scenes of the theatres, where the women, blushing affectedly under the rouge that covered their enamelled cheeks, had eyes but for him. He had soon become familiar with the boulevard slang, its exaggerations and silly affectations; he could say like a perfect *gommeux: "Chic, très chic. C'est infect, on se tord;"* but, in his mouth, spoken with his foreign accent, these expressions lost somewhat of their vulgarity, and gave them a flavour of Bohemianism. There was one word he particularly delighted in: *"rigolo."* He used it at every turn: theatrical plays, novels, public events or private adventures, were or were not *"rigolo."* It exempted Monseigneur from all mental exertion. On one occasion, towards the end of a midnight supper, Amy Férat, who was drunk, and irritated by the constantly repeated word, cried out:

"Hi! I say, *Rigolo!*"

This familiarity pleased him. Here was one, at least, who did not treat him as a king. He made her his mistress, and long after his connection with the actress in vogue was over, the nickname remained to him, as that of *"Queue-de-Poule,"* given to the Prince d'Axel no one knows why, remained in the same way attached to him.

Rigolo and Queue-de-Poule became fast friends. They were always together, hunting the same quarry, mingling in various boudoirs their similar destinies; for the disgrace of the hereditary prince was equivalent to an exile. He spent it as agreeably as he could, and for the last ten years he had been playing his freaks in all the night-haunts of the boulevards, wearing always the same dismal face in the midst of the wildest pranks. The King of Illyria had his apartment in Prince d'Axel's mansion in the Champs Elysées. At first he would sleep there only on rare occasions, but he soon took to spending the night there as often as at Saint-Mandé. These absences, explained with a certain speciousness, left the queen quite calm, but they threw the princess into the greatest despondency. In her mortification at her desertion by the king, she had consoled herself with the hope of regaining his inconstant heart. She used all her skill to do so, a thousand coquettish inventions, new adornments, wonderful combinations of colours and shapes, which should bring out more strikingly than ever the peculiar grace of her beauty. And what bitter disappointment when, at seven o'clock in the evening, the king not having appeared, Frédérique, in her imperturbable serenity, would have little Zara's chair put in the place of honour, saying: "His Majesty will not dine here to-night."

CHAPTER VIII

NERVOUS COLETTE

POOR nervous Colette, obliged to hide her vexation in silence, longed for an outburst from the Queen which should revenge them both; but Frédérique, hardly paler than usual, retained her sovereign composure, though the princess, with true feminine curiosity and consummate art, tried to insinuate ghastly revelations: as to the life in the clubs of Paris, the coarse conversations of men between themselves, and the still coarser amusements to which their idleness and constant absence from home allured them; the terrible gambling which left whole fortunes on the card-tables; the eccentric bets entered in a special register which it would be curious to peruse, true

"golden record" of human aberration. But do what she might, she could not succeed in disturbing the queen by her incessant pricks; the queen did not, or rather would not, understand.

Only once did she betray herself; it was one morning during a ride through the woods of Saint-Mandé.

It was a sharp cold day in March; the wind catching the surface of the lake, ruffled it back towards the hard and still flowerless banks. A few buds only were beginning to show on the tips of the leafless shrubs which still bore the red berries of the winter; the horses, side by side, followed a pathway strewn with dead branches which crackled under their feet, and the noise they made, together with the creaking of new leather and rattling of their curb-chains, were the only sounds that disturbed the silence of the woods. The two women, both equally good riders, rode slowly on, absorbed in the stillness of this intermediate season, which prepares for the renewal of spring, in the heavens still heavy with rain, and on the earth still black with the winter's snow. Colette, however, soon began on her favourite subject, as she did almost always when alone with the Queen. She did not dare to attack the king openly, but she fell upon his surroundings, the men of the Grand Club, almost all of whom she knew through Herbert, or through Parisian gossip, and whom she showed up in masterly style, the Prince d'Axel first and foremost.

Really she could not understand that anyone could be intimate with such a man; a man who spent his life in gambling and feasting, who had no pleasure but in low company; sitting out in the evening with bad women on the boule-vards, drinking like a cabman with the first-comer, hail-fellow-well-met with the lowest sort of play-actors. And to think that such a fellow was an heredi-tary prince! He seemed to take pleas-ure in deg ading, sullying royalty in his own person.

And she talked on and on with towering indignation and anger, while the queen, intentionally absent-minded, looking vacantly ahead, stroked the neck of her horse, hurrying his pace so as to get away from her lady-in-waiting's stories. But Colette pressed her horse on too.

"He has, moreover, a good example to follow. His uncle's conduct is as bad as his own. A man who flaunts his mistress with such impudence be-fore his court, before his wife. What a rôle of sacrificed slave for a queen to play! What kind of nature can she have to put up with such insults!"

This time the thrust had gone home. Cut to the heart, Frédérique lowered her eyelids, and, for a moment, there appeared upon her features, suddenly hollowed and aged, such a worn and painful expression that Colette could not help being moved on seeing the haughty queen whose heart she had never been able to reach, descend to the level of feminine suffering. But the moment was soon past; she quickly regained possession of her dignity:

"The woman you speak of is a queen," she said sharply, "and you would be committing a great injustice to judge her like other women. Other women can be openly happy or un-happy, shed all their tears, and even cry out if their pain is too great. But queens!—alas they must hide every-thing: their sorrows as wife, their sor-rows as mother; they must hide and devour them in silence. Can a queen run away when she is outraged? Can she sue for a separation, rejoicing thereby the hearts of the enemies of her throne? No, at the risk of appear-ing cruel, blind and indifferent, she must preserve a lofty brow to uphold her crown. And it is not pride, but the feeling of our dignity that sustains us. It is this feeling that enables us to drive out in an open carriage be-tween husband and child, under the threatening fire of imminent conspira-cies, that alleviates the dreariness of the land of exile and its murky skies, that gives us the strength to bear cer-tain cruel affronts of which you ought to be the last to remind me, Princesse de Rosen."

She grew excited as she spoke, and the words came hurried towards the end; then she suddenly roused her horse with a vigorous shake of the bridle and dashed off at full gallop through the woods, her blue veil streaming behind her, and the heavy folds of her riding habit flapping in the wind.

From this time forward Colette left the queen in peace; but, as her unquiet nerves needed some distraction and re-lief, she directed her stings and anger against Elysée, and regularly took up the side of the marquise. The royal household was divided into two camps: Elysée had only Father Alphée on his side, and certainly the monk's rugged frankness and ever-ready answer were of immense help in times of need; but he was often absent on frequent mis-sions to Illyria, where he had to manage the affairs of the Franciscan monasteries of Zara and Ragusa, and their arrangements with the mother-house of the rue des Fourneaux.

This, at least, was the pretext of his temporary absences, which he surrounded with the utmost mystery, and from which he always returned more ardent, mounting the stairs with a more furious tramp, rolling his rosary in his fingers, and muttering a prayer, which he seemed to munch like a musket-ball.

He would remain for hours shut up with the queen, then start off again, leaving the coterie of the marquise free to work against the preceptor. From the old duke, whose military and worldly instincts were offended by Méraut's shaggy hair and untidy appearance, down to Lebeau, the valet, and the humblest of the grooms and scullions,—in whom all indepedence creates enemies,—even to the inoffensive Boscovich who, like a coward, followed the others out of respect for numbers, all followed suit, and formed a veritable coalition against the new tutor. This showed itself not so much by overt acts as by words, looks, and attitudes in the little daily skirmishes so common among people who live in the same house while detesting each other. Oh! the indescribable attitudes of Madame de Silvis! In turn disdainful, haughty, ironical, or bitter, she played her part with Elysée, while, at the same time, she assumed an expression of respectful pity, with smothered sighs and eyes rolled up to the ceiling, whenever she found herself with the little prince: "Are you not suffering, Monseigneur?" And she would feel his forehead with her long bony fingers, unmanning him with her tremulous ca-resses. Then the queen in a cheerful tone would reply:

"Come, come, marquise, you will persuade Zara that he is ill."

"I find his hands and forehead rather hot."

"He has just come in from walking. It is the cold air."

And she would take the child away, though slightly disturbed herself at the remarks she so constantly heard repeated around her, and which had created a sort of legend in the house, that Monseigneur was made to study too much. The Parisian portion of the household said so, without believing or attaching any importance to the statement; but not so the servants brought over from Illyria, the tall Petscha, the faithful old Greb: they took the affair in earnest, and cast upon Méraut black looks of hatred, harassing him with their tormenting antipathy in the thousand little pin-pricks which their service put it in their power to inflict upon an absent-minded dependent. He again underwent the petty persecutions and jealousies of the palace at X., the same grovelling subservience that creeps around a throne, and which it appears even overthrow and exile have not the power to remove. His generous and affectionate nature recoiled from the antipathy and resistance which surrounded him; his simple, homely manners, the Bohemian habits of his artist's life were oppressed by the forced ceremonial of the king's household, the imposing candelabras of the brilliantly-lighted dinner-table, where the men in their dress-coats, and the women with bare necks, seated far apart with due formality, never spoke or ate before the king and queen had spoken and eaten; ruled above all by the inexorable etiquette which the Duc de Rosen imposed with more and more rigour as the term of exile extended day by day into the dim future. It would happen occasionally that the old student of the Rue Monsieur-le-Prince would come to the table with a coloured cravat on, and, forgetting all rules, would speak without permission, pitching head foremost into one of the eloquent improvisations so often re-echoed by the walls of the Café Voltaire. But soon called to order by the withering glances thrown at him, the repugnance he felt for the importance attached to the smallest infraction of these petty customs became such, that he longed to throw the whole thing over, and return once more, as he had done before, to his old quarters in the Quartier Latin.

However, his attachment to the queen retained him. As he had become more intimate with Frédérique through her child, he had conceived for her a fanatical infatuation, made up of respect, of admiration, and a sort of superstitious faith. For him, she summed up and symbolised in herself the ideal of his monarchical creed, just as, for the Transteverian peasant, the Madonna represents all religion. It was for her he remained and endeavoured to carry his hard task to a successful end. But it was indeed a tax upon his patience. How difficult to get the least thing into the little head of this king's child! He was a charming little fellow, poor Zara, gentle and good; his will was not wanting; the serious, straightforward soul of his mother was in him, but mingled with a sort of childishness, of fleeting instability in his ideas which his age hardly

accounted for. The mind was evidently undeveloped in this poor, little, old-fashioned, stunted body, never tempted by play, but weighted down by a constant state of dreaminess, which often went as far as torpor. Lulled by the fantastic tales of his governess during his first years, which had been only a long convalescence, the new life, now imperfectly appearing before his eyes, seemed to strike him only by its analogy with his fairy-tales, where the fairies and magicians were confounded with kings and queens, rescued them from enchanted towers and oubliettes, delivered them by a stroke of their golden wands from snares and persecutions, scattering the dragons who spat fire, and the old witches who changed their victims into beasts, and destroying the terrific ramparts of thorns and walls of ice. At his lesson, in the midst of a difficult explanation, he would say: "That is like the story of the little tailor;" or if he was reading the description of a great battle: "The giant Robistor killed more than that." It was this tendency of his mind towards the wonderful which gave him his absent-minded air, and which kept him for hours motionless on the cushions of a sofa, his eyes fixed upon the ever-changing and fleeting phantasmagoria conjured up before them, and dazzled by the blinding light of the fairy scenes in some *Rothomago*, as they unfolded their wondrous prismatic pictures one after the other in his memory. And this was why he found it difficult to reason or apply himself to the serious studies which were expected of him.

The queen assisted at all the lessons, her embroidery which never made any progress in her hand, and in her beautiful eyes the look of deep attention so flattering to the master, who felt her vibrate to all his thoughts, even to those he did not express. This was the bond that united them, unity of dreams, of hopes, the chimeras that float above our convictions and extend them to others. She had adopted him as her counsellor, her confidant, affecting to speak always in the name of the king.

"Monsieur Méraut," she would say, "His Majesty would be glad to have your opinion on such and such a subject."

And great was the surprise of Elysée on finding that the king himself never conversed with him upon these subjects that were supposed to interest him so deeply.

Christian II. treated him with consideration, addressing him in a tone of familiar companionship, most kindly but of a superficial sort. At times, as he passed through the schoolroom, he would pause for a moment to assist at the lesson, and then, laying his hand on the young prince's shoulder:

"Do not press him too much," he would say, in an undertone, which was only an echo of what was thought by all the subordinates of the household. "You surely don't intend to make a scientific man of him?"

"I wish to make him a king," Frédérique would proudly answer.

And on seeing her husband's gesture of discouragement:

"Is he not to reign some day?"

"Oh! certainly, certainly."

And, making a low bow, closing the door behind him to avoid further discussion, he would be heard humming, as he went away, the air of an operetta then in fashion: "*Il règnera, il règnera, car il est Espagnol.*" Altogether Elysée could make nothing of this king, to all appearance so affable, so superficial, so capricious; this perfumed dandy who spent hours lounging, in the weariness of his unstrung nerves, upon the divans of his drawing-room; the man whom he had been led to believe was the hero of Ragusa, the king whose energetic firmness and bravery were described in his *Memorial.* However, notwithstanding Frédérique's skill in disguising the shallowness and emptiness of this crowned head, and the care she took to keep her own personality concealed behind that of the king's, unforeseen events would crop up and reveal the natures of each in their proper light.

One morning after breakfast, just as they entered the drawing-room, Frédérique, on opening the paper, the *Courrier d'Illyrie,* which she was always the first to read, gave vent to such a loud exclamation of grief, that the king, who was ready to go out, stopped short, and all the persons present grouped themselves in one moment around the queen. Frédérique handed the paper to Boscovich:

"Read," she said.

It was the account of a sitting of the Diet of Leybach, and a resolution that had been passed by the Republican Government to return to the dispossessed sovereigns all the domains of the Crown, more than eight millions sterling, on the express condition—

"Bravo!" said Christian, with his nasal voice, "that suits me down to the ground."

"Read on," said the queen severely. "On the express condition that

Christian II. should give up for himself and his heirs all rights to the crown of Illyria."

A burst of indignation followed from all sides. Old Rosen was suffocating, the cheeks of Père Alphée grew deadly white, and his black eyes and beard looked blacker in contrast with the grey pallor that spread over his countenance.

"This must be answered at once," said the queen; "we cannot for a moment stand such an insult," and in her indignation her eyes sought for Méraut, who had been occupied for some minutes writing feverishly at a corner of the table with his pencil.

"This is what I should write," he said as he came forward; and he read, under the form of a letter to a royalist deputy, a spirited proclamation to the people of Illyria, in which the king, scornfully rejecting the insulting proposition made to him, reassured and encouraged his partisans with the impressive accent of a father kept aloof from his children.

The queen, enraptured, clapped her hands, seized the paper, and, handing it to Boscovich, said:

"Quick, translate it and send it off at once. Is not that your opinion?" she added, remembering all at once that Christian was present, and that they were observed.

"No doubt, yes," said the king, nervously biting his nails in his perplexity. "All that is very fine, only this is the question: shall we be able to stick to it?"

She turned upon him, very pale, as though she had received a blow between her shoulders.

"Stick to it! You ask whether we shall be able to stick to it. Is it the king who speaks?"

He answered very calmly:

"When Ragusa was without bread, at last, with the best will in the world, we were, nevertheless, forced to surrender."

"Yes; but this time, when we are without bread, we will lay the beggar's sack on our shoulders and beg from door to door; but royalty shall not surrender."

What a scene in that small drawing-room of a suburb of Paris! This contest between two fallen sovereigns, the one so evidently weary of the struggle, broken down by the want of faith in his own destiny, the other burning with ardour and confidence! How strikingly did their two natures reveal themselves! Yielding versatility written in every line of the king's person, in his very dress, his loose morning suit, his low shirt-collar showing his bare neck; in the effeminacy of his drooping white hands, and the slightly moistened curls on his pale forehead. The queen, slender and superb in her close-fitting riding habit, with its broad lapels, its little straight collar, the plain cuffs that edged with white the sombre mourning of the costume, and set off the splendour of her brilliant complexion, her flashing eyes and auburn tresses. For the first time Elysée had a rapid and true vision of the real state of things between this royal pair.

All at once Christian II. turned to the Duc de Rosen, who was standing against the mantelpiece, his head bent down:

"Rosen!" he said.

"Sire?"

"You alone can tell us that. How

do our money matters stand? Can we hold out?"

The comptroller of the household, with a haughty gesture, answered:

"Certainly."

"How long, do you know? About how long do you suppose?"

"Five years; I have made the calculation."

"Without privations for any one? without any of those we love suffering in any way?"

"Exactly so, sire."

"Are you quite certain?"

"Yes, certain," affirmed the old man, straightening himself up to his full height.

"Well then, all right. Méraut, give me your letter; let me sign it before I go out." And in an undertone he added, as he took the pen from his hand:

"Just look at Madame de Silvis; does she not look as if she were going to sing 'Sombre forêt?'"

And indeed the marquise, just then returning from the garden with the little prince, infected by the dramatic atmosphere of the drawing-room, stood in her green-plumed cap and velvet spencer, with her head thrown back and her hand upon her heart, somewhat in the transported and romantic attitude of an opera-singer about to begin the cavatina of the evening.

The protestation of the king was not only read in Parliament and published in all the papers, but it was also by Elysée's advice autographed and sent in thousands of copies into the country, smuggled through the custom-house by Father Alphée, who concealed them, together with his olive-wood chaplets and roses of Jericho, under the general

name of "articles of piety." The effect was excellent. The royalist party was not only strengthened but augmented. Dalmatia, more particularly where republican ideas had hardly penetrated, was stirred on hearing the eloquent voice of her king delivered in village pulpits by the mendicant friars of the Order of St. Francis who, at the village doors, opened their wallets and paid for the presents of eggs and butter with little bundles of printed papers. Addresses to the king were soon covered with signatures, and those little crosses of the uneducated peasants so touching in their ignorant affection.

Numerous pilgrimages were organized. A stream of deputations flowed into the little house at Saint-Mandé. Groups of fishermen, street porters from Ragusa wearing black cloaks thrown over their bright oriental costumes, half savage Morlachian peasants with their sheep-skin *opankés* tied on to their feet with straps of straw. They descended in troops from the tramways, where their scarlet tunics, their fringed scarves, and the metal buttons of their waistcoats jarred strangely with the grey uniformity of Parisian garb; they crossed the courtyard with firm steps, but faltered as they entered the hall, consulting together in whispers in their shyness and emotion. Méraut, who assisted at their presentation to the king, was moved to the heart; the legend of his childhood rose up again before him as he witnessed the enthusiasm of these pilgrims from afar; it recalled to him the visits to Frohsdorf of the villagers of the *Enclos de Rey*, the privations they imposed upon themselves, the preparations for the journey, the concealed disappointment they brought back; and he bitterly felt the sullen indifference of Christian and the too-evident sighs of relief to which he gave vent at the close of each interview. The king, in truth, hated these visits, which disturbed his every-day habits and pleasures, and obliged him to spend long afternoons at Saint-Mandé. Out of consideration for the queen, however, he received the tearful protestations of all these faithful creatures with a few commonplace words, and then avenged himself for his trouble by some poor joke or other—a caricature pencilled on a bit of paper, with that spirit of malicious mockery which lurked in the corners of his mouth. He once made the caricature of the syndic of the Branizza fishermen, a broad Italian face with flabby cheeks and round staring eyes from which the tears rained down to his chin in the joy and emotion of his interview with the king. The next day this production was circulated round the table amidst the laughter and admiring exclamations of the guests. The Duke himself, in his contempt for the lower classes, puckered up his old face in unrestrained hilarity, and the drawing at last reached Elysée after having passed under the delighted approval of Boscovich. Elysée looked at it in silence, and handed it without a word to his neighbour; and when the king called out to him in his impertinent drawling tone:

"Why don't you laugh, Méraut. Is not my charming syndic to your taste?"

He answered sadly:

"Monseigneur, I cannot laugh. It is the exact portrait of my father."

Shortly after Elysée involuntarily witnessed a scene which enlightene him completely as to the relations o Christian with the queen. It was on Sunday, after mass. The little hous with an air of unusual festivity, ha opened wide its gates upon the ru Herbillon; all the servants stood in double row in the hall which had bee filled with flowers. The reception that day was to be one of extraord nary importance. A royalist deputatio of the members of the Diet of Leyba was expected, the élite of the part come to pay homage of fidelity an devotion to the king, and consult wit him as to the measures to be take for his restoration to the throne. was a long-expected event, and th brilliancy of a glorious winter sun up the solitude of the great receptio room, where the high arm-chair of th king was prepared as a throne; an threw its radiance upon the sparklin gems, the rubies, sapphires, and topaz of the crown.

The whole house was in a state agitation with ceaseless comings an goings, and the rustle of silk dress on the stairs; the little prince was r peating the speech that had been taug him for the last week, while his lo red stockings, velvet suit, and collar Venetian point were being put o Rosen, in full uniform and all his dec rations, stood drawn up taller th ever, ready to receive the deputie while Elysée, keeping away from this stir, alone in the school-roo mused over the possible consequenc of the approaching interview, and the vivid mirage created by his e citable Southern brain, conceived a beheld the triumphal return of princes to Leybach; he saw, amid the roar of cannon, the peal of bells, the streets strewn with flowers, the king and queen holding before them like a promise to their people his beloved pupil, little Zara, the grave and intelligent child whose very gravity told of emotions too violent for his age. And the splendour of this bright Sunday, the cheerful sound of the bells clanging in the brilliant midday sun, were for him enhanced by the hope that in the coming triumph the maternal joy of Frédérique might stray over the head of her child down to him, and beam upon him in a smile of proud satisfaction.

Meanwhile, the chief courtyard resounded with the heavy wheels of the gala carriages which had been sent to fetch the deputies at their various houses, and the loud bell at the gate announced the arrivals one after the other. The carriage doors slammed, subdued sounds of steps as they fell on the carpets of the hall and drawing-room were succeeded by murmurs of reverent voices. Then a long silence which surprised Méraut, who expected to hear the well-known nasal voice which should deliver the king's speech. What could have happened? why this hesitation in the appointed order of the ceremony?

At this moment he perceived the man he supposed to be in the next room presiding over the official reception, skirting the walls, the blackened espaliers of the cold though sun-lit garden, and walking along with a stiff, uncertain gait. He had evidently entered by the private door hidden in the ivy of the Avenue Daumesnil, and was approaching the house slowly and laboriously. Elysée at once imagined there had been some duel or accident, and presently he heard a heavy fall in the room above, which confirmed him in the idea, for long and heavy was it, and accompanied with such a crash of fallen objects, that it sounded like that of a man who had sought to save himself by holding on to the hangings and furniture. He ran up to the king's room. It was a warmly-cushioned nest, situated in the principal wing of the house, hung in dark red, the walls covered with trophies of old weapons, and furnished with divans and low arm-chairs, lions' and bears' skins; and, in the midst of this oriental effeminacy, a camp-bed in which, according to a tradition in his family, the king slept—a piece of originality and affected simplicity common alike to princes and millionaires.

The door was wide open.

Christian stood leaning against the wall, pale and discomposed, with his hat on the back of his head, his long fur coat half opened, and showing underneath his tumbled dress-coat, his white cravat untied, his broad shirt-front creased and soiled, the crumpled linen telling only too plainly of the night's drunken debauch. Before him stood the queen, erect and severe, her stern voice trembling with the violent effort she made to keep calm:

"You must—you must come."

But he, in a low, sheepish voice, replied:

"I can't; don't you see I can't; later, I promise you."

And he stammered out excuses, with a silly laugh and childish deprecation. It was not that he had drunk. Oh, no! it was only the air, the cold air as he came out after supper.

"Yes," said the queen, "I know; but nevertheless you must come down; they must see you, only let them see you. I will do the rest. I know what to say to them."

And as he remained motionless, and a heavy drowsiness began to steal over the ghastly relaxation of his features, Frédérique's anger increased.

"Cannot you understand that your very destiny is in question, that your crown is at stake? Christian, it is your crown, the crown of your son that you are playing with at this moment. Come —come—I beseech you. You must— you shall."

In the force of her powerful will she was superb as she stood galvanizing the king into life, with the magnetism of her ocean-blue eyes. She picked him up with her mesmeric glance; steadied him, helped him off with his hat, his pelisse reeking with the fumes of tobacco and drink. He stiffened out his tottering legs for a moment, made a few staggering steps forward, leaning his burning palms on the marble hands of the queen. But all at once she felt him give way, and, recoiling from his feverish contact, she thrust him violently away with disgust, letting him fall at full length on a divan, and without a look at the crumpled, inert and already snoring mass, she left the room, walking rigidly with eyes half shut, and passed before Elysée without noticing him, murmuring in the disordered, mournful tone of a somnambulist:

"*Alla fine son ostanca de fare gesti de questo monarcaccio!*"

CHAPTER IX

LEVIS' AGENCY

OF all the Parisian dens, of all the thieves' caverns that sap and undermine the great city, there is not a more peculiar or more interesting organisation than that of Levis' Agency. It is known to all, at least from the outside. Situated in the rue Royale, at the corner of the Faubourg Saint-Honoré, in full view of the carriages passing to and from the Bois, so that no one can avoid seeing the glaring advertisement of the sumptuous ground-floor r e a c h e d by eight steps, with its tall plate-glass windows on which are emblazoned, in red, blue, and gold, the escutcheons of the most important powers in Europe: eagles, unicorns, leopards—a complete heraldic menagerie. At a distance of thirty yards, across the whole street which is as wide as a boulevard, Levis' Agency attracts the attention of the least curious of passers-by. Each one asks himself: "What can they sell there?" It would be easier to say "What do they not sell there?" On each window can be read in beautiful gold letters: "Wines, liquors, pale-ale, kummel, raki, caviare, preserved cod" or else: "Ancient and modern furniture t a p e s t r i e s, hangings, carpets from Smyrna and Ispahan." Further on: "Paintings by old masters, marble, terra-cotta, arms and armour, medal panoplies"; or again: "Money change, discount, foreign money." Then: "Universal library, newspapers from every country and in every language, sale and lease of houses, shooting, fishing, seaside residences"; or: "Private inquiries quickly and discreetly carried out."

The crowded inscriptions and brilliant

escutcheons are so mingled that it is impossible to distinguish what is displayed behind the shop window. A vague glimpse is caught of strange and oddly coloured bottles, of carved-wood chairs, of pictures and furs, and, in wooden platters a few half-opened rolls of piastres and bundles of bank-notes are to be seen. But the vast basement of the house, opening on to the pavement by low-grated cellar windows, forms a real solid basis to the garish display of the great flaunting shop, and conveyed the impression of some rich, solid, London warehouse, sustaining the *chic* and show of a shop-window of the boulevard de la Madeleine. In that basement were piles of rich products of all kinds: rows of barrels, bales of materials, heaps of chests, coffers, boxes of preserves, dizzy depths such as are seen on board a loading steamer through the open hatches.

Thus placed, firmly stretched in the very midst of the Parisian eddy, the net catches as they pass every kind of fish—large and small, even the merest fry, the very wariest of all; and at about three o'clock in the afternoon the shop is nearly always full.

At the glass door of the rue Royale, all and light, surrounded by a wide pediment of carved wood, stands a hall porter, covered with gold braid, who turns the handle and holds up an umbrella, if need be, for the customers as they step out of their carriages. The front room is an immense hall divided by wooden barriers and grated wickets into a number of compartments, regular horse-boxes, right and left to the very end. The dazzling light is reflected on the polished floor, the wainscoting, the cat frock-coats and artificially-curled

locks of the clerks, all of them stylish, smart-looking men, but betraying in their accent and manner a foreign origin. Among them are olive complexions, pointed skulls, narrow Asiatic shoulders, light blue eyes and American "goatees," and high-coloured Germans. In whatever language the customer may give his order, he is always certain of being understood, for every language is spoken at this agency, except indeed Russian, which is not necessary, seeing that Russians themselves speak every language except their own. The crowd comes and goes round the wickets, or waits seated on light chairs; ladies and gentlemen in travelling costume, a medley of Astrakan caps, Scotch caps, long veils floating above waterproofs, dust cloaks, check tweeds indiscriminately covering both sexes, with strapped rugs and leathern bags slung across shoulders; in fact, the crowd of a railway station, gesticulating, talking loud, with the indifference and coolness of people in a strange land, producing by a ceaseless jabber in many languages the same confused motley of sound that is heard at a bird-fancier's. At the same time is heard the sound of drawn corks and the rattle of gold pieces on the counters. Then the ring of interminable electric bells, the whistles in the call-tubes, the rustling of some unfolded plans for a house, scales run on a new piano to try it, or the exclamations of a tribe of Samayedes round a gigantic photograph, completes the pandemonium.

From one compartment to another the clerks call out for information, a number, a name, or a street. Now smiling and eager, and again suddenly cold and reserved, appearing completely indifferent to the things of this world, whenever an unfortunate and dismayed customer, sent from wicket to wicket, bends over to whisper into their ear some mysterious affair, which apparently fills them with astonishment. Sometimes, impatient at being stared at as if he were a waterspout or an aërolite, the inquirer would ask to see J. Tom Levis himself, who will, he affirms, certainly understand the matter in question. Then with a lofty smile he is told that J. Tom Levis is engaged, that he is busy with some important client. Not any paltry little business like yours, my dear sir! or such petty folk as you are! Look over there, at the further end of the hall. A door has just opened, and for one moment J. Tom Levis is visible. More majestic than all his clerks put together, with his important round stomach and imposing smooth skull, as shiny as the polished floor of his office, by the toss of his small head and his distant glance, by the despotic gesture of his short arm, and the solemn and loud voice in which he inquires, with an English accent, if "His Royal Highness the Prince of Wales's parcel has been dispatched," keeping at the same time the other hand on the door that he has hermetically closed behind him, as though to indicate that the august personage shut in there, is one who may not be disturbed on any pretext whatever.

Needless to add that the Prince of Wales has never been to this office, and that no parcel has ever been sent to him. But fancy the effect created on the crowd in the hall, and on the solitary customer to whom Tom has just said in his private room: "Excuse me for a moment; I have something to ask about."

All is sham! There is no more Prince of Wales behind the closed door than there is raki or kummel in the strange bottles in the window, nor English or Viennese beer in the casks underground. The emblazoned, gilded, varnished coaches, with J. T. L. or their panels, that pass at a gallop, all the more rapidly that they are empty dashing along through the finest quarters of Paris, are but a noisy and perambulating advertisement, tearing over the pavement with the all-devouring activity that in Tom Levis' Agency characterises both man and beast. Should any poor devil, excited by all this gold, break the glass window and ravenously plunge his bleeding hand into the wooden platters, he would only clutch hold of a handful of counters if he seized an enormous bundle of bank-notes, he would find himself the possessor of a twenty-five pound note on the top of a quire of common paper. There is nothing in the shop-front, nothing in the basement, nothing, absolutely nothing! How then about the port wine the Englishmen are tasting? the French coin the boyard has had in exchange for his roubles? the bronze group carefully packed up for the Greek lady? Nothing is easier. The English beer comes from the tavern next door the gold from a neighbouring money changer on the boulevards; the bronze from "What's his name" in the rue de Quatre-Septembre. Two or three men waiting in the basement, the order transmitted through the speaking-tube, have only to dash off as quickly as their legs will carry them to fetch the required objects.

They go out through a neighbouring courtyard, return in a few minutes and emerge from the spiral staircase, ornamented by a richly-wrought banister and crystal globe that unites the two stories. Here is the article demanded; warranted and labelled J. T. L. If it does not suit his lordship it is of no consequence, it can be changed. The Agency cellars are well-stocked. Maybe it is a trifle dearer than anywhere else, only the double or treble; but is not that preferable to running from shop to shop, where not a word of a foreign language is understood, notwithstanding the alluring promise of *"English spoken"* or *"Man spricht deutsch?"* Better than those shops on the boulevards, where the unfortunate stranger, circumvented and deceived, finds only the dregs, remnants, and refuse of Paris fashions, the "last season's," more tarnished by the date of their make even than by the dust and sun of the shop window. The obsequious, sneering, disdainful, and irrepressible Parisian shop-keeper's day is over, foreigners will have none of him. They are weary at last of being so ferociously defrauded, not only by the shop-keeper, but at the hotel where they sleep, at the restaurant where they dine, by the cab they pick up in the streets, by the theatrical agent who sends them to be bored at the empty theatres. At least at Levis' Agency, this ingenious agency for foreigners, everything wished for could be found, and that without being cheated; for was not J. T. Levis an Englishman, and is not English commercial honesty of wide-world fame?

Nobody could be more English than Tom Levis, from the tips of his square-toed Quaker shoes to his long frock-coat falling over his green plaid trousers, and his tall narrow-brimmed hat, which sets off his round, red, good-natured face so well. British honesty, fed on beefsteaks, can be read in that complexion, in that mouth, slit up from ear to ear, in the flaxen colour of the uneven whiskers, uneven from the habit their possessor has of nibbling one—always the same—whenever he is perplexed; and in the short hairy fingers covered with rings. How loyal also are those eyes, seen behind a great pair of spectacles delicately mounted in gold. So loyal indeed that if perchance J. Tom Levis happens to tell a lie—the best men are exposed to such an eventuality—his eyeballs, by a singular nervous 'tic, turn round rapidly like little wheels twisting and revolving in the vista of a gyroscope.

The finishing touch of Tom Levis' English physiognomy was his cab, the first vehicle of the kind that was seen in Paris, and which seemed the natural shell of this queer being. If at any time he found himself, as often happens in business, hard pressed by some unforeseen complication, Tom would say: "Call the cab!" and he was certain to find some idea as he drove along. He weighed, commented, devised combinations, whilst the Parisians watched the transparent box roll by with the outline of the absorbed man energetically munching his right whisker. It was in this cab that he had conceived and elaborated his most famous strokes of business towards the end of the second Empire. Ah! that was the good time! Paris was crowded with strangers, not mere birds of passage, but exotic fortunes settling down, only craving for pleasure and revelry. There was the

Turk Hussein Bey and the Egyptian Mahomet Pasha, two celebrated Orientals, well-known in the Bois; there was the Princess Verkatscheff scattering all the silver of the Oural mountains from the windows of her first floor in the boulevard Malesherbes; and the American Bergson, whose enormous income, derived from his petroleum wells, Paris was then devouring. Since then Bergson has recovered his wealth. And then there were the nabobs, the swarm of nabobs, of all tints: yellow, brown, red, mottling the theatres and parks, eager to spend, to enjoy life, as though they foresaw that they would soon have to quit this great merry carousal before the formidable explosion that was about to burst through the roof and shatter the mirrors and window-panes.

J. Tom Levis was the indispensable middleman in all these pleasures; not a single napoleon was spent without his having first pared at it. To his foreign customers must be added a few Parisian rakes, amateurs of rare game, poachers of strictly guarded preserves, who applied to Tom as the most shrewd and clever medium, and also because they fancied that his uncouth French and difficulty of expression would keep their secrets safer. J. T. Levis set his seal on all the scandalous stories at the end of the empire.

It was in J. Tom Levis' name that the pit box No. 9 at the Opéra Comique was engaged, behind the grating of which Baroness Mills hid herself an hour every evening to listen to her tenorino, and from which, after the cavatina was over she would carry away, thrust among the lace of her bodice, his handkerchief, stained with perspiration and white lead. In J. Tom Levis' name too,

was the small house hired, Avenue de Clichy, a house that he sublet to the two Sismondo brothers and for the same woman, without their being aware of it, for, as partners in the same bank, they were never free at the same moment. Ah! the agency ledgers at that time contained many a romance in a few lines!

"A house with two entrances on the route de Saint Cloud. Rent, furniture, buying out present tenant—so much.

And below:

"General's Commission—so much.

"A country house at Petit Valtin, near Plombières; Garden, coachhouse, two entrances, buying out tenant—so much.

Always followed by: *"General's commission."*

The general seemed to hold an important place in the agency's accounts!

If, however, Tom made a great deal of money in those days, he also spent a great deal, not in gambling, nor betting, nor on women, but in satisfying the caprices of a most uncivilised and childish nature, of a most fantastic and absurd imagination, which would brook no delay between its dream and the realization. On one occasion he chose to have an avenue of acacia trees at the end of his property at Courbevoie, but, as trees grow but slowly, during eight days all along the banks of the Seine, very bare and black with factories at this spot, huge trucks could be seen toiling along, each one bearing an acacia, the green foliage of which rocked by the slow motion of the wheel was reflected on the water in quivering shadows. This suburban property which according to the English custom, Tom Levis inhabited all the year round and which, at first was but a mere country box composed of a ground floor and attic, soon became for him a source of tremendous expense. By degrees, as his business prospered and extended, he had increased his little estate; adding one building after another, one bit of land to another bit of land, till he finally found himself the possessor of a park made up of annexes, market gardens, and patches of brushwood; a strange property, in which his tastes, ambitions, and English eccentricity revealed themselves, deformed and dwarfed still more, it is true, by the vulgarity of his ideas, and his futile attempts at artistic arrangements.

The old house had been heightened by an additional upper story, over which extended an Italian terrace with marble balustrade, flanked by a couple of gothic towers, and communicating by a covered bridge with another building, a kind of Swiss cottage, with an openwork carved balcony clothed with ivy. All this was built of bricks, plastered in stucco, and looked like a Nuremburg toy, with an abundance of turrets, battlements, weather-vanes, and dormer windows. Then the park bristled all over with kiosks and belvederes, glistened with glass houses, artificial lakes, and the black bastion of an immense reservoir topped by a real mill, the sails of which, stirred by the slightest breath of air, flapped and turned with the perpetual grinding sound of their axle.

As the train rushes through the narrow strip of Parisian suburb traversed by the railway, many a grotesque villa no doubt defiles by the carriage window, like some vision or fantastic nightmare, the effort of some shop-keeper's brain and uncontrolled imagination running

riot. None of them, however, can compare with Tom Levis' folly, except it be the villa of his neighbour Spricht; the great Spricht, the illustrious ladies' tailor! This magnificent personage never stays in Paris longer than his business requires, just the three hours in the afternoon, when he holds his consultations (on finery) in his great laboratory on the boulevards; this over, he at once returns to Courbevoie. The secret of this enforced retreat, is that dear Spricht, the darling of all his customers, although he possesses in his drawers, tossed among the marvellous patterns of his Lyons silks, specimens of most of the delicate scrawls of the aristocracy of Paris, has been obliged to satisfy himself with this intimacy of correspondence; that he is not received by any of the people he dresses, and that his fine business connection has destroyed all intercourse with the commercial world to which he belongs. He therefore leads a very retired life, surrounded only, like all parvenus, by a swarm of poor relatives, and taking a pride in treating them right royally. The only distraction he finds, that imparts the zest necessary to this kind of tabooed existence, is the neighbourhood and rivalry of Tom Levis, a rivalry made up of the hatred and contempt, which they mutually feel for each other, without indeed knowing why, and which therefore is the more irreconcilable.

Whenever Spricht builds a turret— Spricht is a German—he has a passion for the mediæval, for castles, ruins, romantic glades. J. Tom Levis erects a verandah! When Tom knocks down a wall, Spricht cuts down all his hedges. There is a story of a pavilion built by Tom, which blocked Spricht's view in the direction of Saint Cloud. The tailor thereupon added a gallery to his pigeon-house. The other retorted by an additional story; Spricht would not be outdone, and the two buildings by dint of stones and workmen continued their ascension, till one fine night, a gust of wind blew them both down, not a difficult matter, seeing the lightness of the fragile constructions. On one occasion Spricht brought back from Venice a gondola, a real Venetian gondola, and moored it in the little harbour at the foot of his property; a week after, puff! puff! a pretty little steam-yacht came alongside Tom Levis' quay, stirring up in the water all the reflections of the turrets, roofs and battlements of his villa.

Had the empire lasted for ever, this extravagant style of living might have been kept up, but its last hour had come. The war, the siege, the departure of all foreigners were for these two tradesmen a positive disaster, more especially for Tom Levis, whose property was devastated by the invasion, while that of Spricht was spared. But with the peace, the struggle recommenced more fiercely than ever between the two rivals; this time however they did not start fair, for the great tailor saw all his customers come back to him, while poor Tom vainly awaited the return of his clients. The advertisement: "Information, discretion, despatch," brought in next to nothing, and the mysterious general no longer called for his clandestine commissions at the agency. Any other man than Levis would have put the drag on; but this terrible fellow had contracted irresistible habits of expenditure; his hands seemed unable to close. And

then the Sprichts were there, mournful and lugubrious since the catastrophe, loudly proclaiming that the end of the world was nigh; and they had built up at the end of their park, a reduced facsimile of the ruins of the Hôtel de Ville, with its crumbled walls blackened by the flames. On Sunday evenings, it was lighted up with coloured lights, and all the Sprichts raised a chorus of lamentations around it. It was a sinister sight. J. Tom Levis, on the contrary, from hatred of his rival became a republican, celebrated regenerated France organized regattas; crowned *rosières* and at one of these coronations, in a costly explosion of joy, carried off one summer's night at the very hour of the concerts, the band of the Champs Elysées, and brought it steaming up in his own yacht to Courbevoie.

At this rate his debts rapidly increased, but the Englishman did not betray any anxiety. No one better than he, knew how to baffle creditors by cool imposing impudence. No one—not even his well-trained clerks—came up to him, in his manner of curiously examining his creditor's bills, as though they were some strange old manuscript and then tossing them aside in a drawer with an air of superior indifference; nobody knew such tricks to avoid paying to gain time. Time! that was all Tom Levis required to discover some profitable scheme, what he called "a great stroke," in the expressive language of Bohemian financialism. But in vain did he call for his cab, dash feverishly through the streets of Paris, anxiously hungrily, watching for his prey, year passed by, and the great stroke did not come.

CHAPTER X

A LONG, SOFT GLANCE

ONE afternoon, when the agency was swarming with people, a tall young man, with a languid and haughty mien, a mocking eye, thin moustache and pallid puffy good-looking face, went up to the principal wicket, and asked to speak with Tom Levis. The clerk, deceived by the peremptory tone of the request, took him for a creditor, and was already assuming his most disdainful manner, when the young man, in a sharp voice, the nasal inflection of which augmented the impertinent tone, bade the "conceited fool," go at once and tell his master that the King of Illyria wanted to speak to him. "Ah Monseigneur. Yes, Monseigneur." The cosmopolitan crowd turned with a movement of curiosity towards the hero of Ragusa. A swarm of clerks eagerly rushed from their compartments to escort his Majesty and usher him into Tom Levis' private room. The latter had not yet arrived, but could not fail to come in at any moment.

It was the first time that Christian came to the agency, the old Duc de Rosen having hitherto settled all the accounts of the little court. But today the King had to transact such a delicate and private affair, that he had not dared to confide so tender a morsel to the heavy jaws of his aide-de-camp. What he wanted, in fact, was to hire a house for a pretty horse-breaker who had just replaced Amy Férat in his affections, a furnished pavilion with servants and horses, and certain facilities of access, and all this to be ready within twenty-four hours. A feat that could

only be accomplished through Levis agency.

The room into which the king had been ushered contained only two armchairs in moleskin, a narrow silent gasstove, the reflector of which seemed to throw back the fire from an adjacent room, and a small round table covered with a blue cloth on which lay a Paris Directory. Half the room was cut off by the high grating—also draped in blue —of a large bureau, elaborately arranged, whereon was displayed above a great open ledger, with brass-bound corners, surrounded by ink-erasers, sand, rulers and pen-wipers, a long shelf full of books of the same size—the agency ledgers—their green backs forming a straight line like Prussian soldiers on parade. The scrupulous care bestowed on this silent nook, the fresh appearance of everything, did honour to the old cashier, absent at that moment, whose existence was evidently passed there.

While the king waited, stretched out in an armchair, his nose peeping out of his furs, suddenly, without a movement of the glass door leading to the public-room, or of the wide Algerian drapery—with a hole in the middle as in a drop scene—he heard behind the grating the slight scratching of a pen. Some one was seated at the desk; not indeed the old white-headed clerk for whom the den seemed created, but the most delicious little woman that had even turned over the leaves of a ledger. At Christian's gesture of surprise, she turned round, and enveloped him in a long soft glance, that suddenly drowned the sparkle in her eyes. The whole room was illumined by that look, and filled by the musical charm of a voice, almost trembling from emotion, that murmured: "My husband is keeping you waiting very long, Monseigneur."

Tom Levis. her husband! The husband of this sweet creature with such a pale, refined profile, such elegant yet rich contours, like one of Tanagra's statuettes!

How did she happen to be there, alone in that cage, studying those big books, which threw white reflections on her ivory complexion, and of which her little fingers had barely strength enough to turn the pages? And this on such a bright, sunny day; one of those February days, when the sun lights up all the lively gracefulness, the dresses, and the smiles of the ladies strolling down the boulevards. He advanced towards her, turning a compliment in which these varied impressions were mingled; but his heart beat so loudly that he could hardly speak; and he was seized with one of those sudden ungovernable longings, such as he, the spoilt and blasé child, did not remember ever having felt before. In fact this type of woman, between twenty-five and thirty years of age, was utterly unknown to him. It was far removed from the rougish curls of little Colette de Rosen, from the cool impudence and bold painted eyes of Amy Férat, as it was from the noble sadness and embarrassing majesty of the queen. Neither coquetry, boldness, nor proud reserve, nothing that he had ever met with in his own set, or in his relations with the demi-monde. This pretty woman, with her calm and domestic look, her beautiful dark hair, smooth like that of women who dress their hair in the morning for the rest of the day, who, draped in a plain violet-tinted, woollen gown. but for two

enormous diamonds in her rosy ears, might have been taken for any ordinary female accountant; suddenly appeared to him in her industrious captivity behind her wicket, like a Carmelite nun seen through the iron grating of a cloister, or an Oriental slave imploring help through the gilded trellis of her terrace. And she seemed, indeed, to have the submissive bewilderment, the bent profile of a slave; and the amber shade at the roots of her hair, the straight line of her eyebrows, her half-parted lips, imparted an Asiatic stamp to this Parisian woman. Christian stood looking at her, and the figure of the bald-headed, ape-like husband rose up in his mind. How came she in the power of such a clownish fellow? Was it not a shameful robbery, a flagrant injustice!

The voice meanwhile went on slowly softly apologizing:

"I am so distressed. Tom is so long If your Majesty would kindly tell me what you require, I might perhaps——'

The king blushed, feeling slightly embarrassed. Never would he dare confide to this candid and obliging creature the somewhat ambiguous establishment h was meditating. She, however, insisted and said, with a smile: "Oh! your Majesty can quite trust me. I keep the books of the agency."

Her authority in business matters was patent, for at every moment, some clerk or another would come to the little round casement that opened from the private office into the public premises, and ask in a whisper for the most anomalous information: "They have sent for Madame Karitidès' piano' "The individual from the Hôtel Brist has come." She seemed acquainte with everything, answering by one word, or one cypher.

The king, disconcerted, wondered whether this angel in a shop, this ethe-real being was really aware of all the intrigues and swindling of the Englishman.

"No, madam, my business is not urgent. At least, I am no longer in a hurry. My ideas have entirely changed within the last hour."

He leant towards the grating as he stammered out these words, then suddenly paused, regretting his audacity, as he gazes at the placid activity of the woman, her long lashes almost sweeping the paper, while her pen moves along in regular lines. Oh! how he longed to tear her from her prison, to bear her off in his arms, far, far away, to whisper in her ears those soothing, tender words with which little children are lulled. The temptation was so strong, that he felt obliged to run away, and take leave abruptly, without stopping to see J. Tom Levis.

The night was closing in, foggy and cold.

The king, usually so chilly, did not perceive it; but sent away his carriage and went on foot to the Grand Club, through the wide thoroughfares that lead from the Madeleine to the Place Vendôme. His enthusiasm, his delight was so great, that he spoke to himself aloud, his hair flattened down on his eyes, which seemed filled with flickering flames. How many of these exuberant and light-footed joys do we not pass in the streets, and feel as though they left us some of their phosphorescence. Christian arrived at his club in this happy state, and did not notice the melancholy appearance of the long line of reception rooms, which were filled with the gloom of the uncertain, unoccupied hour of twilight, more depressing still in these half-public places where the intimacy of home-life is lacking. The lamps were being brought in. A slow, languid game of billiards was going on at the further end, with the dull sound of the ivory balls upon the cushion; a rustling of newspapers; and the heavy breathing of a sleeper stretched out on the divan of the large drawing-room, whom the king, as he entered, disturbed. He turned round with a yawn that displayed his broken teeth, and stretched out his two lean arms, as he inquired in a dismal tone:

"What is to be the lark to-night?"

Christian gave a cry of delight:

"Ah! prince, I was looking for you."

The Prince d'Axel, more familiarly known as Queue-de-Poule, was evidently better acquainted than he with all the haunts of Parisian life. In the ten years the Prince had spent beating every corner of the boulevards he knew them from top to bottom, in all their length and breadth, from the steps of the Café Tortoni to the very gutter, and would no doubt be able to give him the information he required. Well aware of the only way of getting his Highness to speak, to loosen his dulled and heavy wits, which the wines of France—though he partook of them largely—had never succeeded in rousing; any more than the fermentation of a vintage can inflate and send off like a balloon the huge iron-bound tun that contains it; Christian quickly asked for a pack of cards. As the heroines of Molière are only witty, fan in hand, so d'Axel could only get up a little

spirit in handling his beloved cards.
The fallen majesty, and the heir apparent in disgrace, the two celebrities
of the club, thereupon sat down to a
game of Chinese bezique before dinner,
the most *gommeux* of all games, because it needs no brains and permits the
least skilful player to lose a fortune
without making an effort.

"Tom Levis is married then?" asked
Christian, with assumed negligence, as
he cut the cards. The other gazed at
him with his lack-lustre, red-edged eyes:

"Did you not know?"

"No. Who is the woman?"

"Séphora Leemans, a celebrity."

The king started at the name of
Séphora.

"Is she a Jewess?"

"Probably."

There was a moment's silence. And
indeed the impression left by Séphora
must have been very strong, the smooth,
oval face of the fair recluse, her brilliant eyes, her glossy hair must have
been very bewitching, to triumph over
the prejudice, and to linger in the
memory of this Catholic Slave, haunted
since the days of his infancy by the
petty pillage, the supposed witchcraft
of the Bohemian Jews of his country.
He continued his questions. Unluckily
the prince was losing, and engrossed in
his play, growled in his long, yellow
beard:

"I am awfully bored here—awfully
bored."

It was impossible to get a word more
out of him.

"Capital! here is Wattelet. Come
here, Wattelet," said the king to a
great fellow who just then came into
the room as noisy and full of life as a
playful puppy.

This Wattelet, the favourite painter
of the Grand Club, and of society generally, good-looking enough at a distance, but bearing visibly, on closer
inspection, the marks of a life at high
pressure, represented very exactly the
modern artist who so little resembles
the brilliant traditions of 1830. Dressed
and curled in the height of fashion, this
frequenter of salons and green-rooms
had retained nothing of the student,
save a certain swing and freedom of
gait under the stiffer costume of a
society man, and in his ideas as well
as his language, a somewhat similar
carelessness; a curl of mocking indifference lingering around the corners of
his mouth. Brought to the club one
day to decorate the dining-room, he
had made himself so agreeable, so indispensable to all the members, that he
remained a fixture, and was dubbed the
organiser for life of the hitherto monotonous parties and fêtes; he brought
to these pleasures all the freshness of
a picturesque imagination, and of an
education picked up in his wanderings
through every grade of society. It was
"My dear Wattelet—my dear fellow,"
at every turn. They could not do without him. He was the confidant of all
the members of the club, of their wives,
of their mistresses; he would draw on
one side of a card the costume of the
Duchesse de V—— for the next embassy ball, and on the other side of it
the airy skirt that was to flutter above
the flesh-coloured tights of Mademoiselle Alzire, the duke's plaything of the
moment. On Thursday, his studio was
open to all his noble clients, who enjoyed the freedom, the unceremonious
and eccentric gossip of the place, the
mingled shimmer of colours proceeding

from the tapestries, curiosities, lacquered furniture, and the canvasses of the artist himself; it was a style of painting essentially resembling the man, elegant, but just a trifle vulgar; mostly portraits of women, executed with a profound comprehension of the whole scale of Parisian trickery, false complexions, impossible heads of hair, a style of art in perfect sympathy with that costly bauble trailing its skirts and billowing its laces and gauzes—the modern woman—causing Spricht to say, with the condescending disdain of the parvenu tradesman for the painter who is just making his mark: "No one paints the women I dress as well as that fellow."

At the king's first words Wattelet began to laugh.

"But, Monseigneur, that is little Séphora."

"You know her?"

"Thoroughly."

"Tell us then."

And while the game between the two princes continued, the painter seated astride a chair, and full of pride at the intimacy in which he found himself, coughed, settled himself and assuming the voice of the showman who explains the picture in his booth, he began:

"Séphora Leemans, born in Paris about eighteen hundred and forty-five, six, or seven, in an old curiosity shop of the rue Eginhard, in the Marais, a dirty little musty bye-street between the passage Charlemagne and the church of Saint-Paul, the very heart of the Jews' quarter. Some day, as you drive in from Saint-Mandé, your Majesty should tell your coachman to drive through that labyrinth of little streets, you would see a wonderful bit of Paris Such heads! such houses! a jargon made up of Alsatian and Hebrew; shops, dens full of rubbish, with old clothes and rags stacked high before each door; old hags with hooked noses sorting them, or stripping old umbrellas; and then the dogs and vermin, and smells! a real Ghetto of the middle ages, swarming with houses of the same period, iron balconies, high windows opening into lofts. Father Leemans however is not a Jew. He is a Belgian from Ghent, a Catholic; and it is all very fine to call the girl Séphora, she is only a half-breed, with the skin and eyes of the race, but not the vulture nose; on the contrary, a most charming little straight nose. I don't know where she can have it from; father Leemans' is a jolly ugly one. My first medal at the Salon, that snout of his. Yes, it is quite true the old fellow shows, in a corner of the disgraceful hovel he calls his shop, his full-length portrait, signed Wattelet, and not one of my worst bits of work, either. It was my way of getting inside the place to pay my court to Séphora, for I had a real *béguin* for her just then."

"A *béguin?*" said the king to whom the Parisian dictionary continually presented some fresh surprise. "Ah, yes! I see. Go on."

"I was not the only one in love, I can assure you. All day long there was a procession through the shop in the rue de la Paix; for I must tell you, Monseigneur, that old Leemans had at that time two shops. The old man was sharp enough to have understood the change that had taken place in curiosity dealing during the last twenty years. The romantic bric-à-brac dealer of poky streets, described by Hoffmann and even by Balzac has given way to the dealer in curiosities settled in the midst of the luxurious parts of Paris, with the fine shop front and plenty of lighting. Leemans kept for himself, and real amateurs continued to haunt, his damp and dusty den in the rue Eginhard; but for the public, the idler, for the Parisian who merely follows the lead and can swallow anything, he opened a superb shop in the rue de la Paix, which, with the deep-hued gold, the dark silver of the antique jewellery and the tanned colour of the laces, made the sumptuous modern jewellers and goldsmiths' shops, in the same street, look pale. Séphora was fifteen then, and her serene youthful beauty was well set off by all these antiquities. And how intelligent she was, how clever at selling a thing, with as quick and certain an eye as her father for the value of a curio. Plenty of connoisseurs came to the shop to have the pleasure of touching her fingers, or the wavy silkness of her hair, while leaning over the same glass case.

"The mother was never in the way; the old hag, so black round the eyes that she looked as if she wore goggles, always sat darning, or poking her nose into some old piece of guipure or old scrap of tapestry, and took no trouble whatever about her daughter. And quite right too! Séphora was a serious young person who could not be induced to stray from the paths of virtue."

"Really," said the king, appearing enchanted with the information.

"Your Majesty will judge by this. Old mother Leemans slept at the shop; the daughter on her part, returned at about ten o'clock to the old den, so that her father might not be alone. Well, this splendid creature, whose beauty was celebrated, praised in all the papers, who could with a nod of her head have caused Cinderella's fairy coach to start up before her, used to wait every evening for the Madeleine omnibus and go direct from that to the nest of the paternal owl. In the morning as she started before the omnibus began to run, she walked, in all weathers, her black dress covered by a waterproof, and I can assure you that amid all the crowd of shop-girls who come pouring down the rue de Rivoli-Saint-Antoine, in hood, hat, or bare head, pale faced or smiling, fresh little throats coughing slightly at the early fog, ever pursued by some gallant, not one of them could compare with her."

"At what hour does she walk down?" growled the prince warming up.

Christian grew impatient.

"Let him finish. What next?"

"Then, Monseigneur, I managed to get a footing in the house of my charmer, and I worked my way gently. On a Sunday they would get up a little family game of loto with a few dealers from the passage Charlemagne. Pretty society! I always came back infested by fleas! Only I was able to sit beside Séphora, and tread on her toes beneath the table, while she looked at me with such a limpid and angelic gaze that I fully believed in her ignorance, purity and virtue. Then came a day, when looking in at their den rue Eginhard, I found all the place topsy-turvy, the mother in tears, the father furious, rubbing up an old arquebuse with which he vowed he would take vengeance upon the vile ravisher. The girl had just gone off with Baron Sala, one of old Leemans' richest customers, and the old fellow—I learnt afterwards—had himself sold his daughter just like any old jewel or bit of ancient iron-work. For two or three years Séphora concealed herself and her septuagenarian lover in Switzerland, Scotland, on the borders of many a blue lake. Then I heard suddenly, that she had come back and had started 'a family hotel' at one end of the Avenue d'Antin. I has-tened there. I found my former flame just as adorable and as calm as ever, at the head of a most miscellaneous table d'hôte—Brazilians, English, and ladies of doubtful virtue—a fine mix-ture. One half of the guests would still be eating salad while the other was already turning back the table-cloth to play baccarat. Here it was she first met J. Tom Levis; not handsome, not young, and not a penny to his name into the bargain. How did he attract her? No one can say. What is cer-tain, however, is that for his sake she sold her establishment, married him, helped him to set up the agency—at first prosperous and well-stocked, though now almost gone smash—so that Séphora, of whom one never caught sight, living the life of a recluse in the queer castellated villa Tom Levis had indulged in, made a fresh appearance only a few months ago in the character of a most seductive little book-keeper. By Jove! the business felt the effect immediately. The pick of the clubs began to meet in the rue Royale. There was as much flirtation at the wicket of the office as formerly in the old curios-ity shop, or the office of the 'family hotel.' As for me, I am no longer in it. That woman frightens me. Al-ways the same for the last ten years,

not a wrinkle, not a line, with her long curling eye-lashes cast down, the circle of her eyes always young and fresh, and all that for the grotesque husband she adores! It is enough to puzzle and discourage the most ardent."

The king shuffled the cards with an-noyance:

"Nonsense!" he said, "that is im-possible. An ugly devil, a baboon like Tom Levis, bald, fifteen years older than she is, who talks the slang of a pickpocket."

"Some women like all that, Mon-seigneur."

Here the Prince Royal in his vulgar and drawling accent interrupted:

"Nothing to be done with that woman. All the signals dead set against me. Not a chance. Line blocked."

"Oh! by Jove, d'Axel, we know your way of making signals," said Christian, when he had mastered the meaning of this expression transferred from the lingo of the engine-driver to that of the fashionable *Gomme* of the day. "You have no patience. You like an unde-fended fortress. Hop, skip and a jump. But I declare that for a man who would give himself the trouble to get a little spoony on Séphora, who would not be put off by silence, disdain, and so on, it would only be the affair of a month. Not more."

"Bet you won't," said d'Axel.

"How much?"

"Two thousand napoleons."

"I take you. Wattelet, ask for the book."

This book, in which were entered the bets of the Grand Club, was as curious and instructive in its way, as that other one in the Levis den. The greatest names of the French aristocracy were here found attached to the most grotesque, foolish, and impossible bets; that, for instance, of the Duc de Courson-Launay who bet and lost every hair of his body and was unable for a fortnight to move a step in consequence. There were plenty of other bets yet more extravagant, and the signatures of heroes, inscribed on a hundred glorious deeds, were to be found ill-coupled in this record of folly.

Around the two parties to the wager, were grouped in respectful curiosity several members of the club. This ridiculous and cynical bet, excusable perhaps amid the laughter and intoxication of a parcel of hair-brained youths, assumed a different aspect when sanctioned by the gravity of all these bald heads, the social dignities they represented and the heraldic importance of the signatures to be appended, and the looker-on might have been persuaded he was assisting at the conclusion of some international treaty, regulating the destinies of Europe.

Thus it stood recorded:

"This third day of February, eighteen hundred and seventy-five, his Majesty Christian II, wagers with H. R.H. the Prince d'Axel two thousand napoleons he gains the good graces of Séphora L—— before the end of the present month."

"This would, perhaps, have been the occasion on which to sign Rigolo and Queue de Poule!" said Wattelet to himself, as he carried the book away, the shadow of an evil laugh flitting across his society-clown face.

CHAPTER XI

BOHEMIAN EXILE

"OH yes! we know all that. You old English Goddam. It is only when you wish neither to pay nor to answer that you use that kind of coin. But that won't serve to bamboozle me any longer. We must square accounts, you old rascal."

"Really, Master Lebeau, you speak to me with a vehemence!"

And to give vent to this word "vehemence," which he seems proud to include in his vocabulary, for he repeats it three or four times running, J. Tom Levis throws himself back and seems to disappear within the vast white choker, of old-fashioned clerical type, that swathes his neck. At the same time his shifty glance turns and twists, making behind his wide-open eyes his unfathomable thoughts; while his adversary's glance flickers and cringes beneath his lowered eyelids and replies to the rascally chatter of the Englishman, by the low cunning readable in his narrow weasel-like face. His thin hair, curled and frizzed, his austere black coat close buttoned to the chin, the extreme correctness of his appearance gives Maître Lebeau something of the air of an official prosecutor at the old Châtelet; but as there is nothing like argument, the anger born of interests in danger, to bring out the real character of a man, so it comes about that at this moment the elegant Lebeau, the oily gentlemanly fellow, polished as his own finger nails—the pet of royal ante-rooms, the quondam footman of the Tuileries, betrays himself as the hideous flunkey he really is, eager for gain and prey.

To shelter themselves from a spring shower that was plentifully washing the stones of the courtyard, the two cronies had taken refuge in the great coach-house with whitened wallls freshly washed over, and covered about half-way up with thick matting that protected from the damp the numerous splendid carriages standing there side by side, wheel to wheel, from the state coaches, all glass and gilding, to the unpretending brake used for going to the meet, to the light mail phæton of every-day use, and the sledge even, that the queen drove over the ice and snow when there was a frost; each recalling, in the repose and the dim light of the coachhouse, the superb steeds that bear them forth—briskly or majestically—as the occasion requires. What completed the impression of comfort and luxurious idleness was the neighbour-hood of the stables, whence came a sound of snorting, and resonant kick-ing against the woodwork, and the open saddle-room, showing a well-polished floor and wainscoting, the whips in the racks, the harness and saddles on their blocks, and round the walls the trophies of bridles and bits with their gleam of steel.

Tom and Lebeau argued in a corner and their voices raised in discussion mingled with the rain pattering on the asphalte paving. The valet in particu-lar, feeling himself at home, talked at the top of his voice.

"What a scoundrel this old thief of a Levis was! Who could have supposed he would play such a trick? When their Majesties left the Hotel des Pyra-mides for Saint-Mandé, who arranged the whole job? Was it Lebeau, yes or no? And that in spite of everyone, in spite of the greatest opposition. What was agreed upon in return? Were they not to share all the com-missions, all the tips of the tradesmen? Come now, was that so or not?"

"Well, yes. It was like that."

"Then why try to cheat?"

"No, no, cheat, never," said J. Tom Levis, his hand on his shirt-front.

"Come, come, you old humbug. All the tradespeople have given you forty per cent.; I have proofs of it. And you told me you only had ten. So that, on the forty thousand pounds that setting up the house at Saint-Mandé cost, I have for my part five per cent., that is two thousand pounds, and you, your thirty-five per cent., that is to say, seven times two thousand francs, that is to say, fourteen thousand pounds—fourteen thousand pounds—fourteen thousand pounds."

He was choking with rage, this sum sticking in his throat like a fish-bone. Tom tried to calm him. To begin with, it was all very much exaggerated, and then the agent had had enormous expenses. The rent was raised on his place in the rue Royale; so much money out, so little coming in. Without tak-ing into account that for him it was only a passing affair, could only hap-pen once, while Lebeau was there al-ways, and in a house where the ex-penses were over eight thousand pounds sterling a year, opportunities could not be wanting.

But the valet would not hear of this view of the case. His own affairs were no one's business, and assuredly, he was not going to be robbed by a wretched Englishman.

"Monsieur Lebeau, you are impertinent. I shall not waste any more time on you."

Here Tom Levis turned towards the door. But the other blocked up the way. "Go without paying! Never." His lips were pale. His weasel face quivering with rage was pushed close to the Englishman's, who remained perfectly calm and so exasperating cool that at last the valet, enraged beyond measure shook his fist in his face with a coarse expression. With a backhander, quick as a sword parry, and totally unlike the movement of a boxer, the Englishman knocked his fist away, and in the very purest accent of the Faubourg Saint-Antoine, said:

"No more of that, my boy, or I'll strike."

The effect of these few words was prodigious. Lebeau, stupefied, looked mechanically around him to see if it could really have been the Englishman who spoke; then his glance settling on Tom Levis, with his rolling eyes and a sudden crimson overspreading his features, he was seized with a fit of uncontrollable mirth—in which yet shook a little of his recent anger—a mirth that finally communicated itself to the agent himself.

"Oh, you confounded humbug! I ought to have suspected you. No Englishman could be so terribly English as you are."

They were still laughing, without having yet recovered breath, when the door behind them in the harness-room opened suddenly, and the queen appeared. A few moments ago she had stopped in the neighbouring stable, where she had herself fastened up her favourite mare, and she had not lost a word of the conversation. The trea-son having so low an origin affected her but little. She had long known what to think of Lebeau, the hypocritical valet, witness of all her humiliations, all her misery; the other, the man of the "cab," she hardly knew—a mere tradesman. But from these people she now learned serious matters. So the establishment at Saint-Mandé had cost forty thousand pounds, the existence they fancied so careful, so modest, cost eight thousand a year, and they had but two thousand at the most. How could she have been so long blind to the inadequacy of their real resources to the style in which they lived? Who then furnished the money for all these expenses? Who paid for them, for all this luxury, this house, these horses, carriages, even for her dress and her private charities? Shame burned in her cheeks at this thought while she went straight across the courtyard in all the rain, and rapidly mounted the little flight of steps to the steward's office.

Rosen, busy arranging bills on which lay piles of gold, started to his feet in the surprise of seeing her.

"No, remain seated," she said abruptly, and, leaning over the writing-table, she laid her hand, still in its riding glove, upon it, with a resolute gesture of authoritative insistence:

"Rosen, on what have we lived for two years? Oh! no subterfuges! I know that all I thought only hired, is bought and paid for in our name. I know that Saint-Mandé alone has cost us more than forty thousand pounds, the forty thousand we brought from Illyria. You must tell me now who it is has helped us since then, and from what hands we are receiving alms."

The dismayed countenance of the old man, the piteous quiver of his thousand little wrinkles told Frédérique the truth.

"You!" she said. "It is you!"

She would never have dreamed of that. And the duke, excusing himself, stammered out the words: "duty—gratitude—restitution."

"Duke," said she, violently, "the king does not take away what he has once given, and a queen is not to be kept like a ballet-dancer."

Two tears glittered in her eyes like sparks, tears of pride that did not fall.

"Oh, forgive me, forgive——"

He was so humble and kissed her finger tips with such an expression of sad regret, that she continued somewhat softened:

"You will draw up a list of all your advances, my dear Rosen. A receipt shall be given you, and the king shall pay it off as soon as possible. As to future expenses, I intend to take charge of them, I will see that they do not exceed our income. We will sell both horses and carriages. The establishment shall be reduced. Exiled princes must be satisfied with little."

The old duke started.

"Undeceive yourself, Madam. It is above all in exile that royalty needs all its prestige. Ah! if I had been listened to, it is not here, in a remote suburb with an establishment only fit for a sojourn at some watering-place that your Majesties would have come to live. I would have had you in a palace, in the full tide of Parisian life, convinced as I am that what dethroned kings have most to fear is the indifference that gains upon them, when they have made acquaintance with the level-ling familiarity, the jostling of the streets. I know I have often been thought ridiculous with my points of etiquette, my childish and superannuated stickling for such things. And yet these forms are more important than ever; they help to keep alive the pride of bearing so easily lost in misfortune. It is the unyielding armour that keeps the soldier erect even when wounded to death."

She remained for a moment without replying, her open brow traversed by a thought that had just occurred to her. Then she raised her head and said:

"It is impossible. There is a dignity worth more than this. I intend from this evening that things shall be altered as I have now decided."

Then he became more pressing, almost supplicating:

"But your Majesty does not reflect—a sale of horses, carriages, a sort of royal bankruptcy, what a commotion it would make! What a scandal!"

"What is going on now is still more scandalous."

"Who knows it? Who even suspects it? How should anyone suppose that Rosen, the old miser—. You yourself hesitated to believe it just now. Oh! Madame, Madame, I implore you to accept what you are pleased to call my devotion. To begin with, it would be attempting the impossible. If you only knew,—your revenues for the whole year would hardly supply the king with enough to pay his gambling debts."

"The king shall play no more, duke."

This was said in such a tone, with such a glance that Rosen dared insist no longer. Nevertheless he permitted himself to add one more remark:

"I will do what your Majesty wishes.

But I implore you to remember that all I possess is yours, and that in a case of urgency I have at least deserved to be the first person applied to."

He was perfectly certain the application must come before long.

On the morrow the promised reforms began. Half the servants were dismissed, the useless carriages sent to Tattersall's, where they were sold fairly well, with the exception of the state coaches, too showy and startling in appearance to suit private persons. They were got rid of, however, thanks to an American Circus that had just set up in Paris with a great flourish of trumpets; and the splendid vehicles built by Rosen's orders, to preserve around his princes a little of the vanished pomp, and in the faint hope of a return to Leybach, served to show off the attractions of Chinese dwarfs and learned monkeys, historic processions and apotheoses à la Franconi. Towards the end of the representations, on the trodden and scuffled sand of the arena, these princely carriages, the coats of arms scarcely effaced from their panels, would be exhibited making the round of the circus to the entrancing strains of the orchestra, while out of the half raised windows leant some grotesque and grimacing figure, or the brutal close-cropped head and massive shoulders encased in pink silk fleshings of some famous gymnast bowing to the crowd, his forehead shining with pomatum and perspiration. What an omen for royalty! All these cast-off relics of majesty fallen amid the spangles of a circus, between performing horses and wonderful elephants.

This sale at Tattersall's, coming on while that of the diamonds of the Queen of Galicia at the Hotel Drounot was still advertised on every wall— the two posters hanging side by side —made some noise. But Paris does not linger long over any one subject; ideas are as evanescent as the fleeting sheets of the newspapers. The two sales were talked of four-and-twenty hours The next day, no one gave them a thought. Christian II. accepted without any resistance the reforms determined upon by the Queen; since his last disgraceful freak, he appeared almost confused in her presence, preserving the humble air of a reproved child and even accentuating the very childishness that made the excuse for all his follies. And after all what mattered to him the reforms in the house? His life, given up to dissipation and pleasure, was passed elsewhere. Strange to relate, for six months he did not once have recourse to Rosen's purse. This raised him a little in the Queen's eyes, and it was also a relief to her, not to see the fantastic cab of the English agent waiting perpetually in a corner of the courtyard, and no longer to meet on the stair-case the obsequious smile of this courtier-like creditor.

And yet the King spent a great deal, and plunged into pleasures of all kinds more wildly than ever. Whence did he procure the money? It became known to Elysée in the most singular manner, through old Uncle Sauvadon, the honest fellow whose education as to "ideas upon things," he had formerly undertaken, the only one of his former acquaintances he still continued to visit since he had entered the household in the Rue Herbillon. From time to time he would breakfast with him at Bercy, take him news of Colette, whom the worthy soul complained he never saw. Colette was his adopted child, the daughter of a dearly loved penniless brother whom he had supported till his death. Always deeply interested in her, he had paid for her nurses and her christening robe; later on, for her education in the most fashionable convent in Paris. She was his one vice, the living and moving personification of his vanity, the pretty doll on which he centred all the ambitions that swarmed in his vulgar parvenu millionaire's head; and when in the parlour of the Sacré-Cœur, the little Sauvadon would say in a whisper to her uncle: "That girl's mother is a baroness, or duchess, or marchioness," the millionaire uncle would reply with a shrug of his big shoulders: "We will make something better of you than that." He made her a princess at eighteen. Princes in search of fortunes are not uncommon in Paris; the Levis agency has quite an assortment on hand; all that need be done is to fix the price. And Sauvadon considered eighty thousand pounds was not too much to pay for the privilege of appearing in a corner of the drawing-room on evenings when the young Princesse de Rosen received, for the right of enlivening her guests with the broad smile that turned up the edges of his mouth, and made it look like the rim of a porringer between his short, stumpy, old-fashioned whiskers. Little grey eyes, full of vivacity and intelligence—Colette's eyes—in some sort attenuated the ingenious, ungrammatical stutter that proceeded from the thick, unfinished mouth, with its horny lips, and the too evident vulgarity of those

great square hands, which even in lemon kid gloves could not forget they had rolled casks on a quay.

At first he mistrusted himself, spoke but little—astonished, and even frightened people by his silence. It is not in a warehouse at Bercy, in the traffic of southern wines, doctored with fuscine or logwood, that a man can learn to speak with refinement. Then, thanks to Méraut, he acquired a few opinions ready made, a few bold aphorisms on the events of the day, the last new novel. The uncle spoke, and did not make too great an exhibition of himself, except indeed by a few formidable slips, fit to bring down the chandelier upon his head; and amazement was caused among the guests when this white-waistcoated, lumbering fellow expounded in picturesque language certain theories in the style of de Maistre. But one day the sovereigns of Illyria deprived him both of his provider of ideas and the means of showing them off. Colette, detained by her functions as lady-in-waiting, no longer quitted Saint-Mandé and Sauvadon too well knew the head of the civil and military department to hope for admittance there. He did not even hint at it. Imagine the duke bringing such a man for presentation to the haughty Frédérique! A wine merchant from Bercy! And not a retired merchant even, but on the contrary, one in full swing of business; for, notwithstanding his millions, notwithstanding the entreaties of his niece, Sauvadon was still at work, passed his life at the warehouse, on the quay, a pen behind his ear, his white hair all ruffled, in the midst of carters and barges disembarking and loading up barrels; or else beneath the huge trees of the park, now mutilated and cut up, in which rows and rows of his wealth, in the shape of innumerable casks, lay piled up in sheds. "I should die if I gave up work," he used to say. And, in fact, the noise and commotion of rolling barrels, and the good heady smell of wine rising up from these great stores in the damp cellars, where forty-five years before he had started life as journeyman cooper, were to him the very breath of life.

Here it was that Elysée sometimes came to see his former pupil, and enjoy one of those breakfasts that can only be tasted at Bercy, beneath the trees of the park or the vaulted roof of a cellar, the wine just drawn from the wood, the fish quivering fresh from the fishpool, and local recipes for dressing them *en matelotes*, such as exist in the depths of Languedoc or the Vosges, lending them an extra savour. It was no longer now a question of ideas upon current subjects, since there were no longer any soirées to attend at Colette's; but the worthy man liked to hear Méraut talk, to see him eat and drink freely, for he could never forget the garret in the Rue Monsieur-le-Prince, and treated Elysée as if he were still a waif of humanity, a touching consideration on the part of a man, who had known hunger, towards one whom he knew to be poor. Méraut brought him news of his niece, of her life at Saint-Mandé, and left him a reflection of the grandeur of which, though it cost the good soul so dear, he was never a witness. No doubt he had the proud consciousness that the young lady-in-waiting dined with kings and queens, moved amid the ceremonial

of a court; but the vexation of not seeing her augmented his bad temper and his grievances against old Rosen.

"What has he done to be so proud? His name, his title? Have I not bought them with my money? His crosses, his medals, his stars? Could I not have them if I wished? That reminds me, my dear Méraut, you don't know. Since I last saw you, a piece of good luck has befallen me."

"What may that be, uncle?"

He called him "uncle" with an affectionate familiarity, which, thoroughly southern, came from his wish to give some form to the sympathy he felt for this stout merchant, though no similarity of feeling united them.

"My dear fellow, I have got the Lion of Illyria, the commander's cross. So much for the duke who is so proud of his knight's garter. On New Year's day, when I go to pay my respects, I shall put on my star. That will teach him."

Elysée could not believe him. The order of the Lion! One of the most ancient, the most coveted in Europe, given to Uncle Sauvadon, to "my uncle." Why? For selling adulterated wine at Bercy?

"Oh, it is very simple," said the other, blinking his little grey eyes. "I bought the grade of commander, just as I bought the title of prince. For a little more, I could have had the grand ribbon of the order, for that was for sale too."

"Where?" asked Elysée, turning pale.

"At the Levis agency, to be sure, Rue Royale. There is a little of everything to be found in that confounded Englishman's shop. My cross cost me four hundred pounds. The cordon was priced at six hundred, and I know some one who has purchased it. Guess who. Biscarat, the great hairdresser, Biscarat of the Boulevard des Capucines. But, my good fellow, what I am telling you is well known to all Paris. Just go to Biscarat. At the end of the great hall, where he officiates among his thirty assistants, you will see an immense photograph representing him as Figaro, razor in hand, and the broad ribbon of the order across his chest. The design is reproduced in miniature on all the bottles of the shop. If the general could see that, his moustache would bristle up, I fancy, eh? Like this, you know."

He tried to imitate the general's grimace, but as he had no moustache, the attempt was a failure.

"You have your patent, uncle? Will you let me see it?"

Elysée still cherished a hope that there might at the bottom of this affair be some forgery or cheating trick familiar to the Levis agency. But no! All was regular, labelled in due form, stamped with the Illyrian arms, signed by Boscovich, and bearing King Christian's autograph. Doubt was no longer possible. A trade was carried on in crosses and cordons with the king's sanction: besides, to complete his conviction. Méraut had only on returning to Saint-Mandé to visit the councillor.

CHAPTER XII

THE WORM!

IN the corner of the great hall which took up all the top floor of the house and served as study to Christian—who never studied—as gymnasium, fencing-room, library, he found Boscovich busy over his drawers, with great envelopes of whity-brown paper, sheets laid one above the other, wherein were drying the most lately gathered plants. During his exile the learned councillor had formed the groundwork of a new collection in the woods of Vincennes and Boulogne, which are richly stocked with the flora of France. In addition, he had bought the herbarium of a famous botanist lately dead; and, lost in the examination of his new riches, his bloodless, ageless head bent over the magnifying glass, he raised one by one with infinite precaution the heavy pages between which appeared flattened plants, their colours lost in pressing, and displayed fully from corolla to root. He uttered a cry of admiration and joy when the specimen was intact and well-preserved, gazing at it long, with moist lips, reading aloud its Latin name and the notice written below on a little label. At another moment an exclamation of anger would escape him when he beheld the flower attacked and perforated by that imperceptible worm well-known to herborists, an atom born of the dust of plants and living upon it, which is the danger, often the destruction of collections. The stem yet held, but when the page was shaken all would fall and flutter away—flowers and roots alike, in a frail whirlwind.

"It is the worm, the worm," said Boscovich, his glass to his eye, and with an air expressive of grief and pride, he pointed to a tiny perforation similar to that of the worm in wood, indicating the course the monster had taken. Elysée could no longer harbour a suspicion of him. This poor lunatic was incapable of an infamy, but also incapable of the least resistance. A the first mention of decorations he began to tremble and look askance over his magnifier, distrustful and timid. What did he hear? To be sure the king had lately caused him to prepare a quantity of patents of all grades with a blank for the name, but he knew nothing more, had never allowed himself to ask a question.

"Well, monsieur," said Elysée, gravely, "it is right to warn you as councillor that the king trades in decorations with the Levis agency."

Thereupon he related to him the story of the Gascon barber with which all Paris was just then amused. Boscovich uttered one of his little feminine cries, but in reality was not much scandalized, all that did not concern his mania having but little interest for him. The herbarium he had left at Leybach represented to him his country; that which he was now getting together, exile in France.

"Just think how shocking, a man like you to lend a hand to such abominable jobbery!"

To which the other, annoyed to have his eyes opened for him to what he had no wish to see, replied:

"*Ma che, ma che!* What could I do, my good Monsieur Méraut? The king is the king. When he says, 'Boscovich, write that,' my hand obeys without thinking, above all when his majesty is so kind and generous to me. It is he who, seeing how I grieved over the loss of my herbarium, made me a present of this one. Sixty pounds sterling, a wonderful bargain! And, besides, into the bargain I got the *Hortus Cliffortianus* of Linnæus—first edition."

Quite naïvely and cynically did the poor devil thus lay his conscience bare. It was dry and dead, the colour of a herbarium. His mania, cruel and heartless as the imperceptible insect that plagues the herborist, had perforated every part of his being, eaten away every fibre. He was unmoved till Elysée threatened to tell the queen. Then only the monomaniac pushed his glass aside, and in a low voice, with the great deep sighs of a penitent at confession, he owned all. Many things went on under his eye that he could not prevent, yet that grieved him. The king's surroundings were deplorable. *E poi, che volete?* He had no vocation for being a king, no taste for a throne. He had never had it. For instance, I remember how long ago it is, in the lifetime of the late Leopold, when the king was seized with his first attack as he left the dinner-table, and they came and told Christian he would doubtless soon succeed his uncle, the child—he was barely twelve years old and was playing croquet in the *patio* (courtyard) of the palace—the child began to cry terribly, a regular nervous attack. He said: "I don't want to be king. I don't want to be king. Let them put my cousin Stanislas on the throne instead of me." I have often recalled since, on seeing it again in the glance of Christian II., the terrified and bewildered expression that he had that morning, clinging with all his might to his mallet, as if he were afraid he would be carried off to the throne-room, and crying: "I don't want to be king!"

All Christian's character was expressed in this anecdote. No doubt he was not a wicked man, but a child-man, married too young, with seething passions and hereditary vices. The life he led—the nights at the club, the uproarious suppers, the society of loose women, which in certain circles constitutes the normal life of a husband—all this was aggravated in him by his *rôle* of king, which he was incapable of playing, the responsibilities that were above his strength and conception, and above all by the exile that was slowly and surely demoralizing him. Firmer natures than his cannot always resist the dissolving effects of broken habits, and constantly renewed uncertainty, combined with the groundless hopes, the anguish, the strain of waiting. Like the sea, exile has its moments of torpor; it lowers and benumbs. It is a phase of transition. Only by fixed occupations and regular hours of study can the tedium of a long sea voyage be withstood. But how can a king occupy himself who has neither people, nor ministers, nor council; nothing to decide, to sign; far too much wit or scepticism to amuse himself with the pretense of all these things, and too much ignorance to attempt any diversion in the direction of any other steady work? Then exile, if it resembles the sea, resembles also shipwreck, throwing the privileged saloon passengers overboard pell-mell with the steerage and deck passengers. A truly haughty spirit, a real kingly temperament is needed to avoid the effects of the familiar and lowering promiscuity which afterwards may cause blushes and shame; to remain a king amid the privations and distress that confound all ranks in the uniform misery of humanity.

Alas! that Bohemia of exile from which the Duc de Rosen had so long.

and at the price of such sacrifices, preserved the house of Illyria, began to invade it at last. The king had arrived at all kinds of expedients to pay the expenses of his constant round of pleasure. He began by floating bills, just like any young fellow, finding it just as simple and even easier, with the aid of J. Tom Levis, as those "drafts upon our treasury," that he used formerly to address to the head of the civil and military department. The bills came due, were augmented by a host of renewals, until the day when Tom Levis, finding himself run dry, invented that pretty traffic in patents, since the business of a king without either a kingdom or a civil list presented no other resource. The poor Lion of Illyria, cut up like some common beast for the butcher, was divided into quarters and slices, sold at the stall and by auction at so much the mane, the sirloin, the rib, and the claws. And this was only the beginning. Once in Tom Levis' cab the king was not likely to pause on so fair a road. So said Méraut to himself as he came away from Boscovich. He saw well enough that no dependence could be placed upon the councillor, easy to overrule, as are most people with a mania. He himself was too great a stranger, too newly entered into the household to have any influence over Christian's mind. Should he address himself to old Rosen? But at the tutor's very first words the duke darted upon him the terrible glance of one whose religion is insulted. The king, however low he might fall, was always the king for him. Nothing could be hoped either from the monk, whose wild visage only appeared at long intervals between two journeys, each time thinner and more weather-beaten.

The queen? but she was, he had noticed for months past, sad and feverishly anxious, her beautiful brow always clouded with care, and when she attended the lessons she only listened abstractedly, with absent mind and hand listlessly drooping over her work. She was filled with grave preoccupations, hitherto unknown to her, that touched her to the quick, coming as they did from so low a source, anxieties about money, the shame of all these outstretched hands that she could no longer fill. Tradesmen, the poor and needy, the companions of her exile and misfortune, all remained waiting; for kingship has its duties, even when it has no longer its rights. Those who had learnt their way to the house in its prosperity, waited now for hours in the ante-rooms, and often, tired of waiting, went away with bitter words, which the queen guessed, without hearing, by their discontented step, by the weariness they betrayed, which told of their constant disappointments. She tried in earnest to put some order into their new way of life; but bad luck attended her efforts, bad investments, shares paying no interest. They must either wait or lose all. Poor Queen Frédérique, who thought she had known the whole gamut of suffering, had yet to learn those miseries that wither and fade; the hard wounding contact of common daily life. There were pay-days at the end of the month which kept her awake thinking at night, shivering like a worried business man. Sometimes, when the servants' wages were behindhand, she dreaded to read

in the delayed execution of an order, in a glance less respectful than usual, the dissatisfaction of a domestic. Finally she became acquainted with debt, debt which grows little by little more harassing, and forces open, in the insolence of pursuit, the highest, the most gilded doors. The old duke, grave and silent, watched all the anxieties of his queen, and hovered round her as if to say: "I am here." But she was quite determined to exhaust all other means before taking back her word, before having recourse to him whom she had crushed with so haughty a reprimand.

One evening the little court was assembled in the great drawing-room, a monotonous evening as it always was, while the king as usual was absent. Whist began under the lights of the great silver candelabra,—what they called the queen's play; the duke had the queen for a partner, with Madame Eléonore and Boscovich for adversaries. The princess played softly on the piano some of those "echoes of Illyria" that Frédé ique was never weary of hearing, and which at the least sign of satisfaction the musician converted into a war-song or march. These evocations of the fatherland that called up on the faces of the card-players a tearful or an heroic expression, were the only breaks in the atmosphere of habitual resignation to exile, that prevailed in the luxurious bourgeois drawing-room that chanced to shelter royalty.

Ten o'clock struck.

The queen, instead of retiring to her own rooms, as on other evenings, and thus giving the signal of departure, threw an absent glance around her and said:

"You can retire. I have some work to do with Monsieur Méraut."

Elysée, busy reading by the fireside, bowed and shut up the pamphlet he was perusing, went into the schoolroom in search of pens, ink, and paper.

When he returned the queen was alone, listening to the carriages rolling out of the courtyard, while the great doors were shut, and the lobbies and staircases of the house echoed with the sounds of coming and going, that in a numerous household precede the hour for repose. There was silence at last, silence increased and deepened by two miles of woods, which deadened with the wind and the rustling of the leaves the far-off rumble of Paris. The deserted drawing-room, still blazing with light in this calm solitude, seemed prepared for some tragic scene. Frédérique, her elbow on the table, pushed away with the other hand the blotting-book Méraut had prepared.

"No, no," said she, "we shall not work to-night; it was only a pretext. Sit down and let us talk."

Then, still lower, she added:

"I have something to ask you."

What she had to say probably cost her a great effort to bring forth, for she gathered herself together for a few moments, mouth and eyes half closed, with the profoundly painful and aged expression that Elysée had already noticed sometimes upon her countenance, and which made the beautiful face yet more beautiful in his sight; all the self sacrifices, the devotion, the noble sentiments of the queen and woman engraved on its pure features; and when she looked thus, she inspired him with a respect that was almost religious. At last, summoning all her

courage, in low and timid tones, letting her words fall one after the other like fearful footsteps, Frédérique asked him whether he knew of one of those places in Paris where—one of those places where—money could be borrowed on a pledge.

Imagine such a question put to Elysée, to that thorough Bohemian who knew every pawnshop in Paris, who had made use of them for the last twenty years as store-houses, where he put his winter clothes in summer and his summer clothes in winter. Did he know the *"spout?"* Did he know *"my uncle?"* In the recollections of youth that rose to his mind, this slang of destitution made him smile for a moment. But the queen went on, trying to steady her voice:

"I wished to ask you to take something there for me—some jewels; there are at times difficult moments."

And in her beautiful eyes, now raised to his face, was revealed the unfathomable depths of a calm but overwhelming grief.

Kings in such destitution! so much grandeur humbled to the dust! Was it possible?

Méraut gave her to understand by a bow that he was willing to take charge of anything she pleased.

If he had uttered a word he must have sobbed; if he had permitted himself a gesture, it would have been to fall at the feet of this august distress. And with it all his admiration began to soften into pity. The queen now seemed to him a little less remote, a little nearer drawn to the vulgarities of existence, as if in the sad avowal she had just made, he had felt a touch of Bohemianism that presaged the beginning of a fall, and brought her closer to him.

All at once she rose and took from its crystal case, the antique and neglected relic, which when placed on the table-cover, gleamed like a handful of jewels of all colours. Elysée started. The crown!

"Yes, the crown! For six hundred years it has been in the royal house of Illyria. Kings have died, rivers of noble blood have flowed in its defence. Now it must help us to live. It is all we have left."

It was a magnificent closed crown in the finest old gold, the arches of which, enriched with much ornamentation, were united above the crimson velvet cap. Upon the arches, on the lower circlet of wreathed filigree, in the centre of each flower that imitated the leaves of the trefoil, at the points of the festooned work supporting these flowers, were closely set every variety of known precious stone: here figured the transparent blue of the sapphire, the velvety cerulean of the turquoise, the morning gleam of the topaz, the flame of the oriental ruby, emeralds like drops of water on the foliage, cabalistic opals, pearls of milky whiteness, and surpassing all, diamonds crowded everywhere, catching and reflecting in their facets all these various hues of fire, and like a luminous dust, a cloud crossed by a ray of sunlight, softening and melting together the splendour of the diadem already drilled by the hand of time, yet gleaming with the delicate reflections of a silver-gilt lamp twinkling in the depths of a sanctuary.

The queen placed her trembling finger upon it, here and there:

"Some of the stones must be prized out—the biggest."

"What with?"

They spoke in low tones like two criminals.

But seeing nothing in the drawing-room that would serve their purpose: "Bring a light," said Frédé ique.

They passed into the glass verandah, where the tall lamp held on high threw fantastic shadows and a long trail of light that finally was lost on the lawns, in the black night of the garden.

"No, no, not scissors," she murmured, seeing him turn towards her work-basket. "They are not strong enough; I have already tried."

At last they discovered the gardener's pruning-shears laid on the tub of a pomegranate shrub, the delicate foliage of which caught the moonlight from behind the glass. Both returned to the drawing-room, and Elysée tried with the points of the instrument to raise an enormous oval sapphire that the queen pointed out to him; but the great uncut jewel, firmly set, resisted and slipped under the iron, immovable in the claws that held it. Moreover, the hand of the operator, fearing to spoil the stone, or to break the setting which already bore scratches on its gold, testifying to former attempts, was neither sure nor steady. The poor royalist suffered torments of indignation at the outrage he was compelled to offer to the crown. He felt it quiver, resist, struggle beneath his touch.

"I cannot, I cannot," he said, wiping away the perspiration from his brow.

The queen replied:

"You must, you must!"

"But it will be seen!"

A smile of proud irony crossed her face.

"Be seen! Who so much as glances at it? Who thinks of it, who cares for it here, but I?"

And while he resumed his task, pallor on his bent face, his long locks hanging over his eyes, and held between his knees the royal diadem which his pruning-knife was about to hack and dismember, Frédérique, holding the lamp above him, watched the sacrilege, as cold as the stones that gleamed amid scraps of gold on the table-cover, intact and splendid notwithstanding the violence they had endured.

The following day Elysée, after being out all the morning, came in after the first summons for breakfast, and seated himself silently at table, troubled and agitated, scarcely mingling in the conversation of which he was habitually the main-spring and enlivener. This agitation at last infected the queen without, however, in any way altering her smile or the serenity of her deep contralto voice; and when the meal was ended, it was still a long time before they drew near each other or could talk freely, feeling themselves hemmed in on all sides by the etiquette and rules of custom established in the house, the attendance of the lady-in-waiting, the jealous watchfulness of Madame de Silvis. At last came lesson time. While the little prince got out his books and settled himself:

"What is the matter?" asked Frédérique. "What has happened?"

"Oh, madame! all the stones are false!"

"False!"

"And most carefully imitated in paste. How can that have been done? When?

By whom? There must be a thief in the house!"

She had turned horribly pale at the word "thief." Suddenly from between clenched teeth, with a flash of anger and despair, that smote like a blow in her eyes:

"True! There *is* a thief here. You and I know him well."

Then with a feverish gesture, she seized Elysée's wrist in a vehement grasp, as if to seal a secret compact between them.

"But we shall never denounce him, you promise?"

"Never!" he answered, turning away his eyes, for with one word they had understood each other.

CHAPTER XIII

AT THE FAIR

It was the afternoon of the first Sunday in May, a glorious bright day, fully a month in advance of the season and so warm that Queen Frédérique, the little prince and his tutor were driving in an open carriage in the woods of Saint-Mandé. The first soft caress of springtide, wafted through the fresh foliage, had cheered the queen's heart and infused fresh life into her cheeks. She felt happy without knowing why, and forgetting for a few hours amid the universal kindliness of nature the harshness of life, sat ensconced in a corner of the heavy carriage, her child nestling against her, and conversed in an intimate and friendly manner with Elysée Méraut, who sat opposite them.

"It is strange," she said; "it seems to me that we have already met before becoming acquainted. Your voice, your face, at once awoke some recollection in my mind. Where can we have met for the first time?"

Little Zara remembered well enough that first interview. It was at the convent, far away, in that underground church, where Monsieur Elysée had frightened him so terribly. And in the gentle timid glance the child cast at his master, there was still a little of that superstitious fear. No! even before that Christmas night, the queen felt convinced they had met.

"Unless it was in a former existence," she added half seriously.

Elysée laughed.

"It is true, your Majesty is not mistaken. You saw me, not indeed in a former existence, but in Paris, the very day of your arrival. I was in front of the *hôtel des Pyramides*, standing on the stone basement of the Tuilerie railings."

"And you cried out *'Vive le roi!'* Now I remember. Yes, it was you. Oh, I am glad. It was you who first welcomed us. If you knew how much good your cry did me!"

"And to me also!" replied Méraut. "It was such a time since I had had an opportunity of uttering that triumphant cry: *Vive le roi!* It had hovered so long upon my lips. It is a family cry, associated with all the youthful joys of my childhood, in which at home all our emotions and all our faith was summed up. That cry, as I utter it, recalls to life the southern accent, the gesture and voice of my father; and brings back to my eyes the same emotion I have seen so often in his. Poor man! It was an instinctive cry on his part, a whole creed contained in one word. One day as he was crossing Paris on his return from a journey to Frohsdorff, my father passed on the Place du Carrousel just as Louis-

Philippe was about to come out. A crowd standing close by the railings awaited him,—an indifferent, almost hostile crowd such as is seen towards the end of a reign. My father, hearing that the king is expected, shoves and pushes till he elbows himself into the first rank, in order to have a good stare, and to crush by his contemptuous glance that thieving rascally fellow Louis-Philippe who has stolen the throne from the legitimate king. Suddenly the king appears, crosses the deserted courtyard, amid a death-like silence, a heavy silence that seems to oppress the whole palace, and through which the sounds of the loading of the insurgents' muskets and the crashing of the throne seem to be distinctly heard. Louis-Philippe, already old and very homely looking, advanced slowly, umbrella in hand, with the little short steps of a fat man, towards the gate. Nothing kingly, nothing regal about him. But my father did not see him thus; and at the sight of this representative of royalty, crossing the threshold of the great palace of the kings of France, so full of glorious mementoes, amid the terrible solitude the hatred of a people creates around a prince, something was stirred and roused within him; he forgot all his rancour, suddenly and instinctively snatched off his hat, and cried or rather sobbed out a *'Vive le roi,'* so heartfelt and enthusiastic, that the old king started and thanked him by a long glance full of emotion."

"I must have thanked you in the same way," said Frédérique, and she looked at Méraut with such affectionate gratitude in her eyes that the poor fellow turned pale. Then, absorbed in the narrative she had just heard she added:

"Your father was not of noble birth, was he?"

"Oh, no, madam. He was of the people, a humble weaver."

"Strange," she said, musing.

He made some reply, and their eternal discussion was resumed. The queen did not like, could not understand the people, and had a kind of physical horror of that class. She considered them brutal, terrible in their pleasure as well as in their revenge. Even during the festivities of the coronation, in the honeymoon of her reign, she had feared them, and had shrunk from the thousand hands outstretched to acclaim her, but which she felt held her prisoner. Never had they been able to understand one another; favours and bounties had fallen from her, but had failed to bring forth gratitude, like the accursed seed that cannot germinate, without its being possible to hold the hardness of the soil or the sterility of the grain responsible for the failure.

Among the many fairy tales with which Madame de Silvis had filled the little prince's imagination, there was one about a young Syrian girl, married to a lion, who felt a dreadful terror of her tawny husband, of his roar and his violent way of shaking his mane. The poor lion, however, was full of delicacy and lover-like attentions; he brought honeycombs, and all kinds of choice game to his child-wife, and watched over her while she slept, imposing silence upon the sea, the forest, and the wild beasts. All was in vain! Her repulsion, her offensive dread was incurable; and at last the lion's anger was roused, and he roared a terrific "Go!" with open jaws and bristling mane, as though more inclined to devour her than to set her

free. It was rather the story of Frédérique and her people; and since Elysée had lived in such close intimacy with her, he had vainly striven to make her comprehend the latent kindliness, the chivalrous devotion, the fierce touchiness of this great lion, who roars so often in play before his wrath breaks forth. Ah! if only kings had known! If they had known how to trust their people! And as Frédérique shook her parasol with an incredulous air:

"Ah, yes, I am well aware of your dread of the people. You do not like them, or rather you do not know them. But if your Majesty would but look around in those avenues, through those trees, at these simple, good-natured folk, strolling about and amusing themselves, enjoying to their hearts' content a day of rest, and revelling in the sunlight, they are, nevertheless, the inhabitants of that terrible faubourg of Paris, the terrible faubourg that breeds revolutions, and pours down its infuriated masses through the torn-up streets of Paris."

From the great avenue through which the carriage was slowly making its way, under the still sparse thickets, sprinkled violet with the early wild hyacinths, could be seen luncheons spread out on the ground, white plates dotted over the grass, open-mouthed baskets, and common thick glass from the neighbouring wine-shop stuck among the green shoots like great peonies; shawls and smockfrocks suspended to the boughs; men in shirt-sleeves, women without cloaks, reading, dozing, or sewing as they leant against the trees; bright glades flecked by skirts of cheap fabrics, flitting hither and thither in some game of battledore, blind-man's buff, or quadrilles improvised at the sound of an invisible band, the melody of which reached them in gusts. And children, numbers of children, connecting links between the luncheons, and the games, running together from one group to another, leaping, shouting, filling the whole wood with an immense swallow-like twitter, their endless going and coming through the trees, recalling in their rapidity, the caprice of the birds' shadowy flight. Compared with the carefully tended, neatly kept Bois du Boulogne, and its little rustic palings, this Bois de Vincennes, with all its avenues unobstructed, seemed well suited for the pastimes of a people merry-making, with its green trampled turf, its strong arching trees, as though Nature herself had here chosen to be more kindly and more full of life.

Suddenly a turn of the avenue revealed an open space, with a bright lake and grassy green slopes, and drew an exclamation of delight from the royal child. It was lovely, resembling the sudden glimpse of the sea through the winding stone walls of a Breton village, bringing its ripples to the very foot of the last steep lane. Boats decked out with flags, full of oarsmen in smart red or blue jerseys, covered the lake in every direction, furrowing the surface with the silvery stroke of the oars, and the white foam of the sparkling little waves. Flocks of ducks quacked and swam about, swans in a more stately manner sailed along the banks, their downy feathers filled out by the breeze, while in the distance, hidden behind the green foliage of an islet, a band sent to all parts of the wood a joyous rhythm that re-echoed across the surface of the lake. Over all this reigned a merry disorder, the movement of both wind and water, the flapping of the streamers, the shouts of the boatmen, the groups of people seated on the slopes, of children running about, of two little noisy cafés built almost in the water, their wooden floors as resonant as a bridge, and their disjointed plank walls giving them the appearance of something between a bathing machine and a steamer. Few carriages were to be seen round the lake. From time to time a railway cab, loaded with a workman's wedding party, easily recognisable by the new cloth of the frockcoats and gaudy colours of the women's shawls; or tradesmen's vans full of stout dames in flowery bonnets, who looked with an air of condescension at the passers-by, dragging their steps through the sand. Most of all, little baby carriages, that first outlay of the married workman, perambulating cradles in which the infant faces nod their frilled caps, drowsily gazing at the blue sky through the entwined branches.

Amid all these modest vehicles the queen's equipage, with the Illyrian coat of-arms on its panels, its handsom horses and liveries, could not pass without attracting some notice. Frédériqu had never been there, except on week days; the working men's families, silen and awkward in their Sunday attire nudged each other's elbows, stepping aside at the sound of the wheels, the turned round, unsparing of their adm ration for the haughty beauty of th queen, and the aristocratic air of litt Zara. Now and again a little darin voice would call out from under th trees: "Good day, Madame." Could be Elysée s words, or the splendour the weather, or the joyousness spread even to the horizon, which the silent factories for once left clear and truly rural, or was it the cordiality of these chance greetings? Frédérique could not help feeling a sort of sympathy for these working men on their holiday; for the cleanliness that, considering their hard labours and their rare moments of leisure, was so praiseworthy. As for Zara, he could hardly contain himself; he stamped and fidgeted in the carriage; he would have liked to get out, roll with the other children on the grass, and row about in the boats.

Presently the carriage reached a less noisy part of the wood, where people were reading or sleeping on benches; and loving couples passed along among the shrubs arm in arm. Here the shade was deeper and more mysterious; holding the damp coolness of great forests. The birds twittered in the branches. As they got further from the lake, where the noise of the crowd was concentrated, the echo of another fête reached their ears: shots fired off, beating of drums, the noise of bells and bugles rising above a great clamour that passed like a cloud across the sun. It sounded like the sacking of a town.

"What is that? What sound is that?" asked the little prince.

"It is the gingerbread fair, Monseigneur," said the old coachman turning round on his box, and as the queen consented to go in that direction, the carriage left the park and turned down a set of narrow unfinished streets, where new six-storied houses rose by the side of miserable hovels, with a stable gutter on one side and market-gardens on the other. All around small wine booths,

with their arbours, little tables, and the stands of swings painted in an ugly uniform green. It was crowded with people, shoals of soldiers, in gunners' shakos and white cotton gloves. But there was little noise. An ambulating harpist or violinist was playing between the tables, scraping airs from the *Favorita* or the *Trovatore;* and the people of Paris listened with interest to the sentimental music it is so fond of, always prodigal of alms to those who give it pleasure.

CHAPTER XIV

NOTHING

SUDDENLY the carriage stopped. Vehicles were not allowed to go further than the entrance of this broad avenue of Vincennes, along which the fair was established, and whose background towards Paris was the dusty atmosphere of the suburb with the two columns of the barriè du Trône rising above it. Zara's eyes were lit up with such an intense childish longing at the sight of the happy crowd in that long street of booths that the queen proposed to get out. It was so extraordinary a wish on the part of the proud Frédérique to set foot in the dust of this plebeian Sunday, that Elysée hesitated for a moment.

"Is there any danger?" said the queen.

"Oh, not the least, Madam. Only, if we go into the fair, we had better go alone. The servants' liveries would attract attention."

On receiving the queen's order, the tall footman who was preparing to follow them, got back on to the coach-box and it was arranged the carriage should wait for them. They would certainly not go through the whole fair, and only intended walking a little and looking at a few of the booths.

At the entry they saw small moveable stands, a table covered with a white napkin, shooting galleries with rabbits for prizes, and wheels of fortune. People passed by indifferent and without stopping. Then they came upon open-air frying booths, exhaling a strong smell of burnt fat, great red flames rising up, while scullions dressed in white were busily engaged serving out piles of sugared fritters. Further on was a confectioner, pulling, twisting into gigantic rings the white marshmallow paste perfumed with almonds! The little prince gazed in astonishment. It was all so new to him, poor little caged bird, reared in the upper rooms of a palace, behind the gilt railings of a park, grown up amid terrors and mistrust, who had never gone out unaccompanied, never seen the populace but from some balcony or some carriage surrounded by guards. At first somewhat intimidated, he walked close to his mother, pressing her hand tightly in his, but little by little he became excited with the noise, the odour of the fête, the tunes of the hurdy-gurdies made him long to run wildly about, and he dragged Frédérique forward, at the same time that he wanted every moment to stop, divided between the wish to see everything and a desire to push on and reach the spot where the noise was louder, the crowd denser.

Thus without noticing it, they went further and further from their starting-point, imperceptibly and unconsciously, like a swimmer borne away by a current, the more easily too, that

among all the gaudy dresses flaunting about, the queen's neat costume, dress, mantle and bonnet matching in soft fawnlike tints, passed unnoticed, as did also Zara's big turned-down collar, bare legs and short jacket, the quiet elegance of his attire merely drawing the attention of a few old women who remarked: "That's an English boy." He walked between Elysée and his mother, who exchanged smiles over his head. "Oh mother!" he would exclaim, "look at that! Monsieur Elysée, what are they doing over there? Let us go and see!" From one side of the avenue to the other, describing endless zigzags, they penetrated deeper and deeper into the crowd, following its onward direction.

"Shall we go back?" suggests Elysée; but the child is drunk with excitement. He implores, tugs at his mother's hand and she is so happy at seeing her little drowsy child roused from his torpor, she is herself so excited by the popular ferment, that they go on advancing.

The day becomes warmer, as though the sun in going down caught up with the tips of its rays a stormy mist; and as the sky changes, the fête with its thousand varied colours assumes a fairylike aspect. Now is the time for the shows—the whole staff of the circus and booths are outside, under the entrance awnings, in front of the painted canvas which, swelling and bulging in the wind, impart a semblance of life to the monstrous animals, gymnasts and Hercules painted on it. Here is the display in front of the great military play: an exhibition of costumes of the time of Charles IX and Louis XV, arquebuses, guns, periwigs and plumes mixed up together; the *Marseillaise* clanged out by the brass band, while opposite, the young horses of a circus, with white reins, like bridal horses, prance learnedly about on a platform, count with their hoofs and bow their heads. Next to these a true mountebank show exhibits a clown in motley costume, tiny Astecs in scanty tights, and a big tanned girl in pink ballet-skirt who juggles with gold and silver balls, bottles and glittering tin knives mingling and jingling over her elaborately dressed hair, held together by glass pins.

The little prince is lost in mute contemplation before this magnificent personage, when a queen, a true queen of fairy tales, with a brilliant crown, a short tunic of spangled gauze, her legs crossed over each other, leans upon the balustrade. Zara would never tire of looking at her, but the orchestra claims his attention; an extraordinary orchestra this, composed not of French guards. or Hercules in pink tights, but of real ladies and gentlemen; a gentleman with short whiskers, shining pate and patent leather boots, deigns to play the cornet-àpiston; while a lady, a real lady, almost as solemn as Madame de Silvis herself, in a silk mantle, and nodding flowers in her bonnet, bangs on the big drum, looking right and left with an air of supreme indifference, her violent motions meanwhile tossing the chenille fringe of her mantle high among the roses of her bonnet. Who nows? this may be some royal family also fallen into misfortune. But the fair presents yet other attractions.

In the infinite and perpetually varying panorama were to be seen bears dancing at the end of their chains; negroes in cotton drawers, devils—male and female, with narrow red bands round their heads; gesticulating wrestlers, undaunted combatants, hand on hip, swinging aloft the tights prepared for any volunteer fighter; a fencing-mistress in cuirass-bodice, red stockings embroidered in gold, her face covered by a mask and a leathern gauntlet on her hand; a man dressed in black velvet who looked like Columbus or Copernicus, describing magic circles with a diamond-headed riding-whip, while from behind the platform, amid a sickening odour of stables and wild beasts, was heard the roar of the lions in Garel's menagerie. All these living curiosities mingled in one confused mass with the painted images, giantesses in ball dress, bare necks, and fat, pink, pillow-like arms displayed from the short sleeves down to the tightly-buttoned gloves; figures of somnambulists, seated, with bandaged eyes looking into futurity, by the side of some black-haired doctor; monsters, prodigies, every kind of eccentricity and phenomenon, often sheltered only by two large sheets fastened up by a cord, with the money-box placed on a chair ready for the spectator's coin.

And everywhere, at every turn was seen the king of the fair: gingerbread under all aspects and shapes, in shops draped with red, fringed with gold, wrapped up in shiny picture-paper, tied up with ribbons, ornamented with sugar-plums and burnt almonds; gingerbread flattened and grotesquely shaped like men, representing the Parisian notorieties; Amanda's lover, Prince Queue de Poule and his inseparable companion Rigolo; gingerbread hawked about in baskets. sold on deal planks, spreading a good odour of honey and cocked fruit through the tightly packed crowd, which was becoming too dense for circulation. It was now impossible for the royal party to retrace their steps. They were obliged to follow the despotic current, to advance or retire, unconsciously pushed first towards one booth, then towards another, for the living stream pressed together in the middle of the fair, seeks to overflow on all sides, without finding any issue. Laughs and jokes burst forth in this continuous and compulsory elbowing. Never before has the queen come so closely in contact with the people. Touched almost by their breath and the rough proximity of their powerful shoulders, she is astonished at feeling neither disgust nor terror, and advances with the others, with that hesitating step all crowds have, which resembles the hushed awe of a procession, and retains, even in the absence of vehicles, a kind of solemnity.

The good temper of these folk, the exuberant gaiety of her son, and the quantity of perambulators in the thickest of the crowd, all tends to reassure her. "Don't push there. Don't you see there's a child." Not one, but ten, twenty, hundreds of children, carried in arms by their mothers, or on their father's shoulders; and Frédérique exchanges a smile, when she sees a child of the people of the same age as her own son.

Elysée, however, begins to feel uneasy. He knows what a crowd is, however calm in appearance, and the danger of its sudden movements. If one of those threatening clouds should burst into rain, what disorder and panic would ensue! His imagination, ever on the alert, conjures up the scene: the horrible stifling, the terrible death-struggle on the Place Louis XV, the sinister crowding together of a whole people in the midst of a gigantic Paris, within a stone's-throw of immense, deserted, but inaccessible avenues.

Between his mother and his tutor, who help and protect him, the little prince gets very hot. He complains that he cannot see anything. Then, like the workmen who surround them, Elysée places Zara on his shoulders, and the child bursts into fresh exclamations of delight, for the sight from up there is really splendid. Against a back-ground of setting sun, streaked with light and floating shadows, on the long perspective before them, between the two columns of the barrier, stands out a waving mass of flags and streamers, while the canvas flaps in front of the booths. The light wheels of the gigantic swings raise one by one their little cars full of people; an immense merry-go-round, three-storied, varnished and coloured like a plaything, turns mechanically with its lions, leopards, and fantastic creatures, upon which the children sit as stiff as little wooden puppets. Near at hand clusters of red balloons fly through the air; innumerable twirlings of yellow-paper mills look like artificial suns and above the crowd rise a quantity of little staring eyes and fair-haired heads just like Zara's. The pale rays of the setting sun illumine the clouds, and lend them metallic hues, lighting up or darkening all things by their reflection, and this gives additional movement to the scene. Here they touch up a clown and a columbine, two white patches frisking about opposite each other, like pantomime in white chalk on the background of a black-board; yonder, a lanky mountebank, his head surmounted by a Phrygian shepherd's pointed cap, bends forward, with a gesture as though shoving dough into an oven, and pretends to push into his booth the black stream of people coming up his steps. The mountebank has his mouth open, he must be speaking, roaring indeed, but it is impossible to hear him, any more than the sound of a bell furiously shaken at the corner of a platform over there, or the firing of an arquebus, from which a puff of smoke is seen issuing. Every sound is drowned in the immense uproar of the fair, a clamour made up of every kind of discordant noise rattles, reed-pipes, gongs, drums, speaking-trumpets, the roar of wild beasts, hurdy-gurdies, and the whistles of engines. There is a general struggle to attract the crowd—as bees are attracted by noise—and the most indefatigable, the most deafening instruments are set going; from the swings and whirligigs sharp cries are also heard, while every ten minutes the trains of the circular line pass on a level with the fair, break in and overpower by their whistle a maddening uproar.

All at once, the fatigue and suffocating smell of that human crowd, the dazzling glare of an afternoon sun, slanting and hot, in which so many bright things are turning and twisting make the queen turn giddy and feel faint.

She has but time to seize hold of Elysée's arm in order not to fall, and while she leans clingingly on him, pale though erect, she murmurs in a low voice: "It is nothing—nothing." But her head, in which all the nerves throb painfully; her body, which loses all consciousness of existence, for a moment abandons itself. Elysée will never forget that moment.

It is over. Frédérique is herself again. A breath of fresh air on her brow has quickly revived her, but she does not let go of the protecting arm; and that queen's step, measured on his own, that pressure of that warm gloved hand, produce in Elysée an inexpressible emotion. Danger, the crowd, Paris, the fête, he forgets everything. He is in the magic world where dreams become realities with all their extravagant fancies. Lost in the plebeian crowd, he walks on without hearing it, without seeing it, borne along by a cloud that envelops him, pushes, carries him onward and insensibly brings him out of the avenue. There only does he return to earth and reality. The queen's carriage is far. It is impossible to find it. They are compelled to return on foot to the Rue Herbillon, to follow in the fading daylight the long avenues, the streets lined with wine-shops, full of half tipsy passers-by. It is quite an adventure, but none of them think of the strangeness of their return home. Little Zara talks, rattling on as children do after a treat, eager to relate all the sights, ideas, and events their eyes have beheld. Elysée and the queen are silent. He, quivering still, recalls, and at the same time endeavours to forget, the exquisite and penetrating moment which has revealed to him the secret, the sad secret of his life. Frédérique dwells upon all she has just seen and heard that was new to her. For the first time she has felt the throbs of the people's heart, she has laid her head upon the lion's shoulder. It has left her an impression of powerful sweetness, like a tender and protecting embrace.

CHAPTER XV

THE GRAND STROKE

THE door, slammed to sharply and autocratically, wafted through the Agency a breath of air that fluttered the blue veils and waterproofs, and waved the invoices in the hands of the clerks, and the feathers in the ladies' hats. Hands were stretched out and heads bowed. J. Tom Levis had just entered the hall. A circular smile, two or three orders briefly given to the accountant, and the question asked in a singularly triumphant tone as to whether the parcel had been sent to H.R.H. the Prince of Wales, and he disappeared rapidly into his private office, the clerks signalling to one another by winks that the master was in an extraordinary good humour. Something certainly must be up. Even the calm Sephora behind her grating thought so, and softly inquired as she saw Tom come in:

"What is going on?"

"Such things!" said the other with the wide silent laugh, and the peculiar whirl of eyes habitual to him on great occasions.

He beckoned to his wife to follow him.

They went down the fifteen narrow steps, edged with copper, that led to a little boudoir underground, very tastily furnished with a divan, a dressing-table, and lighted by gas; the little cellar window, that opened on the Rue Royale, being closed by ground-glass as thick as a piece of horn. From this room they could communicate with the cellars and the yards, thus allowing Tom to avoid intruders and creditors, those whom in Parisian slang are called the "pavés," that is to say, people or things that block the circulation. With such complicated affairs as those the Agency dealt in, these Red Indian subterfuges were indispensable. Otherwise life would have been spent in quarrels and wrangling.

The oldest clerks in Tom's office, men who had been in his employ for five or six months, had never been down into this mysterious basement room, where Sephora alone had right of entry. It was the agent's private nook, his very self, his conscience, the cocoon from which he issued each time a transformed being; something like the dressing-room of an actor, which at the present moment, indeed, it greatly resembled, with its gas burners lighting up the marble, the flounced trimmings of the toilet-table, and the strange pantomime that J. Tom Levis, agent for foreigners, was just then performing. In a trice he opened his long English frockcoat and flung it far away, then he tore off one waistcoat, then another, the many-coloured waistcoats of the circus-rider, unwound the ten yards of white muslin that constituted his cravat, the numberless bands of flannel superposed round his waist, and from the majestic and apoplectic rotundity which rushed all over Paris in the first, the only cab known in those days, there suddenly stood revealed, with an "ouf" of relief, a little dried-up, wiry man, no bigger than an empty reel, a frightful quinquagenarian street-arab, who looked as though he had been saved from a fire, drawn from a lime-kiln, with all the wrinkles, scars, and devastating ravages of scalding; and notwithstanding all this, an indescribable appearance of youth, the mischievous look of a *mobile* of '48, the real Tom Levis, no other than Narcisse Poitou, the son of a joiner of the Rue d'Orillon.

After having grown up to the age of ten amid the shavings at the side of the paternal work-bench, and from ten to fifteen received his education in the national school and in the street —that marvellous school of outdoor life, Narcisse had soon felt within him a horror for the populace, and for all manual labour, and, at the same time, became conscious that he was gifted with an all-devouring imagination and an experience which the Parisian gutter and all the nameless things it sweeps along had stocked far more thoroughly than a long voyage could have done. As a child he already planned schemes and projects. Later on his ever-roving imagination prevented his directing his powers towards one settled object, and they remained unproductive. He travelled, began a thousand different trades; a miner in Australia, a squatter in America, an actor in Batavia, a bailiff in Brussels; after having made debts in the two hemispheres, left creditors at the four corners of the earth, he settled down as agent in London, where he lived for a considerable time, and where he might have succeeded if the terrible insatiability of his imagination, ever in quest of something fresh, the imagination of a voluptuary ever forestalling the coming pleasure, had not thrown him back into the deepest and darkest poverty. This time he fell very low, and was picked up one night in Hyde Park as he was trying to steal the swans off the Serpentine. A few months of prison life thoroughly disgusted him with the "land of the free," and he returned like a waif, stranded on the Parisian pavement, whence he had taken his departure.

It was also a whimsical fancy, added to his instincts of actor and mountebank, that had made him dub himself an Englishman, a thing easy enough for him with his knowledge of the manners, language, and ways of the Anglo-Saxons. It was instinctive, a sudden inspiration on the occasion of his first stroke of business, his first "grand stroke."

"Who shall I announce?" had inquired insolently a tall flunky in livery, when he presented himself on this memorable occasion, and Poitou, seeing himself so threadbare, so wretched in the vast ante-room, fearing lest he should be turned away before he was listened to, feeling the imperative necessity of rising above the situation by something abnormal and foreign, had answered:

"Oh! announce Mr. Tom Levis!"

And he at once felt so imbued with confidence under this name, improvised at a minute's notice, and this borrowed nationality, that he took a delight in affecting the peculiarities and manias belonging to it, carefully watching over his accent and manners, correcting his exuberant fancy, and allowing himself time by a hesitation of speech to invent the necessary lies.

Strange as it may seem, of all the innumerable combinations of this inventive brain, this one, that he had the least sought for, was the most successful. To it he owed the acquaintance of Sephora, who at that time kept in the Champs Elysées a kind of *"Family Hotel,"* a pretty three-storied house, with pink curtains and a little flight of stone steps ɔn the Avenue d'Antin, bordered on each side by wide asphalte side-walks, enlivened by trees and flowers. The mistress of the establishment, always neatly attired, displayed her calm seraphic profile at one of the windows on the ground floor, bent over some needlework or ledger. The customers were a strange exotic medley: clowns, bookmakers, circus-riders, horse-dealers, and Anglo-American riffraff, the worst of all, scum of the goldfields and gambling houses. The feminine side was recruited from the quadrilles at Mabille, the violins of which might be heard on summer evenings, mingling with the noisy brawls of the *"family"* and the clatter of counters and gold pieces, for play ran high after dinner. If perchance some respectable family of foreigners, deceived by the appearance of the place, came to settle at Sephora's, the strange look of the guests, the tone of the conversation, drove them away in dismay, their boxes half unpacked, on the very first day.

In the midst of these adventurers and swindlers Monsieur Poitou, or rather Tom Levis, the insignificant occupier of an attic-room, soon acquired an important position by his gaiety, his suppleness, his knowledge of business, of all kinds of business. He invested the servants' savings, and through them gained the confidence of their mistress. How could it be otherwise, with his smiling good-natured frank countenance, with the indefatigable high spirits that made him the most valued guest at the table d'hôte, attracting the customers, exciting expense, the life and soul of the betting and drinking parties. The fair hostess, so cold and reserved with everyone else, was free and unrestrained only with Tom. Often in the afternoon, coming in or going out, he would stop at the little office of the hotel, clean and bright with mirrors and matting. Sephora would relate her affairs, show him her jewels and her ledgers, consult him on the bill of fare, or the care she must bestow on a large arum lily placed by her side in a vase of Minton's earthenware. Together they laughed over the love-letters and proposals of all kinds she received, for she was a woman untouched by sentiment. Of an icy temperament, she kept at all times and under all circumstances an imperturbably cool head, and treated all love affairs in a business-like manner. It is said that a woman's first lover gives the impress to her whole life; Sephora's lover, a sexagenarian chosen by father Leemans, had frozen her blood and perverted her love. This beautiful creature, born in an old curiosity shop, treated everything from a monetary point of view, to which she added the intrigue, cheating, and low cunning acquired by bartering. Little by little a bond was formed between her and Tom, the kind of affection that springs up between guardian and ward. He advised her, guided her, and always with a skill, a fecundity of imagination that charmed her methodical quiet nature, in which Jewish fatalism mingled with the heavy temperament of Flanders. Never did she invent or imagine anything, living only in the present. Tom's fertile brain, his perpetual firework of ready wit therefore completely dazzled her. What put the finishing ouch to her conquest was hearing her boarder, one evening after he had been talking the most comical gibberish all dinner-time, whisper in her ear as he took his key from the office:

"You know, I am no more English than you are!"

From that day she loved him, or rather—for sentiments are known only by their label—she became infatuated with him, like a lady is sometimes infatuated with an actor whom she alone knows as he is away from the footlights, the rouge, and the theatrical get-up; such as he is, and not such as he appears to others; love ever craves for these privileges. Moreover they both came from the same Parisian gutter. In the same gutter that had soiled the edge of Sephora's skirts Narcisse had also wallowed; and they both retained like the taint and the love of the mire whence they sprang. The low stamp, the vicious instincts that would step in at times and raise the mask of the would-be Englishman, are also displayed in the brief flashes that cross Sephora's biblical features, in the irony and the vulgar laugh of her Jewish mouth.

This strange love of Beauty and the east increased in proportion as the woman penetrated more thoroughly into the nature of this mountebank, into the confidence of his tricks, of his apishness; from the invention of the cab down to the numerous waistcoats, by the help of which J. Tom Levis, not being able to add to his stature, strove at least to look imposing; in proportion she associated with this existence, all of surprises and adventures, schemes, dreams, and great and little strokes of fortune. And this apish fellow was so clever, that after ten years of a legitimate and commonplace union, he could still amuse her, charm her, as on the first day they had met. It would have been sufficient to remove all doubt on the subject to have seen her that day, lying back on the divan of the little boudoir, writhing and convulsed with laughter, as she repeated in an ecstacy of delight: "What a ridiculous creature you are!" while Tom, in coloured vest and drawers, reduced to his simplest expression, bald, angular, and bony, danced in front of her a frantic jig, to an accompaniment of spasmodic gestures and mad stamping. When they were both tired, she of laughing and he of jumping, he threw himself down by her side on the sofa, drew his monkeyish head close to her angelic face, and breathed his joy into her ear.

"The Sprichts are squashed! Down with them all! I have hit upon my stroke, my grand stroke."

"Quite sure? Who is it?"

The name he uttered brought to Sephora's lips a pretty disdainful pout.

"What! that great goose? But he has not got a penny. We have sheared him and his Illyrian lion. He has not a scrap of wool left on his back."

"Don't make fun of the lion of Illyria, my dear," said Tom, resuming his habitual seriousness. "His skin alone is worth eight millions sterling." The woman's eyes flashed! He repeated, emphasizing each syllable:

"Eight millions sterling!"

Then coldly, clearly, he explained what he meant. The question was to bring Christian II. to accept the proposition of the Diet, and abandon his rights to the throne for the handsome sum offered to him. After all what was it? merely a signature, nothing more. Christian left to himself would have made up his mind long ago. It was his surroundings, more especially the Queen, that stopped him, and prevented his signing this renunciation. Nevertheless he would have to come to that one day or another. They had not a farthing left in the house. They owed to all the trades-people of Saint-Mandé, to the butchers, to the forage-dealer—for notwithstanding the poverty of the masters, there were still horses in the stables. The establishment was well kept, the table well supplied, all the appearance of luxury concealing sinister privations. The royal linen, embroidered with the crown, lay full of holes in the press, and could not be renewed. The coach-houses were empty, the largest pieces of plate pawned, the servants left hardly sufficed for the work, and their wages often remained several months unpaid. Tom had all these details from Lebeau, the valet, who had at the same time told him the story of the eight millions proposed by the Diet of Leybach and the scene this offer had given rise to.

Since the King knew that eight millions lay there, within reach of his hand, ready to be exchanged for a penful of ink, he was a changed man; he no longer laughed, nor talked, keeping this set idea in his head, like a neuralgic spot aching in one side of his brow. He kept sighing heavily all day, and his temper was that of a surly dog. Nothing however had been changed in his own particular service: he still had secretary, valet, coachman and lacqueys; the same luxurious and costly furniture and dress. Frédérique, in her desperate pride. strove to conceal their distress by dint of haughtiness, and never would allow the King to lack anything. When perchance he dined at the Rue Herbillon, she insisted on the table being royally provided for. One thing, however, she could not supply: that was pocket-money for his expenses at the club, gambling and women. Evidently the King would be overcome by that. Some fine morning, after a long night passed at baccarat or bouillote, unable to pay and unwilling to owe—imagine Christian of Illyria posted up at the club!—he must take up a pen and sign his abdication.

The thing would in fact have already taken place, had it not been for old Rosen, who, secretly, notwithstanding Frédérique's order, had again begun to advance money to His Majesty. The plan was therefore to lead him into fresh expenses, to make him contract such extravagant debts and numberless liabilities as would be beyond the resources of the old duke. This required a considerable amount of money to be laid out.

"But," said Tom Levis, "the thing is so safe that we are certain of finding the necessary funds. The best plan would be to speak of it to father Leemans, and keep the job in the family The only thing I am anxious about i the mainspring—the woman!"

"What woman?" asked Sephora opening wide her ingenuous eyes.

"The woman who will undertake t put the noose round the king's neck We must have a spendthrift of the firs class, a minx who will take up the thin seriously, with the digestion of an os trich, and who won't stick at a larg mouthful."

"Amy Férat, perhaps?"

"No go! used up! utterly used up, and besides not greedy enough. She will sing, sup, kick up a row like any young fool. But she is not the woman to swallow up a quiet little million (forty thousand pounds) a month, without having seemed to put a tooth into it; to hold the prize high, dispute every detail, every square inch, and sell it all dearer than a building lot in the Rue de la Paix."

"Oh! I feel exactly how the thing should be done," said Sephora thoughtfully, "but who is to do it?"

"Ah! indeed who?"

And the laugh that passed between them was equal to a deed of partnership.

"Come! since you have begun!"

"What! you know?"

"Do you suppose I don't see his little game when he gazes at you, and his dawdling by the wicket when he thinks I am out? Besides, he makes no mystery about it, and tells the story of his love to anyone who will listen. He has even written and put his name to it on the club book."

On learning the history of the bet, the tranquil Sephora betrayed some emotion.

"Ah, indeed! Two thousand napoleons that he would be my lover. Well, that is coming it rather too strong."

She rose, took a few steps to shake off her anger, and then coming back to her husband's side:

"You know, Tom, for the last three months I have had that great simpleton hanging round my chair. Well, look, not so much as that—"

Here might be heard the smart crack of a dainty finger-nail against a tooth that asked nothing better than to bite.

She was telling the truth. Notwithstanding the months that had elapsed since the king had first given chase, he was still fain to be content with touching the tips of her fingers, biting the penholders she had used, intoxicating himself with the mere brush of her skirts in passing. Never had such a thing happened before to this Prince Charming, spoilt as he was by the women, assailed on all sides by luring smiles and perfumed billets-doux. His handsome curly head which seemed to bear the impress of a crown, the heroic legend cleverly spread by the queen, and, above all, the indescribable seduction that seems to surround those who are loved already, had procured for him unmistakable success among the ladies of the noble faubourg. More than one of these could have shown, curled up on a corner of the sofa of her aristocratic boudoir, a marmoset from the royal cage, and in the theatrical world, almost always of a royalist and conservative turn of mind, it gave at once a position to an actress to be able to show in her album a portrait of Christian II.

The man, accustomed to find eyes, lips and hearts fly towards him, never to throw a glance without meeting a quivering response, had wasted his time for months before this cold and tranquil woman. She played the part of the model book-keeper, added up columns, turned over the heavy pages, and offered to her sighing wooer nothing but a view of the velvety roundness of her cheek, and the shadow of a smile at the corners of her lips and eyes. The caprice of the Slave had at first been amused by this struggle, then his selfconceit was aroused, the eyes of the whole Grand-Club being riveted upon him; and finally it ended in a real passion, fed by the emptiness of the unoccupied life which permitted the flame to rise straight and high without encountering any obstacle. He came every day at five o'clock, the best moment of the Parisian day, the hour of visits, when the amusement of the evening is decided upon; and little by little all the younger members of the club, who lunched at the agency and hovered round Séphora, respectfully made way for him. This desertion, diminishing as it did the figure of the small running accounts, increased the lady's coldness, and as the lion of Illyria brought in nothing, she was beginning to make Christian feel that he was in the way, that he took possession too royally of the half opened angle of her wicket, when suddenly all was changed, and the change took place on the very day after her conversation with Tom.

"Your majesty was seen last night at the *Fantaisies*."

At this remark, underlined by a sad and anxious glance, Christian II. felt a delightful thrill of emotion.

"Yes," he said, "I was there."

"Not alone?"

"No, but——"

"Ah! some women are very fortunate."

To lessen the provocation of her remark she hastened to add that for a long time she had had a great wish to go to this little theatre to see that Swedish dancer, you know, "But that her husband never took her anywhere."

The king proposed to escort her.

"Oh! you are too well known."

"But if I kept well at the back of a pit-box?" said the king.

In short, an appointment was arranged for the next evening, since, as luck would have it, Tom would then be out.

What a delightful escapade. She in front of the box, in a discreet and becoming gown, expanded into childish joy at the sight of the foreigner who had her little hour of celebrity in Paris—a Swede, dressed all in black with thin face and angular gestures, while from under her fair locks gleamed brilliant black eyes, all iris, eating up the whole face, and in her bounds and noiseless springs lurked the wild affright of a startled bat.

"Oh! what fun! how delightful!" kept repeating Séphora.

The king sitting motionless behind her, a box of sweets on his knee, could not recall a more delicious sensation than that caused by the bare arm under its laces that brushed against his, while the fresh mouth was turned toward him. He insisted upon escorting her to the Saint-Lazare railway station, for she was to return to the country, and in the carriage, in a moment of transport, he impulsively drew her within his arms.

"Oh," said she, sadly, "you will spoil all my pleasure."

The immense waiting-room on the first floor was deserted and badly lighted. Seated together on a bench Séphora, shivering, sheltered herself in Christian's ample fur cloak. Here she was no longer afraid, and letting herself go, talked unreservedly to the king low, tender whispers. From time to time some railway official would pass by, swinging a lantern, or some group of actors living in the suburbs, going home after the play. Amongst them, a couple closely linked, walked together with an air of pleasurable mystery.

"How happy they are!" murmured she. "No ties, no duties. Able to follow the promptings of their own hearts. All the rest is a delusion and a snare."

Alas! she knew something of this. And suddenly, as though carried away by an irresistible impulse, she described to him her sad life with a candour that touched him: the snares, the temptations of the Paris streets for a girl kept poor by the avarice of her father; then at sixteen, the sinister bargain, life at an end; the four years passed by the side of that old man to whom she had been nothing but a sick nurse; afterwards determined not to fall again into the trafficking clutches of old Leemans, the necessity of finding some guide, some support, had induced her to marry this Tom Levis, a man who thought of nothing but money. She had given and devoted herself entirely to him, was deprived of all pleasure, buried alive in the country, and then set to this clerk's work, and all without a word of thanks, or recognition from this ambitious man, who, wholly wrapped up in his affairs at the faintest sign of revolt, at the least wish to see a little more life, crushed her mercilessly by flinging in her face her past, for which she was not responsible.

"That past," she said, rising, "to which I owe the outrageous insult signed with your name in the book of the Grand-Club."

The bell ringing for the start, put a stop exactly in the right place to this little theatrical effect. She glided away, the light folds of her black draperies following her undulating step, and with a parting salute from eyes and hand,

left Christian motionless and stupefied, bewildered by what he had just heard. She knew then? How? Oh! how he abused himself for his baseness, for his boastfulness. He spent the night in writing to ask pardon; his French strewn with all the flowers of his native poetry, in which the beloved was compared to the cooing turtle-dove, or the rosy-tinted fruit of the azarole.

This reproach aimed at the bet was a splendid idea of Séphora's. It gave her a lasting hold over the king. This too, was a sufficient explanation of her protracted coldness, her almost inimical reception of him, and the crafty bargaining she was about to make of her own person. Must not a man put up with anything and everything from a woman to whom he had offered such an insult?

Christian became the timid and obedient cavalier, subservient to all her caprices, the acknowledged lover in the sight of all Paris; and, if the lady's beauty served as his excuse in the eyes of the world, there was, on the other hand, nothing to be proud of in the friendship and familiarity of the husband. "My friend, Christian II.," Tom Levis used to say, drawing up his diminutive figure. The fancy once took him to receive the king at Courbevoie, just to give Spricht one of those fits of jealous rage that must shorten the great tailor's days. The king was shown through the house and park, went on board the yacht, allowed himself to be photographed on the doorsteps, between his hosts, who wished to immortalize the memory of this never-to-be-forgotten day; and in the evening, while a shower of fireworks was let off, and reflected in the Seine as they fell, Séphora, leaning on Christian's arm, murmured in his ear as they skirted the trim beech groves, all white with the Bengal lights:

"Ah! how I could love you, if you were not a king!"

It was a first confession, and a very adroit one. Every mistress he had ever had until now, had adored in him the sovereign, the glorious title, the long line of ancestors. This one loved him for himself alone. "If you were not a king." And he was so little a king, he would willingly have sacrificed to her the shred of dynastic purple that barely clung to his shoulders.

Another time she explained herself yet more clearly. When he expressed uneasiness at finding her pale and tearful. "I am afraid that soon we shall meet no longer," she replied.

"And why?"

"He has just told me that business was too bad in France, and that we must shut up shop here, and start for some other country."

"What! Take you away?"

"Oh! I am only an obstacle to his ambition. He said to me: 'Come if you like.' But I must follow him. What would become of me all alone here?"

"Oh! naughty one. Am I not here?"

She looked at him fixedly, straight in the eyes.

"Yes, it is true, you love me, and I too love you. Would to God I could be yours without shame. But no, it is impossible."

"Impossible?" he asked, breathless at the glimpse of paradise.

"You are too far above Séphora Levis, Monseigneur."

To which he replied, with delightful fatuity:

"I will raise you to my level. I will make you a countess, a duchess. It is one of the privileges that still remain to me; and we can easily find somewhere in Paris a lover's nest, where I can establish you in a manner worthy of your rank, where we will live all alone; no one between us."

"Oh! it would be too much happiness."

She seemed lost in a dream, then raising her childish, candid eyes, in which the hushed tears glittered, said, abruptly:

"No, no, you are king One day, in the midst of happiness, you would leave me."

"Never!"

"But if they recalled you?"

"Where? To Illyria? That is all at an end, broken off for good and all. Last year I missed one of those chances that never come again."

"Really?" said she, with a joy that was not assumed. "Oh, if I were sure of that!"

To convince her, a word hovered on his lips, which he did not pronounce, but which she, nevertheless, understood; and in the evening, J. Tom Levis, duly informed by Séphora of all that had passed, solemnly declared that "the moment had come; the old man must be spoken to at once."

Allured, like his daughter, by the imagination, the infectious, go-ahead spirit, the inventive jabber of Tom Levis, Leemans had several times put money into the agency speculations. After having gained, he had lost, following in that the hazard of play; but when he had been "done," as he expressed it, two or three times, the good man drew the line. He did not recriminate, did not get into a rage, being too well versed in the chances of business and hating useless words; only, when his son-in-law began to talk to him about advancing money for one of those marvellous castles in the air that his eloquence could raise as high as the skies, the dealer smiled gently in his beard, in a significant manner that meant quite clearly, "No go; no more of that," with a sudden lowering of the eyelids that seemed to bring back to reason, to the level of possibility, all Tom's extravagant ideas.

The other knew this; and as he had wisely resolved that the Illyrian affair should not go out of the family, he despatched Séphora to interview the dealer, who in his old age developed a sort of affection for his only child, in whom indeed he recognised a second self.

CHAPTER XVI

SÉPHORA

Since the death of his wife, Leemans had given up his curiosity shop in the Rue de la Paix, and contented himself with his den in the Rue Eginhard. Here Séphora repaired one morning early, in order to be sure of finding him, for the old man remained but little at home. Immensely rich and ostensibly retired from business, he continued to grope and ferret about Paris from morning till night, following the sales, seeking the atmosphere, the stir of business, and above all overlooking with marvellous acuteness the host of little dealers, picture and curio sellers, in whose business he was a sleeping partner, without owning it, lest anyone should suspect his wealth.

Séphora in a moment of caprice, a reminiscence of her youth, came on foot to the Rue Eginhard from the Rue Royale, following very nearly the same road by which she used formerly to return from the shop. It was not yet eight o'clock. The air was keen, there were few vehicles about, and in the direction of the Bastille there lingered a relic of the dawn, an orange mist, in which the gilt figure of the column seemed to dip its wings. On this side, from all the adjoining streets, issued forth a charming population, all the girls of the faubourg going to their work. If the Prince d'Axel could have got up early enough to see this crowd, he would have been well satisfied this morning. In twos and threes, alert and talking as they walked quickly along, they were going to the crowded workshops of the Rues Saint-Martin, Saint-Denis, Vielle-du-Temple, while a few, more elegant than the others, were bound for the shops on the boulevards further off, but opening later.

It was not the animation of the evening, when, the daily task finished, their heads full of the exciting Paris atmosphere, they return homewards, with noisy laughter, and may be some wistful regret of the luxury they have witnessed, which made the garret seem higher perched, and the staircase steeper and more dark. But if some sleep still hung about their youthful eyes, repose had adorned them with a sort of freshness, completed by the neatly dressed hair, the knot of ribbon tied round the neck, and the careful brushing given before starting to the black frocks. Here and there a sham jewel glittered in a little ear pink from the cold, a comb gleamed in the plaits, a buckle sparkled at the waist, or a folded newspaper peeped out of the pocket of a waterproof. And what hurry, what courage was there! Thin cloaks, thinner petticoats, the steps tottering on heels far too high, and trodden away through much usage. In one and all was coquetry innate, not one but had a way of walking along with head erect, eyes never at rest, full of curiosity as to what the day might bring; natures ever ready for what chance might offer, just as their Parisian type—which is no type at all—is open to any sort of transformation.

Séphora was not sentimental, and never saw anything beyond the thing and the moment present; yet this confused tramping, this hurried rustling and bustling around her, amused her. On all these girlish faces, in this morning sky, in the quaint, old quarter, where each street at its corner bore on a framed placard the names of the chief shops, and where nothing had changed for fifteen years, she saw her own youth. Passing beneath the black archway that serves as entry to the Rue Eginhard, on the side of the Rue Saint-Paul, she caught sight of the long robe of the Rabbi wending his way to the neighbouring synagogue; two steps further, she met the rat-killer with his pole and board, from which hung the hairy corpses of many rats, a type of old Paris that is only to be found now amid these mouldy dwellings, in whose walls all the rats in Paris hold their resort; further still, a cabman whom, every morning of her shopgirl's life, she had seen going off thus to his work, moving heavily in his big boots, little fitted for walking, and holding carefully in his had, upright as a communicant's taper, the whip, which is to the coachman as the sword is to the soldier, an insignia of his rank, and which never leaves him. At the door of the two or three shops that compose the whole street, and from which the shutters were being taken down, she saw the same old rags hanging in masses, heard the same gibberish of mixed Hebrew and German, and when, after passing through the low porch of the paternal house, and the little yard with the four steps leading up to the bric-à-brac shop, she pulled the string of the cracked and wheezy bell, it seemed to her that fifteen years were lifted off her shoulders, fifteen years that had not, however, weighed heavily upon her.

Just as in those days, Darnet came to open the door; she was a robust Auvergnate, with a ruddy, shiny colour on her dark complexioned face, who, with her spotted shawl tightly tied behind the waist, and black cap edged with white, seemed to be in mourning for some imaginary coalheaver. Her *rôle* in the house was evident, if only from the way she opened the door to Séphora, and from the sour and frosty smile that the two women exchanged as they stood face to face.

"My father is at home?"

"Yes, Madame, in the workshop. I will call him."

"Needless. I know where it is."

She crossed the ante-room and parlour, took three steps across the garden—a black hole between high walls, in which a few stunted trees vegetated skywards,—encumbered in all its narrow paths by countless odds and ends, old ironwork, leadwork, wrought-iron railings, the great chains of which oxidized and blackened metal matched well with the melancholy box-trees and the greenish hue of the old fountain. On one side was a shed overflowing with rubbish, the carcases of broken furniture of all times and sorts, heaps of tapestry rolled up in every corner; on the other side, a workshop roofed with ground-glass panes to escape prying glances from neighbouring windows. In here, in apparent disorder, an assemblage of riches was piled to the ceiling, their worth only known to the old man himself; lanterns, lustres, old torchstands, panoplies, incense-burners, antique or foreign bronzes. At the further end were two forges and a joiner's and locksmith's bench. It was here that the old dealer mended, copied, and rejuvenated old pieces with marvellous skill and the patience of a Benedictine. Formerly the noise was continuous from morning to night, and five or six workmen surrounded the master; now all that could be heard was the click of a hammer upon the metal, the scratching of a file, all lighted up in the evening by a solitary lamp, just by way of proof that the old dealer was not dead.

When his daughter entered, old Leemans, a leathern apron in front of him, his shirt sleeves tucked up on red and hairy arms, so that they looked as if they had been sprinkled with copper dust from the bench, was busy forging, at a vice, a candelabra in the style of Louis XIV., of which the model stood before him. At the noise of the door he raised his rubicund head, the features buried amid a beard and shock of light red hair, and knit his thick, shaggy eyebrows, whence his glance peered forth as if from under the falling locks of a rough terrier.

"Good morning, pa," said Séphora, pretending not to see the embarrassed gesture of the old man who tried to conceal the candlestick he held; for he did not care to be disturbed or seen at work.

"So it is you, little one."

He rubbed his old face against the delicate cheeks.

"What has happened?" he asked, pushing her towards the garden. "Why have you got up so early?"

"I have something very important to say to you."

"Come in then."

And he hurriedly led the way.

"Oh, but you know I don't want Darnet to be present."

"All right! All right!" said the old fellow, smiling from under his bushy brows, and as he went in he shouted to the busy servant, who was polishing up a Venetian mirror—for she was for ever rubbing and furbishing, even her own forehead, which was as shiny as a waxed floor:

"Darnet, go into the garden and see if I am there."

The tone in which this was said, proved that the old pasha had by no means abandoned his power to the favourite slave. The father and daughter remained alone in the neat, trim little parlour, where the furniture in its white covers, with little wool mats in front of every chair, contrasted oddly with the dusty wealth piled up in the workshop and shed. Like those first-class cooks who for their own part only relish the plainest food, father Leemans, such an expert in objects of art, did not possess in his own house the least vestige of anything of the kind, and in this stood confessed as the mere trader he was, calculating, exchanging, trafficking without passion or regret, not like those real lovers of curiosities, who before parting with some rarity, are concerned to know in what manner the buyer will set it off and display its beauty. In solitary grandeur on the walls, hung his full length portrait by Wattelet, representing him amid his ironwork, at his forge. It was as like him as ever: a little less grey, perhaps, but unchanged otherwise; thin, bent, the doglike head with the flat, reddish, coarse beard and hair hanging long and rough over the forehead, leaving nothing of the features visible but a nose reddened by chronic inflammation, which gave to this tea-drinker's face the look of a drunkard's. Besides a mass-book laid on the mantel-piece, this picture was the only characteristic note in the room. To this book Leemans owed some remunerative strokes of business; by it he distinguished himself from his rivals: from that old rascal Schwalbach, mother Esau, and others, with their Ghetto origin, while he was a Christian, married for love to a Jewess, but a Christian for all that—and a Catholic. This stood him in good stead with his best clients, he attended mass in the oratory of such ladies as the Comtesse Malet, or the eldest Sismondo, and showed himself on a Sunday at the fashionable churches of Saint-Thomas d'Aquin, or Sainte-Clotilde, which were frequented by his richest clients, while by means of his wife he kept in touch with all the great Israelitish financiers. As he grew older, this religious pretence became a habit, and often in the morning, before starting on his rounds, he would enter Saint-Paul's to get, as he said gravely, a tag end of mass, having noticed that he was always more lucky on those days.

"Well, what next?" he said, looking cunningly at his daughter.

"A big thing, pa."

She drew from her bag a bundle of bills and drafts bearing Christian's signature.

"All this has to be discounted. Will you do it?"

At the mere sight of the writing, the old man made a grimace that puckered up his whole face, and made it almost disappear beneath the shock of surrounding hair, with the movement of a hedgehog on the defensive.

"Illyrian paper! Thanks, I know it. Your husband must be mad to send you on such an errand. Do you mean to tell me you have come to that?"

Without being put out at this greeting, which she had expected, she answered:

"Listen," and with her sedate manner she related the affair to him in detail, with proofs in support of it, the number of the *Quernaro* in which was to be found the account of the sitting of the Diet, letters from Lebeau keeping them informed as to the situation. The king, desperately in love, was preoccupied with the sole care of settling his ladylove in a magnificent mansion, Avenue de Messine, with servants, horses and carriages—he wanted all this, and was ready to sign as many bills as necessary, at any rate of interest. Leemans now began to prick up his ears, he raised objections, examined and turned over all the details of the affair so skilfully prepared.

"When would the bills fall due?"

"In three months!"

"Then in three months?"

"Yes, in three months!"

She made a gesture as of tightening a

running noose, compressing her cold lips at the same time.

"And the interest?"

"Whatever rate you please. The heavier the better. He must have no other option than to sign his abdication."

"And once signed?"

"The rest is the woman's business. She will have before her the owner of eight millions sterling to nibble at."

"And if she keeps it all for herself? We must be quite sure of the woman."

"We are sure of her."

"Who is it?"

"No one you know," replied Séphora without flinching, putting back all the bundles of papers into her little handbag.

"Leave those papers here," said the old man sharply. "It's a lot of money, you know; a very large outlay. I must talk to Pichery about it."

"Take care, p'pa. We must not let in too many people. There is already Lebeau, and us, and you. If you let in many others——"

"Only Pichery. You see I am not rich enough to manage it all alone. It is a lot of money—a lot of money."

She replied coldly:

"Oh! we shall require a lot more before we have done."

There was a moment's silence. The old fellow reflected, concealing his thoughts behind his shaggy hair.

"Well, then!" he said at last; "I will do the business, but on one condition. That house, Avenue de Messine, it will have to be stylishly furnished? Well! I shall be entrusted with the furnishing of the works of art!"

Under the usurer, the dealer now asserted himself. Séphora burst into a laugh that displayed all her white teeth.

"Oh! you 'old clo'—'old clo,'" she cried, making use of the common street call suddenly brought back to her mind by her father's bartering, and which jarred with the distinction of her manners and dress. "Well, that's agreed pa. You shall furnish the knick-knacks; but mind, nothing from mamma's collection if you please."

Under this hypocritical title, "Collection of the late Madame Leemans," the second-hand dealer had grouped together a lot of old, damaged, unsaleable things, which, thanks to this sentimental humbug, he sold at enormous prices, never consenting to part with a relic of his dear departed one, except for its weight in gold.

"You understand old man, no tricks, no rubbish, the lady knows what she is about."

"You think she really understands these things?" asked the old dog through his moustaches.

"As well as you and I, I assure you."

"Well, but——"

He put his rugged old face close to the fresh, pretty one; on both the greed of money was written; on the old dried parchment as well as on the delicate rose leaf.

"Well, but who is this woman? You can tell me now I am in the swim."

"It is——"

She stopped for a moment, fastened the broad ribbon of her bonnet-strings under her dainty oval face, cast on the mirror the satisfied glance of a pretty woman, mingled with a new and sudden pride.

"It is the Comtesse de Spalato," she said gravely.

CHAPTER XVII

THE ACADÉMIE

THE classical palace that sleeps under the leaden roof of its cupola, at the end of the Pont des Arts, in the heart of scholarly Paris, had this morning an air of unusual life, and seemed in its animation to step forward on to the quay. Notwithstanding the rain, a pelting summer rain falling in heavy showers, a crowd gathered together on the steps of the principal entrance, forming a trail along the iron railing and the Rue de Seine, a discreet, well-dressed crowd that waited patiently, knowing it would in time get in by means of the little cards of various colours which each one held in his hand. The carriages followed in the same regular file on the deserted Quai de la Monnaie, all that Paris contained in the way of stylish equipages, with magnificent and showy liveries, powdered wigs and gold facings—democratically sheltered under umbrellas or waterproofs—exhibiting on their panels the arms of the greatest houses of France and Europe, even Royal mottoes; a moving and gigantic Peerage stretching out by the side of the Seine. When a ray of sun shone through the rain, a ray of the Parisian sun, which is like a gracious smile upon a serious face, the whole scene was lit up with a wet sheen; the harness, the caps of the police, the globe of the cupola, the castiron lions at the entrance usually dulled with dust, now beautifully polished black by the rain.

At long intervals, on solemn reception days, the old *Institut* suddenly springs into life for the space of a whole afternoon. But this morning there was no reception.

It was too late in the season, and the new members vain—like any actors—would never consent to a *debût* after the Grand Prix had been run, the Salon closed, and trunks packed ready for departure. It was merely a distribution of academic prizes, a ceremony that had never much brilliancy, and which generally attracted only the families of the laureates. The reason of the exceptional and aristocratic affluence at the gates of the *Institut,* was that among the prize essays was the *Memorial of the Siege of Ragusa,* by the Prince de Rosen, and the royalist coterie had seized this occasion to make a sort of protestation against the established government, under the protection of its own republican police. By an extraordinary stroke of good fortune, or perhaps by means of one of those intrigues that mysteriously sap the official and academic foundations, the perpetual secretary being ill, the report on the prize essays was to be read by the noble Duc de Fitz-Roy, and it was well known that this extreme legitimist would startlingly emphasize the most glowing passages of Herbert's volume, that grand historic pamphlet, which had brought together all the scattered devotion and fervour of the royalist party. In a word, it was to be one of the malicious protestations that the *Académie* dared even under the Empire, and which the easy good-nature of the Republic tolerated.

Mid-day. The twelve strokes struck by the old clock caused a murmur and a stir in the crowd. The doors opened. slowly, methodically the crowd advanced towards the entrances of the Place and Rue Mazarine, while the emblazoned carriages turning in the Court deposited their masters—bearers of more favoured cards—under the portico, where amidst the ushers with their silver chains, the affable secretary in his silver-braided coat assiduously received them, smiling and eager like the worthy steward in the Palace of the Sleeping-Beauty, the day she awoke on her bed of state, after her sleep of one hundred years. The carriage doors slammed, the footmen in their long coats jumped from their seats; bows and curtseys are exchanged amid the smiles and whispering of habitual frequenters of the place, and are lost in the noise of the rustling silks as they disappear up the carpeted staircase that leads to the private boxes or in the narrow passage sloping downwards, as if bent with the weight of ages, that leads to the interior of the palace.

The amphitheatre is soon filled on the side set apart for the public. The benches rising in tiers one by one become black with people, till the last rows, standing up, appear in dark outlines against the glass dome above them. Not a single place is empty. It is a surging mass of heads lighted by a dim light like that of a church or a museum, chilled still more by the smooth yellow stucco of the walls, and the marble of the meditating statues; Descartes, Bossuet, Massillon, all the glory of the "great century" congealed in motionless figures. In front of the overflowing semi-circle, a few unoccupied benches, a small green table with the traditional glass of water, await the Academicians and their officials, who will soon enter by the tall doors surmounted by the gilt sepulchral-looking inscription, "LETTERS, SCIENCE, ARTS." All this has a cold, shabby, old fashioned look, which contrasts with the fresh spring costumes that deck the hall. Soft light materials, dove-like greys, tender pinks, cut in the newest tight style, and spangled with jet and steel, bonnets that seem but sprigs of mimosa mingled with lace, humming birds nestling in velvet knots and gold-coloured straw, and over all the regular, continual flutter of enormous fans, wafting delicate perfumes that made the "eagle of Meaux" (Bossuet) blink his eyes. Because they are the representatives of ancient France, there was no reason they should smell musty or be dressed like frights.

All that Paris contains of stylish, well-born, well-bred people is gathered together here; they are smiling to each other with little masonic signs; the flower of the clubs, the cream of the noble Faubourg, a somewhat exclusive society that does not usually mix with the common herd, is not seen on a first night at the play, only appears on certain days at the Opera or the Conservatoire; a discreet society, that tightly closes its many hanging curtains to keep out the light of day, and the noise of the street from its drawing-rooms; and is only spoken of from time to time, when a death or a scandalous separation takes place, or when one of its members —hero of the *Persil* and *la Gomme*— makes himself notorious by some eccentric adventure. In the midst of this choice set, may be seen a few noble Illyrian families, who have followed their prince into exile, fine specimens of men and women, perhaps a trifle too loud and exotic for this extremely refined society; then grouped at certain conspicuous places are the frequenters of the Academic Salons, who long beforehand prepare the elections, count the votes, and whose acquaintance is by far more important to a candidate than his weight in genius. Illustrious but beggared Imperialists striving to creep in among these old partisans, upon whom they had formerly exhausted all the irony of parvenus; then, select as is the company, a few women known for their princely liaisons have managed to slip in, dressed plainly and quietly it is true, and two or three fashionable actresses, faces known to all Paris, trivial and importunate visions, the more so, that other women, indeed, women of every class, tax their ingenuity to imitate them. And the journalists, reporters of foreign newspapers, armed with note-book and pencil, equipped as though for a journey to the centre of Africa.

Below, in the smaller reserved circle at the foot of the benches, the little Princesse Colette de Rosen the laureate's wife, attracts all eyes dressed in a lovely costume of blue-green Indian cashmere and watered silk, looking triumphant, and beaming under the fluffiness of her fair flaxen hair. Near her is a stout man with a vulgar face, old Uncle Sauvadon, very proud to accompany his niece, but who in his ignorant zeal and desire to do honour to the solemnity of the ceremony, has come in a tailcoat. This makes him very unhappy; embarrassed by his white tie as by a *cangue*, he anxiously watches the people coming in, hoping to find a fellow to his coat. There is none!

From the glitter of colour and the excited faces a buzzing sound of voices arises, rhythmical but distinct, that sends a magnetic current from one end of the hall to the other. The slightest laugh spreads, and is contagious; the smallest sign, the mute gesture of two hands spread out ready to applaud is perceived from the top to the bottom of the benches. It is an artificial excitement, the friendly curiosity seen at a first representation when success is certain; and from time to time as some celebrity comes in, an admiring or curious murmur from the assembly goes towards them, dying away only in their immediate vicinity.

Yonder, above Sully's statue, two women, accompanied by a child, have just entered, and have placed themselves in the front of the box. They are the queens of Illyria and of Palermo. The two cousins, proud and erect, dressed in the same mauve silk edged with antique embroidery, the same long, undulating feathers fastened round their diademshaped bonnets, the one over fair hair, the other over dark tresses, forming a charming contrast of two different noble types. Frédérique is paler, the sweetness of her smile is saddened by lines that age her; and the face of her dark cousin also bears traces of the anxieties and worries caused by exile. Between them, the little Comte de Zara shakes the fair curls of his little head, each day held more vigorously erect, and in which both look and mouth have assumed more firmness True royal seed beginning to bear flower

The old Duc de Rosen occupies the back of the box with another personage —not Christian II., who has remained away to avoid too certain an ovation —but a tall fellow with bushy mane an unknown man, whose name, which ought to be in every mouth, will, however, not once be pronounced. It is in his honour that this *fête* is given; it he who has called forth this glorious *requiem* of monarchy, at which the last gentlemen of France and the royal families that have taken refuge in Paris are present; for all the exiled, dethroned princes have come to do honour to their "cousin" Christian, and it has been no little matter to place these crowns according to etiquette. Nowhere are questions of precedence more difficult to settle than in exile, where vanity is on the watch, and susceptibilities rankle like old wounds.

In the Descartes tribune—all the tribunes bear the name of the statue placed under them—the King of Westphalia maintains a proud attitude, which the fixed stare of his eyes makes still more striking—eyes that look, but do not see. From time to time he smiles in one direction, bows in another. His constant preoccupation is to conceal his incurable blindness; and his daughter helps him in the task with unremitting devotion. She is a tall and slender girl; her head seems to bend under the weight of the golden locks, the colour of which she has always hidden from her father. The blind king likes only dark hair: "If you had been fair," he says sometimes, stroking the princess's hair, "I think that I should have loved you less." Admirable pair, treading with dignity the road of exile, as calmly and haughtily as though they were taking a walk through some royal park. In Queen Frédérique's moments of discouragement she thinks of this infirm man guided by this innocent girl, and feels strengthened by the charm of purity that emanates from them.

Further on the eye catches sight of a scarlet satin turban; it is the heavy Queen of Galicia, who, with her massive cheeks and high-coloured complexion, resembles a thick-skinned blood orange. She is in high spirits, puffs, fans herself, laughs and talks to a woman, still young, who wears a white mantilla, a woman of a kindly but melancholy physiognomy, with cheeks that are furrowed by the traces of constant weeping. This is the Duchess of Palma, an excellent creature, little fitted to bear the shocks and terrors constantly occasioned her by the adventuresome monarch of the highway, with whose life she is linked. He, too, is there, restless dare-devil, and pokes familiarly between the two women his glossy black beard and conceited face, bronzed in his last expedition, as costly and as disastrous as the preceding ones. He has played the part of a king: had a court, *fêtes,* women, *Te Deums,* and triumphal entries strewn with flowers. He had pranced, decreed, danced, spilled ink and blood, burnt powder and sown hatred. And once the battle lost, the *suave-qui-peut* ordered, he has returned to France, seeking fresh recruits for his cause, more millions to squander, retaining even now the travelling buccaneer costume, the tight-fitting braided frock-coat that gives him the air of a Zingari. A whole set of noisy youths are talking loud in that box over there, with the impudent carelessness of a barbarian court, and their national tongue, harsh and guttural, flies from one to the other like hard iron balls, accompanied by a familiarity of words and manners, the secret of which is whispered through the hall.

It was a strange thing that, on a day when good seats were so rare, that princes of royal blood were glad to find places in the amphitheatre, one little

box, the Bossuet tribune, should remain
empty. Everybody wonders who is expected there, what great dignitary, what
sovereign passing through Paris, is so
long in making his appearance, and letting the sitting begin without him? Already the old clock has struck one. A
sharp word of command is heard outside: "Present arms!" and amid the
automatic clinking of the rifles, through
the tall wide-opened doors: LETTERS,
SCIENCES and ARTS make their appearance!

A remarkable peculiarity that distinguishes these illustrious beings, all alert
and vivacious,—preserved, it would
seem, by some principle, some traditional force of will—is that the oldest
among them affect a juvenile gait, a
frisky animation, while the younger do
their best to appear solemn and serious
in proportion as their hair 's less grizzly. The general aspect is devoid of
grandeur, the close-cut hair ordained
by modern fashion, the black cloth and
frock-coat of to-day destroying all prestige. Boileau's or Racan's wig must
have had more authority, risen with
more dignity under that high cupola.
The picturesque part of the business is
represented by two or three green palm-
embroidered coats, who settle themselves behind the table and the glass of
sugar and water; and it is one of these
who pronounces the time-honoured
phrase: "Gentlemen, the sitting is
opened." But in vain does he declare
the sitting opened, no one believes him,
nor does he believe it himself. He well
knows that the real business of the sitting is not this report on the Montyon
prizes, that one of the most discursive
members of the assembly is about to

give forth in mellifluous and well-modu-
lated tones.

It is indeed a model Academic discourse, written in true Academic style,
with many "but still's," and "it might
almost seem's," which at each moment
force the mind to retrace its steps, like
a devotee in the confessional, recalling
her faults; a style ornamented with
arabesques and flourishes, like those of
a writing-master running through the
phrases in order to conceal their empti-
ress—a style, in short, which must be
learned, and which everyone here present buckles on at the same time as the
green-palmed coat. Under any other
circumstances, the habitual public of the
place would have gone into raptures
over this homily; and would have pawed
the ground, neighed with delight at all
the little tortuous phrases of which it
would have divined the final point. To-
day, however, everyone is in a hurry;
they had not come for this little literary
treat. With what an air of contemptuous weariness this aristocratic assembly
assists at the procession of humble self-
devotion, of trusty fidelity, of hidden,
jog-trot, bowed down existences, who
wander through this obsolete, hesitating
phraseology, as they have in reality
passed their lives in narrow provincial
corridors, dark, cold, and fireless, wherein they have concealed their self-sacrifice. Plebeian names, threadbare cassocks, old blue smocks, faded by sun
and rain; corners of distant villages
showing for a brief moment their
pointed steeple, low walls built up of
cow-dung,—all these feel ashamed,
abashed, at having been conjured up
from afar, into the midst of such a refined company, under the cold light of
the Institut, as searching as that of a

photographer's studio. The noble society is astonished there should be so many good folk among the lower classes. What more! still more? will they never cease suffering, sacrificing themselves, being heroic? The clubmen declare this is an infernal bore. Colette de Rosen sniffs at her scent-bottle; all these old people, these poor they are hearing about, smell of toil. Ennui is visible on every brow, oozes out from the very walls. The reader begins to understand that he is wearying everyone, and hurries on the humble nomenclature.

Ah! poor Marie Chalaye of Ambérieux-les-Combes, you whom the people of the country call the Saint, who during fifty years have nursed your old paralytic aunt, and have brought up from infancy and provided for eighteen little cousins; and you, worthy Abbé Bourillou, curate of Saint-Maximinle-Haut, who used to go in the most bitter weather carrying consolation and help to the cheese-makers on the mountain-tops, you did not suppose that after having crowned your efforts by a public recognition, the Institut would feel shame and contempt for you, and that your names, hurried and muttered, would disappear unheard in the general inattention and hum of impatient or ironical conversations! The end of the lecture was a positive rout. And as in order to speed his flight, the fugitive soldier throws aside his arms and knapsack, so the reader remorselessly tosses aside into the ditch, records of heroism and of angelic self-abnegation, knowing, moreover, that the papers of the morrow will reproduce his speech in full, and that not one of these delicately wrapped phrases will be lost to the public. At last he has reached the end. A few bravos, and "ah's" of relief greet him. The unfortunate man sits down, sponges his forehead, and receives the congratulations of two or three of his colleagues,—last vestals of the Academic style. Then there is a pause of five minutes, a general buzz in the hall, and, after stretching themselves, the listeners once more settle down.

All at once a great silence prevails. Another green coat has risen.

It is the noble Fitz-Roy, and everyone can admire him as he places his papers in order upon the little table. Thin, bent, wizen, with narrow shoulders and awkward gestures, caused by his long elbowy arms—he is only fifty and appears to be seventy. On this worn-out, badly-shaped body is a little head with distorted, pasty-looking features, between two thin whiskers and a few tufts of fluffy hair. He recalls Montefeltro in *Lucretia Borgia*, who, it will be remembered, drinks Pope Alexander's poison, and is seen passing at the back of the stage, shivering, broken-down, ashamed to live! The noble Fitz-Roy might well represent that personage.

Not that he had ever drunk anything, poor man! neither the Borgia's poison nor anything else; but he is the heir of a terribly old family, that has never been crossed by a *mésalliance*, the off-shoot of a plant that has exhausted its sap, and which it is too late to revive.

The green of his coat makes him look still more livid, accentuates the outline of sick chimpanzee. Uncle Sauvadon thinks he looks divine. Such a fine name! The women say "How distinguished, a Fitz-Roy!"

It is the privilege of this name, of this long genealogy—among whom certainly there has been no lack of fools and contemptible toadies—that has obtained his admission to the Academy far more than his historical studies, a poor compilation, the first volume of which alone showed some talent. It is true that another man had written it for him; and if the noble Fitz-Roy could see up there in the tribune of Queen Frédérique, that powerful, solid head from whence his best work had sprung, he would not perhaps pick up the notes of his speech with such an air of supreme and disdainful peevishness, and would not begin its perusal with that haughty circular glance that takes in all, but sees nothing. First of all, he skillfully and lightly disposes of the lesser works that the Academy is crowning; and in order to show how much this task is beneath him, he takes pleasure in crippling the names of the authors and the titles of the books. Most witty! At last he reaches the Roblot prize, reserved for the finest historical work published in the five preceding years. "That prize, gentlemen, you are aware, has been awarded to Prince Herbert de Rosen for his magnificent *'Memorial of the Siege of Ragusa.'*" A formidable burst of applause greets these simple words thrown out in a resonant voice, with the gesture of a good sower. The noble Fitz-Roy allows this first enthusiasm to subside, then making use of an effective contrast, ingenuous but certain, he calmly, softly resumes: "Gentlemen." He pauses, casts a glance upon the expectant audience, now wholly his, whom he holds at his mercy. He looks as if he would say, "Well! suppose I did not choose to say anything more now. Who would be caught?" But it is he who is caught, for, when he prepares to continue, no one listens to him.

A door up yonder has just slammed to in the box hitherto unoccupied. A woman has entered and has seated herself without seeking to attract attention, but to whom nevertheless the eyes of all present are drawn. Her sober costume, evidently made by the fashionable tailor of the day, embroidered with dark peacock feathers, her bonnet edged with gold lace, set off admirably her supple figure and the delicate oval of this Esther's pale and lovely face—sure of her Ahasuerus. Her name is whispered from ear to ear; all Paris knows her, for her luxury and her love have for the last three months been the topic of all conversations. Her mansion, Avenue de Messine, recalled by the magnificence of its style the most brilliant days of the Empire. The newspapers have given the details of this society scandal, the height of the stables, the price of the paintings in the dining-room, the number of her carriages, the eclipse of the husband, who, more honest than another well-known Menelaus, not having chosen to live by his dishonour, had gone off to sulk abroad, like a betrayed husband of the "great century." It is only the name of the purchaser that the chronicles have left unmentioned. At the theatre, the lady is always seated alone in front of a stage-box, while a pair of delicate moustaches remain concealed in the back-ground. At the races, at the Bois, ever alone in her carriage, the empty place by her side filled by a huge bouquet, and on the panels round an unknown coat of arms, the trivial motto freshly painted, *"Mon droit, mon roy,"* which her lover has bestowed on her together with the title of Comtesse.

CHAPTER XVIII

TO RECOGNISE HER

Now, there can be no doubt as to her rank as favourite. To have placed her there on such a day, amongst the places of honour reserved to sovereigns, to have given her as escort Wattelet, the liegeman of Christian and the Prince d'Axel, ever ready when some discreditable folly is to be committed, is to recognise her before all the world, and to stamp her publicly with the royal seal of Illyria. And yet her presence excites no feeling of indignation. It is the privilege of kings to enjoy immunity; their pleasures are as sacred as their persons in the aristocratic society where the traditions of Louis XIV and Louis XV have been preserved; when the mistresses of kings drove in the queen's carriages, and even took her place in the great hunts. A few fastidious humbugs like Colette de Rosen affect prudish airs, whispering their surprise that the *Institut* should admit creatures of that kind; but it is probable that each of these ladies is in possession of a pretty little marmoset, dying of consumption in her boudoir. On the whole, the impression produced is excellent. The clubmen say, "Quite the thing;" the journalists, "What cheek!"

Approval smiles on all sides, and the immortal themselves complacently eye the beautiful creature who sits without affectation in front of her box, only showing in her velvety eyes the fixed and determined unconcern of women who know themselves to be the centre of attention.

Curious glances are also cast in the direction of the Queen of Illyria, to watch how she accepts the situation. Oh! very well indeed! Not a feature, not a feather of her bonnet has moved. As she never mixes in society, Frédérique cannot know this woman; she has never seen her, and at first only looks at her in a careless manner.

"Who is it?" she asks the Queen of Palermo, who answers very quickly, "I do not know." But in a neighbouring tribune a name pronounced out loud and repeated several times strikes her to the heart, "Spalato, Comtesse de Spalato."

For several months past this name of Spalato had haunted her. She knows it to be that of Christian's new mistress, who has only remembered that he is king to deck this creature of his pleasure with one of the greatest titles of his absent country. This has made her feel his present infidelity more keenly than a thousand others. But this last drop is the bitterest of all. There, opposite his wife and the royal child, sits this creature throning it like a queen: what an outrage! And hardly aware of the cause, Frédérique is stung still more cruelly by the refined and delicate beauty of her rival. The challenge is too evident in the glance of those beautiful eyes, that smooth insolent brow, the red lips of that mouth which defies her. A thousand torturing thoughts rush through her brain: their distress, their daily mortifications; only yesterday the coach-builder clamouring under her windows, whom Rosen had paid, for fear of a scandal. Where does Christian get the money he gives to this woman? Since the discovery of the false stones she knows what he is capable of; and something warns her that this Spalato is to be the dishonour of the king and his race. For one moment, one instant, her ardent nature tempted her to get up and leave the building, holding her child by the hand, to escape violently from this infamous neighbourhood, from this degrading rivalry. But she remembers that she is queen, wife and daughter of kings, that Zara is to be king one day; and she will not give her enemies the joy of such a scandal. A dignity higher than that of the wife—a dignity which she has made the noble, though desperate, rule of her life—keeps her to her rank, here in public, as it does in the privacy of her devastated home. Oh, cruel destiny of these much-envied queens! The effort she makes is so violent that the tears are about to start from her eyes, as the calm water of a lake splashes up under the stroke of the oar. Quickly, to avoid notice, she seizes her opera-glass, and steadfastly, obstinately gazes at the gilded and uninteresting inscription: LETTRES, SCIENCES, ARTS, which through the glasses dimmed by her tears lengthen out and glitter in rainbow tints, over the head of the orator. The noble Fitz-Roy continues reading. It is in a style as colourless as the grey hue of a prison dress, this pompous eulogy of the *"Memorial,"* this eloquent and powerful history, written by the young prince Herbert de Rosen, "who handles the pen as skilfully as the sword," above all the eulogy of the hero who has inspired it, "the chivalrous Christian II who, in his own person sums up the grace, the nobility, the strength, the seductive cheerfulness which is ever found around a throne." (Applause and little cries of ecstasy.) Decidedly a kindly, sensitive, excitable audience, ready to seize the slightest allusions. At times, in the midst of these rounded phrases, a note rings true and striking, a quotation from the *Memorial,* for which the queen has furnished all the documents, everywhere substituting the king's name for her own, sacrificing herself for the benefit of Christian II. Oh, God of Justice, and this is how he rewards her! The crowd hail, as they are uttered, the careless and haughty words of courage, the heroic acts simply performed, set out by the writer in a picturesque prose that reads like an epic tale of the olden times; and perceiving the enthusiastic welcome given to these quotations, the noble Fitz-Roy, who is no fool, gives up his own literature and is content to peruse some of the finest pages of the book.

In the narrow classical building these words are like the vivifying, rapid stroke of a wing; it seems as if the walls widened out, and that through the uplifted cupola a breath of fresh air had come in. They all breathe more freely; the fans no longer betray by their rhythmic flutter the inattention of the public. No, indeed, the whole hall is standing, all heads upraised towards Frédérique's box; they cheer, they hail the conquered but glorious monarchy, in the wife and son of Christian II, the last of kings, the last of knights! Little Zara, intoxicated like all children by the noise and cheers, artlessly applauds, his little gloved hands tossing back his fair hair;

while the queen throws herself slightly back, carried away by the contagious enthusiasm, enjoying the happiness, the moment's illusion it gives her. Thus she has succeeded in surrounding by a halo, this puppet of a king behind whom she lies concealed; she has been able to endow with a new lustre this crown of Illyria that her son will some day wear—a lustre which no one will ever be able to barter. Then what matter exile, misery or treachery? There are dazzling moments in life before which all the surrounding gloom vanishes. Suddenly she turns round to render the homage of her joy to him who, here, quite near her, his head leaning against the wall, his eyes vaguely upturned towards the cupola, listens to these magic sentences, forgetful that he has written them, assisting at this triumph without regret, without bitterness, without for one minute thinking that all this fame has been filched from him. Like those monks of the Middle Ages who grew old in erecting anonymous cathedrals, the son of the weaver is content with doing his work, with seeing it stand out boldly and firmly in the full blaze of noon. And, moved by the self-abnegation and the disinterestedness of his mystic smile, and because also she divines in him something that responds to her own feelings, the queen holds out to him her hand with a soft "Thank you." Rosen, standing near, thinks she is congratulating him on his son's success. He seizes the grateful gesture, and rubs against the royal glove his rough bristling moustache, and the two victims happy at the fête are reduced to exchanging from afar in a look those unmuttered thoughts which bind souls together by mysterious and everlasting bonds.

It is finished. The sitting has come to a close. The noble Fitz-Roy, applauded, complimented, had disappeared as through a trap-door; and "LETTRES, SCIENCES, ARTS" have followed him, leaving their places empty. Through every outlet the crowd that presses out begins to spread those rumours common to the end of a meeting or a play, and which the following day become the opinion of all Paris. Among the good people who are going out, many, pursuing their retrospective dream, expect to find their sedan chairs awaiting them at the gates of the *Institut*, but they find only the rain, pouring down amid the continual rattle of omnibuses and the sound of the tramway horns. Alone a few privileged ones preserve their monarchical illusions as their high-stepping horses bear them rapidly away.

Under the great colonnade, while an attendant calls up the royal carriages in the wet and glistening court, it is amusing to hear the lively exclamations of this aristocratic society as they wait the appearance of the Majesties. "What a success! What a sitting! If ever the Republic recovers from this." The Princesse de Rosen especially is much surrounded. "You must be very happy!" "Oh, yes, very happy." And prettily she prances, and bows right and left, like a little filly in a circus. Her uncle strives to do his best by her side, but still feels very awkward in his white cravat, and butler's shirt-front, which he endeavours to hide behind his hat; he is, nevertheless, very proud of the success of his nephew. Certainly he, better than anyone else, knows what a fraud this success is; he knows that Prince Herbert has not written one word of the prize essay, but at this moment he does not think of that; neither does Colette indeed. She is a true Sauvadon, so far as vanity is concerned; appearances are sufficient for her, and when in the group of *gommeux* who are congratulating her, she perceives the waxed tips of her Herbert's great moustaches, she can hardly help throwing her arms round his neck, there, before everyone, so convinced is she that he had assisted at the siege of Ragusa, that he has written the *Memorial,* and that his handsome moustaches do not hide the jaw of a simpleton. And if the good fellow is delighted and confused at the ovation and admiring glances cast at him,—the noble Fitz-Roy has just solemnly assured him: "When you choose, prince, you will be one of us"—nothing is more precious to him than the unhoped for greeting of his Colette, the loving way in which she leans on his arm, a thing that has not happened since their wedding-day, when they sailed down the nave of Saint-Thomas d'Aquin. amid the burst of sound from the great organ.

But the crowd parts, respectfully uncovering. The guests of the private boxes are coming down, all those fallen Majesties who are about to return into darkness after their brief resurrection of a few hours. A real procession of royal shades, the old blind man leaning on his daughter, the Galician with her handsome nephew, a rustle of stiff materials as on the passage of some Peruvian Madonna. Lastly Queen Frédérique, her cousin, and her son. A carriage draws up, and she steps into it, amid

an admiring and repressed murmur handsome, radiant, and proud. The left-handed wife has departed before the end with d'Axel and Wattelet, so that nothing jars upon this triumphant departure. Now there is nothing more to say, nothing more to see. The tall footmen rush about with umbrellas. For an hour there is a continual pawing of steeds, rolling of carriages, slamming of doors, mingling with the downpour of rain, the names called out, repeated by the echoes that haunt ancient edifices, and which are not often heard at the old French *Institut.*

That evening the coquettish allegories painted by Boucher on the panels of Herbert's room, in the family mansion of the Rosens, must have been roused from their languishing attitudes and rather faded views of life, on hearing a little voice warble: "It is I; it is Colette." It was in truth Colette, wrapped in a dressing-gown trimmed with floating laces, who came to say good-night to her hero, her knight, her genius! At the same hour, Elysée was strolling alone in the garden of the Rue Herbillon, under the light foliage, faintly lit up by a clear bright sky, one of those June skies, in which the sun still seems to linger, and to cast the sharp outline of the trees on the pallid windings of the paths, and to bleach the house and its closed shutters to the paleness of death. Alone on the top story, the king's lamp kept watch. The dropping of water from the fountains. and the thrill of a nightingale to which other nightingales responded, alone broke the silence. These sounds mingled with the penetrating perfume of the magnolias. roses, and sweet-smelling verbena after the rain. And the fever that for two months, ever since the fair at Vincennes, had not left Elysée, which burns in his hands, and scorches his forehead, instead of being soothed by the perfumed and musical surroundings, throbs, vibrates, and fills his heart with emotion.

"Ah, fool, wretched fool," said a voice near him in the grove. Elysée stopped, speechless. It was so true, so precisely what he had been repeating to himself for the last hour.

"Fool, miserable maniac that you are! You ought to be thrown into the fire, you and your dried herbs."

"Is that you, councillor?"

"Do not call me councillor. I am no longer councillor. I am nothing. I have neither honour nor intelligence. Ah, *porco*."

And Boscovich, sobbing with true Italian vehemence, shook his grotesque little head, fantastically illumined by the light that fell through the boughs of the lime-trees. The poor man had become somewhat crazed of late. At times, gay and talkative, he would bore everyone with his herbarium, his famous herbarium of Leybach, which he was soon to recover, he said; then, all of a sudden, in the midst of this whirl of talk he would interrupt himself, throw a side-long glance, and remain motionless and mute. On this occasion, Elysée thought he was going quite mad, when after this childish explosion, he bounded towards him, and seized his arm in a violent grasp, crying out in the night as though he were calling for help:

"This is impossible, Méraut. We must prevent it."

"Prevent what, councillor?" said Ely-

sée, trying to free his arm from the nervous clutch.

Then Boscovich, panting, added in a whisper:

"The deed of abdication is ready. I drew it up myself. At this very moment, His Majesty is signing it. I ought never to. *Ma che, ma che.* But he is the king; and then he promised to have my herbarium of Leybach given back to me. Such magnificent specimens!"

The maniac ran on, but Elysée, stunned by this terrible blow, no longer listened. His first, his only thought, was for the queen. Was this then the reward of her devotion, of her abnegation, the end of this day of self-sacrifice? How idle all the halo of glory so laboriously wreathed round this unconsenting brow! In the garden, now grown dim, he saw nothing but the glimmer of that lamp up yonder, lighting up the mystery of an imminent crime. What can he do? How prevent it? The queen alone; but can he get to her? And indeed, when Elysée presented himself, asking to speak to Her Majesty, the woman-in-waiting, Madame de Silvis already plunged in dreamland, the queen herself, all thought the house was on fire. In all the rooms was heard a chattering of bustling women, like an aviary startled before dawn. At last Frédérique appeared in the boudoir, where the tutor stood awaiting her, wrapped in a long blue dressing-gown, which set off her admirably shaped shoulders and arms. Never had Elysée felt himself so close to her.

"What is it?" she asked, in a low quick voice, with that nervous blink of eyelids that await a blow and see it coming. At his very first word she bounded forward.

"That cannot be. That shall not be while I am alive!"

The violence of her movement loosened the phosphorescent tresses of her hair, and to fasten them up again she raised her arms with a tragic gesture, allowing her sleeves to slip down to her elbows.

"Awake his Highness," she said in an undertone, in the shadowed softness of the adjoining chamber; then, without adding a word, she went up to the king's room.

CHAPTER XIX

WRATH OF A QUEEN!

ALL the magic beauty of that June night poured in through the wide open casement in the great hall. A single lighted candelabra scarcely disturbed the mystery of the moonlight, which streamed in like a "milky way," touching up the polished bar of a trapeze, the arched bow of a suspended guzla, or the glass door of a half empty bookcase, the vacant spaces now filled up by Boscovich's new collection, that exhaled the faint faded smell of a cemetery of dried plants. On the table, across some dusty old papers, lay a crucifix of oxydized silver; for if Christian II. did not write much, he remembered his Catholic education, and surrounded himself with objects of piety; sometimes, indeed, while he was amusing himself in the society of loose women, while around him all was noise and revelry, his hand, already unsteady from drink, would steal into his pocket and tell the beads of the coral rosary, that never left him. By the side of

the crucifix was a thick broad sheet of parchment, covered with a big and tremulous writing. It was the death-warrant of royalty, wanting nothing but the signature, one stroke of the pen, and a strong and violent effort of will to give this; and that was the reason why this weak king hesitated, sitting motionless, his elbows resting on the table, by the lighted candles prepared for the royal seal.

Near him, anxious, prying, yet soft and smooth, like a night-moth or the black bat that haunts ruins, Lebeau the confidential valet, watched him and silently encouraged him; for they had arrived at the decisive moment that the gang had for months expected, with alternate hopes and fears, with all the trepidation, all the uncertainty attending a business dependent upon such a puppet as this king. Notwithstanding the magnetism of this overpowering desire, Christian, pen in hand, could not bring himself to sign. Sunk down in his armchair, he gazed at the parchment, and was lost in thought. It was not that he cared for that crown, which he had neither wished for nor loved which, as a child, he had found too heavy, and that later in life had bowed him down and crushed him by its terrible responsibilities. He had felt no scruple in laying it aside, leaving it in the corner of a room which he never entered, forgetting it as much as possible when he was out; but he was scared at the sudden determination, the irrevocable step he was about to take. However, there was no other way of procuring money for his new existence no other means of meeting the hundred and twenty thousand pounds' worth of bills he had signed, on which payment would soon be due, and which the usurer, a certain Pichery, picture-dealer, refused to renew. Could he allow an execution to be put in at Saint-Mandé? And the queen, the royal child; what would become of them in that case? he must have a scene—for he foresaw the terrible clamour his cowardice must rouse—was it not better to have it now, and brave once for all anger and recriminations? And then—all this was not really the determining reason.

He had promised the Comtesse to sign this renunciation; and on the faith of this promise Séphora had consented to let her husband start alone for London, and had accepted the mansion Avenue de Messine, and the title and name that published her to the world as the king's mistress, reserving, however, anything further till the day when Christian himself would bring her the deed, signed by his own hand. She assigned for this conduct the reasons of a woman in love; he might, later on, return to Illyria, abandon her for the throne and power; she would not be the first person whom these terrible State reasons have made tremble and weep. D'Axel, Wattelet, all the *gommeux* of the Grand Club little guessed when the king, quitting the Avenue de Messine, rejoined them at the club with heavy fevered eyes, that he had spent the evening on a divan, by turns repulsed or encouraged, his feelings played upon, his nerves unstrung by the constant resistance; rolling himself at the feet of an immovable determined woman, who, with a supple opposition, abandoned to his impassioned embrace only the cold little Parisian hands, so skilful in defence and evasion, while she imprinted on his lips the scorching flame of the

enrapturing words: "Oh! when you have ceased to be king, I shall be all yours—all yours!" She made him pass through all the dangerous phases of passion and coldness; and often at the theatre, after an icy greeting and a rapid smile, would slowly draw off her gloves and cast him a tender glance; then, putting her bare hand in his, she would seem to offer it up to his ardent kiss.

"Then you say, Lebeau, that Pichery will not renew?"

"He will not, Sire. If the bills are not paid, the bailiffs will be put in."

How well he emphasized with a despairing moan the word "bailiffs," so as to convey the feeling of all the sinister formalities that would follow: bills protested, an execution, the royal hearth desecrated, the family turned out of doors. Christian saw nothing of all this. His imagination carried him far away to the Avenue de Messine, he saw himself arriving there in the middle of the night, eager and quivering; ascending with stealthy and hurried step the heavily-carpeted stairs, entering the room where the night-light burned mysteriously veiled under lace: "It is done—I am no longer king. You are mine, mine." And the loved one held out her hand.

"Come," he exclaimed, starting out of his fleeting dream.

And he signed.

The door opened and the queen appeared. Her presence in Christian's rooms at such an hour, was so unforeseen, so unexpected, they had lived so long apart, that neither the king, in the act of signing his infamy, nor Lebeau, who stood watching him, turned round at the slight noise she made. They thought it was Boscovich coming up from the garden. Gliding lightly like a shadow, she was already near the table, and had reached the two accomplices, when Lebeau saw her. With her finger on her lips she motioned him to be silent and continued to advance, wishing to convict the king in the very act of his treachery, and avoid all evasion, subterfuge, or useless dissimulation; but the valet set her order at defiance, and gave the alarm: "The queen, Sire!" The Dalmatian, furious, struck straight in the face of this malevolent caitiff with the powerful hand of a woman accustomed to handle the reins; and drawing herself up erect, waited till the wretch had disappeared before she addressed the king.

"What has happened, my dear Frédfrique? and to what am I indebted for—?"

Standing bent over the table that he strove to hide, in a graceful attitude that showed off his silk jacket embroidered in pink, he smiled, and although his lips were rather pale, his voice remained calm, his speech easy, with that polished elegance which never left him when addressing his wife, and which placed a barrier between them like a hard lacquer-screen adorned with flowery and intricate arabesques. With one word, one gesture she put aside the barrier behind which he would fain have sheltered himself.

"Oh! no phrases, no grimacing—if you please. I know what you were writing there. Do not try to give me the lie."

Then drawing nearer, overwhelming his timorous objection by her haughty bearing:

"Listen to me, Christian," and there was something in her tone that gave an impression of solemnity to her words; "listen to me: you have made me suffer cruelly since I became your wife. I have never said anything, but once —the first time, you remember. After that, when I saw that you had ceased to love me, I left you to yourself. Not that I was ignorant of anything you did—not one of your infidelities, not one of your follies remained unknown to me. For you must indeed be mad, mad like your father who died of exhaustion, mad with love for Lola; mad like your grandfather John, who died in a shameful delirium, foaming and framing kisses with the death-rattle in his throat, and uttering words that made the Sisters of Charity grow pale. Yes, it is the same fevered blood, the same hellish passion that devours you. At Ragusa, on the nights of the sortie, it was at Fœdora's that they sought you. I knew it, I knew that she had left her theatre to follow you. I never uttered a single reproach. The honour of your name was saved. And when the king was absent from the ramparts, I took care his place should not be empty. But here in Paris—"

Till now, she had spoken slowly, coldly, in a tone of pity and maternal reproof, as though inspired thereto by the downcast eyes and pouting mouth of the king, who looked like a vicious child receiving a scolding. But the name of Paris exasperated her. A city without faith, a city cynical and cursed, its blood-stained stones ever ready for sedition and barricades! What possessed these poor fallen kings, that they came to take refuge in this Sodom! It was Paris, it was its atmosphere tainted by carnage and vice that com pleted the ruin of the historical houses; it was this that had made Christian lose what the maddest of his ancestors had always known how to preserve: the respect and pride of their race. Oh! When on the very day of their arrival, the first night of their exile, she had seen him so excited, so gay, while all around him were secretly weeping, Frédérique had guessed the humiliation and shame she would have to undergo. Then, in one breath, without pausing, with cutting words that lashed the pallid face of the royal rake, and striped it red as with a whip, she recalled one after the other all his follies, his rapid descent from pleasure to vice, and vice to crime.

"You have deceived me under my very eyes, in my own house; adultery has sat at my table, it has brushed against my dress. When you were tired of that dollish little face who had not even the grace to conceal her tears, you went to the gutter, wallowing shamelessly in the slime and mud of the streets, and bringing back the dregs of your orgies, of your sickly remorse, all the pollution of the mire. Remember how I saw you totter and stammer on that morning when, for the second time, you lost your throne. What have you not done, Holy Mother of angels! What have you not done! You have traded with the royal seal, you have sold crosses and titles."

And in a lower tone, as though she feared lest the stillness and silence of the night might hear, she added:

"You have stolen, yes, stolen! Those diamonds, those stones torn from the crown—it was you who did it, and I allowed my faithful Greb to be suspected and dismissed. The theft being known, it was necessary to find a sham culprit to prevent the real one ever being discovered. For this has been my one, my constant preoccupation: to uphold the king, to keep him untouched; to accept everything for that purpose, even the shame which in the eyes of the world will end by sullying me. I had adopted a watchword that sustained me, and encouraged me in my hours of trial: 'All for the crown!' And now you want to sell it—that crown that has cost me such anguish and such tears; you want to barter it for gold, for the lifeless mask of that Jewess, whom you had the indecency to bring face to face with me to-day."

Crushed, bending low his head, he had hitherto listened without a word, but the insult directed against the woman he loved roused him. Looking fixedly at the queen, his face bearing the traces of her cutting words, he said politely, but very firmly:

"Well, no, you are mistaken. The woman you mention has had nothing to do with the determination I have taken. What I am doing is done for you, for me, for our common happiness. Tell me, are you not weary of this life of privations and expedients? Do you think that I am ignorant of what is going on here; that I do not suffer when I see you harassed by a pack of tradespeople and duns? The other day when that man was shouting in the yard I was coming in and heard him. Had it not been for Rosen I would have crushed him under the wheels of my phaeton. And you—you were watching his departure behind the curtains of your window. A nice position for a queen. We owe money to everyone. **There is a universal outcry against us.**

Half the servants are unpaid. The tutor even has received nothing for the last ten months. Madame de Silvis pays herself by majestically wearing your old dresses. And there are days when my councillor, the keeper of the royal seals, borrows from my valet the wherewithal to buy snuff. You see I am well acquainted with the state of things. And you do not know my debts yet. I am over head and ears in debt. Everything is giving way around us. A pretty state of things, indeed; you will see that diadem of yours sold one day at the corner of a street with old knives and forks."

CHAPTER XX

MOULDED BY THE JESUITS

LITTLE by little, gradually carried away by his own scoffing nature, and the jesting habits of his set, he dropped the moderate tone he commenced with and in his insolent little snuffling voice began to dwell upon the ludicrous side of the situation, with jeers and mockery, borrowed no doubt from Séphora, who never lost an opportunity of demolishing by her sneering observations the few remaining scruples of her lover.

"You will accuse me of making phrases, but it is you who deafen yourself with words. What after all is that crown of Illyria that you are always talking about. It is worth nothing except on a king's head; elsewhere it is obstruction, a useless thing, which for flight is carried hidden away in a bonnet-box or exposed under a glass shade like the laurels of an actor or the blossoms of a concierge's bridal wreath. You must be convinced of one thing, Frédérique. A king is truly king, only on the throne with power to rule; fallen, he is nothing, less than nothing, a rag. Vainly do we cling to etiquette, to our titles, always bringing forward our Majesty, on the panels of our carriages, on the studs of our cuffs, hampering ourselves with an empty ceremonial. It is all hypocrisy on our part, and mere politeness and pity on the part of those who surround us—our friends and our servants. Here I am King Christian II. for you, for Rosen, for a few faithful ones. Outside I become a man like the rest. Monsieur Christian Two. Not even a surname, only 'Christian,' like an actor of the Gaîté."

He stopped, out of breath; he did not remember having ever spoken so long standing. The shrill notes of the night-birds, the prolonged trills of the nightingales broke the silence of the night. A big moth that had singed its wings at the lights flew about, thumping against the walls. This fluttering distress and the smothered sobs of the queen were the only sounds to be heard; she knew how to meet rage and violence, but was powerless before this scoffing banter, so foreign to her sincere nature; it found her unarmed, like the valiant soldier who expects straight blows and feels only the harassing stings of insects. Seeing her break down, Christian thought her vanquished, and to complete his victory he put the finishing touch to the burlesque picture he had drawn of kings in exile. What a pitiful figure they cut all these poor princes in partibus, figurants of royalty who drape themselves in the frippery of the principal characters, and declaim before the empty benches without a farthing of receipts. Would they not be wiser if they held their peace and returned to the obscurity of common life? For those who have money there is some excuse. Their riches give them some right to cling to these grandeurs. But the others, the poor cousins of Palermo for instance, crowded together in a tiny house with their horrid Italian cookery. It smells of onions when the door is opened. Worthy folk certainly, but what an existence! And those are not the worst off. The other day a Bourbon, a real Bourbon, ran after an omnibus. 'Full, sir,' said the conductor. But he kept on running. 'Don't I tell you it is full, my good man.' He got angry, he would have wished to be called 'Monseigneur,' as if that should be known by the tie of his cravat!

"Operetta kings, I tell you, Frédérique. It is to escape from this ridiculous position, to ensure a dignified and decent existence, that I have made up my mind to sign this."

And he added, suddenly, revealing the tortuous Slavonic nature moulded by the Jesuits:

"Moreover, this signature is really a mere farce. Our own property is returned to us, that is all, and I shall not consider myself in the slightest degree bound by this. Who knows? These very thousands of pounds may help us to recover the throne." The Queen impetuously raised her head, looked him straight in the eyes for a moment, then shrugged her shoulders, saying:

"Do not make yourself out viler than you are. You know that when once you have signed—but no.—The truth is, you lack strength and fortitude, you desert your kingly post at the most perilous moment, when a new society, that will acknowledge neither God nor master, pursues with its hatred the representatives of divine right; makes the heavens tremble over their heads and the earth under their steps. The assassin's knife, bombs, bullets, all serve their purpose. Treachery and murder are on every side. In the midst of our pageantry or our festivities, the best of us as well as the worst, not one of us does not start if only a man steps forward out of the crowd. Hardly a petition that does not conceal a dagger. On leaving his palace what king is certain of returning alive? And this is the hour you choose to leave the field!"

'Ah! if fighting could do it," eagerly said Christian II. "But to struggle as we do against ridicule, against poverty, against all the petty meannesses of life, and feel that we only sink deeper every day—."

A ray of hope lit up her eyes:

"Is it true, would you fight? then listen."

Breathlessly, she related in a few rapid words, the expedition she and Elysée had been preparing for the last three months, by letters, proclamations and despatches, which Father Alphée, ever on the move, carried from one mountain village to the other; this time it was not to the nobility they appealed, but to the people; the muleteers, the porters of Ragusa, the market-gardeners of Breno, of la Brazza, the islanders who go to market in their feluccas, the nation which had remained faithful to the monarchical tradition, which was ready to rise and die for its king, on condition that he should lead them. Companies were forming, the watchword was already circulating, only the signal now remained to be given. The Queen hurling her words at Christian to route his weakness by a vigorous charge, had a cruel pang when she saw him shake his head, showing an indifference which was even greater than his discouragement. Perhaps at the bottom of his heart he was annoyed that the expedition should have been so far organized without his knowledge. But he did not believe in the feasibility of the plan. It would not be possible to advance into the country; they would be compelled to hold the islands, and devastate a beautiful country with very little chance of success; a second edition of the duc de Palma's adventure, a useless effusion of blood.

"No really, my dear Frédérique, you are led away by the fanaticism of your chaplain and the wild enthusiasm of that hot-headed Gascon. I also have my sources of information, far more reliable than yours. The truth is, that in Dalmatia as in many other countries, monarchy has had its day. They are tired of it, they will have no more of it."

"Oh! I know the coward who will have no more of it," said the Queen.

And she went out hurriedly, leaving Christian much surprised that the scene should have ended so abruptly. He hastily thrust the deed into his pocket, and prepared to go out in his turn, when Frédérique reappeared, accompanied this time by the little prince.

Roused out of his sleep and hurriedly dressed, Zara, who had passed from the hands of his nurse to those of the queen without a word having been uttered, opened wide his bewildered eyes under his auburn curls, but asked no questions; he remembered confusedly in his poor little dizzy head, similar awakenings for hasty flights, in the midst of pallid faces, and breathless exclamations. It was thus that he had acquired the habit of passive obedience; that he allowed himself to be led anywhere provided the queen called him in her grave and resolute voice, and held ready for his childish weakness the shelter of her tender arms and the support of her strong shoulder. She had said: "Come!" and he had come with confidence, surprised only at the surrounding silence, so different from those other stormy nights, with their visions of blood and flames, roar of cannon, and rattle of musketry.

He saw the king standing, no longer the careless good-natured father, who at times surprised him in his bed or crossed the school-room with an encouraging smile, but a stern father, whose expression of annoyance became more accentuated as he saw them enter. Frédérique, without uttering one word, led the child to the feet of Christian II. and abruptly kneeling, placed him before her, crossing his little fingers in her joined hands:

"The king will not listen to me, perhaps he will listen to you, Zara. Come say with me, 'Father.'" The timid voice repeated, "Father."

"My father! my king! I implore do not despoil your child; do not deprive him of the crown he is to wear one day. Remember that it is not your alone, it comes from afar, from God himself, who gave it six hundred year ago to the House of Illyria. God ha chosen me to be a king, father. It i my inheritance, my treasure, you hav no right to take it from me."

The little prince accompanied hi fervent murmur with the imploring looks of a supplicant; but Christia turned away his head, shrugged his shoulders, and furious though still polite, he muttered a few words between his teeth: "Exaggeration! most improper; turn the child's head." Then he tried to withdraw and gain the door. With one bound the queen was on her feet, caught sight of the table from which the parchment had disappeared, and comprehending at once that the infamous deed was signed, that the king had it in his possession, gave a despairing shriek:

"Christian!"

He continued to advance towards the door.

She made a step forward, picking up her dress as if to pursue him; then suddenly said:

"Well, be it so."

He stopped short, and turned round. She was standing before the open window, her foot upon the narrow stone balcony, with one arm clasping her son ready to bear him into death, the other extended menacingly towards the cowardly deserter. The moon lit up from without this dramatic group.

"To an operetta king, a queen of tragedy," she said stern and terrible. "If you do not burn this instant what you have just signed, and swear on the cross that it will never be repeated, your race is ended, crushed, wife and child, there, on the stones."

Such earnestness seemed to inspire her vibrating tone, her splendid figure bent towards the emptiness of space as though to spring, that the king, terrified, dashed forward to stop her.

"Frédérique!"

At the cry of his father, at the quiver of the arm that held him, the child—who was entirely out of the window—

thought that all was finished, that they were about to die. He never uttered a word nor a moan; was he not going with his mother! Only, his tiny hands clutched the queen's neck convulsively, and throwing back his head with his fair hair hanging down, the little victim closed his eyes before the appalling horror of the fall.

Christian could no longer resist. The resignation, the courage of this child, who of his future kingly duties already knew the first: to die well, overcame him. His heart was bursting. He threw upon the table the crumpled parchment which for a moment he had been nervously holding in his hand, and fell sobbing in an armchair. Frédérique, still suspicious, read the deed through from the first line to the very signature, then going up to a candle, she burned it till the flames scorched her fingers, shaking the ashes upon the table; she then left the room, carrying off her son, who was already falling asleep in her arms, in his heroically tragic attitude.

CHAPTER XXI

THE VIGIL

A MEAL is just over in the bric-à-brac dealer's parlour. Old Leemans, when alone, was accustomed to gobble up a crust at one end of the kitchen table, opposite to la Darnet, without either tablecloth or napkin; when he had company, as on this evening, the careful Auvergnate grumblingly took off the white covers of the furniture, put away the little squares of carpet, and set the table in front of the portrait of "Monsieur" in the little room, as peaceful and tidy as a *curé's* parlour, which for a few hours is filled with the odours of garlic, and resounds with vehement discussions carried on in the slang of low and sordid bartering.

Ever since the "grand stroke" has been in preparation, these dinners at the dealer's shop have been frequent.

It is advisable in affairs of this kind, where profits are shared, that the parties concerned in them should meet frequently and plan their schemes together; and nowhere else could it be done as securely as in the depths of this little street Eginhard—forgotten amid the remains of old Paris. Here, at any rate, talk might be as loud as they pleased, discussion an combination as lively as they fancied. They are drawing near the goal.

In a few days, nay! in a few hours, the deed of renunciation will be signed, and the affair which has already swallowed so much money, will in its turn begin to produce some. The certainty of success kindles the eyes and voices of the guests with a golden hue of joyousness, and makes the table-cloth look whiter, the wine taste better. A real wedding banquet, presided over by old Leemans and Pichery, his fidus Achates —a stiff barber's block of a head well anointed with pomatum, and appearing above a buckram stock, something military, yet not quite above-board about it, the air of an officer degraded from his rank. His profession: usurer in pictures, a new and complicated trade well suited to the art mania of our time. When a young fellow is completely cleared out, and has not a shilling left, he goes to Pichery, picture dealer, in his sumptuous gallery of the rue Lafitte.

"Have you got a Corot? A real good one?" he says. "I am quite cracked about that painter."

"Ah! Corot!" Pichery replies, closing his dead fish-like eyes with rapt admiration; then all at once, changing his tone: "I have the very thing for you," and rolling forward a great easel, he displays a very pretty Corot, a morning scene all tremulous with silvery mists and nymphs dancing under the willows. The fashionable youth puts up his eyeglass, pretends to admire and says:

"Good! very good! How much?"

"Two thousand pounds," says Pichery, without wincing. The other does not wince or blink either.

"At three months?"

"Three months, with security."

The fool puts his name to the bill, carries off the picture to his own rooms or those of his mistress, and during a whole day, gives himself the pleasure of boasting at the club and on the boulevard of the wonderful purchase he has made of a "stunning Corot." Next day, he sends his Corot to be put up at auction, and Pichery buys it again through old Leemans at four or five hundred pounds, its real value. It is usury, and at an exorbitant rate; but it is not illegal, and therefore without danger. Pichery, for his part, is not bound to know whether the amateur has bought in good faith or not. He sells his Corot very dear; has thoroughly "fleeced" his client; and he is within his rights: for the value of an artistic object is arbitrary and changeful. Moreover, he takes care only to deal in thoroughly authentic merchandize, warranted by father Leemans, who furnishes him into the bargain with the whole of his artistic vocabulary, wh ch sounds surprising enough in the mouth of this painted-up old soldier, who stands on the best of terms with the gilded youth and the whole frail population of the Quartier de l'Opéra, whose patronage he courts for the sake of his traffic.

On the other side of the patriarch Leemans, sat Séphora and her husband, their chairs and their glasses drawn close together as if they were two lovers. They see each other but rarely since the beginning of this affair! J. Tom Levis, who is supposed to be in London, lives shut up in his castellated villa at Courbevoie, spends his days in fishing with rod and line for lack of dupes to lay snares for, or occupies himself by playing atrocious practical jokes on the Sprichts. Séphora, watched more strictly than a Spanish queen, obliged to be ever in readiness for the king, at all hours in full war-paint and ceremony, leads the life of the select *demi-monde*—a life so filled with nothings and yet so empty, that these ladies nearly always live two together, in order to be able to endure the long, aimless drives, and the wearisome leisure. But the Comtesse de Spalato has not her equal in the town. She cannot associate with the mixed company of this borderland; nor will respectable women visit her, and Christian II. would not tolerate around her the fluttering crowd of idlers who fill the drawing-rooms frequented only by men. Thus she must remain for ever alone in her boudoirs, amid the painted ceilings, the mirrors garlanded with roses and cupids, that never reflect any other image than her own indolent figure, bored to death with all the insipid sentiment the king pours forth at her feet, like pastilles for sick headaches wasting slowly on golden burners. Ah! how quickly and joyfully would she not exchange this life of princely melancholy for the little low room in the rue Royale, with her merry-andrew beside her, executing his famous jig of the "Grand Strokes." She could hardly even find means to write to him, to keep him informed of the progress of the affairs and the turn it was taking.

Thus it was that she was very happy this evening, pressed close to him, excited him, stirred him up to amuse her! "Come, make me laugh." And indeed Tom bestirred himself well; but his mirth was forced and fell after each burst, gnawed by a tormenting thought that he did not avow, and that no one could have guessed. Tom Levis was jealous! He knew well there could be nothing as yet between Séphora and Christian, and that she was far too crafty and clever to give anything without value received; but the psychological moment was drawing near, and when once the paper was signed, execution could be no longer delayed. And our friend Tom was seized with scruples and qualms that were strange indeed in a man so completely free from all superstition or prejudice. Never had his wife appeared to him so charming, and the title of Comtesse seemed to make her eyes brighter, her features more dainty, while a coronet of pearls almost appeared to his fancy to rest on her bright hair. Evidently J. Tom Levis is not equal to his part, his shoulders are not broad enough for the business. A mere nothing would be enough to make him take back his wife and leave the whole affair stranded. But a feeling of shame holds him back, a fear of ridicule, and then so much money is invested in the speculation. The unlucky wretch struggles with himself, torn by these various scruples of which the Comtesse his wife would never have thought him capable; he affects the wildest gaiety, gesticulates with the dagger twisting in his heart all the while, keeps the table alive with excellent stories of the tricks of the trade, and finally puts old Leemans and even the glacial Pichery himself into such good spirits that they bring forth their best anecdotes, the finest mystifications of the unlucky amateur.

Here, among associates, pals, and in the free and easy atmosphere of after-dinner, anything may be related, all the under-currents of the auction-room, its bye-ways and pit-falls, the ring formed by the great dealers, rivals in appearance only, their greedy exchanges and traffic, the mysterious freemasonry that puts a real barrier of greasy collars and threadbare coats between the rare curio and the buyer's caprice, forcing him to ridiculously high prices. It was a tournament of cynical anecdotes, a tilting to show forth who was the most adroit, the most rascally of them all.

"Did I tell you the story of my Egyptian lantern and Mora?" asks father Leemans, sipping his coffee in little gulps; and for the hundredth time he begins to relate—like an old soldier his favourite campaign—the story of the lantern that a Levantine in difficulties sold to him for eighty pounds and that he sold again the same day for sixteen hundred pounds to the President of the Council, with a double commission—twenty pounds from the Levantine and two hundred pounds from the duke. But what constituted the charm

of the story were the ruses, the dodges, the way in which he had inflamed the fancy of the rich and vain buyer. "Yes, a fine piece, to be sure, but too dear—much too dear. I should really recommend you, Monsieur le Duc, to leave such a piece of folly to someone else. I feel sure that Sismondi! Ah! it is pretty work too, this chasing and this wrought chain." And the old fellow, excited by the laughter that shook the table, turns over the leaves of a little pocket-book, with dog's eared corners that he lays upon the table-cloth, and from whence he renews his inspiration, with a date, a number, an address. In it, all famous amateurs are classed, like heiresses of large fortunes on the books of the famous matrimonial agent, Monsieur Foy: with all their peculiarities and manias, dark or fair: those who require a little bullying, those who only believe an object valuable when its price is high, the sceptical amateur, the naïf amateur to whom you may say, as you sell him an utter fraud: "And you know you should never be persuaded to part with this." In itself this book was a small fortune.

"Look here, Tom," says Séphora to her husband in the wish to make him shine, "suppose you tell them that story of when you first arrived in Paris, you know, your first affair, in the rue Soufflot."

Tom needs no urging, pours himself out a little brandy to give himself a stronger voice, and relates how a dozen years or so ago, on returning from London, ruined and threadbare, one last half-crown in his pocket, he learned through an old comrade he met in an English tavern close to the station, that the matrimonial agencies were at that very moment occupied with a great affair, the marriage of Mademoiselle Beaujars, the daughter of a contractor, who had twelve millions of francs (four hundred and eighty thousand pounds) as her fortune, and had taken into her head that nothing would serve her but to marry some great nobleman. A magnificent commission was promised, and the bloodhounds were many on the scent. Tom, nothing disconcerted, entered a reading-room, turned over all the pedigrees of France, the almanac of Gotha, the directory Bottin, and finally discovered an ancient, very ancient family allied to the greatest houses, and lodged in the rue Soufflot. The disproportion of the title with the name of the street seemed to point to some blemish in the family or to impoverished fortunes. "On what floor does Monsieur le Marquis de X. live?" He sacrificed his last coin and obtained the necessary information from the concierge. Yes, in truth a title of great antiquity—a widower, a son just leaving Saint-Cyr, and a daughter of eighteen very well brought up. "Eighty pounds a year rent, including gas, water, and carpeted stairs," added the concierge, for whom all this added to the dignity of his tenant. "Just the thing for me," thought J. Tom Levis, and up he went, a trifle nervous all the same at the well-to-do look of the staircase— a statue at the entrance, armchairs on every landing, all the luxury of a modern house, with which strongly contrasted his own threadbare coat, his shoes that let the water in, and his very indelicate commission.

"Half-way up," continues the narrator, "I was tempted to go down again. But it seemed to me only plucky to make the attempt. I said to myself: 'You are sharp and cool, and have to earn your living, so here goes. Fortune favours the brave!' and up I went, two steps at a time. I was shown into a great drawing-room, of which the inventory could have been quickly taken. Two or three fine antiques, pompous remains of grandeur; a portrait by Largillière; but under all poverty was visible: the worn-out divan, the barely-stuffed chairs, the chimney-piece cold as its own marble. The master of the house appeared at last, a majestic old fellow in the best style—Samson in *Mademoiselle de la Seiglière.* 'You have a son, Monsieur le Marquis?' At the first words 'Samson' rises indignant; I name the figure, four hundred and eighty thousand pounds! and he calms down, seats himself, and we talk. He begins by owning to me that he has not a fortune equal to his name, twenty thousand francs (eight hundred pounds) at the utmost, and that he would not be sorry to have wherewithal to regild his escutcheon. The son would have a hundred thousand francs (four thousand pounds) on his wedding-day. 'Oh! Monsieur le Marquis, the name would be enough!' Then we fix the rate of my commission, and I hurry away in great haste, being expected at my office. That was good! my office! I did not even know where I should sleep that night. But at the door the old fellow drew me back, and said in a confidential tone: 'Come now! you seem to me a clever fellow. I have something else to propose to you. You ought to find me a husband for my daughter as well. She has no fortune; for to tell the truth, I exaggerated just now in speaking of an income of eight hundred a year.

Take off the largest half. I have, however, a title of Count of the Holy Roman Empire at my disposal for my son-in-law. And, moreover, if he is in the army, my influence and relationship with the Minister of War will enable me to ensure his speedy promotion and advancement.' When I had finished taking my notes: 'Rely upon me, Monsieur le Marquis,' said I and was about to go, when a hand was laid heavily upon my shoulder. I turned round: 'Samson' was looking at me, and laughing with a comical air. 'And then there is myself,' said he. 'What you, Monsieur le Marquis!' 'Yes, indeed; I am not so totally played out, and if I could find a good opportunity——.' He ended by confessing to me that he was overwhelmed with debts, and not a penny to pay them with. 'By Jove! my dear Monsieur Tom, if you can unearth me some good lady in business, owning fair savings, old maid or widow, send her to me, money-bag and all; I will make a marquise of her.' When I left that room, my education was finished. I understood all that could be made out of Parisian society; and the Levis agency was virtually founded."

The story was a marvel narrated or rather acted, by Tom Levis. He rose, sat down again, imitated the majestic air of the old nobleman, with its touch of cynical Bohemianism, and the way in which he spread his handkerchief over one knee before crossing his legs, and the disclosure made in three confessions of the real poverty of his resources. It might have been a scene from the *Neveu de Rameau*, only a Rameau's nephew of the 19th century, without powder, grace, or violin, and with something hard and fierce in the intonation of this English bulldog merged in the jesting loafer of the faubourgs. The others laughed, enjoyed the joke, and drew from Tom's story reflections both philosophical and cynical.

"D'ye see, my dears," said old Leemans, "if dealers could agree among themselves, they would be the masters of the world. Every mortal thing is sold sooner or later, now-a-days. Everything must come to us in time, must pass through our hands, leaving some of its substance behind. Only to think of all the business done for the last forty years in this hole of a shop in the rue Eginhard—of all I have melted, sold, exchanged, patched up. The only thing that had never passed through my hands was a crown, and now I have got that." He rose, glass in hand, with eyes fiercely glittering: "Jobbing for ever, my boys!"

In the background, la Darnet's black Cantal headgear nodded attentively, watching all, listening to everything, drinking in information on bartering and haggling: for she hoped to establish a business for herself whenever "Monsieur" should die, and deal in curiosities on her own account.

Suddenly the cracked door-bell was violently agitated, wheezing like a cold of long standing. Everyone started. Who could it be at such an hour?

"It is Lebeau," said the old father. "It can be no one else."

Loud exclamations welcomed the valet, who had not been among them for some time, and who now entered with set teeth, pale and haggard, looking knocked up and in the worst of tempers.

"Sit there, old chap," said Leemans.

making room for him between himself and his daughter.

"The deuce!" said Lebeau, glancing at their flushed faces, at the table, and remains of the dinner. "You seem to be amusing yourselves famously here."

The observation, and the funereal tone in which it was made, caused them all to look uneasily at each other.

Certainly they are amusing themselves, having great fun. And why not! why should they be melancholy?

"What! you don't know? When did you last see the king then, comtesse?"

"Why this morning, yesterday, every day!"

"And he said nothing to you of the terrible row there has been?"

Then, in a few words he described the scene, the burnt parchment, the affair thus reduced to ashes.

"Ah! the wretch, I am done!" said Séphora.

Tom with great uneasiness gazed into the depths of his wife's eyes. Had she by any chance been imprudently weak? But the lady was in no humour to give explanations, being wholly given over to her rage and indignation against Christian, who for the last week had been entangling himself in a labyrinth of lies to explain how it was that the act of abdication was not yet signed.

Oh! coward! coward and liar! But why had not Lebeau warned them?

"Ah! indeed why?" said the valet with his hideous smile. "Simply because I could not. For the last ten days I have been running hither and thither, five hundred leagues without breathing time, without drawing rein. Not even the chance to write a letter, for I was watched incessantly by an awful monk, a Franciscan Father, who

had the scent of a wild beast, and fingered a dagger like a bandit. He watched my every movement, never took his eye off me for a moment, under the pretext that he did not know enough French to get about alone and make himself understood. The truth is, they suspect me at Saint-Mandé, and have taken advantage of my absence to work a big thing."

"What is it?" asked all eyes.

"An expedition in Dalmatia, I fancy. It is that demon of a Gascon who has worked them up to it. Oh! I was right when I said at the very first that we ought to have got rid of that fellow to begin with."

It was in vain they had tried to hide what was going on from the valet; he had for some time scented preparations in the wind—letters leaving at all hours, mysterious councils frequently held. One day, opening an album of watercolour sketches, which that little fool the Princesse de Rosen had left about, he had seen designs of uniforms, various costumes: *Illyrian Volunteers, Dragoons of the Faith, Blue Garibaldians, Cuirassiers of the Divine Right.* Another day, he overheard a grave discussion between Madame de Silvis and the princess on the shape of the cockades. From all this, from fragments of words he concluded some great expedition was in contemplation; and the journey he had been made to take had in all probability something to do with it.

The little dark man, a sort of hunchback, whom he had been sent to fetch from the mountains of Navarre, must be some great chief destined to lead the army under the orders of the king.

"What! The king goes too?" cried

father Leemans with a contemptuous glance towards his daughter.

A confused torrent of words followed this exclamation.

"And how about our money?"

"And the bills he has signed?"

"It is a shame."

"It is a theft."

And as, nowadays, politics represent the famous dish of Æsop, and are mixed in everything, Pichery, very Imperialist, stiff as his own buckram stock, apostrophizes the Republic:

"Under the Empire such a menace to the tranquillity of a neighbouring state could never have been prepared."

"Certainly," says Tom Levis, gravely, "you may be sure, if this were known at the Presidency, it would not be allowed. We must give notice, we must bestir ourselves."

"Yes, I had thought of that," replied Lebeau; "unfortunately I know nothing precise, nothing for certain. They would not listen to me. And then our people up there are on their guard, all their precautions are taken to turn aside suspicion. For instance, this evening is the Queen's birthday. There is to be a great *fête* at the Rosen's mansion. Not much use going to tell the authorities that all those dancers are busy conspiring and preparing for battle! All the same, there is something unusual about this ball."

Then only did they remark that the valet was in evening dress, thin shoes, white tie; he had the management of the refreshment tables at the ball, and must return as quickly as possible to the Ile-Saint-Louis. Suddenly the Comtesse, who had been thinking deeply for a few moments, said:

"Look here, Lebeau, if the king does go, you would know, would not you? You would be called if only to pack his portmanteau. Well, let me know, only an hour beforehand, and I swear to you, the expedition shall not come off."

She said this in her most tranquil voice, with a slow but decided firmness. And while J. Tom Levis dreamily asked himself by what means Séphora would prevent the king from starting; while the other associates, all crestfallen, were calculating what the failure of the affair would cost them, Master Lebeau, returning to his ball, hastened along on the points of his pumps through the labyrinth of little dark streets, with old-fashioned roofs and escutcheoned doors, that composed this quarter, which in the last century was aristocratic, but is now transformed by workshops and manufactories; and tremulous all day from the passage of heavy drags and the constant movement of the swarming and wretched population, resumes at night its curious appearance of a dead city.

CHAPTER XXII

THE FETE

THE *fête* could be heard and seen from afar in the summer night, and sent over both banks of the Seine widespread echoes of sound, while the lights streamed forth like the red and misty glare of a conflagration from that extreme point of the island which, jutting out into mid-stream, seems to be the rounded and lofty poop of some huge vessel at anchor. On a nearer approach could be distinguished the tall windows gleaming beneath their hangings, the myriad-coloured lights in girandoles atached to the shrubs and venerable trees of the garden, and on the Quai d'Anjou, generally asleep at this hour, the lamps of the carriages pierced the darkness with their little motionless beacons. Since Herbert's marriage, the Rosen's mansion had not witnessed a similar festivity, and that now going on was even more splendid, more overflowing, than the former; all the doors and windows stood open to the splendour of the starry night.

The ground floor was formed of a long gallery of saloons opening one out of the other; lofty as a cathedral, and adorned with paintings and antique gilding; chandeliers of Dutch and Venetian make and lanterns of mosques hung from the ceilings and shed their light upon strange decorations; hangings shimmering with gleams of red and green gold; heavy shrines of massive silver, deeply carved ivories set in frames, old mirrors with blackened faces, reliquaries, standards, treasures from Montenegro and Herzegovina that Parisian taste had known how to assemble and group together without anything appearing too striking or barbaric. The orchestra was ranged upon the tribune of an ancient oratory that called to mind that of Chenonceaux, and was surrounded by streamers that sheltered armchairs reserved for the king and queen; and in contrast with these relics of the past, these magnificent antiques reflected on every side which would have delighted the heart of father Leemans, circled and fluttered the whirlwind of the modern waltz, seductive and dreamy, a vision of long embroidered trains, of fixed and brilliant eyes flashing amid the mist of fluffy tresses, passing and repassing

like a challenge of youth—a delicate vision of fair beauty and dark creamy pallor. Every now and again, out of this circling net-work of dances, of this medley of silken stuffs that adds a coquettish and mysterious murmur to the music of a ball-room, a couple would detach themselves, and stepping out through the lofty French window would receive upon their receding heads, the white glare of the illuminated pediment where the Queen's cipher figured in flaming gas, and advancing through the alleys of the garden, they would continue with some hesitation, caused by the increasing distance from the music, the rhythm of the dance, and finish their waltz in a cadenced step, an harmonious walk among the great balmy clumps of magnolias and roses. Indeed, putting aside the richness and strangeness of the setting, and a few foreign women with wild locks, and the indolent supple movements peculiar to Slavonians, it seemed at first sight to be only one of those fashionable mixed entertainments such as the Faubourg Saint-Germain, represented at the Rosen's mansion by its most ancient and pompous names, sometimes gives in its old gardens in the rue de l'Université, where the dance passes from waxed floors to green lawns, where black coats may be found enlivened by light grey trousers—open air *fêtes* fit for summer weather—freer, and more exuberant in gaiety than others.

In his bedroom on the second floor the old duke, a martyr for a week past to an attack of sciatica, listened to the echoes of his ball, and smothered between his blankets the exclamations of pain and the barrack-room objurgations that escaped him, on the ironic cruelty of the illness that pinned him to his bed on such a day, making it impossible for him to join all this assemblage of youth about to start on the morrow. The word had been given, the posts in the struggle fixed, and this ball was a farewell, a kind of bravado, a defiance offered to the chances of war, at the same time a precaution against the curiosity of the French police. If the duke could not accompany the volunteers, he had the consolation of reflecting that his son Herbert would take part in the affair, and his good gold pieces as well, for their Majesties had graciously permitted him to defray the cost of the expedition. On his bed, mixed with ordnance maps and strategical plans, were strewn bills for stores, cases of guns, boots, blankets, provisions, all of which he carefully checked, with terrible frowns and twistings of his moustache; the heroic feelings of the royalist warring with his parsimonious niggardly instincts. Sometimes a number or a fact was wanting; then he sent for Herbert—a pretext to keep at his side for a few minutes the great son who was to leave him to-morrow for the first time, whom he would perhaps never see again, and for whom he experienced an immense affection, ill-concealed beneath a stately manner and chilly silence. But the prince could not remain long, being in haste to go down again to do the honours of the house, and above all to lose as little as possible of the brief hours he could still pass in the society of his beloved Colette. Standing at his side in the first saloon, she helped him to receive his father's guests, prettier and more elegant than ever in her close-fitting dress, draped with the antique lace of

a Greek alb, of which the creamy tint well set off her delicate beauty, marked this evening by an almost serious air of mystery. It gave repose to her features, depth to her eyes, bringing them to the hue of the blue cockade displayed among her curls beneath a diamond aigrette. Hush! low be it spoken, a cockade for an Illyrian volunteer, a pattern adopted for the expedition and designed by the princess. She had not been wanting in activity any more than the rest during the last three months, the dear little soul. Copying proclamations, carrying them secretly to the convent of the Franciscans, designing costumes and banners, keeping the police —whom she believed to be ever at her heels—off the scent, thus inspired by her readings at the *Sacré-Cœur* did she play her *rôle* as a great royalist lady. One detail only was wanting in this programme of Vendean brigandage; she could not start with the others or follow her Herbert. For now, it was Herbert, nothing but Herbert; by a beautiful provision of nature she thought no more of the other than of the unfortunate marmoset, so cruelly crushed on the neighbouring pavement. The joy of putting on a man's costume, and of wearing miniature jack-boots was denied to Colette for two reasons one the duty that kept her at the queen's side, the other, quite personal and intimate, had been whispered the evening before into the aide-de-camp's ear Yes! if it was not a delusion, in a space of time easily calculated from the day of the academic *séance*, the race of Rosen would be increased by one little representative the more, and it was out of the question to expose so dear and precious a hope to the fatigues of an expedition that could not be expected to terminate without some few rough and bloody sword-thrusts, any more than it was advisable to take a turn of waltz round the splendid rooms. Here were many secrets for the little woman to keep, and notwithstanding the mystery she preserved in speech, her delightfully tell-tale eyes and the languid manner in which she leant on Herbert's arm, betrayed it all without an effort on her part.

Suddenly the orchestra was silent, the dance stopped; everyone stood up for the entry of Christian and Frédérique. They have crossed the three saloons resplendent with national treasures, where the queen may read her cypher everywhere, arranged in flowers, lights, jewels, and see on all sides the souvenirs of her country and its glories; and now they stop at the entrance to the garden. Never had the monarchy been represented more bravely, with greater brilliance; truly a couple to imprint on the coinage of a nation, on the pediment of a dynasty. The queen in particular was magnificent, looking younger by ten years in white dress, and round her neck as her only jewel a magnificent necklace of amber, whence hung a cross. Blessed and presented by the Pope, this necklace had its legend, related in whispers by the faithful. Frédérique had worn all through the siege of Ragusa; twice it had been lost and miraculously found during sorties, under fire. She held a superstition about it herself, a keenly vow was associated with it, and she wore it without troubling herself to the charming effect these pearls of mellow and transparent gold produced so near to her tresses, of which they seemed to catch a reflection.

While the sovereigns stood here radiant, admiring the fête and the garden with its fairy illuminations, three notes sounded from a violin concealed amid a clump of rhododendrons, three wild, strange, soul-stirring notes. Every drop of Slav blood in the assembly quivered and leapt at the sound of its national *guzlas*, with their long necks peeping through the dark verdure. They began with a prelude full of movement, murmuring, humming, ringing with the gradually approaching overflow of far-off waves, sonorous in their advance as they rise and spread. It was like some heavy cloud, full of electricity, that from time to time was torn into zigzag flashes by the keenest note of the bow, and from whence presently poured forth the stormy, voluptuous, heroic national air, hymn and dance at one and the same time; that air of Rodoïtza, which in its country is part of every fête, of every battle, and well represents the two-fold character of its ancient legend: Rodoïtza, fallen into the hands of the Turks, simulates death to escape. They light fire on his chest, the hero stirs not. They place a serpent in his bosom, they drive nails beneath his finger-nails, he preserves a stone-like immobility. Then they bring Haïkouna, the finest, most lovely girl in Zara, who begins to dance while singing the Illyrian national air. At the first bars, when Rodoïtza hears the sequins of the dancer's necklace chink, and the fringes of her sash rattle and shake, he smiles, opens his eyes, and would be lost were it not that the dancer approaching him, in one bound, throws over his face whose animation will betray him, the silken kerchief with which she accentuates and marks the rhythm of her dance. Thus the hero was saved, and this is why for two hundred years the national air of Illyria is called the Rodoïtza march.

Hearing it thus, beneath the skies of exile, all the Illyrians, both men and women, turned pale with emotion. This cry from the *guzlas* with a soft accompaniment from the orchestra in the background within the house, like a murmuring of waters above which resounds the shrill cry of the stormy-petrel, was as the voice of the country itself, overflowing with memories and tears, regrets and unspoken hopes. The huge bows, heavy and shaped like the bow of the archer, were not drawn across commonplace strings, but upon nerves strained to breaking-point, upon the most delicately vibrating and responsive fibres. These young men of proud and hardy temperament, with the stature and figure of heroes, all feel capable of the indomitable courage of Rodoïtza, who thought himself well paid by a woman's love; these handsome Dalmatians, all tall as Haïkouna, have, like her, a tender spot in their hearts for heroes. And the elders, in thinking of the far-distant country; the mothers, as they watched their sons,—all could have sobbed; and all, but for the presence of the king and queen, would have joined their voices to the shrill and strident cry that the guzla-players sent forth with all the force of their lungs as they finished playing, amid a last clash of chords that rose with it towards the stars.

Directly afterwards, dancing was resumed with a vigour and spirit surprising in circles where to amuse oneself is a polite fiction. Decidedly, as Lebeau had said, there was something unusual about this *fête*. Something feverish, passionate, full of ardour, expressed in the closer pressure of the dancers as they flew and crossed, even the cadence of the waltzes and mazurkas, in which sometimes came a note like the clink of stirrups and spurs. Towards the end of most balls, when morning begins to shine through the windows, the last hour of pleasure is marked by this eager haste, these drugged languors. But here the ball had barely begun, and already all hands burned within the gloves that covered them, all hearts beat beneath the flowers of the bodice or the diamonds of the orders; and when a couple passed by, intoxicated by love and the rhythm of the dance, long interested glances followed them with tender and softened smiles. And, indeed, everyone knew that all these fine young men,—scions of Illyrian nobility exiled in company with their prince, French nobility always ready to shed its blood in a good cause—were to start at sunrise on a venturesome and perilous expedition. Even in case of victory, how many of these proud young fellows, who have enlisted without taking count of their numbers, will return? How many in a week's time will be biting the dust, laid low on the mountain sides while the maddening tune of the last mazurka still rings in their ears, mingling with the confused throbbing of the fast ebbing blood! It is the approach of danger that adds to the spirit of the ball the anxiety of a night under arms brings tears and lightning glances shine in the eyes, with so much languor and so much audacity. What can woman refuse to him who is leaving her perhaps for speedy death? And this said death, hovering over all, the rustle of whose wings can be heard almost touching them in the swell of the violins, how it hastens confessions and draws closer the embrace! Light and fugitive loves, chance meeting of ephemeræ crossing the same sunbeam! Perhaps they have never met before, doubtless will never meet again; yet here are two hearts fallen under the spell. A few, the more haughty, try to smile notwithstanding their emotion; but how much sweetness is there beneath this irony. And all this crowd turns and turns, each couple fancying itself alone, shut off from the rest, bewildered amid the magic entanglement of a waltz by Brahms or a mazurka of Chopin's.

Not less moved than the rest was Méraut, in whom the music of the guzlas, by turns of dreamy softness or wild energy, awoke the adventurous gipsy spirit that lies dormant in the depths of all these temperaments of the sunny south, a wild desire to rush away through unfamiliar ways towards light, adventures, battles, to do some valiant and brave action for which women would admire him. He who never danced, and would not have known any better how to fight, was possessed by the witchery of this heroic ball; and to reflect that all these youths were about to start to give their blood, to run the gauntlet of glorious and dangerous enterprise while he remained behind with the old men, the women and children, to think that having organized his crusade he must see it set forth without him, all this caused him an inexpressible sadness and discomfort. The

thought that had conceived felt shame before the action that executed. And perhaps what contributed something to this discouragement, this wish for death inspired by the Slav songs and dances, was the radiant pride of Frédérique as she leant on Christian's arm. How self-evident was her happiness on finding again the king and warrior in her husband! Haïkouna, Haïkouna! at the ring and clatter of arms you can forget all, pardon all—treasons and lies alike! What you love above all things is physical bravery, it is to that you will always throw the handkerchief hot with your tears and the delicate perfume of your own fair face. And while he thus mourned within himself, Haïkouna, perceiving in a corner of the drawing-room the poet's wide brow over which fell in unfashionable style the abundant and rebellious locks, Haïkouna smiled and made a sign to him to approach. One might suppose she had guessed the cause of his sadness.

"What a charming fête, Monsieur Méraut."

Then lowering her voice, she added:

"I owe even this to you. But we owe you so much, it is difficult to know how to thank you."

It was he indeed whose robust and vivifying faith had breathed upon all these extinct embers, brought back hope to despair, and prepared the rising by which they were to profit on the morrow. The queen did not forget it, and there was no one in the illustrious assembly to whom she would have spoken in the presence of all, with that kindly deference, those glances of gratitude and gentleness, in the centre of the respectful circle traced around the sovereigns. But Christian II. drew near, and offering his arm to Frédérique: "The Marquis de Hezeta is here," he said to Elysée. "Have you seen him?" "I do not know him, Sire." "He declares, however, that you are very old friends. Stay, here he is."

This Marquis de Hezeta was the chief who in the absence of the old General de Rosen was to command the expedition. He had shown in the last bold coup of the Duc de Palma's astounding qualities as commander of an army corps, and had he been listened to, the skirmish would never have ended so shamefully and pitiably. When he saw his efforts were in vain and that the pretender himself gave the example and signal for flight, the *cabecilla*, overcome with disappointment and misanthropy, had fled to the depths of the Basque mountains and lived far from the rumour of childish conspiracies, of false hopes, of sword-thrusts in water, that wasted his moral forces. He wished to die obscurely in his own country, but was tempted once more to the game of adventure by the alluring royalism of Father Alphée and Christian II.'s renown for bravery. High rank and ancient family, a romantic existence composed of exile and persecution, chequered with great and startling *coups de main* and the habitual practice of the cruelties of a fanatic, all conspired to surround the Marquis José Maria de Hazeta with an almost legendary interest and to make him the chief personage of the evening.

"How do you do, Ely?" said he, advancing towards Elysée with outstretched hand, and calling him by his childhood's name—that by which he was known in the *enclos de Rey*. "Yes, it is I. Your old schoolmaster, Monsieur Papel."

The evening-dress, covered with orders and crosses, and the white cravat made no change in him, nor yet the twenty years that had passed over the huge dwarf's head, so burnt by the smoke of battle and the keen weather of his mountain home, that the great vein of the forehead, frightful and characteristic as it was, could scarcely be seen. With it seemed to have faded the royalist fervour, as if the *cabecilla* had left in the crown of the Basque biretta, thrown into a torrent at the end of the campaign, a portion of his ancient beliefs, of the illusions of his youth.

Elysée was strangely surprised to hear the voice of his old master, he who had made him what he was.

"You see my little Ely——"

Little Ely was a good two feet taller than his old master, and his locks were plentifully sprinkled with grey.

"It is all over; there are no more kings. The principle exists still, but the men are wanting. Not one of these dismounted horsemen is capable of getting into the saddle again; not one really wishes it. Ah! what I have seen, what I have seen, during the war!"

A gory mist seemed to float round his head, and filled his fixed and stony eyes, which, growing larger and larger, appeared to gaze upon visions of shame, cowardice, and treasons.

"But all kings are not alike," protested Méraut, "and I am sure that Christian——"

"Yours is worth no more than ours—a child, a mere dabbler. Not a idea, not a vestige of will in those pleasure-loving eyes. Only look at him!"

He indicated the king, who just then waltzed into the saloon, his little round head bent with swimming eyes over the bare shoulder of his partner, that his lip seemed on the point of touching. In the increasing animation of the ball the couple passed without noticing them, so close that they almost felt the warmth of their panting breath; and as the gallery filled rapidly to watch Christian II. dance—for he was the best waltzer in his kingdom—Hezeta and Méraut took refuge in one of the deep recesses of the great open windows overlooking the Quai d'Anjou. There they remained a long time, half-way between the noise and commotion of the ball and the refreshing darkness, the calm silence of the night.

"Kings no longer believe in themselves; kings no longer have any strength of will. Why should we give ourselves any trouble about them?" said the Spaniard, gloomily.

"You no longer have faith in them, and yet you go!"

"Yes, I go."

"Without hope?"

"One only. That of breaking my head, my poor head, that I no longer know where to lay."

"And the king?"

"Oh! that fellow! I am quite easy about him!"

Did he mean to say that Christian II. was not yet in the saddle, and that like his cousin, the Duke of Palma, he would always be sure of returning safe and sound from the battle? He did not explain himself further.

Around them the ball continued to whirl in mad circlings, but Elysée now looked at it through the discouraged vision of his old master and his own disillusions. He felt a boundless pity for all this valiant troop of youths, who were so gaily preparing to fight under chiefs devoid of faith in their undertaking; and already the *fête*, its confused bustle, its shaded lights, seemed to him to disappear in the smoke of the battlefield, the vast scuffle of disaster in which the unknown dead are gathered up. Once, for a moment, to escape this sinister vision, he leant upon the window-sill, turning towards the deserted quay, whereon the palace threw lengthened squares of light that stretched away to the Seine. And the water, as he listened to it tossing and tumultuous at this point of the island, mingled the noise of its currents, its furious shocks against the arches of the bridges, with the sighs of the violins, the thrilling cry of the guzlas; and sometimes bounded onwards with short gasping sounds, like the sobs of an afflicted spirit; and sometimes spread itself forward in great exhaustive waves, like the blood welling from a wide-open wound.

CHAPTER XXIII

THE NIGHT TRAIN

"WE start this evening at eleven o'clock from the Gare de Lyons. Destination unknown. Probably Cette, Nice, or Marseilles. Do as you think best."

When this note, rapidly pencilled by Lebeau, reached the Rue de Messine, the Comtesse de Spalato, fresh, sweet, and supple, had just left her bath, and was busy in her room and her boudoir, watering and tending her flowers and hothouse plants, with light Suède gloves drawn up to the elbow, for this her daily walk through her artificial garden. She was not in any degree affected by the news, but paused a moment to reflect, in the softened light admitted through the lowered blinds, and with a little decided gesture, a shrug of her shoulders which meant: "Pooh, who wants the end takes the means;" she rang for her maid that she might be ready to receive the king.

"What dress does madame wish to put on?"

Madame threw an inquiring glance at her mirror.

"None," she said: "I will remain as I am."

Nothing, indeed. could be more becoming than the long clinging pale flannel robe with its soft pleats, the large neckerchief crossed on her bosom and tied behind her waist, and the curly tresses of her black hair, twisted and raised high in heavy coils on her head, revealing the curve of her neck and the line of her shoulders, which were evidently of a darker hue than her face,— of the warm, smooth tint of amber.

She thought, with good reason, that no amount of dressing could equal this simple négligée, that set off the ingenuous, childlike air which the king liked so well in her; but this obliged her to breakfast in her room, for she could not go down into the dining-room in such a costume. She had put her household on an eminently respectable footing; it was no longer the fanciful Bohemian style of Courbevoie. After breakfast, she settled herself in her boudoir, from which a covered verandah gave a prolonged view of the avenue, and began her watch for the king, peaceably seated under the rosy-tinted blinds, just as in former days she had sat at the window of the "family hotel." Christian never visited her before two, but from that moment began an anguish of waiting quite new to this placid nature; an expectation, which was no more at first than the tremor of water that is about to boil, but which presently becomes fevered, agitated, persecuting. Hardly any carriages passed at this hour on the quiet avenue, with its double rows of plane-trees bathed in sunlight, and of new mansions coming to an end at the gilded gates, and sparkling lamp-posts of the Parc Monceaux. At every sound of wheels, Séphora drew aside the blind to look out, and disappointment or each new hope was aggravated by the luxurious serenity and provincial calm of the avenue.

What could have happened? Would he really leave without seeing her?

She sought for reasons, for pretexts; but expectation is a state that keeps the whole being in suspense; our very ideas float undecided, and remain as unfinished as the words that hover or stammering lips. The Comtesse endured this torment, the sickly faintness in which the nerves are in turn strained and relaxed. Once more she raised the rose-tinted blind. A soft breeze was rustling in the green tufts of the branches, a fresh air rose from the avenue, which was washed in sharp and rapid jets by the water-carts, interrupted at every moment by the passing carriages, now more numerous, going up towards the Bois de Boulogne for the five o'clock drive. She now began to be seriously alarmed at the desertion of the king. and sent off two letters, one addressed to the house of Prince d'Axel, the other to the club. Then she dressed herself, for she could not remain till evening in the costume of a little girl who has just left her bath; and she resumed her walk from her room to her boudoir, to her dressing-room, and soon throughout the whole house, in her attempt to baffle the torment of waiting by dint of agitation.

It was not a mere bijou residence the Spalato had bought, nor one of those huge mansions that millionaire financiers have crowded into the aristocratic new quarters of the Parisian West end, but an artistic home worthy of the names borne by the surrounding streets: Murillo, Velasquez, Van Dyck; and very unlike its neighbours from the top of its façade to the knocker on the door. Built by Comte Fotnicki for his mistress, an ugly woman to whom he every day presented a thousand franc note (forty pounds) which he placed folded in four on the marble toilet-table, this marvellous dwelling, had been sold for eighty thousand pounds with all its artistic furniture at the death of the rich Pole, who had left no will, and Séphora had purchased it with all its treasures.

The Comtesse Spalato descends the massive staircase of sculptured wood fit to support a coach and pair, which gives to the severe beauty of the lady the dark background of a Dutch picture; she enters the reception rooms of the ground floor: the first is called the Dresden china-room, a small Louis XV. room, which contains an exquisite collection of enamelled vases and statuettes in the fragile style of the 18th century, looking as if it were kneaded by the rosy finger-tips of the king's favourites and animated by the fascination of their smile; the second, called the Ivory room, where, within glass cases lined with crimson, collections of Chinese carved ivories are displayed, representing human figures, trees laden with jewelled fruits, fishes with eyes of jade, by the side of ivory crucifixes of the middle ages with passionately mournful expression of face, and red wax imitation of blood looking like a stain on the pallor of a human skin; the third, lighted up like a studio and hung with Cordova leather, is as yet incomplete and awaits father Leemans' finishing touch.

The heart of the *bric-à-brac* dealer's daughter habitually exults in the midst of these her precious possessions, made more precious in her eyes by the wonderful bargain she had made, but to-day she goes and comes without looking at them; she sees nothing, for her thoughts are far away, lost amid a thousand irritating reflections. What! he would leave her thus. Did he not love her then? she who thought she had so successfully caught and captivated him.

The footman returns. No news of the king. He has not been seen anywhere That was just like Christian. Aware of his own weakness he had fled. A fit of uncontrollable rage for a moment seizes hold of the woman and breaks down her wonderful self-control.

She would have dashed to pieces all that surrounds her in an instant if her long habit of traffic, which mentally labelled the price of every separate article, did not restrain her. Plunged in an arm-chair, while the closing day draws its veil over her newly-acquired riches, she sees them all vanish and disappear together with her colossal dreams of fortune. Suddenly the door opens, and the servant announces: "Dinner is on the table."

She must sit at her table alone in the majestic dining-room, its light panels filled with portraits by Franz Hals valued at thirty-two thousand pounds, pale and solemn figures in their stiff ruffles, not so solemn, however, as the butler in his white cravat, who carves at the side-table the dishes that are handed to the Comtesse by two impassive flunkeys in gorgeous livery. The irony of this pompous service, contrasting with the solitude and desertion that menace Madame de Spalato, wrings her heart with vexation; it might even be thought that the servants suspect something, for they accentuate more than usual the ceremonious attitude of disdain with which they wait on her till she has finished, standing motionless and severe, like a photographer's assistant after having fixed the customer in front of the camera. Little by little, however, the deserted woman cheers up and returns to her normal condition. No, she will not allow herself to be cast off like this. Not that she cares for the king. But the scheme, the grand stroke, the good opinion of her associates, all her self-love is at stake. Her mind is soon made up! She goes to her room, writes a letter to Tom; then, while the servants in the basement are dining and gossiping about the lonely and agitated day their mistress has spent, the Comtesse with her clever little hands prepares a travelling-bag that has often made the journey to and fro between the agency and Cour-

bevoie, throws a grey woollen cloak over her shoulders as a protection against the cold night air, and furtively quits her palace, going off in the direction of the nearest cabstand on foot, her little bag in her hand, just like a lady's-companion who has been dismissed from her place.

On his side, Christian II. had passed a no less anxious day. He had, with the queen, remained very late at the ball, and had awoke with his head and heart re-echoing with the heroic strains of the guzlas. The preparations for the expedition, his arms to look over as well as the costume of lieutenant-general that he had not put on since Ragusa, all this took up his time till eleven o'clock, under the watchful and anxious gaze of the perplexed Lebeau, who did not dare to hazard too many questions or insinuations. At eleven the court assembled to assist at a low mass said by Father Alphée in the drawing-room, transformed into a chapel for the occasion, the mantelpiece being turned into an altar and its velvet draperies covered over by an embroidered altar-cloth. The Rosens were absent, the old duke still in bed, and the princess having accompanied Herbert as far as the station, whence he had started with some young men. Hezeta was to follow by the next train, and the little band was thus to leave in detachments throughout the day in order not to attract attention. This secret mass, that recalled the former troubled times, the fanatical face of the monk, the martial energy of his voice and gesture, all seemed to call up a mingled smell of incense and powder—a religious ceremony solemnized by the approach of battle.

All these mixed emotions cast a gloom over the breakfast-table, although the king affected a certain coquet y in leaving nothing but pleasant recollections behind him, and adopted a respectfully tender attitude towards the queen, which, however, was received with a suspicious coolness by Frédérique. The child glanced timidly from one to the other, for the terrible scene of that other night haunted his young memory, and gave him a nervous intuition above his age. The Marquise de Silvis heaved beforehand deep sighs of farewell. As for Elysée, all his faith had returned, and he could not contain his joy as he thought of the counter-revolution he had so long dreamed of, made by the people; of the insurrection which would break open the gates of a palace to reinstate a king. For him success was not doubtful. Christian, however, did not feel the same confidence; but except for a certain feeling of uneasiness that accompanies every departure, when a sudden sensation of solitude is cast over all, the premature separation from the beings and surroundings habitual to every-day life, he felt no sinister apprehensions, rather a sort of release from a false position, oppressed as he was by pecuniary embarrassments and debts of honour. In case of victory, the civil list would settle everything. Defeat, on the contrary, would bring with it a general collapse; death, a bullet through the head while facing his enemies! He thought of this, as a definite solution for his monetary and love affairs, and his careless indifference did not jar too much with the preoccupations of the queen, and the enthusiasm of Elysée. However, while they were talking together, all three in the garden, a footman happened to pass by.

"Tell Samy to bring the carriage round," ordered Christian. Frédérique started.

"You are going out?" she inquired.

"Yes, I think it more prudent," he replied. "Yesterday's ball must have set all Paris talking. I must show myself, be seen at the club, on the boulevards. Oh! I shall return and dine with you."

He ran up the steps, joyous and free, like a schoolboy leaving the class-room.

"I shall be anxious till he is gone!" said the queen; and Méraut, knowing as much as she did, could not find a word of encouragement.

The king had, nevertheless, taken strong resolutions. During mass, he had vowed to himself that he would not see Séphora again, knowing well that if she chose to detain him, if she passed her arms round his neck, he would be powerless to leave her. In all good faith he had himself driven to the club, found there some bald-pates absorbed in silent whist, or slumbering majestically round the great library table. Everything looked deserted and dead; the more so, that play had run high on the previous night. In the morning, as the whole set of clubmen were leaving H.H. Prince d'Axel at their head, a troop of she-asses passed in front of the club, trotting and jingling their bells. Monseigneur had sent for the driver, and the whole party, after having drank the warm milk in champagne glasses, had mounted the poor beasts in spite of their kicks and the driver's vociferated remonstrances, and had ridden the most ridiculous races all along the Rue de la Paix.

It was amusing to listen to the pompously affected account of Monsieur Bonœil, the manager of the Grand Club: "No! it was too funny! Monseigneur was on a tiny she-ass, obliged to tuck up his long legs—for Monseigneur is admirably gifted in legs; and his imperturable coolness. Ah! if his Majesty had been there."

His Majesty indeed regretted having missed such a delightful madcap freak. Lucky Prince d'Axel! On bad terms with the king his uncle, turned out of his country by some court intrigues, he will probably never reign, since the old monarch talked of marrying again some young woman, who would bear him a host of little presumptive heirs. All this did not disturb his equanimity. To amuse himself in Paris seemed far more interesting to him than being engaged in politics at home. And little by little the bragging, sceptical, scoffing spirit once more took possession of Christian, as he lay back on the divan on which the Prince Royal had left the impress of his contagious indolence. In the idle atmosphere of the club, all the heroic impulses of the previous day and the morrow's expedition appeared to him equally devoid of glory, magic, and grandeur. The longer he remained there, the more he became demoralized; and to escape the torpor that seemed to invade his whole being like a stupefying poison, he rose and went down into the living, active, bustling life of the boulevards.

Three o'clock! The hour at which he usually went off to the Avenue de Messine, after having breakfasted at the club or at Bignon's. Mechanically his footsteps led him in the habitual direction of that summer quarter of Paris, larger but less heady than the other, full of such charming views, such airy perspectives, with its green masses against stone walls, and the shadows of foliage cast on the white asphalt of the avenues.

What a number of pretty women glide under the trees, half hidden by their parasols, with all the gracefulness and seductive charm of their sparkling good-humour! What other women can walk, drape themselves in the grace of their very step, talk, dress, or undress themselves like these? Ah! Paris, Paris, city of pleasure and fleeting hours! To think that to make more sure of losing all this, he was, perchance, going to have a bullet put through his head! And yet what a good time he had had! what thorough and complete voluptuousness he had enjoyed!

The fervour of his gratitude threw a bright look into the Slav's eyes as he gazed at all these passing women, who by one flutter, one fan-like sweep of their dress, captivated him. There was a vast difference between the knightly king who that morning, by the side of his wife and child, bent low in his oratory before starting for the conquest of his kingdom, and this pretty lady-killer, with his nose in the air, and his hat placed with a conquering swagger on his round, curly head, fevered by the pursuit of pleasure. Frédérique was not wrong in cursing the Parisian hotbed, in dreading its effect upon this vacillating nature, ever in fermentation, like certain wines that have no body.

At the corner of the Boulevard Haussmann and the Avenue de Messine Christian paused for a moment, and le several carriages pass by. Here, reason recalled him to himself. How had he got there, so quickly?

The Hôtel Potnicki stood out in the vaporous sunset with its two little turrets and its balcony draped like an alcove. What a temptation! Why should he not go in? why should he not see once more the woman who would henceforth remain in his life as the dry, parched remembrance of an unsatisfied desire?

At last, after a moment's terrible debate, after a hesitation visibly betrayed by the reed-like swaying of his weak body, he took an heroic decision, jumped into an open cab that was passing by, and gave the address of his club. Never would he have had this courage, if it had not been for the oath he had taken that very morning during mass. For his effeminate, pusillanimous soul this was stronger than anything.

At the club he found Séphora's letter, which by its odour of musk, communicated the fever that had dictated it. The prince handed him her other note: a few hurried, imploring phrases, written in a very different handwriting from that of Tom Levis's ledgers. But here Christian II., sustained by the observant looks around him, felt stronger: for he was one of those whose attitude depends very much upon an audience. He crumpled up the letters into his pocket. The fashionable youth of the club were now arriving, full of the story of the donkey race, that had been given at full length in one of the morning papers. The paper passed from hand to hand, and it was greeted with the weak, foolish laugh of unamused and worn-out men.

"Are we going to have a lark to-night?" inquired these young scions of nobility as they absorbed soda-water or the mineral waters with which the club was as well stocked as a chemist's shop.

Carried away by their high spirits, the king consented to dine with them at the Café de Londres: not in one of the saloons which had so often been witnesses of their drunken debauchery, whose mirrors bore their names written, crossed, and mixed like a winter's frost upon window-panes: but in the cellars, those admirable catacombs of casks and bottles which stretch out their long regular lines of bins marked with china labels, as far underground as the Opéra Comique. All the vintages of France slept there. The table had been laid at the further end, amid the Château-Yquem, whose greenish recumbent bottles, spangled by the reflection of the gas and coloured glass chandeliers, softly glistened in their bins. This fancy had been inspired by Wattelet, who wished to mark, by an original repast, the departure of Christian II., which was known only to him and to the prince. But the effect was lost by the dampness of the walls and the ceilings, which soon penetrated the guests, wearied by the preceding night's gaieties. Queue-de-Poule could hardly keep his eyes open, and every now and then awoke with a start. Rigolo spoke little, laughed, or rather pretended to laugh, and pulled out his watch every five minutes. He might, perhaps, be thinking of the queen, and of the anxiety she must be undergoing at his delay.

At dessert there appeared a few women who had been dining at the

Café de Londres, and who, hearing that the princes were downstairs, had left their tables, and, guided by the waiters carrying lighted candlebras, crept down into the cellars, holding their long skirts over their arms, with the little screams and the frightened airs usual on these frolicksome occasions. Nearly all were bare-shouldered.

In five minutes they were all coughing and shivering with cold by the side of the men, who at least had the collars of their coats to turn up. "A freak fit to send them all into a galloping consumption," said one of them, more chilly or less of a madcap than the others. It was decided to go and take coffee upstairs in the saloons, and, during the move, Christian disappeared. It was barely nine o'clock. He found his brougham waiting at the door.

"Avenue de Messine," he said, in a low tone, through his clenched teeth.

The craze had seized upon him like a sudden fever. During the whole of the dinner he had been haunted by her, only her, breathing in the rapturous vision conjured up by the naked shoulders of the women around him. Oh! to clasp her in his arms, deaf to her tears and prayers.

"Madame is gone out."

The words fell like a cold douche on a fiery brazier. Madame had gone out! The sight of the house, left to the discretion of the servants whom Christian had seen flying in every direction at his entrance, could leave him no doubt. He asked no further questions, and suddenly recalled to his senses, he realized the appalling depth of the abyss into which he had so nearly fallen. A perjurer to his God! a traitor to his crown!

His burning fingers met his little rosary. He muttered *Aves* to return thanks for his escape, while the carriage rolled off in the direction of Saint-Mandé, through the fantastic views and mysterious nocturnal aspects of the wood.

"The king," cried Elysée, who was watching at the drawing-room windows and saw the two lamps of the brougham dash into the courtyard like flashes of lightning. The king! It was the first word that had been uttered since dinner. As by magic all faces brightened, all tongues were loosed. The queen herself, notwithstanding her self-control and apparent calm, could not keep back her cry of joy. She had thought that all was lost; that Christian had been taken possession of by that woman; that he had abandoned his friends, and had dishonoured himself for ever. And there was not a being around her who, during those three mortal hours of suspense, had not had the same thought, the same anxiety; even little Zara, whom she had kept sitting up, and who, comprehending the anguish, the dramatic meaning of the general silence, never ventured a question —those cruel, telling questions which children will make in their sweet clear voices. Sheltered behind the leaves of a large album, he suddenly raised his pretty face when the king was announced, a face bathed with th tears that had been flowing silently fo the last hour. Later on, when he wa questioned as to this great grief, b confessed that he was in despair at th thought that the king had left withou embracing him. Loving little soul. t whom this young, witty, ever-smilin father appeared like a big brother, delightful brother whose wild pranks, however, caused the despair of their mother.

Christian's voice was heard, sharp and hurried, giving his last orders. Then he went up into his room, and five minutes later appeared ready equipped for the journey in a little round hat with blue band and coquettish buckle, and dainty gaiters, like one of those sea-side tourists painted by Wattelet. The monarch was, however, to be discerned beneath the garb of the dandy, by his air of authority, and the ease of manner he showed under every circumstance. He approached the queen, and murmured an apology for his dilatoriness. Still white with emotion, she said, in a low voice:

"If you had not come, I should have gone with Zara in you stead." He felt that she spoke the truth, and for a moment there flashed across his brain the vision of the queen with the child in her arms, in the midst of the bullets, just as on the balcony during that last terrible scene, when the little fellow had so resignedly closed his eyes before impending death. Without saying a word, he raised Frédérique's hand fervently to his lips; then with a youthful impetuosity, drew her towards him, saying: "Forgive me, forgive me!"

The queen no doubt would still have forgiven him, but she caught sight of Lebeau, the knavish valet, the confident of his master's pleasures and faithlessness, standing near the door ready to accompany the king; and a horrible idea at once crossed her mind while she quietly freed herself from his embrace. "If he lied. If he were not starting after all!" Christian divined her thought, and turning to Méraut

said: "You will accompany me to the station, Samy will bring you back." Then as time pressed, he hurried his adieux, said an amiable word to each, to Boscovich, to the Marquise, took Zara on his knee, spoke to him of the expedition that he was undertaking to reconquer his kingdom, bade him never be a subject of grief to the queen, and if he should never see his father again, to remember that he had died for his country fulfilling his kingly duty. Quite a little speech in Louis XIV.'s style, really well turned, which the little prince listened to gravely, rather disconcerted at the solemn words issuing from the lips he had always seen smiling. But Christian was indeed the man of the present moment, changeable, and fickle beyond measure, and now full of his leavetaking, of the chances of the expedition, more moved than he wished to show, he hurriedly tore himself away from the emotion of the last minute. He waved an "Adieu! adieu!" with his hand to all around, bowed low before the queen, and went out.

CHAPTER XXIV

A DIVINE INTERVENTION

TRULY, if Elysée Méraut had not known what had taken place in the royal household for the last three years, if he had not seen the profligacy and disgraceful weakness of Christian II., he would have found it difficult to recognize the Rigolo of the Grand Club, in the proud and heroic prince who explained to him his plans, his schemes, his intelligent and liberal political views as they rolled rapidly along in the direction of the Lyons station.

The royalist and somewhat superstitious faith of the tutor, saw in this a divine intervention, a privilege of caste, a king necessarily always returning to kingly sentiments at the supreme moment, by the grace of God and by the immutable laws of heredity; and, without being able to explain to himself the reason, this moral regeneration of Christian, preceding and presaging the other that was nigh at hand, caused him an inexpressible feeling of discomfort, a haughty jealousy, the motives of which he would not analyse. While Lebeau took the tickets and booked the luggage, they paced up and down in the great waiting-room, and in the solitude of this nightly departure, the king could not help thinking of Séphora, and the tender farewells at the Saint-Lazare station. Under the influence of these thoughts, a woman passed by and attracted his notice, the same figure, a touch of that staid but coquettish step.

Poor Christian, poor king in spite of himself!

At last he is in a carriage, of which Lebeau holds the door open for him, an ordinary first-class carriage, in order not to attract attention. He throws himself into a corner, anxious to get off, to have finished with it all. This slow process of tearing himself away is very painful to him. The engine whistles, the train begins to move, to draw out to its full length, darts noisily over the bridges, through the sleeping suburbs, dotted by long lines of lamps, and dashes off into the open country. Christian II. breathes again, he feels strong, safe, sheltered; he could almost hum a tune if he were alone in his compartment. But over there at the opposite window, a little shadowy figure

buried in black, shrinks back modestly in the corner, with the obvious intention of avoiding notice. It is a woman; young, old, ugly, pretty? The king, a matter of habit, casts a sidelong glance at her. Nothing stirs but the two little wings in the hat, which seem to turn back and fold together for sleep. "She sleeps. I will do the same." He stretches himself out on the seat, wraps himself up in a rug, looks out vaguely at the confused soft outlines of the trees and bushes, which seem to run one into the other as the train passes them; at the signal posts; the drifting clouds in the balmy sky; and his eyelids heavy with sleep are about to close when he feels on his cheek a caress of soft hair, of long eyelashes, of a violet-scented breath, and of two lips, murmuring close to his own lips: "Cruel man! Leaving me without saying good bye!"

Ten hours later, Christian II. awoke to the roar of cannon, in the dazzling light of a resplendent sun, softened by the surrounding verdure. He was just dreaming that at the head of his troops, under a storm of grape shot, he was scaling the rapid ascent leading from the port at Ragusa to the citadel. But he found himself lying motionless in a large bed, his eyes and brain confused, and his whole being exhausted by a delicious languor. What had happened? Little by little he roused himself and remembered. He was at Fontainebleau, at the Hotel du Faisan, in front of the forest, its close green summits rising up against the blue sky; the cannon was the sound of the artillery practice. And the living reality the visible link of his ideas—Séphora—seated in front of a writing desk, such as is always to be found in an hotel but never anywhere else, was writing diligently with a bad, scratchy pen.

She saw in the mirror the admiring, grateful look of the king, and replied to it, without turning round or betraying the slightest emotion, by a tender glance of her eyes and a motion of her pen, then went on quietly writing, with a smile hovering at the corner of her seraphic mouth.

"A despatch I am sending home to reassure them," she said, rising; and the telegram given, the waiter gone, relieved from some secret anxiety, she opened the window to the golden rays of the sun that poured into the room like the water from a sluice. "Oh dear! What beautiful weather." She came and sat down on the edge of the bed by the side of her lover. She laughed, delighted at the idea of finding herself in the country, of rambling through the wood on such a lovely day. They had plenty of time till the night train that had brought them should pick up Christian the following night; for Lebeau, who had continued the journey, was to warn Hazeta and his companions that the landing was to be delayed for a day. The enamoured Slave would fain have remained indoors, and have drawn the great curtains over a happiness that he would willingly have prolonged to the last hour, the last minute. But women are gifted with more ideality, and directly breakfast was over, an open carriage carried them off through the magnificent avenues, bordered by lawns, and clumps of trees that give to the forest a look of some glade in the park at Versailles, before the rocks are reached that divide it into bold, wild sites. It was the first

time they had gone out together, and Christian revelled in this brief joy, which was to have such a terrible morrow of battle and death.

They rolled on under immense arches of verdure, under the delicate foliage of the beech-trees spreading out light and motionless, the distant sun barely penetrating the dense greenery. Sheltered from all eyes, without any other horizon than the profile of the loved one, without any other hope, any other souvenir or desire but that of her caresses, the poetical side of the Slave's character overflowed. Oh! to live there together all alone they two, in a keeper's tiny cottage, covered with thatch and mosses, and luxuriously furnished with every comfort! Then he wanted to know how long she had loved him, what impression he had made on her the first time they had met. He translated for her the poetry and songs of his country, rhythmically showering kisses on her neck and on her eyes; and she listened, pretended to understand and answer him, her eyelids, meanwhile, closing, heavy and sleepy after her broken night's rest.

The eternal discordance of love-duets! Christian wished to plunge into the isolated, unexplored parts of the forest; Séphora, on the contrary, sought out all the famous spots, the labelled curiosities of the forest, with the inevitable tea-gardens, booths full of carved juniper wood, and guides who show the rocking stones, the lightning-struck trees: a whole tribe of nondescripts, who dash out from huts or caverns at the least sound of a wheel. She hoped in this manner to escape from the wearisome and monotonous love-ditty; and Christian admired the kindly patience with which she listened to the interminable stories of the worthy country folk, who always seem to have both time and space for all they do.

At Franchart she insisted on drawing water from a renowned well of the old monks, so deep that the bucket is nearly twenty minutes coming up. Most entertaining for Christian! There, a good woman covered with medals like an old dragoon, showed them the beauties of the place, the old ponds, on the banks of which the deer used to be cut up and served to the hounds; having told the same story for so many years past in exactly the same words, she fancied she had herself lived in the convent, and, three hundred years later, had been present at the sumptuous picnics given under the First Empire when the court came to reside here: "It was here, ladies and gentlemen, that the great Emperor sat in the evening, surrounded by his court." She pointed to a stone bench in the midst of the heather. Then, in a proud tone, she added: "Opposite, the Empress with her ladies." There was something sinister in this evocation of imperial pomp in the midst of fallen rocks, distorted trunks of trees, and burnt-up broom. "Are you coming, Séphora?" inquired Christian; but Séphora was looking at an esplanade, where according to the cicerone, the little King of Rome used to be carried by his nurse, to kiss his hand from afar to his august parents. This vision of the child-prince reminded the King of Illyria of his little Zara. He seemed to stand up in front of him in the arid landscape, held aloft in Frédérique's arms, watching and gazing sadly at him, as though to ask what he was

doing there. It was, however, but a vague reminder quickly repressed; and they continued their stroll under the great fantastic oak-trees—hunting rendezvous, dubbed with high-sounding names—through the green vales, on the ledges that overlooked fallen masses of granite and sand-pits, where the pine-trees furrowed the red ground with their powerful projecting roots.

Now they followed a dark avenue of impenetrable shade, ploughed by deep, damp ruts. On each side rows of trees like the pillars of a cathedral formed silent naves, through which was heard only the step of a startled deer, or the fall of a golden-tinted leaf. An immense sadness fell from these high archways, these branches without birds, resonant and hollow like deserted houses. As the day wore on the enamoured Christian felt his passion deepened, with a shade of melancholy at the approaching separation. He told her how he had made his will before starting, and the emotion he had felt at writing when in the full vigour of life words that would only be read after his death.

"Yes, it is very tiresome," said Séphora, in the absent tone of a person thinking of something else. But he fancied himself so beloved, he was so accustomed to be loved, that he did not notice her abstraction. Indeed, he even consoled her beforehand in case anything should befall him, tracing out her existence for her; she must sell her house and retire into the country and live on the recollection of their love. All this was delightfully conceited, naïve, and sincere: for he felt his heart seized with the sadness of farewells, which he mistook for the presentiment of death. In a low whisper, their hands entwined, he spoke of a future life. He wore round his neck a little medal of the Virgin, which never left him; he took it off, and gave it to her. Fancy how delighted Séphora must have been!

Shortly after, they came upon an artillery camp, and the glimpse caught through the trees of rows of grey tents, light smoke, and horses unbridled, hobbled for the night, gave the king's thoughts another direction. The moving hither and thither of uniforms, the fatigue parties, all the activity of life carried on in the open air in the warm light of the setting sun, the merry aspect of the soldier's encampment, roused the instincts of his wandering and warlike race. The carriage, as it rolled over the green moss-covered avenue, aroused the attention of the soldiers occupied in pitching the tents or making their soup. They laughingly followed the pretty couple with their eyes, and Christian longed to speak to them, to harangue them, as he examined the camp under the trees to its farthest extremity. A bugle sounded, and others answered from afar. Before an officer's tent, a little aside from the others, on rising ground, a beautiful Arab horse, with nostrils open and flowing mane, pranced and neighed at the sound of the bugles. The Slave's eyes sparkled. Ah! what grand days were now before him! What mighty sword-thrusts he would give! But what a pity Lebeau had gone on to Marseilles with his luggage; he would have been so proud to show himself to her in his uniform of lieutenant-general. And in his excited imagination he saw the gates of the town forced

open, the republicans routed, his own triumphant entrance into Leybach through the gaily-decked streets. She should be there, by Gad! He would have her there, and give her a superb palace at the gates of the town. They would continue to see each other as freely as in Paris. To all these wonderful plans Séphora did not answer much. No doubt she would have preferred to keep him all to herself; and Christian admired her silent abnegation, which so well befitted her position as mistress of the king.

Ah! how he loved her, and how quickly that evening passed at the Hotel du Faisan, in their crimson-hung room, with the great curtains drawn upon the fading light of a summer's evening; in the little, sparsely-lit town, buzzing with the hum of the conversations before the doors and of the passers-by, dispersing at the sound of the drums and bugles of the garrison. How many kisses, and follies, and passionate vows went to rejoin the kisses and vows exchanged the previous night. In their delicious languor and their close embrace they listened to the quick beating of their own hearts; while a soft breeze shook the curtains after having murmured in the trees, and a fountain played, like in a Moorish court, in the middle of the little garden of the hotel, where the only light was the red and flickering reflection of the office lamp.

One o'clock! It is the hour of parting. Christian dreaded the wrench of the last moment for he thought he would have to struggle against the caresses and prayers of Séphora, and would have to summon up all his courage.

But she was ready before he was,

and insisted on accompanying him to the station, placing the honour of her royal lover before his love. If he could have heard the sigh of relief the cruel creature gave, when, alone on the platform, she watched the two green eyes of the train winding away in the distance; if he could have known how happy she was at the idea of finding herself alone in the hotel; while as the empty omnibus rattled her over the old pavement of Fontainebleau, she said to herself in a quiet tone free from all thrill of passion: "If only Tom has done the needful in time!"

Yes, most assuredly the needful had been done, for when the train reached Marseilles, great was the surprise of Christian II. when he alighted from the railway carriage with his little portmanteau in his hand, to see a flat silver-braided cap approach him and very politely beg him to step for one moment into his office.

"What for? Who are you? asked the king, haughtily.

The flat cap bowed and replied: "Government inspector!"

In the office, Christian found the prefect of Marseilles, a former journalist, with a red beard and bright and witty countenance.

"I am sorry to have to inform your Majesty that your journey must end here," said he in a tone of exquisite politeness. "My Government cannot allow a prince to take advantage of the hospitality afforded to him by France to conspire and arm against a friendly power."

The king tried to protest, but the prefect was acquainted with the minutest details of the expedition.

"You were to embark at Marseilles, and your companions at Cette on a Jersey steamer. The place chosen for the general landing was the shore of Gravosa, the signal two rockets, one from the ship, the other on land. You see we are well informed. They are the same at Ragusa, and I am saving you from a regular trap."

Christian II. was astounded, and wondered who could have betrayed secrets known only to himself, to the queen, to Hezeta, and one other, whom he certainly did not dream of suspecting. The prefect smiled in his fair beard.

"Come, Monseigneur, you must make the best of it, you have failed this time. On the next occasion you will be more fortunate and more prudent also. Now I beg your Majesty will accept the shelter of the *préfecture*. Anywhere else you would be the object of a troublesome curiosity, for your projected expedition is known all over the town."

Christian did not answer immediately. He looked around the little official room, filled by a green armchair, green portfolios, an earthenware stove, and great maps marked with the lines of railway, the miserable corner in which his heroic dream, and the last echoes of the March of Rodoïtza lay stranded. He was like a traveller in a balloon, who, having started for dizzy heights, had fallen down at once upon a peasant's hut, with his empty balloon, a mere bundle of crumpled silk, cast aside under a stable roof.

He, however accepted the invitation, and found the prefect's home a truly Parisian one; his wife a charming woman and a thorough musician, who after dinner, when they had talked over all the topics of the day, seated herself at the piano, and ran through the newest opera. She had a pretty voice and knew how to sing; so after a while Christian drew near her and discussed music and operas. The *Echoes of Illyria* were lying on the music-stand between the *Reine de Saba* and the *Jolie Parfumeuse*. The lady asked the king to show her the rhythm and style of the ballads of his country. And Christian II. hummed one or two popular airs: *"Beaux yeux, bleus comme un ciel d'été,"* and again: *"Jeunes filles qui m'écoutez en tressant des nattes."*

And while this captivating king stood leaning against the piano affecting the melancholy tones and attitudes of an exile; far away, on the Illyrian Sea, of whose foam-tipped waves and flowered shore the *Echoes* sang, a troop of young and enthusiastic men, whom Lebeau had calmly neglected to warn, scudded joyously towards the fatal shores, into the very jaws of death. to the cry of: "Long live Christian II.!"

CHAPTER XXV

THE CONDEMNED CELL!

"My darling wife, we have just been brought back to the citadel of Ragusa, Monsieur de Hezeta and I, after ten hours passed in the theatre of the Corso, where a court-martial has been sitting upon us. We have been unanimously condemned to death.

"I confess that I prefer this. At least we now know what to expect, and are no longer in solitary confinement. I can read your dear letters and can write to you. The complete silence utterly crushed me. I was without any news of you, of my father, of the king

whom I fancied killed, the victim of some ambush. Fortunately His Majesty is spared, and has but the failure of the expedition and the lives of a few loyal servants to deplore. Things might have been worse.

"The newspapers, no doubt, have told you what took place. Owing to some incredible fatality, the king's counter-order had not reached us, and at seven o'clock in the evening we were to leeward of the islands at the appointed rendezvous. Hezeta and I were on deck, the others in the cabin, all armed and ready, your pretty little cockade stuck in our hats. We cruised about for two or three hours. There was nothing within sight but some fishing smacks and some big feluccas belonging to the coasting trade. Night fell, and with it a sea-fog, adding to the difficulties of our meeting with Christian II. After waiting about a long time, we came to the conclusion that his Majesty's steamer had probably passed by without seeing us, and that the king had landed. Just then, from the shore where they were to await our signal, a rocket was fired into the air. That meant: 'Land at once.' We had no more doubts, the king was evidently there. And we started to join him.

"As I am thoroughly acquainted with the country—I have so often shot wild-duck in that neighbourhood—I was put in command of the first launch, Hezeta was in the second, and Monsieur de Miremont was in the third with our Parisian adherents. In my boat we were all Illyrians, and how our hearts beat high. It was our motherland that lay before us. that dark coast rising through the fog, bearing the little red revolving light of the Gravosa lighthouse. The complete silence on the beach, however, astonished me. Nothing was to be heard but the waves breaking on the shore, a long rippling, clapping sound, nothing of that mysterious sound that arises from the most silent crowd, that always resembles a clink of arms, or the panting of subdued respirations.

"'I see our men!' said San-Giorgio in a whisper to me.

"We perceived on landing that what we had taken for the king's volunteers were clumps of cactus, and Barbary fig-trees planted in rows on the beach. I advanced. Nobody. But there were the footmarks of a trampling crowd, and furrows in the sand. I said to the Marquis: 'This looks very suspicious. Let us get back to the boats.'

"Unfortunately, the Parisians had just landed; you know how impossible it is to hold them. They scattered themselves all along the shore, beating the bushes and thickets. All at once there was a line of fire, the cracking of musketry. The cry is raised: 'Treason! treason! To the boats!' We rush towards the launches; jostling, and hustling like a herd of mad, bewildered cattle, through sand and water. There was a moment of terrible panic when the moon shone out and showed us the sailors pulling away as hard as they could to the steamer. However, that did not last long. Hezeta dashed forward, revolver in hand. *'Avanti! Avanti!'* What a voice! The whole shore echoed again with the sound. We followed on his heels. Fifty against a whole army. We had but to die. And that is what our men did with true

courage. Pozzo, Mélida, young Soris your admirer of last winter, Henri de Trébigne who in the midst of the scuffle, called out to me: 'I say, Herbert, this lacks *guzlas!*' And Jean de Véliko, who, while he slashed right and left, sang the 'Rodoïtza' at the top of his voice; all fell, and I saw them stretched out on the sand, their faces turned towards the heavens. It is there that the rising tide will have ingulfed and shrouded them, the gay dancers of our last ball! Less fortunate than our comrades, the marquis and I alone survived that hailstorm of bullets; we were seized, bound, fastened on to mules' backs and carried to Ragusa, your unhappy Herbert howling with impotent rage, while Hezeta calmly repeated: 'It was fated. I knew this would happen.' What a strange fellow! How could he know that we should be betrayed, abandoned to our enemies, and on landing be received by musket and grapeshot; and if he did know it, why did he lead us on? However, the result is the same, the thing is a failure, and when another attempt is made, greater precautions must be taken.

"I understand now, by your dear letters that I never tire of reading and re-reading, why our trial has been put off for so long, and the meaning of all the going and coming of the lawyers' gowns through the citadel, the haggling over our lives, all the ups and downs, all the delay. The wretches were treating us like hostages in hopes that the king, who refused to renounce the throne for millions, would give way when the lives of two of his faithful servants were at stake. Blinded by your affection, you are surprised and exasperated, my darling, that my father refused to say a word to save his son. A Rosen could not betray such weakness! He loves me no less dearly, poor old man, and my death will be a terrible blow to him. As for our sovereigns, whom you accuse of cruelty, we must not judge them: we have not the same high standpoint they have, which enables them to govern men. They have duties and rights beyond those of the common herd. Ah! how eloquently Méraut would discourse on this theme. As for me, I feel all these things but am unable to express them; the words stick in my throat. I do not know how to bring them out; my jaws are too heavy. How often have I felt this difficulty with you, whom I love so tenderly, and to whom I have never known how to tell it! Even here, when I am separated from you by hundreds of miles and such thick iron bars, the thought of your pretty grey eyes, your arch smile, and your little nose turned up in laughing mockery, intimidates and paralyses me.

"And yet, before leaving you for ever, I must try and make you understand, once for all, that I have never loved anybody in the world but you, and that my life only began from the day I first met you. Do you remember, Colette? It was at the agency Rue Royale; at that fellow, Tom Levis'. We were supposed to be there by chance. You tried a piano; you played, sang something very lively that, without knowing why, almost made me weep. I was caught! Who would have thought it? A marriage made through a matrimonial agency become a love match! And since that I have never, never met, either in or out of society, a woman half as charming as my Co-

lette. You may rest easy, you have always been present in my heart, even when absent from me; the very thought of your pretty little face kept me happy. I laughed alone as I recalled it. It is true, your image is always associated with the joyousness of laughter. At this moment our situation is terrible, and nothing has been spared to increase its horror. Hezeta and myself are *en chapelle*, that is to say, in the little cell with its whitewashed walls an altar has been prepared for our last mass, a coffin has been placed in front of each bed, and on the walls are hung cards inscribed with the words 'Dead—Dead.' Well, notwithstanding all this, the room seems to me very cheerful. I take refuge from these gloomy threats by thinking of my Colette: and when I raise myself up to our grated window, the sight of this lovely country, the road that leads down from Ragusa to Gravosa, the aloes, the cactus rising against the blue sky and sea, all recalls to me our wedding trip, the Corniche road between Monaco and Monte-Carlo, and the tinkle of the mule bells bearing along our happy love, joyous and light-hearted as those bells. Oh! my dear little wife, how pretty you were, how I should have wished the journey through life to have lasted longer with such a companion!

"You see that your image remains triumphant, even on the threshold of death, even in death itself; for it will be on my heart as a scapulary, over there at the Porte de Mer, where in a few hours we are to be taken; and it will enable me to meet death with a smile. Therefore my loved one, do not grieve too much. Think of the little

one, the child who will soon be born.
Keep yourself for him, and when he is
at an age to understand, tell him that
I died like a soldier, erect, with two
names on my lips: my wife and my
king.

"I should have wished to leave you a
souvenir of this last moment, but I
have been robbed of every jewel,
watch, wedding-ring, and pin. I have
nothing left but a pair of white gloves
that I meant to wear on our entry at
Ragusa. I shall put them on presently
to do honour to my execution; and
the chaplain of the prison has faithfully promised me to send them to you
when all is over.

"And now, farewell, my darling Colette. Do not weep. I tell you not to
weep, and my tears are blinding me.
Comfort my father. Poor old man!
He who so often scolded me for coming late for the orders of the day.
Well, I shall never come again now.
Farewell, farewell! And yet I had so
much more to say to you. But no, I
must die. Alas! Cruel destiny. Colette, good-bye!

"HERBERT DE ROSEN."

CHAPTER XXVI

ABDICATION

"THERE is still one course left open
to you, Sire."

"Speak, my dear Méraut. I am
ready to make any sacrifice."

Méraut hesitated. What he was
about to say seemed to him too serious
a matter to be discussed in the billiard-
room, whither the king had brought
him to play a game after breakfast.
But the strange irony that presides over
the destiny of dethroned sovereigns re-

quired that the fate of the royal race
of Illyria should be decided there, before the green cloth on which the balls
rolled with a hollow and sinister sound
amid the silence and mourning of the
Saint-Mandé establishment.

"Well? What is it?" asked Christian
II., stretching himself over the table to
strike the ball.

"Well, Monseigneur," replied Elysée,
and he paused till the king had made
his cannon, till Councillor Boscovich
had piously marked it, and then continued in a slightly embarrassed tone:
"The people of Illyria are like other
peoples, Sire. They admire success and
power, and I fear lest the fatal issue
of our last enterprise——"

The king turned round, his cheeks
aglow.

"I asked you for the plain truth,
my dear Méraut, do not try to disguise it."

"Sire, you must abdicate," said the
Gascon, bluntly.

Christian stared at him with astonishment.

"Abdicate what?" he said. "I have
nothing left. A fine present to make
to my son. I think he would prefer
a new bicycle to the vague promise of
this crown at his majority."

Méraut quoted the precedent of the
Queen of Galicia. She too had abdi-
cated in favour of her son during her
exile, and if Don Léonce was on the
throne now, it was owing to that abdication.

"Eighteen to twelve!" said Christian,
sharply. "Councillor, you are not
marking."

Boscovich bounded like a startled
hare, and rushed up to the board, while
the king, his whole body and mind in-

tent on a difficult stroke, appeared absorbed in his play. Elysée watched him, and his royalist faith was put to a rude test as he looked at this specimen of the used-up dandy, this inglorious victim—his thin long neck displayed by the wide-open collar of his flannel shirt, his eyes, mouth, and nostrils still tinged with the jaundice that he had just recovered from, and which had kept him for about a month in bed. The disaster at Gravosa, the terrible death of all those young men, the fearful scenes the trial of Herbert and Hezeta had given rise to at Saint-Mandé; Colette dragging herself on her knees before her former lover to obtain her husband's life; the days of anguish and dread expectation, in which he was ever haunted by the sound of the platoon firing, for which he seemed himself to give the word of command; and added to this, money cares, Pichery's bills coming to maturity; the restlessness of his evil destiny, all this without being able to overcome the careless indifference of the Slave, had nevertheless physically prostrated him.

He stopped after making a cannon, and chalking his cue most carefully, asked Méraut, without looking at him:

"What does the queen say about this plan of abdication? Have you mentioned it to her?"

"The queen is of my opinion, Sire."

"Ah!" he said drily, with a slight stare.

Strange inconsistency of human nature! He did not love this woman, whose cold distrust and sharp glance he feared; this woman whom he reproached with having treated him too much as a king, and wearied to death by her continual reminders of duty and

prerogatives, and yet he was indignant now at the idea that she no longer believed in him, at her abandonment of him for the benefit of the child. He felt—not a blow to his love, not one of those stabs at the heart that make it cry out, but the chill of a treacherous thrust on the part of a friend, of confidence lost.

"And you, Boscovich, what do you think of it?" he suddenly asked, as he turned to his councillor, whose smooth anxious face reflected convulsively the various phases of his master's countenance.

The botanist made a slight pantomimic gesture expressing doubt, his arms wide open, his head sunk between his shoulders, a mute "*Chi lo sa?*" so timid, so little compromising, that the king could not help laughing.

"With the advice of our council," he said scoffingly, in his nasal tones, "we will abdicate whenever we are requested to do so."

Whereupon His Majesty returned with greater eagerness than ever to his billiards, to Elysée's intense despair, who was dying to go and inform the queen of the success of a negotiation she had not ventured upon herself, for this shadow of royalty still overawed her, and it was with a trembling hand that she dared take up this crown he refused to wear.

The abdication took place a short time after. Stoically the chief of the civil and military household proposed that the ceremony, which is usually surrounded with as much solemnity and authenticity as possible, should take place in the splendid galleries of the Rosen mansion. But the catastrophe of Gravosa was too recent for these reception halls, still re-echoing with the music of the last ball; it would have been too sad and evil an omen for the new reign. It was therefore resolved to invite to Saint-Mandé the few noble Illyrian or French families whose signatures were necessary at the foot of such an important document.

At two o'clock the carriages began to arrive, the rings at the bell succeeded each other, while on the long carpets rolled from the door to the bottom of the stairs the guests slowly ascended, and were received at the entrance of the drawing-room by the Duc de Rosen, tightly buttoned up in his general's uniform, wearing all his decorations, and around his neck the broad ribbon of Illyria, which he had laid aside without a word, when he had learned that the barber Biscaret wore the same insignia as himself over his Figaro's vest. Around his arm and on his sword hilt the general wore a fresh crape bow, and what was still more significant than the crape, was the senile shake of his head, a sort of unconscious protest, "no, no," which he had kept ever since the terrible debate that had taken place in his presence with regard to Herbert's reprieve, a debate in which he had energetically refused to take part, notwithstanding Colette's entreaties and the revolt of his paternal love. It seemed as though his little, shaky hawklike skull paid the penalty of his inhuman refusal, and was condemned henceforth to say no to every impression, every sentiment, even to life itself; for nothing more now could ever interest him, nothing exist for him after the tragical end of his son.

Princess Colette was also there, wearing a fashionable mourning that became her fair hair, her widowhood somewhat consoled by the hope apparent in her slower gait and heavier appearance. Even in the midst of her sincere grief, her little frivolous mind, ever taken up with trifles, and which the cruelty of fate had not modified, was still occupied with a variety of coquetish trifles for her child if not for herself. The ribbons, laces, and magnificent trousseau she was having made for her infant and embroidered with an original monogram under her coronet, mitigated her sorrow. The baby should be called Wenceslas or Witold, Wilhelmine if it were a girl, but certainly its name should begin with a W., because it was an aristocratic letter and looked pretty embroidered on linen. She was explaining her ideas on the subject to Madame de Silvis, when the doors were thrown open, and preceded by a blow of the halberd on the floor, the names of the guests were called out: the Princes and Princesses de Trébigne and de Soris, the Duc de San-Giorgio, the Duchesse de Mélida, the Comtes Pozzo, de Miremont, de Véliko, etc. It sounded like the death roll, re-echoed from the bloody strand, of all those youthful victims fallen at Gravosa. And what lent a terrible, fatal, and funereal aspect to the ceremony, notwithstanding all the precautions taken, the sumptuous liveries and the state hangings, was that all the new comers were in deep mourning, dressed and gloved in black, smothered in those woollen materials that impart such a dreary look, seeming to place a restraint upon the women's gait and gestures, the mourning of old people, fathers and mothers, sadder, more heartrending, and more unjust than any other mourning. Many of these unhappy creatures had come out to-day for the first time since the catastrophe, drawn from their solitude and seclusion by their devotion to the dynasty. They straightened themselves as they entered, summoning up all their courage; but as they gazed at one another, sinister reflections of the same grief, with bowed heads and quivering shoulders, they felt their eyes fill with the tears that welled in those of the others, while to their lips rose the sighs that were so painfully restrained at their side; soon the nervous tension became contagious, and the room was filled with a long, broken sigh, a stifled exclamation of grief. Old Rosen alone did not weep, erect and inflexible he continued to shake his head, as though saying:

"No, no. He must die!"

That evening, at the Café de Londres, H.R.H. the Prince d'Axel, who had been invited to sign the abdication, related that he might have fancied he was attending a first-class funeral, all the family assembled and waiting for the corpse to be taken away. In truth the royal prince cut a sorry figure when he made his entrance there. He felt chilled, embarrassed by the silence and despair, and looked with terror at all those old women, till he caught sight of the little Princesse de Rosen. He quickly went and sat near her, curious to know the heroine of that famous breakfast of the Quai d'Orsay; and while Colette, at heart very much flattered by his attention, received His Highness with a sad and sentimental smile, she little suspected how those

dull lifeless eyes bent on her, were considering the exact fit of the little pastry-cook costume moulding her inviting little person.

"Gentlemen, the king!"

Christian II., very pale and careworn, walked in first, holding his son by the hand. The little prince had a befitting air of gravity which suited him well, heightened by the black jacket and trousers which he wore for the first time with the pride and serious gracefulness of a youth. The queen followed, looking very handsome in a magnificent mauve dress covered with lace, too sincere to be able to conceal her joy, which contrasted with the surrounding sadness, as the bright colour of her dress with that of the mourning garments around her. She was so happy, so egotistically happy, that she had not a look of sympathy for the sublime affliction which encompassed her, any more than she noticed the desolation of the garden, the moisture on the widow-panes, and the sombre November fog, floating under the dark and lowering sky, full of misty torpor. For her this gloomy day was to remain in her memory warm and luminous. So true is it that all lies within us, and that the exterior world is transformed for us by our own impressions, and assumes the colour that our passions lend it.

Christian II. placed himself in front of the fire place in the centre of the drawing-room, with the Comte de Zara on his right and the queen on his left; a little further off Boscovich, in his ermine cloak as Aulic Councillor, was seated at a small writing-table. When each one had taken his place, the king, in a low voice, announced himself ready to sign his abdication and give his motives for so doing to his subjects. Upon which Boscovich rose, and in his little, weak, indistinct voice read Christian's manifesto to the nation, the brief history written in broad lines, of the expectations of the first years of his reign, of the disappointments, the misunderstandings that had followed, and finally the king's resolution to retire from public affairs, and confide his son to the generosity of the Illyrian people.

This short letter, in which the hand of Elysée Méraut was visible in every line, was read so badly, and sounded so much like a tiresome botanical nomenclature, that it allowed full time for reflection, and for the hearers to see all that was vain and derisive in this abdication of an exiled prince, this transmission of a power that did not exist, of rights that were disowned and unheeded. The document itself which was read by the king ran as follows:—

"I, Christian II., King of Illyria and Dalmatia, Grand Duke of Bosnia and Herzegovina, etc., etc., hereby declare that of my own free will, and not yielding to any foreign pressure whatever, I leave and transfer to my son Charles-Alexis-Leopold, Count of Goetz and Zara, all my political rights, reserving only my civil rights as his father and guardian."

Then at a sign from Rosen, all those present approached the table and signed. For a few minutes only a sound of shuffling of feet and rustling of dresses was heard, and the scratching of trembling or heavy pens, with pauses every now and again necessitated by the ceremonial. Then the ceremony of kissing hands began.

CHAPTER XXVII

CANDID EYES

CHRISTIAN II. opened the ball, and acquitted himself of his delicate task— the homage of a father to his son— with more sprightly grace than respect. The queen on the contrary kissed her child's frail hand with a passionate, almost reverential effusion; the protecting mother had become the humble subject. Now Prince d'Axel's turn came, and that of the noble lords, who came forward in an order of precedence which the little king soon found very tedious; but he maintained a charming air of dignity in his candid eyes as he held out his little white transparent hand, the square nails and disproportioned wrist of which betrayed the child whose playing days are not yet over. Notwithstanding the gravity of the occasion and the sinister preoccupation of their mourning hearts, all these nobles were still full of the importance of their rank, and jealously guarded their rights of precedence, which were measured according to their titles and their dignities; and when Méraut made an attempt in his enthusiasm to rush up to his pupil, he found himself stopped by a stern, "By your leave, sir!" which made him step back and find himself face to face with the indignant Prince of Trébigne, a terribly asthmatic old fellow, who breathlessly opened his eyes like round balls, as if he were trying to breathe through them. Elysée, ever respectful of tradition, deferentially gave way before this remnant of the past, and came up the last to kiss hands. As he was retiring, Frédérique, standing beside her son, like the mother of a young bride, who in the vestry receives her share of the surrounding homages and smiles, said in a low but exultant tone:

" 'Tis done!"

There was in her intonation an unutterable relief and a fulness of joy that was almost ferocious.

" 'Tis done!" That is to say the diadem was henceforth safe, beyond the reach of traffic and contamination. Now she could sleep, breathe, live free from the terrible apprehensions which seemed to warn her in advance of the approaching catastrophes, and would have enabled her to say like Hezeta after each fatal dénouement, "I knew it." Her son would not be despoiled, her son would be king. What! was he not king already by his majestic attitude, his affable and condescending kindliness.

However, as soon as the ceremony was over, the child's nature asserted itself, and Leopold V. darted joyfully towards old Jean de Véliko to announce his great news: "You know, godfather, I have got a pony, a dear little pony, all to myself. The general is going to teach me to ride, and mamma also." All eagerly flocked around the child, and bent upon him looks of adoration; while Christian, somewhat lonely and deserted, felt a strange, indefinable impression, as though his brow were lightened, as if the removal of his crown left a chill. He actually felt light-headed. And yet he had longed for this hour, he had cursed the responsibilities of his position. Then what was the meaning of this uneasiness, this depression, now that he saw the shore recede, and new perspectives open before him?

"Well, my poor Christian, I am afraid you have received your marmoset."

This was Prince d'Axel's whispered consolation.

"You are a lucky dog, indeed! Would not I be happy if the same lot fell to me; if I could be exempted from the obligation of leaving this charming Paris to go and reign over my people, a set of white-stomached seals!"

He went on for a moment in the same tone; then, taking advantage of the tumult and inattention of the assembly, they both disappeared. The queen saw them go out, she heard the sound of the phæton wheels as they rolled away, those light wheels she had never heard before without a pang. But what matter now? It was no longer the King of Illyria those women of Paris were leading astray.

After Gravosa, in the first moment of his shame, Christian had sworn he would never again see Séphora. As long as he was in bed, with the dread of illness so common to the Southerner, he never thought of his mistress but to curse her, and inwardly accuse her of all his faults; but when he became convalescent, and his blood flowed more freely through his veins, his recollections, mingling with his dreams during his enforced idleness, changed the course of his ideas. He first began to excuse the woman, timidly; and then only saw in what had happened a fatality, one of the thousand designs of Providence, on whom true Catholics throw the whole burden of responsibility.

One day, at last, he ventured to ask Lebeau if no letters had come from the Comtesse. The valet answered by bringing him a quantity of little notes which had arrived during his illness; tender, passionate, timid notes; a shower of white turtle-doves cooing love.

Christian's heart was aglow in a moment; he answered at once from his bed, longing to resume the romance interrupted at Fontainebleau.

Meantime, J. Tom Levis and his wife were enjoying themselves in their mansion, Avenue de Messine. The foreigners' agent had not been able to endure the dulness of Courbevoie. He missed the bustle of business, of traffic, and, above all, the admiration of Séphora.

Moreover, he was jealous,—a stupid, obstinate, throbbing jealousy that stuck like a fish-bone in his throat. He fancied it gone, and yet felt the prick; and not a person to whom he could complain and say: "Just look at what I have here sticking in my throat." Unfortunate Tom Levis, caught in his own trap, inventor and victim of his Grand Stroke. Séphora's journey to Fontainebleau caused him the most uneasiness. On several occasions he tried to lead her to the subject, but she would always stop him with such a natural burst of laughter: "What is the matter with you, my poor Tom? How funny you look!" Then he was forced to laugh also, for he knew that between them there could be no deep feeling, only fun and nonsense, and that Séphora's fancy for him, the fancy of a circus girl for a clown, would quickly cease if she thought him jealous and sentimental—a plague like the rest.

In reality he suffered at being away from her, and went so far as to write verses. Yes, the man of the cab, the imaginative Narcisse, had discovered this solace for his anxieties, a poem to Séphora, one of those queer lucubrations, scanned with pretentious ignorance, such as are often found at Mazas on the table of a prisoner. Truly, if Christian II. had not fallen ill, Tom Levis would have done so.

The joy of the clown and his love at spending these few weeks together, may be imagined. Tom danced his most fantastic jigs, and stood on his head on the carpets. He was like a monkey in a good humour: like Auriol the clown, let loose in the house. Séphora writhed with laughter, though made somewhat uncomfortable by the servant's hall, where "the husband of Madame" was decidedly disapproved of. The butler had indeed declared that if "the husband of Madame" ate at table, he would decline to serve him; and as he was quite an exceptional servant, given and chosen by the king, she did not press the point, but had the meals brought up to her boudoir by a housemaid. When she received a visitor—Wattelet, or the Prince d'Axel for instance—J. Tom would disappear and hide himself in a dressing-room. Never did a husband find himself more strangely situated; but he adored his wife, and had her all to himself in a setting that made her appear ten times prettier in his eyes. In short he was the happiest of the whole set, for the constant delays and evasion were beginning to cause much disquietude amongst them.

Each one felt a knot, a hitch in this affair that had been so well started. The king never paid the bills that fell due, but on the contrary kept drawing fresh ones, to the dismay of Pichery and father Leemans. Lebeau endeavoured to keep up their courage: "Patience, have patience; we shall succeed, it is a dead certainty." But he was not out of pocket, while the others had piles of reams of Illyrian paper in their desks. The poor "father," who had lost a great deal of his confidence, would come every morning to the Avenue de Messine in search of reassuring words from his daughter and son-in-law.

"Then you still think we shall succeed?" and he went on discounting bills, again and again, since the only way to recover his money, was to throw more after it.

One afternoon, the Comtesse was getting ready for a drive in the Bois; tripping from her room to her dressing-room under the paternal eye of J. Tom, who lounging on a sofa, cigar in mouth and thumbs in armholes, enjoyed the pretty spectacle of a lovely woman dressing, putting on her gloves before her mirror, and studying her attitudes. She was bewitching in her pretty autumnal dress and her hat, with the veil stopping short just below her eyes, while the jingle of her bracelet, the sparkle of the jet trimming on her cloak, harmonised with the appearance of the carriage waiting under the windows, with the click of the harness and the pawing of the horses, the whole forming part and parcel of the King of Illyria's establishment.

She was going out with Tom for a drive round the lake, taking advantage of a fine day in the already advanced season, under the low sky which brings into relief the new fashions, and the faces refreshed by a long stay in the country or seaside.

Tom, elegantly dressed in English fashion, was charmed at the prospect of this drive in the close luxurious brougham, half-hidden by his pretty Comtesse, like a pair of lovers.

Madame is ready, they are about to start, after a last loving look cast at the mirror, when suddenly the hall door opens, the bell rings hurriedly: "The king!" And while the husband dashes into the dressing-room, with his eyes rolling savagely, Séphora runs to the window just in time to see Christian II. coming up the stone steps with a conquering air. He soars, he has wings. "How happy she is going to be!" he says to himself as he rapidly enters the house.

The fair one guesses that something has happened, and prepares to receive the news. To begin with, she utters a cry of joyful surprise on seeing him, falls into his arms and allows herself to be carried to an armchair, in front of which he falls down on his knees and exclaims: "Yes, it is I, it is I, for ever yours!"

She gazes at him with wide open eyes, frantic with love and hope. And he, bathed, drowned in her glance, says:

"The deed is done. It is no longer the King of Illyria who loves you, but a man who will give up his whole life to you!"

"Ah! this is too much happiness! I dare not believe it."

"Look, read!"

She took the parchment, and slowly unfolded it.

"Then it is true, my Christian, you have renounced——"

"I have done more than that."

And while she perused the deed, he stood twirling his moustache, and looked at Séphora with an air of triumph; then, finding that she did not understand fast enough, he explained to her the difference between a renunciation and an abdication,—that he would be just as free from his duties and responsibilities, without in any way compromising his son's future. It is true, the money—but they did not require so many millions to be happy.

She stopped reading, and listened to him with lips apart, her pretty teeth showing in an acrid smile, as though to seize what he was telling her. She had understood, however; oh yes, indeed; she saw at a glance the ruin of their ambition, the total loss of all the piles of gold invested in the affair; the rage of Leemans, of Pichery, of all the set: robbed by the wrong manœuvre of this fool. She thought of all the useless sacrifices, of the six months of dreary *ennui* she had undergone, made up of sickening dissimulation and mawkishness; of her poor Tom, even now holding his breath in the dressing-room, while that other fellow in front of her awaited an explosion of tender feeling on her part, certain of being loved,—an irresistible, overpowering conqueror. The situation struck her as absurd: the irony was so complete, so absolute. She rose, seized with a fit of uncontrollable laughter—an insulting and scornful laugh, which brought to her cheeks a transient red, all the dregs of her coarse nature stirred up; and passing before Christian, who remained stupefied: "You fool!" she cried out to him, as she dashed into her room and drew all the bolts behind her.

Without a penny, without a crown, without a wife or a mistress, he looked indeed a pitiful object as he went down the stairs.

CHAPTER XXVIII

LITTLE KING

OH, the magic of words! No sooner had Méraut's pupil exchanged the name of Comte de Zara for that of Leopold V. than a complete transformation took place in him, as if the four letters of the word *king* possessed a cabalistic power. The painstaking, attentive child, tractable and ready to receive any impress, without, however, showing any superiority of intelligence, seemed suddenly to shake off all drowsiness, to be roused by some singular mental excitement; his body even appearing to gain strength from the interior flame that quickened him. His natural indolence, his lazy habit of lying about on sofas and chairs while he was read to, or while stories were related to him; that craving for other people's thoughts, to which he idly listened, was changed into an activity that the mere games of his age failed to satisfy. The old General de Rosen, crippled with rheumatism, had to summon up all his strength to give him his first lessons in fencing, shooting, and riding; and it was a touching sight, every morning at nine o'clock, to see the former Pandour, dressed in a blue coat, whip in hand, standing in the middle of an open space transformed into a lunging-ring, and with the manners of an old Franconi respectfully, but persistently, correct his pupil's errors, and perform all the duties of a riding-master. Little Leopold trotted and galloped, proud and serious, attentive to the smallest observation; while the queen looked on from the top of the stone steps, occasionally throwing in a word of advice: "Hold yourself straight, Sire. Slacken the reins." And sometimes, in order to be more quickly understood, the mother—herself a splendid horsewoman—would run down and join example to precept. How happy she was the first day they rode out together, regulating her mare's step or that of the prince's pony; they went as far as the neighbouring wood, the child's figure overshadowed by the mother's, who, ignoring any maternal fears, urged on the animals at full speed, and galloped off with her son till they reached Joinville! She, too, had undergone a great change since the abdication. In the eyes of this superstitious believer in divine right, the title of king henceforth protected and defended the child. Her tenderness, strong and deep as ever, no longer manifested itself outwardly, or in affectionate caresses; and if in the evening she still entered his room, it was no longer to "see Zara put to bed," nor to tuck him up. A valet now attended to all this, as though Frédérique feared to make her son effeminate and retard his manliness by keeping him too much under her gentle care. She only came to hear him repeat the beautiful prayer, taken from "The Book of Kings," that Father Alphée had taught him:

"O Lord, my God, Thou hast placed Thy servant on the throne; but I am only a child, knowing not how to guide myself, and charged with the guidance of the people Thou hast given unto me. Vouchsafe to me, O Lord, the necessary wisdom and intelligence. . . ."

The small voice of the prince would rise clear and firm, with a tinge of authority and conviction, which, in his present state of exile, in the corner of a suburb far away from the problematic throne beyond the seas, was most touching. But in the eyes of Frédérique, her Leopold reigned already, and she threw into her evening kiss a proud subjection, an indefinable respect and adoration, that reminded Elysée, when by chance he observed this strange mixture of maternal feelings, of the old carols of his country, in which the Virgin sings, as she rocks Jesus in the stable: *"I am Thy servant, and Thou art my God."*

Several months passed in this way, indeed the whole winter, during which the queen felt only one shadow pass over the serenity of her life. And it was Méraut who unconsciously was the cause. Dreaming ever the same dream, mingling their onward glances and aspirations, walking together closely united towards the same goal, a certain familiarity and community of thought and life had arisen, which suddenly gave to Frédérique, without well knowing why, a sense of uneasiness. When she found herself alone with him she was embarrassed, and startled at the influence this stranger had acquired over her most private decisions. Did she divine the feelings that agitated him? the passion smouldering so close to her? which each day became more absorbing and more dangerous. A woman is seldom mistaken in such matters. She would have wished to protect herself, to regain her impassibility; but how? In her doubt and emotion she had recourse to the guide.

the adviser of a Catholic wife—to her confessor.

When he was not wandering all over the country on his royalist propagandism, Father Alphée was the queen's director. To see the man, was to recognize him at a glance for what he was. This Illyrian priest, with his pirate's countenance, had something of the blood, appearance, and features of one of those birds of prey and tempest who formerly swept the Latin seas. The son of a fisherman of Zara, brought up amongst sailors, in the midst of tar-brushes and fishing-nets, he had one day been picked out by the Franciscans for his pretty voice, and from cabin-boy had been raised to the rank of chorister. He grew up in the convent, and became one of the heads of the confraternity; but he had retained the impetuosity of the sailor and the complexion tanned by the sea-breeze, which the cloisters of the convent had not been able to bleach. Moreover, neither bigoted nor over-scrupulous, ready to draw his knife (cotellata) in the good cause; the monk, when political affairs pressed upon him, would dispatch at early morning in a lump all the orisons of the day, and even of the morrow: "to get ahead," as he would gravely say. Ardent in his affection as well as in his hatred, he had vowed a boundless admiration to the tutor he had himself introduced into the royal establishment.

To the queen's first avowal of the agitation of her soul, of her scruples, the good priest turned a deaf ear; but when she insisted, he got angry, and rebuked her harshly, as if she were an ordinary penitent, some rich shopkeeper's wife of Ragusa.

Was she not ashamed to bring forward such childish nonsense in face of the great things at stake? What did she complain of? Had anyone been wanting in respect towards her? Fancy letting this man go—this man whom God had certainly sent to their aid for the triumph of royalty—on account of some foolish scruples, or the sentimentality of a woman who thinks herself irresistible! And in his sailor-like language, and his Italian emphasis toned down by a priestly smile, he added: "Pray do not let us cavil at the fair wind that is blown to us from heaven. We must set our sail and go ahead." The most upright of women will always give in to such plausible arguments. Conquered by the casuistry of the monk, Frédérique persuaded herself that she had no right to deprive her son of such a powerful auxiliary. It now depended upon herself alone to be strong and wary. What did she risk after all? Soon she became thoroughly convinced that she was mistaken about Elysée's devotion, about his enthusiastic friendship. The truth was that he loved her passionately. A strange deep love, which he had often thrust aside, but which each time had returned more ardent than ever, and which now asserted itself with all the despotism of a conqueror.

Hitherto Elysée Méraut had thought himself incapable of love. There had been moments when, stirred by the fire of his royalist speeches, some girl of the Quartier Latin, without understanding a word of his harangue, would fall desperately in love with him, attracted by the music of his voice, the flash of his fiery glance, the passion of the ideal that emanated from him—the magnetic fascination of a Magdalen for an apostle. He would smilingly and condescendingly bend down to her, pluck the proffered flower, veiling with kindness and gentle affability the incorrigible contempt for women that lies at the bottom of every southerner's heart. For love to penetrate into his heart, it had first to take possession of his powerful mind; and it was thus that his admiration for the haughty beauty of Frédérique, for that royal adversity so nobly borne, had slowly but surely become a real passion, heightened by the narrow existence and familiarity enforced by exile, by the daily, hourly intercourse, and the anxieties they had shared,—a humble, discreet, hopeless passion, which was content to burn at a distance, like the poor man's taper lighted on the lowest step of the altar.

Life went on, however, in appearance much as usual, heedless of this mute drama, and the first days of September arrived. Bathed in the rays of a warm sun that seemed to harmonize with the happy disposition of her mind, the queen was taking her daily stroll after breakfast, followed by the duke, Elysée and Madame de Silvis, who replaced the little princess as lady-in-waiting during her enforced absence. They all followed in the shady ivy-bordered paths in the little park, and every now and then the queen would turn round to throw them a word or phrase, with the graceful decided air, which, however, took away nothing of her feminine charm. On that day she was particularly bright and lively. Good news from Illyria had been received that

morning, telling of the excellent effect which had been produced by Christian's abdication, and the popularity of Leopold V., already far spread among the country people. Elysée Méraut was triumphant.

"Did I not tell you, Monsieur le Duc, that they would soon adore their little king? Childhood, you see, has the power of re-awakening love. We have infused into their hearts a new religion, with all its simplicity and fervour."

And, pushing back his hair with his two hands, by a violent gesture familiar to him, he dashed into one of the eloquent improvisations that always transfigured him; just as the dejected Arab, cowering in his rags on the ground, becomes transformed into a spirited cavalier when on horseback.

"We are in for it," whispered the marquise, with a bored look, while the queen seated herself on the edge of the path under a weeping ash, in order to hear him better. The others stood respectfully around her, but by degrees the audience diminished. Madame de Silvis was the first to go, ostensibly to protest, as she never failed to do; presently the duke was called away for some detail of his service. They remained alone. Elysée was not at first aware of this, and continued his discourse, standing in the sunlight, which brought out the irregularities of his noble features like the angular surfaces of a hard stone. He was handsome thus, with an intelligent, taking, irresistible beauty, which struck Frédérique so forcibly that she had not time to conceal her admiration. Did he read her thoughts in those sea-green eyes? Did he receive in return the electric shock communicated by this sentiment so vivid and so near? He stammered at first, then stopped short, his whole being trembling with emotion, and threw upon the queen's head, upon her golden hair spangled with a shimmer of light, a long look, burning with love—almost an avowal. Frédérique felt the warmth of this flame run through her, like a more blinding, more dazzling sun than the one in the heavens, but she had not the strength to turn away. And when, terrified at the thoughts that were rising to his lips, Elysée tore himself away from her, she remained penetrated to the very core by the magnetic power of this man and felt as if life were leaving her; her soul fainted within her, and she sat there, on that bench, helpless and crushed. Pale shadows floated over the gravel of the winding paths. The water trickled over the edges of the fountain, refreshing the lovely summer's day. Nothing could be heard in the flower-garden but a far-spread murmur of wings and the buzz of insects over the fragrant flower-beds, and the sharp crack of the little prince's rifle at the further end of the park, near the wood.

In the midst of this silence the queen recovered herself, first in a movement of anger and revolt. She felt the offence, the outrage of that look. Was it possible? Had she not been dreaming? She, the proud Frédérique who, in the dazzling brilliancy of courts, had disdained the homage of the most noble, the most illustrious hearts; she, who had so jealously guarded her own, throw it thus to a man of nought, to this son of the people! Tears of wounded pride blinded her eyes. And in the whirl of her thoughts, the prophetic words of old Rosen rang in her ears: "The Bohemia of Exile." Yes, exile alone, with its dishonouring promiscuities, could have emboldened this underling. But as she overwhelmed him with her contempt, the recollection of the services he had rendered rose before her. What would they have done without him? She remembered her emotion on their first meeting, how her hopes had revived as she listened to him. Since then, while the king took his pleasure, who had taken the direction of their destiny, repaired the blunders and the crimes? And the indefatigable devotion of each day, all the talent, the ardour, the genius that he had applied to the self-sacrificing task he had undertaken, devoid of all profit and glory for himself! Was not the result her little king, so truly king, of whom she was so proud, the future master of Illyria! An invincible gush of tenderness and gratitude filled her heart, recalling that moment of the past when at the Vincennes fair, she had leaned upon the strong arm of Elysée; she closed her eyes now, as she had done then. and abandoned herself to delicious thoughts of him, of the great, devoted heart which she almost fancied she could feel beating against her own.

Suddenly, after a shot which had sent the birds flying through the branches, a terrible cry, one of those cries that mothers hear in their dreams when harassed with anxiety; a fearful cry of distress darkened the heavens, expanded the garden to the measure of an immense grief. Hurried steps were heard in the alleys; the hoarse, altered voice of the tutor was heard calling near the shooting-range. In one bound Frédérique was there

It was at the end of the park, against a wall of verdure made up of hops, vines, wistaria and the tall vegetation of rank soil, in the green shade of an arbour. The targets hung against the trelliswork, pierced with little round regular holes She saw her child stretched on his back motionless on the ground, his white face stained with red near the right eye, which let fall from under its closed lids drops of blood like tears. Elysée on his knees beside him, was wringing his hands and crying: "It is I! It is I!" He was passing. Monseigneur had begged him to try his rifle, and by a horrible fatality the ball had rebounded from some bit of iron in the trellis. But the queen did not hear him. Without a cry, without a word, wholly given up to her maternal instinct, to the one thought of saving her child, she snatched him up in her arms, carried him wrapped in her dress to the fountain, then waving away the people of the house who hurried to help her, she placed her knee on which the little king lay inert, against the stone ledge, and held under the overflowing basin the beloved little pale face with the fair hair clinging to it in long damp locks, and allowed the water to stream down on to the discoloured eyelid, on the sinister red stain that the water washed away, but which continued to ooze out, brighter and brighter, from between the lashes. She did not speak, she did not even think. In her rumpled, dripping cambric dress, that clung to her beautiful form, she looked like a marble naiad as she bent over her child and watched.

What a moment of anguish! Little by little, revived by the immersion, the wounded child moved, stretched his limbs as if awaking, and began to moan.

"He lives!" she cried in a delirium of joy.

Then as she raised her head, she perceived Méraut standing opposite to her, who by his pallor and dejection seemed to crave for pardon. The recollection of all she had felt on the bench in the garden mixed with the terrible shock of the catastrophe, the thought of her weakness so quickly followed by chastisement on her child, roused in her a fearful rage against this man and against herself.

"Go! go! Let me never see your face again!" she cried with a terrible glance. It was her love that she confessed before all, to punish and cure herself at the same time; the love which she threw as an affront in his face in the insulting tyranny of her command.

CHAPTER XXIX

DARK ROOM

"ONCE upon a time, there lived in the Duchy of Oldenburg, a Countess Ponikau, who on her wedding-day had received three little golden loaves from the elves——"

It is Madame de Silvis who is thus relating a fairy tale, in a dark room, with windows and shutters hermetically closed, and heavy curtains let down to the floor. The little king is stretched on his small bed, while the queen, seated near him pale as a ghost, applies to his bandaged brow, pieces of ice which she has renewed every two minutes, day and night, for the last week. How has she managed to live without sleep, almost without food, seated by that narrow bedstead, holding her son's hands in her own whenever not busied in tending him, passing from the alternative of icy cold to the fever heat, which she anxiously watches for and dreads to feel in that poor little pulse?

The little king wants his mother near him, always by his side. The darkness of the great room is for him peopled with sinister shadows, terrifying apparitions. Then the impossibility in which he finds himself of reading or playing with his toys has thrown him into a torpor that alarms Frédérique.

"Are you in pain?" she asks at every moment.

"No. But it is so dull," replies the child in a spiritless voice; and it is to drive away this dulness and fill the gloomy shades of the room with brighter visions that Madame de Silvis has reopened the fairy-tale book full of old German castles, of sprites dancing at the foot of the turreted keep where a princess spins with her glass distaff and awaits the arrival of the blue bird.

The queen is in despair as she listens to these interminable stories; it seems to her that the work she has so laboriously accomplished is being slowly undone, and that she assists at the crumbling, stone by stone, of an upright triumphal column. It is this she sees before her in the darkened chamber during her long hours of seclusion, more troubled at the idea that her child has fallen back into women's hands, has returned to his childish little Zara days, than anxious about the wound itself, the full gravity of which she is not yet aware of. When the doctor, lamp in hand, disperses for a moment the surrounding gloom, takes off the bandage, and tries by a drop of atropine to revive the sensibility of the injured eye, the mother is reassured at seeing that the little patient does not utter a cry, does not put his hand up to repel the doctor. Nobody dares to tell her that this insensibility, this quietude of the nerves betokens the complete death of the organ. The bullet in its rebound, although it had spent a good deal of its strength, had struck and loosened the retina. The right eye is irretrievably gone. All the remedies now applied are directed solely to the preservation of the other eye, threatened on account of the organic co-relation which makes sight like a single instrument with double branches. Ah! if the queen knew the extent of her misfortune!—she who firmly believes that thanks to her care, her tender vigilance, the accident will leave no traces, and who already speaks to her child of their first drive.

"You will be pleased to take a nice long drive in the forest, will you not, Leopold?"

Yes, Leopold will be very pleased. He asks to be taken again to that fair where he went once with his mother and his tutor. Then suddenly interrupting himself he inquires:

"Where is Monsieur Elysée? Why does he never come to see me?"

They tell him that his tutor is away on a long journey. This explanation satisfies him. It tires him to think even to speak; and he falls back into a dull indifference; returns to the vague misty country that envelopes the sick mingling their dreams and surrounding with those actualities of life, the noise and movement of which are so dreaded for them by those who tend them. People come and go; whispers and soft steps glide about. The queen hears nothing, heeds nothing but bathing the wound. At times Christian pushes open the door, ever ajar on account of the heat in the confined room, and in a voice that he strives to render joyous and careless, comes and tells his son some funny story, something to make him laugh or talk. But his voice rings false in this recent catastrophe, and the father intimidates the child. The young memory, smothered, filled with confusion by the gun-shot, has retained some strange recollections of past scenes, of the despairing expectations of the queen, of her revolt and indignation that evening when she had been so near throwing herself with him from the window. He answers the king in a low tone, through his clenched teeth. Then Christian turns to his wife: "You should take a little rest, Frédérique; you will kill yourself. In the interest of the child himself." Imploringly the little prince presses his mother's hand, who reassures him in the same mute and eloquent manner. "No, no, do not fear. I shall not leave you." She exchanges a few cold words with her husband and leaves him to his own gloomy thoughts.

The accident that has happened to his son is for Christian the final blow after a long series of misfortunes. He feels stunned and despairing, alone in the world. Ah! if his wife would only try him again! He has the craving the weak feel in misfortune to lean on someone, the longing for some friendly bosom on which to lay his head and pour out his tears, his remorse; only to return afterwards more light-hearted than before to new pleasures

and new faithlessness. But Frédérique's heart is for ever lost to him, and now the child in his turn repulses his caresses. He says all this to himself as he stands at the foot of the bed in the gloom of the dark room, while the queen, counting the minutes, takes ice from a bowl, applies it to the wet bandage, raises and kisses the little sick brow in order to ascertain its temperature, and Madame de Silvis gravely goes on with the story of the three little golden loaves to amuse the legitimate sovereign of Illyria and Dalmatia.

Without his exit being more noticed than his entry, Christian leaves the room, wanders sadly about the silent, orderly house, kept up to its usual ceremonial by old Rosen, who is to be seen coming and going from the pavilion to the mansion, ever erect, notwithstanding the perpetual shake of his head. The hothouse, the garden, continue to bloom; the marmosets, revived by the warmer atmosphere, fill their cage with chatter and capers. The little prince's pony, led up and down by a groom in the courtyard strewn with litter, stops at the steps, and sadly turns its hazel eyes in the direction from whence the little king formerly used to issue forth. The aspect of the mansion is still elegant and comfortable; but an air of expectancy hangs over all, there is a suspense in its very life, a silence such as reigns after the blast of a great storm. The most striking spectacle are the three closed shutters up yonder, hermetically sealed, even when all else opens to fresh air and light, shutting in behind them the mystery of suffering and disease.

Méraut, who, dismissed from the royal household, has taken lodgings hard by, ceaselessly prowls round, and despairingly watches these closed windows. It is his torture and his condemnation. Hither he returns each day, dreading lest he may one morning find them wide open, with the last vapour of an extinguished wax-taper floating out upon the air. The inhabitants of that quarter of Saint-Mandé begin to know him. The woman who sells the cakes drops her rattle when the big unhappy-looking fellow passes by, the players on the bowling-green, the tramway clerk shut up in his small wooden hut, think he is slightly crazed; and in truth these is madness in his despair. It is not the lover who suffers. The queen has done well to dismiss him, he deserved that, he thinks; and his passion vanishes in the greatness of the disaster that has engulfed all his hopes. To have dreamed of making a king, to have devoted his life to such a magnificent task, and to have broken and destroyed everything with his own hands! The father and the mother, more cruelly struck in their tenderness, were not more desperately afflicted than he. He had not even the consolation of tending and devoting himself at all hours to the sufferer; hardly could he obtain news, the servants bearing deep resentment since the accident. One of the forest-rangers, however, who had access to the house, repeated to him the gossip of the servants' hall, magnified by that love of the terrible that is innate in the people. At times, the little king was said to be blind, at others, ne had brain-fever, and the queen, it was added, had resolved to let herself die

of hunger; and the unhappy Elysée would live a whole day musing over this dismal rumour, wandering through the wood as long as his legs would carry him, and then returning to his watch at the edge of the grounds, amid the tall flowery grass, so trampled on Sundays, but which, deserted on the weekdays, resumed its rural and picturesque aspect.

One evening, as the night was falling, he had stretched himself down in the fresh meadow, his eyes turned towards the house, on which the rays of the setting sun were dying away among the entwined branches. The bowlers were leaving the green, the keepers beginning their evening round, and the swallows flew in great circles above the tallest grasses, in pursuit of the gnats that had descended lower with the setting sun. It was a melancholy hour. Elysée seemed overwhelmed, weary both in mind and body; and all the recollections, all the anxieties of his past life were awakened within him, as though, in the silence of nature, his inward struggle found vent more easily. Suddenly, his vague glance was arrested by the sight of the awkward gait, the Quaker hat, the white waistcoat, and gaiters of Boscovich. The councillor, walking rapidly, with little, hurried feminine steps, looked very agitated, and held an object carefully wrapped up in his pocket-handkerchief. He did not appear surprised at seeing Elysée, but went up to him as if nothing had happened, and said to him, in the most natural manner in the world:

"My dear Méraut, you see a very happy man."

"Ah! Good Heavens! What! Is Monseigneur's state——?"

The botanist's face assumed a serious expression suitable to the occasion, and replied that Monseigneur was in just the same condition: kept in bed, in a dark room. Oh! a very painful state of suspense, very painful indeed. Then, abruptly changing his tone, he said: "Guess what I have got here. Take care, it is very delicate, you might loosen the earth. A clematis root; not the common clematis of our gardens, but the *Clematis Dalmatica,* a particular dwarf kind only found in my country. When I first saw it, I had doubts. I have watched it grow ever since the early spring. But look at the stalk, the corolla; smell the perfume of crushed almonds."

He opened his handkerchief with infinite precautions, and produced a weak, crooked, milky-white flower, shaded green, the blossom hardly distinguishable from the pale leaves. Méraut strove to question him, to obtain other news; but the eccentric old fellow was completely absorbed by his discovery. It was, indeed, a strange thing that this little plant should—the only one of its kind—have grown six hundred miles from its native soil. Flowers have their history, and also their romance; and it was the probable romance that the old man repeated to himself, thinking the while that he was relating it to Méraut.

"By what peculiarity of the soil, what geological mystery, has this little wandering seed germinated at the foot of an oak at Saint-Mandé? Such cases are sometimes met with. A friend of mine, a botanist, found, I remember, a Lapland flower in the Pyrenees. It is no doubt due to atmospherical currents, to some stray vein of soil peculiar to the spot. But the wonderful thing in the present case is that the plant should have grown in the immediate neighbourhood of its compatriots, exiles also. And look how it has thriven! A little pale, no doubt, from its exile, but its tendrils are all ready to climb up."

He stood there, in the twilight, his clematis in his hand, motionless and happy in his admiration. Suddenly he said:

"The deuce! It is getting late. I must go in. Good bye."

"I will come with you," said Elysée.

Boscovich was thunderstruck. He had witnessed the scene, known how the tutor had been dismissed, although, however, he attributed his dismissal only to the accident. But what would be thought? What would the queen say?

"No one will see me, Monsieur the Councillor. You will let me in by the avenue, and I can creep up quietly as far as the room."

"What! you want to——?"

"To be near Monseigneur, to hear his voice for one moment, without his even guessing that I am there."

Boscovich remonstrated and weakly opposed him, but he still walked on, urged on by Elysée's desire, who eagerly followed, regardless of his protestations. Oh! what cruel emotion Méraut felt when the little door on the avenue opened amid the thick ivy, and he found himself once more on the spot where his whole life had foundered!

"Wait here for me," said the councillor, trembling; "I will come and tell you when the servants are at table. In that way you will avoid meeting anyone on the stairs."

CHAPTER XXX

A STIFLED SOB

No one had ventured back to the shooting-ground since the fatal day. The trampled borders and paths still bore the impress of the distracted footsteps. The same pierced targets hung to the trellis, the water flowed from the basin like an inexhaustible spring of tears, grey in the sad hour of twilight, and it seemed to Elysée that he again heard the voice of the queen sobbing, and the "Go, go!" which ever re-echoed through his memory, bringing with it the sensation of a wound and a caress. When Boscovich returned, they glided along the shrubbery as far as the house. In the glass gallery opening on to the garden, which they used as a school-room, the books still lay upon the table, the two chairs for master and pupil stood ready, waiting for the next lesson with that cruel inertia of inanimate objects. It all wore a poignant aspect, the aspect of a place that a child brightens with his presence, dashing about in his narrow circle, filling it with laughter and songs, and which when the child is gone seems desolate and mournful.

Boscovich, followed by Elysée, went up the brilliantly-lighted stairs, and led him into the room which preceded the king's, and which, in order that not the slightest ray of light should penetrate his chamber, was also kept in obscurity. A night-light alone burned in a recess, and shone through the surrounding physic bottles and draughts. "The queen and Madame de Silvis are with him. Mind you do not utter a word, and come back quickly."

Elysée no longer heard him, his foot was already on the threshold, and his heart beat with a feeling of awe. His eyes, unaccustomed to the darkness, could not pierce the gloom. He could distinguish nothing; but from the further end of the room, a childish voice arose, repeating the evening prayers—a voice that he could hardly recognize as that of the little king, so weary, dismal, and tired did it sound. After one of the numerous "Amens," the child paused, and said:

"Mamma, must I also say the king's prayer?"

"Yes, darling," replied a noble, grave voice, the tone of which was very much changed too, wavering, like a metal that has had its edges worn by the constant dripping of a corrosive acid.

The prince hesitated, and said:

"I thought—it seemed to me that it was hardly worth while now."

The queen asked sharply:

"Why not?"

"Oh!" said the child-king thoughtfully, in the tone of an old man, "I think there are many other things I have to ask of God than what are in that prayer."

But, his kindly little nature reasserting itself, he added:

"I will say it at once, mamma, at once, as you wish it."

And slowly he began in a resigned and shaky voice.

"*O Lord, my God, Thou hast placed Thy servant on the throne, but I am only a child, knowing not how to guide myself, and charged with the guidance of the people Thou hast given unto me.*"

A stifled sob was heard at the end of the room. The queen started:

"Who is there? Is it you, Christian?" she added, as she heard the door shut.

At the end of the week, the doctor announced that the little patient was no longer to be condemned to a dark room, and that the time had come to admit a little light.

"Already?" said Frédérique. "You had said that this darkness must last for a month."

The doctor dared not tell her that the eye being dead, irretrievably lost, without the slightest chance of recovery, the confinement became useless. The queen did not understand, and no one had the courage to tell her the truth. They awaited Father Alphée's return, religion being the solace of all wounds, even of those that it cannot cure. In his rough, gruff manner, the monk, who was in the habit of using God's word like a cudgel, dealt her the terrible blow which was to crush and annihilate all Frédérique's pride. The mother had suffered on the day of the accident, all her maternal fibres wrung by the cries, the fainting, the blood that ran from the poor little fellow. This second grief fell more directly on the queen. Her son disfigured, mutilated! She who had longed for him to be handsome for the day of triumph, was she to present this cripple to the Illyrians? She could not forgive the doctor for having so deceived her. Thus, even in exile, kings are always the victims of their own grandeur and of human cowardice!

In order to avoid too abrupt a transition from darkness to light, the windows had been covered with green baize blinds; later on full daylight was admitted. and when the actors of the melancholy drama could once more see each other in the full light of day, they perceived the terrible changes wrought by this sad seclusion. Frédérique had grown old, and was obliged to change the style of doing her hair, to smooth it down on her brow to hide the grey locks. The little prince, very pallid, wore a bandage over his right eye, and his whole face, marked with premature wrinkles, seemed to bear the weight of this bandage. How strange too, was this new existence of an invalid! At table he had once more to learn how to eat; his spoon or his fork, awkwardly handled, touched his forehead or his ear, the deficiency of one sense affecting all the others.

He would laugh a sick, weakly laugh, and the queen at each moment turned away her head to hide her tears.

As soon as he could go into the gardens, fresh anxieties assailed her. He would hesitate, stumble at every step, walk askew instead of in a straight line, fall even; or else draw back timidly at the least obstacle, clinging to his mother's hands or skirts; turning round the familiar angles of the park as though they were so many ambushes laid for him. The queen strove to rouse his mind, but no doubt the shock had been too great; and with the sight of one eye, a ray of intelligence seemed also lost. He understood, poor little fellow, how painful his state was for his mother; and in speaking to her, he raised his head with an effort, casting a timid and awkward glance at her, as though to implore pity for his weak state. He could not, however, overcome certain instinctive terrors. Thus, the sound of a shot fired on the edge of the wood, the first he had heard since his accident, nearly brought on an attack of epilepsy. The first time they spoke to him about riding his pony, he trembled from head to foot.

"No, no, I entreat you," he said, pressing close to Frédérique's side. "Take me with you in the carriage. I am too afraid."

"Afraid of what?"

"I'm afraid—dreadfully afraid."

Neither reasoning nor entreaties could prevail.

"Well then," said the queen, with subdued anger, "get the carriage ready."

It was a beautiful autumnal Sunday, very like that Sunday in May when they had gone to Vincennes. In contradistinction, however, to that day, Frédérique felt harassed by the plebeian crowd spread over all the avenues and grass plots. This open-air rejoicing, the smell of the victuals nauseated her. Now she saw but the poverty and distress that lay beneath the laughter and holiday clothes. In vain did the child strive to bring a smile on the beautiful face, which he thought he had saddened, and to propitiate his mother with passionate, yet timid coaxings.

"You are angry with me, mamma, because I would not ride the pony?"

No, she was not angry with him. But how would he manage on the day of his coronation, when his subjects should have recalled him? A king ought to know how to ride.

The little wrinkled face turned round to look inquiringly at the queen, with his only eye.

"Do you really think they will care to have me as I am now?"

He looks very puny, very wizen. Frédérique, however, was indignant at the doubt, and mentioned the King of Westphalia, who was quite blind.

"Oh! He is not a real king. They sent him away."

Then she related to him the story of John of Bohemia, at the battle of Crecy, how he charged his knights to lead him far enough into the battle to strike with his sword; and so far had they led him, that the following day they were all found dead side by side, their bodies stretched out, and their horses fastened together.

"Oh! that was terrible—terrible!" said Léopold.

And he shuddered, pondering over the heroic deed, as though it were one of Madame de Silvis's fairy-tales; a poor, weak child, with little of a king about him! At that moment the carriage left the shores of the lake, and turned down a narrow road, where there was barely room for it to pass. Someone quickly drew back—a man whom the child, hindered by his bandage, did not notice, but whom the queen recognized at once. Grave, with a hard look, with a motion of her head, she showed him the poor cripple, nestling in her skirts, their masterpiece shattered; this fragment and wreck of a great race. It was their last meeting; after this, Méraut definitely left Saint-Mandé.

CHAPTER XXXI

FIDES, SPES

THE Duke of Rosen was the first to enter.

"It is a little damp," he said gravely. "It has not been opened since my son's death."

And indeed a great chilliness filled

the air; the cold damp of a tomb struck upon the senses in this magnificent suite of rooms, where the guzlas had sounded so proudly, and where nothing had changed place since the night of the ball. The two carved chairs of the king and queen still presided over the scene from their place by the musician's gallery, magnificent desks in wrought iron standing beyond them. Armchairs set together in circles formed aristocratic nooks. Ribbons, scraps of flowers, crumpled gauze, the dust of the dance, lay scattered on the floors. It was evident that the decorators had hurriedly taken down the hangings and the garlands of flowers, and had hastened to shut both doors and windows upon these saloons which recalled scenes of festivity only in this house of mourning. The same neglect was visible in the garden littered with dead leaves, over which had passed first the winter, and then an uncared-for and uncontrolled springtime with its invasion of weeds. In his grief, which insisted that all around him should be as mournful and barren as his own life, the duke had allowed nothing to be touched, any more than he would himself consent to occupy his magnificent home.

Since the affair of Gravosa, and since Colette, in very delicate health after the birth of her little W., had gone off to Nice with the child for change of air, he had given up his solitary home-life at the Quay d'Anjou, and had caused a bed to be put up for him at the office. It was evident he would one day or other sell the family mansion, and even now was preparing the way by getting rid of the sumptuous relics of antiquity with which it was crowded. The Venetian mirrors, which had reflected the images of loving couples whirling in Hungarian mazourkas, the flashes darted by bright eyes and sparkling chandeliers, had nothing else to reflect to-day in the grey chill light of a Parisian sky but the queer profiles, the lucre-loving eyes and greedy lips of old Leemans and of Pichery his acolyte, with side curls and moustaches stiff with cosmetics on the dirty pallor of his face.

Truly it needed all the long force of habit on the dealer's part, his constant experience of trade and of those comedies which bring into play every expression of the human countenance, to keep back the cry of joy and admiration that almost escaped him when the general's servant, as old and stiffly upright as his master, had opened the tall shutters, throwing them back against the northern wall with a noisy clatter, letting in the light upon the precious treasures of a collection gleaming with all the subdued hues of wood, ivory, and bronze, not labelled or cared for like that of Madame de Spalato, but in far more luxurious abundance, of a more barbaric kind, though of more recent date. Not a flaw anywhere! Old Rosen had not looted at random, after the fashion of those generals who pass through a summer palace like a hurricane, carrying off with the same violence bell-turreted roofs and bits of straw. Here were none but marvels of taste. And it was curious to note the dealer's decisions, as he fixed his glass on first one object then another, tenderly scratching the enamels, ringing the bronzes, with an air of indifference, even of contempt, while all the time, from head to foot, from the tips of his fingers to the point of his flat beard, every nerve within him vibrated and quivered as if put in communication with an electric battery. Pichery was no less amusing to watch. Having no notion of art himself, he modelled his impressions upon those of his comrade, paraded the same scornful airs, quickly turned to stupefaction when Leemans whispered low in his ear, as he bent over the pocket-book in which he unceasingly made notes: "Worth four thousand pounds, if it's worth a farthing." Here was an unique opportunity for both to recoup themselves from the effects of that "grand stroke" in which they had been so ignominiously done. But it was necessary to be well on guard, for the old general of Pandours, just as suspicious and as impenetrable as the whole bric-à-brac-dealing community put together, followed them step by step, and planted himself behind them, not for a moment duped by their antics and gestures.

Thus they reached at last the end of the reception-rooms. and stopped before a little room raised two steps, and charmingly decorated in the Moorish style, with very low divans, and carpets and cabinets of the most genuine antiquity.

"Is this included?" asked Leemans.

The general hesitated imperceptibly before replying. It was Colette's favourite boudoir, the refuge to which she resorted in her rare moments of leisure to write her letters. For a moment the thought occurred to him to save these Eastern decorations she had liked; but he did not linger over the idea; all must be sold.

"Yes, included," he said coldly.

Leemans, attracted at once by the rarity of a piece of Moorish furniture, carved, gilt, with miniature arcades and galleries, began to examine its endless drawers and secret hiding places, opening one out of another by means of concealed springs, narrow little drawers smelling freshly of orange flowers and sandal wood as their polished surfaces met the air. Plunging his hand into one of them, something crackled beneath his touch.

"There are some papers here," he said.

The inventory finished, the two dealers shown to the door, the duke bethought him of these papers forgotten in the dainty piece of furniture. There was a whole packet of letters, tied round with a well-worn ribbon and impregnated with the delicate perfume of the drawer. Mechanically he glanced at them and recognised the writing, the large, fantastic, irregular writing of Christian, which for many months he had had ample opportunities of studying on bills and drafts. No doubt they were letters from the king to Herbert. Alas, no! "Colette, my darling." With an abrupt gesture he tore off the band and scattered the bundle on a divan; some thirty notes, appointments of rendezvous, thanks, delays, all the correspondence of an intrigue in its sad sameness, terminating finally in excuses for appointments not kept, in missives growing cooler and scarcer like the last fluttering papers on the tail of a kite. In all and every one of these letters were numerous allusions to a tiresome and persecuting bore, whom Christian jestingly called "Courtier of misfortune," or merely "C. of misfortune," and on whom the duke was unable to put a name until, on the turn of one of these mocking pages, invariably more libertine than sentimental, he beheld a caricature of himself, his tiny pointed head perched above long stilt-like legs and claws. It was himself, his wrinkles, his eagle nose, his blinking eyes; and beneath, in order to leave no room for doubt: *Courtier of misfortune keeping guard on the Quai d'Orsay.*

The first surprise over, the outrage comprehended in all its baseness, the old man ejaculated "Oh!" and remained motionless and stunned.

That his son had been betrayed was not what astonished him. But that this Christian, for whom they had sacrificed everything, for whom Herbert had given his life when only twenty-eight years of age, for whom he was in a fair way of ruining himself, on the point of selling even his trophies of victory that the royal signature should not be dishonoured——. Ah! if he could only avenge himself, if he could only take down from those panoplies of arms two weapons, no matter which. But he was the king! And suddenly the magic of the sacred word cooled his anger, and he reflected that, after all, his Majesty, in trifling with one of his fair subjects, was not so culpable as he, the Duc de Rosen, who had married his son to a Sauvadon. He must now pay the penalty of his cupidity. All those reflections lasted but a minute. Putting the letters under lock and key he went out, and returned to his post at Saint-Mandé in the pavilion, where notes and papers of all sorts were awaiting him, among which he recognised more than once the large, irregular hand-writing of the love-letters; and Christian could not have guessed that the old man was ware of all that had taken place, when,

passing through the yard on the following days, he perceived behind the window panes the tall, gaunt profile, ever upright, devoted and watchful, of the "Courtier of misfortune."

It is the privilege of kings, with the halo of national traditions and superstitions which surrounds them, to inspire devotion such as this, even when totally unworthy of it. Now that his child was out of danger, Christian II. plunged afresh into dissipation more madly than ever. He had at first tried to regain Séphora. Yes, even after having been brutally and cynically turned away, after having had every proof of her treachery, he still loved her enough to fly to her feet at the least sign. The fair lady was at this moment wholly given up to the joys and delights of a renewed honeymoon. Cured of her ambitions, fallen back into the wonted tranquillity of her nature from which the alluring bait of millions had drawn her, she would fain have sold her mansion, have realised everything, and have gone to live at Courbevoie with J. Tom as wealthy retired tradespeople, and have satisfied her vanity by crushing the Sprichts with her superior luxury. J. Tom Levis on the contrary dreamed of new speculations; the pompous grandeur of his wife's surroundings gave him little by little the idea of another agency, under a more luxurious and worldly form, business in white kid gloves, amid the flowers and music of balls and parties, around the lake, on the race-course; the cab, now out of date and relegated to the ranks of hired vehicles, should be replaced by a handsome carriage with servants in livery, and bearing the motto and monogram of the countess.

He had not much difficulty in persuading Séphora, in whose house he had now definitely taken up his abode. The reception rooms of the Avenue de Messine were in consequence opened for a series of balls and dinners, the invitations for which were sent out in the names of the Comte and Comtesse de Spalato. At first the guests were few and far between. Then, after a while, the female element, rebellious in the beginning, ended by treating J. Tom Levis and his wife as one of those wealthy foreign couples come from far lands, whose luxury and splendour cause their exotic origin to be forgiven. All the gilded youth pressed round Séphora, whom her adventures had made the fashion of the day, and Monsieur le Comte from the very first winter was able to put some excellent affairs in hand.

It was impossible to refuse Christian admission to the salons that had cost him so dear. At first, this title of king lent éclat to the house and gave it a certain standing. He came there like a coward, with the vague hope of once more reaching the Comtesse's heart, not by the grand staircase but by the back stairs. After having for awhile displayed himself in this rôle of dupe or victim, having shown his pale face, white as his shirt-front, once a week in the gilded recess of a window where the whirling eyes of Tom Levis riveted him to the spot with their ceaseless watch, he became discouraged, came no longer, and to divert his thoughts, took to bad company and low women. Like all men in search of a type once lost, he wandered everywhere, lost himself often, descended lower and lower,

guided by Lebeau, a fellow well inured to Parisian vice, who thought nothing of taking his master's portmanteau in the morning to very strange haunts indeed. It was a real descent of Avernus, easier day by day to this weak soul, made weaker still by the voluptuary's life he had led; and the melancholy calm of his home was not calculated to turn him from it. There was very little gaiety in the Rue Herbillon now that neither Méraut nor the princess were there. Léopold V. was recovering gradually, confided during his convalescence to the care of Madame de Silvis, who was thus at last able to apply the precepts of the Abbé Diguet on the six methods of knowing men. and the seven methods of turning aside flatterers. Sad lessons they were, the child's attention distracted by the bandage which covered one side of his head, and the queen presiding as she had been used to do, but with a heart-broken glance directed towards the *Clematis Dalmatica,* the little flower of exile, pining away its life against the glass of the conservatory. For some time past the Franciscans had been in search of another tutor; but it was not easy to find two Elysée Mérauts among the youth of the day. Father Alphée for his part had a definite idea, which he took care to keep to himself for the present, for the queen would not permit the former tutor's name to be mentioned in her presence. Once, however, under circumstances of great gravity, the monk ventured to speak of his friend.

"Madame, Elysée Méraut is dying," he said as they left the table, after grace had been said.

CHAPTER XXXII

ELYSEE'S ROOM

DURING the whole time he was at Saint-Mandé, Méraut had kept on his room in the Rue Monsieur-le-Prince, being moved thereto by a sort of superstition, just as a man sometimes keeps on the top shelf of a wardrobe some old-fashioned garment of his youth that he will never wear again. He never came there, allowing forgetfuiness to fold over the books and papers, and the mystery of this retreat ever silent and closed in the midst of the noisy furnished lodgings which surrounded it. One day at last he returned to it, aged, weary, his locks almost white. The fat landlady, roused from her torpor by hearing a searching among the keys hung on their hooks, scarcely recognised her former lodger.

"What *have* you done to yourself, my poor Monsieur Méraut? What a shame to ruin your nealth in this way? It should not be allowed."

"It is true, I am rather used up;" answered Elysée smiling, and up he mounted to his fifth story with rounded stooping back, utterly crushed.

The room was unaltered; the same melancholy horizon appeared through its dull windows—the roofs of the square courtyards of the monastery, of the *École de Médecine,* the amphitheatre, chilly monuments, communicating to the gazer something of the melancholy of their destined uses; and on the right, towards the Rue Racine, the two great water reservoirs of the city, gleaming in their vast stone basins and reflecting the wan sky and smoky chimneys. Nothing was changed, but for him was lost for ever the noble ardour and vivacity of youth that gives colour and warmth to all things and only increases in face of difficulties and distress. He tried to set himself steadily to work, to read, he shook the dust from the unfinished work. But between his thoughts and the page before him, glided the queen's look of reproach, and it seemed to him as if his little pupil was seated at the other end of the table waiting for his lesson and listening to him. He felt too lonely, too heartbroken, and hurriedly went down stairs again and hung his key on its nail. From that time he was to be seen, as in bygone days, with his great ungainly figure, his hat well at the back of his head, a bundle of books and reviews under his arm, wandering about the Quartier Latin, beneath the arcades of the Odéon, on the Quai Voltaire, bent over the odour of fresh print and the great clumsy cases of second-hand literature, reading as he passed along the streets, or the alleys of the Luxembourg, or gesticulating as he leant against some statue in the garden in the keenest weather, in front of the fountain's frozen basin. In this centre of study and of intelligence, which the hand of the demolishers of old Paris has not yet reached nor driven away, he regained his ardour and spirit. Only his audience was no longer the same, for the stream of students changes and is often renewed in this home of birds of passage. The meetings, too, had changed their head-quarters; the political cafés were now deserted for the taverns where the attendants are girls dressed in fancy costumes Swiss, Italian, Swede, in spruce tinselled garb designed by some fashionable artist. Of Elysée's old rivals, of the fine orators of his time, Pesquidoux of the *Voltaire,* Larminat of the *Procope,* there remained nothing but a vague souvenir in the minds of the waiters, as of actors long since withdrawn from the footlights. Some few had mounted high and were now in power, well to the front in public life; and sometimes as Elysée strolled along among the shops, his hair streaming in the wind, from a passing carriage some illustrious member of the Senate or the Chamber of Deputies would call to him: "Méraut, Méraut." Then they would talk together: "What are you doing? are you working?" Méraut, with knitted brow, talked vaguely of some great undertaking that "had not succeeded." Not a word more. They would gladly have drawn him out, utilized this lost power thrown away. But he remained faithful to his monarchical ideas and his hatred of the Revolution. He asked for nothing, had need of no one; nearly all the money he had gained in his tutorship was still untouched, he did not even seek to give lessons, and wrapped himself up in a disdainful sorrow, too great, too profound to be comprehensible, without any other distractions than a few visits to the convent of the Franciscans; there he had news of Saint-Mandé, and he loved the quaint chapel with its Jerusalem cavern and bleeding and highly coloured Christ. This naïve mythology, these almost pagan representations delighted him—a Christian of the first centuries of faith. "Philosophers place God too high," he would say sometimes, "they have made him invisible." He, for his part, could see Him well in the dark gloom of the crypt, and among all the images undergoing barbaric penance, beside the Margaret d'Ossuna scourging the marble of

her shoulders, he recalled the vision of that Christmas Eve—the Queen of Illyria, before the manger with clasped hands and outstretched arms that held her son, with a gesture that was imploring and protecting at the same time.

One night Elysée was awakened with a start by a singular sensation of heat mounting upwards from his chest slowly like a rising tide, without shock or pain, but with a sensation of approaching death, and in his mouth an insipid taste of blood. It was a mysterious and sinister approach of disease after the fashion of an assassin who steals in noiselessly in the dark. He was not alarmed, but consulted the young medical students of his table d'hôte. They told him he must be very ill. "What is the matter with me?" "Everything." He had reached forty years, that climacteric of Bohemia, when infirmities lie in wait, and watch their man, making him pay dear for the excesses or privations of his youth; a terrible age, above all when the moral spring is broken, when the wish to live no longer exists. Elysée led the same existence, always out in rain and wind; passing from the overheated rooms, the vitiated atmosphere of gas-lit rooms, to the cold of the street in mid-winter, continuing —long after all lights were out—to discuss on the edge of the pavement, and walking half through the night. The hæmorrhages became more frequent: fearful langour followed them. In order not to take to his bed, for the melancholy solitude of his room weighed upon him, he settled himself at the *Rialto,* a tavern next door to the hotel and there read his papers and dreamed his dreams in a corner. The spot was quiet enough till the evening, and bright with its furniture in polished oak, its walls covered with frescoes representing Venice, with bridges and cupolas in perspective over a liquid rainbow. The Venetian attendants themselves, who in the evening were so alert, swinging their leather money bags between the benches, while their coral necklaces were reflected in the glasses, were at this hour asleep with their heads on the table, crumpling their high lace caps and their puffed cambric sleeves, or else were seated around the stove at work upon their sewing, which they left every now and then to drink with some student. One of them, a tall powerful girl, had thick auburn hair twisted on the top of her head, and her hands moved with grave, slow gestures over her embroidery while she paused at times in the act of listening. Méraut watched her for hours till she spoke, when a hoarse and vulgar voice broke the spell. But soon strength failed him even for these hours spent behind the tavern curtain. He could no longer come downstairs, but was obliged to remain in bed surrounded by books and papers, leaving his door wide open, so that some echo of life, some of the swarming busy movement of the hotel might reach him.

Above all he was forbidden to speak. Then the Southerner resigned himself to writing, and with fevered and trembling hand took up his book again, the famous book upon monarchy, and worked at it while shaken by a cough that scattered the pages wide over the bed. Now he only dreaded one thing—that he should die before he had finished. and steal away from life as he had lived, hidden, unknown and unexpressed.

Sauvadon, the old uncle at Bercy, whose coarse vanity suffered a shock in seeing his old master in such a garret, visited him often. Directly after the catastrophe he had hastened to Elysée's side, with open purse, in search as before, of "ideas upon things." "Uncle, I have no longer any," Elysée had answered wearily. To draw him from his apathy, the worthy man talked of sending him to the South, to Nice, to share the sumptuous quarters of Colette and her little W.

"It will cost me no more," he said naïvely, "and it may cure you."

But Elysée was not anxious to be cured, wishing only to finish his book in the same spot where the idea of it had germinated, amid those profound murmurs of Paris in which each hears the dominant note that he seeks. While he wrote, Sauvadon, seated at the foot of the bed, maundered on about his pretty niece, and worked himself into further irritation against that old lunatic the General who was about to sell his house on the Ile Saint-Louis.

"What in the world can he do with all that money? He must hide it away in holes, in little heaps. After all, it is his own look out. Colette is rich enough to do without him."

And the wine-merchant slapped a side pocket on the tight and drum-like rotundity of his stomach.

Another time, throwing on the bed the bundle of daily papers he brought to Elysée, he said: "It seems they are making a stir in Illyria again. They have just returned a royalist majority to the Diet of Leybach. Ah! if they only had a man there! But that poor little Léopold is very young yet, and Christian sinks lower and lower every day. Now he frequents the lowest dancing saloons and houses with his valet." Elysée heard, and shivered all over. Poor queen! The other went on, without noticing the pain he caused:

"They go a rare pace, our noble exiles. There is the Prince d'Axel horribly compromised in that disgraceful affair of the Avenue d'Antin. You know, that 'family hotel' which, with its patriarchal name, serves as a shelter for debauched young girls. What a scandal! An heir presumptive. One thing however about it puzzles me. At the very moment of the 'family' scandal, Colette wrote me word that Monseigneur was at Nice, and that she had been at the regatta in a yacht hired for her by his Highness. There must be a mistake somewhere. I should be very glad of it, for between ourselves, my dear Méraut——"

Here the good soul with great mystery confided to his friend that the prince royal "had been paying great attention to Colette, and as she was not a woman to——, as you can suppose, it might be, that before long——"

The wide peasant face of the parvenu lighted up with a smile:

"Just think of that: Colette, Queen of Finland! and Sauvadon of Bercy, her old uncle, becoming uncle to a king. But I am tiring you."

"Yes, I should like to sleep," said Elysée, who had for some moments lain with closed eyes, a polite way of getting rid of this worthy, but vain chatterbox.

The uncle once gone, he gathered his papers together, and settled himself to write, but without being able to trace a single line, so overcome was he by extreme weariness and disgust of life. All these hideous stories made his heart sink. In face of the pages lying scattered over his head, this pleading fo royalty, in which he was using up the little life-blood that remained to him looking upon himself in that sordid room with the whitened hair of an aged scholar, reviewing the lost ardour the spent forces, he for the first time doubted, and asked himself if he had not been all his life a dupe. A defender, an apostle! Of what? O these kings who were wallowing in degraded pleasures, and deserted their own cause. And while his eyes wandered sadly over the bare walls, within which the setting sun reached him only by reflections from the windows opposite he beheld in its dusty old frame the reseal "Fides, Spes," that he had take from his father's bedside. Suddenly th fine old Bourbon head of father Mérau appeared to him as he had last seen it rigid and calm in the slumber of death fallen asleep in the midst of his sub lime confidence and fidelity; and the rose before him too, the narrow an steep lanes, the horizon of crumblin windmills standing high between the dr sunburnt rock of the hill side, and th implacable deep blue of the souther sky. It was a moment of hallucina tions; the enclos de Rey, all his yout floated through a memory over whic the mists were already stealing.

All at once the door opened with murmuring of voices and rustling o skirts. He thought it was some neigh bour, some kindly attendant of th Rialto, bringing a refreshing drink fo his parched mouth. Quickly he shu his eyes, that readily feigned sleep tha dismissed unwelcome visitors. But li tle hesitating footsteps drew near ove the cold, polished floor of the narrow room. A soft voice murmured: "Good morning, Monsieur Méraut." Before him stood his pupil, a little grown, gazing with his sickly and constitutional timidity at the poor pale tutor, so sadly changed, stretched on his wretched bed. In the background, by the door, a woman, proud, erect, and deeply veiled, stood awaiting. She had come; she had mounted the five stories, passed up the staircase alive with sounds of debauchery, brushed with her immaculate skirts by the doors labelled: "Alice— Clémence." She could not let him die without seeing his little Zara again; and, without entering the room herself, sent him her forgiveness by the little hand of her child. That hand Elysée Méraut took and pressed against his lips; then, turning towards the august apparition whose presence he guessed upon his threshold, he summoned his remaining strength, and, with his last breath, his last effort of life, he said, in a low voice and for the last time: "Long live the King!"

CHAPTER XXXIII

LAST OF A RACE

THERE was a well-contested match going on that morning at the tennis-court. Around the immense court, the well-beaten and trodden arena was enclosed by a great net which with its narrow meshes protected the evolutions of six players in white jackets and tennis shoes, bounding, shouting, and striking at the balls with their heavy rackets. The light falling from the ceiling, the stretched net, the hoarse cries, the jumps and erratic springs of the white jackets, the cool, impassive manner of the attendants—every one of them English—slowly pacing the surrounding gallery, all contributed to give the impression of a circus during the rehearsal of the gymnasts' or clowns' performance. Among the clowns, His Royal Highness the Prince d'Axel, to whom the noble game of tennis had been recommended by the doctors to counteract his habitual state of coma, was one of the noisiest players. He had only arrived the previous day from a month spent at Nice at Colette's feet, and this game was his re-entry into Parisian life. He struck the ball each time with a "*han*" that seemed to proceed from a butcher-boy's lungs, and a display of muscles that would have excited admiration in a slaughter-house; when, at the very height of the game, he was informed that some one wanted to speak to him.

"Go to the devil!" answered the heir presumptive, without even turning his head.

The attendant insisted, and whispered a name in his Highness's ear, at which he calmed down and showed a certain astonishment.

"All right; ask him to wait; I will come directly this game is over."

When at last he went into one of the bath-rooms arranged round the gallery, furnished with bamboo seats and daintily hung with Japanese matting, he found his friend Rigolo sunk down on a divan looking the picture of dejection.

"Oh, my dear Prince, such an affair," began the ex-King of Illyria, raising a face that betrayed his extreme agitation.

He stopped at the sight of the servant laden with towels and horsehair gloves who was preparing to sponge and curry his highness, streaming with perspiration like a Mecklenburg horse that has just reached the top of a hill. When the operation was over, Christian continued with pale, trembling lips:

"This is what has happened. You have heard of the adventure at the Family Hotel?"

His Highness turned his dull gaze on him and inquired: "Caught?"

The king nodded affirmatively, and turned his handsome, shifty eyes aside. Then, after a pause, he resumed:

"You can fancy the scene: the police coming in, in the middle of the night; the girl crying, rolling on the ground, resisting the police, clinging to my knees: 'Monseigneur, Monseigneur, save me.' I tried to make her hold her tongue; too late. When I gave the first name I could think of, the police agent laughed in my face: 'It is useless: my men have recognized you. You are the Prince d'Axel!'"

"That's good!" growled the prince from his basin, "and then?"

"By Jove! my dear fellow, I was so taken aback, so surprised—Other motives which I will also tell you—In short, I let the man believe that I was you, being persuaded that the affair would not go any further. But nothing of the kind. They are beginning to work it up, and as you might be called before the *Juge d'Instruction*, I have come to beg you——"

"To stand in the dock in your place?"

"Oh, it won't come to that. Only the newspapers are sure to get hold of it, names will be mentioned. And just now, with the royalist movement preparing in Illyria, our possible restoration, this scandal would have a most disastrous effect."

Poor Rigolo presented a truly piteous appearance, as he stood awaiting his cousin d'Axel's decision while the latter silently combed his sparse yellow locks over his prematurely bald head. At last the royal prince condescended to speak:

"You really think the papers——? then suddenly in his weak, sleepy ventriloquist voice he added: "Capital! awfully funny! My uncle will be in a fine rage when he hears of it!"

By this time he was dressed; he took up his stick, stuck his hat on one side, and said: "Let us go and breakfast." Arm in arm, they went across the *terrasse des Feuillants,* and got into Christian's phæton that was waiting at the gates of the Tuilerie Gardens, wrapped themselves up in their furs, for it was a fine winter morning, illuminated by a cold rosy light, and the elegant equipage started off like the wind, bearing the inseparable pair towards the café de Londres; Rigolo relieved and beaming, Queue-de-Poule less drowsy than usual, exhilarated by his tennis and the thought of this last freak of which all Paris would believe him to be the hero. As they crossed the Place Vendôme, at this hour nearly deserted, young and elegant woman holding child by the hand, stopped at the edge of the pavement and seemed to be examining the numbers. His Royal Highness, who from his seat stared at all the women with the avidity of a townsman famished by three weeks of provincial life, caught sight of her and started: "Look Christian, how like— But Christian did not hear him, his attention entirely absorbed by his mare which was very frisky that morning and when they turned round in the narrow carriage to look at the fair passer-by, she and her child had disappeared under the archway of one of the houses in the neighbourhood of the *Ministère de la Justice.*

The lady walked hurriedly, her veil down, hesitating and timid, as if going to a first rendezvous; if, however, the sombre and somewhat too handsome dress and the mysterious gait were calculated to arouse suspicions, the name she inquired from the porter, the deep sadness of her voice when she pronounced it—the name of the most celebrated man in the medical world—dissipated all ideas of a love affair.

"Doctor Bouchereau?" replied the porter. "First floor, door facing the stairs. If you have not an appointment it is useless going up."

She did not answer, but dashed up the stairs, dragging the child after her, as though she were afraid of being recalled. On the first floor they told her the same thing: "If Madame did not send in her name yesterday—."

"I will wait," she said.

The servant did not insist, but led them first through an ante-room, crowded with people seated on the boxes where the firewood was kept, then through a second room likewise filled, and lastly he solemnly opened the door of a large drawing-room, which he closed immediately after the mother and child had entered as though to say: "You choose to wait; well, wait."

It was an immense room, very high, like all the first floors of the place Vendôme, sumptuously decorated with painted panels, wainscoting and ceiling. The sparse, old-fashioned crimson velvet furniture scattered about the room, the curtains and hangings of the same colour, and a few chairs and settees in worsted work, jarred with the surroundings. A chandelier in Louis XV. style hung over a small table dating from the First Empire, on the mantelpiece a common clock surmounted by a group stood between two candlesticks, and a complete absence of taste and of any artistic objects revealed the character of the modest, hard-working doctor who had suddenly become the fashion, and had made no efforts either to attain or to retain it. And what renown it was! It was, indeed, the renown that Paris alone can confer, extending to all classes, from the highest to the lowest strata of society, overflowing the provinces, foreign lands, all Europe in fact; and this had already lasted ten years, without slackening, without diminishing, with the unanimous approbation of his colleagues, who admitted that this time, for once, success rewarded true merit, and not quackery in disguise. Bouchereau owed this fame, these extraordinary crowds of patients, less to his marvellous skill as an operator, his admirable lectures on anatomy, and his knowledge of the human frame, than to the light, the species of divination which guided him more clearly and more surely than the steel of his instruments; and to the genial eye common to all great thinkers and poets, which endows science with a magical power of seeing into the very depths and beyond! He was consulted like a Pythoness, with a blind, unreasoning faith. When he says, "It is nothing," the lame walk, the dying go away cured; hence his popularity, the tyrannical pressure of the crowd, which gives this great man neither rest nor peace. Consulting physician to a large hospital, each morning he makes a long, slow, and minute examination of the patients, followed by an attentive escort of students, who watch the master as a god, wait on him, hand him his instruments, for Bouchereau never carries his case, but borrows from anyone at hand the instrument he may require, and as invariably forgets to return it. When he quits the hospital, he pays a few visits. Then returns quickly to his study, without stopping to snatch a mouthful, and at once begins his consultations, which last far into the evening.

That day, although it was but twelve o'clock, the drawing-room was already full of anxious, gloomy faces, seated round the walls, or grouped near the table, bending over the books and illustrated papers, and hardly turning when the door opened to note the freshcomers, so absorbed is each one in himself and his ailments, so anxious are they to know what the oracle will say.

The silence of these patients is sinister, and their countenances furrowed with suffering lines, their dull, listless eyes are at times lighted up with cruel glances. The women still betray a kind of coquetry, some, indeed, wore a mask of haughtiness to hide their sufferings; but the men, torn away from their toil, from the physical activity of life, seem more depressed, more struck down and dejected. Among all this selfish misery, the mother and her little companion form a touching group; he looks so frail, so pale, with his little face void of expression and colour, in which only one eye seems alive; she, so motionless, transfixed by a terrible anxiety. One moment, weary with waiting, the child rose to fetch an engraving or two on the table: with the timid awkward movements of a cripple as he stretched out his arm he touched a patient, and received such an angered, ill-tempered look in return, that he went back to his place empty-handed, and remained there without stirring, his head bent on one side, in that uneasy attitude of a bird on a branch, so often seen in blind children.

These long hours of waiting at the door of the physician's study are like a suspension of life, a state of hypnotism, interrupted only by an occasional sigh, a cough, the rustling of a skirt a smothered groan, or the ringing of the bell which at each moment heralds some fresh arrival. Sometimes the newcomer opens the door and as quickly shuts it again, horrified at finding the room so crowded, then, after a short colloquy and a slight remonstrance, he returns again, resigned to await his turn. No favour is ever shown at Bouchereau's. The only exceptions made are for any of the Parisian or country doctors when they themselves accompany their patient. These alone have the right to send in their card and pass in before their turn. They can be recognized by a certain familiar, authoritative air, as they pace nervously up and down the drawing-room. pulling out their watches, wondering that it is already past twelve, and that nothing as yet stirs in the physician's study. More and more people continue to pour in people of all classes, from the fat heavy banker who, in the early morning, has sent a servant to keep two chairs for him, down to the humble clerk, who says to himself: "Whatever it costs, I must consult Bouchereau." All kinds of costumes. all sorts of attire. fashionable bonnets, and linen caps, shabby little black dresses by the side of rich satins; but the same equality reigns in the reddened eyelids, the careworn brows, the anguish and sadness that haunt those who wait in the drawing-room of the great doctor.

Amongst the last comers, a fair-haired, tanned peasant, broad faced and wide shouldered, accompanies a small puny child who leans upon him on one side and on the other upon a crutch. The father takes touching precautions, bends his back, already arched with tilling the ground, under his new smock, and strives with his big fingers to handle and seat the child comfortably: "Are you comfortable like that?" he says. "Steady yourself; wait, I'll put this cushion under you." He speaks in a loud tone, unmindful of the other people, and disturbs everybody to get a chair or a stool. The child abashed, refined by his sufferings, remains silent, his whole body awry, holding his crutches between his legs. At last, when he is settled, the peasant begins to laugh, but there are tears in his eyes.

"Well! here we are! He is a wonderful man this doctor! You'll see he will soon cure you."

Then he smiles round at the company, a smile, however, that meets with nothing but an icy hardness on all faces. The lady in black, accompanied also by a child, alone looks at him kindly; and although she has a somewhat haughty air, he speaks to her, tells her his story; that his name is Raizon, market-gardener at Valenton, that his wife is almost always ailing, and that unfortunately their children take after her, and not after him, a strong, healthy man.

The three eldest have died of a disease they had in the bones. The last one looked as if he were going to grow up all right, but a few months ago, his hip had got bad like the others. So they had put a mattress in the cart and had come off to see Bouchereau.

He says all this quietly, in the slow, methodical manner of country folk, and while his neighbour listens kindly, the two little infirm children examine each other with curiosity, drawn together by their suffering, which throws, for the moment, over the little fellow in his smock and woollen comforter, and the child wrapped up in rich furs, the same tinge of melancholy. A shiver suddenly runs through the assembled patients, faces redden, and all heads are turned towards a door behind which is heard a sound of steps, and of chairs scraping the floor as they are moved. The doctor is there, he has at last arrived. The steps draw nearer. On the threshold of the suddenly opened door appears a thick-set man of medium height, square shouldered, bald headed, with hard features. In a glance that meets all these anxious looks, his eyes run round the room and scrutinize all the new or old sufferers. Some one goes in with him and the door closes again. "He does not look very inviting," whispers Raizon, and to reassure himself, he looks at all the people who will pass in before him to the consulting room. A crowd indeed, and the weary hours of waiting are only broken by the slow, resounding strokes of an old provincial clock, ornamented by a figure of Polyhymnia, and the rare apparitions of the doctor. Each time he appears one turn is gained; there is a movement, a little life in the room, and then once more everything resumes its dull, motionless aspect.

From the moment of her entry the mother has not spoken a word nor raised her veil, and there is something so imposing in her silence, perhaps in her mental prayer, that the peasant does not dare to address her again, but remains mute, and heaves deep sighs. At one moment he draws from his pocket, indeed, from the multitude of his pockets, a little bottle, a goblet, and a biscuit wrapped up in paper, that he carefully and slowly undoes to give a "sippet" to his boy. The child moistens his lips, and pushes aside the glass and biscuit: "No, no, I'm not hungry," and as he gazes at the poor worn-out little face, Raizon thinks of his three eldest children, who, like this one, were never hungry. His eyes grow dim, his cheeks twitch nervously at this thought, and he says abruptly: "Don't move, my pet. I'll just go down and see if the cart is all right." How often he goes down to see if the cart is still waiting on the square, by the side of the pavement! And when he comes back smiling and beaming, he fancies that no one can notice his swollen, red eyes, and his cheeks purple from the rubbing and violent blows he has given them to drive back his tears.

CHAPTER XXXIV

OH! MY DARLING!

THE hours pass on slowly and sadly. In the drawing-room, which is getting dark, the faces appear paler, more anxious, more supplicatingly turned towards Bouchereau, as he impassively appears at regular intervals. The man from Valenton is in despair, as he begins to fear it will be night before they reach home again, that his wife will be anxious, and that the little one will catch cold. His concern is so great, and expressed aloud with such touching simplicity, that, when after five mortal hours of expectation, the mother and child's turn is come, they give it up in favour of Raizon. "Oh, thank you, Madame." His effusiveness has not the time to become intruding, for the door has just opened. Quickly he catches up his son, gives him his crutch, so upset and confused that he does not see that the lady has slipped something into the hand of the poor cripple saying: "It is for you, for you."

Oh! how long both mother and child find this last waiting, made more dreary by the coming night and the apprehension that chills them to the heart. At last their turn has come, and they enter a large study, lighted by a tall, wide window, which opens on to the square, and which, notwithstanding the late hour, still admits a good deal of light. Bouchereau's table is placed in front,— a simple unornamented piece of furniture such as a country doctor or registrar might have. He sits down, the light at his back falling on the faces of the new comers;—on the woman, whose uplifted veil reveals a youthful and energetic countenance, a brilliant complexion and eyes fatigued with constant watching, and on the little fellow who bends down his head as though the light in front were painful to him.

"What is the matter with the child?" inqui.es Bouchereau kindly, drawing the boy towards him with a fatherly gesture for the ragged features conceal an exquisite tenderness that forty years' practice have not yet blunted. Before answering, the mother motions to the child to leave them, then, in a grave voice and foreign accent, she relates how her son had lost his right eye, a year ago, by accident. A short time ago some perturbations have been noticed in the left eye, the sight has become misty, with flashes every now and again, the visual power seeming to decrease. To avoid complete blindness, she has been advised the extraction of the right eye. Is the operation feasible? Is the child in a fit state to bear it?

Bouchereau listens attentively, leaning forward in his arm-chair, his two keen eyes fixed on the scornful mouth, on the full blood-red lips, unsullied by any paint. Then, when the mother has finished all she has to say, he replies:

"The ablation that has been recommended, Madame, is of daily occurrence, and entirely devoid of danger, unless there are some exceptional circumstances in the case. Only once in the twenty years I practised at the hospital Lariboisière did I have a case that did not survive the operation. It is true that he was an old man, a raggatherer, badly fed, addicted to drink. Here the case is different. Your son does not look very strong, but his mother is a fine healthy woman, who has no doubt given him a good constitution. We shall soon ascertain this, however."

He called the child, placed him between his knees, and to occupy his attention while he examined him, asked him with a smile:

"What is your name?"

"Léopold, Monsieur."

"Léopold who?"

The child looks at his mother without answering.

"Well, Léopold, you must take off your jacket and waistcoat," continues the doctor: "I must examine and sound you all over."

The child slowly and awkwardly undresses, assisted by his mother's trembling hands, and by the fatherly old Bouchereau, who is more handy than either of them.

Oh! what a poor, puny, rickety little boy, what narrow shoulders drawn in towards the flat chest, like the wings of a bird folded before its flight, and what flesh! so pallid, so bloodless, that the scapulary and medals hanging from the neck stand out in the evening light as on a plaster *ex-voto* tablet. The mother casts down her eyes, as though ashamed of her child, while the physician sounds and listens, pausing occasionally to ask a question.

"The father is an old man, is he not?"

"No, Monsieur. About thirty-five years of age."

"Often ill?"

"No, hardly ever."

"All right; you may put on your clothes, my little man."

He leans back in his great arm-chair thoughtfully, while the child, after having put on his blue velvet jacket and furs, goes back to his seat at the further end of the room without being told. For a year he has been surrounded by so much mystery, so many whispered conversations have been held around his sick bed, that he no longer minds them, no longer tries to understand, but abandons himself to his fate. Who, however, can describe the anguished look the mother casts upon the physician!

"Well, doctor?"

"Madame," replies Bouchereau in a low voice, emphasizing each word, "your child is in truth threatened with the total loss of his sight. And yet—if he were my son—I would not operate upon him. Without quite understanding as yet his constitution, I notice such strange organic disorders, such a perturbation in his whole being, above all such worn-out, vitiated, impoverished blood——"

"Say royal blood!" exclaims Frédérique, abruptly rising in an outburst of indignation. She has a sudden recollection, a vision of the pale face of her little first-born lying in its tiny coffin covered with roses. Bouchereau also has risen, suddenly enlightened by these three words, and recognizes in the woman before him the Queen of Illyria, whom he has never seen, as she goes nowhere, but whose portraits are in every shop window:

"Oh, Madame, had I known——"

"Do not apologize," says Frédérique, already calmer.

"I came here to hear the truth—that truth we never hear, even in exile. Ah! Monsieur Bouchereau, how unhappy queens are! To think that everybody is persecuting me to allow my child to be operated upon! And yet they know his life is at stake! But State reasons! In a month, perhaps in a fortnight, or sooner even, the Diets of Illyria will be sending a deputation. They want to be able to show them a king. As he is at present, he might do; but blind! Nobody will have him. Therefore, at the risk of killing him, he must be operated upon! Reign or die! And I had almost become accomplice of this crime. My poor little Zara! My God, what matter if he reigns or not! Let him live, my child, let him live!"

Five o'clock! The night is closing in. In the Rue de Rivoli, crowded by the carriages returning from the Bois de Boulogne and the approaching hour of dinner, the vehicles slowly follow each other along the side of the Tuileries iron railings, which, lighted by the quickly setting sun, seems to cast long dark iron bars over the passers-by. On the side of the Arc de Triomphe the sky is still bathed in a red boreal light, while in the opposite direction it is of a dark mourning violet, thickened and shaded black at the edges. It is in this direction that the heavy carriage with the Illyrian arms on its panels rolls off. At the turn of the Rue de Castiglione the queen suddenly catches sight of the Hotel des Pyramides and remembers all the illusions of her first arrival in Paris, singing and surging like the music of the brass band that resounded on that day through the dense foliage. Since then, what deceptions! what struggles! Now it is all over, quite over. The royal race is ended. A deathlike chill falls upon her shoulders as the carriage plunges deeper into the shadow, ever going deeper into gloom.

She does not therefore see the tender, timid, imploring look that the child turns towards her.

"Mamma, if I am not a king any more will you love me just the same?"

"Oh! my darling!"

She passionately grasps the little hand outstretched towards hers. The sacrifice is made! Warmed and comforted by that clasp, Frédérique becomes nothing but a mother, and while the Tuileries, their solid ashes gilded by a ray of the setting sun, rise suddenly before her as though to recall the past, she gazes at them without emotion, without a remembrance, looking at them as at some ancient monument of Assyria or Egypt—mute witness of men and manners long since disappeared —some grand old thing—now dead.

A Passion of the South

CHAPTER I

THE ARENA

On that Sunday, a white-hot Sunday in July, there was a great festival in the arena of Aps, in Provence, on the occasion of the district competitions. The whole town had come: the weavers of the Chemin-Neuf, the aristocracy of the Calade quarter, even some people from Beaucaire. "Fifty thousand persons at least!" said the *Forum* in its next day's chronicle; but allowance should be made for Southern exaggeration.

The truth is that an enormous crowd were crushed together in rows on the burning steps of the old amphitheatre, as in the good old times of the Antonines, and that the festival itself counted for nothing in bringing these masses together. Something else was needed than the local races, the wrestling, the jumping, the competition of flute-players and drummers, spectacles more familiar to them than the red sand of the arena, to make them stand two hours on those flaming flagstones, two hours in that killing, blinding sun, breathe in the scorching heat and the dust smelling like gun-powder, brave ophthalmia, sunstroke, deadly fevers, all the dangers, all the tortures of what is there called a day's fête.

The great attraction for the crowd was Numa Roumestan.

Ah! the proverb which says: "No one is a prophet"—is certainly true of artists, of poets, whose superiority their compatriots are ever the last to recognize, altogether ideal as it finally is, and without visible results; but it could not be applied to statesmen, to political or industrial celebrities, to those strong, influential men who have favours at their command, overflow with blessings of all kinds on their town and its inhabitants.

It is ten years that Numa, the great Numa, the deputy and leader of the parliamentary Right, has been a prophet in the land of Provence, ten years that the town of Aps has shown for this illustrious son the tenderness, the effusive affection of a mother, and of a Southern mother, by its demonstrations, its shouts, its gesticulating caresses. As soon as he arrives in summer after the sittings of the Chamber have broken up, as soon as he appears at the railway station, the ovations begin: the orpheon-players are there, swelling out their embroidered banners amid heroic choruses; porters, sitting on the steps, wait till the old family coach, gone to fetch the Leader, has made three turns of the wheel among the broad plane-trees of the Avenue Berchère, then put themselves in the shafts and draw the great man along, amid "vivats" and raised hats, to the house of the Portals, where he gets out. This enthusiasm has so passed into a tradition, into the ceremonial of his arrival, that the horses stop of their own accord, as at a relay station, at the corner of the street where the porters are wont to unharness them, and all the whipping in the world would not make them budge a step further. The aspect of the town changes from the first day: it is no longer the dull prefecture, with long siestas lulled by the shrill noise of the grasshoppers on the withered trees of the Cours. Even during the hot hours, the streets, the promenade are lively and crowded with busy people, in visiting hats, black cloth dress, distinct in the brilliant light, casting on the white walls the epileptic shadow of their gestures. The carriage of the bishop, of the president, shakes the road; then delegates from the suburbs, where Roumestan is worshipped for his Royalist convictions, deputations of warpers come in bands along the whole breadth of the Boulevard, their heads held proudly with their Arles ribbons. The inns are full of country folk, farmers from Camargue or Crau, whose unharnessed waggons encumber the little squares, the streets of the populous quarters, as on market days; in the evening, the cafés, crammed with people, remain open till late at night, and the windows of the White Club, lit up at unconscionable hours, quiver beneath the tones of the god's voice.

Not a prophet in his own country! One had only to look at the arena on that blue Sunday in July, 1875, the indifference of the public to what happened in the circus, every face turned in the same direction, that cross-fire of all eyes towards the same point: the municipal platform where Roumestan sat amid holiday dresses and many-coloured silks, sunshades brought out on ceremonious occasions. One had only to listen to the chatter, the shouts of rapture, the simple observations of this good-natured populace of Aps uttered aloud, some in Provençal, others in a barbaric French, seasoned with garlic, all in that accent, implacable as the sun there, which cuts off and emphasizes every syllable, does not omit a single dot on an "i."

"God! how handsome he is!"

"He's got a bit stouter during the past year."

"He looks all the more imposing like that."

"Don't push so.—There's room for everybody."

"You see him, little one, our Numa.— When you are grown up, you'll be able to say you saw him."

"There's always his Bourbon nose.— And he hasn't lost a tooth."

"And no white hair either——"

"Gracious!—He's not as old as that! He was born in 1832, the year Louis-Philippe——"

"Ah! the beggarly Philippe!"

"He doesn't look forty-three."

"No, he certainly doesn't.—You splendid man!"

And, with a bold gesture, a tall girl with flashing eyes sent him, from a distance, a kiss that sounded in the air like the cry of a bird.

"Take care, Zette—if his lady saw you!"

"It's the one in blue, his lady?"

No, the one in blue was his sister-in-law, Mademoiselle Hortense, a pretty girl who had only just left the convent and was already going the pace like a dragoon. Madame Roumestan was more sedate, in better style, but she looked far prouder. Those Parisian ladies, they do think a lot of themselves! And, in the bold picturesqueness of their half-Latin tongue these women, standing up, their hands shading their eyes, criticised aloud the two Parisians in detail, their little travelling hats, their tight-fitting dresses, without jewels, so great a contrast with local toilettes: golden chains, skirts of green, of red, rounded off with huge circumferences. The men enumerated the services rendered by Numa to the good cause, his letter to the Emperor, his speech for the white flag. Ah! if they had a dozen like him in the Chamber, Henry V would have been on the throne a long time.

Intoxicated by this gossip, excited by the surrounding enthusiasm, the worthy Numa could not keep still. He threw himself back on his broad armchair, his eyes shut, his face smilingly turned from one side to the other; then he jumped up, took long strides over the tribune, bent a moment towards the circus, inhaled that light, those cries and returned to his place, in a familiar, good-natured way, with his cravat loose, knelt on his seat, and with his back and the soles of his feet to the crowd, talked to his Parisians sitting behind and above him, tried to communicate his delight to them.

Madame Roumestan was bored. It could be seen in an expression of aloofness, of indifference on her beautifully featured face, which had a rather haughty, chilly look, when the vivid flash of her grey eyes, eyes of pearl, real Parisian eyes, with a half-smile showing her fine teeth, did not give life.

These southern gaieties, composed of turbulence, of familiarity, this wordy race, all outside, on the surface, the opposite of her own nature which was deep and serious, chilled her, per-

haps, without her exactly accounting to herself for it, because she found again in this people the multiplied, vulgarised type of the man by whose side she had lived for ten years, and whom she had learnt to know at her own cost. The sky, with its excessive brightness, with its scorching heat, did not enrapture her either. How did they manage to breathe, all those people? Where did they get the breath for so much outcry? And she began to speak dreamily of a nice Parisian sky, grey and misty, with a fresh April shower on the shining pavements.

"Oh! Rosalie, how can you talk like that——"

Her sister and her husband were indignant; her sister especially, a tall young lady blooming with life, with health, standing as upright as possible so as to see better. She had come to Provence for the first time, and yet one might have said that all these cries, gestures under an Italian sun stirred in her a secret fibre, a slumbering instinct, the southern origin revealed by her long eyebrows united over her houri-like eyes, and by the paleness of a complexion in which summer set no red.

"Come, my dear Rosalie," protested Roumestan, who was bent on convincing his wife, "get up and look around.— Did Paris ever show you anything like that?"

In the huge, elliptical theatre, which cut off a big piece of the blue sky, thousands of faces were packed together on the terraced steps, with the lively animation of appearance, the varied colouring, the lavish display of gala toilettes and picturesque costumes Thence, as from a gigantic cellar, issued joyous halloos, loud voices and sounds, volatilised, as it were, by the intense sunlight. This noise, which in the lower trees, which were powdered with dust and tainted with many breaths, was hardly distinguishable, grew louder as it mounted, till it vanished in the pure air. One could especially distinguish the cry of the sellers of milk-loaves who carried from terrace to terrace their basket draped with white linen: *"Li pan ou la!—Li pan ou la!"* And the women, selling fresh water, balancing their green, varnished pitchers, gave you a thirst to hear them calling: *"L'aigo es fresco. Quau voù beùre?"*—"The water is fresh. Who wants a drink?"

Then, up at the top, children, running and playing on the edge of the amphitheatre, raised over the deafening clamour a crown of shrill sounds, on the plane of air where martins fly, in the kingdom of birds. That sky so pure, that sun of vaporous silver, those Latin intonations preserved in the Provençal idiom, the motionless poses which the vibration of the air made antique, almost sculptural, the type of the place, those heads struck like medals, with their short, bold noses, the broad shaven chin, Roumestan's upturned chin, all completed the illusion of a Roman spectacle, even to the lowing of the Landes cows echoing in the subterranean parts, whence issued of old the lions and elephants for fighting.

It was now the turn of the harnessed mules, led by hand, covered with sumptuous Provençal trappings, holding high their small heads adorned with silver bells, rosettes, ribbons, bows, and not frightened by the loud, sharp whip-

cracks of the muleteers standing one on each of them. Among the crowd, each village recognized its champions, shouted out:

"There's Cavaillon.—There's Maussane."

The long sumptuous file went right round the arena, filling it with a bright jingling, with luminous sounds of ringing, stopped before Roumestan's box, according him a minute of whip-cracks and jinglings in his honour. But, except a few country people, nobody looked at it. They only had eyes for the municipal platform, which was invaded by a number of persons come to greet Numa, friends, clients, old schoolfellows, proud of their relations with the great man and of showing themselves off on the platform, well in public view.

And how Roumestan welcomed them, without distinction of fortune or origin, with the same inexhaustible effusion!

"Te! Monsieur d'Espalion! and how are you, marquis——?"

"Hé bé! my old Cabantous, and how goes the piloting?"

"I greet with all my heart M. le président Bédarride."

Then handshakes, embraces, those kindly taps on the shoulder which double the value of words, which are always too cold to suit southern sympathy. Certainly the interview did not last long. The Leader only listened with one ear, with an abstracted look and whilst talking said good-day with his hand to the new-comers; but nobody was offended by his abrupt way of dismissing them with friendly words. "All right, all right—I'll see to it. Send in your request—I'll have it granted."

There were promises of tobacco

shops, of receiver's situations; what they did not ask for, he guessed, encouraged timid ambitions, excited them. No medal, old Cabantous, after twenty lives saved! "Send me your papers.—They worship me at the Admiralty!—We shall repair that injustice!" His voice sounded warm and metallic, striking, detaching the words. One would have thought he was coining new gold pieces. And they all went away ravished by this glittering coinage, came down from the platform with a radiant face, as of a schoolboy carrying off his prize. The finest thing about this devil of a fellow was his prodigious suppleness in assuming the manners, the tone of the people to whom he talked, and that in the most natural, the most unconscious way in the world. Unctuous, with rounded gestures, his mouth compressed, with President Bédarride, his arm magisterially extended as if he were shaking his gown at the bar; his air martial, his hat bellicose, when talking with Colonel de Rochemaure, and when dealing with Cabantous, his hands in his pockets, his legs bent, with the roll of shoulder of an old sea-dog. From time to time, between two greetings, he would return to his Parisians, radiant, wiping his dripping forehead.

"But, my good Numa," whispered Hortense with a pretty laugh, "where'll you get all the tobacco-shops you've promised?"

Roumestan bent his big, curly head, little thin at the top: "It's promised, little sister; it's not given."

And guessing a reproach in his wife's silence:

"Don't forget we're in the South, among compatriots speaking the same language. Those worthy fellows all know the value of a promise, and have no more positive expectation of their tobacco-shop than I myself reckon on giving it them. Only they speak of it, it amuses them, their imagination travels. Why deprive them of that joy?— Besides, you see, among Southerners words have but a relative sense—it's a matter of standpoint."

As the phrase pleased him, he repeated it twice or thrice, emphasising the final words "of standpoint—of standpoint."

"I like those people," said Hortense, who was certainly much amused. But Rosalie was not convinced. "Yet words mean something," she murmured very seriously, as if speaking to herself from her own deepest depths.

"My dear, that depends on latitudes!"

And Roumestan affirmed his paradox by a shrug of the shoulder, which was habitual to him, the forward movement of a pedlar taking up his pack again. The great orator of the Right retained some bodily habits like that, of which he had never been able to get rid, and which, in a different parliamentary party, would have made him pass for a vulgar man; but at the aristocratic summits where he sat between the Prince d'Anhalt and the Duke de la Rochetaillade, it was a sign of power and vigorous originality, and the Faubourg Saint-Germain went wild about that shrug of the shoulder on the broad, great back which carried the hopes of the French monarchy. If Madame Roumestan had once shared the Faubourg's illusions, they were all gone now, to judge by the disenchantment of her gaze, the slight smile that curled her lip as the Leader spoke, a smile paler even with melancholy than with disdain. Her husband, however, left her abruptly, drawn by the sounds of a strange music that rose from the arena among the shouts of the crowd, who stood up excitedly, crying: "Valmajour! Valmajour!"

Victor in the competition of the day before, the renowned Valmajour, the first tabour-player in Provence, came to welcome Numa with his prettiest tunes. He was really handsome, this Valmajour, standing in the centre of the circus, his yellow woollen vest on his shoulder, his light red scarf round his waist, contrasting with the white starch of the linen. He held his long, light tabour hanging by a strap on his left arm, and with the hand of the same arm carried to his lips a small fife, while with his right hand he played the tabour, with a bold look, his leg advanced. Small as it was, the fife filled the space like a swarm of grasshoppers, well suited to the limpid, crystalline atmosphere, where everything vibrates, whilst the tabour, with its deep voice, supported the chant and its flourishes.

At the sound of that shrill, barbaric music, Roumestan saw rising before him his childhood as a Provençal boy going to the country fêtes, dancing beneath the leafy plane-trees of the village squares, in the white dust of the high-roads, on the lavender of the scorched hills. A delightful emotion pricked his eyes; for, in spite of his forty years and more, the sterilizing effect of political life, he still retained, owing to the goodness of Nature, much imagination, the surface sensitiveness which deceives one as to the true character. And, besides, that Valmajour

was not an ordinary tabour-player, one of those vulgar minstrels who pick up odds and ends of quadrilles, music-hall refrains at country fêtes, vulgarizing their instrument whilst trying to suit it to modern taste. Son and grandson of tabour-players, he never played but national tunes, tunes sung quaveringly by grandmothers during the evenings; and he knew them, he did not tire of them. After the Christmas carols of Saboly rhythmed as minuets, as rigadoons, he intoned the "Marche des rois," to which Turenne in the great century conquered and burnt the Palatinate. Along the terraces the electrified masses marked time with their arms, with their heads, followed the superb rhythm, which swept like a mistral through the deep silence of the arena.

When Valmajour had finished, frantic acclamations burst forth. Hats, handkerchiefs waved in the air. Roumestan called the musician to the platform and flung himself on his neck: "You've made me cry, my dear chap!" And he showed his eyes, big brown, golden eyes, filled with tears. Very proud of seeing himself among official embroideries and mother-of-pearl swords, the other accepted the congratulations, the greetings, without much embarrassment. He was a fine looking fellow, with a regular-shaped head, a high forehead, a beard and moustache shining black on his sunburnt complexion, one of those proud peasants of the Rhone valley who have none of the cunning humbleness of the villagers of the centre. Hortense at once noticed how handsome his hand was in its glove of sun-burn. She looked at the tabour, with its ivory tipped stick, was astonished at the lightness of the instrument which had been two hundred years in the family, and whose walnut case, adorned with delicate sculptures, polished, slender, sonorous, seemed as if made supple by the hand of time. She admired especially the *galoubet*, the simple, rustic, three-holed flute of the old tabour-players, to which Valmajour had returned out of respect for tradition, and which he had mastered by skill and patience. Nothing could be more touching than the little story he told of his struggles, of his victory.

"It came to me," he said in his bizarre French, "it came to me one night as I listened to the nightingale singing. I thought in myself: What! Valmajour, there is the bird of the good God whose throat suffices him for all the trills, and what he does with one hole, can't you do with the three holes of your flute?"

He spoke deliberately, confidently and softly in a fine tone of voice, without any feeling of being ridiculous. Moreover, nobody would have dared smile in the presence of Numa's enthusiasm, lifting his arms, stamping enough to break through the tribune. "How magnificent he is!—What an artist!" And, after him, the mayor, the general, President Bédarride, M. Roumavage, a big brewer at Beaucaire, Peruvian vice-consul, and others besides, carried away by the Leader's authority, repeated in convinced accents: "What an artist!" It was also Hortense's feeling, and she expressed it with her expansiveness: "Oh! yes, a great artist!"—whilst Madame Roumestan murmured: "But you'll turn his head, the poor man." Still, it hardly appeared so, from the calm manner of Valmajour, who did not even show emotion when Numa told him abruptly:

"Come to Paris, my dear chap, your fortune's made."

"Oh! my sister wouldn't like to let me go," he answered smiling.

His mother was dead. He lived with his father and sister in a farmhouse bearing their name, three leagues from Aps, on Mount Cordoue. Roumestan swore he would visit him before going. He would speak with his relations; he was sure to settle the matter.

"I will help you, Numa," said a small voice behind him.

Valmajour bowed without a word, turned on his heel, and went down the broad platform carpet, his case on his arm, his head upright, with the slight hip-movement of the Provençal who loves rhythm and dance. His comrades below were waiting for him, shook hands. Then a shout resounded: "The farandole!" an immense clamour, doubled by the echo of the vaults, the passages. In a moment the circus was full, full enough to burst the barriers, with a mass of villagers, a mixture of white neckerchiefs, loud skirts, velvet ribbons fluttering on lace caps, braided blouses, woolen vests.

At a rolling of the tambourine, the crowd formed in line, defiled in bands, legs extended, hands joined. A trill of the flute made the whole circus undulate, and the "farandole," led by a youth from Barbantane, the country of famous dancers, slowly marched along, unwinding its rings, cutting capers, filling with a confused din, with a noise of rustling and breathing, the enormous gulf of the exit in which it was gradually swallowed up. Valmajour followed at an even, solemn pace, pushed the big tambourine with his knee as he walked, and played louder and louder as the compact heap in the arena, already half lost to sight in the blue ashes of the twilight, unravelled itself like a bobbin of gold and of silk.

"Look up there!" said Roumestan suddenly.

It was the foremost part of the dancers emerging between the vault arches of the first terrace, whilst the tabour-player and the last dancers were still footing it in the circus. And the farandole went up, went up, reached the higher galleries, which the sun was still illuminating with a tawny light.

Down below, on the emptied platform—for people were going, and the ranks of dancers were growing larger above the empty stone steps—worthy Numa asked his wife, as he threw a small lace shawl over her shoulders against the coolness of the evening:

"Well, isn't it fine?—isn't it fine?"

"Very fine," quoth the Parisian, stirred this time to the depths of her artist nature.

And the great man of Aps seemed prouder of this approval than of the noisy homage with which he had been deafened during two hours.

CHAPTER II

LOVE

NUMA was twenty-two, when he went to Paris to finish the legal studies he had begun at Aix. He was at that time a good-natured fellow, full of high spirits, noisy, florid of complexion, with fine gold-brown eyes, and a shock of black curly hair that fell over half his forehead like an otter-skin cap without

a peak. Not the shadow of an idea, of an ambition, beneath that sumptuous covering. A regular student of Aix, very good at billiards and pool, without an equal at drinking a bottle of champagne at a party, at hunting cats with torches till three in the morning in the broad streets of the old aristocratic and parliamentary town, but interested in nothing, never opening a paper or a book, steeped in the provincial foolishness which shrugs its shoulders at everything and clothes its ignorance with a reputation of plain good sense.

The Quartier Latin brisked him up a bit, but there was no reason why. Like his compatriots, he lived at the Café Malmus. It was at the corner of the Rue du Four-Saint-Germain, with three storeys of windows as big as those of a draper, and was full of noise from the billiard-room and the cries of a *clientéle* of young savages from the South. Apart from the lectures, which they attended assiduously, they spent their time there.

There were few women among them. Scarcely two or three on each floor, whom their sweethearts brought there with a shame-faced look, and who spent the evening beside them and a "bock," glancing over the big cartoons of the illustrateds, dumb and out of place among these Southern youths, brought up in contempt "of the female" (dou fémélan). Mistresses! *pardi*, they knew where to get them, at night or on the instant, but never for long. Bullier, the music-halls, the late suppers did not tempt them. They much preferred to stay at Malmus's, talk patois, wander between the café, the lecture-room, and the table d'hôte.

In this limited *milieu* Numa was easily an eagle. He was more noisy than the others, and he enjoyed a superiority, at any rate a reputation for originality because of his lively liking for music. He went to the pit of the Opera two or three times a week, and returned full of recitatives and tunes, which he sang with a fairly good throat-voice which was quite untrainable. When he reached Malmus's, when he advanced theatrically among the tables, singing some Italian finale, shouts of delight welcomed him from every storey; they cried: *"Hé!* what an artist!"* And, as happens in bourgeois environment, the word drew to him a caressing curiosity in women's looks, a curl of envious irony on the men's lips. This artistic reputation was afterwards of use to him in his career.

As for the lectures, he was similarly easy-going; though only half-prepared, for he was lazy, feared work and solitude, he passed rather brilliant examinations, thanks to his boldness, his southern subtlety, which always enabled him to discover the weak point of a professor's vanity. Moreover his face, with its frank, amiable expression, helped him and, as a lucky star, lighted the way before him.

When he became advocate, his parents summoned him home, because the moderate allowance they made cost them too bitter privation. But the project of shutting himself up at Aps had nothing in it to attract the indefinite ambition which the Provençal felt underlay his taste for the stir and bright intelligence of Paris. With great difficulty, he was allowed to take two more years to prepare for his doctor's degree. This time was passed and he

was about to return home, when he met at the house of the Duchess de San-Donnino, at one of those musical parties which were open to him owing to his good voice and his musical bent, Sagnier, the great Sagnier, the Legitimist advocate, brother of the Duchess and a confirmed melomaniac, whom he had enraptured by his nerve, breaking into society monotony, and by his enthusiasm for Mozart. Sagnier offered to take him as his fourth secretary. The salary was nothing, but it was no slight advantage to get a berth in the office of the first lawyer in Paris, as Sagnier had a huge amount of Parliamentary work and many influential clients in the Faubourg Saint-Germain. Roumestan *père* was unfortunately determined to cut off his allowance, expecting in that way to bring back his only son, an advocate of twenty-six, who was of an age to earn his living. The café-proprietor Malmus then intervened.

He was a type, this Malmus, a fat, asthmatic, pale man, who, from a mere café waiter, had become proprietor of one of the biggest establishments in Paris, by giving credit and by usury. He used at one time to advance students their month's allowance, which he made them pay thrice over when the ship arrived. Now he was rich, had perfected his method of business, based it entirely on credit, unlimited credit. The information he got from Aps gave him full confidence in Roumestan, whose father, once a cotton-spinner, had been ruined by speculations and inventions, and now lived modestly on an inspectorship of insurances; but his sister, Madame Portal, the childless widow of a wealthy magistrate, was sure to leave her nephew her whole fortune. That is why Malmus wanted to keep him in Paris: "Go to Sagnier's—I'll help you." The secretary of a well-known man could not live in a student's lodging, so he furnished him some bachelor's rooms on the Quai Voltaire, and undertook to pay his expenses; and in this way the future leader began his campaign, apparently comfortably off, in reality terribly impecunious, in want of ready money. Sagnier's friendship brought him splendid connections. The Faubourg welcomed him. But these social successes, these invitations to town and country-houses, only resulted in increasing his necessary expenses. His Aunt Portal helped him now and then, but accompanied her contributions with long lectures and Biblical threats against ruinous Paris. The position was untenable.

At the end of the year, Numa was looking out for something else; Sagnier, besides, needed hard workers, and that was not Numa's line. He was invincibly indolent, and especially dreaded steady, constant office life and work. He was radically wanting in concentration, owing to the vivacity of his imagination, the continual surging of ideas in his brain, the mobility of mind which could be seen even in his writing, which was always different. He was all outside, in voice and in gesture like a tenor.

"When I'm not speaking, I'm not thinking," he would say very naïvely; and it was true. With him the words did not spring from the idea, but the idea from the words. He was himself amused and amazed at his own fluency. In speaking, he revealed to himself a sensibility he did not know he possessed, was moved by the vibration of his own voice, by certain tones that stirred his heart, filled his eyes with tears. There were in him, assuredly, the qualities of an orator; but he was unaware of them, hardly ever having a chance of using them at Sagnier's.

Yet this period of a year with the great Legitimist advocate was decisive in his life. He won there convictions, a party, a taste for politics, a thirst for fortune and glory. The glory came first.

Some months after leaving his employer, the title of "Sagnier's secretary," which he retained, gave him the chance of defending a small Legitimist paper, Le Furet, much circulated in the well-to-do world. He did so with much success and good luck. He came unprepared, his hands in his pockets spoke two hours with an insolent verve and so much liveliness that he made the judges listen to the end. His accent, the terrible drawling of which his idleness had prevented his getting rid, lent something biting to his irony. It was a force, the rhythm of that very Southern eloquence, theatrical and familiar, with its especial light and clearness, such as are found in the work of the Southerners even as in their utterly limpid landscapes.

The newspaper was of course condemned, and paid for the advocate's big success in fines and imprisonment. Sagnier, who had come to hear him speak, embraced him in court. "Go and be a great man, my dear Numa," he declared, rather surprised at having hatched a falcon's egg. The most astonished, however, was Roumesta, who went away as in a dream, his ov words echoing in his buzzing ears, as he went down the vast, banisterless staircase of the Palais, quite dazed.

After this success, this ovation, a shower of panegyrical letters, the yellow smiles of his *confrères*, the advocate thought himself fairly started, waited patiently for briefs in his office, but nothing came, except a few more invitations to dinner and a pretty bronze from Barbédienne's, presented by the staff of the *Furet*. The new great man had to face the same difficulties, the same uncertainties as to the future. He was reduced to giving lessons in law in the Legitimist and Catholic society; but the work seemed beneath his reputation, his successes at the Conférence, the praises with which his name was garlanded in the party journals.

Some years thus passed, during which his name became better known, but always without profit except a few of Barbédienne's bronzes, then he was called upon to defend a shopkeeper of Avignon, who had had some seditious *foulards* manufactured, with a design displaying a deputation standing round the Count de Chambord, which was confused through the clumsiness of the printing, but was emphasized by an imprudent "H. V." surrounded by an escutcheon. Roumestan played an excellent comedy scene, grew indignant that the least political allusion could be seen there. "H. V.!" Why, it was Horace Vernet, presiding over a commission of the Institute!

This tarasconade had a local success which did more for his future than all the Parisian puffs, and above all won for him the active sympathies of Aunt Portal. It expressed itself first by a despatch of olive oil and white melons, then followed a crowd of other provisions: figs, pepper, *canissons* from Aix, *poutargue* from Martigues, jujubes, *azeroles*, carobs, common, insignificant fruits, of which the old lady was madly fond, and which the advocate allowed to rot at the bottom of a drawer. Some time after, a letter arrived, which showed in its thick, goose-quill writing the aunt's brusqueness of accent, her quaintnesses of expression, and revealed her slipshod mind in the utter lack of punctuation the quick leaps from one idea to another.

However, Numa thought he could gather that the worthy woman wanted to marry him to the daughter of a Councillor of the Paris Court of Appeal, M. le Quesnoy, whose wife—a Demoiselle Soustelle of Aps—had been brought up with her at the convent of La Calade—large fortune—pretty, spirited, with a rather constrained air, but marriage would clear it away. And if the marriage took place, what would Aunt Portal give her Numa? A hundred thousand francs in good money down on the wedding-day?

Beneath the provincialisms of the language, there was a serious proposal, so serious that two days after Numa got an invitation to dine with the Quesnoys. He went there, rather excited. The Councillor, whom he often met at the Palais, was one of the men who impressed him most. Tall, thin, a proud face, of morbid pallor, a keen, piercing eye, a mouth as if sealed, the old magistrate, who came from Valenciennes and seemed himself like a fortification of Vauban's, embarrassed him with his cold Northern manner.

The high position he owed to his splendid works on the penal law, to his large fortune, to the austerity of his life, a position which would have been still higher, had it not been for the independence of his opinions and the stern isolation in which he shut himself since the death of a son of twenty, all these facts passed before the eyes of the Southerner, as, one evening in September, 1865, he went up the broad, stone staircase, with carved iron banisters, of the *hôtel* de Quesnoy, one of the oldest in the Place Royale.

The large drawing-room into which he was shown, the solemnity of the high ceilings, the light painting on the panels of the doors, the hangings of striped damask framing the windows which looked on to an old balcony and an entire red corner of the brick buildings of the *place*, were not likely to dissipate the impression. But Madame Le Quesnoy's welcome soon put him at his ease. This little woman, with her sad kindly smile, closely shawled and weighed down with rheumatism, from which she suffered since she lived in Paris, kept the accent, the habits of her dear South, the love of everything that reminded her of it. She made Roumestan sit by her, and said, looking at him tenderly in the half-light: "He is quite the portrait of Evélina." The Christian name of Aunt Portal, which Numa was not accustomed to hear, touched him like a memory of childhood. Madame Le Quesnoy told him she had long wanted to know her friend's nephew: they were however, so dull now: they had not gone into society since their melancholy loss. But they had now made up their minds to receive a little, not that they grieved less, but

because of their daughters, the eldest of whom was nearly twenty; and turning to the balcony, which rang with youthful laughter, she called: "Rosalie—Hortense—come here. Here is M. Roumestan."

Ten years after this evening he remembered the calm, smiling appearance, in the frame of the high window and the tender light of the setting sun, of the beautiful young girl smoothing her hair, which the younger sister had disarranged in her play, and coming to him, with bright eyes, straight glance, without the least coquettish shyness.

He felt himself at once in confidence, in sympathy with her.

Once or twice, however, during dinner, whilst they were talking, Numa thought he caught sight, in the expression of the beautiful, clear-hued profile near him, of a disdainful passing shiver, no doubt the "constrained look," of which Aunt Portal spoke, and which Rosalie had from her likeness to her father. But the parted lips soon began to smile, and the deep-blue eyes softened into a kindly attentiveness, a delight of surprise which she did not even try to hide. Born and educated in Paris, Mademoiselle Le Quesnoy had always felt a resolute aversion from the South, whose accent, manners, landscape, partly known through holiday journeys, were all alike antipathetic to her. There was in it a kind of instinct of race, and it was a subject of affectionate quarrels between mother and daughter.

"I will never marry a man from the South," Rosalie would say laughingly and she had imagined to herself a type of him, noisy, coarse and empty-brained, a sort of operatic tenor or traveller in

Bordeaux wines, with expressive and regular head. Roumestan was certainly a trifle like this clear image conjured up by the mocking little Parisian; but his warm, musical words, which that evening had an irresistible power amid the environing sympathy, exalted, refined his countenance. After a few words in a low voice between those sitting next each other at table, those *hors-d'œuvre* of conversation which go round with the *marinades* and the caviare, the talk became general. The recent fêtes at Compiègne were mentioned, and those travesties of hunts, in which the guests figured as lords and ladies of Louis XV's time. Numa, who knew old Le Quesnoy's Liberal ideas, launched out in a superb, almost prophetic improvisation, showed up the Court as a circus, with its horsemen and women prancing beneath a stormy sky, rushing to the death of the stag mid lightning and distant thunder-claps; then the deluge when the fête is at its highest, the hunt entirely drowned, the whole monarchical carnival ending in a splash of blood and of mud!

Perhaps the speech was not quite new, perhaps Roumestan had already tried it at the Conférence. But never had his vividness, his accent of honourableness in revolt ever excited the enthusiasm suddenly visible in the limpid, deep look he felt turned towards him, whilst the Madame Le Quesnoy's sweet face was lit up with a ray of malice, and seemed to ask her daughter: "Well! what do you think of him, the man of the South?"

Rosalie was captured. The beautiful, deep voice stirred the inmost parts of her temperament, and the generous ideas expressed with such eloquence found an echo in her passion for truth and justice. Like women, who at the theatre identify the singer with the song, the actor with the rôle, she forgot the allowance that must be made for the virtuoso. Oh! if she had only k n o w n how empty the advocate's phrases were, how little he cared for the galas at Compiègne, and how it would only have required an Imperial invitation to decide him to take part in those cavalcades, in which his vanity, his instincts as a player would have been agreeably satisfied! But she was entirely under his spell. The table seemed magnified to her, the tired, sleepy faces of the few guests, a president of a chamber, a neighbouring doctor, seemed transfigured: and when they passed into the drawing-room, the lustre, illuminated for the first time since her brother's death, dazzled her with a warmth as of a real sun. The sun was Roumestan. He brought back life to the stately house, banished the mourning, the black that haunted every corner, those atoms of grief which float about in old dwellings, brought light into the big mirrors and life into the delicate panels which had faded during a century.

"You like painting, monsieur?"

"Oh! mademoiselle, there's nothing I like better——"

The truth is, he knew nothing at all about it; but on this, as on every other subject, he had a stock of excellent phrases ready, and, while the card-tables were being prepared, painting was as good an excuse as any other for a pleasant talk with the beautiful girl Anybody seeing them together and noticing the eloquent assurance of his talk, together with Rosalie's attentive air, would have said the advocate was some famous master giving his pupil a lesson.

"Mamma, may we go into your room?—I should like to show monsieur the hunting panel."

They crossed a passage lined with books, and came to the room which was as stately and old as the drawing-room. The hunting panel was over a small, finely-sculptured door.

"We can't see anything," said the young girl.

She lifted up the two-branched candelabra, which she had taken from a card-table, and holding her hand high, with her bust stretched forth, she lit up the panel representing a Diana, with the crescent on her brow, among her huntresses, in an Elysian landscape. But with that upright gesture of a canephora, which cast a double flame over her simple head-dress, her bright eyes, with the disdainful smile, the lithe symmetry of her virgin body, she was more Diana than the goddess herself. Roumestan gazed at her, and smitten by her modest charm, by the whiteness of her real youth, he forgot who she was, what he was doing there, his dreams of fortune and ambition. A mad impulse came upon him to hold in his arms that supple waist, to kiss that lovely hair, whose exquisite odour intoxicated him, to carry off that beautiful girl, and to make her the charm and happiness of his whole life; and something suggested to him that, if he attempted it, she would let him do so, that she was his, quite his, vanquished,

conquered the first day. Flame and wind of the South, you are irresistible.

CHAPTER III
ROUMESTAN!

IF there were ever two persons unsuited to live together, they were indeed these two. Opposite in instincts, education, temperament, race, not having the same ideas about anything, it was a case of North and South, without hope of possible fusion. Passion lives on such contrasts, it laughs when they are pointed out, feeling itself superior; but in daily life, in the monotonous return of days and nights under the same roof, the mist of the intoxication that constitutes love is scattered, and people see and judge each other.

In the new household the awakening did not come at once, to Rosalie at least. Clear of sight and sensible in everything else, she was long blind about Numa, without understanding how far she was his superior. He had soon recovered himself. The passions of the South are swift, in direct proportion to their violence. Besides, the Southerner is so convinced of woman's inferiority, that when once married, assured of happiness, he establishes himself as master, as a pasha, accepting love as homage, and thinking it kind of him even to accept it; because in fact it takes up time to be loved, and Numa was very busy, with the new mode of life necessitated by his marriage, his large fortune, his high position at the Palais as Le Quesnoy's son-in-law.

Aunt Portal's hundred thousand francs had served to pay Malmus and the upholsterer, to pass the sponge over his heart-breaking, endless bachelor's life, and the transition seemed pleasant from the lowly plush bench to the dining-room in the Rue Scribe, where he presided, opposite his elegant little Parisian, over sumptuous dinners to the princes of law and song. The Provençal liked a brilliant life, pleasure of the luxurious and magnificent kind; but he liked it especially at home, with that amount of free-and-easiness which allows of a cigar and a dubious story. Rosalie accepted everything, accommodated herself to the inconvenience of keeping open house, with the table laid for ten or fifteen guests, every night. She endured it without complaint, carried away in the impetuosity of her terrible great man, who agitated her by all his turbulences, and now and then smiled at his little wife between two thunders. She only regretted one thing, it was that she did not have him enough to herself. Even at breakfast, at that early lawyer's breakfast cut short by the hour of consultation, there was always the friend between them, that companion whom the Provençal could not dispense with, the everlasting talker necessary to the spouting forth of his ideas, the arm on which he liked to lean, to which he confided his too heavy portfolio on his way to the Palais.

Ah! how gladly she would have accompanied him over the bridges, how happy she would have been, on rainy days, to come and wait from him in their *coupé* and to return with him, closely shut in, behind the quivering mist of the windows. But she did not venture now to ask him, sure that he would always have a pretext, an appointment, in the Salle des Pas-Perdus,

with one of the three hundred intimates of whom the Southerner said affectionately—

"He worships me.—He would throw himself into the fire for me."

It was his way of understanding friendship. For the rest, no selection in his companions. His easy temper, the liveliness of his caprice, threw him at the head of the first comer and took him away as readily. Every week a new fancy, a name that recurred in all his phrases, which Rosalie carefully wrote down, at every meal, on the small menu card, and which then suddenly vanished, as if the gentleman's personality was as fragile, as easily burnt up, as the little coloured cards.

Among these friends of passage, one alone stayed less as a friend than a custom of childhood, for Roumestan and Bompard were born in the same street. He formed part of the household, and at her marriage the young wife found installed in her house, in the place of honour, like a piece of family furniture, that lean person, with a brigand's head, a big aquiline nose, eyes like agate balls in a dry, saffron skin, a piece of Cordova leather wrinkled by continual contortions. Yet Bompard had never been a comedian. At one time he sang in the chorus at the Italian opera, and it was there Numa had found him again. Apart from this detail, it was impossible to get anything precise about his undulating existence. He had seen everything, carried on every trade, had been everywhere. If anybody spoke before him of a celebrated man, a famous event he would observe: "That's a friend of mine," or "I was there—I've just come from there," and at once would follow a story in proof.

His present was no less obscure and mysterious than his past. Where did he live? On what? Now he spoke of a big business in asphalte, of a portion of Paris to be covered after an economical system; then suddenly, absorbed in his discovery of an infallible remedy for phylloxera, he would be only waiting for a letter from the minister to win the prize of a hundred thousand francs.

This delirious Southerner was Roumestan's joy. He took him with him everywhere, using him as a butt, drawing him out. When Numa stopped to talk to anybody on the Boulevard, Bompard went a few paces off on the pretext of lighting a cigar. He was to be seen at funerals, at first nights, asking hurriedly: "Have you seen Roumestan?" He became as well known. But Rosalie could not tolerate this sharer of her happiness, always between herself and her husband, filling up the rare moments when they might have been alone. The two friends spoke a dialect which left her in the cold, laughed at local, untranslatable jokes. What she particularly urged against him was his need of lying, his inventions in which she had at first believed, so foreign was imposture to her straight, frank nature, whose greatest charm was the harmonious accord of word and thought, an accord perceptible in the sonorousness, the assurance of her crystal voice.

"I don't like him—he's a liar," she would say in a deeply indignant tone, which greatly amused Roumestan. And, defending his friend, he would reply—

"But no, he is not a liar—he's a man of imagination, an awakened dreamer, who speaks his dreams. My country is full of such people.—It's the sun, it's the accent. Look at my aunt Portal, and myself, at every instant, if I did not watch over myself——"

A little hand protested, shut his mouth: "Hush, hush—I shouldn't like you any more, if you were of that South."

But he was; and despite the Parisian manner, the society polish that checked him, she was about to see that terrible South, narrow, brutal, illogical, come out in him. The first time it was a matter of religion; Roumestan followed the tradition of his province in that as in everything else. He was the Provençal Catholic, who does not act up to his faith, never goes to church except to look for his wife at the end of the Mass, remaining near the holy water, with the superior air of a pater familias at a pantomime, confess only in time of cholera, but would let himself be hung or martyred for the faith he does not feel, which moderates nothing of his passions or his vices.

When he married, he knew his wife was nominally of the same creed as himself; he asked no further. All the women he knew, his mother, his cousin Aunt Portal, as well as the Duchess of San-Donnino, were ardent Catholics. He was therefore much surprised, after some months of marriage to notice that Rosalie did not practise her religion. He observed—

"So you never go to confession?"

"No, my friend," she said, without

emotion—"nor you either, so far as I see."

"Oh! I! it's not the same thing."

"Why?"

She looked at him with eyes so sincerely, so luminously amazed; she had so little the air of suspecting her womanly inferiority, that he found no answer, and left her to explain. Oh! she was not a free-thinker, an "intellectual." Educated in an excellent Paris boarding-school, with a priest of Saint-Laurent for religion, up to seventeen years of age, up to her leaving school, and even at home for a few months more, she had continued her religious practices with her mother, a devout Southerner; then one day something broke inside her, she had declared to her parents the insurmountable repugnance caused her by confession. Her mother had tried to overcome what she thought a caprice; but M. Le Quesnoy had interposed.

"Let her be, let her be—I was taken like her, at the same age."

And thenceforth she had only had her young conscience to take advice and guidance from. Still, as a Parisian, a woman of the world, who had a horror of acts of independence which were in bad taste; if Numa insisted on going to Church she would accompany him as she had long accompanied her mother, without, however, agreeing to the lie, the grimace of belief she no longer possessed.

He heard her with stupefaction, frightened at hearing such things spoken by her, and with an energetic assertion of her moral being which routed all his native ideas on feminine dependence.

"Then you don't believe in God?"

he asked in his finest advocate style, his finger solemnly raised toward the moulding of the ceiling. She cried: "Is it possible?" so spontaneously, so sincerely that it was equal to a declaration of faith. So he fell back on society, social conventions, the solidarity of the religious and monarchical idea. All these ladies confessed, the Duchess, Madame d'Escarbès; they received their confessor at table, at their parties. It would have a deplorable effect if people knew—— He stopped, feeling that he was muddled, and the discussion ended. The next two or three Sundays he made a great point of taking his wife to Mass, which gave Rosalie the luck of a walk on her husband's arm. He soon tired of the habit however, made an excuse of business, and stopped his Catholic manifestation.

This first misunderstanding did not trouble the household at all. As if wishing to earn forgiveness, the young wife redoubled her attentions, her ingenuous and ever-smiling submission. Perhaps, less blind than during the earlier days, she confusedly had a pre-sentiment of things she did not even dare to avow to herself, but she was nevertheless happy, because she wanted to be, because she was living in that paradise into which the change of life, the revelation of their woman's destiny, casts young married women, still envel-oped in those dreams, those uncertainties which are like the floating white *tulles* of their wedding-dress. The awakening could not be delayed. In her case it was fearful and sudden.

One summer's day—they were spending the fine season at Orsay on the Le Quesnoys' estate—Rosalie, when her father and husband had gone off to

Paris, as they did every morning, she found she wanted a little pattern for the small outfit at which she was working. Yes, *mon Dieu!* a baby's outfit. Superb ones, ready made, are on sale; but true mothers, those who are mothers beforehand, love to sew, to cut out themselves. On no account whatever did Rosalie wish to deprive herself of this joy, nor would she have allowed any other hand at the gigantic work undertaken five months since, when she had become sure of her happiness—and the pattern was wanting.

"Send your maid," said the mother. The maid, forsooth!—How would she know? "No, no, I'll go myself.—I'll buy my things before twelve. Then I'll go and surprise Numa and eat half his lunch."

The idea of this bachelor meal with her husband in the apartment in the Rue Scribe amused her like an escapade. She was smiling all to herself at it, when, her errands finished, she went up the carpetless staircase of the Parisian house, and said to herself, cautiously putting the key in the lock so as to surprise him: "I've come a bit late.—He will have lunched."

There was nothing in fact in the dining-room but the remains of a choice little banquet, with covers for two, and the valet in his check jacket installed at the table, finishing the bottles and dishes. She saw at first nothing but her failure, through her own fault. Ah! if she hadn't loitered so long in the shop, with the pretty trifles in embroidery and lace.

"Monsieur has gone?"

The valet's slowness in reply, the sudden pallor of that broad impudent face, flattened down between the long whiskers, did not then strike her. She only saw the dismay of the servant who had been caught at his thieving and gluttony. Still, he had to say that his master was there—and at business—and would be a long time. But what a time he took to stammer it out, what trembling hands he had, the man, as he cleared the table and laid his mistress's cover.

"Did he lunch alone?"

"Yes, madame—that is—with M. Bompard."

She was looking at some black lace thrown on a chair. He also saw it, and, as their eyes met, it was like a flash of lightning to her. At once, without a word, she darted forward, crossed the small ante-room, reached the door of the study, opened it wide, and fell unconscious. They had not even shut themselves in.

And if you had seen the woman, her forty years of faded blonde, her thin lips, her eyes haggard and wrinkled like the skin of an old glove; violet marks under the lids, scars of a life of pleasure, square shoulders, hideous voice. Only, she was noble—the Marquise d'Escarbès!—and, for the Southerner that took the place of everything, the coat-of-arms concealed the woman. Separated from her husband by scandalous trial, embroiled with her family and the great houses of the Faubourg, Madame d'Escarbès had rallied to the Empire, had opened political, diplomatic, dubiously police attended *salon*, which was visited by the most prominent personages of the time, without their wives; then, after two years of intrigues, when she had created a party and influence for herself, she thought of appealing. Roun stan, who had pleaded for her in the first instance, could hardly refuse to follow her. He hesitated, however, because of his very pronounced opinions. But the marquise flattered the advocate's vanity in such ways, that he resisted no more. The appeal being now near at hand, they met every day, sometimes in his rooms, sometimes at her house.

Rosalie nearly died of this horrible discovery. The child was still-born, the mother survived. But when, after three days of agony, she recovered her memory for suffering, she had a crisis of weeping, a bitter flood nothing could stop. Without a cry, without a complaint, when she had finished weeping at her friend's, her husband's treason, her tears redoubled at the sight of the empty cradle, in which slept, alone, the treasures of the baby-outfit under transparent blue curtains. Poor Numa was about as despairing. The great hope of a little Roumestan, of "the eldest," always endowed with prestige in Provençal families, destroyed, nullified by his fault, his wife's pale face buried in an expression of renunciation, her grief with teeth clenched, with dull sobs that pierced his soul, so different from his own outbursts and the violent superficial sensibility he displayed, sitting at the foot of his victim's bed, his eyes haggard, his lips trembling.

"Rosalie—come now!" that was all he could find to say, but what a meaning was there in the "Come now!" uttered in the Southern tone, readily moved to pity! They meant: "Don't keep on sorrowing, my poor creature.— Is it worth while? Does it prevent my loving you?"

Truly he loved her, as far as his shallowness allowed him a lasting attachment. He did not dream of anybody but her to direct his household, look after him, fondle him. He who said so ingenuously: "I have need of devotion around me!" was certain that his wife's was the most complete, the most loving he could desire, and the idea of losing her frightened him. If that is not love!

Alas! Rosalie imagined a quite different thing. Her life was broken, her idol overset, her confidence destroyed for ever. And yet, she forgave. She forgave out of pity, as a mother gives way to a child who cries, who humiliates himself; also because of the dignity of their name, her father's name, which the scandal of a separation would have tarnished, and because, as her family believed her happy, she could not disillusion them. She warned him that he could not count upon forgiveness if he renewed the outrage. Never again! In that case their two lives would be cruelly, radically parted, before the world!—This was signified in a tone, with a look, in which the wife's pride took its revenge on all the social conventions and shackles.

Numa understood, swore never to do so again, and sincerely. He still grieved at having risked his happiness, the repose he held so dear, for a pleasure which only gratified his vanity. And the relief at having rid himself of his *grande dame,* this raw-boned marquise who, apart from the coat-of-arms, had no appeal for his senses, was almost as pleasing to him as his wife's clemency, the restored peace in the house.

He was as happy as before. There was no change in the appearance of their life. The table was always spread, the same parties given, at which Roumestan sang, declaimed, entertained without suspecting that near him two beautiful eyes were watching, wide open, made clearer in sight by real tears. She really saw him now, her great man, all gesture, all speech, kindly and generous by starts, but of a brief kindliness, composed of caprice, of ostentation and a coquettish desire to please. She felt what little substance there was in that nature which hesitated in its convictions as in its hates; above all she was frightened on her own and on his account at his weakness hidden beneath big words and boisterous tones, a weakness that excited her indignation, but at the same time attached her to him by the need of maternal protection, on which a wife bases her devotion when love has departed. And, ever ready to give herself, to devote herself to him in spite of his treason, she had only one secret fear: "provided he does not discourage me!"

Clear of perception as she was, Rosalie soon noticed the change taking place in her husband's opinions. His relations with the Faubourg grew strained. Old Sagnier's nankeen waistcoat, the fleur-de-lys of his scarf-pin, no longer inspired him with the same veneration. He thought his great intelligence was waning. Numa was slowly evolving, gradually opening his doors to Imperialist instabilities, to be met with in Madame d'Escarbès's *salon,* whose influence had prompted the change of front. "Look after your great man, I believe he is wobbling," said the Councillor to his daughter, one day, when the advocate had amused himself at table about the Frohsdorf party, which he

compared to Don Quixote's wooden Pegasus which was motionless and nailed to its place, whilst the cavalier with eyes bandaged imagined he was making a long journey through the sky. She had not to put many questions. Though he could be a dissembler, his lies, which he disdained to back up with any subtleties, had an abandon about them which immediately convicted him. Coming one morning into his study, she surprised him much absorbed in the composition of a letter, bent her head to the level of his:

"To whom are you writing?"

He stammered, tried to invent something, and penetrated by her look, which haunted him like a conscience, he had an outburst of compulsory frankness—it was a letter to the Emperor written in a bold emphatic style in which he accepted the post of Councillor of State. It began: *As a Vendéan of the South, grown up in the monarchical faith, and the respectful veneration of the past, I believe I am doing no violence to honour or to my conscience——*

"You will not send that!" she said impetuously.

He began by getting angry, speaking loudly, brutally, like a regular Ap bourgeois laying down the law in his household. What was she interfering for? What did she mean? Did he bother her about the shape of her hat or the makers of her new dresses? He thundered forth, as if in court, whilst Rosalie remained humbly quiet, almost contemptuous.

"You will not send that letter," she resumed. "It would be giving the lie to your life, to your promises."

"Promises?—To whom?"

"To me. Remember how we got to know each other, how you captured my heart with your rebellious, your lofty indignations against the Imperial masquerade. And I cared still less for your opinions than for a straightforward line of conduct, once adopted, a man's will that I admired in you."

He defended himself. Ought he to bury himself all his life in a party that was frozen up, without resources, a camp abandoned under the snow? Besides, it was not he that went to the Empire, but the Empire that came to him. The Emperor was an excellent man, full of ideas, very superior to his *entourage.*—And all the usual good excuses for leaving anybody in the lurch. Rosalie accepted none, and showed him his clumsiness in his felony. "So you don't see how uneasy all those people are, how they feel the ground is ruined, sapped around them. The least shock, a loosened stone, and the whole crumbles—into what an abyss!"

She gave details, such as a silent woman culls and ponders on, of the after-dinner talk, when the men gathered apart leave their wives, intelligent or not, to languish in those banal conversations which toilette, society ill-natured gossip are not always enough to make lively. Roumestan was astounded: "Funny little woman!" Whence had she taken all she had just said? He could not get over the fact that she was so acute, and in one of those ardent impulses which are the charm of such impetuous characters, he took that clever, beautiful young head of hers in his hands and covered it with rain of tender kisses.

"You're right, a hundred times right—I must write the exact opposite."

He was about to tear up his rough draft, but there was a phrase at the beginning which pleased him and which might be used again, by modifying it somewhat as follows: *A Vendéan of the South grown up in the monarchical faith and the respectful veneration of the past, I am convinced I should be doing violence to honour and my conscience, if I accepted the post which your Majesty——*

This refusal, very politely, but very decidedly worded, was published in the Legitimist journals, put Roumestan in a quite new position, made his name synonymous with incorruptible loyalty. Some time after, the Empire went to pieces; and when the Bordeaux Assembly met, Numa Roumestan had three Departments of the South to choose from, which had elected him deputy solely on account of his letter. His first speeches had soon made him leader of all the Right parties.

Councillor-General of his Department, the idol of the entire South, exalted yet further by the magnificent position of his father-in-law, passed First President of the Court of Cassation since the fall of the Empire, Numa was evidently destined to become a minister one day or other.

CHAPTER IV

PORTAL HOUSE

PORTAL HOUSE, in which the great man of Aps lodges during his sojourns in Provence, is reckoned among the curiosities of the place. It figures in the guide-books with the temple of Juno, the amphitheatre, the old theatre, the tower of the Antonines, ancient remains of Roman rule of which the own is very proud. But it is not a great heavy door of the old provincial house embossed with huge nails, nor the windows barred with bristling spikes that strangers are asked to admire; only the balcony on the first floor, a narrow balcony with iron railings over the porch. From there Roumestan speaks and exhibits himself to the crowd when he arrives, and as the whole town could bear witness the orator's heavy fist it is that has given those capricious curves to the balcony which was once straight as a yard measure.

"*Té! Vé!*—he's bent the iron."

They tell you that, with their eyes staring out of their heads, with a rolling of the r's, which does not allow a shadow of a doubt.

The race is proud in the land of Aps and good-natured; but with a vivacity of impressions and intemperance of language of which Aunt Portal, a true type of the local *bourgeoisie*, can give a distinct idea. Enormous in size, apoplectic, with all her blood flowing into her flaccid purple cheeks, which are contrasted with her skin, which is that of one who was a blond, imposing and majestic in appearance, with an agreeable smile, such is a first impression of Madame Portal in the twilight of her drawing-room which is always hermetically closed, in Southern fashion. You would say she was like a family portrait. an old Marquise de Mirabeau, well suited to the old house built a hundred years before by Gonzague Portal, leading Councillor at the Parliament of Aix.

But if when talking with the aunt you unhappily claim that Protestants are as good as Catholics, or that Henri V is not near to ascending the throne, the old portrait dashes violently from its frame, and with the swollen veins of her neck, her irritated hands deranging her carefully-ordered frills and furbelows, it yields to a frightful outburst of rage mingled with abuse, threats, curses, one of those rages that are notorious in the town.

In any other spot in the world she would have been treated as a madwoman, but in Aps, a land of hotheads, they agree to find Madame Portal "hasty tempered." In the long run an excellent person, passionate, generous, with that need of pleasing, of giving herself, which is one of the sides of the race and of which Numa had experienced the benefits. Since his nomination as deputy the house in the Place Cavalerie belonged to him, his aunt reserving to herself merely the right to live in it till her death. And what a fête for her was the arrival of her Parisians, the festivities. the serenades, the receptions, the visits with which the visits of the great man filled her life greedy of exuberance. Then she adored her niece Rosalie with all the contrast of their two natures, with all the respect imposed on her by the daughter of President Le Quesnoy, the first magistrate of France.

And truly the young wife had need of a singular indulgence of that family cult which she had from her parents to endure for two long months the fancies, the wearying surprises of that disordered, always over-excited imagination which was as active as the gross body was idle. Luckily, Rosalie through living with her Numa was accustomed to such frenzies of speech, she hardly asked herself how it was that she, reserved, discreet as she was, had been found able to enter such a family of comedians, draped with phrases, overflowing with gestures; and the story had to be very "strong" for her to interrupt by absent-mindedly exclaiming, "Oh! aunt."

"Yes, you're right, my little one. I'm perhaps exaggerating a bit."

It was a Friday morning during lunch, a Southern lunch, fresh and gay to the eye, but rigorously in keeping with the fast, for Aunt Portal was a martinet in such matters. In the middle of the table two splendid cutlets for Numa were smoking on a hot plate. Although his name was blest in the congregations, mingled with all their prayers, or perhaps even because of that fact, the great man of Aps alone of the family had a dispensation from fasting from Monseigneur, and serenely cut up the underdone meat with his strong hands, without troubling about his wife and sister-in-law, who, like Aunt Portal, were making do with figs and watermelons. Rosalie was accustomed to it, the orthodox fasting two days a week, as a part of her annual burden, like the sun, the dust, the mistral of the South, the stories of the aunt and the services on Sunday at Sainte-Perpétue. Hortense, however, began to revolt with all the strength of her young stomach, and it needed the authority of the elder sister to close the mouth of the spoilt child, which would have upset all Madame Portal's ideas regarding the education, the proper conduct of young ladies. The girl contented herself with eating what was before her, rolling her eyes in a comical way, expanding her nostrils despairingly towards Roumestan's cutlet, and murmuring in a low tone for Rosalie's benefit—

"What luck!—I've just been riding this morning.—I'm as hungry as a traveller."

She still had on her riding habit, which fitted well her long supple figure, as the little collar suited her piquant, irregular features enlivened by the riding in the open air. And her morning promenade having given her a taste for an excursion—

"Apropos, Numa—And Valmajour, when are we going to see him?"

"Who's that Valmajour?" asked Roumestan, whose fickle brain had already forgotten the tambourinist. "Té, of course, Valmajour—I wasn't thinking of him; what an artist!"

He saw again the arena and the people dancing the farandole to the dull rhythm of the tambourine which excited him in the memory of it. And with sudden decision:—

"Aunt Portal, lend us the berlin—we're going off after lunch."

The aunt frowned like a Japanese idol.

"The berlin—avai!—And what are you going to do?—At any rate, I hope you're not going to take your ladies to this tutu-panpan player."

The words "tutu-panpan" rendered the double instrument, fife and tabour, so well, that Roumestan began laughing. But Hortense took up the cudgels for the old Provençal tabour with much briskness. Of all she had seen in the South, that had especially impressed her. Besides, it would not be right to break one's word with that fine fellow. "A great artist, Numa—you said so yourself!"

"Yes, yes, you're right, little sister—we must go there!"

Aunt Portal, suffocated with indignation, could not understand how a man like her nephew, a deputy, should put himself out for common peasants, people who played on the flute from father to son at village fêtes. Absorbed in her idea, she scoffingly mimicked the musician's gestures, her fingers extended on an imaginary flute, whilst her other hand tapped on the table. Nice sort of people to show to young ladies!—No, it was only that Numa.—Go to the Valmajours! good holy Mother of Angels! —And, growing excited, she began to charge them with every crime, to make of them a family of monsters, notorious and blood-thirsty as the Trestaillon family, when she perceived, on the other side of the table, Ménicle, who belonged to the Valmajour country and was listening opposite her, his features all distorted with amazement. Immediately she ordered him in a fearful voice to "go and change" quickly, and have the berlin ready at a quarter to two. All the aunt's fits of choler ended in the same fashion.

Hortense threw down her napkin and ran and kissed the fat woman on both cheeks. She was laughing, jumping with delight: "Let's hurry, Rosalie."

Aunt Portal looked at her niece—

"Ah ça! Rosalie! I hope you're not going on trip with these children?"

"No, no, aunt—I'll remain with you," answered the young wife, smiling at the rôle of elderliness which her indefatigable obligingness, her loving resignation had finally bestowed on her in the house.

At the appointed hour, Ménicle was ready; but he was let go in advance, the rendezvous being fixed at the Place des Arènes, and Roumestan set off on foot with his sister-in-law, who was curious and proud to see Aps, leaning on the arm of the great man, the house where he was born, to recall with him in the streets the memories of his early childhood and youth.

It was the hour of siesta. The town was asleep, deserted and silent, rocked by the mistral, blowing great guns, aërating, vivifying the warm summer of Provence, but making walking hard, especially along the *Cours*, where there was nothing to check it, where it could rush whirling, encircling the small city with its howls as of a bull let loose.

They chatted together, following a labyrinth of dark, oriental streets, where old women were sleeping on their doorsteps, other streets less gloomy, but crossed in their breadth by big, flapping strips of printed calico bearing such signs as: *Grocers, linen-drapers, bootmakers;* and so they reached what is called at Aps the Placette, a square of asphalte melting beneath the sun, surrounded by shops now shut and mute. An unfinished monument adorned the centre of the Placette. As Hortense wanted to know what was going to be set on the white marble Roumestan smiled in some embarrassment——

"It's a long story!" said he, hastening on.

The municipality of Aps had voted him a statue, but the Liberals of the *Avant-garde* having severely censured such an apotheosis of a living person his friends had not dared to go on with it. The statue was quite ready people were waiting probably for his death to set it up. The empty pedi ment, gleaming in the sun, gave Roumestan, whenever he passed it, the feeling of a stately family tomb, and the sight of the amphitheatre was needed to draw him from his funereal thoughts. The old building, vacant of Sunday's noisy animation, restored to its solemnity as a useless, grandiose ruin, displayed through the serried openings its broad, damp, cold corridors.

"How cheerless it is!" cried Hortense regretting Valmajour's tambourine; but it was not cheerless for Numa. His childhood had there lived its best hours in delights and desires. Oh! the bullfights on Sundays, the lounging about the railings with other children poor as himself, who had not ten *sous* for a ticket. In the burning sun of the afternoon, the mirage of forbidden pleasure, they looked at the little they could see between the heavy walls, the corner of the circus, the legs of the toreros encased in loud-coloured stockings, the furious onslaughts of the animal, the dust of the combat. The desire of going in was too strong for them; accordingly the boldest watched for a moment when the sentinel was going away; and they slipped with some little effort between two of the bars.

"As for me, I always used to get through," said Roumestan expressively. His life's whole story was summed up in those two words: whether it was due to chance or skill, however narrow the opening might be, the Southerner had always got through.

"It's all the same now," he added sighing, "I was thinner than I am to-day." And his glance passed with an expression of comic regret from the narrow railings of the arches to the broad white waistcoat, which testified

decisively to his more than forty years.

Behind the huge monument the berlin was awaiting them, sheltered from the wind and sun. They had to wake up Ménicle who was asleep on his seat between two baskets of provisions in his heavy livery of royal blue. Hortense, who began to fear they would never get out of the town where the great man discovered some eloquent memory in every stone, urged him gently into the berlin—

"Let's get in, Numa—we should talk quite as well on the way."

CHAPTER V

THE REDS

It hardly takes more than two hours to go from Aps to the Mont de Cordoue. Drawn by its two old Camargues horses the berlin went along quite by itself, pushed by the mistral which shook it, lifted it up, dented the leather of its hood or swelled it like a sail. Here it no longer roared as it did round the ramparts, but free, unshackled, driving before the immense undulating plain, where a few isolated farms, all grey in a green setting, seemed the scattering of a village by the tempest, it passed as mist over the sky, as a swift darkness on the tall grains, on the fields of olive trees, whose silver leaves it shook in a dance, and in great gusts that raised light floods of dust that crackled beneath the wheels; it lowered the heads of close-grown cypresses, the Spanish reeds with long wavy leaves giving the illusion of a fresh streamlet by the side of the road. When it was hushed for a minute as if short of breath, you felt the burden of summer, an African heat, coming from the sun, which very speedily dissipated the healthy, vivifying whirlwind that extended its merry progress to the furthest point of the horizon, towards those small greyish hills which are found at the back of every Provençal landscape which the setting sun irises with fairy hues.

They did not meet many people. At long intervals a carter coming from the quarries with a cargo of enormous blocks of stones, blinding in the sunlight, an old peasant woman of the Ville-des-Baux bent beneath a great load of aromatic herbs, a mendicant friar, wallet on back, rosary hanging by his thigh, his skull sweating and glistening, or a carriage full of women and girls returning from a pilgrimage in full dress, with fine black eyes, big chignons, bright fluttering ribbons, coming from La Sainte-Baume or from Notre-Dame de-Lumière.

"Hé! Ménicle!—Ménicle——"

"Monsieur Numa?"

"What is that building down there on the other side of the road?"

"That, Monsieur Numa, is the dungeon of Queen Jeanne."

"Ah, yes, that's true—I remember."

He then related to Hortense the story of the royal dungeon, for he was thoroughly at home in Provençal legends—and working himself into excitement, forgetting that his only audience was his sister-in-law and Ménicle's blue livery, he soared into one of those ingenious and brilliant improvisations, which truly made him a descendant of the Provençal trouvères.

"There's Valmajour!" suddenly said Aunt Portal's coachman, bending back to show them the height with the end of his whip.

They had left the high road and were following the zig-zag narrow path up the sides of the Mont de Cordoue, slippery because of the tufts of lavender whose perfume was exhaled at every turn of the wheel. On a plateau, half-way up the hill at the foot of a ruined black tower, the roofs of the farm were to be seen. The Valmajours had lived there from father to son for years and years, on the site of the old castle whose name had remained to them. And who knows? Perhaps those peasants were actually descended from the princes of Valmajour who were allied to the Counts of Provence and the house of Baux This hypothesis imprudently suggested by Roumestan was altogether to Hortense's liking, who thus explained to herself the really noble manners and mien of the tabour-player.

As they talked about it in the carriage Mènicle on his seat listened to them in stupefaction. The name of Valmajour was widely spread in the district. "So they would be at tha rate all of them grands seigneurs!" But the astute Provençal kept his observation to himself. And whilst they were slowly advancing into this bare rugged country, the girl upon whom Roumestan's lively conversation had cast the spell of a historical novel in its coloured dream of the past, perceiving up above a peasant woman seated at the foot of the ruins, half turned to look at them arriving, with her hand over her eyes, imagined she saw some Princess on the summit of her tower.

The illusion scarcely ceased when the travellers, getting out of the carriage, found themselves face to fac with the tabour-player's sister, who was busily engaged in plaiting osier twigs for the silkworms. She did not rise, though Mènicle had cried to her from far off: "*Vé!* Audiberte, here are some visitors for your brother." Her clever, regular, oval face, dark as an olive, showed neither joy nor surprise, retained the concentrated expression that knotted her thick, straight, black eyebrows, under her obstinate forehead, as with a very tight band. Roumestan, rather taken aback by her reserve, introduced himself—

"Numa Roumestan—the deputy."

"Oh! I know you well," she said gravely, and leaving her work beside her in a heap: "Come in for a moment—my brother will be here soon."

When she stood up, the mistress of the castle lost prestige. Very short, her figure entirely developed in bust only, she walked awkwardly, inharmoniously with her pretty head, which was finely set off by the small Arles cap and the broad muslin *fichu* with bluish folds They went in. This peasant abode had a fine appearance, leaning against a ruined tower, with a coat-of-arms in the stone over the gate. Two or three images, the Saints Mary, Martha and La Tarasque, the red copper of a small, antique lamp, with the salt-cellar and the flour-box on each side of the chimney-piece, completed the adornment of the huge room. The long table was spread lengthways, flanked by benches and chaplets of onions hung from the ceiling, all black with flies which buzzed about whenever the door was opened.

"Refresh yourselves, monsieur, madame—pray, have the *grand-boire* with us."

The "grand-boire" is the appetizer of the Provincial peasants. It is served in the fields, even at the place of work, under some tree, in the shade of a mill, in the hollow of a ditch. Valmajour and his father, however, who worked quite near, on their property, came home to have it. And the table was already awaiting them, with two or three little yellow plates, preserved olives, and a *salade de romaine* glistening with oil. In the osier basket in which the bottle and glasses were placed, Roumestan thought he saw wine.

"So you have still vines here?" he inquired in an affable way, trying to tame the strange little savage woman. But at the word "vines," she at once leapt up and her voice sounded in a diapason of fury. Vines! Ah! yes, fine vines!—Plenty of them!—They could only save one out of five, the smallest, and even that they had to keep under water six months in the year. And whose fault was all that? The fault of the Reds, those pigs, those monsters of Reds and their republic without religion which had let loose hell-abominations on the country.

As she talked with such passion, her eyes became blacker, with a murderous black, her pretty face was convulsed and grimacing, her mouth contorted, the knot of her eyebrows drawn tight so as to make a big fold in the middle of her forehead. The funniest part of it was that she continued busy amid her wrath, prepared her men's fire, coffee, got up, sat down, holding in her hand the bellows, the coffee-pot, or burning embers, which she brandished like the torch of a fury. Then suddenly she calmed down: "Here's my brother."

The rustic blind parted and there entered Valmajour's tall figure, followed by a little old man, clean-shaven, wizened, black as the foot of a diseased vine. Neither father nor son were more excited than Audiberte at their visitors, and after the first greetings took their seats round the "grandboire," reinforced by the victuals taken from the berlin, at which old Valmajour's eyes flamed up. Roumestan, who did not recover from the slight impression he made on these peasants, spoke at once of the great success at the amphitheatre on Sunday. That ought surely to have pleased the old father!

"Certainly, certainly," grumbled the old man, "but I have also taken tabour prizes in my time." And his malicious smile showed the same contortion of the mouth as did his daughter quite recently. Very quiet at the moment, the peasant woman was seated almost on the ground on the hearth-stone, her plate on her knees; for although absolutely mistress of the house she obeyed the Provençal custom which forbids women to sit at table with the men. Still, from her lowly posture, she attentively followed what was said, moved her head. She herself did not like the tambourine. Ah! *nani!*—Her mother had died of it, from blood-poisoning, through her papa's music. It damaged work and cost more than it brought in.

"Well! let him come to Paris," said Roumestan. "I'll answer for it that he'll make money there by his instrument."

He tried to explain that Parisians paid dear for their caprices. He told of the success of old Mathurin, the player of the bag-pipe, in the "Closerie des Genêts." And what a difference between the shrill, vulgar Breton bag-pipe and the *svelte,* elegant Provençal tambourine! All the Parisian ladies would lose their heads, would want to dance the "farandole." Hortense also became excited, said a few words, whilst the tabour-player smiled vaguely and twisted his brown moustache with the vanishing gesture of a self-conscious, handsome man.

"But what exactly d'you think he would earn with his music?" asked the peasant girl.

Roumestan thought a bit. He could not say precisely.—About 150 to 200 francs.

"A month?" said the father enthusiastically.

"*Hé!* no! a day——"

The three rustics quivered, then gazed at each other. Had it been anybody else than "Moussu Numa," deputy, member of the General Council, they would have believed it a joke! But, as it was, the matter was becoming serious—200 francs a day! The musician himself was quite ready. The sister, more prudent, would have liked Roumestan to sign a paper; and deliberately, with eyes downcast, lest they should betray her greed for gain, she went on discussing in a hypocritical voice. Valmajour was very necessary to the house, *pécaïré!* He managed the property, toiled, pruned the vines, as his father was not strong enough. What should they do if he went? All alone in Paris, he would grow home-sick. And his money, his 200 francs a day, what would he do with it in that big town?—Her voice grew hard as she spoke of that money, whose keeping she would not have, which she would not be able to shut up in the lowest of her drawers?

"Well, then," said Roumestan, "come to Paris with him."

"And the house?"

"Let it, sell it—when you return, you'll buy a finer one."

Upon an uneasy look from Hortense he stopped, and as if remorseful at disturbing the repose of these worthy people—

"After all, you're happy as you are."

Audiberte broke in vivaciously: "Oh! happy! Life is very hard! It's not as it once was." She began again to groan about the vines, the silk-worms, the vanished wealth of the district. They had to work like satyrs.—True, they had in the future expectations from Cousin Puyfourcat, who had been in Algeria thirty years as a colonist, but Algeria is so far away in Africa. And all at once the astute little person, in order to excite again the enthusiasm of "Moussu Numa," which she reproached herself for having chilled rather too much, told her brother felinely, in her caressing, singing ones—

"Qué, Valmajour suppose you gave us a little tune to please this beautiful young lady?"

Ah! the cunning rogue! She was not mistaken. At the first beat of the stick, at the first trill, Roumestan was again captivated and rapturous. The young man played in front of the farm, leaning on the edge of an old well, whose arched iron railings, entangled in a wild fig-tree, wonderfully framed his elegant figure and dark complexion. His arms bare, his chest open, in his dusty working dress, he

looked even somewhat prouder and nobler than in the arena, when his grace was stiffened by a theatrical artificiality. And the old tunes of the rustic instrument, poeticized by the silence and solitude of a fine landscape, awakening the gilded ruins from their stone sleep, flew like larks over those stately inclines, all grey with lavender or variegated with grain, with dead vines, with large-leaved mulberries, whose shadows began to lengthen as it became lighter. The wind had fallen. The setting sun was flaming on the violet line of the Alpilles, was casting into the hollow of the rocks a mirage of pools of liquid porphyry, of molten gold, and a luminous vibration on the whole horizon, the tense chords of a burning lyre, the sounds of which seemed to be the continuous song of the grasshoppers and the beats of the tabour.

Hortense, sitting in meek rapture on the parapet of the ancient dungeon, listened and admired, gave rein to her romantic little head, full of the legends gathered during the journey. She saw the old castle arising from its decay, lifting up its towers, its cloister-like arches peopled with lovely ladies of that pale complexion which great heat does not affect. She herself was a Princess des Baux; and the musician who was serenading her was a prince also, the last of the Valmajour, in peasant's attire.

"Adona, the song is ended," as they say in the chronicles of the courts of love; and she broke off a spray of pomegranate over her head, to which hung a heavy, bright purple flower, and handed it as a reward for his serenade to the handsome musician, who gallantly tied it to the strings of his tambour.

CHAPTER VI

TRANSFIGURED

THREE months have passed since the trip to the Mont de Cordoue.

Parliament has just opened at Versailles amid a November deluge which unites the fountain basins of the park with the low, foggy sky, envelopes the Chambers with damp gloom and darkness, but does not cool political animosities. The session promises to be a terrible one. Train-loads of deputies, of senators, cross, follow, whistle, groan, shake their threatening smoke, animated in their own way with the hates and intrigues they are bearing along under torrents of rain; and, during that hour of travelling, the discussions go on with the same bitterness, the same fury as in the tribune The most excited, the noisiest of all, is Roumestan He has already made two speeches since the Chambers have met again. He speaks in the committee-rooms, in the passages, at the station, at the refreshment bars, shakes the glass roofs of the photographic saloons in which all the Right are assembled. You can only see his moving, heavy silhouette, his big head, his broad shoulders which are feared by the ministry whom he is about to "throw" according to the rules, like a supple, vigorous wrestler of the South. Ah! the blue sky, the tabours, the grasshoppers, all the bright scenery of his holidays, how far away it is! Numa does not think of it one moment, absorbed in the whirl of his double life as barrister and politician; for, like

his old master Sagnier, he did not give up the Courts when he entered the Chamber; and every evening, from 6 to 8, there is a crowd at the door of his room in the Rue Scribe.

You would think it was a legation, that room. The first secretary, the leader's right arm, his councilor, his friend, is an excellent business advocate called Méjean, a Southerner like all Numa's *entourage*, but from the Cévennes South, the South of rocks, which takes more after Spain than Italy, and retains in its manner, in its speech, the wise reserve and practical good sense of Sancho. Squat-built, robust, already bald, with the bilious tint of hard workers, Méjean carries on the office business by himself alone, gets up the *dossiers*, prepares the speeches, tries to insert facts into the sounding phrases of his friend, his future brother-in-law, say the well-informed. The other secretaries, MM. de Rochemaure and de Lappara, two young men related to the most ancient provincial nobility, are only there for show, and are accomplishing their political novitiate at Roumestan's.

Lappara, a tall, handsome, sturdy-limbed young fellow, with a warm complexion, yellow beard, son of the old Marquis de Lappara, head of the party in the Bordeaux district, is a good type of the créole South, boastful, adventurous, keen at duelling and escapades Five years of Paris, 100,000 franc gambled away at the club and paid for with his mother's diamonds, have given him the genuine accent of the boulevard. Quite different is the Viscount Charlexis de Rochemaure, a compatriot of Numa, brought up among the Pères de l'Assomption, who studied law the provinces under the care of his mother and an abbé, and retained from his upbringing a certain candour, shyness that contrasted with his Louis XIII. beard, his appearance at once refined and *Jocrisse*.

The tall Lappara tries to initiate the young Pourceaugnac into Parisian life. He teaches him to dress, what is "good form" and what is not, to walk with his head stretched forward, his mouth stiffened up, to sit down in one piece, with his legs extended so as not to crease his breeches at the knee. He would like him to get rid of his *naïve* belief in men and things, his taste for scribbling. But no, the Viscount likes his work, and when Roumestan does not take him to the Chamber or the Palais, he remains writing for hours at the long table installed for the secretaries beside the master's cabinet. Lappara, smoking a cigar, with his legs outstretched, is looking through the rain at the long line of carriages drawn up at the pavement for Mme. Roumestan's Thursday.

What a lot of people! And that is not all; there are still carriages arriving. Lappara, who boasts he knows his Paris by heart, announces: "The Duchess de San Donnino—Marquis de Bellegarde—*mazette!* The Mau-conseils also! *Ah ça!* what's up?"

Méjean had suddenly arrived from the Palais, quite out of breath.

"Great news!" he cried, throwing his portfolio on the table. "The ministry is beaten."

"You don't mean to say so!"

"Roumestan takes the Ministry of Public Instruction."

Roumestan a Minister!

"Ah! my dear fellow, what a rascal he is!" repeated the tall Lappara, slipping down in his armchair till his legs touched the ceiling. "He knows how to play the game!"

Rochemaure was scandalised.

"Don't let's be malicious, my dear sir.—Roumestan is a conscience. He goes right ahead like a bullet."

"To begin with, my little man, there are no longer any bullets. There are only shells.—And shells go like this."

He showed the trajectory with the tip of his boot.

"Fool!"

"Idiot!"

"Gentlemen—gentlemen——"

And Méjean reflected to himself on the singular nature of this complex Roumestan, who, even when viewed from quite near, could be judged so differently.

"A rascal"; "a conscience."

The public were similarly divided in opinion. He, who knew him best, knew what depths of levity and idleness modified this ambitious temperament which was both better and worse than its reputation. But was the news of the portfolio true? Curious to be assured of it, Méjean glanced at his dress in a glass and crossed over to Madame Roumestan's.

In the ante-chamber, where the footmen were waiting, with fur cloaks on their arms, a murmur of voices could be perceived dulled by the high ceilings, the heavy luxury of the hangings. As a rule Rosalie received in the small drawing-room, furnished as a winter garden with light seats, dainty tables, the daylight penetrating between the glistening leaves of the green plants near the windows. But today the two reception rooms were crowded; and people were continuously arriving, friends and acquaintances, faces to which Rosalie could not have given a name.

Very simple, in a short violet dress which showed off well her *svelte* figure, the elegant harmony of her whole being, she welcomed every one with the same rather haughty smile, the chilly air of which Aunt Portal once spoke. Not the least bedazzlement at her new good fortune, some surprise and uneasiness rather, which, however, did not betray itself in everything. She was busy among the various groups, whilst the sun was rapidly setting in this Parisian first floor, and the servants brought lamps, lit the chandeliers, so that the room appeared as it did on evening fêtes with its rich glittering stuffs, its oriental carpets coloured like jewels.

"Ah! Monsieur Méjean——" Rosalie freed herself for a moment, went to meet him, happy in an intimacy discovered amid the society horde. Their natures understood each other.

"I came to assure myself if the news was true—I no longer doubt now," he said, pointing to the full rooms. She handed him the telegram she had received from her husband. And she whispered: "What do you say to it?"

"It's a burdensome post, but you will be there."

"And you, too," she said, shaking his hands and leaving him for fresh visitors. Nobody went away. They were waiting for their Leader, they wanted to hear from his lips the details of the meeting, how he had upset them all with a shrug of the shoulders. Some of the new-comers were already reporting some rumours from

the Chamber, some tit-bits of speeches. There was a stir, a pleasing excitement around them. The women especially appeared inquisitive, passionate; beneath the big hats that were in fashion that winter, their pretty faces had that light pink fire, that fever on the cheek, which is seen on those of the players of *trente-et-quarante* at Monte Carlo. They all seemed very strong in politics, they celebrated the glory of Roumestan, and there was on all hands the same cry: "What a man! What a man!'

In one corner, old Béchut, Professor at the Collège de France, very ugly, a nose, a huge scientific nose spreading over his lips, took Roumestan's success as a text for propounding one of his favourite theses: that the weakness of the modern world comes from position held in it by women and children. Seeing people approaching to listen, he raised his voice, quoted historical examples, Cæsar, Richelieu, Frederick, Napoleon, proved scientifically that woman was several stages below man as a thinking being. "In fact, if we examine the cellular tissues——"

Suddenly Roumestan came in. In the midst of loud welcomings he quickly crossed the *salon*, went straight to his wife, kissed her on the cheeks before she was able to prevent the somewhat embarrassing manifestation, which however emphatically belied the assertion of her physiologist. All the ladies exclaimed: "Bravo!" There was again an exchange of handshakes, effusive greetings, then an attentive silence whilst the Leader, leaning on the chimney-piece, began a rapid account of the day.

The great *coup* prepared during the

week, the marches and counter-marches, the mad rage of the Left at the moment of defeat, his own triumph, his amazing invasion of the tribune, even to the tones of his fine answer to the Marshal: "That depends on you, Monsieur le Président,"—he remarked on everything, detailed everything with a communicative gaiety and warmth. Next, he became grave, reckoned up the heavy responsibilities of his office: the University to be reformed, the youth to be prepared for the realization of the great hopes—the phrase was understood, greeted with applause—but he would surround himself with enlightened men, would appeal to all good-will and devotion. And, with a moistened eye, he looked round the circle crowded about him: "I shall appeal to my friend Béchut—to you also, my dear de Böe."

The hour was so solemn that nobody asked how University reform could be thus served. For the rest, the number of persons of that calibre, whom Rougestan that afternoon had begged to collaborate with him in the terrible duties of public instruction, was truly incalculable. As for the fine arts, he felt more at his ease, and doubtless they would not refuse him—A flattering murmur of laughter, of interjections, prevented his continuing. There was but one opinion in Paris, even among the most hostile. Numa was the man for the post. At length they were about to have a jury, lyric theatres, an official art. But the minister cut short the dithyrambs and observed in a familiar jocular way, that the new cabinet was almost entirely composed of Southerners. Out of eight ministers, the Bordeaux, the Périgord, the Lan-guedoc districts had furnished six. And growing excited: "Ah! the South is rising, the South is rising—Paris belongs to us. We hold everything. Take your choice, Messieurs. For the second time, the Latins have conquered Gaul."

He was indeed himself a Latin of the conquest, with his sculpturesque head, broad cheeks and warm complexion, and his rough, easy-going manner that were out of place in so Parisian a *salon*. Amid the laughter and applause raised by his last *mot*, he left the chimney-piece quickly like a good comedian who knows how to retire after making his point, beckoned to Méjean to follow, and disappeared by one of the interior doors, leaving Rosalie to make his excuses. He was dining at Versailles, with the Marshal; he had hardly the time left to get ready, to write a few signatures.

"Come and dress me," he said to the servant who was about to lay the three covers for monsieur, madame and Bompard, around the basket of flowers, fresh every day, which Rosalie liked on the table at every meal. He felt quite pleased at not dining there. The tumult of enthusiasm he had left at his heels extended behind the closed door, encouraged him to seek yet more people and illuminations. And besides, the Southerner is not a home man. It is the people of the North, the poor climates who have invented "home," the intimacy of the family circle to which Provence and Italy prefer the terraces of ice-shops, the noise and excitement of the street.

Between the dining-room and the barrister's study, a small ante-room had to be crossed, usually full of people at that hour, of restless folk watching the clock, with their eyes en the illustrated papers, whilst absorbed in the preoccupations of legal proceedings. Méjean had dismissed them that evening, rightly thinking Numa could not give any consultations. Still, a person had remained behind, a tall young man, dressed up in ready-made clothes, awkward as a non-commissioned officer dressed as a civilian.

"*Hé!* good-day—Monsieur Roumestan—how are you?—I've been hoping to see you for some time."

Numa remembered well having come across that accent, that dark complexion, that conceitedly triumphant expression somewhere, but where?

"Con't you know me?" asked the other—"Valmajour, the tabour-player!"

"Ah! yes, very well—perfectly."

He was about to go on. But Valmajour barred his way, saying he had arrived the evening before. "Only, you know, I couldn't come earlier. When a man transports a whole family like that into a country he doesn't know, it's difficult to settle down."

"A whole family?" inquired Roumestan. with wide-open eyes.

"*Bé!* yes, my father, sister—we've done what you said."

Numa made an embarrassed, angry gesture. as he did whenever he was confronted with one of his bills to pay, which he had taken up enthusiastically, out of a need to speak, to give, to be agreeable. Mon Dieu! He wanted nothing better than to help such a fine fellow. He would look out for the means. But he was very pressed that evening. Exceptional circumstances. The favour with which the Chief of the State——Seeing that the peasant did not go off, he said quickly: "Come into the cabinet"—and they passed in.

Whilst sitting at the bureau, he hastily read and signed several letters. Valmajour gazed at the huge room suptuously carpeted and furnished, the library going round it, surmounted by bronzes, busts, works of art, souvenirs of glorious cases, the King's portrait signed with a few lines, and he felt impressed by the solemnity of the place, the stiffness of the sculptured seats, the quantity of books, especially by the presence of the footman, correct, dressed in black, coming and going, carefully laying suits and clean linen on arm chairs. However, in the lamp's warm shadow, Roumestan's kindly broad face, his well-known profile reassured him a trifle. The great man next passed into his valet's hands, and with his leg extended for the drawing off of his trousers and boots, he questioned the tabour-player, learnt with terror that before coming the Valmajours had sold everything, the mulberries, the vines, the farm.

"Sold the farm, you unfortunate man!"

"Ah! my sister was a bit frightened at it. But the papa and I insisted on it. As I said: What risk is there, when Numa is at hand, as it was he who told us to come?"

He had need of all his innocence to dare to speak of the minister, in his presence, in that unceremonious way But that was not what most struck Roumestan. He pondered on the numerous enemies he had already procured himself by his incorrigible mania for promising. Why go and trouble the lives of these poor people? And the smallest details of his visit to the Mont de Cordoue came back to him the opposition of the peasant girl, his decisive phrases. Why? What demon had he within him? He was dreadful, that rustic! As for his talent, Numa hardly recollected it, seeing only what a burden he had laid on himself.

He heard beforehand his wife's reproaches, felt the cold of her severe look. "Words mean something." And in his new position, at the source of all favours, how much embarrassment he was going to create for himself by his fatal goodwill.

The idea, however, that he was a minister, the consciousness of his power almost immediately reassured him. Can these follies still preoccupy one at such heights? As sovereign master at the Beaux-Arts, with all the theatres to his hand, it would cost him nothing to help this poor man. Having recovered his self-esteem, he changed his tone with the countryman, and in order to prevent his familiarity he solemnly informed him in a very loud voice of the important dignities to which he had been raised that morning. Unfortunately, at that moment he was half-dressed, standing in his silk socks on the carpet, with his stomach prominent in the white flannel of a pink-ribboned hose; and Valmajour did not seem to be moved, the magic word "minister" not being connected in his mind with this fat man in shirt sleeves. He went on calling him "Moussu Numa," spoke to him of his "music," of the new tunes he had learnt. Ah! he wasn't afraid now of one of the Parisian tambourinists!

"You wait—you'll see."

He darted out to take up his tambourine in the ante-room. But Roumestan held him back:

"But I tell you I am pressed for time, qué diable!"

"All right—all right—it'll do for another time," said the peasant with his good-natured air.

And, seeing Méjean approaching, he thought he ought to tell the story of his three-holed flute for his wonder:—

"It occurred to me one night, as I listened to the nightingale singing. I thought within myself: What! Valmajour——"

It was the same tale he had told at the amphitheatre. He had remembered it word for word. But this time he told it with a certain shy hesitation, an emotion increasing from minute to minute, as he saw Roumestan being transformed before him under a broad shirt front of fine linen with pearl buttons, the black dress of severe cut which the valet handed him.

At the time, "Moussu Numa" seemed to him to have grown. His head, which his endeavour not to derange the knot of white muslin made stiff and solemn, was lit up by the pale reflections of the great cordon of Sainte-Anne round his neck, and the broad plaque of Isabella the Catholic. And suddenly the peasant, struck with a great, frightened respect, at last understood he had before him one of the privileged of the earth, that mysterious, almost chimerical being, the powerful idol, towards whom prayers, wishes, desires, entreaties, are only extended on large sheets of paper, so high that the lowly never see him, so proud that they never utter his name but in a whisper, with a sort of reverent fear and ignorant emphasis: "The Minister!"

He was so put out by it, poor Valmajour, that he scarce heard the kindly words with which Roumestan dismissed him, asking him to call again in a fortnight, when he was installed at the ministry.

"All right—all right, Monsieur le Ministre."

He regained the door, stepping backwards, dazzled by the brilliance of the official Orders and the extraordinary expression of the transfigured Numa. The latter was much flattered by the sudden timidity which gave him a high opinion of what he henceforth termed "his ministerial air."

CHAPTER VII

THE PASSAGE

WHILST waiting to set up housekeeping on a more complete scale, which could only take place after the arrival of their furniture which was on the way by baggage train, the Valmajours had put up in the renowned Passage du Saumon, where travellers from Aps and the district had put up at all times. They occupied there under the roof a room and a cabinet, the latter being without light or air, a sort of coffer in which the two men slept, the room being scarcely bigger, but it appeared splendid to them with its mahogany, its worn hangings, and its attic window cutting off a portion of the sky as yellow, as foggy as the long plate-glass at the entrance of the Passage. In this *niche* they kept up their country's memory by a strong odour of garlic and onions, cooking their exotic food themselves on a small stove. Old Valmajour being a great *gourmand*, loving company, would have preferred to descend to the table d'hôte, whose white linen and plated cruets warmed his enthusiasm, to enter into the noisy conversation of the commercial travellers they heard laughing at meal-times even as high as their fifth floor. The little Provençale, however, definitely opposed it.

Exceedingly astonished at not finding on their arrival that Numa's fine promises had been realised namely, the 200 francs a night which, since the visit of the Parisians, caused her little imaginative head to swim in a pile of amassed gold, frightened by the exorbitant price of everything, she had been seized on the first day with that panic which the Paris crowd calls "the fear of failure." Had she been alone, with some anchovies and olives, she would have got out of the mess, but her men had wolves' teeth, much longer here than in the country because it was less warm, and she had at every turn to open her money-bag, in which rang the 3,000 francs, the product of the sale of their property. With each louis she changed, there was a struggle, a wrench, as if she were parting with the stones of her farm, the fruit of the last vine.

Never did a traveller lost in a haunted wood cling to his valise more energetically than she to her money-bag, when she was crossing the road with her green skirt, her Arles coif, at which passers-by turned back to glance when she went into the shops, where her out-of-the-way names for things made her, a French woman of the South, as bewildered, as much a stranger in the capital of France, as if she had come from Stockholm or Nijni-Novgorod.

At first very humble in manner, soft in tone, she would at times, when some shopman was scoffing or brutal, suddenly have fits of fury which found vent in convulsions of her pretty brown face, in the gestures of a madwoman, in a chattering quarrelsome vanity. And then out would come the story of cousin Puyfourcat and his legacy, the 200 francs a night, their patron Roumestan of whom she spoke, disposed of as something belonging entirely to her, calling him now Numa, now the "minister," all this would be outpoured, till the moment when, mistrust taking the upper hand again, the peasant would stop, attacked by a superstitious fear at her own talkativeness, suddenly dumbstruck, her lips tight-shut like the strings of her money-bag.

At the end of a week she became a stock figure at that entry of the Rue Montmarte, all fitted with shops, spreading through their open doors the life and secrets of the houses of the quarter, together with the odours of vegetables, fresh meat of colonial produce. And it was that—the questions mockingly put to her in the morning when she got the change for her slender purchases, the allusions to her brother's constantly delayed *début*, to the Bedouin's heritage, those wounds to self-love yet more than the fear of poverty, that excited Audiberte against Numa, against those promises of which she was at first rightly mistrustful, like a true daughter of the South where words fly quicker than elsewhere, through the lightness of the air.

"Ah! if he had been made to draw up a paper."

It had become her fixed idea, and every morning, when Valmajour set off for the ministry, she took great care to see that the perforated sheet was in the pocket of his overcoat.

But Roumestan had other papers to sign besides that, other business in his head than the tabour. He was installed at the ministry, with the bustle, the fever of upset, the generous ardours of people taking possession. Everything was new to him, the vast rooms of the administrative *hôtel* as well as the broadened views of his lofty post. To reach the first rank, "to conquer Gaul," as he said, was not the difficult task; but to maintain himself, to justify his good luck by intelligent reforms, attempts at progress! Full of zeal, he gathered information, consulted, conferred, surrounded himself with shining lights of knowledge. With Béchut, the eminent professor, he studied the faults of university education, the methods of extirpating the Voltairean spirit of the *lycées;* helped himself by the experience of his Chargé of the Beaux-Arts, M. de la Calmette, who had been twenty-nine years in the office; of Cadaillac, the Director of the Opera, who had survived three bankruptcies, to reconstruct the Conservatoire, the Salon, the Académie de Musique, on new plans.

The worst was that he did not listen to these gentlemen, talked for hours, and suddenly, looking at his watch, got up, dismissed them hurriedly—

"The deuce! And I was forgetting the Council. What a life, not a second to oneself. Very good, dear friend. Send me your report soon."

The reports were piled up on Méjean's bureau, who, despite his intelligence and good-will, had not too much time to spare for current business, and let the great reforms slumber.

Like all ministers just appointed, Roumestan had brought his people with him, the brilliant *personnel* of the Rue Scribe: the Baron de Lappara, the Viscount de Rochemaure, who gave the new cabinet an aristocratic flavour, though for the rest they were quite at sea and ignorant in every question. The first time Valmajour presented himself at the Rue de Grenelle, he was received by Lappara, who was more particularly busied with the Fine Arts, sending at all hours staff messengers, dragoons, cuirassiers, to take the young ladies of the minor theatres invitations to supper in big official envelopes. M. le Baron greeted the tabour-player good-humouredly, rather haughtily, like a great lord receiving one of his tenants. With his legs extended for fear of spoiling his French blue trousers, he spoke to him without stopping polishing, filing his nails.

"Very difficult at the moment. The minister so busy. Soon, in a few days. You will be informed, my good man."

And when the musician naïvely confessed it was a matter of some urgency, that their resources would not last for ever, M. le Baron, speaking with his most serious air, put him off with a joke.

The next time, Valmajour had to do with the Viscount de Rochemaure. He raised his curled head from a dusty book in which it had quite vanished, had explained to him conscientiously the mechanism of the flute, took notes, tried to understand, and finally declared that he was more specially concerned with the religious sections. Then the poor peasant found nobody in, as the whole cabinet had gone to attend the Minister in the inaccessible regions where His Excellency took shelter. Still, he lost neither coolness nor courage; to the evasive replies of ushers and their shrugs of shoulders he always opened bright, astonished eyes of raillery—

"All right. All right. I'll come back."

And he returned. Had it not been for his gaiters and his instrument, he might have been taken for an employee of the house, so regular was his arrival there, though more painful each morning.

The mere sight of the high door now made his heart beat. Yet, he feared still more the scenes at the lodgings, Audiberte's fearful frowns, and so he returned despairingly. The *concierge* at last had pity on him, advised him, if he wanted to see the minister, to wait for him at the Saint-Lazare Station, when the train left for Versailles.

He went there, entered the big, lively room on the first floor, at the time of the Parliamentary train. After five minutes he saw Numa Roumestan arrive, leaning on the arm of a secretary carrying his portfolio, his big coat open his face beaming, even as it had appeared to him on the first day on the steps of the amphitheatre, and, from a distance, he recognized his voice, his good-natured words, his protests of friendship: "Rely on it—trust to me. It is as if you'd got it."

The minister was then in the honeymoon of power. Apart from political enmities, often less violent in Parliament than might be imagined, the rivalry of fine speakers, quarrels of barristers defending opposite causes, he knew of no enemies, not having had the time, during the three weeks since his taking office, of wearying out the askers of favours. He was still given credit. Scarcely two or three began to grow impatient, to watch for him as he passed. To them he shouted a loud "Good morning, friend," whilst hastening his steps, a phrase which anticipated reproaches and refuted them at the same time, kept requests familiarly at a distance, left the petitioners deceived and flattered. A windfall was that "Good morning, friend," and of a quite instructive duplicity.

At the sight of the musician coming towards him, showing his white teeth in a smile, Numa had a great desire to launch forth this "Good morning"; but how could he treat as a friend this rustic in a small otter-skin cap, in a grey jacket, whence his hands showed forth brown as on village photographs? He preferred to assume his "ministerial air" and to pass stiffly on, leaving the poor devil stupefied, dumb-foundered, hustled about by the crowd pressing behind the great man. However, Valmajour appeared next day and the following days, but without venturing to approach, sitting on the edge of a seat, one of those resigned, sad silhouettes, such as one sees them at railway stations, among soldiers and emigrants, ready for all the hazards of an evil destiny. Roumestan could not avoid that dumb apparition which was ever in his path. It was all very well for him to feign to ignore him, to turn his eyes away, to talk louder whilst passing; his victim's smile was there and remained till the train went off. Assuredly, he would have preferred some brutal shouting scene, in which the police would have intervened and he would have been freed. It occurred

to him, the minister, to change his station, to go sometimes by the left bank in order to get rid of this living remorse.

The other was not discouraged.

"He's ill," he said to himself, on those days; and he returned obstinately to his post. At the lodgings his sister was awaiting him feverishly, watching for his return.

"*Eh! bé*, you saw him, the minister? He signed it, the paper?"

And what exasperated her more than the everlasting: "No—not yet," was her brother's phlegm. as he dropped in a corner the box that left its mark on his shoulder, a phlegm of indolence and carelessness as frequent among Southern natures as their liveliness. Whereupon the strange little creature flew into her furies. What had he got in his veins? Was there never to be an end of it? "Take care, if I suddenly put my finger in the business!" He very coolly drew from their case the flute, the ivory-tipped stick, rubbed them with a piece of wool, for fear of the damp, and promised to manage better next day, to try again at the ministry, and if Roumestan was not there, to ask to see his lady.

"Ah! *vaï*, his lady. You know well she doesn't like your music. If it was the young lady—she, yes, truly!"

And she nodded her head.

"The lady or the young lady, they are both scoffing at you," said old Valmajour, ensconced before a fire which his daughter economically covered with cinders, and which was an eternal subject of quarrel between them.

In point of fact, owing to trade jealousy, the old man was not sorry at his son's failure. At first he was delighted at the journey, at the idea of seeing Paris, "the Paradise of women and the hell of hosses," as the waggoners say in those parts, with fancies about houris in light veils, and horses mutilated, writhing in the midst of flames. On arrival he had found cold, privations, rain. Out of fear of Audiberte, out of respect for the minister, he had been contented with grumbling, shivering in his corner, slipping in his word, winking with his eyes; but Roumestan's desertion, his daughter's fits of anger opened for him also the way to recriminations. He revenged himself for all the wounds to his self-love inflicted by the young man's success during ten years, shrugged his shoulders when listening to the flute.

"Music—music's all very well. It won't do you much good."

And he asked out loud if it was not pitiful that a man of his age should have carried him so far from home, to that Siberia, for him to die of cold and want; he invoked the memory of his poor holy wife, whom he had by the way killed with grief, "made her like a rabbit," to use Audiberte's expression, remained for hours groaning by the fire, till his daughter, tired of his laments, got rid of him with two or three sous to drink at the wine-shop. There his despair soon calmed down. It was comfortable, the stove roared. He amused the gallery with his gasconnades, bragged of his son's tabour, which cost them all kinds of annoyances at their lodgings; for Valmajour, in expectation of his *début*, practiced till midnight, and his neighbours complained.

"Never mind, go on," said Audiberte to her brother; and the landlord gave notice.

The evening before leaving, Audiberte, after the tambourinist's daily and fruitless quest was over, gave the men a hasty dinner, without speaking, but her eyes shining, her air determined with a resolve taken. When the meal was over, she left to them the task of cleaning the table, threw her long cloak on her shoulders.

"Two months, two months soon we'll have been in Paris!" she cried with clenched teeth. "That's enough. I'm going to speak to him myself to that minister!"

She adjusted the ribbon of the terrible little coif, which, mounted on her head in broad waves, moved like a helmet, and violently quitted the room. The father and son looked at each other frightened, without trying to keep her, knowing well they would only increase her choler; and they spent the afternoon in a *tête-à-tête,* hardly exchanging three words, whilst the rain dripped below on the window-panes, the one cleaning his stick and flute, the other cooking on a fire he made as hot as possible, to make up for Audiberte's long absence. At last, her hurried footstep was heard in the corridor. She came in; she was beaming.

"A pity the window doesn't give on to the street," she observed, taking off her cloak, which was quite dry. "You would have seen below what a fine carriage I came in."

"A carriage! you're joking?"

"And lackeys, and liveries. It's made quite a sensation here."

Then, amid their admiring silence, she related her expedition, in mimicry. Firstly, instead of asking for the minister, who would never have received her, she got the address—if you speak politely, you can get anything—the address of the sister, the tall young lady who came with him to Valmajour. She did not live at the ministry, but with her parents, in a quarter of small, badly-paved streets, with odours of druggeries, recalling to Audiberte her province. And it was far, and she had to walk. At last she found the house, in a square where there were arches, like around the Placette at Aps. Ah! the fine young lady! how well she had received her, without haughtiness, although everything looked very rich in her house, the room full of splendid gilding and silk curtains hanging up on every side—

"Eh! good-day. So you're in Paris? Since when?"

Then when she learnt how Numa made them come, she at once rang for her housekeeper—a lady also with a hat—and they all three went off to the ministry. You should have seen the eager courtesy and humble respect of all the old beadles who ran before them to open the doors.

"So you saw him, the minister?" inquired Valmajour timidly, whilst he recovered his breath.

"If I saw him! And polite, I warrant you! Ah! poor fool, when I told you to see to the young lady in your job! It was she who quickly managed the business, and without discussion. In a week there will be a grand musical fête at the ministry to introduce you to the various directors. And immediately afterwards, cra-cra, the document and the signature."

The best of it was, the young lady had just accompanied her back there, in the minister's carriage.

"And how she wanted to come up here," added the Provencale, winking her eye at her father and twisting her pretty face with a meaning grimace. The old man's whole face, his cracked, dried-fig skin, contracted as if to say: "Understood!" He no longer laughed at the tabour. Valmajour himself, very cool, did not grasp his sister's perfidious allusion. He only thought of his coming *début,* and taking down the instrument began playing all his tunes over again, so as to send an adieu in trills from one end to the other of the Passage du Saumon.

CHAPTER VIII

EQUAL TO BEAUTY

THE minister and his wife were finishing lunch in their first-floor dining-room which was ostentatious and too vast, and this could not be concealed by the thickness of the hangings, the heating-apparatus all over the *hôtel,* nor the steam of a copious repast. That morning they happened to be alone. On the tablecloth, among the dessert, which was always very abundant at the Southerner's table there was his cigar-box, the cup of vervain which is the tea of the Provençal, and big boxes with many-coloured labels in which were inscribed the senators, deputies, rectors, professors, Academicians, society people, the ordinary and extraordinary *clientèle* of the ministerial *soirées*—some cards higher than others, for the privileged guests, necessary to the first series of "little concerts." Mme. Roumestan was turning them over, stopping at certain names observed furtively by Numa, who, whilst choosing his after-dinner cigar, was watching for a sign of disapproval on the calm physiognomy, a check to the rather hazardous manner in which these first invitations had been made.

But Rosalie made no inquiry. All these preparations were indifferent to her. Since their establishment at the ministry, she felt herself yet further from her husband, separated by incessant obligations, a too numerous *personnel*, a breadth of life that destroyed intimacy. To that was added the ever-harrowing regret at having no children, at not hearing around her those tireless little steps, those hearty, ringing laughs which would have relieved their dining-room of the icy look of an inn room, where they seemed only to be sitting as passengers, together with the impersonality of the linen, furniture, plate, the whole luxurious apparatus of public position.

In the embarrassed silence ensuing at the end of the meal were heard stifled sounds, outbursts of harmony broken into by hammer-blows, the tapestry, the stand which was being nailed together downstairs for the concert, whilst the musicians rehearsed their pieces. The door opened. The chief of the cabinet entered, with papers in his hand—

"Some more requests!"

Roumestan was furious. No, by Jove! Were it the Pope himself, there was no more room. Méjean coolly laid before him a bundle of letters, cards, perfumed letters—

"It's very hard to refuse—you promised."

"I? Why, I never spoke to any one."

"See here: 'My dear Minister, I beg to remind you of your kindly word'; and this: 'The general told me you had been so kind as to offer him'; and again: 'Remind the Minister of his promise.' "

"Well, then, I'm a sleep-walker, *allons!*" cried Roumestan, amazed.

The truth is that hardly had the fête been decided on when he had told people he met in the chamber, in the Senate: "You know, I rely on you for the tenth," and as he added: "Quite an intimate affair," they would not have taken care to forget the flattering invitation.

Amazed at being caught red-handed before his wife, he attacked her as always in such cases—

"It's your sister, busy with her tambourinist. I didn't think of beginning the concert so early. But that girl was so impatient: 'No, no—at once.' And you were as urgent as she. The deuce take it if that tabour has not turned your head!"

"Oh; no, not mine," said Rosalie merrily. "And I'm even afraid such exotic music won't be understood by Parisians. It should be accompanied by the horizon of Provence, the costumes, the farandoles—but above all"—her voice grew serious—"it was only a question of keeping a promise."

"A promise—a promise," repeated Numa. "Soon I'll not be able to say a word."

And turning to his secretary, who was smiling—

"*Pardi!* my dear sir, all Southerners are not like you, cold and deliberate, greedy of their words. You're a sham Southerner, you are, a renegade, a *Franciot*, as the saying is with us. A

Southerner! pooh! A man who has never lied and doesn't like vervain!" he added with comic wrath.

"Not so *Franciot* as I seem, M. le Ministre," replied Méjean, very calmly. "On my arrival at Paris twenty years ago, I smelt terribly like my country. I had cheek, an accent, gesticulated— chattered and invented like ——"

"Like Bompard," suggested Roumestan, who did not like other persons to laugh at his intimate, but did not mind doing so himself.

"Yes, faith, almost as much as Bompard—an instinct urged me never to speak the truth. One morning I felt ashamed, I laboured to correct myself. The exterior exaggeration one can readily get the better of by lowering one's voice, for instance. But the inward, that is what boils up, what wants to come out. So I took a heroic resolution. Whenever I surprised myself at a lie, my condemnation was not to speak for the rest of the day—that's how I was able to reform my nature. Nevertheless the instinct is there, at the bottom of my coldness. Sometimes I stop right in the middle of a phrase. It's not the word that's missing; on the contrary, I hold myself in, because I feel I'm about to lie."

"Terrible South! there's no means of escaping it," observed easy-going Numa, despatching the smoke of his cigar to the ceiling in philosophic resignation. "In my case it holds me particularly by the mania of promising, the itch I have to throw myself at people's heads, to wish them happiness despite themselves."

The usher on duty interrupted him by observing significantly and confidentially from the threshold:

"M. Béchut has come."

The Minister had an impulse of ill-humour.

"I'm lunching. I want to be left quiet!"

The usher excused himself. M. Béchut stated it was His Excellency ——. Roumestan quieted down.

"Well, well, I'm going to him. Let people wait in my cabinet."

"Ah! but no," said Méjean. "It is full. The Superior Council, you know. You fixed the time yourself."

"Then at M. de Lappara's."

"I put the Bishop of Tulle there," timidly declared the usher. "M. le Ministre had told me." Every room was full of people; petitioners he had confidentially asked to come at that time so as to be sure not to miss him; and for the most part people of mark.

"Take my little drawing-room. I'm going out," said Rosalie getting up.

And whilst the officer and the secretary went to look after these persons, the minister quickly gulped down his vervain, burnt himself as he repeated: "I'm overwhelmed with them—overwhelmed."

"What does that gloomy Béchut want now?" asked Rosalie, instinctively lowering her voice. The house was so full that there was a stranger behind every door.

"What he wants? His directorship, té! He is Dansaert's shark! He waits for him to be thrown overboard for him to devour."

She went up to him quickly:

"M. Dansaert is leaving the Ministry?"

"You know him?"

"My father has often spoken of him to me. A compatriot, a friend from childhood. He considers him an honourable man of great intellect."

Roumestan stuttered a few reasons: "Bad tendencies—Voltairean. It interferes with a plan of reforms. And besides, he is old."

"And you are replacing him by Béchut?"

"Oh! I know the poor man has not the gift of pleasing ladies."

She smiled a fine, disdainful smile.

"I care as little for his impertinences as for his homage. What I don't pardon in him are his clerical grimaces, his display of orthodoxy. I respect all creeds. But if there's one thing ugly in the world, which one should hate, Numa, it's lying, it's hypocrisy."

In spite of herself, her voice rose, warm, eloquent, and her rather cold visage took on a glory of honourableness, of straightforwardness, a pink burst of generous indignation.

"Sh! Sh!" cried Roumestan, pointing to the door. Doubtless, he admitted, it was not very just. Old Dansaert rendered great services. But what should he do? He had given his word.

"Take it back," said Rosalie; "come, Numa—for me—I beg you."

It was an affectionate command, supported by the pressure of a small hand on his shoulder. He felt moved. For a long while his wife seemed uninterested in his life, with a dumb forgiveness when he confided to her his ever-changing schemes. The entreaty flattered him.

"Can one resist you, my dear?"

And the kiss he gave her on the tip of her fingers mounted quiveringly up to just beneath the tight lace sleeve. She had such lovely arms. He was pained nevertheless by being obliged to say something disagreeable to somebody, and rose with an effort.

"I shall follow you! I'll listen," she said, threatening him with a pretty gesture.

He went into the little drawing-room hard by, leaving the door half-open to give himself courage and that she might hear. Oh! the beginning was clear, energetic.

"I am in despair, my dear Béchut— what I wanted to do for you is impossible."

The savant made some replies, of which only the lachrymose tones could be heard. However, to Rosalie's great astonishment Roumestan did not yield, and went on defending Dansaert with surprising conviction for a man to whom the arguments had just been suggested. Certainly it cost him something to take back his word when given; but was it not better than to perpetrate an injustice? It was his wife's idea, modulated, set to music, with big, stirring gestures that made the wind disturb the tapestry.

"For the rest," he added, changing his tone suddenly, "I intend to recompense you for the little disappointment."

"Ah! *mon Dieu!*" murmured Rosalie. There was at once a hail of astounding promises, the Cross of Commander for the 1st January next, the first seat vacant in the Superior Council, the—the — The other tried to protest, as a matter of form. But Numa:—

"Be quiet! be quiet! It's an act of justice. Men like you are too rare."

Intoxicated with this good feeling, stammering under his own affectionateness, if Béchut had not departed, the Minister would have positively offered him his portfolio. At the door, he called him back again—

"I count on you on Sunday, my dear sir. I'm starting a series of little concerts—among friends, you know."

And turning back to Rosalie—

"Well! what d'you say? I don't fancy I yielded at all to him."

It was so funny that she greeted it with a loud burst of laughter. When he knew the reason and all the new promises he had just made, he seemed frightened.

"Well, well. They're grateful all the same."

She left him, smiling as she used to of old, quite light-hearted at her good deed, happy also perhaps to feel her heart stirred by something she believed had long died.

"Go, you angel!" exclaimed Roumestan, who looked at her as she went, stirred in heart, with tender eyes; and when Méjean returned to remind him of the Council—

"You see, my friend, when one has the happiness to possess such a woman—marriage is paradise on earth. Hasten and marry."

Méjean shook his head, without answering.

"What! Isn't your affair going all right?"

"I fear not, indeed. Mme. Roumestan had promised me to ask her sister, and as she does not talk to me any more about anything——"

"D'you want me to take charge of it? I'm on the wonderfully best of terms with my sister-in-law. I bet you I settle her."

There was a little more vervain in the tea-pot. Whilst pouring out a fresh cup, Roumestan flowered forth into protestation on behalf of his chief of the

cabinet. Ah! his high position had not altered him. Méjean was ever his excellent, his best friend. Between Méjean and Rosalie, he felt himself more solid, more complete.

"Ah! my dear man, that woman, that woman! If you knew how kind, forgiving she has been. When I think I was actually capable"——

It positively cost him something to refrain from the confidence which was on his lips, with a deep sigh. "If I didn't love her, I should be exceedingly culpable——"

The Baron de Lappara entered hastily, with a mysterious air—

"Mademoiselle Bachellery is here."

Numa's face went at once a deep red. The sparkle of his eyes concealed the affection revealed in them.

"Where is she? In your room?"

"I already had Monseigneur Lippmann," said Lappara, rather amused at the notion of a possible meeting. "I put her downstairs—in the big drawing-room. The rehearsal is over."

"Good. I'll go to her."

"Don't forget the Council," Méjean tried to say. But Roumestan without hearing dashed down the small staircase leading from the minister's private apartments to the ground-floor reception room.

Since the affair of Mme. d'Escarbés, he had always avoided serious *liaisons*, affairs of the heart or of vanity that might have ruined his home for ever. He was truly not a model husband; but the contract was still valid. Rosalie though awakened, was too straight, too honest, for jealous watchings, and though always uneasy never arrived at any proofs. Even at that hour, if he could have suspected the place this new caprice was about to take in his existence, he would have hurried to climb again up the stairs quicker than he had gone down; but our destiny is always amusing itself by intriguing us, by coming to us wrapt up and masked, doubling the charm of first meeting by mystery. How could Numa have distrusted the young girl, whom he had seen from his carriage some days before, crossing the court of the *hôtel*, skipping to cross the flags, her skirt tucked up in one hand, and with the other lifting her nether garb with a quite Parisian boldness? All he had seen of her was two big arched eyebrows above a roguish nose, blonde hair knotted down the back in American fashion, and which the dampness of the air was curling at the tip, a full, well-turned leg, self-possession on high heels that whirled about and in the evening he asked Lappara without attaching any more importance to it—

"I'll bet she was going to you, that little rascal I met in the court this morning."

"Yes, M. le Ministre, she was; but she was coming for you."

And he named the little Bachellery. "What! the *débutante* at the Bouffes —how old is she? Why, she's a child!"

The papers mentioned that winter a good deal about Alice Bachellery whom the caprice of a fashionable maëstro had found in a small provincial theatre, and whom all Paris wanted to hear sing the song of the *Petit Mitron*, the refrain of which she gave with an irresistible vulgarity of fascination: "Chaud! Chaud! Les p'tits pains d'g'uau!" One of those divas the Boulevard swallows down half-a-dozen of each season, glorious on paper, swollen with gas and puffing,

reminding one of the little pink balloons that have only one day of sun and dust in the public gardens. And do you know what she had come to ask the minister? The favour of figuring in the programme of the first concert. The little Bachellery at the Ministry of Public Instruction? It was so gay, so wildly mad, that Numa wanted to hear her ask it of him herself; and by ministerial letter smelling of the cuirassier's gloves let her know he would receive her next day. Next day Mlle. Bachellery did not come.

"She must have changed her mind," said Lappara. "She's so childlike!"

The Minister was piqued, did not speak of her for two days, and on the third sent for her.

Now she was waiting in the drawing-room of the fêtes, red and gold, so imposing with its high windows on a level with the bare garden, its Gobelins tapestry and the great marble Molière sitting and dreaming at the furthest end. A Pleyel, some desks for the rehearsals, hardly took up a corner of the vast room, whose cold aspect, as of a deserted museum, would have impressed any but the little Bachellery; but she was so child-like! Tempted by the large floor glistening with wax, she amused herself with sliding from one end to the other, close-fitted by her furs, her arms in the cuffs which were too short, her nose in the air under the toque, with the manner of a coryphée dancing the "ballet on the ice" in the "Prophète."

Roumestan surprised her at this exercise.

"Ah! Monsieur le Ministre."

She was taken aback, her eyes opening and shutting, rather out of breath.

He had come in, his head held high, walking gravely, to find out if there was anything abnormal in the interview, and to give a lesson to this illbred girl who bandied terms with Excellencies. But he was at once disarmed. How could it be otherwise? She explained her little affair so well, the ambitious desire she had suddenly felt to perform at that concert which was so much talked of, an opportunity for her to make herself heard otherwise than in operetta and comic songs. Then, thinking it over, the impulse had taken her.

"Oh! but it was one of those impulses. Wasn't it, mama?"

Roumestan then caught sight of a fat lady in a velvet mantle, with a plumed hat, who advanced bowing in three time from the end of the room. Mme. Bachellery, an old star of the *cafés-concerts*, with a Bordeaux accent, with her daughter's small nose drowned in a broad monkey face, one of those awful mamas who appear beside their young ladies like the disastrous future of their beauty. But Numa was not in a studiously philosophic mood, was absorbed in the grace of capricious youth, in an adorably framed body, in the theatre argot mingled with an ingenuous laugh—the laugh of sixteen, said these ladies.

"Sixteen years! But at what age did she start on the boards?"

"She was born there, M. le Ministre. Her father, now retired, was director of the Folies-Bordelaises."

"A child of the ball, eh?" said Alice chaffingly, displaying thirty-two glistening teeth ranged close in a straight line, as if on parade.

"Alice! Alice! You're not respectful to His Excellency."

"Never mind. She's a child."

He made her sit near him on the sofa, with a good-natured, almost fatherly gesture, complimented her on her ambition, her tastes for high art, her desire to escape the facile and fatal successes of operetta, only she must work, work hard, study seriously.

"Oh! as for that," said the young girl flourishing a roll of music. "Every day two hours with La Vauters!"

"La Vauters? Perfect. Excellent method." He opened the roll like a connoisseur.

"And what shall we sing? Ah! ah! the valse in 'Mireille,' the song of Magali. Why, that comes from my part of the country."

He began to hum, with his head on one side, his eyes in front of him—

O Magali, ma bien-aimée,
Fuyons tous deux sous la ramée,
Au fond du bois silencieux—

She went on—

La nuit sur nous étend ses voiles
Et tes beaux yeux—

And Roumestan, at full pitch—

Vont faire pâlir les étoiles.

She broke in—

"Just wait—mama will accompany us."

And the desks being upset, the piano opened, she forcibly installed her mother. Ah! a determined little person!—The minister wavered a second, his finger on the page of the duet. If any one heard them!—Bah! they had been rehearsing every day for three mornings in the grand saloon. They began.

The two standing up followed on the same page of the music which Mme. Bachellery accompanied by heart. Their foreheads approaching nearly touched, their breaths mingled with the caresses of the rhythm. And Numa grew excited, gave expression, extended his arms, at the high notes. For some years, since his big political rôle, he had more often spoke than sung; his voice had become heavy like his person, but he still took much pleasure in singing, especially with this child.

Actually, he had quite forgotten the Bishop of Tulle, and the Superior Council assembled round the big green table. Once or twice the usher's palace face had appeared with the clicking of his silver chain, to retire at once, frightened at having seen the Minister of Public Instruction and Worship singing a duet with an actress of the minor theatres. Numa was no longer minister, but Vincent pursuing Magali in her coquettish transformation. And how well she ran, how she escaped with her child-like mischievousness, the pearly brilliance of her sharp-toothed laughter, till the moment when, vanquished, she abandoned herself, her wild little head bewildered by the running, on her friend's shoulder!

It was mama Bachellery, who broke the charm by turning round, as soon as the piece was ended—

"What a voice, M. le Ministre, what a voice!"

"Yes—I sang in my youth"—he said with a certain fatuousness.

"But you still sing magnificently.—

Hein, Bébé! what a contrast with M. de Lappara!"

Bébé, who was rolling up her piece, slightly shrugged her shoulders as if so indisputable a truth deserved no other answer. Roumestan asked a little uneasily—

"Ah! M. de Lappara——?"

"Yes, he comes sometimes to eat *bouillabaisse* with us; then, after dinner, Bébé and he sing their duet."

At that moment the usher, hearing no more music, resolved to go in, with the precautions of a trainer entering a wild-beast's cage.

"I'm coming—I'm coming," said Roumestan, and addressing the girl, in his most ministerial tone, in order to let her feel the hierarchical distance separating him from his attaché—

"I compliment you, mademoiselle. You have much talent, much, and if you like to sing here on Sunday, I gladly grant you the favour."

She exclaimed like a child—"Really? —oh! how nice you are!" and at once flung her arms round his neck.

"Alice!—Alice!—good gracious!"

She was however already far away, running through the *salons*, where she seemed so little in the high rooms, a child—quite a child.

He was stirred by the caress, waited a minute before going up again. Before him, in the withered garden, a sunbeam was traversing the lawn, warming and quickening the winter. He felt himself penetrated to the heart by a similar sweetness, as if that body, so full of life, so supple, as it touched him, had communicated to him a little of its spring warmth. "Ah! it's beautiful, is youth." He looked at himself in a glass, mechanically; an anxiety came to

him which he had not had for years.—
What changes, *boun Diou!* Very stout
owing to his sedentary life, the carriages he abused, the muddy complexion of sleepless nights, the temples already thinned and g ey, he was further
frightened at the breadth of his cheeks,
of the flat distance between his nose
and ear. "If I let my beard grow to
hide it"—Yes, but it would grow white.
And he was not forty-five. Ah! politics
ages.

He then knew for a moment a
woman's dreadful sadness, who sees
herself ended, incapable of inspiring
love, though she can still feel it. His
reddened pupils dilated; and, in this
palace of power, such deeply human
bitterness, in which ambition was as
nothing, held something more cutting
still. But, with his fickleness of impression, he soon comfo ted himself, by
thinking of glory, of his talent, his high
position. Was not that equal to beauty,
youth, in making oneself loved?

"Allons donc!"

He thought himself very silly, banished his grief by a shrug of the shoulder, and went up to dismiss the Council, because he had no time left to pre-
side over it.

"What's the matter with you to-day,
my dear Minister?—You seem quite
rejuvenated."

More than ten times during the day,
he was addressed with this compliment
on his very marked good-humour in the
corridors of the Chamber, where he
surprised himself humming: "O Magali,
ma bien-aimée." Seated on the ministerial bench he listened with an attentiveness very flattering to the orator to
an endless discourse on the customs
tariff—smiled happily, with his eyes
bent down. And the Left, who were
terrified by his reputation for astute-
ness, whispered trembling: "Let's look
out—Roumestan is up to some game."
It was simply the silhouette of little
Bachellery, which his fancy was amused
to evoke in the vacuum of the buzzing
speech, to make appear before the ministerial bench, with all her attractions
in detail, her hair dividing her forehead with blond tresses, her tint of
pink hawthorn, her alluring manner as
of a girl already a woman.

Yet, towards night, he had another
fit of gloom on returning from Versailles with some of his colleagues of
the cabinet. Amid the stuffiness of a
carriage full of smokers, they were chatting, in the tone of gay familiarity
which Roumestan carried with him
everywhere, about a certain velvet hat
framing a creole pallor in the diplomatic tribune where it had caused a
happy diversion from customs tariffs
and set all the hon. members agog, as
in a school-class when a butterfly flutters lost during a Greek lesson. Who
was it? No one knew.

"You must ask the general," said
Numa gaily, turning towards the Marquis d'Espaillon d'Aubord, War Minister, an old worn-out scamp where love
was concerned — "Good — good—don't
defend yourself; she only had eyes for
you."

The general made a grimace that carried his yellow old goat's beard up to
his nose, as with a lever.

"It's ages since women don't look
at me.—They've only eyes for those—
there."

The man indicated in such easy-going terms, particularly dear to all aristocratic soldiers, was young De Lappara, sitting in a corner of the carriage, and preserving a respectful silence among the big-wigs. Roumestan felt himself hit without precisely knowing how, and gave a lively retort. According to him there were many other things women preferred to youth in a man.

"They tell you so."

"I appeal to these gentlemen."

All bepaunched, with coats lumped over their stomachs, or withered and thin, bald or quite white, toothless, their mouths attacked by some disorder of health, these gentlemen, ministers, under-secretaries of State, were of Roumestan's opinion. The discussion grew lively amid the noise of the wheels, the loud creakings of the Parliamentary train.

"Our ministers are having a row," said the neighbouring compartments.

And the journalists tried to catch a few words through the walls.

"What they love," thundered Numa, "is the known man, the man in power. To tell themselves that he who is there before them, rolling his head on their knees, is famous, powerful, one of the levers of the world, that is what excites them!"

"*Hé!* quite so."

"Right—right——"

"I'm of your opinion, my dear colleague."

"*Eh bien!* I tell you, I, that when I was a simple little lieutenant, and when I used to go out on Sundays in full dress, with my twenty-five years, with new aiguilettes, I used to gather as I passed some of those women's looks that envelope you in a blow of the whip from nape to heel, some of those looks which they have not for a big epaulet of my age. So, now, when I want to feel the warmth, the sincerity of one of those glances, a dumb declaration in the open street, d'you know what I do? I take one of my aides-decamp, young, with good teeth, broad chest, and I pay myself for going out on his arm, s—n—d—D—!"

Roumestan was silent till Paris. The melancholy of the morning seized him again, but with some anger added, an indignation against women's blind silliness, who can go mad about fools and handsome blockheads. After all, what rare quality had that Lappara? Without interrupting the discussion, he stroked his blond beard with a foppish air, his garments worn fastidiously, the neck part very open. And little Bachellery—his mistress, quite sure—the idea revolted him; but at the same time he wanted to know, to be convinced.

Hardly were they alone, whilst his *coupé* rolled towards the ministry, than he asked brutally, without looking at Lappara—

"Have you known those women long?"

"What women, M. le Ministre?"

"Why, those Bachellery ladies, of course!" His brain was full of them. He thought every one thought about them like him. Lappara began laughing.

Oh! yes, it was a long time; they lived in the same country parts. The Bachellery family, the Folies-Bordelaises, all the jolly memories of eighteen years. His heart as a Lycée youth had beaten hard enough for the name to burst the buttons off his tunic.

"And to-day it beats for the daughter?" asked Roumestan carelessly, wiping the glass with the tip of his glove to look at the wet dark street.

"Oh! the daughter, that's a different story altogether. In spite of her little flirty ways, she's a very cool, very earnest young lady. I don't know what she's trying for, but she's trying for something, which I suppose I am not in a position to give her."

Numa felt comforted:

"Ah! really? And yet you go again to them?"

"Why, yes—it's so amusing, the inner life of the Bachellerys. The father, the ex-director, composes comic couplets for the *café-concerts*. The mama sings and gesticulates them, whilst making *bouillabaisse* and fricassees. Shouts, disorder, scraps of music, the Folies-Bordelaises at home. Little Bachellery leads the uproar, whirls about, sups, plays the giddy, but doesn't lose her head an instant."

"Eh! You young rascal, you're reckoning on her losing it one day or another, and to your profit."

Becoming suddenly grave, the minister added: "A bad set for you, young man. You must be more serious than that, the devil! The Bordeaux madness can't last all your life."

He took his hand.

"You're not thinking of marrying, are you?"

"Faith, no, M. le Ministre—I'm very well as I am—unless an astounding windfall turns up."

"The windfall will be found for you. With your name, your relations——" And suddenly, impetuously: "What would you say to Mlle. Le Quesnoy?"

Lappara, despite his audacity, paled with rapture, with amazement.

"Oh! M. le Ministre, I'd never dared ——"

"Why not? Yes, yes—you know how I like you, my dear boy—I should be happy to see you in my family—I should feel myself more complete, more——"

He stopped right in the middle of his phrase, which he recognized having already remarked to Méjean in the morning.

"Ah! so much the worse! It's done."

He shrugged his shoulders and leant back in the carriage. "After all, Hortense is free, she will choose. In any case I shall have dragged this young fellow out of a bad set." In his own conscience, Roumestan was sure this sentiment alone had inspired his act

CHAPTER IX

A SOIREE

THAT evening the Faubourg Saint-Germain had an unusual appearance. Small streets, usually quiet, that went to bed early, were awakened by the rumbling of omnibuses disturbed from their routes; other streets, on the other hand, suited to the ceaseless noise of the big Parisian arteries, showed like the bed of a river turned from its course, silent, empty, magnified, guarded at the entrances by the lofty silhouette of a Paris mounted guard or the gloomy shadow—across the asphalt—of a band of policemen signing to the carriages— "No thoroughfare."

At a distance the illumination of the ministry on its two façades, the fires lit on account of the cold in the middle of the road, the slowly filtering gleam of rows of lanterns concentrated on a single point, encircled the district with a fire-halo enlivened by the blue limpid ness, the icy dryness of the air. But on approaching you were quickly reassured by the fine ordering of the fête, the even white sheet of light soaring to the top of the neighbouring houses, whose inscription in gold letters: "Mairie du VIIe Arrondisement — Ministère des Postes et Télégraphes," could be read as in daylight, and melted away in Bengal fire, in fairy lighting of the scene in a few large, bare, motionless trees.

Among the passers-by who stopped despite the cold and formed an inquisitive hedge at the *hôtel* door, was a peasant woman wrapt in a long cloak who only let two sharp eyes be seen of her. She came and went, bent in two, her teeth chattering, but not feeling the frost, in an excitement of fever and intoxicating triumph.

Audiberte wanted to see for herself how it would all go off. With what pride she gazed at the crowd, the lights, the soldiers on foot and on horseback, the whole of a quarter of Paris turned upside down for Valmajour's tabour. For it was in his honour that the fête was being given, and she was convinced that those fine gentlemen, those fine ladies had only Valmajour's name on their lips. From the door in the Rue de Grenelle, she ran to the Rue Bellechasse, by which the carriages were leaving, went near a group of Paris guards, of coachmen in great-coats, round about a brazier flaming in the middle of the road, was astonished to hear them talk of the cold, very severe that winter, of potatoes freezing in the cellars, of matters quite unconnected with the fête and her brother. Especially was she irritated at the slowness of that endlessly defiling row of car-

riages; she would have liked to see the last of them go in, to say to herself "It's all ready.—They're beginning.— This time it's once for all." But the night was getting on, the cold becoming more piercing; her feet were freezing so as to make her cry with pain—it rather too absurd to cry when you have so glad a heart! Finally she determined to go home, not without gathering together in a last look all those splendours, which were carried through deserted streets during that icy night in her poor wild head, when the fever of ambition was beating in her temples congested with dreams, with hopes, her eyes for ever dazzled and blinded by that illumination to the glory of the Valmajours.

What would she have said, had she entered, had she seen those white and gold *salons* following one the other under their arched doors, magnified by mirrors in which was reflected the fire of the lustres, the glitter of the diamonds, the aiguillettes, the Orders of all kinds, in the shape of palms, of aigrettes, of brochettes, large as fire work suns or small as brelogues, or hung round the neck by those broad red ribands that make one think of bloody beheadings.

There were there, pell-mell with the great names of the Faubourg, ministers generals, ambassadors, members of the Institute and of the Superior Council of the University. Never in the arena at Aps, not even at the great meeting of tambourinists at Marseilles, had Valmajour had such an audience. His name, it is true, did not occupy much space in this fête whose occasion it was. The programme announced indeed: "Airs with variations on the ta bour," with the name of Valmajour combined with that of several lyrical illustrations; but no one looked at the programme. Only intimates, people who are *au courant* of everything, remarked to the minister, standing at the entrance to the first *salon*:—

"So you have a tabour-player?"

And he, abstractedly.—

"Yes, it's a fancy of these ladies."

Poor Valmajour hardly occupied his thoughts. There was to-night another *début*, more serious for him. What would people say? Would she succeed? Had not his interest in the child deceived him about her talent as a singer? And being hard hit, although he did not yet want to confess it to himself, bitten to the bone by the passion of a man of forty, he felt the anguish of a father, a husband, a lover, one of those painful anxieties such as one sees on first nights at the theatre. That did not hinder him from being amiable, obliging, from welcoming his guests with open arms—and how many guests, *boun Diou!*

Suddenly abandoning, almost repulsing, the dear guest to whom he was about to promise in a whisper a crowd of invaluable favours, the minister dashed to meet a lady high of colour, with an authoritative gait: "Ah! Madame la Maréchale!" and took under his arm an august arm strangled in a twenty-button glove, and led the noble visitor from room to room, between a double row of black suits respectfully bowed, through to the concert room, where Mme. Roumestan and her sister were doing the honours. Returning he distributed more handshakes, cordial words: "Rely on it—it's as good as done!"—or uttered very quickly his

"Good-day, friend," or again, in order to stir up the company, to set a current of sympathy going amidst all this society solemnity, he introduced people to each other, threw them into each other's arms without warning: "What! You're not acquainted?—M. le Prince d'Anhalt—M. Bos, Senator," and did not notice that, hardly had their names been uttered, when the two men, after a sudden deep bow, "Monsieur, Monsieu-," merely waited for him to go in order to turn their backs ferociously on each other.

"It's the devil to get the stiffness and dullness out of these *salons* of the Education Ministry. The shade of Fraysinous will certainly return to-night."

This reflection in a loud voice came from a group of young musicians crowding round Cadaillas, the director of the Opera, who was philosophically seated on a velvet stool, with his back to Molière's statue. Very corpulent, half deaf, with his moustache bristly and white, it was hard to distinguish the supple, light-hearted impresario of the Nabob's fêtes in that majestic idol with its swollen, impenetrable mask, whose eye alone betrayed the parisian *blagueur*, his fierce science of life, his mind like a thorn-stick iron-shod, hardened in the fire of crawling. But, contented, fearing above all to be dislodged from his directorship, he drew in his claws, spoke little, especially here, was satisfied to underline his remarks about the official society comedy with Bas-de-Cuir's silent laugh.

"Boissaric, my lad," he asked in a whisper of an intriguing youth of Toulouse who had just had a ballet performed at the Opera after only ten years' trial, which nobody thought of believing—"Boissaric, you who know everything, tell me the name of that solemn moustached person who talks familiarly with everybody and walks behind his nose with a devout air as if he were going to the funeral of that accessory.—He must belong to the household, because he talked theatre to me with some authority."

"I don't think so, sir.—Rather a diplomatist. I heard him just now tell the Belgian Minister they had long been colleagues."

"You are wrong, Boissaric.—He must be a foreign general. He was preaching only a moment ago in a group of big epaulets, and said very loud: 'One should never have had a great military command!'"

"Curious!"

Lappara, consulted in passing, began laughing—

"Why, it's Bompard."

"Who's he?"

"The minister's friend. How is it you don't know him?"

"From the South?"

"*Té!* by Jove!"

Bompard it was truly, who, strutting in a superb new suit with velvet adornments, his gloves in his half-open waistcoat, was trying to enliven his friend's soirée by a varied and sustained conversation. Unknown in the official world, where he was produced for the first time, he may be said to have created a sensation by promenading from one group to another his inventive faculties, his lightning visions, tales of royal amours, adventures and fights, triumphs at the federal shooting meetings which lent all the faces around him the same look of amaze-

ment, annoyance and uneasiness. There was a certain amount of fun in it, but understood only by a few intimates, powerless to dispel the boredom that penetrated even to the concert hall—an immense room, very picturesque with its two floors of galleries, and its glass ceiling which seemed like the open sky.

A green decoration of palms, of bananas with long leaves motionless under the chandeliers, constituted a background of freshness to the dresses of the women lined and packed together on innumerable rows of chairs.

The discomfort on the faces here was complicated by the prospect of being two hours motionless before the concert platform. Oh! the tortures of the musical craze! They knew it all! It counted among the wearinesses of their winter and the cruel society burdens. Which is why, if you had sought throughout the immense hall, you would have found only a single contented, smiling countenance, that of Mme. Roumestan, and it was not the ballet-dancer smile of mistresses of households, so easily altered to an expression of hateful weariness when it feels itself no longer regarded, the face of a happy woman, a loved woman, about to begin life again. O inexhaustible affection of an honest heart that had only beat for one! There she was, beginning again to believe in her Numa so kind, so gentle, for some time. It was like a return, the embracing of two hearts reunited after long absence. Without searching whence this renewal of kindness could come, she saw him again, loving and youthful as he was one night before the hunting panel, and she was ever the desirable Diana, supple and neat in her dress of white br cart, her chestnut hair in bands over her pure forehead without an evil thought in it, when her thirty years seemed five-and-twenty.

Hortense was very pretty also, all in blue; a blue tulle which engirt in a cloud her long figure slightly stooping, shaded her visage with a brown softness. But her musician's *début* preoccupied her. She asked herself how that refined public would like the local music, whether, as Rosalie said, they ought not to have framed the tabour in a horizon grey with olive-trees and hills in lace; and silently, agitatedly, she counted on the programme the items before Valmajour, amid a semi-rustle of fans, of whispered conversations, with which mingled the tuning of the various instruments.

A tapping of bows on desks, a rustling of paper on the platform where the choir has risen, parts in hand, a long gaze from the victims, like a desire to run away towards the high door obstructed by black suits; and Glück's chorus sends its first notes towards the glass above, where the winter's night superimposes its blue sheets:

"Ah! dans ce bois funeste et sombre——"

It has begun.

Boredom!

That was indeed the prevailing note in that concert at the Ministry. Beneath the required admiration, the ecstatic physiognomies which are part of the stock-in-trade of the sincerest women, it penetrated little by little, fixed the smile and the brightness of the eyes, spoilt their pretty poses as of birds perched on branches or sipping water drop by drop. One after the other, on the long rows of chairs, they struggled against it, with "Bravo!—Divine!—Delicious!"—in order to revive themselves, and succumbed to the invasive torpor which disengaged itself like a fog from that pool of sound.

Yet there were there the most famous, the most illustrious artists in Paris, interpreting classical music with all the science it needs, and which is only gained, alas! at the cost of years. For thirty years has La Vauters been singing that beautiful *romance* of Beethoven. "L'Apaisement," and never with more passion than to-night. Who other than Mayol, the handsome Mayol has ever sighed the serenade in "Don Giovanni" with such airy delicacy! Unhappily they cannot hear his voice now; it is not good his rising on tiptoe, his neck outstretched, so as to eke out the worn voice with gesture; there is no result, none. Paris applauds in spite of it, grateful for past pleasures. But these used-up voices, these faded, too well-known faces, medals whose constant circulation has consumed the effigy, will not banish the fog hovering over the minister's fête, in spite of his efforts to revive it.

At one moment, Alice Bachellery's entry on the stage awakens and stirs up everybody. At the two doors of the hall there is a curious pushing forward to catch a glimpse of the little diva in her short skirts on the platform, with her mouth half-open, her eyelids fluttering as with surprise to see so large a crowd. "Chaud! Chaud! les p'tits pains d'gruau!" hum the young clubmen. Old gentlemen of the University approach eagerly, stretching forth their heads on the side of their sound ears, so as not to lose a suggestion in the song of the hour. And it is a disappointment when with her shrill little voice she sings a great aria from "Alceste," prompted by La Vauters, who encourages her from the wings. Faces lengthen, black costumes desert, begin again to roam the room freely because the minister is not watching, as he has gone off to the other end of the last saloon on the arm of M. de Boë, quite dazed by such an honour. Eternal childlikeness of Love! Pass twenty years in the Palais, fifteen in the tribune, be sufficiently master of yourself to preserve amid the stormy meetings and savage interruptions the fixed idea and coolness of the penguin fishing in a howling tempest; and if passion has once anything to say to you, you will find yourself weak among the weak, trembling and cowardly to the pitch of desperately hanging on to an imbecile's arm rather than of hearing the least criticism of your idol.

"Pardon me, I must leave you—it's the entr'acte"—and the minister rushes away. People are pushing towards the buffet; and the comforted looks of all those unfortunate persons who have been restored to movement and speech, may give Numa the idea that his protégée has just had a very great success. They crowd about him, congratulate, him—"Divine!—Delightful!" but nobody speaks positively of what interests him, and at last he gets hold of Cadaillac, who is passing near, walking on one side, thrusting off the human billow with his enormous shoulders like a lever.

"Well!—How did you like her?"

"Whom?"

"The girl," says Numa in a tone he tries to make indifferent. The other,

sharp as a needle, understands, and without turning a hair:

"A revelation!"

The amorous man blushes as he did at twenty, at Malmus's.

"So then you believe that at the Opera—?"

"No doubt! But she needs a good showman," answered Cadaillac with his mute laughter; and whilst the minister runs and congratulates Mlle. Alice, the good showman goes on his way towards the buffet visibly framed by a large mirror at the end of a room decked out with brown and gold woodwork Despite the austereness of the tapestry, the heavy aspect of the refreshment apparatus, ill-humour and boredom are here dissipated, in the presence of the huge bar laden with fine crystallised fruit, fresh fruit, sandwiches in pyramids, and give place—humanity resuming its rights—to greedy and voracious attitudes. People talk, they get animated, eyes flash, laughter rings out under the influence of the fine wines. A thousand things are said, words broken off, answers given to questions already forgotten. In one corner there are little indignant cries: "What a horror!—It's dreadful!" round about the savant Béchut, the foe of women, who goes on with his invective against the weak sex. A quarrel among musicians.

"Ah, my dear chap, take care—you deny the augmented fifth."

"Is it true she's only sixteen?"

"Sixteen years since the vintage and a few years in bottle."

"Mayol!—Allons donc, Mayol!— ended, done for. Fancy the Opera giv ng two thousand francs every night for that!"

"Yes, but he takes one thousand francs in tickets for warming his room, and Cadaillac snaps up the rest at écarté."

"Bordeaux—chocolate—champagne."
"—to come to explain his conduct in the bosom of the Committee."

"—by remounting the ruche a little with loops of white satin."

Elsewhere, Mlle. Le Quesnoy, surrounded on all sides, recommends her tambourinist to a foreign correspondent, an impudent flathead, begs him not to go before the end, scolds Méjean for not backing her up, calls him a sham Southerner, *Franciot*, renegade. In the group at the side, a political discussion. An odious mouth projects itself, foaming at the teeth, chewing at words like balls, to poison them—

"All that the most subversive demagogy——"

"A Conservative Marat!" shouts a voice, but the talk is lost in the confused sound of plates, glasses, conversations, which Roumestan's metallic tones suddenly dominate: "Quick! mesdames, mesdames,—You will miss the Sonata in *fa!*"

Deathlike silence. The long procession through the saloons begins again. Concertos, symphonies succeed one another. The handsome Mayol starts again trying to make sounds, La Vauters to touch the relaxed chords of her voice. Suddenly, a somersault of life, of curiosity, as just now on the entry of little Bachellery. It is Valmajour's tabour, the appearance of the splendid rustic, his soft otter's cap on his head, the red sash on his loins, his country cloak on his shoulder. An idea of Audiberte's, an instinct of her woman's taste, of dressing him thus to produce more effect among the black garments. Really, it is all new, improvised, that long tabour balanced on the musician's arm, the small flute on which his fingers run, and the pretty airs whose movement, lively and inspiring, awakens with a shiver the satin of beautiful shoulders. The *blasé* public is amused at the entirely fresh ballads, embalmed in rosemary, at the refrains of old France.

"Bravo!—Bravo!—Encore!"

And when he attacks the "Marche de Turenne" in a broad, victorious rhythm which the orchestra accompanies *en sourdine*, inflating, sustaining the rather weak notes of the instrument, there was a delirious outburst. He had to come back twice, ten times, summoned by Numa, whose zeal has been re-warmed by the success, and who now takes to his own account "the fancy of those ladies." He relates how he discovered the genius, explains the wonder of the three-holed flute, gives details about the Valmajours' ancient castle.

"He's really called Valmajour?"

"Certainly—Princes des Baux—he's the last."

And the legend circulates, spreads, intensifies, a regular George Sand romance.

"I have the parchments at my house!" affirms Bompard in a tone admitting of no reply. But, amid the society enthusiasm, more or less factitious, a poor heart is excited, a young head is nearly intoxicated, takes se riously the bravos, the legends. Without saying a word, without even clapping, her eyes staring, abstracted, her long supple figure following in dream-rhythm the measures of the hero-march, Hortense finds herself again down there in Provence on the high platform commanding the sunburnt country, whilst her musician plays her the serenade as to a lady of the Courts of Love, and fits the pomegranate-flower to his tabour with a wild grace. The memory stirs her deliciously, and she whispers, leaning her head on her sister's shoulders: "Oh! how well I feel!" in a deep, heartfelt tone which Rosalie does not at once remark, but which will later become more defined, will haunt her like the murmured news of a misfortune.

"*Eh! bé!* my brave Valmajour, when I told you—What a success!—*Héin?*" cried Roumestan in the small saloon where a standing supper had been served to the artistes. The other stars of the concert thought the success a trifle overdone. Little Bachellery however had no bitter feeling in the matter like Mayol and La Vauters. She played at children amid a group of young "mashers," laughing, fluttering about, biting with her white teeth. She tried Valmajour's flute.

"See here, M'sieu le Ministre!"

Then, noticing Cadaillac behind His Excellency, she gave him with a piroutte her childlike forehead to kiss.

"B'j'ou, m'n'oncle.'—It was an imaginary relationship, a stage adoption.

"A sham giddy girl!" growled the good showman beneath his white moustache, but not too loud, because she

was probably about to become an employee of his, and an influential.

Valmajour, with a foppish air, much run after by ladies, by journalists, stood before the fireplace. The foreign correspondent was putting to him brutal questions, not in the fawning tone he used towards ministers in private audiences; but without troubling, the peasant answered by the story stereotyped on his lips: "It came to me one night, on hearing the nightingale sing——" He was interrupted by Mlle. Le Quesnoy, who handed him a glass and a plate filled as he had required.

"Good-day, monsieur.—And I too, I am bringing you the *grand-boire*." She had missed her effect. He answered with a slight nod, pointing to the chimney-piece: "Very good—very good—put it there," and went on with his story. "What the bird of the good God does with one hole——"

Without being disheartened, Hortense awaited the end, then spoke to him of his father, of his sister.

"She will be contented?"

"Yes, it hasn't gone badly."

With his conceited smile he twirled his moustache, looking restlessly about him. He had been told the director of the Opéra wanted to make proposals to him. He watched him from afar, feeling already an actor's jealousies, was astonished people could trouble so much about that little good-for-nothing singer; and, full of his thought, he did not trouble to answer the beautiful girl who had stopped before him, fan in hand, in the pretty half-bold attitude which the habit of society gives. She however, preferred him thus, disdainful and cold towards everything but his art. She admired him receiving condescendingly the compliments with which Cadaillac bombarded him with his rough outspokenness:—

"Yes—yes—I tell you I think so. Much talent—very original, very new. —I don't want any theatre but the Opera to have you. I shall seek an opportunity of 'presenting' you. From today consider yourself as one of the staff."

Valmajour thought of the perforated paper he had in his vest pocket; but the other, as if he had seen through him, held out his supple hand. "This is our mutual engagement, my dear sir" —and pointing to Mayol, La Vauters, who were luckily occupied with something else, for they would have laughed too much: "Ask your comrades what Cadaillac's word is worth."

Whereupon he turned on his heels, and returned to the ball. It was now a ball that stirred in the rooms that were less full, but more lively; and the admirable orchestra revenged itself for three hours of classical music by suites of valses of the purest Viennese. Hortense, much sought after, as the minister's sister-in-law, the First President's daughter, beheld a flight of waistcoats hovering around her big dowry and her influence.

Lappara, greatly excited, declared to her whilst dancing that His Excellency had given permission for him—But the valse ended, she left him without waiting for the sequel, and went to Méjean who did not dance, and yet could not make up his mind to go.

"What a face you have, you grave man, you man of reason!"

He took her hand: "Sit down there, I have something to tell you. Authorised by my minister——" He smiled in great emotion, and Hortense, under-

standing by the trembling of his lips, quickly sprang up; "No, no—not to-night—I can't listen to anything, I'm dancing."

She escaped on Rochemaure's arm. who came for her for the cotillon. He also, extremely smitten, the worthy young man, always imitating Lappara, ventured to utter a phrase which made her go into a fit of merriment, that whirled with her all round the saloon; and, the figure ended, she went to her sister, whispered: "We're in for it— Numa has promised me to his three secretaries!"

"Which are you going to take?"

Her reply was cut short by the rolling of the tabour.

"The farandole!—The farandole!"

A surprise of the minister for his guests. The farandole to wind up the cotillon. And Hortense in the the forefront, the farandole unrolls through the long enfilade of the drawing-rooms followed by Valmajour playing with superb gravity, proud of his success and of the looks won for him by his masculine and sturdy figure in an original costume.

"How fine he is!" exclaimed Roumestan, "how fine!—A Greek shepherd!"

CHAPTER X

FELINITIES

BETWEEN President Le Quesnoy and his son-in-law there never was any great sympathy. Time, frequent intercourse, the bonds of relationship had not diminished the apartness of their natures, so as to conquer the intimidating cold felt by the Southerner in the presence of the tall, silent man with the haughty, pale head, whose blue-grey eyes, the eyes of Rosalie, minus their affection and indulgence, lit upon his vicacious energy and froze it. Numa, fickle and mobile, ever at the mercy of his own speech, at once ardent and complex, revolted against his father-in-law's logic, straightforwardness, rigidity; and whilst envying his qualities, set them to the account of the coldness of the man of the North, of the extreme North, whom the President represented in his eyes. "Further on, there's the white bear.— Then nothing more, the Pole and death."

Still, he flattered him, tried to fascinate him with adroit felinities, his snares to capture the Gaul; but the Gaul, subtler than he, did not let himself be enveloped. And when they talked politics on Sundays in the dining-room in the Place Royale; when Numa, cheered by the good fare, tried to persuade old Le Quesnoy that in truth they were very near an understanding, as they both wished the same thing—freedom: you should have seen the repellent head-shake with which the President shook off all his arguments.

"Ah! but no, not the same!"

In four precise, hard-headed reasonings, he re-established the distances, unmasked the words, proved he was not letting himself be caught by such humbug. The barrister retreated jocularly, at heart much vexed, especially because of his wife, who, without ever interfering in politics, listened and looked. Accordingly, when returning at night in their carriage he tried to show her that her father had no common-sense. Ah! if it had not been for her, he would have had a nasty retort. Rosalie, not to irritate him, avoided taking sides:—

"Yes, it's unlucky—you don't understand each other," but in her heart of hearts she held the President to be in the right.

With the entry of Roumestan into the ministry, the coldness between the two men had been accentuated. M. Le Quesnoy refused to show himself at the receptions in the Rue de Grenelle, and explained himself very clearly to his daughter:—

"Tell your husband—to continue coming to my house and as often as possible, I shall be very glad; but I'll never be seen at the ministry. I know what those people are up to; I don't want to seem to be an accomplice."

For the rest, the situation was saved in the eyes of society by the profound mourning that kept the Le Quesnoys within their own four walls so long a time. The Minister of Public Instruction would probably have been very much embarrassed to know that his salons were frequented by that vigorous contradictor in whose presence he remained a little boy; however, he affected to seem wounded by his decision, made an attitude of it, a thing always most precious to a comedian, and a pretext for only coming very unpunctually to the Sunday dinners, excusing himself with committees, reunions, obligatory banquets, which give husbands in politics such vast liberty.

Rosalie on the other hand did not miss one Sunday, arrived early in the afternoon, happy to recover in her parents' home the taste of family life which official existence scarce left her leisure to satisfy. With Mme. Le Quesnoy still at Vespers, Hortense at church with her mother, or taken by friends to some musical matinée, Rosalie was sure to find her father in his library, long room tapestried with books from top to bottom, shut in with those dumb friends, those intellectual confidants, the only ones at which his sorrow had never taken umbrage. The President did not sit down to read, he used to inspect the shelves, would stop at a beautiful binding, and standing up, without suspecting it, would read for an hour, not noticing either time or fatigue. He smiled palely when he saw his eldest daughter come in. After a few words exchanged, for neither of them was talkative, she also passed her beloved authors in review, selected, dipped into them beside him, under the rather darkened light of a large court of the Marais, where fell in heavy notes, amid the Sunday quiet in the commercial quarters, the sounds of vesper bells. At times he would give her a half-open book—

"Read that!" underlining with his nail; and when she had read:—

"It's beautiful, isn't it?"

There was no greater pleasure for this young wife, to whom life offered such brilliance and luxury, than this hour with her old sad father.

She owed him her rectitude of thought, her feeling of justice which made her so valiant, also her artistic taste, the love of painting and the fine arts. Her mother Rosalie loved, worshipped, not without some revolt against a nature, which was too simple, too soft, annihilated in her own house, whom grief, which uplifts certain souls, had bent to earth to the most vulgar feminine preoccupations, practical piety, the small household details.

In the middle of their quiet chatting, the noise of a door was heard, the *frou-frou* of silk. Hortense had returned.

"Ah! I knew I'd find you there."

She did not care for reading. Even novels bored her; they were never romantic enough for her imagination. After going up and down for five minutes, keeping her hat on—

"It smells musty here, with all these papers—don't you think so, Rosalie?—Come along with me a little—father has had enough of you. Now it's my turn."

And she would drag her off into her room, their room, for Rosalie had also lived in it till she was twenty.

There she saw, during a charming hour of chat, all the objects that had formed part of herself, her bed with cretonne curtains, her desk, the library where a little of her childhood remained in the titles of the volumes, in the puerility of a thousand nothings preserved with love. She found again all her thoughts in all the corners of the room, more coquettish and ornate than in her time, a carpet on the floor small frail tables for sewing, for writing. More elegance and less order, two or three pieces of work begun, on the backs of chairs, the desk open with a quantity of writing material. When they entered there was always a brief minute of scurry.

"It's the wind," Hortense would say, bursting with laughter; "It knows I adore it, so it came to see if I was there."

"The window must have been left open." calmly replied Rosalie. "How can you live in there?—I am unable to think, myself, when nothing is in its place."

She got up to put straight a frame nailed to the wall, which worried her eye.

"Well, with me it's quite the opposite, it excites me—I fancy I am on a journey."

This difference of nature recurred in the countenances of the sisters. Rosalie, regular of feature, with a great purity of lines, calm eyes and colour changing like running water whose spring is deep; the other, with irregular traits, a clever look. on a pale creole complexion. The North and South of father and mother, two temperaments of great diversity which had joined without fusion, each perpetuating its race. And that in spite of the life in common, the similar education in a big boarding-school where Hortense, under the same masters, a few years later, took up again the school tradition which had made of her sister a serious, careful woman, absorbed in her every act, and turned out Hortense a warped, chimerical creature, of restless mind, always agog about something. Sometimes, seeing her so excited, Rosalie would cry:—

"I am myself very happy—I have no imagination."

"I have nothing else!" Hortense would say; and she reminded her that in M. Baudoy's course of lectures—he had to teach them style and the development of thought, what he pompously called his "imagination class"—Rosalie had no success, as she expressed everything in a few terse words, whilst she herself would scribble volumes if she had as many ideas.

"That's the only prize I ever got, the prize of imagination."

They were however united in tender affection, one of those affections of a big for a little sister, into which there enters something of the filial and of the motherly. Rosalie took her everywhere with her, to balls, to her friends, to her rounds of shopping which refine the tastes of Parisian ladies. Even after their leaving school, she remained her little mother. And now she was busied about marrying her, of finding the calm level-headed companion who was indispensable to that madcap, the firm arm with which her impetuosity must be kept in balance. Méjean was obviously indicated; but Hortense, who at first had not said no, suddenly displayed an evident antipathy. They had an explanation the day after the ministerial soirée, when Rosalie had surprised her sister's emotion, agitation.

"Oh! he is kind, I like him well enough," said Hortense. "He is a loyal friend, such as one would wish to have near all one's life.—But he is not the husband I want."

"Why?"

"You will laugh.—He does not speak enough to my imagination, there you are!—Marriage with him gives me the impression of a middle-class, rectangular house at the end of an avenue straight as a poker. And you know I prefer other things, the unforeseen, surprises."

"Who, then? M. de Lappara?"

"Thanks! for him to prefer his tailor to me."

"M. de Rochemaure?"

"The model paper-cutter—I who have a horror of paper."

And when the disquiet of Rosalie pressed her hard, wanting to know questioning her intimately: "What I would like," said the girl, whilst a slight flame, like a straw fire, rose into the pallor of her complexion, "what I would like——," then in an altered voice, with a comic look—

"I'd like to marry Bompard; yes, Bompard, that's the husband of my dreams. At least he has imagination, resources against monotony."

She got up, paced the room, with her rather bent posture, which made her seem even taller than she was. People really did not know Bompard. What pride, what dignity in his life, and logic in his madness! "Numa wanted to give him a berth near him; he didn't want it. He has preferred to live his chimera. And the South is accused of being practical, industrious. There's one who belies the legend. Why at this very moment—he was telling me at the ball the other night—he is hatching ostrich eggs—an artificial hatcher; He is sure to get millions. He is far happier than if he had them.—But a man like that is a perpetual fairy-tale! Bompard for me! I want Bompard only."

"Well, I shan't get to the bottom to-day," thought the elder sister, who guessed there was something lurking beneath this badinage.

One Sunday Rosalie on arriving found Mme. Le Quesnoy, who was waiting for her in the anteroom and said mysteriously:—

"There's somebody in the drawing-room—a lady from the South."

"Aunt Portal?"

"You will see."

It was not Mme. Portal, but a lovely Provençale, whose rustic bow ended in a burst of laughter.

"Hortense!"

With her skirt reaching down to her flat boots, the corsage widened by folds of tulle, her features framed by falling waves of hair kept in its place by the small headdress adorned with velvet chiselled, embroidered by jet butterflies, Hortense looked much like the "chato's" to be seen on Sunday flirting on the Lice at Arles, or walking two and two, with lowered eyelids, between the colonnettes of the cloister of Saint Trophyme.

"Would you believe she's so pretty!" cried the mother, enraptured at the living personification of the country of her youth. Rosalie on the contrary grieved with an unconscious sorrow as if that costume were carrying her sister far away, very far.

"There's a fancy dress!—It suits you, but I prefer you as a Parisian. And who has dressd you so well?"

"Audiberte Valmajour. She has just gone from here."

"As she comes often," said Rosalie, going into their room to take off her hat, "what a friendship—I shall be jealous!"

Hortense defended herself, somewhat put out. The Southern coif gave the mother pleasure.

"Isn't it fine, mother?" she exclaimed from one room to the other. Besides, the poor girl was so disorientalised in Paris, and so interesting with her blind devotion to her brother's genius.

"Oh! genius!" said the elder sister, shaking her head.

"Dame! You saw the other night at our house what effect—it's everywhere the same."

And when Rosalie replied that one must estimate at their true value such society successes, which were composed of complaisance, of chic, of the caprice of a soirée, Hortense burst out:—

"Well, then, he's at the Opéra."

Moreover, the Valmajours were not ordinary peasants, but the last representatives of a decayed family!

Rosalie, standing before a pier-glass, turned round laughing.

"What! you believe that legend?"

"Why of course! They descend directly from the Princes des Baux—the parchments are there like the coat of arms on their rustic door. The day they wished——"

Rosalie shivered. Behind the peasant flute-player was the prince. With a prize for imagination, that might become dangerous.

"There's nothing fine in all that"—and she no longer laughed this time—"there are round about Aps ten families of the so-called princely name. Those who have told you otherwise have lied out of vanity, out of——"

"But it's Numa, it's your husband—the other night at the ministry he gave all sorts of details."

"Oh! with him you know—you must make allowances, as he says."

Hortense was no more listening. She had returned to the drawing-room, and sitting at the piano she began singing in a loud voice—

Mount 'as passa la matinado
Mourbieu, Marioun.

It was an ancient popular song of Provence set to an air as serious as plain-song, which Numa had taught his sister-in-law, and which he amused himself by listening to her singing, with her Parisian accent, which reminded one of Italian pronounced by an Englishwoman.

Hortense went on singing, but presently broke off to rap out with the gesture and intonation of Numa when he was getting excited: "That, you see, my children. It's good as Shakespeare!"

"Yes, a picture of morals," observed Rosalie approaching. "The husband gross, brutal, the wife feline and a liar —a regular Southern household."

"Oh! my daughter," said Mme. Le Quesnoy in a tone of gentle reproach, the tone of old quarrels that have passed into a habit. The piano-stool turned briskly on its pivot and confronted Rosalie with the cap of the wrathful Provençale.

"It's too bad. What has the South done to you? As for me, I adore it. I did not know it, but my last journey with you has revealed to me my real country. It's all very fine that I was baptized at Saint-Paul; I belong myself to the other part. A child of the Placette! You know, mama, one of these days, we shall leave these cold Northerners and go and live, we two, in our beautiful South, where people sing, where they dance, the South of the wind, the sun, the mirage, of all that poeticises and broadens life. 'C'est là que je voudrais vi-i-vre.' " Her agile hands fell again on the piano, scattering the end of her dream in a confusion of resounding notes.

"And not a word about the tabour," thought Rosalie, "that's serious!"

Still more serious than she fancied.

From the day Audiberte had seen the young lady tie a flower to her brother's tabour, at that very minute there had risen in her ambitious mind a splendid vision of the future, which had not been foreign to their transplantment. Hortense's welcome when she came to her to complain, her eagerness to rush off to Numa, strengthened her in her still vague hope. And since then, slowly, without opening her thoughts to her men-folk otherwise than by hints, with the duplicity of an almost Italian peasant girl, she made ready their paths by gliding, by creeping. From the kitchen in the Place Royale, where she began by waiting timidly in a corner on the edge of a chair, she struggled through to the drawing-room established herself, always neat and well-coifed, in a poor relation's position. Hortense was wild about her, showed her to her friends like a pretty trinket brought from that Provence of which she spoke with passion. And the other, making herself out simpler than nature, exaggerated her barbaric bewilderments, her clenched fits of anger against the muddy sky of Paris, cried 'Boudiou!' very nicely and watched its effect like any theatre ingénue. The President himself smiled at it, at the 'Boudiou.' And to make the President smile!

But it was with the young lady, when alone with her, that she put all her caressing artifices in motion. She would suddenly fall down on her knees, take her hands, go into ecstasies over the least graces of her toilette, her way of tying a ribbon, of dressing her hair, emitting those leaden compliments to a person's face which give pleasure despite everything, so simple and spontaneous they appear. Oh! when the young lady had got out of the carriage at the farm, she believed she saw the queen of the angels in person, so that she could not speak for stupefaction. And her brother, *pecaïré!* When he heard the carriage in which the Parisian was returning creaking on the stone of the down-path, he said it was as if the stones were falling one by one on his heart. She made play with the brother, and of his pride, of his uneasiness. Uneasiness, why? I just ask you a moment. Since the minister's soirée they were talking of him in all the papers, his portrait appeared everywhere. And so many invitations in the Faubourg Saint-Germain that he could not manage them all. Duchesses, countesses wrote him perfumed notes, coronetted just like the carriages they sent to fetch him. *Eh! bien,* he was not contented, the poor fellow!

All this whispered to Hortense impressed on her some of the peasant woman's feverishness and magnetic will. Then, without looking, she asked if Valmajour had not perhaps down there in the country a bride waiting for him.

"He, a bride! *Avaï,* you don't know him. He thinks too much of himself to want a peasant girl. The wealthiest of them have run after him, that girl of the Colombettes, and another one, and fine girls, you know! He didn't even look at them! Who knows what he's got in his head? Oh! those artists!"

And the word, which was new to her, assumed on her ignorant lips an indefinable expression, like the Latin of the Mass or some cabalistic formula culled from Albertus Magnus. The heritage of Cousin Puyfourcat also very often recurred in her cunning chatter. She believed in the legacy and mentioned it to the girl, less in order to dazzle her than to decrease the social distance separating them. On the death of Puyfourcat, her brother would buy back Valmajour, would have the castle rebuilt and his titles of nobility confirmed, since they all said the documents were in existence.

At the end of these talks, prolonged sometimes till twilight, Hortense would remain silent a long time, her forehead touching the window-pane, seeing the lofty towers of the rebuilt castle rising in a rosy winter's setting sun, the platform streaming with lights and serenades in honour of the châtelaine.

"*Boudiou,* how late it is!" the peasant would cry, perceiving she had reached the desired mood. "And my men's dinner not ready! I'm off!"

Often Valmajour came and waited for her downstairs; but she never let him come up. She knew him to be so awkward and so vulgar, besides being indifferent to any notions of trying to fascinate. She had not need of him.

A person who also bothered her much, but difficult to avoid, was Rosalie, with whom her felinities, her sham simplicities did not take. In her presence Audiberte, with her terrible black eyebrows knitted at the forehead, said not a word; and in her dumbness there arose, together with a race-hatred, the sullen and vindictive anger of the weaker against the most serious obstacle to her plans. Her real grievance was that; but she avowed to the younger sister there were others. Rosalie did not like the tabour; then "she did not keep up her religion. And a woman who does not do so, you see—." Audiberte herself kept it up, and furiously; she never missed a service and communicated on the appointed days. Which did not check her in anything, liar, hypocrite, violent even to crime as she was, seeking nothing in scriptural texts but precepts of revenge and hate. Only

she remained honest, in the feminine sense of the word. With her twenty-eight years, her pretty face she preserved in the low environments in which they now lived the severe chastity of her thick peasant's *fichu,* pressed against a heart that had never beaten but with ambition for her brother.

"Hortense disquiets me! Look at her."

Rosalie, to whom her mother uttered this confidence in a corner of the *salon* at the ministry, thought Mme. Le Quesnoy shared her mistrust. The mother's remark, however, applied to Hortense's condition, who had not succeeded in getting rid of a very bad cold. Rosalie looked at her sister. She had still her dazzling complexion, her vivacity, her cheerfulness. She coughed a bit, but, well! like all Parisian ladies after the dancing season. The fine weather would very soon set her right.

"Have you spoken about it to Jarras?"

Jarras was a friend of Roumestan's, one of the old ones of the Café Malmus. He gave assurance it was nothing, advised the waters of Arvillard.

"*Eh bien!* She must go there," said Rosalie swiftly, enchanted at the pretext for sending Hortense away.

"Yes, but your father will be alone."

"I'll visit him every day."

Whereupon the poor mother confessed, sobbing, the fear caused her by this voyage with her daughter. For a whole year she had had thus to go the round of the watering-places with the son they had lost. Was she about to start on the same pilgrimage, with the same fearful end in prospect? In his case also, he was seized in the fulness of health, in the fulness of strength.

"Oh! mama, mama—please be silent."

And Rosalie scolded her gently. Hortense was not ill, you see; the doctor said so. The journey would be a simple distraction. Arvillard, in the Dauphinese Alps, a wonderful country. She would have liked to accompany Hortense in her place. Unluckily, she could not. Serious reasons.

"Yes, I understand. Your husband, the ministry."

"Oh! no, it isn't that."

And in her mother's arms, in the heart-intimacy they rarely enjoyed together: "Listen, but keep it to yourself alone, for nobody knows it, not even Numa," she confessed to the still very frail expectation of a great happiness of which she had despaired, which made her mad with joy and fear, the new hope of a child who was perhaps about to come.

CHAPTER XI

ARVILLARD

ARVILLARD-LES-BAINS,
August 2, 1876.

"WELL, it's very queer, the place from which I am writing to you. Imagine a square hall, very high, flagged, stuccoed, echoing, where the light from two large windows is veiled by blue curtains even to the last panes, further darkened by a kind of floating steam, tasting like sulphur, which sticks to the dresses, tarnishes gold ornaments; within, people sitting against walls on benches, chairs, stools, round small tables, people that look at their watches every minute, get up, go out to give place to others, revealing each time through the half-open door the crowd of visitors, walking about in the bright vestibule, and the white fluttering apron of hurrying servants. No noise, despite all this movement, a constant murmur of whispered conversations, of newspapers being unfolded, of bad rusty pens scratching on the paper, a church-like meditativeness, bathed, refreshed by the great jet of mineral water installed in the centre of the hall and whose spring is broken against a metallic dish, scatters itself in sprays, pulverizes itself over broad streaming basins. That is the inhalation room.

I may tell you, my darling, that every one does not inhale in the same way. Thus the old gentleman now opposite me follows literally the doctor's orders: I know them all. Feet on a stool, chest out, keep the elbows in, and the mouth always open to facilitate breathing. Poor dear man! How he inhales, with what trust, what small, devout, and credulous eyes, that seem to say to the spring—

"O spring of Arvillard, cure me properly, see how I inhale, what trust I put in you."

Then we have the sceptic who inhales without inhaling, his back turned, shrugging his shoulders and gazing at the ceiling. Then the disheartened ones, the real sick who feel the uselessness and nullity of it all; a poor lady, my neighbour, whom I see, after each cough, quickly put her finger to her mouth, look whether the glove is not stained at the tip with a red point. And yet the people find the means of being merry.

Some ladies of the same hotel bring their chairs together, group themselves, embroider, whisper, comment on the *Visitors' Journal* and the list of foreigners. The young persons read English novels with red covers, some priests read their breviary; as for me, you know novels are not in my line, especially novels of to-day, where everything happens as in life. Besides, I correspond with two or three victims, Marie Tournier, Aurélie Dansaert, and you, my big sister, whom I adore. Look out for regular diaries. Just think! two hours' inhalation four times every day! No one here inhales as much I do; that is, I am a real phenomenon. I am much looked at on that account and I am rather proud of it.

Apart from this, no other treatment, except the glass of mineral water I go and drink at the spring morning and evening, and which is bound to conquer the obstinate hoarseness that bothersome cold has left in my voice. It's the speciality of the waters of Arvillard; so the singers have a rendezvous here. The handsome Mayol has just left us with quite new vocal chords. Mlle. Bachellery, you know, the little diva of your fête, is so well under the treatment that after finishing the three regular weeks, she is beginning three more, for which the *Visitors' Journal* praises her highly. We have the honour of living in the same hotel as this young and illustrious person, attended by an affectionate mother from Bordeaux who at *table d'hôte* makes a request for "appetites" in the salad and speaks of the 140 franc hat worn by her young lady at the last Longchamps. A delightful couple and extremely admired among us. People swoon away at Bébé's pretty ways, so her mother says, at her laugh, at her liftings of

a brief skirt. They crowd before the sanded court of the hotel to see her play croquet with the little boys and girls—she only plays with quite little ones—run, jump, throw a ball like a regular street urchin.

Every one says: "She's so childlike!" For me, I believe her sham childlikeness is part of a rôle, like her skirts with broad knots. Then she has such an extraordinary way of kissing that fat Bordeaux woman, hanging round her neck, making her rock her before everybody! You know how caressing I am, well! true, it embarrasses me to kiss mama.

A very curious, but less cheerful family also is Prince and Princess d'Anhalt, their daughter, governess, servants and suite, who occupy the whole first floor of the hotel of which they are the personages. I often meet the princess on the staircase, climbing step by step on her husband's arm, a fine-looking fellow, dazzling in health. She only goes to the establishment carried in a chair; and it's heart-rending that hollowed, pale head behind the small window-pane, the father and child who walk beside it, the girl looking very poorly, with all her mother's features, and also perhaps her illness. She is bored, this little one of eight years, who is forbidden to play with the other children and looks sorrowfully from the balcony at the games of croquet and the hotel riding-parties. They think her blood too blue for such common amusements, they prefer to keep her in the mournful atmosphere of a dying mother, with a father who promenades his sick wife haughtily about, or to leave her to the servants.

The other night there were a lot of

us in the big drawing-room on the ground floor where we meet to play games, sing, even dance sometimes. Mama Bachellery had just accompanied Bébé in a cavatina from an opera—we want to enter the Opéra, we've even come to Arvillard to "recuperate the voice for that," according to the mother's elegant phrase. Suddenly the door opens and the princess appears, with her grand air, dying, elegant, wrapt in a lace shawl that conceals the fearful and significant emaciation of the shoulders. The child and husband followed.

"Go on, please," coughs the poor woman.

And lo and behold! that beast of a little singer goes and chooses out of all her repertory the most heart-rending, the most sentimental romance, "Vorrei morir," something like our "Dead leaves" in Italian, a sick woman who fixes the date of her death in autumn, in order to give herself the illusion that all nature will die with her, covered by the first fog as by a shroud.

"Vorrei morir nella stagion dell 'anno."

The tune is graceful, of a sadness that prolongs the caress of the Italian words; and in the big drawing-room, into which, through the open windows, penetrated the perfumes, the light flitings of birds, the refreshingness of a lovely summer night, that longing to live still to autumn, that truce, that surcease demanded from evil took on something poignant. Without saying word, the princess rose, went out suddenly. In the black of the garden heard a sob, a long sob, then a man's voice which scolded, and those wailings

wept by a child who sees sorrow for her mother.

To Arvillard they only send convalescents like me, or desperate cases in which nothing does any good. Luckily we only have at our hotel, the *Alpes Dauphinoises,* three patients of the latter kind, the princess and two young Lyonnese, brother and sister, orphans, very rich, they say, who seem to be at the worst; the sister especially, who has the white-pale hue of Lyonnese women, wrapt up in peignoirs and knitted shawls, without a jewel, a ribbon, any care for coquetry. She smells of poverty, this rich girl. She is done for, knows it, despairs and gives up. There is on the contrary in the young man's hollowed figure, closely fitted by a jacket in the fashion, a terrible will to live, an incredible resistance to evil.

"My sister has no spring. I have!" he said the other day at the *table d'hôte,* in a hoarse voice which can no more be heard than La Vauters' "ut" when she sings. And the fact is he has a tremendous amount of go. He is the heart and soul of the hotel, the organizer of the games, parties, excursions: he rides on horseback, in sledges, a kind of small sledges laden with branches, on which the mountaineers of these parts shoot you down the steepest inclines, he valses, fences, shaken by dreadful attacks of coughing, which do not stop him one moment. We have further a medical celebrity, Dr. Bouchereau, you remember, the doctor whom mama had gone to consult about our poor André. I don't know if he recognized us, but he never salutes. An old wolf.

We have a very simple establishment,

very convenient, two rooms on the second floor, the whole valley in front of us, a circle of mountains black with firs at the foot, and which are shaded off, lightened up as they climb with masses of eternal snow.

In the evening there is the drawing-room; in the day-time we roam in the park for the treatment which, connected with this existence at once so busy and so empty, takes hold of you and absorbs you. The amusing hour is after lunch, when we group ourselves at little tables for coffee, under the big limes, at the entrance of the garden. It is the hour of arrivals and departures.

All this stir amuses me, but our dear mama remains very sad, much absorbed, in spite of the smile she essays when I look at her. I divine that every detail of our life brings her a heart-rending recollection, an evocation of lugubrious images. She has seen so much of those caravanserais of sick persons, during the year when she followed her dying one from watering-place to watering-place, in the plain or on the mountain, under the pines at the edge of the sea, with a hope always deceived and the eternal resignation she was obliged to show in her martyrdom.

Really, Jarras might well have prevented this renewal of her sorrows; because I am not ill, I hardly cough at all any more, and, apart from my nuisance of a cold which gives me a voice like a hawker's, I have never felt so well. An appetite like Hades, fancy! one of those awful appetites that can't wait. Yesterday after a lunch of thirty courses, with a menu more complicated than the Chinese alphabet, I see a woman picking strawberries before her door. All of a sudden a longing seizes me. Two bowls, my dear, two bowls of those big strawberries, so fresh, "the fruit of the country," as our waiter at table says. And that's my stomach!

All the same, my darling, how lucky it is neither you nor I have taken the illness of that poor brother I hardly knew, and whose haggard features, disheartened expression (such as he has it in his portrait in our parents' room), I find here on other countenances! And what an original is that doctor who once tended him, the renowned Bouchereau! The other day mama wished to introduce me to him, and in order to get a consultation we prowled in the park around the tall old man with his brutal and harsh physiognomy; but he was entirely surrounded by the doctors of Arvillard, listening to him with the humility of schoolboys. So we waited for him at the exit of the inhalation. Time wasted. Our man began walking at a pace as if he wanted to run away from us. With mama, you know, one can hardly walk quickly, and we missed him again. Finally, yesterday morning Fanny went to ask his housekeeper, on our behalf, if he could receive us. He sent reply that he was here to look after himself and not to give consultations. There's a churl for you! It's true I have never seen such a pallor wax-like. Father is a high-coloured gentleman compared with him. He lives only on milk, never comes down to the dining-room, much less to the *salon*. Our fussy little doctor, he whom I call Monsieur "That's All Right," declares he has a very dangerous heart disease, and that it is the waters of

Arvillard that have enabled him to endure for the last three years.

"That's all right! That's all right!"

6th *August.*

So it's true, Numa is coming to see us. Oh, how glad I am, how glad I am! Your letter arrived by the one o'clock courier, and the distribution takes place in the hotel bureau. A solemn moment, decisive for the hue of the day. The bureau full, people form in a semi-circle round fat Mme. Laugeron, very imposing in her blue flannel peignoir, whilst her authoritative voice, rather affected, as of a former lady companion, announces the many-coloured addresses of the budget. Each person goes forward as his name is called, and I must tell you there is a certain *amour-propre* involved in having a large batch. On what do we here not set some self-love in this perpetual friction of vanities and follies? When I think I have managed to get proud of my two hours' inhalation! "M. le Prince d'Anhalt—M. Vasseur—Mlle. Le Quesnoy." Disillusion. It's only my fashion paper. "Mlle. Le Quesnoy." I look to see if there is nothing else for me, and run off with your dear letter to the further end of the garden, to a bench shut in by great nut-trees.

That is my bench, the corner in which I isolate myself in order to dream, to weave my romances; for, an astonishing thing! in order to invent well, to develop according to M. Baudoy's rules, large horizons are not needful for me. When it is too big, I lose myself, I am scattered. The only annoyance about my bench is the neighbourhood of a swing, where that little Bachellery spends half her days in having herself launched into space by the young man with elasticity. I should rather think he must have a spring to push her like that for hours! And there are the cries of Bébé, the little screams: "Higher! still higher!" *Dieu!* How that girl exasperates me. I wish the swing would despatch her into the clouds and that she would never come down again.

I feel so well, so far apart from the others, on my bench, when she is not there. I tasted your letter there, the postscript of which made me cry out with delight.

Oh! blessed be Chambéry and its new *lycée,* and that foundation stone to be laid, which brings in to our regions the Minister of Public Instruction. He will be very comfortable here for the preparation of his speech, either walking in the avenue or under my nut-trees when Mlle. Bachellery does not spoil them. My dear Numa! I understand him so well, he is so living, so cheerful. How we are going to talk together about our Rosalie and of the serious motive preventing her from travelling at the moment. Ah! *mon Dieu,* it's a secret. And mama made me swear so—she is also glad to welcome dear Numa. On a sudden she is losing all bashfulness, all modesty, and you should have seen her stateliness as she entered the hotel bureau to engage the rooms for her son-in-law the Minister. No! but the face of our hostess when she heard the news!

"What! mesdames, you are—you were?"

"We were—we are——"

Her broad face grew lilac, purple, an impressionist palette. And M. Laugeron and all the servants! Since our arrival, we have asked in vain for an extra candle; immediately there were five on the mantelpiece. Numa will be well served, I will answer for it, and put up. He will be given the Prince d'Anhalt's first floor, which will be free in three days. It seems the waters of Arvillard are deadly to the princess; and the little doctor himself is of opinion she should go as soon as possible. "That's all right," because if a misfortune happened, the *Alpes Dauphinoises* would not recover from it.

It is piteous the haste displayed in connection with the leaving of these unfortunates; how they are urged, how they are pushed, with the help of the magnetic hostility exuding from places when one is inopportune. Poor Princess d'Anhalt, whose arrival was so fêted here! For a trifle, she would be taken back to the borders of the Department between two gendarmes. The hospitality of watering-places!

Apropos, and Bompard? You don't tell me if he will be one of the company. Dangerous Bompard! if he comes, I am quite capable of eloping with him on some glacier. What developments we should discover for ourselves, towards the summits! I laugh, I am happy. And I inhale and I inhale, rather put out by the neighbourhood of the dreadful Bouchereau, who has just come in and sat down two places away from me.

What a hard look he has, that man! His hands on the handle of his stick, his chin leaning on it, he speaks out loud, looking straight ahead, without addressing any one. Ought I to take it to myself what he says about the imprudence of visitors, about their dresses of bright cambric, about the foolishness of going out after dinner in a country where the evenings are deadly cool? The malicious fellow! One would fancy he knows I am going to beg to-night at the church of Arvillard for the work of the Propagation. Father Olivieri is to relate in the flesh his missions in Tibet, his captivity, his martyrdom, Mlle. Bachellery to sing Gounod's "Ave Maria." And I am making myself a fête of the return through all the small dark streets with lanterns, like a real torchlight procession.

If M. Bouchereau has given me a consultation in those words of his, it is too late: I don't want any. First of all, monsieur, I have *carte blanche* from my little doctor, who is far more obliging than you and has even allowed me a little valse in the drawing-room to wind up with. Oh! only one, you know. Besides, when I dance a little too much, everybody is after me. They don't know how strong I am with my figure like a tall reed, and that a Parisian lady is never ill from overdancing. "Take care. Don't tire yourself." The one brings my shawl; another shuts the windows at my back, for fear I catch cold. But the most attentive of all is the young man with the spring, because he finds I have a deuced lot more of it than his sister. It's not difficult, poor girl. Between ourselves I believe the young gentleman, desperate at Alice Bachellery's coolness, has fallen back on me and is paying me his court. But, alas! he is losing his pains, my heart is captured, Bompard has it all. *Eh, bien!* no, it is not Bompard, and you yourself suspect it is not Bompard. Who is the hero of my romance? It is—it is

—Ah! So much the worse, my hour is gone by. I shall tell you another day, Mademoiselle "Chilly."

CHAPTER XII

HER EYELIDS

THE morning on which the *Visitors' Journal* announced that "Son Excellence M. le Ministre de l'Instruction publique," Bompard attaché, and their suite, had arrived at the *Alpes Dauphinoises,* the consternation in the neighbouring hotels was great.

La Laita had been actually keeping in reserve during the past two days a Catholic Bishop of Geneva in order to produce him at a favourable moment, as well as a Councillor-General of the Isère Department, a Lieutenant-Judge at Tahiti, an architect from Coston, a whole swarm in fact. *La Chevreite,* too, was expecting a "Deputy of the Rhône and family." But the Deputy, the Lieutenant-Judge, all vanished, carried away, swallowed up in the furrow of glorious flame that followed Numa Roumestan everywhere. He alone was talked about, busied about. Every pretext was good enough to introduce oneself into the *Alpes Dauphinoises,* to pass over the lawn before the little drawing-room on the ground floor, where the Minister was eating between two ladies and his attaché, to see him play *boule,* dear to Southerners, with Father Olivieri of the Missions, a holy, dreadfully hairy man, who through living among savages had assumed some of their ways, uttered awe-inspiring cries and brandished the *boules* above his head like a tomahawk.

The minister's handsome face. the affability of his manners won him all hearts; and particularly his sympathy for the humble. On the day after his arrival the two waiters who served the first floor declared at the office that the minister would take them with him to Paris for his personal service. As they were good servants, Mme. Laugeron made a grimace, but did not let His Excellency see any of it, whose stay was such an honour to her hotel. The prefect, the rector arrived from Grenoble in full dress, to present their homage to Roumestan. The Abbé of the Grande Chartreuse—he had pleaded for them against the Praemonstratensians and their elixir—sent him with great pomp a case of extra-fine liqueur. Finally the Prefect of Chambéry came for his orders for the ceremony of laying the foundation stone of the Lycée, an occasion for a declaratory speech and a revolution in the ways of the University. The minister, however, requested a little respite: the labours of the session had fatigued him, he wanted to get his second wind, to quiet down among his family, to get ready at leisure this Chambéry discourse, which was to be of such considerable import. And M. le Préfet perfectly understood that, asking only to be warned forty-eight hours beforehand, in order to lend the brilliance necessary to the ceremony. The stone had waited two months, it could well wait further for the illustrious orator's good pleasure.

In reality, what kept Roumestan at Arvillard was neither the want of repose nor the leisure necessary to that marvellous improvisation, on which time and reflection had the effect of damp on phosphorus, but the presence of Alice Bachellery. After five months of a passionate flirtation Numa was no further advanced with his "little one" than the day of their first meeting. He frequented the house, tasted Mme. Bachellery's *bouillabaisse,* the *chansonettes* of the ex-director of the Folies-Bordelaises, recognized those trifling favours by a mass of presents, bouquets, despatches of ministerial boxes, tickets for the meetings of the Institute of the Chamber, even the palms of officer of the Academy for the song-writer, all that without forwarding his projects. He was not, however, one of those novices who go fishing at all hours, without having first tried the water and baited it properly. Only he had to do with a most subtle carp, who amused herself at his precautions, nibbled at the bait, gave him at times the illusion of capture, and suddenly escaped, leaving his mouth dry with desire, his heart whipt by disturbances of his supple, undulating and enticing fish. Nothing more enervating than that game. It was in Numa's hands to stop it by giving the little one what she asked, her nomination as *première chanteuse* at the Opéra, an agreement for five years, a big salary, the whole drawn on perforated paper, and not by a simple handshake of Cadaillac's. She no more believed in that than in the "I answer for it—it's as if you had it," by which Roumestan had been trying for five months to hook her.

The latter found himself on the horns of a dilemma. "Yes," said Cadaillac, "if you renew my lease." Now, Cadaillac was burnt out, done for; his presence at the head of the first theatre of music, a scandal, a blemish, a purulent inheritance from the Imperial administration. The Press would assuredly cry out against the gambler, thrice bankrupt, who could not wear his cross as an officer, and the cynical showman, shamelessly squandering the public money. Weary at last of being unable to let herself be caught, Alice broke the line and ran away, dragging the hook.

One day the minister arriving at the Bachellery, found the house empty and the father who, to comfort him, sang him his last refrain—

"Donne-moi d'quoi q't 'as, t'auras d'quoi qu'j'ai."

He forced himself to patience for a month, then returned to see the fertile song-writer who wanted to sing him his new one—

"Quand la saucisson va, tout va"—

and to inform him that the ladies, finding themselves admirably put up at the watering-place, had the intention of doubling their sojourn. It was then that Roumestan recalled that he was expected for that foundation stone of the Lycée at Chambéry, a promise "made in the air" and which would probably have remained there, if Chambéry had not been near Arvillard, where, by a providential chance, Jarras, the minister's doctor and friend, had just sent Mlle. Le Quesnoy.

They met, on his arrival, in the hotel garden. She, very surprised to see him as if that very morning she had not read the pompous note in the *Visitors Journal,* as if for the last week the whole valley through the thousand voices of its forests, of its fountains, its innumerable echoes, had not announced His Excellency's coming—

"You, here?"

He, with his imposing ministerial air—

"I came to see my sister-in-law."

He was besides astonished to find Mlle. Bachellery still at Arvillard. He thought her gone a long time ago.

"*Dame!* I must take great care of myself, as Cadaillac pretends my voice is so unsound."

Thereupon a little Parisian salute from the end of her eyelids, and she went off, singing brightly, a pretty lark-trill, which you hear long after the bird is out of sight. Only, from that day, she changed her ways. She was no longer the precocious child, always romping about the hotel, sporting on the swing, playing innocent games, who was only amused with the little ones, disarmed the severest mamas, the most morose ecclesiastics by the frankness of her laugh and her punctuality at services. They saw now appear Alice Bachellery, the diva of the Bouffes, the pretty, free-and-easy young woman of the world, surrounding herself with young fops, improvising fêtes, parties, suppers, which her mother, always present, only half protected from evil interpretations.

Every morning there started from the perron a merry cavalcade of which she was the centre attraction, joined by all that was free, that was bachelor, at the *Alpes Dauphinoises* and the neighbouring hotels, the Lieutenant-Judge, the American architect, and especially the young man with the spring, whom the diva no longer seemed to drive to despair with her innocent infantilities. And the day was not complete except when the whole party had been drenched on their trip by one of those mountain storms, varied with lightning and hail, which frightened the horses, dramatized the landscape, prepared a sensational return, with the little Bachellery in a man's overcoat, her toque adorned with a woodcock's feather, holding the reins, whipping hard to warm herself, and when once on the ground relating the peril of the trip with the keen voice, the flashing eyes, the lively reaction of her youth against the chill shower and a slight shiver of fear.

If at least she had then felt the need of a good sleep, one of those sleeps of stone which are procured by excursions in the mountains! No, even till morning there was in those women's rooms a succession of laughs, songs, uncorked bottles, suppers which were taken up at such unheard-of hours, tables rolled along for baccarat, and over the head of the minister, whose apartment was just underneath.

He complained several times to Mme. Laugeron, who was much divided between her desire to be agreeable to His Excellency and the fear of discontenting clients of such connexions.

These sleepless nights, heavy July nights, which Roumestan passed in feverishly turning over and over in his bed certain importunate thoughts, whilst up above rang his neighbour's clear laugh, mingled with singing and scraps of tunes, he might have employed at his Chambéry speech; but he was too excited, too furious, restraining himself from mounting to the floor above in order to kick out the young man with the spring, the American, and the infamous Lieutenant-Judge, a dishonour to the French magistracy in the

Colonies, in order to seize by the neck that wicked little scamp, telling her once for all—

"Will you soon have finished making me suffer like that?"

One afternoon, at the hour when the band played, the coquettish and talkative hour in the life of baths, whilst all the visitors, crowded in front of the establishment as on the deck of a ship, were coming and going, turning in a round or taking their places on the seats packed together in three rows, the minister, in order to avoid Mlle. Bachellery, whom he saw arriving in a dazzling blue and red costume, escorted by her staff, had retired to a lonely alley, and seated alone at the corner of a bench, penetrated in his preoccupations by the melancholy of the hour and of the distant music, was mechanically fending off with the end of his parasol the scintillations of fire with which the setting sun was flooding the alley, when a slow shadow passing over his sun caused him to raise his eyes. It was Bouchereau, the celebrated doctor, very pale, haggard, dragging his feet along. They knew each other even as at a certain height of life all Parisians know one another. By accident, Bouchereau, who had not gone out for several days, felt in a sociable temper. He sat down, they talked.

"So you are ill, doctor?"

"Very ill," said the other in his wild-boar manner. "A hereditary evil—a hypertrophy of the heart. My mother died of it, my sister also—only I shall not last as long as they, because of my dreadful profession; I may last one year, two at the very utmost."

To that great scientist, to that infallible diagnoser speaking about his death with such tranquil assurance, there was no reply to be made but futile banalities. Roumestan understood it, and in silence he thought that there were sorrows in that case very differently serious from his own. Bouchereau went on without looking at him, with the vague eyes, the implacable sequence of ideas, which the habit of the professional chair and of lecturing gives to the professor—

"We doctors, because we have the appearance of it, people think we feel nothing, that we only pay heed to the sickness in the sick person, never the human and suffering being. Great mistake!—I have seen my master, Dupuytren, who yet passed for hard as iron, sobbing aloud before a poor little diphtheritic patient who said gently that it worried him to die. And those heart-rending appeals of motherly anguish, those passionate hands which clutch your arm: 'My child! Save my child!' And the fathers who stiffen themselves in order to tell you in a very manly voice, with big tears running down their cheeks: 'You will get him out of that, won't you, doctor?' It is all very well to harden oneself, such despairs wound the heart; and that is all right, when the heart is always attacked! Forty years' practice, to become each day more vibrating, more sensitive. It is my patients who have killed me. I am dying of others' sufferings."

"But I thought you no longer gave consultations, doctor," observed the minister, who was moved.

"Oh! no, never again, not for anybody. Were I to see a man fall down there before me, I should not even bend down. You understand, it is revolting in the long run, that sickness I have fostered from all sickness. I want to live, I—there's nothing but life."

He grew animated in his pallor; and his nostril, marked with a morbid stigma, drank in the light air impregnated with warm aromas, vibrating fanfares, cries of birds. He resumed with a heart-broken sigh—

"I practise no more, but I always remain a doctor, I retain that fatal gift of diagnosis, that horrible second-sight of the latent symptom of the suffering about which one wishes to be silent, which, hardly regarded at all in the passer-by, in the being who walks, speaks, acts in full vigour, shows me the dying man of to-morrow, the dull corpse—and that as clearly as I see the syncope coming on to which I shall succumb, the last swoon from which nothing will bring me back."

"It's terrifying," murmured Numa, who felt himself paling, and, a coward in the presence of illness and death, like all Southerners, those maniacs in favour of life, turned away from the redoubtable savant, dared no longer to look him in the face, for fear of allowing him to read on his rubicund face the sign of an early end.

"Ah! that terrible diagnosis which they all envy me, how it saddens me, how it spoils for me the little of life that yet remains. Look here! I know here a poor woman whose son died ten, twelve years ago, of laryngeal phthisis. I had seen him twice, and I alone of all asserted the seriousness of the illness. To-day I find the mother again with her young daughter; and I can say that the presence of these unfortunates ruins my stay at the watering-place, causes me more harm than my treatment will

do me good. They pursue me, they wish to consult me, and I, I refuse to do so absolutely. No need to auscultate the child to condemn her. It was enough for me to have seen her the other day throw herself voraciously on a bowl of strawberries, to have looked during the inhalation at her hand lying on her knees, a thin hand on which the nails are swollen up, are raised above the fingers as if ready to detach themselves. She has her brother's phthisis, she will die before a year is out—but let others tell it them. I have had enough of those stabs which recoiled on me. I don't want any more."

Roumestan had risen, greatly frightened.

"Do you know the ladies' names, doctor?"

"No. They sent me their card; I did not even want to see it. I only know they are at our hotel."

And suddenly, gazing at the end of the alley—

"Ah! *mon Dieu*, there they are! I'm off."

At the end, when the band was playing its final accord, there was a movement of umbrellas, of gay dresses fluttering among the branches at the first sounds of the dinner-bells ringing round about. Out of an animated, gossiping group, the ladies Le Quesnoy detached themselves, Hortense tall and *svelte* in the light, a dress of mousseline and valenciennes, a hat garnished with roses, in her hand a bouquet of those same roses bought in the park.

"With whom were you talking, Numa? It looked like M. Bouchereau."

She was in front of him, dazzlingly bright, in so favourable an aspect of happy youth, that the mother herself began to lose her terrors, allowing some of that bewitching gaiety to be reflected on her old face.

"Yes, it was Bouchereau, who told me of his wretched life—he is very down in the mouth, poor man!"

And Numa, gazing at her, was reassured.

"The man is mad. It is not possible, it is his own death he takes with him and diagnoses eve ywhere."

At that moment Bompard appeared, walking very swiftly, flourishing a newspaper.

"What now?" inquired the minister.

"Great news! The tambourinist has made his début."

Hortense was heard murmuring: "At last!" and Numa, who was beaming, asked—

"Success, wasn't it?"

"You bet!—I haven't read the article, but three columns in the first position in the *Messager!*"

"Yet another one I have invented," remarked the minister, who had sat down again, his hands in the armholes of his waistcoat, "Come, read it to us."

Mme. Le Quesnoy, observing that the dinner-bell had rung, Hortense answered quickly that it was only the first time; and with her cheek on her hand, in a pretty pose of careful attention, she listened.

"Is it to the Minister of Fine Arts, is it to the Director of the Opéra that the Parisian public owes the grotesque mystification of which it was the victim last night?"

They all started, except Bompard, who in his vivacity as a fine elocutionist, soothed by the *ronron* of his own phrasing, without understanding what he was reading, looked at them one after the other, much surprised at their astonishment.

"But go on," said Numa, "go on!"

"In any case, it is M. Roumestan whom we hold responsible. It is he who brought us from his province this bizarre and barbaric booby, this——"

"There are some very wicked people," broke in the girl, paling beneath her roses. The reader went on, his eyes rounded by the enormities he saw coming—

"—— to whom our Academy of Music owes it that for one night it resembled a return from the fair at Saint Cloud. And verily he had to be a famous booby, to believe that Paris——"

The minister tore the paper violently from him.

"You're not going to read us that tomfoolery right to the end, I suppose—it's quite enough to have brought it to us."

He ran through the article, with the quick glance of a publicist accustomed to Press invectives. "Provincial Minister—the Roumestan of Valmajour—hissed the ministry and burst his tabor." He had enough of it, hid the mischievous sheet at the bottom of his pocket, then got up, suppressing the rage which swelled his face, and taking Mme. Le Quesnoy's arm—

"Let's go and dine, mama. That will teach me not to interpose again for a lot of good-for-nothing people."

They were going all four in a line, Hortense with her eyes on the ground, in consternation.

"It concerns an artist of great talent," she said, trying to strengthen her rather

muffled voice, "he must not be held responsible for the injustice of the public, for the irony of the newspapers."
Roumestan stopped.

"Some talent—some talent—*bé*, yes
I don't say otherwise—but too exotic."
And raising his sunshade—

"Let's beware of the South, little sister, let's beware of the South—don't
let's overdo it—Paris would get tired."

He continued walking with deliberate
steps, calm and cold as an inhabitant of
Copenhagen, and the silence was only
disturbed by the crackling of the gravel
under their steps, which in certain circumstances seems like the crushing, the
annihilation of a fit of anger and of a
dream. When they were in front of the
hotel, whose immense hall sent forth by
its ten windows the hungry noise of
spoons at the bottom of the plates, Hortense stopped, and raising her head—

"So, this poor fellow—you're going
to desert him?"

"What am I to do? It's no good
struggling—since Paris won't have him."

She had a look of almost contemptuous indignation.

"Oh! it's awful, what you say—*Eh
bien*, I—I am prouder than you, and
I oyal to my enthusiasms."

She crossed in two bounds the perron
of the hotel.

"Hortense, the second bell has gone."

"Yes, yes, I know—I shall come
down."

She went up into her room, shut herself in, with the key inside, so as not
to be disturbed. Opening her desk, one
of those coquettish *bibelots* by means
of which the Parisian woman gives personality even to an inn room, she drew
out of it one of the photographs she

had had taken of herself with the ribbon and the fichu of Arles, wrote a line
at the bottom and signed it. Whilst she
was addressing it, the hour sounded at
the clock tower of Arvillard in the violet
sombreness of the valley, as if to sol-
emnize what she was daring to do.

"Six o'clock."

A mist was rising from the torrent,
in wandering, fleecy patches of white.
The amphitheatre of forests, of mountains, the silver aigrette of the glacier
in the rose-hued evening, she noted the
least details of that silent, quiet minute,
as one notes in the calendar one date
among all others, as one underlines in a
book the passage that has stirred one
most, and thinking out loud—

"It is my life, all my life that I bind
at this moment."

She took to witness of it the solemnity
of the evening, the majesty of nature,
the grand peacefulness of everything
around her.

Her whole life which she bound!
Poor little woman, if she had known
how small a thing it amounted to!

A few days later Mesdames Le
Quesnoy left the hotel, Hortense's cure
being finished. The mother, though reassured by her child's healthy appearance and by what the little doctor told
her of the miracle worked by the
nymph of the waters, was in a hurry to
end that form of existence, the least details of which re-awakened her former
martyrdom.

"And you, Numa?"

Oh! he, he reckoned to remain a week
or two longer, to go on with a certain
amount of the "cure," and to profit by
the quiet in which their departure would
leave him, in order to write the famous

discourse. That was going to make a fine row, of which they would have news in Paris. *Dame!* Le Quesnoy would not be satisfied.

And suddenly Hortense, who was ready to go, though so happy to return home, to see again the dear absent ones whom the distance made still dearer to her, for she had imagination even in her heart, Hortense felt a sorrow at leaving the beautiful country, the hotel society of three weeks' friends to whom she did not know she was so attached. Ah! loving natures, how you give yourselves, how everything lays hold of you, and what pain then to break the invisible and sensitive threads! They had been so good to her, so obliging; and at the last hour there crowded about the carriage so many extended hands, affectionate faces. Some girls kissed her.

"It won't be gay now without you."

They promised to correspond, they exchanged souvenirs, perfumed boxes, mother-of-pearl paper-cutters with the inscription, "Arvillard, 1876," in a blue reflection of the lakes. And whilst M. Laugeron slipped into her bag a phial of superfine chartreuse, she saw up above, behind the window-pane of her room, the mountaineer woman who served her, stanching her eyes with a big purple handkerchief, she heard a worn-out voice murmuring at her ear: "Elasticity, mademoiselle—always elasticity." Her friend, the consumptive, who was sending her a farewell look, his eyes hollow, haggard, feverish, but sparkling with energy, with will, and with some emotion too. Oh! the kind people, the kind people.

Hortense did not speak for fear of crying.

"Good-bye, good-bye all!"

The minister, who accompanied the ladies to the distant station, took his place opposite them. The whip cracks, the bells ring out. Suddenly Hortense exclaims: "My parasol!" She had it only a moment ago. Twenty persons dash for it. "The parasol—the parasol." In the room, no, in the *salon.* The doors open and shut, the hotel is rummaged from top to bottom.

"Don't look for it—I know where it is."

Always lively, the girl leaps out of the carriage and runs into the garden towards the cradle of nut-trees where that very morning she added a few chapters to the romance running through her ebullient little head. The parasol was there, thrown across a bench, something of herself left at her favourite spot and resembling her. What delightful hours spent in that nook of bright verdure, what confidences flown away with the bees and the butterflies! Doubtless she would never return there; and the thought panged her heart, kept her there. Even to the long creaking of the swing, which at that hour she thought charming!

"*Zut!* you're bothering me."

It was the voice of Mlle. Bachellery who, furious at seeing herself deserted for the departing visitors, and thinking herself alone with her mother, spoke to her in her usual language. Hortense thought of the filial caressings which had so often irritated her nerves, and laughed to herself as she returned to the carriage, when at the turning of an avenue she found herself face to face with Bouchereau. She was giving way, but he held her by the arm.

"So you're leaving us, my child?"

"But yes, sir."

She did not know exactly what to say, upset by the meeting and the fact that he was speaking to her for the first time. So he took her hands in his, kept her thus in front of him, with his arms apart, considered her deeply with his piercing eyes under their white, bristling eyebrows. Then his lips, his grasp, all trembled, a wave of blood empurpling his paleness—

"Well, good-bye—a good journey!"

And without more words, he drew her to him, pressed her against his chest with a grandfather's tenderness, and went off, his hands pressed on his heart, which was bursting.

CHAPTER XIII

NUMA'S SPEECH

Non, non, je me fais hironde-c-elle
Et je m'envo-o-le à tire d'ai-ai-le.

WITH her tart voice, which had that morning been originally quite clear and good-humoured, the little Bachellery was singing before her mirror whilst she finished buttoning her gloves. Attired for the trip, her cheerful little person had a pleasant odour of fresh toilette and new costume, strictly trim, in contrast with the disorder of the hotel room, where the remains of a supper were visible on the table among odds and ends, cards, candles, close to the uncovered bed and a big basin full of that marvellous Arvillard essence which is unsurpassable for calming the visitors' nerves and making their skins like satin.

Below, the basket-carriage, shaking its bells, and a youthful escort prancing before the perron, were waiting for her.

As her toilette was about ready, there was a knock at the door.

"Come in!"

Roumestan entered, much excited, handed her a big envelope.

"Here it is, mademoiselle. Oh! read —read."

It was her engagement at the Opéra for five years, with the required salary, the right to have her name in capitals, everything. When she had deciphered it article by article, coldly, deliberately, even to Cadaillac's flat-fingered signature, then, but only then, she made a step towards the minister, and, lifting her veil, already put down against the dust of the excursion, raised up to him the rosy mouth—

"You are good—I love you——"

Nothing more was needed to make the publicist forget all the worries the appointment was bound to cause him. He restrained himself, however, remained upright, cold, supercilious as a roc.

"Now I've kept my word I retire— I don't want to derange your party."

"My party? Ah! yes, it's true— we're going to Château-Bayard."

And passing her arms round his neck, coaxingly—

"You'll come with us. Oh! yes—oh! yes——"

She touched his face with her big, pencilled eyelashes, and even nibbled at his statue-like chin, not very hard, with the tips of her child's teeth.

"With young people?—but it's impossible. You are not thinking of it?"

"Those young men?—I have a good joke with them—I'll get rid of them— mama will tell them. Oh! they're used to it—you understand, mama?"

"I'm going," said Mme. Bachellery, who could be observed in the side-room, her foot on a chair, trying to get her merino boots, a size too small, over her red stockings. She gave the minister a most elaborate theatrical bow, and ran down to dismiss the gentlemen.

"Keep a horse for Bompard—he'll come with us," cried the little one; and Numa, touched by this attention, tasted the delicious joy of hearing, with this pretty girl in his arms, the impertinent youths whose caracolings had so often wounded his heart, departing slowly with ears lowered. A kiss long pressed on a smile that promised everything, then she drew away.

"Go quick and dress—I'm in a hurry to be off."

What a murmur of curiosity throughout the hotel, what an eager peeping through the blinds, when it became known that the minister was going on the trip to Château-Bayard, and he was seen to get into the carriage and sit opposite the singer, with his broad white waistcoat and his big Panama hat. After all, as Father Olivieri observed, who was much toned down by his voyages, what harm was there in that, did not the mother accompany them? Is not Château-Bayard a spot of historical interest, calculated to draw the attention of the Minister of Public Instruction? Do not therefore, let us be so intolerant, *mon Dieu*, especially in speaking about men who give their lives to the defence of the sound doctrines and our holy religion.

"Bompard is not coming, what is he doing?" murmured Roumestan, impatient at waiting there, with so many inquisitive eyes watching, for he could be seen from the windows, in spite of the carriage-hood. At a first-floor window something extraordinary appeared, white, round, outlandish, which shouted in the tones of the former chief of the Circassians—

"Go in advance—I'll catch you up."

As if they had only been awaiting this signal, the two mules scampered away, shaking their bells, and had crossed the park in incredibly short time, and reached the bath establishment.

"Look out! Look out!"

The frightened bathers and the sedan-chairs had to get out of the way as well as they could, whilst the women with their big pockets full of money and colored tickets appeared at the end of the gallery, and the shampooers, with no more clothing than Bedouins under their woolen shawls, appeared on the staircase leading to the heated room, the curtains of the air-baths were lifted, to see the minister and the singer pass. They were, however, already at a distance, galloping at full speed through the dark, narrow streets of Arvillard, over the sharp pebbles veined with sulphur, which emitted sparks as the carriage sped over them, shaking the ramshackle old houses where leprosy still lingers, and bringing the inmates to door and window, bowing and waving hats in the minister's honour. The ladies sat proudly on their seats opposite him, enraptured to be with so great a man, did not put themselves at ease till they were in the country on the long Pontcharra road, when the mule had a rest at the foot of the Tower of Treuil, which Bompard had fixed as the rendezvous.

The minutes go by, no Bompard. They know he is a good horseman, he has so often bragged about it. They are amazed, they are irritated. Numa especially, who was impatient to be far away on that white, straight road, whic reems endless, to go forward into that day which opens like a vein, full of hopes and adventures. At length, from a whirlwind of dust amid which pants a frightened voice, "Ho!—la—ho!—la," emerges Bompard's head, surmounted by one of those cork helmets covered with white cloth worn by the Anglo-Indian army, and which Bompard had assumed in order to aggrandize, to dramatize his voyage, making his hatter believe he was off to Bombay or Calcutta.

"Come on, dawdler."

Bompard nodded with a tragic air. Evidently many things had happened since his departure from the hotel, and the Circassian must have given the hotel people a poor idea of his equilibrium, for large patches of dust soiled his sleeves and his back.

"Bad horse," he said, greeting the ladies, "bad horse, but I made him step out."

So effectually had he done so that the strange beast would not now move an inch farther, pawing the ground and turning round like a sick cat despite his cavalier's efforts. The carriage was already far away.

"Are you coming, Bompard?"

"Go in advance—I'll catch you up," he cried again in his finest Marseilles accent; then he made a despairing gesture and he vanished in the direction of Arvillard in a cloud of flying hoofs. Every one thought: "He must have forgotten something," and did not trouble about him any more.

The road now wound about high ground, mountains rising up as far as could be seen on either side of the French high-road bordered with walnut-trees, while on the other side great chestnut and pine forests variegated the landscape. Deep down in the glen were smiling villages, encircled by vineyards, corn and maize-fields, mulberry and almond-trees, patches of golden broom whose pods, bursting open with the heat, made a constant crackling, as if the earth were on fire. Such might have been thought to be actually so, because of the excessive sultriness of the air, which appeared to proceed not so much from the sun, now almost invisible behind a veil of mist, as from the soil, so parched and dried up as nearly to be in a state of combustion, so that the view of the Glayzin and its summit coifed with snow, which, it seemed, one could almost touch with the end of a parasol, was deliciously refreshing.

Roumestan did not remember any landscape comparable to that, no, not even in his dear Provence; he could not imagine any happiness more complete than his. Neither care, nor remorse. His loyal and believing wife, the hope of a child, Bouchereau's prediction about Hortense, the disastrous effect that would be produced by the appearance of the Cadaillac decree in the *Officiel*, nothing of the kind now existed for him. His whole fate hung on this beautiful girl, whose eyes were reflecting his eyes, her knees touching his, and who beneath her azure veil, tinted pink by her blond skin, sang whilst pressing his hand—

Fuyons tous deux sous la ramée,
Maintenant je me sens aimée.

Whilst they were being carried along in the wind, the scenery on the road was rapidly enlarging, bringing to view an immense semi-circular plain, lakes, villages, then mountains, shaded according to distance, the beginning of Savoy.

"How beautiful it is! how great it is!" the singer was exclaiming; he was whispering, "How I love you!"

At the last halt, Bompard again joined them, on foot, very pitiable, leading his horse by the bridle. "The beast is astonishing," he said, without adding more, and the ladies asking if he had fallen: "No—it's my old wound re-opened." Wounded, where, when? He had never mentioned it, but, in the case of Bompard, one had to expect surprises. They made him get into the carriage, his very peaceful horse being docilely tied behind, and they set off for the Château-Bayard, whose crumbling towers, restored in Vaudal style, could be distinguished on a plateau.

A female servant came out to them, an astute mountaineer, at the orders of an old priest formerly officiating in the neighbouring parishes, who lives at Château-Bayard, on condition of allowing visitors to visit it freely. When they are seen approaching, he shuts himself in his own room, unless they happen to be eminent persons; but the minister took care not to let it be known who he was, and the new-comers were, therefore, escorted by the attendant, who showed them over all that remains of the ancient manor of the brave knight without fear and without reproach, explaining the details of the ruin in phrases learnt by heart, in the singing tone usual with guides, while the coachman laid lunch beneath an arbour in the small garden.

"Here is the ancient chapel where the good knight morning and evening—I beg mesdames and messieurs to notice the thickness of the walls."

They noticed nothing. It was dark, they stumbled against heaps of rubbish only faintly lit up by the light from a loophole entering over a hayloft made among the rafters. Numa, with the little one's arm under his, scoffed a bit at the Chevalier Bayard and "his respectable mother, the Dame Hélène of the Germans." The odour of old things bored them; and even one moment, in order to try the echo of the kitchen vaults, Mme. Bachellery having begun her husband's last song, there on the spot, quite freely, "J'tiens ça d'papa—j'tiens ça d'maman," no one was scandalized; on the contrary.

But outside, the lunch having been served on a massive stone table, and when the first hunger was appeased, the calm splendour of the horizon about them, the valley of the Graisivarden, the Bauges, the severe outlines of the Grande-Chartreuse, and the contrast, in this scenery on large lines, of the little terraced orchard where this old recluse lived, absorbed entirely in God, in his tulip-trees, in his bees, penetrated them gradually with something grave, sweet, which resembled religious reverence. At dessert, the minister, opening the guide-book to refresh his memory, spoke of Bayard, "of his poor lady mother who tenderly wept," the day when the child, going off to Chambéry as page to the Duke of Savoy, made his small roan horse prance before the northern gate on the very spot where the shadow of the great tower was lengthening, majestic and frail, like the phantom of the old vanished castle.

And Numa, warming to his subject read to them Madame Hélène's splendid words to her son, at the moment of departure: "Pierre, my friend, I recommend you that before all things you love fear and serve God, without in any wise

offending Him, if it is possible to you."
Standing on the terrace, with a broad
gesture that extended as far as Chambéry: "That's what ought to be said to
children, that's what all parents, what all
masters——"

He stopped, smote his brow.

"My speech!—it's my speech!—I have
it—superb! The Château-Bayard, a
local legend—I've been looking for the
thing for a fortnight—and there it is!"

"It's providential," cried Mme. Bachellery, full of admiration, thinking,
nevertheless, the end of the lunch rather
serious, "What a man! what a man!"

The little one seemed also much excited; but the impressionable Numa paid
no heed. The orator burned beneath
his forehead, in his breast, and taken up
with his idea.

"The fine thing," he said, seeking
about, "the fine thing would be to date
the speech from Château-Bayard——"

"If M. l'avocat would like a small
corner for writing——"

"Oh! merely a few notes to jot down.
You allow me, ladies—whilst they're
serving you the coffee—I'll come back.
It's to be able to write the date without
lying."

The servant put him up in a very ancient, little, ground floor room, whose
dome-shaped roof still retained some
fragments of gilding, and which is
claimed to have been Bayard's oratory,
just as the vast neighbouring hall with
its big old-fashioned four-post bed with
chintz curtains is represented as his
sleeping-room.

It was good to write between those
thick walls, which the closeness of the
weather did not pierce, behind the glass
door, half-open, casting across the page
the light. the perfumes of the little or-

chard. At first, the orator's pen was
not quick enough for the enthusiasm of
the idea; he sent one sentence crowding
on another's heels in the quick march of
the words along the lines of the paper,
mostly phrases such as the Southern
barrister revelled in, rather hackneyed
perhaps, but always eloquent. Suddenly
he stopped, his skull empty of words or
burdened with the fatigue of the journey
and the vapours of the lunch. He then
roamed from the oratory to the chamber, speaking loud, exciting himself, listening to the sound of his own step, as if
it were that of an illustrious ghost, and
sat down again without power to trace
a line. Everything was turning round
about him, the walls whitened with chalk,
that hypnotizing beam of light. He
heard a noise of plates and laughing in
the garden far off, very far off, and ended
by going into a deep sleep, his nose on
his rough draft.

A violent thunderclap started him to
his feet. How long had he been there?
Rather confused, he went out into the
deserted, motionless garden. The odour
of the tulip-trees scented the air. In
the empty arbour the wasps were flying
heavily round the champagne glasses,
and sucking the dregs of sugar left in the
coffee-cups, which the servant girl was
clearing away without noise, overcome
by a nervous animal fear at the approach
of the storm, and crossing herself at each
flash of lightning. She informed Numa
that the young lady had a bad headache
after lunch, so she had put her in Bayard's chamber to sleep a little, closing
the door "very softly" so as not to disturb the gentleman in his work. The
two others, the fat lady and the white
hat, had gone down into the valley, and

would get wet for certain, for there was going to be a—"Look!"

In the direction she indicated, on the jagged crest of the Bauges, the chalky summits of the Grande-Chartreuse enveloped in lightnings like a mysterious Sinai, the sky was darkening with an enormous splash of ink which grew as they looked, and under which the whole valley, with its groves of trees, its golden corn, the roads marked by their lines of white rising dust, the silver waters of the Isère, assumed an extraordinary value of light, the brightness of a slanting, white reflection, in proportion as the sombre and rumbling menace projected itself. In the distance, Roumestan perceived Bompard's canvas helmet, gleaming like a lighthouse.

He went in again, but could not set himself again to his task. Drowsiness did not in this instance paralyse his pen; he felt himself, on the contrary, strangely excited by Alice Bachellery's presence in the neighbouring room. Was she actually still there? He half-opened the door and did not dare to close it again, for fear of disturbing the pretty slumber of the singer, who had thrown herself quite undressed on the bed, in a fascinating disorder of curly tresses, open materials of costume, half-seen white forms.

"Come now, Numa—Bayard's room, what the deuce!"

He positively took himself by the collar like a malefactor, pulled himself together, forcibly seated himself at his table, his head between his hands, stopping up his eyes and his ears, in order the better to absorb himself in the last phrase, which he repeated in a low voice—

"And, gentlemen, those supreme recommendations of Bayard's mother that have come to us in the so sweet language of the middle ages, we would wish that the University of France——"

The storm was enervating him, so heavy, numbing like the shade of certain tropical trees. His head was whirling, intoxicated by an exquisite odour exhaled by the little flowers of the tulip-trees or that mass of blond hair scattered over the bed at the side. Unfortunate minister! It was all very well for him to nail himself to his speech, to invoke the knight without fear and without reproach, the Ministry of Public Instruction, the Religions, the Rector of Chambéry, nothing availed. He had to enter again into Bayard's chamber, and this time so close to the sleeper that he heard her light breathing, touched with his hand the stuff of the curtains which had fallen, enframing that provocative sleep, that flesh pearly in the shadows and outside them pink with a roguish sanguine tint of Fragonard's.

Even there, on the border of his temptation, the minister still struggled, and the machine-like murmur of his lips mumbled the supreme recommendations which the University of France—when the sudden rolling of an approaching thunderclap awoke the singer with a start.

"Oh! how frightened I have been— Well now! is it you?"

She recognized him with a smile in her bright eyes like an awakened child, without any embarrassment at her disorder and they remained tongue-tied, without moving, the silent flames of their desire meeting. The room was, however, unexpectedly plunged into a black night by the wind shutting the high blinds one after the other. They heard the door slamming, a key fall, whirlwinds of leaves and flowe.s rustling on the sand up to the threshold where the tempest blew plaintively.

"What a storm!" she whispered to him, taking his burning hand and drawing him almost beneath the curtains.

"And, gentlemen, these supreme recommendations of Bayard's mother, that have come to us in the so sweet tongue of the middle ages——"

It was at Chambéry, in view of the old Château of the Dukes of Savoy and of that wonderful amphitheatre of green hills and snowy mountains of which Châteaubriand thought in the presence of Taygetus, that the Grand Master of the University spoke this time, surrounded by embroidered costumes, palms, ermines, big epaulets, dominating a huge crowd gathered by the power of his *verve,* his strong hand still holding the little ivory-handled trowel which had just cemented the first stone of the Lycée.

"We would wish that the University of France should address them to each of its children. Pierre, my friend, I recommend you above all things——."

And whilst he cited those touching words, an emotion caused his hand, his voice, his broad cheeks to tremble, at the memory of the large sweet-smelling room where, in the excitement of a memorable storm, the Chambéry speech had been composed.

CHAPTER XIV

VICTIMS

A MORNING. Ten o'clock. The anteroom of the Minister of Public Instruction, a long passage, badly lighted, with sombre hangings and oak wainscoting, is encumbered by a mass of petitioners, sitting or tramping about, more numerous from minute to minute, each new-comer giving his card to the solemn usher with the chain, who takes it, inspects it, and religiously places it without a word by his side on the little table where he writes in the haggard light of the loophole windows dripping with a fine October drizzle.

One of the last arrivals has, however, the honour of stirring up this august impassiveness. He is a big, sunburnt man, with two miniature silver anchors as ear-rings and a voice like a hoarse seal, such as it is heard in the clear morning vapour of Provençal ports.

"Tell him it's Cabantous the pilot. He knows what it's about—he expects me."

"You're not the only one," replies the usher, who smiles discreetly at his own pleasantry.

Cabantous does not see the cleverness of it; but he laughs confidently, his mouth stretched to the anchors, and shouldering his way through the crowd which makes way for his soaked umbrella, he goes and sits on a bench beside another patient almost as tanned as himself.

"*Té! vé!* It's Cabantous—*Hé!* goodday."

The pilot excuses himself, he does not recognize the person.

"Valmajour, you know—we knew each other down there, in the arena."

"Good gracious, true!—*Bé!* my lad, you can say Paris has altered you."

The tambourinist is now a gentleman with very long black hair, brushed back behind the ears, artist fashion, which, taken together with his olive tint, his bluish moustache which he is continually fingering, makes him resemble a gipsy of the fair. On the top of that, a crest always raised like a village cock's, the conceit of a handsome fellow and the vanity of a musician, in which is betrayed and overflows the exaggeration of his Southern nature which is apparently calm and untalkative. The failure at the Opéra has not chilled him. Like all actors in like cases he assigns it to a cabal, and in the eyes of his sister and himself the word assumes barbarous, extraordinary proportions, a Sanscrit orthography, the *Kkabbale,* a mysterious animal connected with the belled serpent and the horse of the Apocalypse. And he relates to Cabantous that in a few days he is making his bow at a big *café-concert* on the Boulevard, "an *eskating,* come now!" where he is to figure in some tableaux vivants at 200 francs a night.

"Two hundred francs a night!"

The pilot rolls his eyes.

"And, besides, my biography which will be cried in the streets and my portrait life-size on all the walls of Paris, with the costume of a troubadour of ancient times which I shall put on at night when I play my music."

It is that especially which flatters him, the costume. What a pity he was not able to put on his helmet and mailed boots to come and show the minister the magnificent engagement, on proper paper this time, which has been signed without his aid! Cabantous looks at the perforated paper blackened on both sides and sighs.

"You're very lucky—why, I've been waiting more than a year for my medal. Numa has told me to send in the papers about it. I sent in my papers—since then I've heard nothing about the medal or the papers or anything. I wrote to the Admiralty; they don't know me at the Admiralty. I wrote to the Minister; the Minister did not answer. And the——part of it is that now, without my papers, when I have an interview with the sea-captains about the piloting, the fellows don't want to listen to my reasons. So, seeing that, I thought to myself: let's go and see Numa."

He nearly cried over it, the unlucky pilot. Valmajour comforts him, reassures him, promises to speak to the minister for him, this in an assured tone, his finger at his moustache, like a man who can be refused nothing. Besides, this haughty attitude is not peculiar to him. All these persons awaiting an audience, old priests with smiling manners in visiting dress, methodical and authoritative professors, dandified painters, with Russian head-dresses, thickset sculptors with spade-shaped fingers, have the same triumphant demeanour. Special friends of the minister, sure of their business, all on arriving have told the usher—

"He's expecting me."

All have the conviction that if Roumestan knew they were waiting there! Which gives the ante-room of the Ministry of Public Instruction a very special physiognomy, without anything of those feverish pallors, of those trembling anxieties, which are found in ministerial waiting-rooms.

"With whom is he?" asks Valmajour aloud, approaching the little table.

"The Director of the Opéra."

"Cadaillac—all right, I know—it's about my business."

After the tambourinist's failure at his theatre, Cadaillac refused to let him have a fresh hearing. Valmajour wanted to go to law; but the minister, who fears the advocates and the minor papers, begged the musician to withdraw his appointment, guaranteeing a large indemnity. It is that indemnity which they are doubtless discussing at that moment, and not without some animation, for Numa's clarion voice pierces every instant the double door of the cabinet which is at last opened brutally.

"It is not my protégée, it's yours."

The stout Cadaillac goes out with these words, crosses the ante-room with furious paces, jostling against the usher who advances between two rows of recommendations.

"You've only to give my name."

"Let him only know I'm here."

"Tell him it's Cabantous."

The other listens to nobody, walks very gravely, with some visiting-cards in his hand, and, behind him, the door which he leaves half-open displays the ministerial cabinet, full of light from its three windows looking on to the garden, a whole panel being covered by the mantle doubled with ermine of M. de Fontanes painted at the foot.

With some surprise on his cadaverous face, the usher returns and calls—

"Monsieur Valmajour."

The musician is not astonished, not he, at passing in thus before the rest.

Since the morning he has his portrait advertised on the walls of Paris. He is now a public character and the minister would not let him now languish in the draughts of a station. Conceited, fatuous, smiling, there he is planted in the centre of the sumptuous cabinet where some secretaries are in course of taking down cardboard boxes and drawers in a frightened search. Rou-

mestan, furious, thunders, scolds, his hands in his pockets—

"But really those papers, *qué diable!* They've been lost, that pilot's papers. Really, gentlemen, there's a want of order here."

He perceives Valmajour. "Ah! it's you," and he jumps at him at a bound, whilst the backs of secretaries flee panic-stricken by the side-doors, carrying off piles of cardboard boxes.

"*Ah, ça,* when are you going to stop persecuting me with your dog-music—you haven't enough with one oven? How many d'you want? There you are now, they tell me, on the walls in costume—and what is this nonsense that's come to my ears? That your biography!—A tissue of stupidities and lies. You know well you're no more a prince than I am; that these parchments of which people speak have never existed but in your imagination."

With a brow-beating and brutal gesture he held the unhappy man tight by the middle of his jacket and shook him as he spoke. To begin with, that skating rink had not got a *sou.* It was a mere puffing show. He would not get his pay, whilst he would involve his patron's name in the shame of that dirty advertisement. The papers would begin their jokes again, Roumestan and Valmajour, the booby of the ministry. And warming up at the remembrances of the insults, his broad cheeks swollen by a family fit of choler, an Aunt Portal attack, more terrifying in the solemn and administrative surroundings where personalities are bound to disappear before situations, he shouted to him at the top of his powerful lungs—

"But go, you scoundrel, go!—Nobody wants to have anything more to do with you; they've had enough of your tomfoolery."

Valmajour, stunned, was powerless, stammering: "All right—all right," with an imploring look at the pitying face of Méjean, the only one whom the master's wrath had not put to flight, and at the big portrait of Fontanes who seemed scandalized by such violences, emphasizing his ministerial air the more Roumestan lost it. At last, loosened by the strong wrist that had held him tight, the musician was able to reach the door, to run off in bewilderment, he and his skating-rink tickets.

"Cabantous, pilot!" said Numa reading the name presented by the impassive usher. "Another Valmajour!—Ah! but no—I have enough of being their dupe. Finished for to-day. I'm no longer to be seen."

He went on pacing the study, banishing what remained of the violent fit of temper of which Valmajour had unjustly borne the brunt. That Cadaillac, what impudence! to come and reproach him about little Bachellery, at his own place, in the home of the ministry, in the presence of Méjean, in the presence of Rochemaure!

"Ah! decidedly I'm too weak. That man's nomination to the Opéra is a grievous mistake."

His chief of the cabinet shared the opinion, but he would have been the last to say so; because Numa was no longer the good-natured fellow of yore, who was the first to laugh at his entanglements, accepted chaffing and remonstrances in good part. Having become the effective head of the Ministry, owing to the Chambéry speech and some other oratorical prowesses, the intoxication of altitudes, that royal atmosphere in which the strongest heads come to grief, had changed him, made him nervous, arbitrary, irritable.

A door under the hanging opened, Mme. Roumestan appeared, ready to go out, elegantly hatted, an ample cloak hiding her figure. And with that air of serenity which had illumined her pretty face during the last five months, she asked: "Have you a Council today?—good-day, M. Méjean."

"But yes—Council—meeting—everything!"

"I wanted to ask you to come as far as mama's—I'm lunching there—Hortense would be so glad."

"You see, it is not possible."

He looked at his watch.

"I must be at Versailles at noon."

"Then I'll wait for you, I'll take you to the station."

He hesitated a second, merely a second.

"Good—I'll sign here, and we'll be off."

Whilst he was writing Rosalie whispered to Méjean news of his sister. The return of winter affected her, she was forbidden to go out. Why didn't he go and see her? She had need of all her friends. Méjean gave a gesture of discouraged sorrow: "Oh! I——"

"But yes—but yes! It's not all over with you. It's only a whim: I'm sure it won't last."

She saw things in a rosy light, and wished all her people to be happy like herself. Oh! so happy and with so perfect a happiness that she fostered the discreet superstition of never admitting it. Roumestan himself talked about his good fortune on all sides, both to the indifferent and to intimates, with a comical pride: "We shall call him the child of the ministry!" and he laughed at his phrase till he cried.

Verily, for anybody who knew of the life he led outside, the town-house shamelessly inaugurated with receptions and an open table, this husband, so attentive, so affectionate, who spoke with tears in his eyes of his coming paternity, appeared indefinable, at peace in his lie, sincere in his effusiveness, routing the opinions of any one who did not know the dangerous complications of Southern natures.

"I'll take you, certainly," he said to his wife, getting into the carriage.

"But if they're waiting for you?"

"Ah! so much the worse—they will wait—we shall be longer together."

He took Rosalie's arm under his, nestling against her like a child, observed—

"*Té*, you see, it's only then I feel well. Your gentleness soothes me, your coolness fortifies me. That Cadaillac has put me in a hole—a man without conscience, without moral."

"You didn't know him then?"

"He carries on that theatre; it's shameful!"

"It's true the engagement of that Mlle. Bachellery—why did you let him do it? A girl who has everything false about her, her youth, her voice, even to her eyebrows."

Numa felt himself reddening. It was he now who fixed them on, with the tips of his big fingers, the little one's eyebrows. The mama had taught him.

"To whom, pray, does she belong, this nothing of anything? The *Messager* spoke the other day of high influences, of mysterious protection."

"I don't know—to Cadaillac, no doubt."

He turned away to hide his embarrassment, and suddenly threw himself back in his seat, panic-stricken.

"What is it now?" inquired Rosalie, looking also through the window.

The skating-rink advertisement, immense, in loud tones, which stood out in the rainy, greyish sky, repeated at every street corner, at every place free on a bare wall or on enclosure-planks, a gigantic troubadour, surrounded by tableaux vivants, in yellow, green, blue, with the ochre of a tabor thrown across.

"My executioner!" remarked Roumestan with comic despair.

And Rosalie gently chiding—

"No—your victim—and if he were the only one! But another has taken fire at your enthusiasm."

"Who's that?"

"Hortense."

She then told him about what she was at last certain of, despite the mysteries made by the girl, her love for the peasant, which she had at first thought a mere fantasy, and which now disquieted her as a moral aberration on the part of her sister.

The minister grew indignant.

"Is it possible?—that rascal, that bumpkin!"

"She sees him with the imagination, and especially in the light of your legends, your inventions for which she has not been able to make allowance. That's why this advertisement, this grotesque illustration which irritates you fills me on the contrary with joy. I fancy that her hero will seem so ridiculous to her that she will no longer venture to love him. Without that, I don't know what would happen to us. Consider my father's despair—see yourself, you, as Valmajour's brother-in-law! Ah! Numa, Numa—poor involuntary dupe-maker."

He did not defend himself, being irritated at himself, at his "accursed South" which he could not control.

"Well, you must remain ever as you are, nestling against me, my dear council, my holy protection. You are the only kind, indulgent one, who understands me and loves me."

He held her small gloved hand under his lips, and spoke with such conviction that tears, real tears, reddened his eyelids. Then, warmed up again, expanded by this effusion, he felt better; and when, on arriving at the Place Royale, he had helped his wife to get down with a thousand tender cares, it was in a pleased tone, free from any remorse, that he called to his coachman: "Rue de Londres—quick!"

Rosalie, slow in walking, vaguely heard the address and it pained her. Not that she had the least suspicion; but he had just told her he was going to the Saint Lazare station. Why did his acts never answer to his words?

A further disquiet awaited in her sister's room, where she perceived on entering that she had stopped a discussion between Hortense and Audiberte, who kept her stormy expression, the ribbon quivering on her fury-like hair. Rosalie's presence restrained her, as was visible at her lips, at her sullenly contracted eyebrows; however, as the young wife asked for news, she was obliged to answer, and then talked feverishly of the "eskatin," of the fine terms proposed to them,

then, amazed at her calmness, asked almost insolently—

"Won't madam come to hear my brother? It's worth the trouble, at least, merely to see him in his costume!"

As described by her in her peasant phraseology, from the cap to the curved point of the shoes, this ridiculous costume inflicted tortures on poor Hortense, who did not dare raise her eyes to her sister. Rosalie excused herself; the state of her health did not admit of the theatre. Besides, there were in Paris certain places of amusement where all women could not go. The peasant checked her at the first words.

"Pardon—I shall go there myself and I think I am as good as another woman. I have never done any ill, I haven't; I have always fulfilled my duties of *religion*."

She raised her voice, with none of her former timidity, as if she had acquired rights in the house. But Rosalie was much too kindly, too far above this poor ignorant person, to humble her, especially as she thought of Numa's responsibilities. Then, with all the wit of her heart, all her delicacy, with those words of truth which heal whilst burning a little, she tried to make her understand that her brother had not succeeded, that he would never succeed in that implacable Paris, and that rather than engage in a humiliating struggle, descending into degrading depths, they would do much better to return to the country, to buy back their house, everything, for which means would be provided them, and to forget in their laborious life, in the bosom of nature, the bitterness of this unlucky expedition.

The peasant let her go right to the end, without once interrupting, merely darting at Hortense the irony of her malevolent eyes as if to excite her to reply. Finally, seeing that the girl did not wish to say anything yet, she declared coldly that they would not go away, that her brother had engagements at Paris of every kind—of every kind—which it was impossible for him to miss. Thereupon she threw on her arm the heavy wet cloak, which had remained on the back of a chair, made a hypocritical bow to Rosalie—"A real good-day, madam—and thank you, at least"—and made off, followed by Hortense.

In the ante-room, lowering her voice because of the servants—

"Sunday night, qué?—half-past ten, without fail."

And she added, urgently, authoritatively—

"You certainly owe him that, come now, to your poor friend, to hearten him up. First of all, what d'you risk? I shall come myself for you—I shall myself bring you back."

Seeing her still hesitate, she said further, almost out loud, in a diapason of menace—

"I say, are you his betrothed, yes or no?"

"I'll come—I'll come," said the girl, frightened.

When she came back, Rosalie, who saw her absent-minded and gloomy, asked her—

"What are you thinking of, my darling? Is it still your romance that continues? It must be well advanced for the long time you've been at it!" she cried gaily, taking her by the waist.

"Oh, yes, very far advanced."

With a dull tone of melancholy Hortense went on, after a silence—

"But it's my conclusion that I don't see."

She loved him no more; perhaps even she had never loved him. Transformed by absence and the "sweet brilliancy" which misfortune lent to Abencerage, he had appeared to her at a distance as the man of her destiny. She had thought it a proud thing to engage her life to him who was being abandoned by all, success and his patrons. But on her return, what pitiless clarity, what terror at seeing how she had been mistaken!

Audiberte's first visit shocked her, to begin with, by her new manners, too free, too familiar, and the conspirator's glances with which she informed her in a whisper: "He's coming to fetch me—sh!—say nothing!" It seemed to her very prompt, very bold, especially the idea of introducing the young man into her parents' house. But the peasant woman wanted to hasten matters. And suddenly Hortense understood her mistake, at the sight of that vulgar fellow brushing his hair back, with an inspired movement, shaping the Provençal sombrero on his head in character, always handsome but with a visible anxiety to appear so.

Instead of humiliating himself a little, of getting himself forgiven for the generous impulse she had had towards him, he kept his victorious, fatuous air of conquest, and without speaking —for he would hardly have known what to say—he treated the refined Parisian as he would have treated the Combette girl in a similar case, took her by the waist with the gesture of a soldier-troubadour and wanted to draw her to him. She drew away with a repulsion of all her nerves, leaving him bewildered and silly, whilst Audiberte quickly interposed and scolded her brother in very forcible language. What were those manners? Had he learnt them in Paris, in the Faubourg Saint-Germeïn, no doubt, among his duchesses?

"At least wait till she's your wife! There now!"

And to Hortense—

"He loves you so much—his blood's going all rotten, pécaïré!"

From that time, when Valmajour came for his sister, he thought he must assume the sombre and fatal mien of melodrama. The girl might have been touched by it; but the poor fellow seemed decidedly too much of a nonentity. He only knew how to stroke the fur of his otter-skin cap as he related his successes in the noble Faubourg or the rivalries of the stage. He spoke to her one day for an hour on the commonness of the handsome Mayol, who had abstained from congratulating him after a concert, and he repeated the whole time—

"That's him, your Mayol—Bé! He's not polite, your Mayol."

And always the vigilant attitudes of Audiberte, her severity as gendarme of morality, in the presence of these two cold lovers. Ah! if she had been able to divine in Hortense's soul the terror, the disgust at her frightful mistake!

However, she had promised, and every day she was harassed with new demands; for instance, the première of the skating rink, whither the peasant woman wanted to drag her by sheer

force, counting on the success, the enthusiasm of the applause to carry her off her feet. And after a long resistance the poor girl had at last consented to this sortie at night without her mother's knowledge, involving at the same time humiliating lies and complicities; she had yielded through fear, through weakness, perhaps also in the hope of regaining there her original vision, the vanished mirage, of rekindling the flame so hopelessly extinguished.

CHAPTER XV

HORTENSE'S ROMANCE

WHERE was it? Where was she going! The cab had travelled a long time, a long time, Audiberte sitting by her side, stretching out her hands to her, reassuring her, speaking with a feverish warmth. She looked at nothing, heard nothing; and the shrillness of that thin voice amid the creaking of the wheels had no meaning for her any more than those streets, those boulevards, those façades appeared to her in their known aspect, but discoloured by her lively interior emotion, as if she saw them from a hearse or bridal carriage.

At length a shock, and they stopped before a broad pavement flooded with a white light, cutting the gathered crowd into black, swarming shadows. A wicket-gate for the tickets at the entrance of a broad corridor, a screen-door of red velvet, and immediately the ball, an immense hall, which reminded her of an Anglican Church where she had once gone for a marriage. Only here the walls were covered with advertisements, with varied announcements, hats, shirts on measure at 4 fr. 50, puffs of dressmakers, alternating with the portraits of the tabor-player, whose biography was being hawked about amidst a deafening din, in which the murmuring of the crowd, the knocking of the balls on the cloth of the English billiard table, the calls for refreshments, the scraps of music blended with patriotic fusillades that came from the bottom of the hall, were dominated by a perpetual clinking of roller skates going to and fro on a broad asphalted space, surrounded by balustrades.

Anxious, dazed, now paling, now blushing beneath her veil, Hortense walked behind the Provençale, followed her with difficulty through a labyrinth of small round tables round which sat women, two and two, and drank, their elbows on the table, a cigarette at their lips, with a bored look. Here and there, against the wall, a laden counter, and behind it a girl standing, her eyes circled with kohl, her mouth rouged. And this white, this red of painted flesh, this vermilioned smile, were reproduced in all the women, like a livery which they wore of pale, nocturnal apparitions.

Sinister also the slow promenade of those men who pressed themselves, insolent and brutal, between the tables, sending to right and left the smoke of their big cigars, the insult of their chaffering, approaching to see the display nearer. And what best gave the impression of a market was the cosmopolite public talking broken French, an hotel public, that had arrived the day before and came there in travelling costume, Scotch caps, threadbare jackets, tweeds still steeped in the fogs of the Channel, and the Muscovite furs hastening to unfreeze, and the long black beards, the boorish airs from the borders of the Spree masking the grins of fauns and the barbarities of Tartars, and Ottoman fezzes on collarless coats, negroes in full dress, shining like the silk of their hats, little Japanese in European dress, neat and correct.

"*Boun Diou!* How ugly he is!" suddenly cried Audiberte before a grave Chinaman, his long pigtail down the back of his blue costume; or she stopped, and nudging her companion's elbow—

"*Vé, vé!* a bride"—she showed her, stretched on two chairs, one of which supported her white satin boots with silver heels, a woman all in white, with corsage open, her train unrolled, and the orange flowers piercing in her hair the lace of a short mantilla. Then, suddenly scandalized at words that enlightened her about this fortuitous orange-tree, the Provençale added mysteriously: "*One* poison, you know!" Quickly, in order to get Hortense away from the pernicious example, she drew her into the enclosure in the middle, where right at the further end, holding the place of the choir in a church, the theatre arose under intermittent electric flames falling from two globes.

Here people rested from the tumultuous scandal of the promenades; families of small *bourgeois*, storekeepers of the district. Few women. You might have thought yourself in some kind of theatre, had it not been for the horrible, pervading noise which always predominated with a regular, obsessing roll over the skating on the asphalt, drowning even the brass, even the drums of the orchestra, making everything impossible but the mimicry of the tableaux vivants.

The curtain was being lowered at that moment on a patriotic scene, the lion of Belfort, enormous, in cardboard, engirt with soldiers in triumphant poses on crumbled ramparts, their *képis* at the end of their guns, following the measure of an inaudible "Marseillaise." The Provençale grew excited; her eyes started out of her head, and as she put Hortense in her seat, she exclaimed—

"We're all right here, *qué?* But lift up your veil—don't tremble—you're trembling. There's no risk with me."

The girl answered nothing, haunted by that slow, outrageous promenade into which she had been plunged, among all those pallid masks. And there in front of her she found them again, those horrible masques with bleeding lips, in the grimaces of two clowns, with a bell in each hand, carolling a tune from "Martha" amid their gambols; a real gnome music, formless, well suited to the harmonic babelism of the rink. Then the curtain fell again, and the peasant, who had got on her feet ten times sat down again, excited, adjusting her headdress, exclaimed suddenly as she followed the programme, "The Mont de Cordoue—the *cigales*—Farandole—it's beginning. *Vé, vé!*"

The curtain going up again revealed on the canvas a lilac hill, where white masonry of bizarre construction, half castle, half mosque, arose in minarets, in terraces, with aloes, palm-trees of zinc at the foot of towers motionless beneath the indigo of a very crude sky. Despite all, despite the loud tones of the slopes blooming with thyme and exotic plants which had strayed there for the Mont de Cordoue, Hortense ex-perienced an emotion of uneasiness in the presence of that scenery whence sprang her most happy memories; and that Osmanli *casbah* on that mount of pink porphyry, that rebuilt castle seemed to her the realization of her dream, but grotesque and burdensome, as when dream is near to falling into the oppression of nightmare. At the signal of the orchestra and an electric jet, long rows, represented by girls un-dressed in the clinging silk of their emerald green tights, darted forth, flut-tering long wings.

"Those, grasshoppers! Nothing of the kind!" said the Provençale, indig-nantly.

The sadness that anguished Hor-tense's feelings was yet increased, when she heard coming, at first in the dis-tance, then growing louder and louder, the dull rumbling of the tabor.

She would have liked to run away, not to see the man who was about to enter. The flute in its turn was sound-ing its thin notes; and, shaking beneath the cadence of its steps the dust from the earth-coloured carpet, the farandole defiled, with fantastic costumes, loud, short skirts, red gilt-edged stockings, padded vests, sequin coiffures, with a fine Parisian contempt for local truth. Behind came with deliberate steps, pushing from his knee a tabor covered with gilt paper, the great troubadour of the advertisements, in close-fitting tights, one leg yellow with blue foot-gear, the other blue with yellow foot-gear, and a satin vest, a velvet cap shading a face that had remained brown in spite of the grease-paint and of which you could only clearly see a moustache stiffened with Hungarian pomade.

"Oh!" cried Audiberte in ecstasy. The farandole was drawn up on both ides of the stage in front of the big-winged *cigales*, the troubadour in the entre saluted, with assured and van-quishing mien. The serenade began, ustic and faint of sound, scarcely pass-ng beyond the stage. The public ooked on without understanding. Val-ajour began another piece, which was eceived f om the first bars with laugh-er, murmurs, exclamations. Audiberte ook Hortense's hand—

"It's the cabal—you watch!"

The cabal here uttered a few cries f "Sh!—louder!" and jokes like that hich a hoarse-voiced girl shouted at almajour's complicated mimicry—

"Have you done, you performing rab-it?"

Then the skating and the billiards ent on again, the noise overpowering he flute and tabor which the musician ersisted in playing right to the end of he serenade. After which he saluted, ad-anced to the footlights. His lips were en moving, sketching out some words.

"It came to me—a hole—three holes. he bird of good God——"

His desperate gesture, understood by e orchestra, was the signal for a llet in which the *cigales* were enlaced ith houris for the purpose of poses astiques, undulating lascivious dances, der rainbow Bengal-fire that reached en the troubadour's pointed shoes, o continued his tabor mimicry before e castle of his ancestors in a glory apotheosis.

And that was Hortense's romance! at is what Paris had made of it.

The clear note of the old clock hang-
 in her room having struck one, she got up from the easy-chair, into which she had fallen exhausted on her return, glanced around her sweet virgin's nest, with the comforting warmth of a dying fire.

"What am I doing here? Why haven't I gone to bed?"

She no longer remembered, feeling only a wounding of her whole nature, and a buzzing in her head that beat upon her brow. She walked two paces, noticed she had still her hat on, her cloak, and the whole scene returned to her. The departure from that place after the fall of the curtain, their re-turn through the hideous market more brightly illuminated towards the end, drunken bookmakers fighting at a bar, cynical voices whispering a price as she passed, then the scene with Audiberte on their going out, she wishing her to go and congratulate her brother, her anger in the cab, the insults that crea-ture hurled at her in order presently to humble herself, to kiss her hands in excuse; all that, confused and dancing in her memory with clowns' antics, dis-cordances of bells, of cymbals, soarings of many-coloured flames about the ridiculous troubadour to whom she had given her heart. A physical horror overcame her at the idea.

"No, no, never—I'd rather die!"

Suddenly she observed in the glass in front of her a hollow-cheeked spec-tre, with narrow shoulders thrust for-ward in a gesture. It looked rather like her, but much more like the Princess d'Anhalt, whose sad symptoms she de-tailed at Arvillard with pitying curios-ity, and who had just died at the begin-ning of the winter.

"Come! Come!"

She bent forward, approached again, recalled the inexplicable kindness they had all showed her there, her mother's fear, the tender affectionateness of old Bouche eau at her departure, and she understood. At last she had it, her conclusion. It came quite by itself. She had been seeking for it long enough.

CHAPTER XVI

AUDIBERTE'S REVENGE

"MADEMOISELLE is very ill. Madame will not see anybody."

For the tenth time in ten days Audiberte received the same answer. Motionless before that heavy door, such as one hardly finds any nowadays except under the arcades of the Place Royale, and which being shut seemed to bar to her for ever the Le Quesnoy's old dwelling.

"All right," she said. "I shall not come back any more. It's they who'll call on me now."

And she went away thoroughly upset, amid the animation of that commercial quarter. She did not take notice of the infernal noise; her malevolent brain was conceiving brutal thoughts, terrible reactions of her defeated will. And she went along, not feeling the fatigue, traversed on foot, so as to economize the omnibus, the long distance from the Marais to the Rue de l'Abbaye-Montmartre.

Quite recently, after travelling through lodgings of all kinds, hotels, furnished apartments, from which they were each time expelled on account of the tabor, they had come and let themselves down there, in a new house which was occupied at bricklayers' prices by a gang of loose women. Bohemians,

agents, families of adventurers such as you see in seaports, watching the waves from which they always expect something. Here it is fortune they are spying for. The rent was very dear for them, now especially as the skating rink was bankrupt. However, in this freshly painted bark, its door open at every hour for the different unavoidable professions of the lodgers, together with the quarrels taking place the tabor disturbed nobody. It was the taborist who was disturbed. The puffs the advertisements, the close-fitting tights and his fine moustaches had made havoc among the ladies of the skating rink. He knew some actors of the Batignolles, some café-concert singers, quite a nice company that met in an inn along the Boulevard Rochechou art called the "Paillasson."

This Paillasson, where his time was spent, in a boozy lounging, in messing about cards, drinking bocks, was the foe, the terror of Audiberte, the occasion of savage tempers under which the two men bent their backs as under tropical storm, free to curse their bi skirted despot in company, speaking her in the mysterious and hateful tor of schoolboys or of servants: "What did she say? How much did she gi you?" and having an understanding go out behind her heels. Audiber knew it, watched them, worked outside impatient to return, and that day espe ally, as she went away in the mornir She stopped a second as she was goi up, and heard neither tabor nor flu

"Ah! the idle scamp—he's still at Paillasson."

But, as soon as she entered, father ran up to her and averted the plosion.

"Don't shout! There's some one for you. A gentleman from the *ministery*."

The gentleman was awaiting her in the "drawing-room," a drawing-room of which the peasant woman was very proud. And Méjean was considering, full of compassion, the Provençal furniture buried in that dentist's waiting-room, in the crude light of two curtainless windows. Audiberte's haughty, very pure, profile, in her Sunday ribbon, itself too de-countryfied in that Parisian fifth floor, put the finishing touch to his pity for these victims of Roumestan; and he began gently the explanation of his visit. The minister, wishing Valmajour to avoid fresh misconceptions for which he felt himself responsible to a certain point, was sending them 5,000 francs to compensate them for their disturbance and to repatriate them. He took the orders from his pocket, placed them on an old walnut coffer.

"Then we'll have to go?" asked the woman, meditatively, without moving.

"M. le Ministre desires it to be so as soon as possible. He is eager to hear you are at home again, happy as before."

Valmajour senior risked a glance at the orders.

"As for me, it seems reasonable. *Dé qué n'en disés?*"

She said nothing, waited for the sequel, which Méjean was getting ready, turning his portfolio on this side and that. "To these 5,000 francs we shall add another 5,000—as here—in order to get back—in order to get back—" He was strangling with emotion. It was a cruel commission Rosalie had given him in that matter. Ah! It often costs something to pass for a quiet,

strong man; people ask much more of you than of others. He added very quickly: "The portrait of Mlle. Le Quesnoy."

"Well, at last—now we've come to the point. The portrait. I knew quite well, *pardi!* So you think you can make us come from the other end of France, that you could promise everything to us who asked for nothing, and that then we could be put out like dogs who have misbehaved themselves. Take back your money, sir. You can tell them for certain we're not going, and we shall not give them back the portrait. It's a document, that. I keep it in my bag. It never leaves me; and I shall show it in Paris, with what is written on it, that the world may know all those Roumestans are a family of liars—of liars."

She foamed at the mouth.

"Mlle. Le Quesnoy is very ill," said Méjean very grave.

"*Avaï!*"

"She is about to leave Paris and will probably never come back—alive."

Audiberte did not answer, but the mute laughter of her eyes, the implacable refusal of her antique forehead, low and obstinate, under the little, pointed coif, indicated sufficiently the firmness of her rejection. A temptation then came over Méjean to throw himself on her, to tear the bag from her girdle and run away with it. He contained himself, however, tried some useless entreaties, then himself too quivering with rage, "You'll be sorry for it," said he, and he left, to old Valmajour's great regret.

"Look out, little one—you'll bring us some harm."

"Not so! We'll do them some. I'm going to consult Guilloche."

"GUILLOCHE, AGENT."

Behind that yellowed card, stuck on the door opposite theirs, there was one of those dreadful "business agents" whose whole material of installation consists in an enormous leather portfolio, containing *dossiers* of purulent histories, some white paper for the denunciations and blackmailing letters, paste, a false beard, and even sometimes a hammer to knock down the milk-women, as we have seen in a recent trial. This type, very common in Paris, would not deserve a line of portraiture if the said Guilloche had not added to his profession a new and characteristic detail. Guilloche did the punishment tasks of the youths of the Lycée. A poor devil of a clerk went and collected the punishments when the classes went out and sat up very late at night to copy out the verse of the Æneid or the three moods of λύω. When contentious matters were lacking, Guilloche, who was a B.A., harnessed himself to this original work, from which he drew some profit.

Placed *au courant* of the affair, he declared it excellent. The minister would be brought to book, the newspapers would be given the tip; the portrait of itself alone was worth a gold mine. Only he required time, and advances of money in hard cash for running about the town, as the Puyfourcat inheritance seemed to him a pure mirage. The peasant woman's rapacity, already put cruelly to the ordeal, was racked with anguish, the more so as Valmajour, who was in great request at the *salons* during the first winter, no

longer set foot in the Faubourg Saint Germeïn.

"So much the worse—I'll work. I'll make things hum, *zou!*"

The energetic little coif of Arle moved actively in the big new build ing, went up and down stairs, hawking from floor to floor its sto y about the minister, it grew excited, it shook, it leapt, and suddenly in a mysterious voice was heard: "Besides, there's the portrait." With a furtive, dubious look, like the hawkers of certain photo graphs in back streets, she would show the thing.

"A pretty girl, at any rate! An you've read what's written at the bo tom? I think that with that we've g them," she would add with a furiou gesture of strangling.

One day Audiberte was invited to g to the police commissary of the di trict. She ran there with all spee persuaded that the matter referred Cousin Puyfourcat, went in smiling, h coif set high, and departed at the e of a quarter of an hour upset by t very peasant-like fear of the gendarm who at the first words had made h give up the portrait and sign a recei for 10,000 francs by which she aba doned all proceedings. Certainly s obstinately refused to leave the tow persisted in believing in her brothe genius, ever retaining at the back her eyes the dazzling effect of that lo line of carriages, one winter's evening, the court of the illuminated minist

On her return, she hinted to her me folk, who were more timorous than h self, that they must not talk any mo about the affair; but said no syllal about the money received. Guilloc who suspected it, that money, used his methods to get his share of it, and having only got the minimum compensation cherished a terrible rancour against the Valmajours.

"Well!" he said one morning to Audiberte, whilst she was brushing on the banister the best suit of the musician who was still in bed. "*Eh bien!* you should be content. He's dead at last."

"Who?"

"Why, Puyfourcat, the cousin. It's in the paper."

"Father! Brother! Quick the legacy!"

They were all stirred to their souls, panting around the infernal Guilloche, who unfolded the *Officiel* and read to them very slowly as follows: " 'Under date of 1st October, 1876, the tribunal of Mostaganem has, at the request of the administration of the domains, ordered the publication and advertising of the legacies hereinafter. — Popelino (Louis) labourer.'—That's not it.— Puyfourcat (Dosithée).' "

"That's him," said Audiberte.

The old man thought it his duty to wipe his eyes.

"*Pécaïré!* Poor Dosithée!"

" 'Puyfourcat, deceased at Mostaganem the 14th January, 1874, born at Valmajour, Commune of Aps."

The peasant woman grown impatient inquired—

"How much?"

"Three francs, thirty-five *cintimes!*" cried Guilloche with the voice of a coalheaver; and leaving them the paper that they might verify their mistake, he went off with a burst of laughter which went from floor to floor even into the street, afforded merriment to the whole of the great village of Montmartre where the legend of the Valmajours circulated.

Three francs thirty-five the legacy of the Puyfourcats! Audiberte affected to laugh at it louder than the others; but the frightful desire of vengeance that brooded in her against the Roumestans, responsible in her eyes for all their misfortunes, only grew fiercer and fiercer, seeking a vent, a means, the first weapon within reach.

The papa's face was singular during this disaster. Whilst his daughter was exhausted with fatigue and rage, he, looking blooming, careless, no longer cherishing even his former professional jealousy, seemed to have arranged for himself somewhere outside a tranquil existence apart from his own kin. He decamped immediately after lunch; and sometimes in the morning when brushing his clothes he let drop from his pockets a dry fig, a *berlingot, canissons,* the origin of which the old man explained away somehow.

He had met a peasant woman in the street, some one from down there, who would come and see them.

Audiberte shook her head.

"*Avaï!* if I followed you!"

The truth is that whilst sauntering about Paris he had discovered in the Saint-Denis quarter a big provision shop, where he had entered, lured by the inscription and by the temptations of an exotic shop-front, with coloured fruits, with silver paper, shining bright in the fog of a populous street. The store, in which he had become a regular diner and friend, well known to Southerners become Parisians, was entitled—

"AUX PRODUITS DU MIDI."

And never a truer label. There, everything was a product of the South, from the masters, M. and Mme. Mèfre, two products of the Midi Gras, with the prominent nose of Roumestan, the flashing eyes, the accent, the phrases, the demonstrative welcome of Provence, down to their shop assistants, familiar, thinking nothing of shouting out to the office in drawling tones: "I say, Mèfre, where have you put that sausage, eh?" Down to the little Mèfres, impish and dirty, running at every instant the risk of being disembowelled, scalped, put in the soup, dipping their fingers nevertheless in all the open barrels; down to the buyers gesticulating, chatteing for hours, for the acquisition of a *barquette* of two sous, or sitting on chairs in a circle to discuss the qualities of the garlic sausage and the sausage with pepper, Aunt Portal's whole vocabulary in boisterous exchange, whilst a "dear brother" in black dress, a friend of the house, would buy some salt fish, and the flies, a quantity of flies, attracted by all the sugar of these fruits, of these sweets, of these almost oriental pastries, would buzz about even in mid-winter, kept alive by the cooking warmth. And when a Parisian got impatient at the dawdling of the shopmen, at the absentminded indifference of the shopkeepers continuing their chat from one place to another, whilst weighing and measuring all wrong, you should have heard the talk—

"*Té, vé,* if you're in a hurry, the door it is open, and the tramway it passes in front, you know well."

In this environment of compatriots, old Valmajour was received with open arms. M. and Mme. Mèfre remembered having seen him at the fair of Beaucaire, at a tabor competition.

Among old people of the South, this fair of Beaucaire, to-day vanished, existing only in name, has remained as a bond of masonic brotherhood. In our Southern provinces, it was the fairy time of the year, the distraction of all those stunted existences; preparations were made for it long in advance, and it was talked about long after. It was promised as a reward to the wife, to the children, always bringing them back, if they could not be taken with one, a Spanish lace, a toy which one found at the bottom of the bag. The fair of Beaucaire, it was still, under a pretext of commerce, a fortnight, a month of free, exuberant, unforeseen life, of Bohemian camping out. People slept here and there at a native's house, in the shops, on the desks, in the open street, under the stretched canvas of the wagons, in the warm light of the July stars.

Oh! for the business without the wearisomeness of the shop, business despatched whilst dining, at the door, in shirt-sleeves.

At the Mèfres' every one felt at ease, rather like at the Beaucaire fair; and indeed, the shop resembled in its picturesque disorder an improvised caravan and store of produce of the South. The old man would go inside, his nostrils distended, overflowing with greedy eagerness, greatly excited. He who in the case of his children shirked the least work and when he had sewn a button on his waistcoat wiped his brow for hours, boasting of having performed a labour of Hercules, was here ever ready to lend a hand, to take off his coat to nail, to unfasten boxes, picking up here and there a *berlingot,* an olive enlivening the work by his monke tricks and his tales; and once a week, the day of the *brandade,* he even worked late at the shop so as to help to send off the consignments.

This Southern dish among all the rest, the *brandade* of turbot, can hardly be got except at the "Produits du Midi"; it is the genuine, white, fine-flaked, creamy, with a dash of *aïet,* such as it is manufactured at Nîmes, whence the Mèfres get it. It arrives on Thursday evening at seven by the "Rapide" and is distributed on Friday morning in Paris to all the good clients inscribed in the big ledger of the firm. It is on that journal of commerce with its worn pages, smelling of spices and spotted with oil, that the history is written of the conquest of Paris by the Southerners, that you may see in file high fortunes, political, industrial situations, celebrated names of advocates, deputies, ministers, and among all, that of Numa Roumestan, the Vendéan of the South, pillar of the altar and of the throne.

For that line in which Roumestan is inscribed, the Mèfres would throw the whole book in the fire. It is he who best represents their ideas in religion, in politics, in everything. As Mme. Mèfre says, and she is even more impassioned than her husband—

"That man, you see, one would damn one's soul for him."

They like to recall the time when Numa, already on the road to glory, did not disdain to come himself to lay in his provisions. And how well he understood the choosing of a "grastègne à la tâte," a sausage properly sweating under the knife! Moreover, such kindness, that fine, imposing face, always a compliment for madame, a good word for the "dear brother," a caress for the little Mèfres who escorted him right to the carriage, carrying the packets. Since his elevation to the ministry, since those villains of Reds gave him so much to do in the two Chambers, they did not see him any more, *pécaïré!* but he remained the loyal customers of the "Produits"; and he was always the first attended to.

One Thursday night, about ten, all the pots of *brandade* being prepared, sealed up, in fine order on the bench, the Mèfre family, the assistants, old Valmajour, all the products of the South, in their entirety, sweating, panting, were resting with that expansive air of people who have well accomplished a hard task and were refreshing themselves with *biscottes* in mulled wine, with syrup of barley, "something sweet, you know!" for Southerners do not much like anything strong. Among the town populace as in the country parts, alcoholic intoxication is almost unknown. The race has an instinctive fear and horror of it. It feels itself drunk from birth, drunk without drinking.

And it is very true that the wind and the sun distill into it a terrible alcohol of nature, whose effects all those who are born down there feel more or less. Some have only a little extra amount of it, which unloosens the tongue and gestures, makes life look rose-coloured with sympathies everywhere, lights up the eyes, broadens the streets, levels obstacles, doubles boldness and comforts the timid; others, more affected, like the little Valmajour, Aunt Portal, reach at once a blind delirium. You should see our votive fêtes in Provence, peasants standing on the tables, howling, stamping with their big yellow shoes, calling: "Waiter, the gassy stuff!" a whole village rolling drunk after a few bottles of lemonade. And those sudden prostrations of the intoxicated, those collapses of the whole being following on anger, on enthusiasm, with the suddenness of a sunstroke or of a shadow in a March sky; who is the Southerner who has not felt them?

Without being deliriously affected like his daughter, old Valmajour was born with a considerable amount of the alcohol in him; and that night his barley drink transported him with a mad mirth that made him grimace in the middle of the shop, glass in hand, his mouth distorted, all his amusing tomfoolery. The Mèfres, and their assistants were writhing with laughter on the grain sacks.

"Oh! that Valmajour!"

Suddenly the old man's hilarity disappeared, his clownish gesture was broken off short by the appearance before him of a Provençal coif, all quivering.

"What are you doing there, father?" Mme. Mèfre raised her arms to the ceiling—

"What! it's your young lady? You didn't tell us. Hé! How tiny she is! but very nice, certainly. Sit down, pray, mademoiselle."

Owing to a habit of lying as well as in order to keep himself freer, the old man had not mentioned his children, gave himself out for an old bachelor living on his income; but among Southerners, an invention or so does not count. Had a whole cargo of little Valmajours blossomed forth after Audiberte, the welcome would have been the same, demonstrative and warm.

They were attentive to her, made room for her—

"*Différemment*, you will have a drink, you too."

The Provençale was taken aback. She came from the outside, from the cold, from the black of the North, a December night, where the feverish life of Paris, continuing in spite of the time, was being wildly pursued in the thick fog torn in all directions by rapidly moving shadows, the coloured lanterns of the omnibuses, the hoarse horn of the tramways; she came from the North, she came from winter, and suddenly, without transition, she found herself in the midst of Italian Provence, in the Mèfre shop, glittering at the approach of Christmas with sunny, *gourmand* riches, among well-known accents and perfumes. It was her country suddenly re-discovered, the return to the country after a year of exile, of trials, of distant struggles among the Barbarians. A gentle warmth invaded her, soothed her nerves, in proportion as she steeped her biscuit in an inch full of Carthagena wine, replying to all these worthy people who were at ease and familiar with her as if they had known her for twenty years. She felt she had entered again into her life, into her habits; and tears rose to her eyes, those hard eyes veined with fire that never wept.

Roumestan's name uttered near her at once dried up her emotion. It was Mme. Mèfre inspecting the addresses of her consignments and advising them not to make a mistake, not to take the *brandade* of Numa to Rue de Grenelle, but to Rue de Londres.

"Seems that at Rue de Grenelle the *brandade* is not in the odour of sanctity," remarked one of the "products."

"I should think so," said M. Mèfre. "A lady of the North, the most North imaginable. Cooks with butter, *allons!* Whilst at the Rue de Londres, it's the pretty South, gaiety, songs, and everything with oil. I understand how Numa finds himself more comfortable there."

They spoke lightly about the minister's second household in a small, very convenient *pied-à-terre* quite near the station, where he could rest from the fatigues of the Chamber, free from receptions and the great to-dos. Quite certain that the excitable Mme. Mèfre would have given vent to some fine shrieks if such a thing had happened in her own household; but, in the case of Numa, it was only sympathetic and natural.

He liked skirts; but didn't all our kings run after women, and Charles X, and Henri IV, that gallant of gallants? It came from his Bourbon nose, *té pardi!*

And with this levity, with this tone of raillery with which the South treats all amorous affairs, was blended a race-hatred, antipathy against the woman of the North, the stranger and the cooking with butter. They grew excited, they gave detailed *anedotes*, they descanted on the charms of the little Alice and her successes at the Grand-Opéra.

"I knew Mama Bachellery at the time of the fair of Beaucaire," said old Valmajour. "She used to sing ballads at the Café Thibaut."

Audiberte listened without breathing, not losing a word, fixing in her head the name, address; and her little eyes gleamed with a diabolical intoxication in which the wine of Carthagena counted for nothing.

CHAPTER XVII

ROSALIE'S TRIAL

MADAME ROUMESTAN started at the light knock at the door of her room, as if surprised in some guilty act, and pushing back the delicately shaped drawer of her Louis XV commode, before which she was bending, almost kneeling, she asked—

"Who is there? What do you want Polly?"

"A letter for madame — it's very urgent," answered the Englishwoman. Rosalie took the letter and quickly shut the door again. An unknown, vulgar handwriting, on the commonest paper, with the "Personal and Urgent" of requests for help. Never would a Parisian chambermaid have disturbed her for so little. She threw it on the commode, deferring the reading of it till later, and returned quickly to her drawer which contained the marvels of the previous baby outfit. For eight years, since the drama, she had not opened it, fearing to find her tears again there; nor even since her pregnancy, owing to a very motherly superstition, for fear of yet again bringing misfortune on herself, with that premature caress given to the child who is going to be born, over its little trousseau.

She had, that valiant woman, all the nervousnesses of a woman, all her tremblings, her delicate shrinkings as of a mimosa; society, which judges without understanding, thought her cold, even as the ignorant imagine flowers do not live. Now, however, her hope being six months old, it was necessary to take all those little objects from their folds of mourning and enclosure, to visit them, perhaps to transform them; because fashion changes even for the newly born, they are not always beribboned in the same way. It was for this intimate work that Rosalie had shut herself in carefully; and in the big, busy, scribbling ministry there was certainly nothing as serious, as moving as that woman on her knees before an open drawer, her heart beating and her hands trembling.

She lifted the somewhat yellowed lace which preserved with perfumes all that white of innocent toilettes, the dress for the baptism, the doll stockings. She saw herself again down there at Orsay, gently languid, working for entire hours under the shade of the tall catalpa whose white calices fell into the work-basket among her materials and her fine embroidery scissors, all her thought concentrated on a point of cutting-out which bounded her dreams and hours. What illusions then, what beliefs! What a joyous branching in the leaves over her head! In herself, what an awakening of tender, new sensations! In one day life had taken it all back from her, suddenly. And her despair came back to her heart, her husband's treachery, the loss of the child, in proportion as she unfolded her "layette."

The sight of the first little garment, all ready to pass, that which is got ready on the cradle at the moment of birth, the sleeves one in the other, the arms separated, the caps swollen in their roundness, made her burst into tears. It seemed to her that her child had lived, that she had kissed and known it. A boy. Oh! certainly, a boy, and strong, and handsome, and even at the outset possessing his grandfather's serious, deep eyes. He would

be eight to-day, with long curly hair falling over a big collar: at that age they still belong to the mother who marches them about, dresses them, makes them work! Ah! cruel, cruel life.

But gradually as she drew out and handled the small objects, their flowered embroideries, their snowy laces, she grew calm. Well, no, life is not so malevolent; and as long as it lasts one must keep up one's courage. She had lost all her courage at that deadly turning, imagining it was all over with her in respect to belief in loving, in being a wife and mother, that the only thing left for her was to observe the luminous past going far away like a passing riverbank one looks at with regret. Then, after mournful years, beneath her heart's cold snow the revival had slowly blossomed, and here it was flourishing again in that quite little one which was about to be born, which she felt to be already vigorous by the terrible little kicks it used to give her during the night. And her Numa, so changed, so kind, cured of those brutal violences! There were, indeed, still in him weaknesses she did not like, those Italian peculiarities from which he could not defend himself; but "that's politics," as he would say. Further, she no longer cherished the illusions of the early days; she knew that in order to live happily one must be contented with the approximate in all things, carve for oneself full happiness in the half-happiness existence gives us.

There was another knock at the door. M. Méjean, who wanted to speak with madame.

"Good. I'm coming."

She joined him in the small drawing-room which he was pacing up and down, greatly agitated.

"I have a confession to make to you," he said in the rather brusque tone of familiarity which a friendship already old authorized, of which they had made a brotherly bond. "I ended that wretched affair a few days ago. I did not tell you, so as to keep this longer."

He handed her Hortense's portrait.

"At last! Oh! how happy she will be, poor darling."

She grew tenderly affectionate as she beheld the pretty face of her sister sparkling with health and youth under her Provençale disguise, read at the bottom of the portrait the very fine and very firm handwriting: "I believe in you and I love you.—Hortense Le Quesnoy." Then, reflecting that the poor lover had also read it and that he had in this case been entrusted with a mournful commission, she shook his hand affectionately.

"Thanks."

"Don't thank me, madame. Yes, it was hard. But I have lived with that for a week. 'I believe in you and I love you.' At moments I fancied it was for me."

And in a low voice, shyly—

"How is she?"

"Oh! not well. Mama is taking her to the South. Now she wishes everything one wishes. There is as it were a spring broken in her."

"Changed?"

Rosalie made a gesture: "Ah!"

"Au revoir, madame," said Méjean very quickly, rushing away at a great pace. At the door he turned and squaring his solid shoulders under the half-lifted curtain—

"It's real luck. I have no imagination. I should be too unhappy."

Rosalie re-entered her room, much saddened. In spite of defending herself from it, invoking her sister's youth, Jarras's encouraging words that persisted in only reckoning on a crisis to be overcome, black ideas came to her which no longer departed with the festal whiteness of her "layette." She hastened to arrange, to put away, the little scattered things, and as she rose she perceived the letter resting on the commode, took it, read it mechanically, expecting a commonplace request such as she received every day from so many different hands, and which would have arrived suitably at one of those superstitious junctures when charity seems to bring good luck. That is why she did not understand quite at first, was obliged to read again those lines written as a punishment task with the pen of a schoolboy, Guilloche's young man.

"If you are fond of *brandade* of turbot, there is some excellent to be eaten to-night at Mme. Bachellery's, Rue de Londres. Your husband is standing the treat. Ring three times and enter at once."

From these stupid phrases, from this filthy and perfidious background, the truth rose up, appeared to her, aided by coincidences, memories; the name of Bachellery, so often uttered during the last year, the enigmatic articles about her engagement, this address which she had herself heard him give, the long stay at Arvillard. In a second doubt for her had passed into certainty. Besides, did not the past throw light on the present with all its actual horror? Lie and grimace, he was not, could not be anything but that. Why should that constant maker of dupes have spared her? It was she who had been mad to let herself be caught by his deceitful voice, by his banal tenderness; and some details recurred to her which in the same second caused her to blush and to grow pale.

This time it was no more the despair accompanied by the big, pure tears of the first deceptions; an anger was mingled with it against herself for being so weak, so cowardly as to have been able to forgive, against him who had deceived her, in contempt of his promises, his oaths regarding the past error. She would have liked to convict him there, at once; but he was at Versailles, at the Chamber. The idea came to her to summon Méjean, then it went against the grain to oblige an honest man to lie. And, compelled to stifle a whole violence of contrary feelings, in order not to shriek, to abandon herself to the terrible nerve-crisis which she felt was attacking her, she walked here and there on the carpet, her hands—with a familiar pose—on her waist freed from her peignoir. Suddenly she stopped, quivered with a mad fear.

Her child!

He was suffering, he too, and recalled himself to his mother with all the strength of a life which is struggling. Ah! *mon Dieu*, if he were to die, this one, like the other—at the same period of pregnancy, in similar circumstances. Destiny, which is called blind, has sometimes these ferocious combinations. And she reasoned to herself in half-uttered words, in tender cries, "dear little one—poor little one," tried to view things coolly, so as to behave with dignity and especially not to compromise the being that alone remained to

her. She even took up a piece of work, that Penelope's embroidery which the activity of the Parisian always keeps going; because she had to wait for Numa's return, to have an explanation with him or rather gather from his attitude the conviction of his guilt, before the irremediable sensation of a separation.

Oh! those brilliant wools, that regular, colourless canvass, what confidences they receive, what regrets, joys, desires, form the complicated, knotted reverse, full of broken threads, in those feminine works with the flowers quietly interlaced.

Numa Roumestan, on arriving from the Chamber, found his wife plying the needle beneath the narrow brightness of a single lighted lamp, and the tranquil picture, the beautiful profile softened by chestnut hair, in the luxurious shadow of the wadded hangings, where lacquered screens, old coppers, ivories, faïences, attracted the wandering gleams, warm with a wood fire, struck him by contrast with the noisiness of the Assembly, the bright ceilings enveloped with dust floating over the debates like a cloud of powder hovering over a field of manœuvres.

"Good-day, mama. It's nice here with you."

The meeting had been hot. Always that dreadful budget, the Left hanging for five hours on the heels of that poor General d'Espaillon, who could not sew two ideas together consecutively, when he did not say s— n— d— D—. In fact, the cabinet was escaping this time again; but it was after New Year's Day, when the question of the Fine Arts came on, that it would be decided. "They count a great deal on the

Cadaillac affair to give me a basting. Rougeot will speak. Not accommodating, that Rougeot. He has pluck and boldness!"

Then, with a shrug of the shoulders— "Rougeot versus Roumestan. The North versus the South. So much the better. It will amuse me. There'll be hard hitting."

He talked in monologue, absorbed in the fire of business, without noticing Rosalie's dumbness. He came quite near her, sitting on a cushion, making her leave go her work, trying to kiss her hand.

"Is it then very urgent what you're embroidering there? Is it a present for me? As for me, I have already bought yours. Guess!"

She drew herself back gently, gazed at him so as to embarrass him, without replying. His features were wearied by the days of full-dress meeting, the tired relaxation of his face betraying at the corner of his eyes and his mouth a nature at once soft and violent, all the passions and nothing to resist them. The faces of the South are like its scenery, they must only be looked at in the sunshine.

"You're dining with me?" asked Rosalie.

"But no. I'm expected at Durand's. A boring dinner. Té! I'm already late," he added, rising. "Luckily there is no dressing."

His wife's gaze followed him. "Dine with me, I beg you." And her harmonious voice hardened as she insisted, became threatening, merciless. But Roumestan was not an observer. And besides, business, isn't it so? Ah! Those existences of public men are not spent as one would wish.

"Good bye, then," she said gravely, signifying by the good bye, "since that is our fate."

She heard the coupé rolling under the archway; then, carefully folding her work, she rang.

"A carriage at once. A cab. And you, Polly, my cloak, my hat. I'm going out."

Quickly ready, she inspected with a look the room she was leaving, where she regretted nothing, left nothing of hers, a regular room in furnished lodgings, under the pomp of its cold yellow brocade.

"Take this big box down to the carriage."

The "layette," everything she was taking away of the common property.

At the door of the cab, the Englishwoman, very inquisitive, asked if madame would not dine. No, she was dining at her father's, she would also sleep there, probably.

On her way a doubt still came to her, rather a scruple. If nothing of it was true! If that Bachellery did not live in the Rue de Londres! She gave the address, without much hope; but she must have certainty.

They stopped at a small hôtel of two stories, surmounted by a terrace like a winter garden, the old pied-à-terre of a Cario Levantine who had just died ruined. The aspect was that of a little house, windows shut, curtains down, a strong smell of cookery rising up in the lighted, noisy basements. Merely by noting the way in which the door obeyed the three rings of the bell, turned of itself on its hinges, Rosalie was fully informed. A Persian tapestry in the middle of the ante-room gave a view of the staircase, its deep-piled carpet, its lamps, the gas of which burnt on every landing. She heard laughing, advanced two steps and saw that which she never forgot—

Numa was bending over the banister on the first floor, red in the face, inflamed with excitement, in shirt-sleeves, holding by the waist that girl, also very excited, whose hair was down her back on the frills of a dishabille of pink foulard. And he cried in his boisterous tones—

"Bompard, bring up the *brandade*."

That was when he ought to have been seen, the Minister of Public Instruction and of Religions, the great merchant of religious morality, the defender of sound doctrines, there where he showed himself without a mask and without grimaces, all his Southern blood exposed, at ease and careless of appearances as at a Beaucaire mart.

"Bompard, bring up the *brandade!*" repeated the curious creature by his side, expressly exaggerating the Marseillaise intonation. Bompard, it was no doubt that improvised lackey, coming up from the kitchen, with his arms spread round a big dish, who was startled and turned round at the loud slamming of the door.

CHAPTER XVIII

SINS OF YOUTH

"Gentlemen of the Central Administration!"

"Gentlemen of the Direction of Fine Arts!"

"Gentlemen of the Academy of Medicine!"

As the usher, in full dress, short breeches, sword by his side, announced

them in his mournful voice in the solemnity of the reception rooms, rows of black coats crossed the huge gold and red *salon* and went and ranged themselves in a semi-circle before the minister, who was leaning against the mantelpiece, having near him his Under-Secretary of State, M. de la Calmette, his chief of cabinet, his attachés, and some directors of the ministry, Dansaert, Béchut. To each body presented by its president or its oldest member, His Excellency addressed compliments for the decorations, the academic palms awarded to some of its members; then the body made a half-turn, gave place, and whilst they retired, others came up rapidly; for it was late, past one, and everybody was thinking of the family lunch awaiting him.

In the concert hall, transformed into a robing-room, the groups were impatiently looking at their watches, buttoning their gloves, readjusting their white ties beneath drawn faces, yawns of boredom, ill-temper and hunger. Roumestan, he also, was feeling the fatigue of the great day of the New Year. He had lost his splendid warmth of the preceding year on the same occasion, his faith in the future and in reforms, made flabby speeches, pierced by the cold to his marrows in spite of the heating apparatuses, the enormous flaming log; and the little fleecy flecks of snow, that whirled at the windows, fell lightly and freezingly on his heart as on the lawn of the garden.

"Gentlemen of the Comédie-Française!"

Clean-shaven, solemn, bowing just as in Louis XIV's time, they stood in noble attitudes round their *doyen* who, in a hollow voice, introduced the Company, the Company without epithet, without qualification, just as one says "God," just as one says the "Bible," as if there existed no other Company in the world but that one; and poor Roumestan would have had to be in the last stage of exhaustion if this Company, of which he seemed to form part, with his blue chin, his poses of conventional distinction, had not re-awakened his eloquence in big grand theatrical phrases.

The fact is that during the past week, since Rosalie's departure, he was like a gambler who has lost his mascot. He was afraid, suddenly felt himself inferior to his good fortune, and well nigh being crushed by it. The mediocrities whom luck has favoured have these faintings and these giddinesses, enhanced in his case by the frightful scandal which was about to break out, by the separation proceedings which the young wife absolutely insisted on, in spite of letters, influences of all kinds, his grovelling prayers and his oaths. For form's sake, it was stated at the ministry that Mme. Roumestan had gone to live with her father owing to the approaching departure of Mme. Le Quesnoy and Hortense; but nobody was taken in by it, and on all the faces defiling before him, at certain emphasized smiles, at certain excessively vibrating handshakes, the wretched man saw his misadventure reflected in pity, in curiosity, in irony. Even the humblest employers, who had come to the reception in jacket and overcoat, were "in the know"; couplets were going the round of officers in which Chambéry was rhymed with Bachellery and which more than one of the employees, discontented with his Christmas box,

hummed within him whilst bowing low to the supreme head.

Two o'clock. And the constituted bodies were still being presented, and the snow was being heaped up, whilst the man with the chair introduced pellmell, without hierarchic order—

"Gentlemen of the School of Law!"

"Gentlemen of the Conservatoire of Music!"

"Messieurs, the Directors of the subventioned theatres!"

Cadaillac came at the head, with the lead of his three bankruptcies; and Roumestan had far more desire to use fisticuffs on the cynical showman whose nomination was causing him such grave troubles, than to listen to his fine elocution which was belied by the fierce bluffing of his look and to pay him in reply a forced compliment half of which remained in the folds of his cravat—

"Very touched, gentlemen—*mn mn mn*—progress of art—*mn mn mn*—shall do yet better."

And the showman, as he went off, commented to himself—

"He has some lead in his wing, our poor Numa."

When they had gone, the minister and his assessors did honour to the usual collation; but the lunch, so cheerful the previous year and full of effusion, was affected by the master's gloom and by the ill-humour of his household, who were all rather angry with him for the compromising of their situation. These scandalous proceedings, falling right in the middle of the Cadaillac debate, would make Roumestan impossible in the cabinet; that very morning, at the reception at the Elysée, the Marshal had said two words about it with his brutal and laconic eloquence, like the old trooper he was—"A dirty affair, my dear minister, a dirty affair."

Without precisely knowing about these august words, whispered in the ear in an embrasure, these gentlemen saw their disgrace coming behind that of their chief.

"O women! women!" grumbled the scientist Béchut into his plate. M. de la Calmette and his thirty years of office grew melancholy in thinking of retirement like Tircis; and the tall Lappara, in a whisper, amused himself by throwing Rochemaure into consternation: "Viscount, we must look out for ourselves. We shall be chucked out within a week."

After the minister's toast to the New Year and his dear fellow-workers, given in a voice in which were tears, the company dispersed. Méjean, remaining last, paced up and down once or twice with his friend, without their having the courage to say a single word to each other; then he went away. In spite of all his longing to retain beside him that day the upright nature which intimidated him like a reproach of conscience, whilst sustaining, comforting, him, Numa could not prevent Méjean from running away to his visits, distributions of good wishes and presents, any more than he could forbid his usher from going and freeing himself in his family circle of his sword and his short breeches.

What a solitude, that ministry! And in all the rooms, below, above, in his study where he vainly tried to write, in his room which he was filling with sobs, everywhere the little January snowflakes were whirling by the broad windows, were veiling the horizon,

were accentuating a steppe-like silence. O wretchedness of grandeurs!

A clock struck four, another answered, and yet others in the desert of the vast palace. The notion of remaining there till night, face to face with his grief, frightened him. He wanted to unfreeze himself with a little friendship, affection. All those heating-apparatuses, haloes of trees in combustion, did not make a hearth. For a moment he thought of the Rue de Londres. But he had sworn to his advocate, for proceedings were already begun, to keep quiet till they came on. Suddenly a name crossed his mind: "And Bompard?" Why had he not come? Usually, on fête mornings, he would arrive the first, his arms laden with bouquets, bags of bonbons for Rosalie, Hortense, Mme. Le Quesnoy, on his lips a smile expressive of grand-papa, of Santa Claus. Be it understood that Roumestan paid the expenses of those surprises; but friend Bompard had enough imagination to forget it, and Rosalie, despite her antipathy, could not prevent herself feeling softer towards him, as she reflected on the privations the poor devil must have imposed on himself to be so generous.

"If I went and fetched him, we could dine together."

He was reduced to that. He rang, took off his black suit, his plaques, his Orders, and went on foot by the Rue Bellechasse.

The quays, the bridges were quite white; but when the Carrousel had been crossed, there was no trace of snow on the ground or in the air. It disappeared in the traffic of the street, in the swarming of the crowd hurrying on the pavements. The tumult of the festive night, the cries of the coachmen, the shouts of the street-porters, amid the luminous confusion of the windows, the yellow winking of gas-jets and the last reflections of the pale daylight, soothed Roumestan's chagrin, merged him with the bustle of the street, whilst going towards the Boulevard Poissonnière where the ex-Circassian, who was very sedentary, like all people of imagination, had sojourned for twenty years, since his arrival in Paris.

After going up innumerable floors, wandered in vast passages, and tumbling on invisible stairs, Roumestan, put out of breath by the ascent to which his illustrious legs as of a successful man were no longer adapted, knocked up against a large wash-basin hanging on the wall.

"Who's there?" drawled an accent he knew.

The door turned slowly, because on it hung all the winter and summer clothing of the lodger; for the room was small and Bompard did not lose a millimetre of it, being reduced to establishing his dressing-room in the corridor. His friend found him lying on a small iron bedstead, his forehead adorned with a scarlet coiffure, a sort of Dantesque headdress which bristled up with astonishment at the sight of the illustrious visitor.

"Not possible!"

"Are you ill?" asked Roumestan.

"Ill?—never."

"Then what are you doing there?"

"You see, I'm collecting my wits," he added, to explain his thought: "I have so many schemes in my head, so many inventions. At moments, I am scattered, I am dazed. It's only in bed I recover myself a bit."

Roumestan looked for a chair; but there was only one, serving as a night-table, laden with books, with papers, and a candle was guttering on it. He sat at the foot of the bed.

"Why haven't I seen you again?"

"But you're joking. After what happened, I couldn't meet your wife again. Think a bit! I was there, in front of her, the *brandade* in my hands! I must have been amazingly cool not to let it drop."

"Rosalie is no longer at the ministry," observed Numa, in consternation.

"So the matter was not arranged? You astonish me."

It did not seem possible to him that Mme. Numa, a person of so much good sense.—Because, after all, what was there in the whole thing? "An escapade, a spree!"

The other broke in—

"You don't know her. She's a ruthless woman—the spit of her father. Northern race. my dear fellow. They're not like us, whose most violent wrath evaporates in gestures, in threats, and nothing else. They remember everything, it s dreadful."

He did not say she had already forgiven him once. Then, in order to escape such dreary broodings—

"Dress. I'll take you to dinner."

Whilst Bompard was proceeding with his toilet on the landing, the minister inspected the attic, lit by a small window, on to which fell the melting snow. He was seized with pity in the presence of the bareness, the damp walls, the bleached paper, the little stove, fireless in spite of the season, and asked himself, accustomed to the sumptuous comfort of his palace, how any one could live there.

"Have you seen the garden?" cheerfully cried Bompard from his basin.

The garden! it was the leafless top of three plane-trees which could only be seen by clambering on the sole chair in the room.

"And my little museum?"

He gave this name to some labelled débris: a brick, a short pipe in hard wood, a rusty blade, an ostrich egg. But the brick came from the Alhambra, the knife had served in the vendettas of a famous Corsican bandit, the pipe bore the inscription: "Pipe of Moorish convict"; finally, the hardened egg representing the abortion of a beautiful dream, all that remained—of the Bompard hatcher and artificial culture. Oh! he had a better scheme than that now. A marvellous idea, with millions in it, which he could not mention yet.

"You madman!" said Roumestan, with a shade of envy for that miserable victim of chimeras, so happy in his tatters and rags. "You have a splendid imagination. Are you ready? Come! Let's go down. There's a black frost in your room."

A few turnings, amid the merry masses of the Boulevard, and the two friends were seated in the heady, beaming heat of a *cabinet* in a grand restaurant, oysters opened, the Château-Yquem carefully uncorked.

"Your health, comrade. May it be good and lucky!"

"*Té!* that's right," said Bompard, "we have not yet kissed each other."

They embraced over the table, their eyes moist; and tanned though the Circassian's hide was, Roumestan felt quite revived. He had been longing to embrace some one since the morning. Then, it was so many years since they knew each other, thirty years of their lives spread before them; and amid the steaming of delicate dishes, with luxurious wines, they recalled the days of youth, of brotherly memories, races, parties, saw again their faces as boys, interlarded their effusions with *patois* words which brought them yet nearer together.

"*T'en souvênés, digo?* I say, you remember?"

In a side-saloon, shrill laughing, little cries could be heard.

"To the deuce with females!" said Roumestan, "only friendship counts."

And they again drank to each other. But all the same their talk took a fresh turn.

"And the little one?" asked Bompard, winking. "How's she?"

"Oh! I haven't seen her again, you understand."

"Of course, of course," replied the other, suddenly very grave, with a consequential nod.

Now, behind the hangings, a piano was playing fragments of fashionable valses, quadrilles, refrains of operettas, alternatively boisterous or languid. They were silent so as to listen; and Numa began thinking of his wife, of his child, of his lost happiness, poured forth his heart out loud, with his elbows on the table.

"Eleven years of intimacy, of trust, of affection. All that burnt out, vanished in a moment. Is it possible? Ah! Rosalie, Rosalie——"

Nobody would ever know what she had been for him; and he did not himself understand it properly until her departure. Her mind so upright, her heart so honest. And what shoulders she had, and what arms! Not a sawdust doll like the little one. Something full, white, delicate.

"Besides, you see, comrade, it can't be denied that when one is young, one wants surprises, adventures. The hasty meetings, made more pleasing by the fear of being caught, the staircases descended four at a time, all that forms part of love. But at our age what we desire more than anything else is peace, what the philosophers call security in pleasure. Only marriage gives that."

He got up with a start, threw down his napkin: "Let's be off, *té!*"

"We're going?" asked Bompard, impassive.

"To pass under her window, like twelve years ago. That's the point he has reached, my dear chap, the Grand Master of the University."

Under the arches of the Place Royale, the friends walked a long time.

"To think she's there," sighed Roumestan, "so near, and that I can't see her!"

Bompard was shivering, with his feet in the slush, did not understand clearly this sentimental excursion. To put an end to it, he used a trick, and knowing him to be a molly-coddle, frightened at the least symptom of illness—

"You'll catch cold, Numa," he traitorously suggested.

The Southerner was afraid, and they got back into the carriage.

She was there, in the drawing-room where he had seen her the first time and whose furniture remained the same in the same places, having reached the age when furniture, like character, does not renew itself any more. Perhaps a few faded folds in the tawny hangings, a mist on the brilliance of the mirrors as

on desert pools which nothing disturbs. The faces of the old parents bending beneath the two-branched lamps, in company with their habitual partners, had also something more worn out about them. Mme. Le Quesnoy, with her features swollen and sagging, as if defibred, the President accentuating yet more his pallor and the proud revolt he kept in the bitter blue of his eyes. Seated near a large armchair whose cushions were hollowed by a slight impression, Rosalie, her sister having gone to bed, was continuing in a low voice the reading which she had only just been doing out loud, amid the silence of a game of whist, interrupted by the half-words, the exclamations of the players. It was a book of her youth, one of the poets of nature whom her father had taught her to love; and from the white of the strophes she saw rising her whole past as a young woman, the fresh and penetrating impression of the first reading.

La belle aurait pu sans souci
Manger ses fraises loin d'ici,
Au bord d'une claire fontaine,
Avec un joyeux moissonneur
Qui l'aurait prise sur son cœur.
Elle aurait eu bien moins de peine.

The book slipped from her hands to her knees, the last verses resounding in sad harmony with the deepest of her being, reminding her of her misfortune which for a moment had been forgotten. That is the cruelty of poets; they soothe you, they calm you, then with a single phrase they quicken the wound they were about to heal.

She saw herself again at this spot, twelve years before, when Numa was paying her court, and when adorned with her twenty years, with the desire of being beautiful for him, she saw him coming by that window, just as one watches one's fate. There remained in every corner echoes of his warm, tender voice, so ready at lying. With a little search among the music lying on the piano, she could have found the duets they sang together; and all her surroundings seemed to her to have conspired in the disaster of her failure in life. She pondered over what it might have been, that life, beside an honourable man, a loyal companion, not a brilliant, ambitious life, but simple and obscure, in which they would have valiantly borne together their sorrows, their mournings, even to death—

Elle aurait eu bien moins de peine.

She was so absorbed in her thoughts that, when the whist was over, the habitual guests had gone away without her having almost observed it, as she replied mechanically to the friendly and compassionate greeting of each, not noticing that the President, instead of accompanying his friends to the door, as he was in the habit of doing every night whatever the weather or season, was walking with long strides up and down the drawing-room, stopped at last in front of her to question her in a voice that made her suddenly tremble. "Well, my child, what have you arrived at? What is your decision?"

"But always the same, father."

He sat down by her, took her hand, tried to be persuasive.

"I've seen your husband. He consents to everything. You'll live here with me the whole time your mother and sister are away; afterwards also if your resentment still lasts. But I say again, these proceedings are impossible. I venture to hope you won't go on with them."

Rosalie shook her head.

"You don't know the man, father. He will use his cunning to envelop me, to get me back, to make a dupe of me, a voluntary dupe, accepting a degraded existence, without dignity. Your daughter is not one of those women. I wish for a complete irreparable rupture, proclaimed aloud to the world."

From the table where she was putting the cards in order, Mme. Le Quesnoy intervened gently, without turning—

"Forgive, my child, forgive."

"Yes, it's easy to say so when one has a loyal, straightforward husband like yours, when one does not know the stifling atmosphere of lies and treachery around one. He's a hypocrite, I tell you. He has his Chambéry morals and his Rue de Londres morals. Words and deeds always conflicting. Two words, two faces. All the catlike nature and seductiveness of his race. A man of the South, in fact!"

And forgetting herself in an outburst of anger—

"Besides, I had already forgiven once. Yes, two years after my marriage. I didn't tell you about it. I didn't tell any one about it. I was very unhappy. We then only remained together after he had sworn an oath. But he only lives on perjuries. Now, it's finished, finished once and for all."

The President no longer insisted, got up slowly and came to his wife. There was a whispering like an argument, surprising, between the authoritative man and the humble, annihilated creature, his wife: "She must be told. Yes—yes —I want you to tell her." Without another word, M. Le Quesnoy went out, and his sonorous, regular footstep, as on every night, echoed up from the deserted arches to the solemnity of the great drawing-room.

"Come here," said the mother to her daughter with an affectionate gesture, "Nearer, still nearer." She would never venture on it in a loud voice. And even, when so near, heart against heart, she still hesitated—"Listen, he wishes it. He wants me to tell you that your fate is that of all women, and that your mother has not escaped it."

Rosalie was frightened by that confidence which she guessed at the first words, whilst a dear old voice, broken with tears, spelt out with difficulty a sad, very sad story in every respect similar to her own, the husband's adultery in the first days of marriage, as if the device of these poor coupled beings were "deceive me or I'll deceive you," and the man hastened to begin so as to keep his superior rank.

"Oh! enough, enough, mama, you are hurting me."

Her father whom she admired so much, whom she set above every one else, the upright, firm magistrate! She who had not wept for her husband's treachery, felt a flood of tears at this humiliation of her father. And they reckoned on it to overcome her! No, a hundred times no, she would not pardon. Ah! that was marriage, was it? Well, all the more shame and contempt for marriage! What mattered the fear of scandal and the convention of society, since the point was who would brave them the best?

Her mother had taken her, pressed her against her heart, trying to quiet the revolt of this young conscience wounded in its beliefs, in its dearest superstitions, and gently she fondled, as if rocking her.

"Yes, you will pardon—you will do as I did. It's our lot, you see. Ah! at the first moment I, too, I had a great grief, a great longing to jump out of the window. But I thought of my child, my poor little André who was born, who grew up after, who died laughing, respecting all his family. You likewise, you will pardon in order that your child may enjoy the happy calm which my courage procured you, in order that he may not be one of those half-orphans whom the parents share, whom they bring up in hatred and contempt the one of the other. You will reflect also that your father and your mother have already suffered much and that other despairs are threatening them."

She stopped, overwhelmed. Then in solemn accents—

"My daughter, all griefs become appeased, all wounds may heal. There is only one irreparable misfortune, that is the death of those whom one loves."

In the state of emotional exhaustion that followed the last words, Rosalie saw her mother's face growing the greater by all that her father was losing in her eyes. She was angry with herself at having misunderstood her so long under the apparent weakness resulting from blows of anguish, from sublime and resigned self-renunciation. And accordingly it was to obey her, and to obey only her, that in gentle words, almost of forgiveness, she abandoned her proceedings of vengeance.

'Only don't ask me to go back to him. I should be too ashamed. I shall accompany my sister to the South. Afterwards, later, we shall see."

The President returned. He saw the impulsive affection of the old mother throwing her arms round her child's neck and understood that their cause was won.

"Thanks, my daughter," he murmured, deeply touched. Then, after hesitating a little, he approached Rosalie for the usual "good-night." But the forehead so affectionately offered as a rule was not offered to be caressed, the kiss slipped into her hair.

"Good-night, my father."

He said nothing, went away with bent head, with a convulsive shudder of his high shoulders. He who in his life had accused so much, condemned so much, he found a judge in his turn, the first magistrate of France!

CHAPTER XIX

A PRETTY VOICE

By one of those sudden dramatic strokes, so frequent in Parliamentary comedy, the meeting of January 8, at which Roumestan's lucky star seemed bound to set, turned out a famous triumph. When he mounted the tribune to reply to Rougeot's hard-hitting satire on the management of the Opéra, the scandal about the Beaux-Arts, the emptiness of the reforms so loudly clarioned forth, Numa had just learned that his wife had gone away, renouncing all proceedings, and the good news, known to himself alone, gave an effulgent assurance to his answer. He showed himself disdainful, familiar, solemn, made allusions to whispered calumnies, to the expected scandal— "There will be no scandal, gentlemen!"

And the tone in which he said it caused lively disappointment, in the tribunes crowded with toilettes, to all the pretty inquisitives, greedy of strong emotions, who had come there to witness the devouring of the tamer. Rougeot's interpellation was reduced to rags, the South seduced the North, Gaul was once more conquered, and when Roumestan went down again, exhausted, voiceless, he had the pride of seeing his party, which recently was so cold, almost hostile, his colleagues in the cabinet who accused him of compromising them, surround him with acclamations, with enthusiastic flatteries. And in the intoxication of the success there always recurred to him, as a supreme deliverance, his wife's renunciation.

He felt satisfied with all the world, calmed down, expansive, so much so that on returning to Paris he had the idea of going to the Rue de Londres. Oh! only as a friend, to comfort the poor child who was as uneasy as himself at the consequences of the interpellation, and who endured their mutual exile with so much courage, sent him in her naïve handwriting dried with rice-powder nice little letters in which she told him about her daily life, exhorted him to patience, to prudence.

"No, no, don't come, poor dear— write to me, think of me—I shall be strong."

It just happened there was no performance at the Opéra that night, and during the short drive from the station to the Rue de Londres, whilst clasping in his hand the little key that had tempted him more than once during the past fortnight, Numa was thinking—

"How happy she will be!"

The door being opened and shut without noise, he found himself suddenly in darkness; the gas had not been lit. This negligence lent the little house an aspect of mourning, of widowhood, which flattered him. The carpet on the staircase deadening his steps as he quickly went up, he arrived without anything to proclaim his presence, in the drawing-room adorned with Japanese stuffs in deliciously false shades to suit the factitious gold of the little one's hair.

"Who's there?" asked a pretty, irritated voice from the divan.

"I, *pardi!*"

There was a cry, and leap, and in the twilight the singer got up, frightened, whilst the handsome Lappara, motionless, overcome, stared at the flowers of the carpet so as not to meet his chief's eyes. Nothing could be denied.

"Dirty scamps!" said Roumestan in his throat, strangled by one of those furies in which the beast roars in the man with the desire of tearing to pieces, of biting, rather than of striking.

He found himself outside without knowing it, carried away by fear of his own violence. At the same place, at the same time, some days before, his wife had received, like him, a treacherous blow, an outraging, dastardly wound, cruel in another way, undeserved in another way than his own; but he did not think of it an instant, being absorbed in indignation at the personal insult. No, never had such villainy been seen under the sun. That Lappara whom he loved like a son, that creature of a singer for whom he had

compromised even his political fortunes!

"A dirty lot!—a dirty lot!" he repeated out loud in the lonely street, under a penetrating drizzle which calmed him more effectively than the finest reasonings.

"*Té!* but I am drenched!"

He ran to the cab-rank in the Rue d'Amsterdam.

Instead of the rest he reckoned on taking when he returned, a fresh blow awaited him at the ministry, a telegram which Méjean had opened in his absence and which he handed to him, greatly agitated.

"Hortense is dying. She wishes to see you. Come quickly. Portal."

All his fearful selfishness was vented in a desolate cry—

"I shall lose a being devoted to me!"

Next he thought of his wife who was present at the death agony and let Aunt Portal sign the message. Her resentment was not abated, would probably never be abated. But if she had only wished it, how he would have begun life again by her side, cured of imprudent follies, a family man, honourable, almost austere! And thinking no more of the harm he had done her, he reproached her for her hardness as an injustice. He spent the night in correcting the proofs of his speech, interrupting himself to write sketches of letters, furious or ironical, scolding and hissing, to that rascally Alice Bachellery. Méjean, too, was awake at the secretariate, eaten up with sorrow, seeking forgetfulness in excessive work; and Numa, tempted by his being near, felt a real punishment at not being able to tell him of his deception. But it would have been necessary to confess he had returned to the woman and the ridiculousness of his part in the drama.

He did not, however, stick to his point; and in the morning, when his chief of cabinet accompanied him to the station, he left him among other instructions the business of dismissing Lappara. "Oh! He's expecting it right enough. I caught him red-handed in an act of the blackest ingratitude. When I think how kind I have been to him, even to the extent of wanting to make him—" He broke off short. Was he not about to relate to the lover that he had promised the hand of Hortense twice? Without further explanation, he declared he did not wish to meet again at the ministry so sadly immoral a character. For the rest, the duplicity of the world disheartened him. Ingratitude, egoism. It was enough to make anybody throw up the whole thing, honours, affairs, to make him leave Paris and become the keeper of a lighthouse on a wild rock, in the open sea.

"You've slept badly, my dear chief," said Méjean with his quiet air.

"No, no—it's as I told you—Paris gives me the nausea."

Standing on the departure platform, he turned with a gesture of disgust towards the great city where the provinces pour out all their ambitions, their covetousnesses, their seething and filthy excess, and which they then accuse of perversity and infection.

Roumestan got into his carriage, pierced to the bones by the cold of his sleepless night, shivering as he saw at the windows the gloomy prospects of the *faubourg*, the iron bridges over wet streets, the high houses, barracks of miserable poverty, with innumerable windows furnished with rags, those morning faces, haggard, mournful, sordid, those bent backs, those arms clasped round the chest for concealment or for warming, those publichouses with all kinds of signboards, that forest of factory chimneys spewing forth their heavy smoke. He closed his eyes at the sight of that heartrending Northern winter, which the whistle of the train traversed with long calls of distress; but beneath his shut eyelids his thoughts were not more smiling. Whilst so close to that beast of a woman, the severing of his bond with whom still stabbed his heart, he thought of what he had done for her, of what the keeping of a "star" for six months had cost him. Everything is false in theatre life, especially the success which is not worth buying. Expenses of the *claque*, management tickets, dinners, receptions, presents for the reporters, publicity in all its forms, and those magnificent bouquets at which the artiste blushes, is stirred with emotion as she loads her arms, her bare breast, the satin of her dress; and the ovations, the escorts to the hotel, the serenades at the balcony, those continual stimulants of the dull indifference of the public, all that had to be paid for and very costly it is. For six months he had kept his purse open, never haggling with the little one about her triumphs.

He ended by going to sleep, his features drawn with disgust, with fatigue, his whole body shaken by the rushes, by the metallic leaps of an express going at full speed.

"*Valeince! Valeince!*"

He opened his eyes again, like a child whom its mother is calling. The South was already beginning, the sky was hollowed by blue abysses between the clouds which the wind drove away. A sunbeam warmed the glass, and some meagre olive trees whitened among the pines. There was a calming in the Southerner's whole sensitive being, a change of Pole in his ideas. He was sorry he had been so hard to Lappara. To spoil in that way the poor young man's future, to distress a whole family, and why? "An escapade, come now!" as Bompard said.

There was only one way of reparation, of removing any appearance of disgrace from this dismissal from the ministry—the Cross. And the minister began laughing at the idea of the name of Lappara in the *Officiel* with the mention, *exceptional services*. It was one, after all, to have delivered his chief from a degrading *liaison*.

Orange! Montélimar and its *nougat!* The voices vibrated, emphasized with lively gestures. The waiters at the buffet, the newspaper hawkers, the inspectors were rushing about, their eyes staring out of their heads. They were certainly a different people from those thirty leagues higher up; and the Rhône, the broad Rhône, billowy as the sea, glittered beneath the sun which gilded the crenelated ramparts of Avignon whose bells, working since Rabelais's time, greeted with their clear carillons the great man of Provence. Numa sat down at a buffet table with a small white roll, a croustade, a bottle of that wine of La Nerte ripened between the rocks, which is capable of giving even a Parisian a Southern accent.

But where his native air revived him most was when, having left the main line at Tarascon, he took his seat in the small, patriarchal, single-lined railway, which penetrates the heart of Provence between the branches of mulberry and olive trees, whilst the flowers of wild rose bushes brush against the windows. There was singing in all the carriages, they stopped every instant to let a flock of sheep pass, to get a laggard on board, to take a package which a farm-hand was bringing at a run. And there were greetings, gossipings between the people in the train and the farmers' wives in Arles coifs, on the steps of their doors or washing with soap on the stone of the well. At the stations there were cries, hustling, a whole village gathered together as escort to a conscript or to a girl who is going out to service in the town.

"*Té! vé*, good-bye, darling—be very brave now, come!"

They weep, they kiss.

Leaning back in his carriage to escape ovations, Roumestan enjoyed himself at all this good humour, at the sight of those brown faces lit up with passion and irony, of those tall, knowing-looking youths, of those women coloured like the long grains of the muscat, who would become, as they grew old, similar to those grandmothers there, black and dried up by the sun, shaking off some dust of the tomb at each of their emphatic gestures. He found his people again there, his mobile and nervous Provence, a race of brown crickets, always at the door, and always singing!

He was himself the prototype of them, already cured of his deep despair of the morning, of his disgusts, of his love, swept away at the first breath of the mistral which blew strong in the Rhône valley, lifting the train, checking its advance, driving everything before it, the trees bent in an attitude of flight, the Alpilles retreating in the distance, the sun shaken by sudden eclipses, whilst afar off the town of Aps, under a ray of whipped light, grouped its monuments at the foot of the ancient tower of the Antonines, even as a herd of oxen in the middle of Camargue gathers round the oldest bullock, so as to make headway against the wind.

And it was to the sound of that grandiose fanfare of the mistral that Numa made his entry into the station. From a feeling of delicacy equivalent to his own, the family had kept his coming secret, in order to avoid the orpheons, banners, solemn deputations. Aunt Portal was waiting alone for him, pompously installed in the station-master's armchair, a foot-warmer under her feet. As soon as she caught sight of her nephew, the pink face of the fat lady, which had expanded during his rest, took on a desolate expression; and stretching out her arms, she burst into sobs and laments.

"Aïe de nous, what misfortune! Such a pretty little one, péchère! And so brave! so gentle! that one would have taken the bread out of one's mouth for her."

"Mon Dieu! Is it over then?" thought Roumestan, recalled to the reality of his journey.

Under the bare trees of the Avenue Berchère, amid a whirlwind of branch and dry pieces of bark which the mistral hurled at the illustrious traveller, the horses advanced slowly; and Ménicle, at the turning where the porters were in the habit of unharnessing them. was obliged to crack his whip several times,

so surprised seemed his animals by this indifference to the great man. Roumestan himself only thought of the horrible news he had just learnt; and holding his aunt's doll-like hands, who continued wiping her eyes, he asked softly—

"When did it happen?"

"What?"

"When did she die, the poor little thing?"

Aunt Portal bounded on her piled-up cushions.

"Dead! Bou Diou! Who told you she was dead?"

She immediately added with a deep sigh—

"Only, péchère, she can't last long."

Oh! no, not very long. She did not get up now, she did not leave her lace pillows any more, on which her shrunken little head became daily less recognizable, her cheeks glowing with a hectic spot, her eyes, her nostrils darkened with a blue tint. Her ivory hands stretched out on the cambric of the bed-clothes, near her a small comb, a mirror for brushing her beautiful brown hair from time to time. She remained for hours without speaking, owing to the painful hoarseness of her voice, her eyes gazing abstractedly towards the tops of trees, the dazzling sky of the old garden of the Portal house.

That night her dreamy motionlessness lasted so long, under the flames of the setting sun which empurpled the room, that her sister grew disquieted

"Are you sleeping?"

Hortense shook her head, as if to drive away something.

"No. I wasn't sleeping: and yet ?

was dreaming—I dreamt I was going to die. I was just on the borders of this world, leaning towards the other—oh! leaning and about to fall. I still saw you and bits of my room; but I was already on the other side, and what struck me was the silence of life compared with the great noise made by the dead. The noise of a beehive, of beating wings, the roar the sea leaves at the bottom of big shells. As if death was peopled, encumbered in a different way from life. And that so intense, it seemed to me that my ears heard for the first time, that I was discovering a new sense for myself."

She spoke slowly with her raucous, hissing voice. After a silence, she went on with the utmost vivacity of which the broken, worn-out instrument was capable.

"My head's always travelling. First prize for imagination, Hortense Le Quesnoy, of Paris!"

They heard a sob, stifled in the noise of a door shutting.

"You see," said Rosalie, "that's mama going away. You give her pain."

"On purpose—every day a little—so that she may have less all at one time," replied the girl in a whisper. Through the great passages of the old provincial house the mistral was galloping, groaning under the doors, shaking them with furious blows. Hortense smiled.

"D'you hear? Oh! I like that. It seems to me I'm far off—in different countries! Poor darling," she added, taking her sister's hand and carrying it with an exhausted gesture to her mouth, "what a bad turn I have done you without intending it. There's your baby who will belong to the South

through my fault. You will never forgive it me, *Franciote.*"

Amid the howling of the wind, a locomotive whistle came to her ears, made her quiver.

"Ah! the seven o'clock train."

Like all sick persons, all captives, she knew the least noises of the environment, mingled them with her motionless existence, like the horizon in front of her, the pine woods, the old Roman tower outlined on the hill. From this moment she was anxious, agitated, watching the door at which a servant at last appeared.

"That's right," said Hortense in a lively way, smiling at her elder sister. "One minute, will you? I'll call you."

Rosalie thought it was the visit of a priest bringing his parochial Latin with him and his terrifying consolations. She went down to the garden, a Southern enclosure, without flowers, with alleys shaded by high resisting cypresses. Since she had been nurse, she had gone there to breathe the fresh air, to hide her tears, to relax all the nervous concentrations of her grief. Oh! how well she understood now her mother's words.

"There is only one irreparable misfortune, it is the loss of what one loves."

Her other grief, her destroyed happiness as a wife, all vanished. She only thought of that horrible, inevitable thing, nearer day by day. Was this the hour, this red, fugitive sun which left the garden in the shadow and lingered at the windows of the house, that sorrowful wind blowing from on high, which could be heard without going out? At that moment she endured a sadness, an anguish inexpressible. Hor-

tense, her Hortense! more than a sister
for her, almost a son, her first joys of
precocious motherhood. Sobs stifled
her, without tears. She would have
wished to cry out, to call for help, but
whom? The heavens, to which the desperate look, was so high, so far, so cold,
as if polished by the hurricane. A
flight of travelling birds was hastening
there, whose cries and sail-like creaking of wings one could not hear. How
could a voice from the earth reach
those mute, indifferent depths?

There was a call from the house. She
ran up trembling, having reached that
state of nervous fear in which the least
noise re-echoes even to the inmost of
one's being. With a smile the sick
woman drew her near the bed, having
no more any strength or voice, as if
she had just been talking a long time.

"I have a favour to ask you, my
darling. You know, that last favour
which is granted to one who is condemned to death. Forgive your husband. He has been wicked, unworthy
with you but be indulgent, return to
him. Do that for me, my big sister,
for our parents whom your separation
desolates and who will have need for
people to gather closely round them,
for them to surround them with loving
affection. Numa is so full of life, he
alone will be able to cheer them up a
little. It's finished, isn't it? You forgive?"

Rosalie answered: "I promise it you."
What availed this sacrifice of her pride,
at the cost of irreparable misfortune?
Standing near the bed she closed her
eyes a moment, drinking her tears. A
hand that trembled was placed on hers.
He was there before her, agitated,

piteous, tortured by a need of affec
tion he dared not show.

"Kiss each other!" said Hortense.

Rosalie offered her forehead, and
there Numa timidly put his lips.

"No, no—not like that—with open
arms, like people who love each other."

He took hold of his wife, pressed her
close to him with a long sob, whilst
night fell in the large room, out of pity
for her who had thrown them into one
another's arms. It was her last sign of
life. Afterwards she remained absorbed,
distracted, indifferent to all that happened around her, without answering
those griefs at departure to which there
is no answer, retaining on her young
face the expression of sullen, haughty
rancour characteristic of those who die
too early for their ardour of living, and
to whom the disillusions of life had
not said their last word.

CHAPTER XX

A BAPTISM

THE great day in Aps is Monday,
market day.

Well before dawn the roads leading
to the town, those deserted highways
of Arles and Avignon where the dust
looks calm as a fall of snow, are stirred
by the slow creaking of wagons, the
cackling of fowls, the barking of dogs,
the bleating of sheep, the shouts of
oxherds panting after their beasts.
Then, on awaking, the town finds itself
occupied on every side by a huge, animated, noisy market, as if the whole
of rural Provence, men and cattle, fruit
and grains, had risen, assembled together in a nocturnal inundation.

On the morning in question, the third
Monday in February, the animation was

lively and the crowd compact as on the finest days in summer, an illusion of which was given by a cloudless sky, gilded by a hot sun. People were talking, gesticulating in groups; but there was less question of buying and selling than of an event which suspended the traffic, turned all looks, all heads towards the church of Sainte-Perpétue. The rumour had just spread in the market, where it caused extraordinary emotion, that on this very day was being baptized Numa's baby boy, that little Roumestan whose birth three weeks before had been welcomed by transports of joy in Aps and in all the Provençal South.

Unfortunately the baptism, delayed on account of the deep family mourning, was bound, for the same reasons of seemliness, to remain of an incognito character; and had it not been for some old witches of the district of the Baux who establish every Monday on the steps of Sainte-Perpétue a little market of aromatic herbs, of dried and perfumed simples culled in the Alpilles, the ceremony would probably have passed unnoticed. On seeing Aunt Portal's carriage stop at the church, the old saleswomen gave the word to the aïet-sellers who wander about everywhere, from one end to the other of the Cours, their arms laden with their gleaming chaplets. The aïet-sellers told the fishdealers, and soon the little streets leading to the church poured upon the Place all the noise, all the excitement of the market. They pressed round Ménicle, sitting upright on his seat, in deep mourning, crape on arm and hat, who answered questions by a dumb and indifferent play of the shoulders. In spite of all, they persisted in waiting,

and under the calicot bands stretched across the marketing street, they piled themselves on each other, stifled each other, the boldest mounting on stone pillars, all eyes fixed on the big door, which at last opened.

There was an "Ah!" as at a firework display, triumphant, modulated, then cut short by the sight of a tall old man, dressed in black, exceedingly haggard, exceedingly mournful for a god-father, giving his arm to Mme. Portal, who was very proud at having served as godmother with the First President, their names united on the parochial register, but who was sombre in feeling from her recent mourning and the sad impressions she had just received again in the church. There was a deception of the crowd in the aspect of that severe-looking couple, who were followed, all in black, too, and gloved, by the great man of Aps, chilled by the loneliness and cold of that baptism between four wax-tapers, without other music than the whinings of the baby on whom the Latin of the Sacrament and the lustral water on its tender little head, as of a plicked bird, had made the most disagreeable impression. But the appearance of a buxom nurse, broad, heavy, be-ribboned like a prize animal at a cattle-show, and the bright little parcel of lace and white embroideries which she dandled in her arms dissipated the spectator's depression, gave rise to a fresh outcry as at a mounting rocket, a cheery mirthfulness scattered in a thousand enthusiastic exclamations.

"Lou vaqui, there he is—vé! vé!"

Surprised, dazzled, blinking in the sun, Roumestan stopped a moment on the high perron to look at those brown faces, whence a wild emotion of affection rose up to him; and though used to ovations, he felt one of the liveliest emotions in his existence as a publicist, a proud intoxication which was ennobled by a quite new and already very vibrating sentiment of fatherhood. He was going to speak, then reflected that that was not the place for it.

"Get in, nurse," he said to the quiet Burgundian whose milch-cow-like eyes were opened in bewilderment, and whilst she engulfed herself with her light burden in the carriage, he told Ménicle to drive back quickly by the side street. But an immense clamour was the reply.

"No, no—the grand tour—the grand tour."

The market was to be traversed through all its length.

"Well, then, the grand tour!" said Roumestan, after having consulted with his eyes his father-in-law, for whom he would have wished an avoidance of this merry-making part; and the carriage moving on with loud creakings of its ancient carcass entered the street, on the Cours, amid the vivats of the crowd which warmed up at its own outcries, reached a delirium of enthusiasm, checked at every moment the movement of the horses and the wheels. The windows being lowered, they went at a foot pace, among acclamations, the raising of hats, the waving of handkerchiefs, and the odours, the hot breaths of the market that arose as they passed on. The women thrust forward their fiery, bronzed heads, even into the carriage, and after merely having seen the clothes of the baby exclaimed—

"*Diou! lou bèu drôle!* Heavens! the lovely child!"

"He's like his father, *qué!*"

"Already his Bourbon nose and his kind manners!"

"Show it, my dear, show it; your lovely man's face."

"He's pretty as an egg."

"You could drink him in a glass of water."

"*Té!* my treasure."

"My partridge."

"My lambkin."

"My fine pearl."

And they enveloped him, licked him with the brown flame of their eyes. He, a month-old baby, was not at all frightened. Awakened by the noise, resting on his red-ribboned cushion, he looked on with his cat's eyes, the pupil dilated and staring, with two drops of milk at the corners of his lips, and remained calm, visibly happy at those appearances of heads at the windows, at those growing shouts and noises. Whilst all in the carriage were holding their hands to their ears, the tiny man remained impassive, and his coolness made even the old President smile as he said: "If that baby is not born for the forum."

They hoped to be quit of the affair on leaving the market, but the crowd followed, swelled by the weavers of the Chemin-Neuf, bands of factory women, porters of the Avenue Berchère. The merchants ran to the doorsteps of their shops, the balcony of the White Club was filled with people, and soon the orpheons with banners debouched from all the streets, intoning choruses, fanfares, as if Numa had just arrived, together with something gayer, something improvised, beyond the usual festival.

In the finest room in the Porta house, whose white woodwork, whose silks dated back a century, Rosalie, reclining on an easy-chair, gazing from the empty cradle to the lonely, sunny street, was impatiently expecting her child's return. On her refined features, bloodless, hollowed with fatigue and tears, in which there nevertheless appeared, as it were, a happy calm, one could read the story of her life during the last months, anxieties, agonies, her rupture with Numa, the death of her Hortense, and finally the birth of the child, which surpassed everything. When this great happiness had come to her, she no longer was reckoning on it, broken by so many blows, thinking herself unable to give life to anything. During the last days she fancied she no longer felt the impatient movements of the little imprisoned being; and she hid the cradle, the "layette," which was all ready, from a superstitious fear, telling only the Englishwoman who served her: "If you are asked for baby's clothes, you'll know where to get them."

At last, after a bed of torture, her eyes shut, her teeth clenched, after long hours broken every five minutes by a harrowing cry, half-killed, she heard that attempt at a voice, that crying respiration, that call to the light, of the child which is born. She answered it, oh! with what overflowing tenderness.

"My little one!"

He was alive. They brought him to her. To her belonged that tiny creature with the short breath, dazed, bewildered, almost blind; that thing of flesh attached her again to existence, and merely by pressing it against her, the whole fever of her body was drowned in a feeling of comforting freshness. No more mourning, no more wretchedness! Her child, her boy, that desire, that regret she had endured for ten years, which burnt her eyes with tears when she looked at others' children, that baby she had kissed beforehand on so many darling pink cheeks! He was there and caused her a new rapture, a surprise, each time she leaned from her bed towards the cradle, parted the muslin resting on the slumbering child with its scarcely audible breathing. She wanted it always near her. When it went out she was restless, counted the minutes, but never with such anguish as on that baptism morning.

"What time is it?" she asked every moment. "How late they are! Heavens! how long it is."

Mme. Le Quesnov, who had remained with her daughter, reassured her, though herself a little anxious, for this grandson, the first, the only one, was very strongly bound up with the hearts of the grandparents, brightened their mourning with a hope.

A distant uproar, which was approaching, redoubled the women's disquiet.

They go and see, they listen. Songs, detonations, shouts, bell-ringing. And suddenly the Englishwoman, who was looking outside, exclaimed—

"Madame, it's the baptism!"

It was the baptism, that uproarious tumult, those cannibalistic howlings round a warrior's meal.

"Oh! that South—that South!" repeated the frightened young mother. She trembled lest they should stifle her baby in the midst of them.

But no. There he was, very much

alive, in splendid condition, moving his short little arms, his eyes wide open in the long baptismal robe.

"He didn't cry once, nor take the breast once the whole way;" affirms Aunt Portal, who relates in her flowery way the triumphant circuit of the town, whilst the old *hôtel* becomes again the house of ovations, and the servants hasten to the porch to serve the musicians with "something gassy." Trumpets blare forth, windows shake. The old Le Quesnoys have gone down into the garden, far from that merry-making which rends their hearts; and as Roumestan is about to speak on the balcony, Aunt Portal, and English Polly go quickly into the drawing-room to hear him.

"If madame would kindly hold the baby!" asks the nurse, who is inquisitive as a woman of the wilds, and Rosalie is quite happy to be alone, her baby on her knees. From her window she sees the banners gleaming in the wind, the close-packed crowd, intent upon the words of its great man. Some words of the speech reach her in snatches; but she hears especially the *timbre* of that captivating, stirring voice, and a painful shudder passed through her at the memory of all the evil that has come to her from that eloquence which is skilled to lie and to dupe.

At present, it is over; she feels herself sheltered from deception and wounds. She has a child. That sums up all her happiness, all her dreams. And making herself a buckler of the dear little creature, whom she presses over her breast, she asks him in a low voice, quite close, as if she sought an answer or a resemblance of one in that little shapeless face, those slight lineaments which seem impressed by a caress in wax and already indicate a sensual violent mouth, a nose curved for adventure, a dimpled, square chin.

"Will you be a liar, you too? Will you spend your life in betraying others and yourself, in breaking simple hearts which shall have done no other harm than to believe in you and love you? Will you be light-heartedly and cruelly fickle, taking life as a virtuoso, as a singer of cavatinas? Will you make a traffic in words, without disquieting yourself about their value, about their agreement with your thought, provided they shine and they sound?"

And her mouth kissing the little ear surrounded by wandering curls—

"Will you be a Roumestan, say?"

On the balcony, the orator was exciting himself, was gushing forth into the effusivenesses of which one could only hear the beginnings, emphasized in Southern manner: "My soul—My blood — Morality — Religion — Country" — punctuated by the hurrahs of an audience made in his image, which he summed up, in its qualities and in its vices, an effervescent, mobile South, tumultuous as a sea with many billows, each of which reflected it.

There was a last *vivat*, then the crowd was heard dispersing slowly. Roumestan entered the room wiping his forehead, and intoxicated with his triumph, warmed by the inexhaustible affection shown him by a whole people, approached his wife, kissed her with sincere effusion. He felt kind to her, tender as on the first day, without remorse as without rancour.

"*Bé!* Don't they fête him, monsieur your son!"

Kneeling by the canopy, the great man of Aps played with his child, looked for its little fingers which hold on to everything, its little feet beating the air. Rosalie looked at him, a fold on her forehead, trying to define that contradictory, inexplicable nature.

Then she observed in a lively tone, as if she had found out—

"Numa, what's that proverb of your race which Aunt Portal mentioned the other day?—'Joy of street'—what was the rest?"

"Ah! yes—'Gau de carriero, doulou d'oustau—Joy of street, grief of house.'"

"That's it," she said with a deep expression.

And dropping the words one by one like stones in an abyss, she repeated slowly, putting into it the complaint of her life, that proverb in which a whole race has been painted and fo mulated—

"Joy in street, grief in house."

La Belle Nivernaise

CHAPTER I

A RASH ACT

THE street Des Enfants-Rouges is in the Temple quarter—a very narrow street, with stagnant gutters and puddles of black mud, with foul water and mouldy smells pouring from its gaping passages The houses on each side are very lofty, and have barrack-like windows, that show no curtains behind their dirty panes. These are common lodging-houses, and dwellings of artisans, of day-laborers, and of men who work at their trade in their own rooms. There are shops on the ground floor; many pork-dealers, wine-retailers, vendors of chestnuts, bakers of coarse breads, butchers displaying viands of repulsive tints. In this street you see no carriages, no flounced gowns, no elegant loungers on the pavement; but there are costermongers crying the refuse of he market-places, and a throng of workmen crowding out of the factories with their blouses rolled up under their arms.

This is the eighth of the month, the day when poor people pay their rents, the day when landlords who are tired of waiting any longer turn Want out of doors. On this day you see removal carts going past with piles of iron bedsteads, torn mattresses, kitchen utensils, and lame tables rearing up their legs in the air; and with not even a handful of straw to pack the wretched things, damaged and worn out as they are by being knocked about on dirty staircases, and tumbled down from attic to basement.

It is now getting dark, and one after another the gas-lamps are lighted, and send their reflections from the gutters and the shop windows. The passers-by, however, hasten onward; for the fog is chilly.

But there, in a warm, comfortable wine-shop, is the honest old bargeman, Louveau, leaning against the counter, and taking a friendly glass with the joiner from La Villette. The bargeman's big, weather-beaten face dilates into a hearty laugh, that makes the copper rings in his ears shake again, as he exclaims:

"So it's settled, friend Dubac, that you take my load of timber at the price I have named."

"Agreed."

"Your good health."

"Here's to yours."

They clink their glasses together, and Louveau drinks with his head thrown back and his eyes half closed, smacking his lips in order to taste better the flavor of his white wine.

It can't be helped, look you, but every one has his failing; and white wine is the special weakness of our friend Louveau. Not that he is a drunkard. Far from it. Indeed, his wife, who is a woman of sense, would not allow fuddling; but when one has to live like our bargeman, with his feet in the water, and his pate in the sun, it is quite necessary to quaff off a glass now and then.

Louveau is getting more and more elated; and he smiles at the shining zinc counter—which he now sees rather indistinctly—for it brings to his mind the heap of new, bright coins he will pocket to-morrow when he delivers his timber.

After a parting glass, and a shake of the hands, our friends separate.

"To-morrow without fail?"

"You may depend on me."

Louveau, at least, will not fail to keep the appointment. The bargain is too good, and has been too hard driven for him to be behind.

So in high glee, our bargeman turns down towards the Seine, rolling his shoulders and elbowing his way along, with the exuberant delight of a schoolboy who has a franc piece in his pocket.

What will mother Louveau say—the wife with a head-piece—when she learns that her husband has sold his timber right off, and that at a good profit? Two or three more bargains like this, and then they can afford to buy a new boat and drop the *Belle Nivernaise,* for she is beginning to get much too leaky. Not that she is to blame for that, for she was a fine boat when she was new; only, you see, everything gets old and goes to decay; and Louveau himself feels that even he is not now as active as when he used to assist in steering the timber-rafts on the Marne.

But what is going on down there? The gossips are collected before a door, and people are stopping, and engaging in conversation, while the policeman standing in the middle of the gathering is writing something in his note-book. Like everybody else, our bargeman crosses the road to satisfy his curiosity,

and see whether a dog has been run over, or a vehicle has stuck fast, or a tipsy man has fallen into the gutter, or what other equally uninteresting event has occurred. Something different this time! A small child with disordered hair, and cheeks all over jam, is sitting on a wooden chair, rubbing his eyes with his hands, and crying. The tears that have streamed down his rather dirty face have left upon it fantastically shaped marks. The officer is questioning the little fellow, with a calm and dignified air, as if he were examining a prisoner, and he is taking notes of the answers.

"What is your name?"

"Totor."

"Victor What?"

No answer; only the poor little brat cried more, and sobbed "Mamma! Mamma!"

At this moment, a very plain and untidy woman of the laboring class was passing by, dragging her two children after her. She advanced through the group, and asked the police-officer to allow her to try what she could do. She knelt down, wiped the little fellow's nose, dried his eyes, and kissed his sticky cheeks.

"What is your mammy's name, my dear?"

He did not know. Then the policeman addressed himself to one of the neighbors:

"Now you should know something about these people, as you are the door-keeper."

No, he had never heard their name, and then there were so many tenants going backwards and forwards in the house. All that could be ascertained was that they had lived there for a month, that they had never paid a farthing of rent, that the landlord had just turned them out, and that it was a good riddance.

"What did they do?"

"Nothing at all."

The father and mother used to spend the day in drinking, and the evening in fighting. They never agreed together in anything, except in thrashing their other children, two lads that used to beg in the streets, and steal things there exposed for sale. A nice family, as you may believe.

"Do you think they will come to look for their child?"

"I am sure they will not."

The removal had, in fact, afforded them an opportunity of abandoning the child. That was not the first time such a thing had happened on the term days.

"Did nobody see the parents leaving?" asked the policeman.

Yes! they went away in the morning, the husband pushing the hand-cart, while his wife carried a package in her apron, and the two lads had nothing, but their hands in their pockets.

The passers-by, after indignantly exclaiming that these people should be caught, continued on their way.

The poor little brat had been there since noon, when his mother had set him in the chair and told him to "be good," and all that time he had been waiting. But when he began to cry for hunger, the fruit-woman over the way had given him a slice of bread with jam on it. This had long ago been devoured, and the little wretch was beginning to cry again.

The poor innocent, too, was nearly dying with fear. He was afraid of the dogs prowling round him—afraid of the night that was coming on—afraid of the strangers talking to him—and his little heart was beating violently in his bosom, like that of an expiring bird.

As the crowd round him continued to increase, the police officer, tired of the scene, took the child by the hand to lead him to the station.

"Come now; does anybody claim him?"

"Stop a moment!"

Every one turned round, and saw a great ruddy face wearing a silly smile that extended from one copper-ringed ear to the other.

"Stop a minute! if nobody wants him I will take him myself."

Loud exclamations burst from the crowd: "Well done,"—"That's right,"—"You are a good fellow."

Old Louveau, excited by the white wine, the success of his bargain, and the general approbation, stood with folded arms in the middle of the admiring circle.

"Oh, it's a simple matter."

Those who were curious went on with him to the police magistrate's, without letting his enthusiasm cool. When he got there he was asked the questions usual in such cases:

"Your name?"

"Francis Louveau, your Honor, a married man, and if I may say so, well married, to a wife with a head-piece. And that is lucky for me, your Honor, for you see I am not very clever myself, ha! ha! not very clever. I'm not an eagle. 'Francis is not an eagle,' my wife says."

He had never before been so eloquent, but now he felt his tongue loosened, and all the assurance of a man who had just concluded a good bargain

—anr who had drunk a bottle of white wine.

"Your occupation?"

"Bargeman, your Honor, master of the *Belle Nivernaise*, rather a rough boat, but manned by a smartish crew. Ah! now mine is a famous crew. . . . Ask the lock-keepers all the way from the Pont Marie to Clamecy. . . . Has your Honor ever been there, at Clamecy?"

The people about him were smiling, but Louveau went on, spluttering and clipping short his syllables.

"Well, now, Clamecy is a nice place, if you like! It's wooded from top to bottom; and with good wood, workable wood; all the joiners know that. . . . It is there I buy my timber. He! he! I am famous for my timber. I see a thing at a glance, look you! Not because I am clever; as my wife says, I am by no means an eagle: but in fact I do see a thing at a glance. . . . For instance, now, I take a tree as thick as you—asking your Honor's pardon—and I lap a string round it, this way. . . ."

He had drawn a cord from his pocket, and seizing hold of the officer standing by, had encircled him with it.

The officer struggled to disentangle himself:

"Please leave me alone."

"Yes . . . yes . . . I want to show his Honor how I pass the string round it, and then when I have the girth, I multiply it by . . . I multiply by . . . I forget now what I multiply by . . . My wife does the calculation. She has a good head-piece, has my wife."

The audience was highly amused, and the magistrate himself could not refrain from smiling behind his table. When the laughter had subsided a little, he asked:

"What will you make of this child?"

"Certainly not a gentleman. We have never had a gentleman in our family. But he shall be a bargeman, a smart barge lad, like the rest."

"Have you any children?"

"I should think I have! I have one able to walk, another at the breast, and there is a third one coming. That's not so bad, is it, for a man who is not an eagle? With this one there will be four; but pooh! where there is enough for three, there is enough for four. Packed a little closer, that's all. One must pull one's belt a little tighter and try to get more for one's wood."

And his laughter again shook the earrings, as he turned a complacent look on those present.

A big book was put before him, but as he could not write he had to sign with a cross.

The magistrate thereupon gave the lost child up to him.

"Take the little fellow away, Francis Louveau, and mind you bring him up well. If any inquiries are made about him, I will let you know. But it is not likely that his parents will ever claim him. As for you, you seem to be an honest man, and I have confidence in you. Always be guided by your wife; and now good-bye, and don't you take too much white wine."

A dark night, a cold fog, a lot of unconcerned people hurrying away home—that all tends to quickly bring a man to his senses.

Hardly had our bargeman got into the street by himself, leading by the hand the child he had taken under his care, and carrying his stamped document in his pocket, than he felt his enthusiasm suddenly cool down and he became aware of the serious import of his act.

Is he then always to be like this? Always to be a simpleton and a braggart? Why could not he go on his way like other people without meddling in what did not concern him?

Now, for the first time, he pictured to himself the wrath of mother Louveau. Just fancy the kind of reception he will meet with!

What a dreadful thing it is for a simple, kind-hearted man to have a shrewd wife! He would never have the courage to go home, and yet he dared not go back to the police magistrate's. Whatever should he do?

They went on through the fog, Louveau gesticulating and talking to himself. He was getting a speech ready.

Victor was dragging his shoes in the mud and letting himself be pulled along like a dead weight. At length, he could go no farther, and then Louveau stopped, lifted him up and carried him, wrapping his overall round him. The twining of the little arms round his neck caused our bargeman to resume his journey with a rather better heart.

Faith, bad as it was, he would run the risk. If mother Louveau turned them out, there would still be time to carry the little brat back to the police-office; but if she would keep him only for one night, he would be the gainer by a good meal.

They came to the Bridge of Austerlitz, where the *Belle Nivernaise* was moored, and the faint, pleasant odor from the loads of newly-cut wood filled the night air. A whole fleet of boats was rocking in the dark shade of the river's bank, and the movement of the water made the lamps swing and the chains grate together.

To get to his boat, Louveau had to pass over two lighters connected by planks. He went on with timid steps and trembling limbs, hampered by the hug of the child's arms about his neck.

The night was extremely dark, and the only signs of life about the *Belle Nivernaise* were the little lamp shining in the cabin window, and the ray of light that found its way beneath the door.

Mother Louveau's voice was heard chiding the children, while she was cooking the evening meal:

"Be quiet, Clara!"

It was now too late for retreat, and the bargeman pushed the door open. Mother Louveau had her back towards it, and was leaning over her frying-pan, but she knew his footstep, and without turning round, said:

"Is it you, Francis? How late you are in getting back!"

The frying potatoes were dancing about in the crackling oil; and as the steam from the pan passed towards the open door, it dimmed the panes of the cabin windows.

Francis had put the poor brat on the floor, and the little fellow, impressed by the warmth of the place, and feeling his reddened fingers restored to animation, smiled and said in a rather soft and sweet voice:

"Warm here. . . ."

Mother Louveau turned round, and, pointing to the ragged child standing in the middle of the room, asked her husband in angry tones:

"What is that?"

But even in the best of households there are such moments.

"A surprise for you, he! he! a surprise."

The bargeman grinned from ear to ear, in order to keep himself in countenance; but he very much wished that he was still in the street. However, as his wife was waiting for an explanation, and glaring at him with a dreadful look, he faltered out his story in a jumbled way, with the supplicating eyes of a dog threatened with the whip.

His parents had abandoned him, and he had found him crying on the pavement. Some one had asked if anybody would take him. He said he would. And the police magistrate had told him he might take him away.

"Didn't he, my child?"

Then the storm burst upon him:

"You are mad, or drunk! Did ever any one hear tell of such a piece of folly! I suppose you want us to die of starvation? Do you think we are too well off? That we have too much to eat? Too much room to lie in?"

Francis contemplated his shoes without answering a word.

"Think of yourself, you wretch and think of us! Your boat is holed like my skimmer, and yet you must go and amuse yourself by picking up other people's children out of the gutter!"

But the poor fellow knew all that too well already, and did not attempt to deny it. He bowed his head like a criminal listening to the statement of his guilt.

"You will do me the favor of taking that child back to the police magistrate, and if any objections are made about receiving him back again, you must say

that your wife won't have him. Do you understand?"

She advanced toward him, pan in hand, with a threatening gesture, and the bargeman promised to do all she wished.

"Come, now, don't get vexed. I thought I was doing right. I have made a mistake. That's enough. Must he be taken back at once?"

Her good man's submission softened mother Louveau's heart. Perhaps, also, there arose in her mind the vision of a child of her own, lost and alone at night, stretching out its hands towards the passers-by.

She turned to put her pan on the fire, and said in a testy tone:

"It cannot be done to-night, for the office is closed. And now that you have brought him, you cannot set him down again on the pavement. He shall remain to-night; but to-morrow morning. . ."

Mother Louveau was so enraged that she poked the fire first with one hand and then with the other.

"But I vow that to-morrow you shall rid me of him!"

There was silence.

The housewife laid the table savagely, knocking the glasses together, and dashing the forks down. Clara was frightened, and kept very quiet in one corner.

The baby was whining on the bed, and the lost child was looking with wonder at the cinders in the stove getting red hot. Perhaps he had never seen a fire in all his life before.

There was, however, another pleasure in store for him, when he was put to the table with a napkin round his neck, and a heap of potatoes on his plate. He ate like a robin-redbreast picking crumbs off the snow.

Mother Louveau helped him furiously, but at heart she was a little bit touched by the appetite of the starved child. Little Clara was delighted, and stroked him with her spoon. Louveau was dismayed and dared not lift an eye.

When she had removed the table things and put her children to bed, mother Louveau seated herself near the fire, and took the child between her knees to give him a little wash.

"We can't put him to bed in that dirty state."

I lay he had never before seen either sponge or comb. Under her hands the poor child twirled round like a top.

But when once he had been washed and tidied up, the little lad did not look bad, with his pink poodle-like nose, and hands as plump as rosy apples.

Mother Louveau looked upon her work with a certain degree of satisfaction.

"I wonder how old he is?"

Francis laid down his pipe, delighted once more to be an actor in the scene. This was the first time he had been spoken to all the evening, and a question addressed to him was almost like a recall to grace. He rose up and drew his cords from his pocket.

"How old? He! he! I'll tell you in a minute."

He took the little fellow in his arms, and wound lines round him as he did to the tree at Clamecy.

Mother Louveau looked on with amazement.

"Whatever are you doing?"

"I am taking his dimensions."

She snatched the cord from his hands, and flung it to the other end of the apartment.

"My good man, how silly you make yourself with these mad tricks! The child is not a young tree."

No chance for you, this evening, poor Francis! Quite abashed he beats a retreat, whilst mother Louveau puts the little one to bed in Clara's cot.

The little girl is sleeping with closed hands and taking up all the room. She is vaguely conscious that something is put beside her, stretches out her arms, pushes her neighbor into a corner, digs her elbows into his eyes, turns over and goes to sleep again.

In the meantime the lamp has been blown out, and the Seine rippling round the boat gently rocks the wooden habitation.

The poor cold child feels a gentle warmth steal over him, and he falls asleep with the new sensation of something like a caressing hand upon his head, just as his eyes are closing.

CHAPTER II

YES OR NO?

MADEMOISELLE CLARA used always to awake early, and this morning she was surprised at not seeing her mother in the cabin, and at finding another head on the pillow beside her. She rubbed her eyes with her little fingers, then took hold of her bedfellow by the hair and shook him.

Poor "Totor" was roused by the strangest sensations, for roguish fingers were teasing him by tickling his neck and seizing hold of his nose.

He cast his wondering eyes round about him, and was quite surprised that his dream still continued. Above them there was a creaking of footsteps, and a rumbling sound caused by the unloading of the planks upon the quay. Mademoiselle Clara seemed greatly perplexed. She pointed her little finger to the ceiling with a gesture that seemed to ask her friend:

"What is that?"

It was the delivery of the wood beginning. Dubac, the joiner from La Villette, had come at six o'clock with his horse and cart, and Louveau had very quickly set to work, with a hitherto unknown ardor.

The good fellow had not closed an eye all night for thinking that he would have to take that child, who had been so cold and hungry, back to the police-magistrate.

He expected to have a scene in the morning again; but mother Louveau had some other notions in her head, for she did not mention Victor to him; and Francis thought that much might be gained by postponing the time for explanations.

He was striving to efface himself, and to escape from his wife's view, and he was working with all his might, lest mother Louveau should see him idle, and should call out to him:

"Come now, as you have nothing to do, take the little boy back where you found him."

And he did work. The pile of planks was visibly diminishing. Dubac had already made three journeys, and mother Louveau, standing on the gangway with her nursling on her arm, had her time fully taken up counting the lots as they passed.

Working with a will, Francis selected for his burdens rafters as long as masts and as thick as walls. If the beam were too heavy, he called the Crew to help him to load.

The Crew was a boatman with a wooden leg, and he alone formed the personal equipment of the *Belle Nivernaise*. He had been picked up from charity, and retained from habit.

This maimed one would prop himself up on his peg, or raise up the log with great effort, and Louveau, bending beneath the load, with his belt tight round his waist, would pass slowly over the movable bridge.

How could a man so busily occupied be interrupted in his work? Mother Louveau could not think of it. She went up and down on the gangway, intent only on Mimile who was at her breast.

He was always thirsty, that Mimile, like his father. But Louveau, thirsty? . . . he certainly was not so to-day. He had been working since morning, and the question of white wine had never been raised. He had not even taken breathing time, or wiped his brow, or drunk a drop at the edge of a counter. Even when, after a little, Dubac proposed to go and have a glass, Francis heroically replied:

"We shall have time later on."

Refuse a glass! the housewife could not understand it at all; this could not be her Louveau, but must be some substitute.

Her Clara now seems a changeling also, for eleven o'clock has struck, and the little girl, who would never remain in bed, has not stirred the whole morning.

Mother Louveau hastens into the cabin to see what is going on. Francis remains on deck, swinging his arms, and gasping for breath, as if he had just received in his stomach a blow from a joist.

Now for it! His wife has bethought herself of Victor; she is going to bring him on deck, and he must start for the police office. . . . But no; mother Louveau reappears all alone. She is laughing and she beckons to him:

"Just come and look here, it is so funny!"

The good man cannot understand this sudden hilarity, and he follows her like an automaton, the fulness of his emotion almost depriving him of the use of his legs.

The two monkeys were sitting on the edge of the bed, in their shirts, and with bare feet. They had possessed themselves of the bowl of soup that the mother left within reach of their little arms when she got up. As there was only one spoon for the two mouths, they were cramming each other in turns, like fledglings in a nest; and Clara, who used always to be averse to taking her soup, was laughing and stretching out her mouth for the spoon. Although some crumbs of bread might have got into eyes or ears, the two babies had broken nothing, had upset nothing, and they were amusing themselves so heartily that it was impossible to find fault with them.

Mother Louveau continued to laugh.

"As they are agreeing so well as that, we need not trouble ourselves about them."

Francis immediately returned to his work, quite delighted with the turn things were taking.

Usually, at the unloading time, he would take a rest during the day; that is to say, he would go the round of all the bargemen's taverns, from the Point-

du-Jour to the Quai de Bercy so that the unloading used to drag on for a whole week, during which mother Louveau's wrath would continue unappeased.

But this time there was no idleness, no white wine, but a passionate desire to do well by ardent and sustained labor.

On his part the little fellow, as if he understood that his cause must be won, was doing all that he possibly could to amuse Clara.

For the first time in her life, this little girl passed a whole day without tears, without dashing herself about, without making holes in her stockings. Her companion amused her, soothed her. He was always willing to make a sacrifice of his hair to stop Clara's tears on the edges of her eyelids.

And she tugged at her big friend's rough poll by handfuls, teasing him like a pug-dog nipping a poodle.

Mother Louveau observed all this from a distance, and inwardly remarked that this child was just as useful as a little nurse. So they might keep Victor until the unloading was finished. There would be time to take him back afterwards, just before their departure.

For this reason, she did not that evening make any allusion to sending him back, but gorged him with potatoes and put him to bed as on the night before.

One would have thought that Louveau's little friend was a member of the family, and to see the way Clara put her arm round his neck as she went to sleep, would lead one to suppose that she had taken him under her special protection.

The unloading of the *Belle Nivernaise*

lasted three days. Three days of impetuous labor, without any relaxation, without any break. About midday the last cart was laden and the boat was empty.

They could not take the tug until the morrow, and Francis passed the whole day between decks, repairing the planks, but still haunted by those words that for three days had been ringing in his ears:

"Take him back to the police-magistrate."

Ah! that magistrate! He was not more dreaded in the house of wicked Mr. Punch than he was in the cabin of the *Belle Nivernaise*. He had become a kind of bogle that mother Louveau availed herself of to keep Clara quiet.

Every time she pronounced that name of fear, the little fellow fixed upon her the restless eyes of a child who has too early had experience of suffering.

He vaguely understood all that this word meant of dangers to come. The magistrate! That meant no more Clara, no more caresses, no more warmth, no more potatoes; but a return to a cheerless life, to days without bread, to slumbers without bed, to awakening in the morning without kisses.

How he therefore clung to mother Louveau's skirts on the eve of the boat's departure!—when Francis, in a trembling voice, asked:

"Come now, shall we take him back, yes or no?"

Mother Louveau did not answer. You would even fancy she was thinking of some pretext for keeping Victor.

As for Clara, she rolled on the floor, choking with sobs, and determined to have convulsions if she were separated from her friend.

Then the wife with a head-piece spoke seriously:

"My good man, you have done a foolish act, as usual. And now you have to pay for it. This child has become attached to us, Clara is fond of him, and every one would be grieved to see him leave. I am going to try and keep him, but I will have each one to bear a part. The first time that Clara works herself up into a fit of passion, or that you get drunk, I shall take him back to the police-magistrate's."

Old Louveau became radiant.

It was done. He would drink no more.

He smiled right up to his ear-rings and sang away as he coiled his cable on the deck, whilst the tug towed along the *Belle Nivernaise* together with quite a fleet of other boats.

CHAPTER III

UNDER WAY

VICTOR was under way. Under way for the suburban country, where the water mirrors little houses and green gardens—under way for the white land of the chalk hills—under way beside the flagged, resounding towing-paths—under way for the uplands, for the canal of the Yonne, slumbering within its locks—under way for the verdure of winter, and for the woods of Morvan.

Francis leant against the tiller of his boat, firm in his resolution not to drink, and turned a deaf ear to the invitations of the lock-keepers, and of the wine-dealers, who were astonished to see him passing free. He was obliged to cling to the tiller to keep the *Belle Niver-*

.naise from going alongside of the taverns. The old boat, from the time she had made the same voyage, seemed as if she knew the stations, and wanted to stop at them of her own accord, like an omnibus horse.

The Crew was perched on one leg in the prow, where, handling an immense boat-hook in a melancholy way, he pushed back the bushes, rounded the turns, and grappled the locks.

It was not much work he used to do, although the noise of his wooden leg on the deck might be heard day and night. Resigned and silent, he was one of those for whom everything in life had gone wrong. A school-fellow had caused him the loss of an eye; an axe had lamed him at the saw-mill; a vat had scalded him at the sugar refinery.

He would have been a beggar dying of hunger at the edge of a ditch, if Louveau—who always saw a thing at a glance—had not, as he was coming out of the hospital, engaged him to help in working the boat.

This was, at the time, the occasion of a great quarrel—exactly as for Victor. The wife with a head-piece was vexed, whereupon Louveau gave in.

In the end, the Crew remained, and at this time he formed part of the household of the *Belle Nivernaise*, on the same footing as the cat and the raven.

Old Louveau steered so exactly, and the Crew worked the boat so well, that after having ascended the river and the canals, the *Belle Nivernaise*, twelve days after her departure from Paris, got moored at the bridge of Corbigny, there to rest peacefully in her winter sleep.

From December to the end of Febru-

ary, the bargemen make no voyages, but repair their boats, and look through the forests to buy the spring cuttings as they stand.

As wood is cheap, they keep good fires in the cabins; and if the autumn sale has been successful, this idle time is made into a very enjoyable holiday.

The *Belle Nivernaise* was laid up for wintering; that is to say, the rudder was detached, the jury-mast was stowed away between decks, and the whole space was clear for playing and running about on the upper deck.

Wha*.* a change in his life for the foundling! During all the voyage, he had continued in a state of astonishment and fear. He was like a cage-bird surprised by being set free, that in the suddenness of the change. forgets its song and its wings. Though too young to enjoy the charms of the landscape spread before his eyes, he had nevertheless been impressed by the grandeur of that passage up the river between two ever-changing horizons.

Mother Louveau, seeing him shy and silent, kept on all day saying:

"He is deaf and dumb."

But the little Parisian from the Temple district was not dumb! When he got to understand that he was not dreaming. that he should no more go back to his garret, and that, in spite of mother Louveau's threats, there was really not much to fear from the police-magistrate, his tongue was loosed. It was like the blossoming of a plant grown in a cellar and then put upon a window shelf. He ceased to cower timidly down in corners like a hunted ferret. His eyes, deeply set under his projecting brow, lost their uneasy restlessness, and although he remained rather pale and had a thoughtful look, he learned to laugh with Clara.

The little girl passionately loved her play-fellow, as people do love each other at that age—for the pleasure of falling out and making it up again. Although she was as self-willed as a little donkey, she had a very tender heart, and the mention of the magistrate was enough to make her do as she was bid.

They had hardly arrived at Corbigny, when another sister came into the world. Mimile was just eighteen months old, and that made cots enough in the cabin —and work enough likewise; for, with all the encumbrances they had, they could not afford a servant.

Mother Louveau grumbled so much that the Crew's wooden leg quaked with fear. But nobody in the place had any pity for her. Even the peasants did not hesitate to say what they thought about it to the priest, who used to hold up the bargeman as a pattern.

"Say what your Reverence likes, there's no common sense in a man who has three children of his own picking up those of other people. But the Louveaus have always been like that. They are full of vanity and conceit, and no advice you can give them will alter them."

People did not wish them ill, but were not sorry they had got a lesson.

The vicar was a kind, well-meaning man, who easily adopted the opinions of others, and always wound up by recollecting some passage of Scripture, or sentence from the Fathers, with which to keep his own mind easy about his sudden turns and changes.

"My parishioners are right," said he to himself, as he passed his hand under his badly shaven chin, "we must not tempt divine Providence.'

But as the Louveaus were, on the whole, good honest people, he made his pastoral call on them as usual.

He found mother Louveau cutting breeches for Victor out of an old jacket. for the little brat had brought no clothes with him, and she could not beat rags and tatters about her.

She placed a seat for his Reverence, and when he spoke to her about Victor, hinting that with the influence of the Bishop they might perhaps get him into the orphanage at Autun, mother Louveau who would speak her mind to everybody, abruptly answered:

"The little fellow may be a burden to poor folks like us, certainly; I think that when he brought him home, Francis gave one more proof that he is not an eagle. I am not harder hearted than my husband; if I had met Victor, I should have been sorry for him, but yet I would have left him where he was. But now that we have taken him, it is not in order to get rid of him; and if we should some day find ourselves in a difficulty through nim, we shall not go and ask charity from anybody."

At this moment Victor came into the cabin with Mimile in his arms.

The little monkey, angry at having been weaned, was seeking his revenge by refusing to be set down, and was showing his teeth and biting everybody.

Touched by this sight, the vicar put his hand on the foundling's head and gravely remarked:

"God's blessing is on large families."

And away he went, delighted with himself for having recollected a sentence so appropriate to the situation.

Mother Louveau but told the truth

when she said that Victor was now one of the family.

While continually grumbling, and talking about taking the little fellow back to the police-magistrate's, this woman with a head-piece was getting to like the pale-faced child that clung so persistently to her skirts.

When old Louveau thought they were making too much of him, she always replied:

"Then you should not have taken him."

As soon as he was eight years of age, she sent him to school with Clara.

Victor would always carry the books and the basket. He would fight bravely in defending their luncheon against the unscrupulous appetites of the young Morvandians.

Nor did he show less spirit in his work than in his fighting, and although he attended the school in winter only, when no voyages were made, he knew more on his return than the little peasants, who, dull and noisy as their wooden shoes, would yawn over their alphabet for twelve months together.

Victor and Clara used to come back from the school through the forest, and it amused the two children to see the wood-cutters hewing down the trees.

As Victor was light and nimble, they would get him to climb to the top of the pines in order to fasten the rope that served to pull them down. He would appear smaller and smaller as he clambered higher up, and when he got to the top, Clara would be very frightened. But he was fearless, and would sometimes swing on a branch purposely to plague her.

At other times, they would go to see M. Maugendre in his wood-yard. The wood-dealer was a thin man and as dry as a stick. He lived alone, away from the village, amid the forest.

Nobody ever knew him to have any friends; and the curiosity of the village had for a long time been balked by the seclusion and reserve of the unknown, who had come from the farthest part of the Nièvre to set up a wood-yard away from others.

For six years he worked in all weathers, never taking a holiday, and like a very drudge. Yet it was supposed he had plenty of money, for he did a large trade, and often went to Corbigny to consult the notary about the investment of his savings.

He once told the vicar that he was a widower, but beyond this nothing was known of him.

When Maugendre observed the children coming he used to lay down his saw, and leave his work to have a chat with them. He took a great liking for Victor, and taught him to cut hulls of boats out of splinters of wood.

He once said to him:

"You remind me so much of a child I lost."

Then, as if afraid he had told too much, he added:

"Oh! it is a long time ago—a very long time ago."

Another day he said to Louveau:

"When you get tired of Victor give him to me. I have no heirs, and I will deny myself something to send him to college in the town. He shall pass examinations, and be entered at the School of Forestry."

But Francis was still in the flush of his good action, and he declined. Maugendre resolved to wait patiently until the progressive increase of the Louveau family, or some money difficulty, should have put the bargeman out of conceit with adoptions.

It seemed as if Fate wished to grant his desires. For one might almost believe that ill-luck had embarked on board the *Belle Nivernaise* at the same hour as Victor.

From that moment everything went wrong. The wood did not sell well. The Crew always broke some limb on the eve of the unloading. And at length, one fine day, just as they were setting out for Paris, mother Louveau fell ill.

Francis nearly lost his senses amidst the yelling of the little brats. He mistook soups for draughts, and draughts for soups, and so annoyed the sick woman by his stupidity, that he had to give up attending to her, and let Victor do it.

For the first time in his life, the bargeman bought his wood by himself. It was in vain he lapped his strings round the trees, and took thirty-six times in succession the same measure, for he always went wrong in his calculations. You know the famous calculation:

"I multiply by—I multiply by . . ."

It was mother Louveau that knew how to do that!

He executed his orders all wrong, set out for Paris in a very uneasy state of mind, and fell in with a dishonest purchaser, who took advantage of the circumstance to cheat him.

He came back to his boat with a very full heart, sat down at the foot of the bed, and said in a despairing tone:

"My dear, you must try to get well, r we shall be ruined."

Mother Louveau recovered slowly.

She strove against ill-fortune, and did unheard-of things to make both ends meet.

If they had something to buy a new boat with, they would have been able to get their trade back again; but during her illness they had expended all their savings, and the profits were now going to fill up the holes in the *Belle Nivernaise*, which was worn out.

Victor became a heavy burden for them. He was no longer a child of four years of age that could be dressed out of an old jacket, and his food never missed.

He was now twelve years of age, and he ate like a man, although he remained a thin, nervous child, such as they could not think of requiring to handle the boat-hook,—when the Crew had broken any limb.—

Everything kept going from bad to worse. On their last voyage they had great difficulty in getting up the Seine as far as Clamecy. The *Belle Nivernaise* was letting in water at every part, and patching up would no longer suffice; it would be necessary to repair the entire hull, or rather to put the vessel aside to be broken up, and replace her by a new one.

One evening in March, on the eve of getting under sail for Paris, as Louveau, full of care, was taking leave of Maugendre after having settled his account for wood, the timber-merchant asked him to come and drink a bottle in his house.

"I want to talk to you, Francis."

They went into the cottage, and Maugendre filled two glasses as they placed themselves opposite each other at the table.

"I have not always led a lonely life

such as you see now, Louveau. I can remember the time when I had everything that is necessary for happiness; a little money and a wife who loved me. I have lost all—by my own fault."

The wood-merchant stopped; the confession that was sticking in his throat was nearly choking him.

"I have never been a wicked man, Francis; but I had a vice."

"You?"

"I have it still. I love the 'rhino' above everything. That has been the cause of my misfortunes."

"How is that, my dear Maugendre?"

"I am going to tell you. When we were married and had our baby, the idea came into my head of sending my wife to Paris to seek a nurse's place. That pays well when the husband is an orderly man, and knows how to manage his house by himself. But my wife was unwilling to be separated from her infant. She said to me—'But, husband, we are earning money enough as it is. The rest would be money accursed, and would not profit us. Leave such resources as these to poor households already burdened with children, and spare me the pain of leaving you.' I would not hear of it, Louveau, and I compelled her to go."

"Well?"

"Well, when my wife had found a situation she gave her child into the charge of an old woman to take it back to our place. She saw them to the railway station, and they have never been heard of since."

"And your wife, my dear Maugendre?"

"When this news was told her, it caused her milk to turn, and she died."

They were both silent, Louveau touched by what he had just heard, Maugendre overcome by his remembrances. The wood-merchant spoke the first:

"For my punishment, I am condemned to the existence I now lead. I have lived for twelve years apart from every one. I can endure it no longer. I have a dread of dying alone. If you have any pity for me, you will give me Victor, that he may take for me the place of the child I have lost."

Louveau was much embarrassed. Victor was costing them much; but if they parted with him at the time he was about to make himself useful, all the sacrifices that they made would be thrown away. Maugendre guessed his thoughts:

"I need not say, Francis, that if you give him to me, I shall recoup you what he has cost. It would, moreover, be a good thing for the lad. I can never see the forestry pupils in the wood, without saying to myself: 'I should have been able to make a gentleman of my boy, like those gentlemen.' Victor is industrious, and he pleases me. You know I shall treat him like my own son. Come, now, is it agreed?"

When the children had been put to bed in the cabin of the Belle Nivernaise, this matter was talked over. The wife with the head-piece attempted to reason.

"You see, Francis, we have done for that child all that we could. God knows, one would like to keep him, but now that there is an opportunity of parting from him, without making him wretched, we must try to have courage."

Despite themselves, their eyes turn towards the bed, where Victor and Mimile are sleeping the deep and calm sleep of childhood.

"Poor little fellow," said Francis, in a low voice. They heard the river rippling along the planks, and the occasional whistle of the railway engine piercing the stillness of the night. Mother Louveau burst out in sobs: "God help us, Francis, we will keep him."

CHAPTER IV

LIFE IS HARD

VICTOR was nearly fifteen years of age. He had grown up all at once; the little pale-faced child had become a stout lad, with big shoulders and a quiet carriage.

Since he first sailed on the *Belle Nivernaise*, he began to find his way like an old bargeman, knowing the clear channels, guessing the depths of the water, passing from the handling of the pole to that of the rudder. Now he had a red waist-band, and wore a striped vest about his hips.

When Louveau gave up the tiller to him, Clara, who was growing a big girl, would come and knit beside him, much taken by his calm face and robust movements.

This time, the passage from Corbigny to Paris had been a hard one. The Seine, swollen by the autumn rains had carried away the weirs, and was rushing towards the sea like a wild beast let loose.

The anxious bargeman hurried on with their deliveries, for the stream was already rolling by at the level of the quays, and messages sent from the lock stations, hour after hour, brought bad news. It was reported that the tributary streams were breaking down their banks and overflowing the country, and that the flood was getting higher and higher.

The quays were filled with a busy crowd, a swarm of men, carts and horses; while up aloft the steam-cranes were working their huge arms. The wine-market was already cleared out, and drays were carrying away cases of sugar. The mooring-men were leaving their cabins; the quays were getting empty; and a file of wagons was ascending the slope of the incline, retreating from the flood like an army on the march.

The Louveaus were so hindered by the roughness of the water, and the intermission of work in the moonless nights, that they despaired of delivering their wood in time. Everybody had taken his share of the work, and they labored till very late in the evening, by the light of lanterns and of the gas lamps on the quay.

At eleven o'clock, all the cargo was piled up at the foot of the incline; and, as Dubac the joiner's cart did not reappear, they went to bed.

It was a dreadful night, with much grinding together of chains, creaking of planks, and bumping of boats. The *Belle Nivernaise*, with her timbers loosened by the shocks, groaned like one in pain.

It was impossible to close an eye. Louveau, his wife, Victor, and the Crew rose up at daybreak and left the children in bed.

The Seine had risen still higher during the night, and rough and surging like a sea, its green waters were rushing on under a heavy sky. On the quays there was no movement of life—on the river not a boat; nothing but the remains of roofs and fences borne along in the current of the stream. Beyond the bridges the outline of Notre-Dame was shadowed out against the fog.

There was not a moment to be lost, for the river had already got over the parapets of the lower quay, and the little waves that lapped the ends of the planks had caused the stacks of wood to tumble down.

While Francis, mother Louveau, and Dubac were loading the cart, with the water half-way up to their knees, they were startled by a loud crash on one side of them. A lighter laden with millstones had parted its mooring chain, and had come against the quay and foundered, being split up from stem to stern. It sank with a dreadful noise, and a strong eddy took its place.

They were standing motionless, impressed by this sudden wreck, when they heard shouts behind them. The *Belle Nivernaise*, unmoored by the agitation was leaving the quay. Mother Louveau raised a cry:

"My children!"

Victor had already rushed into the cabin, and he now reappeared on deck with the little one in his arms. Clara and Mimile followed him, and all stretched out their hands towards the quay.

"Take them!"

"A boat!"

"A rope!"

What was to be done? It was impossible to take all of them to shore by swimming. The Crew was running from one plank to another, bewildered, useless. They must get alongside at any cost.

In presence of this bewildered man, and of these sobbing little children, Victor, thus unexpectedly made into a captain, felt within himself the energy that was needed to save them. He gave his orders:

"Come, throw a cable! Quick!"

This was done three times over, but the *Belle Nivernaise* was already too far from the quay, and the cable fell into the water.

Victor then ran to the rudder, and they heard him shout:

"Don't be afraid. I'll see after them."

And, in fact, by a vigorous movement of the tiller, he brought the craft right, for having been taken by the water broadside on, she was drifting in the current.

On the quay, poor Louveau quite lost his senses, and wanted to leap into the water in order to reach his children; but Dubac threw his arms round him, whilst mother Louveau covered her face with her hands to shut out the dreadful sight.

The *Belle Nivernaise* was now keeping in the current, and shooting towards the bridge of Austerlitz with the velocity of a tug-boat.

Composedly leaning against the tiller Victor steered, encouraged the little ones, and gave his orders to the Crew. He knew he was in the right channel, for he had steered for the red flag that hung in the middle of the centre arch to show the bargemen the way.

But, good heavens! would there be height enough to pass through! He saw the bridge approaching very quickly.

"Get your boat-hook ready. Crew! You. Clara, don't leave the children."

He was clinging to the rudder, and already he felt the wind from the arch moving his hair. They are in it! Carried on by her impetus, the *Belle Niver-*

naise disappeared under the span with a dreadful sound, yet not so fast but that the crowd collected on the bridge of Austerlitz saw the wooden-legged boatman miss the stroke with his boat-hook and fall flat down, whilst the lad at the helm cried out:

"A grapnel! a grapnel!"

The *Belle Nivernaise* was under the bridge. In the shade of the arch Victor distinctly observed the enormous rings made fast to the layer of piles, and the joints of the vault above his head, and in the distance the line of other bridges, inclosing their pieces of sky.

Then it seemed as if there were an enlargement of the horizon, a dazzling glare as when one comes out of a cellar into the light, a sound of hurrahs above his head, and the vision of the cathedral, like a frigate anchored in the stream.

The boat abruptly stopped. The bridgemen had succeeded in throwing a hook on board, and Victor ran to the mooring-line and wound the rope firmly round the timber-head.

The *Belle Nivernaise* was seen to put about, turn round on the mooring-line, and, obeying the new impulse that was given to her, slowly come alongside the quay of the Tournelle, with her crew of little children and her captain of fifteen years.

Oh! what joy when they found themselves all assembled in the evening round the steaming stew in the cabin of the boat—this time well anchored, well moored.

The little hero had the place of honor—the captain's seat. They had not much appetite after the experiences of the morning with its violent emotions,

but their hearts were expanded as after a period of anguish, and they breathed freely.

There was a wink across the table, as much as to say:

"Ha! if we had taken him back to the police-magistrate's?"

Louveau laughed from ear to ear, as he cast his moistened eyes over his brood. You would have supposed that some good luck had befallen them, that they had gained a big prize in the lottery, or that the *Belle Nivernaise* had no longer any holes in her sides.

The bargeman kept knocking Victor about with punches in the ribs. It was his way of showing his affection. "What a chap Victor is! What a pull of the tiller! Did you see that, Crew? I could not have done better myself, *he! he!* master as I am."

For a fortnight the good fellow could do nothing else but express his admiration, and go along the quays to describe this pull of the tiller. "You know, the boat was drifting. Then he . . . Ah!" And he showed by a gesture how it was done.

In the meantime the Seine was getting lower, and the time for setting out was again at hand. One morning, as Victor and Louveau were pumping on the deck, the postman brought a letter.

It had a blue seal on the back. The bargeman opened the letter with a rather trembling hand, and, as he could not trust to his own ability in reading more than in arithmetic, he said to Victor:

"You spell that out for me."

And Victor read:

"OFFICE OF THE COMMISSARY OF POLICE
"12th Arrondissement

"Monsieur Louveau (Francis), master bargeman, is requested to call at the Office of the Commissary of Police with as little delay as possible."

"Is that all?"

"That is all."

"What can he want with me?"

Louveau was away all day.

When he came back in the evening all his cheerfulness had disappeared; he was gloomy, cross, sullen.

Mother Louveau could make nothing of it; and as the youngsters had gone to play on the deck, she asked him:

"Whatever has happened?"

"I am weary of it."

"What, of unloading?"

"No, about Victor."

And then he told her about his visit to the police-magistrate.

"You must understand that the woman who abandoned him was not his mother."

"No, really?"

"She had stolen him."

"How do they know that?"

"She herself confessed it to the police-magistrate before she died."

"Then they told you the name of his parents?"

Louveau gave a start.

"Why do you think they would tell me?"

"Well, because they had sent for you."

Francis got vexed.

"If I knew it, you think, perhaps, I should tell you!"

He was quite red with anger, and he went out, slamming the door after him.

Mother Louveau was overcome with astonishment.

"Whatever is the matter with him?"

Yes, what could have been the matter with you, Francis. From that time his ways, his words, his character were quite changed. He could not eat, he slept badly, he talked all night. He even answered his wife back! He fell out with the Crew. He spoke harshly to everybody, and to Victor most of all. When mother Louveau, quite amazed, asked him what was the matter, he answered savagely—

"Nothing at all. Do I look as if anything was the matter with me? You are all plotting against me."

The poor woman got nothing for her pains:

"Take my word for it, he is going out of his senses."

She thought he was quite cracked, when one evening he made a dreadful scene for them about Maugendre.

They were at the end of the voyage, and had got nearly to Clamecy. Victor and Clara were talking about the school, and the youth having said that he should be glad to see Maugendre again, Louveau flew into a passion:

"Don't talk to me about your Maugendre. I want to have nothing more to do with him."

Mother Louveau interposed:

"What has he done to you?"

"He has . . . he has . . . It does not matter to you. I am the master, I suppose."

Alas! He was so much the master now, that instead of making fast at Corbigny, as usual, he went two leagues higher up, into the heart of the forest.

He declared that Maugendre thought of nothing else than duping him in all their bargains, and that he could do business on better terms with another vendor.

They were now too far from the village to think of attending the classes, and therefore Victor and Clara rambled through the woods all day, gathering sticks.

When they were tired carrying their burden they would put it down beside a ditch, and sit down on the ground amidst the flowers. Victor would pull a book out of his pocket, and would get Clara to read.

They liked to see the sun peeping through the branches, and throw a flickering light on the page and on their hair, while about there was the hum of millions of little creatures, and surrounding all reigned the silence of the woods.

When they got late, they had to return very quickly, all along the great avenue, barred by shadows of the tree trunks. The mast of the *Belle Nivernaise* would be visible in the opening at the end, as well as the gleam of a fire through the slight fog rising from the river.

It was Mother Louveau cooking, in the open air at the margin of the stream, over a fire of waste rubbish.

Mimile would be sitting close by her, with his hair all ruffled, his shirt bursting through his breeches, and he would be lovingly contemplating the pot, while his little sister rolled about on the ground, while Louveau and the Crew smoked their pipes.

One evening, at supper time, they saw some one come out of the wood and advance towards them.

"Ha! Maugendre!"

It was the timber-merchant. He looked much older, and much grayer. He had a stick in his hand, and seemed to talk with difficulty.

He came forward to Louveau and held out his hand.

"Well, you have left me then, Francis?"

The bargeman stammered out a confused reply.

"Oh! I am not vexed at you."

He had so wearied a look that mother Louveau was touched by it, and without giving any heed to her husband's bad humor, she handed him a seat.

"You are not ill, I hope, M. Maugendre?"

"I have got a bad cold."

He spoke slowly, almost in a whisper. Suffering had softened him. He told them that he was about to leave the neighborhood, to go to live in the distant part of the Nièvre.

"It's all done with. I have given up business. I am now rich; I have money, plenty of money. But what is the good of it? I cannot buy back the happiness I have lost."

Francis listened with knit brows.

Maugendre continued:

"The older I get, the more keenly do I suffer from being lonely. Formerly, I used to forget all when I was working; but now, I have no longer any heart for work. I have lost interest in everything. So I am going to banish myself; that may perhaps give me some distraction."

And, in spite of himself, his eyes turned towards the children. At this moment Victor and Clara issued from the avenue with their load of branches, and seeing Maugendre, they threw down their bundles and ran to him.

He received them as cordially as usual, and said to Louveau, who remained sullen:

"You are a happy man to have four children. I have none now."

And he sighed: "I must not complain, it is my own fault."

He rose up, and everybody did the same.

"Good-by, Victor. Be industrious, and love your parents; you ought to."

He had put his hand on the boy's shoulder, and was looking at him fixedly.

"Ah, if I had a child, he should be like him."

Louveau opposite to him, with compressed lips, bore an expression that seemed to say: "Begone from hence."

Yet at the moment the timber-merchant was leaving, Francis felt an impulse of sympathy towards him, and he called him back, saying—

"Maugendre, won't you take soup with us?"

This was said as if against the grain, and in a gruff tone of voice that did not encourage acceptance. The old man shook his head.

"No, I thank you, I am not hungry. When one is melancholy, look you, other people's happiness does not do one much good."

And he departed, bending over his stick.

Louveau did not speak a word the whole evening. He passed the night in walking up and down the deck, and in the morning he went away without saying a word to any one.

He went to the vicarage, which was close to the church. It was a large square building, with a court in front and a kitchen garden behind. Fowls were foraging at the threshold, and a cow was lowing in the grass.

Louveau felt his heart lightened by the resolution he had taken. As he opened the gate, he said to himself with a sigh of satisfaction, that when he came out of it again he should be relieved of his care.

He found the vicar seated in his cool dining room. The good priest had finished his breakfast, and was dozing lightly with his head leaning over his breviary. Aroused by Louveau's entrance, he turned down the page, and having closed the book, he motioned to the bargeman, who was twirling his cap in his fingers, to sit down.

"Well now, Francis, what can I do for you?"

He wanted advice, and he asked to be allowed to tell his story from the beginning.

"Because, as your Reverence knows, I am not very clever. I am not an eagle, he! he! as my wife tells me."

And having put himself at his ease by this preamble, he told his business, very much out of breath, very red, and all the while gazing intently at the peak of his cap.

"Your Reverence will recollect that Maugendre told you he was a widower? He has been so for the last fifteen years. His wife went to Paris to be a nurse. She showed her child to the doctor, as the custom is, gave it the breast for the last time, and then she intrusted it to a *meneuse*."

The priest interrupted him.

"What is a *meneuse*, Francis?"

"A *meneuse*, your Reverence, is a woman who is employed to take back home the children of the wet nurses. She carries them away in a creel or basket like kittens."

"That's a queer trade!"

"There are some honest people that carry it on, your Reverence; but mother Maugendre had fallen in with a woman that nobody knew, a witch who stole children and let them out to other idle vagabonds to drag them about the streets in order to excite commiseration."

"You do not mean to say that, Francis?"

"It is the simple truth, your Reverence. This wretch of a woman carried off a lot of children, and Maugendre's little one among the rest. She kept him for four years. She wanted to teach him to beg; but as he was the son of an honest man, he refused to hold out his hand. Thereupon she abandoned him in the street, and then—become what you can! But now, six months ago, on her deathbed in the hospital, she was stricken with remorse. I know what that is, your Reverence, it is devilish hard to bear. . ."

And he turned his eyes up to the ceiling, poor man, as if to call Heaven to witness the truth of his statement.

"Then she asked for the police-magistrate and she told him the name of the child. The magistrate has informed me. It is Victor."

The vicar let his breviary fall: "Is Victor Maugendre's son?"

"He is."

The ecclesiastic was taken all aback. He muttered a phrase in which the words "poor child," "finger of God" were distinguishable. He got up, walked about the room, went near the window, drank a glass of water, and ended by stopping in front of Louveau with his hands in his waist-band. He was trying to recollect a sentence that would apply to the circumstance, but as he could not find one, he simply said:

"Ah, well, but he must be restored to his father."

Louveau started.

"That is exactly my trouble, your Reverence. For the six months that I have known all this, I have never had the courage to tell anyone, not even my wife. We have denied ourselves so much to bring up that child, we have endured so much poverty together, that now I do not know how I can bring myself to part from him."

All this was true, and if Maugendre seemed to deserve compassion, some pity should also be felt for poor Francis. Possessed by these contradictory sentiments, the vicar was perspiring visibly, while mentally he was requesting light from on high. And forgetting that Louveau had come to ask for his advice, he murmured in a subdued voice:

"Come, now, Francis, if you were in my place, what would you advise?"

The bargeman looked down.

"I quite understand, your Reverance, that Victor must be given up. I felt that the other day, when Maugendre came upon us unexpectedly. It cut me to the heart to see him so old, so sad, and so broken down. I was as ashamed as if I had his money, stolen money, in my pocket. I could no longer keep this secret to myself, and I have come to tell it you."

"And you have done right, Louveau," said the vicar, delighted at seeing the bargeman find him a solution of the question. "It is never too late to repair an error. I am going with you to Maugendre's, and there you will confess all to him."

"To-morrow, your Reverence."

"No, Francis, immediately."

And observing the poor fellow's grief, and the nervous twisting about of his cap, he entreated in a softer voice:

"I beg of you to do it now, Louveau, whilst we are both resolved."

CHAPTER V

MAUGENDRE HAS A SON!

A SON! Maugendre has a son!

He is gazing at him complacently, as he sits on the opposite cushion in the buzz and hum of the railway carriage that is bearing them towards Nevers.

It was really an abduction. The old man had taken his son away, almost without saying thank you, like a rustic who has won the big prize in the lottery, and runs straight off with it.

He did not want to leave his child open to the old attachments. He was now as greedy for affection, as he formerly was for gold. No borrowing, no sharing; but his treasure is to be for himself only, without the peering eyes of others.

There was a buzzing in Maugendre's ears like that of the express. His head was hot like the locomotive. But his dreams were hastening on faster than any locomotives or express trains, and passing at a dash over days, and months, and years.

His dreams were of a Victor dressed in dark-green faced with silver; a student of the School of Forestry! One might even say that this student Maugendre had a sword at his side, and the two-cornered hat on his head, like a student of the *Ecole Polytechnique*— for all the schools and all the uniforms were a little mixed in Maugendre's dreams.

No matter! Embroidery and gold lace are not spared by the wood-merchant. He has the "rhino" to pay for all that . . . and Victor shall be a gentleman covered with gold lace from head to foot.

Men will speak to him with their hats off.

Fine ladies will be madly in love with him.

And, in one corner, there will be an old man with horny hands, who will say, bridling up:

"This is my son."

"Come now, my son."

"My son" also is dreaming, with his little cap over his eyes—until he gets the two-cornered gold-laced hat.

He would not like his father to see him weeping. But it was sudden, that separation. Clara had given him a kiss that still glowed on his cheek. Old Louveau turned away, and mother Louveau was very pale.

And Mimile brought him his porringer of soup, to console him. All! even to little Mimile. Oh! how will they live without him? And how will he live without them? The future student of the School of Forestry is so troubled by these thoughts, that every time his father speaks to him, he answers:

"Yes, monsieur Maugendre."

And he is not yet at the end of his tribulations, our little bargeman of the *Belle Nivernaise*. For it costs not only money to become a gentleman, but also sacrifices and sorrows.

Some of these Victor is conscious of, as the quick train passes with a whistle over the bridges above the suburbs of Nevers. It seems to him that he has before seen somewhere, in a sad and distant past, these same narrow streets.

and those windows small as the air-holes of a prison, with raveled rags hanging out of them.

Now they have the pavement beneath their feet, and round them there is the station rout, the crowd of lookers-on, the press of people laden with parcels, the roll of cabs and of heavy railway omnibuses, which travelers, carrying rugs tied up with straps, noisily take by assault.

Victor and his father go out of the station gates in a carriage. The wood-merchant sticks to his idea. He must have an immediate transformation. So he takes his son straight away to the college tailor's.

The shop is new, the counters lustrous, and well-dressed gentlemen, like those shown in the colored engravings hung on the wall, open the door for the customers with a patronizing smile.

They put before old Maugendre the choicest of the fashion plates, where a collegian is smoking in company with a lady in a riding-habit, a gentleman in a complete hunting suit, and a bride dressed in white satin.

The tailor happens just to have in hand a pattern tunic, padded back and front, with square skirts and gilt buttons. He displays it to the wood-merchant, who beaming with pride, cries:

"In that, you will look like a soldier."

A gentleman in his shirt sleeves, with a tape round his neck, now comes up to the student Maugendre, and takes the measure of his legs, his waist, and his back-bone.

This operation brings to the mind of the little bargeman remembrances that call the tears to his eyes! The ways of dear old Louveau, the tempers of the wife with the head-piece—all that has he left behind him forever.

It is all past and gone now. The correct young man in the regulation uniform, that Victor beholds in the big looking-glass, has nothing in common with the ship-lad of the *Belle Nivernaise*.

The tailor with his toe contemptuously pushes the dishonored boat garments under his bench like a bundle of rags.

Victor feels that he has been made to leave there all his past life. How much is there in that word "leave"! Here now is he forbidden even to retain the memory of it.

"You must detach yourself from all the errors of your early education," said the Principal sternly, without concealing his distrust.

And in order to facilitate this regeneration, it is decided that the student Maugendre shall go out of the college only on the first Sunday in each month.

Oh! how he weeps the first night, at the end of the cold, dreary dormitory, while the other scholars are snoring on their iron bedsteads, and the assistant-master is devouring a romance on the sly, by the glimmer of a night-light.

How he suffers during the hated hour of recreation, whilst his comrades hustle and mob him!

How weary he is in the study, with his head bent over his desk, trembling at the anger of the usher as the latter, with all his might, hits his table, repeating over the same phrase:

"Silence there, sirs."

That shrill voice, by stirring up in Victor the bitter dregs of sad memories, blights his whole life.

It reminds him of the dark days of

"He is not going to die, is he?"

For it is plain that the doctor is not confident, at least his gray hairs are not, for they say "no" faintly, as if they were afraid of committing themselves.

No mention now of green coats or of two-cornered hats. It is solely a matter of saving the student Maugendre's life.

The doctor told them frankly that if he should recover, they would do well to restore him to his country freedom.

If he should recover!

The idea of losing the child just restored to him annihilated all the ambitious desires of the rich father. It is all over with his dream, he renounces it forever. He is quite ready to bury the student of the School of Forestry with his own hands. He will nail up the coffin, if desired. He will wear no mourning for him. Only but let the other one consent to live! Let him but speak to him, get up, throw his arms round his neck, and say:

"Be comforted, father, I am getting well now."

And the wood-merchant leant over Victor's bed.

It is done. The old tree is cleft to the core. Maugendre's heart has been softened.

"I will let you leave here, my lad. You shall return to them, you shall sail again. And it will be good enough for me to see you sometimes in passing."

At this time, the bell no longer rings the hours for recreation, for study, and for meals. It is the vacation, and the great college is deserted. Not a sound is heard save that of the fountain in the courtyard, and the sparrows chirping on the grassplots. The rattle of an occasional carriage sounds dull and distant, for they have laid down straw in the street.

It is in the midst of this silence and this solitude, that the student Maugendre comes to himself again.

He is surprised to find himself in a very white bed, surrounded by large muslin curtains that spread about him the seclusion of subdued light and quietude.

He would much like to raise himself up on the pillow, and draw them apart a little, to see where he is; but his strength is unequal to the effort, although he feels himself most delightfully refreshed. So he waits.

But there are voices whispering near him. One would fancy there were feet walking on tiptoe over the floor, and even a well-known stumping, something like the promenade of a broom-handle over the boards. Victor had heard that before. Where? Surely on the deck of the Belle Nivernaise. That's it!

And the patient, collecting all his strength, cries out with a feeble voice, which he, however, means for a loud one:

"Yeho! Crew! yeho!"

The curtains are withdrawn, and in the dazzling burst of light, he sees all the dear ones he has so often called on in his delirium.

All? Yes, all! They are all there. Clara, Maugendre, Louveau, mother Louveau, Mimile, the little sister; and the scalded old heron, as thin as his own boat-hook, was smiling immensely his silent smile.

And every arm is stretched towards him, every head is bent, there are kisses from everybody, smiles, shakes of the hand, questions.

"Where am I? Why are you here?"

But the doctor's orders are precise, and the gray hairs were in downright earnest when thus prescribing:

"He must keep his arms under the bed-clothes, be quiet, and not get excited."

And in order to prevent his child from talking, Maugendre goes on speaking all the time.

"Would you believe that it is ten days ago—the day you fell ill—that I had just seen the Principal to speak to him about you? He told me you were making progress, and that you were working like a machine. . . . You may imagine how pleased I was! I asked to see you, and you were sent for, when at that moment your master rushed into the Principal's study quite frightened. You had just had an attack of high fever. I ran to the infirmary; you did not recognize me, your eyes were like tapers, you were in delirium! Ah! my dear lad, how ill you were! I did not leave you for a moment. You kept raving on. You were talking about the *Belle Nivernaise*, about Clara, about the new boat, and I know not what else. Then I recollected the letter— Clara's letter; it had been found in your hands, and they had given it to me, and, for the time, I had forgotten all about it, you know! I drew it from my pocket, I read it, I shook my head, and I said to myself: 'Maugendre, your disappointment must not make you forget your friends' trouble.' Then I wrote to al' these good people to come and see us. No answer. I took advantage of a day on which you were rather better, to go and find them, and I brought them to my house, where they are now living and where they will

live, until some means of settling their affairs has been found. Is it not so, friend Louveau?"

Every one has a tear in his eye, and, on my word!—so much the worse for the doctor's gray hairs,—the two arms come out of the bed-clothes, and Maugendre is embraced as he has never been before.—the real kiss of an affectionate child.

Then, as it is impossible to take Victor home, they arrange their future life —Clara will remain with the patient in order to sweeten his draughts and chat with him; mother Louveau will go to keep house; Francis shall go and superintend a building that the timber-merchant has contracted for in the *Grande Rue*.

As for Maugendre, he is going to Clamecy. He is going to see some acquaintances who have a large contract for wood. These people will be delighted to engage so clever a bargeman as Louveau.

No! no! No objections, no opposition. It is an understood thing, quite a simple matter.

Certainly it is not for Victor to object.

He is now lifted up and rolled in his big arm-chair to the window.

He is alone with Clara, in the silent infirmary.

And Victor is delighted. He blesses his illness. He blesses the sale of the *Belle Nivernaise*. He blesses all the sales and all the illnesses in the world.

"Do you remember, Clara, when I used to hold the tiller, and you would come and sit beside me, with your knitting?"

Clara remembered so well that she

cast down her eyes, and blushed, and both of them were rather embarrassed.

For now, he is no longer the little lad in a red cap, whose feet could not reach to the deck when he climbed up on the tiller, and sat astride it.

And she, when she comes in the morning and takes off her little shawl, and throws it on the bed, appears quite a handsome young woman; her arms are so round, and her waist is so slender.

"Come early, Clara, and stop as long as you can."

It is so nice to have breakfast and dinner, the two together, near the window in the shade of the white curtains.

They are reminded of their early childhood, of the pap eaten at the edge of the bed with the same spoon. Ah! those memories of childhood!

They flit about the college infirmary like birds in an aviary. No doubt they make their nest in every corner of the curtains, for each morning there are fresh ones newly opened for their flight.

And truly, if you heard their conversations about the past, you would say that they were a couple of octogenarians looking back only on the distance behind them.

Now, is there not a future, which also may have some interest for them?

Yes, there is such a future: and it is often thought of, if it is never mentioned.

Besides, it is not absolutely necessary to use phrases in conversing. There is a certain way of taking hold of a hand, and of blushing at every turn, which says a great deal more than words. Victor and Clara talk in that language all day long.

That is probably the reason why they are so often silent. And that, too, is why the days pass so quickly that the month glides by noiselessly and imperceptibly.

That is the reason why the doctor is obliged to make his gray hairs bristle up, and to turn his patient out of the infirmary.

Just at this time, Maugendre the elder returns from his journey. He finds them all assembled in his house. And he cannot help smiling, when poor Louveau very anxiously asks him:

"Well, will they have anything to do with me down there?"

"Will they not, old man? . . . They wanted a master for a new boat, and they thanked me for the gift I was giving them."

Who can these people be? Old Louveau was so delighted he did not inquire further. And everybody set off for Clamecy without knowing anything more about it.

What a pleasure, when they get to the banks of the canal!

There, on the quay, a magnificent boat, adorned with flags from top to bottom, and brand new, raises her polished mast amid the green fields.

They are giving her the last touch of varnish, and the stern on which the name of the craft is painted, remains covered with gray canvas.

A cry breaks from every mouth:

"What a fine boat!"

Louveau does not believe his eyes. He has a deuced queer feeling of smarting in the eyelids, of a splitting open of his mouth about a foot wide, and of a shaking of his ear-rings like a couple of salad paniers.

"That is too grand! I would not dare to undertake to steer a boat like that. She was never made to sail. She should be put under a glass case."

Maugendre had to push him by force on the foot-bridge, where the Crew was making signals to them.

How is this! Has the Crew himself been repaired? Yes, repaired, refitted, caulked afresh. He has a boat-hook, and a wooden leg, both quite new.

These are the gift of the contractor, a man of intelligence, who has done the thing well. As, for example, the deck is of waxed wood, and is surrounded by a handrail. There is a seat for resting yourself, and an awning to afford shade from the sun.

The hold is big enough to carry a double cargo. And the cabin!—oh, the cabin!

"Three apartments!"

"A kitchen!"

"Mirrors!"

Louveau drew Maugendre aside on the deck. He was touched, shaken by his feelings—as were his ear-rings. He stammered out:

"Dear old Maugendre . . ."

"What's the matter?"

"You have forgotten one thing."

"Yes?"

"You have not told me the name of the firm on account of whom I am to sail."

"You want to know?"

"Certainly!"

"Well, then, on your own account!"

"How? . . . but then . . . the boat . . ."

"Is yours!"

What an event, my friends! What close pressings of breast to breast!

It is fortunate that the contractor—who is a man of intelligence—had be-

thought himself of putting a seat upon the deck.

Louveau drops upon it like a man felled by a blow.

"It is impossible. . . . we cannot accept."

Maugendre has an answer ready for everything:

"Come, now, you are forgetting our old debt, the money you have laid out for Victor. Keep your mind easy, Francis; it is I who owe you the most."

And the two companions kissed each other like brothers. No mistake this time; they wept.

Assuredly Maugendre has arranged everything to make the surprise complete, for whilst they are embracing each other on the deck, behold his Reverence, the Vicar, issuing from the wood, with a band behind him and a banner floating on the wind.

What can this be for? It is for the benediction of the boat, most certainly. All Clamecy has come in procession to be present at the celebration.

The banner is floating out in the breeze.

And the band is playing—

"Rum,—dum—dum."

Every face looks happy, and over all there is a bright sun that makes the silver of the cross and the brass of the musicians' instruments flash again.

What a celebration! They have just taken away the canvas that covered the stern; and the name of the boat shows up in gold letter on an azure ground:

"LA NOUVELLE NIVERNAISE."

Hurrah for the *Nouvelle Nivernaise*! May she have as long a life as the old one, and a happier old age!

The Vicar steps up to the boat. Behind him, the singers and the musicians are drawn up in a row, while the banner forms a background.

"Benedicat Deus. . . ."

Victor is the godfather, Clara the godmother. The Vicar asks them to come forward to the edge of the quay close to himself.

They hold each other's hand, and are bashful, trembling. They confusedly stammer out the words that the choirboy whispers to them, whilst the Vicar is shaking the holy-water sprinkler over them:

"Benedicat Deus. . . ."

Would you not have taken them for a young couple at the altar? That thought occurs to everybody. Perhaps it occurs to themselves, also, for they dare not look at each other, and they get more and more confused as the ceremony proceeds.

At length, it is finished. The crowd retires. The *Nouvelle Nivernaise* has received her benediction.

But you cannot let the musicians go away like that, without any refreshments.

And, whilst Louveau is pouring out bumpers for the musicians, Maugendre, winking at mother Louveau, takes the godfather and godmother by the hand and turning towards the Vicar, asks:

"Here is the baptism finished, your Reverence; when will the marriage come off?"

Victor and Clara become as red as poppies. Mimile and his little sister clap their hands.

And, in the midst of the general enthusiasm, old Louveau, very excited, leans over his daughter's shoulder, and laughing up to his ears in anticipation of his joke, the honest bargeman says, in a bantering tone:

"Well now, Clara, now's the time. . . . shall we take Victor back to the magistrate's?"

The Third Low Mass

CHAPTER I

TWO TURKEYS

"Two truffled turkeys, Garrigou?"

"Yes, reverend sir, two magnificent turkeys, crammed with truffles. I know something about it, since it is I who helped to stuff them. One would think that their skins must burst in roasting, they are stretched so tight—"

"Jesu-Maria! I who so love truffles! Quick! give me my surplice, Garrigou. And what else did you see in the kitchen beside the turkeys?"

"Oh! all sorts of good things. We have done nothing since noon but pluck pheasants, lapwings, pullets, and grouse. Their feathers were flying everywhere. Then they have brought from the pond eels, golden carp, trout, and—"

"How big were the trout, Garrigou?"

"As big as that, reverend sir. Enormous!"

"Oh, ye gods! It seems to me that I can see them. Have you put the wine in the cruets?"

"Yes, reverend father, I have put the wine in the cruets. But, pshaw! it is not so good as that which you will drink presently, when you come from the midnight Mass. If you could see in the château dining-room all those blazing decanters, full of wine of every colour! And the silver plate, the chased epergnes, the flowers, the candelabra! Never again will be seen such a supper! The marquis has invited all the nobles in the neighbourhood. There will be at least forty of you at table, without counting the bailiff or the notary. Ah, you are very happy to be one of them, reverend father! Simply from having smelled those fine turkeys, the odour of the truffles follows me everywhere. Meuh!"

"Come, come, my child. Let us beware of the sin of gluttony, especially on the night of the Nativity. Go light the tapers quickly, and ring the first bell for Mass; for it is almost midnight, and we must not be late."

This conversation was carried on one Christmas Eve in the year of grace sixteen hundred and something, between the Reverend Dom Balaguère, ex-prior of Barnabites, now salaried chaplain of the lords of Trinquelage, and his little clerk Garrigou, or at least what he believed to be his little clerk Garrigou, for you must know that the devil, that night, had taken on the round face and the unformed features of the young sacristan, that he might the better lead the reverend father into temptation, and cause him to commit an appalling sin of gluttony. Therefore, while the suppositious Garrigou (hum! hum!) was lustily ringing the bells of his lordship's chapel, the reverend father finished putting on his chasuble in the little sacristy of the château, and, with his mind already

excited by all these gastronomic descriptions, kept repeating to himself as he robed,—

"Roast turkeys! Golden carp! Trout as big as that!"

Without, the night wind blew, scattering the music of the bells; and gradually lights appeared in the shadows on the sides of Mont Ventoux, from whose flanks rose the old towers of Trinquelage. They were carried by the families of farmers who were coming to hear the midnight Mass at the château, and who climbed the hillside singing, in groups of five or six, the father in front, lantern in hand, the women wrapped in their great brown cloaks in which the children nestled for shelter. In spite of the hour and the cold, all these good people walked cheerfully, supported by the thought that after the Mass there would be, as every year, a table set for them below in the kitchens. Now and again, on the steep road, the windows of some great lord's carriage preceded by torch-bearers would glitter in the moonlight, or a mule trotted along with its bells tinkling, and by the light of the fog-dimmed lanterns, the farmers recognized their bailiff, and greeted him as he passed,—

"Good evening, good evening, Master Arnoton!"

"Good evening, good evening, my children!"

The night was clear, and the stars shone the brighter for the cold. The wind was sharp, and a fine sleet, sliding off from their garments without wetting them, preserved faithfully the traditions of a Christmas white with snow. At the top of the hill appeared the château, their goal, with its enormous mass of towers and gables, the belfry of its chapel rising in the blue-black sky; while a crowd of little lights flickering, going, coming, and shifting in all the windows, resembled, against the dark background of the building, sparks running through the ashes of a burned sheet of paper. When one has passed the drawbridge and postern, it was necessary, in order to reach the chapel, to traverse the first court, full of carriages, footmen, and sedan chairs, and bright with the light of torches and the kitchen fires. One could hear the rattle of the jacks, the clatter of saucepans, the clash of glass and silverware being arranged for the supper; while over all, a warm vapour, with a good smell of roast meat and the strong herbs of complicated sauces, caused the farmers to say, with the chaplain, the bailiff, and everybody else.—

"What a good supper we are going to have after the Mass!"

CHAPTER II

MIDNIGHT

Ting-a-ling-a-ling! Ting-a-ling-a-ling!

It was the midnight Mass beginning. In the château chapel—a cathedral in miniature, with intersecting arches and oak woodwork rising to the tops of the walls—tapestry has been hung and all the tapers lighted. And what a crowd, what toilettes! Here, in the first place, seated in one of the carved stalls which surround the choir, is the Lord of Trinquelage, in a suit of salmon-coloured taffeta, and beside him all the noble lords whom he has invited. Opposite, at Prie-Dieus, hung with velvet,

are the marquise dowager in her flame-coloured brocade, and the young lady of Trinquelage, wearing a high headdress of fluted lace in the latest fashion of the Court of France. Below can be seen the Bailiff Thomas Arnoton and the notary, Master Ambroy, clad in black with huge periwigs and smooth shaven faces, two dark notes amid the gaudy silks and brocaded damasks. Then come the stout major-domos, the pages, the huntsmen, the stewards, and Dame Barbe, with all her keys hanging at her side upon a key-chain of massive silver. At the bottom, on the benches, are the lower servants, the maids, and the farmers with their families; and finally, below, and close to the door, which they open and close carefully, are the scullions who come in between the confection of two sauces, to catch a breath of the Mass, and to bring a whiff of the supper into the church, warm with the flames of so many candles and decked in its gala array.

Is it the sight of these little white caps which distracts the officiating priests? Is is not rather Garrigou's bell, that mad little bell which is ringing at the foot of the altar with infernal haste, and seems to be continually saying,—

"Come, hurry, hurry; the sooner we are finished, the sooner we shall be at table."

The fact is, that every time that it rings—this devil's bell—the chaplain forgets his Mass and thinks only of the supper. He pictures to himself the bustling cooks, the furnaces burning like forge-fires, the steam rising from the half-lifted lids, and in this steam two magnificent turkeys, stuffed, bursting, mottled with truffles.

Or again he sees passing files of pages bearing dishes enveloped in tempting vapours, and with them he enters the great hall, already prepared for the feast. Oh, delicious! There is the immense table, all set and dazzling, the peacocks dressed in their feathers, the pheasants spreading their russet wings, the ruby-coloured flagons, the pyramids of brilliant fruit amid the green leaves, and those marvellous fish of which Garrigou spoke (ah, yes, Garrigou!), laid out upon their beds of fennel, with their scales as pearly as when they came from the water, and a bunch of fragrant herbs in their monstrous nostrils. So vivid is the vision of these marvels that it seems to Dom Balaguère that all these wonderful dishes are served before him upon the embroidery of the altar-cloth; and twice or three times, instead of the *Dominus Vobiscum*, he catches himself saying the *Benedicite*. Apart from these slight mistakes, the worthy man reads his office very conscientiously, without skipping a line or omitting a genuflection and everything goes well enough until the end of the first Mass; for you know that on Christmas Day the same priest must celebrate three consecutive Masses.

"One!" said the chaplain to himself, with a sigh of relief; then, without losing a minute, he makes a sign to his clerk, or to him whom he supposes to be his clerk, and—

"Ting-a-ling-a-ling! Ting - a - ling - a - ling!"

It is the second Mass beginning; and with it also begins the sin of Dom Balaguère.

"Quick, quick, make haste!" cries Garrigou's bell in its shrill little voice; and this time the unhappy celebrant, wholly given up to the demon of gluttony falls upon his missal, and devours its pages with the ravenousness of his over-excited appetite. He kneels and rises in frantic haste, cuts short his signs of the cross and genuflections, hurries all his gestures in order to be the sooner finished. He s c a r c e l y stretches out his arms at the Gospel, or beats his breast at the *Confiteor*. The service is a race between him and the clerk. Versicles and responses rush along and jostle each other. Words half pronounced without opening their mouths, which would take too much time, are lost in incomprehensible murmurs,—

Oremus ps—ps—ps—
Mea culpa--pa—pa—

Like hurried vintagers treading the grapes in the vat, they both paddle in the Latin of the Mass, sending splashes of it on every side.

Dom—scum! says Balaguère.

Stutuo! replies Garrigou: and all the while the accursed bell is there, ringing in their ears like those bells which are put on post-horses to make them gallop the more swiftly. You can fancy that at such a rate a low Mass is quickly over.

"Two!" says the chaplain, quite winded; then, without taking time to catch breath, purple and perspiring, he trots down the steps of the altar, and—

"Ting-a-ling-a-ling! Ting - a - ling - a - ling!"

It is the third Mass beginning. There are only a few more steps to take in order to reach the dining-room; but, alas! the nearer the supper comes, the more the unfortunate Balaguère feels himself possessed by a madness of impaience and gluttony. The apparition grows more lifelike; the golden carp, the roast turkeys are there, there. He touches them; he—Oh, heavens! The dishes smoke, the wines spread their fragrance; and shaking its mad clapper, the little bell cries to him,—

"Quick, quick. still faster!"

But how could he go faster? His lips scarcely move. He no longer pronounces the words. Unless he were to cheat the good Lord altogether, and rob him of his Mass. And that is precisely what he is doing, the unhappy wretch! From temptation to temptation, he begins by skipping a versicle, then two. The Epistle is too long, he does not finish it; he skims over the Gospel, passes before the *Credo* without entering, jumps the *Pater,* bows to the Preface from a distance, and thus, by leaps and bounds, precipitates himself into eternal damnation, always followed by the infamous Garrigou, *vade retro Satanas!* who seconds him with marvellous skill, raises his chasuble, turns the leaves two at a time, hustles the desks about, overturns the vases, and ceaselessly rings the little bell louder and faster and faster.

You should have seen the frightened faces of the congregation! Obliged to follow by the motions of the priest this Mass of which they could not hear a word, some were rising as others knelt, some sitting while others stood; and at every stage of this singular service, there were a host of different attitudes in the pews. The star of Christmas on its way along the heavenly road toward the little table turned pale with horror on seeing his confusion.

"The abbé is going too fast; it is impossible to follow him," murmured the old dowager, feebly shaking her head-dress.

Master Arnoton, with his great steel spectacles on his nose, tries to find in his prayer-book where the deuce they are. But in their inmost hearts all these good people, who are also thinking of supper, are not sorry that the Mass is thus going post-haste; and when Dom Balaguère, with radiant face, turns to the congregation, crying with all his strength, *Ite, missa est!* there is but one voice in the chapel answering him with so joyous and hearty a *Deo gratias!* that one would fancy himself already at table, at the first toast of the supper.

CHAPTER III

THE VISION

FIVE minutes later, the crowd of nobles sat down in the great hall, the chaplain in their midst. The château, illuminated from top to bottom, rang with songs, cries, and laughter; and the venerable Dom Balaguère planted his fork in the wing of a pullet, drowning the remorse for his sin in waves of the Vin du Pape and of the good juices of meat. He ate and drank so much, the poor holy man, that he died during the night of a terrible attack, without having had even time to repent; then, in the morning, he arrived in heaven, still in a flutter over the festival of the night before, and I leave you to guess how he was received there.

"Out of my sight, bad Christian!" said the Sovereign Judge, the master of us all. "Your fault is great enough to efface a whole life of virtue. Ah, you stole from me a midnight Mass! Well, you shall pay me three hundred in place of it, and you shall not enter

Paradise until you have celebrated in your own chapel these three hundred Christmas Masses, in the presence of all those who have sinned by your fault and with you."

And that is the true legend of Dom Balaguère, as it is told in the land of the olive. Now the château of Trinquelage no longer exists, but the chapel still stands on the top of Mont Ventoux in a grove of evergreen oaks. The wind shakes its riven door, the grass blocks up the archway; there are nests in the angles of the altar and in the embrasures of the tall windows, from which the coloured glass has long since disappeared. Still, it appears that every year, at Christmas, a supernatural light strays amid these ruins, and that on their way to Mass or supper the peasants see this spectre chapel lighted with invisible candles which burn in the open air, even amid the snow and wind. You may laugh if you like, but a vine-dresser of the neighbourhood named Garrigue, no doubt a descendant of Garrigou, has affirmed to me that one Christmas night, having had a drop too much, he lost his way upon the mountain in the neighbourhood of Trinquelage; and this is what he saw. Up to eleven o'clock, nothing. All was silent, dark, motionless. Suddenly, near midnight, a chime of bells was heard from the top of the belfry,—an old, old chime, which sounded as if it were ten leagues away. Soon, on the road up the mountain, Garrigue saw lights flickering and un-certain shadows moving. People were walking beneath the porch of the chapel, and whispering,—

"Good evening, Master Arnoton."

"Good evening, good evening, my children."

When every one had gone in, my vine-dresser, who was very brave, went softly up, and looking through the broken door, saw a singular sight. All the people whom he had seen passing were ranged around the choir and in the ruined nave, as though the old pews had still existed. Beautiful ladies in brocade with lace headdresses, lords bedizened from head to foot, peasants in flowered jackets like those worn by our grandfathers, all had an old, faded, dusty, wearied air. From time to time, nightbirds, the wonted lodgers in the chapel, flew around the candles, whose flame rose straight and indistinct, as if it had burned behind gauze; and what greatly amused Garrigue was a certain person with large steel spectacles, who kept shaking his tall black periwig, on which one of these birds stood upright, with his feet entangled in it, and silently flapped its wings.

At the back a little old man of the size of a child, kneeling in the middle of the choir, was despairingly ringing a bell without tongue or sound; while a priest, dressed in old gold, went and came before the altar, reciting orisons of which not a word could be heard. It was certainly Dom Balaguère, saying his third low Mass.

A Violet!

Monsieur the Sous-Préfet is on his circuit. With coachman in front and lackeys behind, the carriage of the sous-préfecture is bearing him majestically to the district fair of La Combe aux Fées. For this memorable day the sous-préfet has put on his fine embroidered coat, his little cocked hat, his tight breeches with silver stripes, and his dress-sword with its mother-of-pearl hilt. Upon his knees lies a large portfolio of embossed shagreen, at which he is looking mournfully.

The sous-préfet looks mournfully at his embossed shagreen portfolio; he is thinking of the address which he will shortly have to deliver before the inhabitants of La Combe aux Fées.

"Messieurs et chers administrés,"—

But in vain does he twist the blond silk of his whiskers, and repeat twenty times over, *"Messieurs et chers administrés";* the rest of the address will not come.

The rest of the address will not come. It is so hot in this carriage! As far as the eye can reach, the road to La Combe aux Fées lies dusty beneath the Southern sun. The air is on fire, and upon the roadside elms thousands of cicadæ call to one another from tree to tree. Suddenly the sous-préfet starts. He has just seen in the distance at the foot of a hill a grove of evergreen oaks which seems to beckon to him.

The little wood of evergreen oaks seems to beckon to him.

"Come this way, Sous-Préfet; you will find it much more comfortable to write your address beneath my trees."

Monsieur the Sous-Préfet yields to the temptation; he jumps down from his carriage, and tells his servants to wait for him, because he is going to write his address in the little oak wood.

In the oak wood there are birds, violets, and springs beneath the tender grass. When they saw the sous-préfet with his fine breeches and his embossed shagreen portfolio, the birds were frightened and stopped singing, the springs no longer dared to make a noise, and the violets hid in the turf. No one of this little world has ever seen a sous-préfet, and they ask one another in undertone who is this fine gentleman who goes about in silver breeches.

In undertones, beneath the leaves, they ask one another who is this fine gentleman in silver breeches. Meanwhile, the sous-préfet, delighted with the silence and coolness of the wood, parts the tails of his coat, lays his cocked hat upon the grass, and sits down on the moss at the foot of a young oak; then he opens upon his knees his large embossed shagreen portfolio, and takes from it a great sheet of foolscap paper.

"He is an artist," says a warbler.

"No," says the bullfinch, "he is not an artist, for he has silver breeches; he must be a prince."

"He must be a prince," says the bullfinch.

"Neither artist nor prince," interrupts an old nightingale which has sung a whole season in the sous-préfecture gardens. "I know what he is; he is a sous-préfet."

And all the little grove falls a-whispering,—

"He is a sous-préfet! He is a sous-préfet!"

"How bald he is!" remarks a huge crested lark.

The violets ask: "Is it cross?"

"Is it cross?" ask the violets.

The old nightingale replies: "Not in the least."

And upon this assurance the birds resume their singing, the springs their bubbling, and the violets their fragrance, as though the gentleman were not there at all. Unmoved amidst this pretty tumult, the sous-préfet invokes the Muse of District Fairs, and, pencil in hand, begins to declaim in his official voice:—

"*Messieurs et chers administrés*"—

"*Messieurs et chers administrés*," says the sous-préfet in his official voice.

A peal of laughter interrupts him; he turns and sees nothing but a large woodpecker, which looks at him laughing, perched upon his hat. The sous-préfet shrugs his shoulders and tries to go on with his address; but the woodpecker interrupts him again, and calls to him from a distance,—

"What's the use?"

"What! What's the use?" says the sous-préfet, who becomes very red; then, driving away the impudent creature with a wave of his hand, he begins afresh:—

"*Messieurs et chers administrés—*"

"*Messieurs et chers administrés*," the sous-préfet begins afresh.

But then the little violets, a-tiptoe on their stalks, say to him softly,—

"Monsieur the Sous-Préfet, smell how sweet we are!"

And the springs play him divine music beneath the moss; and in the branches, above his head, a flock of warblers come and sing him their prettiest airs; and all the little wood conspires to prevent him from writing his address.

All the little wood conspires to prevent him from writing his address. The sous-préfet, intoxicated with perfumes, drunk with music, tries in vain to resist the new charm which takes possession of him. He leans back upon the grass, unbuttons his fine coat, again murmurs twice or thrice:—

"*Messieurs et chers administrés. Messieurs et chers admi—Messieurs et chers—*"

Then he consigns his *administrés* to the devil; and the Muse of District Fairs can now but veil her face.

Veil thy face, O Muse of District Fairs! When, at the end of an hour, the servants of the sous-préfecture, anxious about their master, entered the little wood, they saw a spectacle which caused them to recoil with horror. The sous-préfet was lying on his face in the grass, as slovenly as a Bohemian. He had taken off his coat, and with a violet between his teeth the sous-préfet was writing verses.

The Two Inns

It was on my way home from Nimes, one afternoon in July. The heat was overwhelming. As far as the eye could reach, the white, scorching, dusty road ran between gardens of olives and little oaks, beneath a great sun of dead silver which filled the whole sky. There was not a patch of shade or a breath of wind,—nothing but the quivering of the hot air and the strident voice of the cicadæ, — a mad, deafening music in hurried time, which seems the very voice of this immense luminous vibration. I had been walking through a desert for two hours, when suddenly before me a group of houses detached itself from the dust of the road. It was what they call the *relaise de Saint-Vincent*,—four or five farms, long barns with red roofs, a waterless drinking-trough in a clump of scraggy fig-trees, and, at the end of the village, two large inns staring at each other from opposite sides of the road.

There was something striking in the propinquity of these inns. On the one side was a large, new building, full of life and animation, with every door open, the diligence before it, the smoking horses being unharnessed, the travellers who had dismounted drinking hurriedly in the road in the scanty shadow of the walls. The courtyard was crowded with mules and carts, and wagoners lay beneath the mangers awaiting the cool of the e v e n i n g. Within were cries, oaths, the pounding of fists on tables, the clink of glasses, the click of billiards, lemonade corks popping, and, dominating all this up-roar, a joyful, resonant voice, which sang so that the windows rattled,—

La belle Margoton
Tant matin s'est levée,
A pris son broc d'argent,
A l'eau s'en est allée.

The inn opposite, on the other hand, was silent and as if abandoned. There was grass beneath the archway, the shutters were broken, over the door a faded branch of holly hung down like an old plume, and the doorsteps were propped up with stones from the road. It was all so poor and pitiful that it seemed really a charity to stop there to drink a glass.

When I entered, I found a long room, deserted and dismal, which the dazzling sunlight from three large, curtainless windows caused to appear still more dismal and deserted. A few halting tables on which stood dusty glasses, a broken billiard-table which stretched forth its four pockets like alms-basins, a yellow divan, and an old desk slept there in an unwholesome and heavy heat. And the flies, the flies! Never had I seen so many,—on the ceiling, glued to the windows, in the glasses, in clusters. When I opened the door, there was a buzzing and a whir of wings, as though I had been entering a beehive.

At the end of the room, in the recess of a window, a woman was standing close to the glass, busily occupied in looking out. I called twice,—

"Here, hostess!"

She turned about slowly, and showed me the commonplace face of a peasant, wrinkled, pitted, earth-coloured, framed in a cap of reddish lace such as is worn with us by old women. She was not, however, an old woman; but tears had quite faded her.

"What do you wish?" she asked me, wiping her eyes.

"To sit down and drink something."

She looked at me greatly astonished, without moving from her place, as though she did not understand me.

"Is not this an inn?"

The woman sighed.

"Yes, it is an inn, if you like— But why do you not go opposite, like the rest? It is much more gay."

"It is too gay for me. I prefer to remain here."

When she was quite sure that I was speaking seriously, the hostess began to come and go with a very busy air, opening drawers, rattling bottles, wiping glasses, and disturbing the flies. One could feel that serving this traveller was a real event. Once in a while the poor woman would stop and take her head in her hands, as though she despaired of comprehending it.

Then she passed into the room behind. I could hear her rattling the keys, working at the locks, feeling in the bread-box, blowing, dusting, washing plates. Now and then I would hear a heavy sigh or a half-stifled sob.

After a quarter of an hour of this, I had before me a plate of *passerilles* (raisins), an old loaf from Beaucaire, as hard as sandstone, and a bottle of the sourest kind of wine.

"You are served," said the strange creature; and she hastily returned to her place before the window.

As I drank, I tried to make her talk. "You do not often have customers, do you, my poor woman?"

"Oh, no, sir, never any one! When we were alone in the village, it was different; we had the relays, the meals for hunters during the teal season, and wagons the year around. But since our neighbours have settled here we have lost everything. People prefer to go opposite. They find it too gloomy here. The truth is that the house is not very agreeable. I am not handsome, I have the fever, and my two litle girls are dead. Over there, on the contrary, they are always laughing. It is an Arlésienne who keeps the inn,—a handsome woman who wears lace and three turns of a gold chain about her neck. The conductor, who is her lover, takes her the diligence; and besides she has a lot of wheedling girls for chambermaids. Consequently, no end of business comes to her. She has all the young men of Bezouces, of Redessan, of Jonquières. The wagoners go out of their way to stop at her house. As for me, I remain here all the day, without any one, eating my heart out."

She said this in a listless, indifferent voice, with her forehead always pressed against the glass. There was evidently something in the inn opposite which held her attention.

Suddenly there was a great bustle on the other side of the street. The diligence started off in the dust. We could hear the cracking of the whips, the postilion's fanfares, and the maids who had run to the door, crying,— "Adiousias! Adiousias!" and over all the formidable voice heard a few moments before, singing louder than ever.—

A pris son broc d'argent,
A l'eau s'en est allée;
De là n'a vu venir
Trois chevaliers d'armée.

At this voice the hostess shivered from head to foot, and, turning to me, said in a low voice,—

"Do you hear? It is my husband. Does he not sing well?"

I looked at her in amazement.

"What? Your husband? So he goes there too?"

Then she replied, with a heart-broken look but very gently,—

"What can you expect, sir? Men are like that,—they do not care to see one

weep, and I do nothing but weep since the death of my little girls. And then it is so lonely in this great barrack, where there is never any one. So, when he is too dreary, my poor José goes opposite to drink; and as he has a fine voice, the Arlésienne makes him sing. Hush! he is beginning again."

And trembling, with outstretched hands and great tears which made her still uglier, she stood there before the window, as if in ecstasy, listening to her José sing for the Arlésienne,—

Le premier lui a dit:
"Bonjour, belle mignonne!"

The Elixir

"DRINK this, neighbour, and tell me what you think of it."

And drop by drop, with the scrupulous care of a lapidary counting pearls, the curé of Graveson poured me out two fingers of a green, golden, warm, sparkling, exquisite liqueur. It brought a flood of sunshine into my stomach.

"It is Père Gaucher's elixir, the joy and the health of our Provence," said the good man, with a triumphant air; "it is made at the convent of Prémontrés, a couple of leagues from your mill. Is it not worth all the Chartreuse in the world? And if you knew how amusing the story of this elixir is! Just listen!"

Then, quite simply, and without seeing the joke of it, the abbé began in the dining-room of the *presbytère*, so quiet and calm, with its Way of the Cross in little pictures, and its pretty white cur-

tains starched like surplices, a somewhat sceptical and irreverent story, of the fashion of a tale by Erasmus or D'Assoucy.

Twenty years ago the Prémontrés—or rather the White Fathers, as our Provençaux call them—had become wretchedly poor. If you had seen their house in those days, you would have pitied them.

The great wall and the Pacôme Tower were crumbling away. All about the grass-grown cloister the colonnades were falling, and the stone saints toppling over in their niches. There was not a whole window, or a door which would shut. The Rhone wind blew in the closes and in the chapels, extinguishing the candles, breaking the lead of the casements, and spilling the holy water from the basins. But saddest of all was the convent belfry, as silent as an empty dove-cote; and the fathers, for lack of money to buy a bell, were obliged to ring matins on rattles made of almond wood!

Poor White Fathers! I can still see them at the Corpus-Christi procession, marching sadly in their patched gowns, pale, thin, fed on a diet of lemons and watermelons; and behind them the abbot, who walked with hanging head, ashamed to show his ungilded crosier and his moth-eaten mitre of white cloth. The ladies of the sisterhood wept with pity in the ranks, and the fat banner-bearer sneered in their midst under his breath as he pointed at the poor monks:

"Starlings go thin when they go in flocks."

The fact is that the unfortunate White Fathers had themselves reached the point of questioning whether it would not be better for them to take their flight into the world, each to seek his food in his own direction.

Well, one day when they were debating this grave question in the chapter, word was brought to the prior that Frère Gaucher asked to be heard by the council. You must know, for your better comprehension, that this Frère Gaucher was herdsman of the convent; that is to say, he spent his days wandering from arcade to arcade in the cloister, driving before him two lean cows which sought for grass in the cracks of the pavement. The poor herdsman, who had been cared for till the age of twelve by a crazy old woman of Baux called Aunt Bégon, and who since then had been taken in by the monks, had never been able to learn anything but to drive his cattle and to say his Pater Noster; and even that he said in Provençal, for his brain was impenetrable, and his wit like a leaden dagger. For the rest he was a fervent Christian, though somewhat visionary, comfortable in his hair shirt, flagellating himself with hearty sincerity, and with such arms!

When they saw him enter the chapter house, simple and awkward, bowing to the company with a scrape of the foot, the prior, canons, and treasurer all began to laugh. It was the effect he always produced whenever he went anywhere, by his good face with its grayish goat-like beard and his somewhat wild eyes, and therefore Frère Gaucher was not disturbed by it.

"Reverend Fathers," said he, good-humouredly, twisting his olive-wood rosary, "they are right when they say that empty hogsheads sing the loudest. By digging in my poor head, which is already so hollow, I think that I have discovered the means of getting us out of our difficulties.

"This is how. You remember Aunt Bégon, that good woman who took care of me when I was little? (May God keep her soul, the old sinner! she sang terrible songs when she had been drinking!) I must tell you then, Reverend Fathers, that Aunt Bégon knew as much about the herbs of our mountain as—yes, more than an old Corsican blackbird. Among other things she had composed toward the end of her life an incomparable elixir by mixing five or six kinds of simples which we used to go together and gather on the Alpilles. That is many years ago; but I think that with the help of Saint Augustine and the permission of our father the abbot, I might, if I tried hard, recover the composition of this mysterious elixir. Then we would have nothing to do but to put it into bottles and to sell it somewhat dear, which would allow the community to grow rich quietly, like our brothers of La Trappe and the Grande—"

He had not time to finish. The prior had risen and fallen upon his neck. The canons clasped his hands. The treasurer, more deeply moved than any of the others, kissed with respect the tattered border of his robe. Then each one returned to his stall to deliberate, and on the spot the chapter decided that they would intrust the cows to Frère Thrasybule, in order that Frère Gaucher might give himself up wholly to the confection of his elixir.

How did the good brother succeed in recovering Aunt Bégon's receipt? At the cost of what efforts, what vigils? History does not say. Only, what is certain is that at the end of six months the elixir of the White Fathers was already very popular. In the whole county, in the whole neighbourhood of Arles, there was not a *mas* nor a grange, which had not, in the depths of its cupboard, between the bottles of mulled wine and the jars of picholine olives, a little brown earthenware flagon, sealed with the arms of Provence, with a monk in ecstasy on a silver label. Thanks to the popularity of its elixir, the house of the Prémontrés grew rich very rapidly. They rebuilt the Pacôme Tower. The prior had a new mitre, the church pretty stained-glass windows; and within the fine lace of the belfry, a whole covey of bells, big and little, alighted one fine Easter morning, pealing merrily.

As for Frère Gaucher, that poor lay brother whose clownishness had so amused the chapter, he was no more heard of in the convent. Henceforth they knew only the Reverend Père Gaucher, the man of intellect and of great learning, who lived completely isolated from the many and trifling occupations of the cloister, and shut himself up all day in his distillery, while thirty monks scoured the mountain in search of fragrant herbs for him. This distillery, into which no one, not even the prior, had the right to enter, was an old, abandoned chapel, at the very end of the canon's garden. The simplicity of the good fathers had made of it something mysterious and terrible; and if by chance a bold and curious young monk, clinging to the climbing vines, reached the rose-window over the door, he would slip down hastily, frightened by the sight of Père Gaucher, with his wizard's beard, leaning over his furnaces, hydrometer in hand, and surrounded by retorts of rose-coloured sandstone, gigantic alembics, crystal worms, and a whole weird apparatus which shone as if bewitched in the red light of the windows.

At nightfall, when the last angelus rang, the door of this abode of mystery would be opened cautiously, and the reverend father would betake himself to the church for the evening service. What a reception they gave him whenever he walked through the monastery! The brothers would form a lane for him as he passed, and whisper,—

"Hush! he has the secret."

The treasurer would follow him and speak to him in an undertone. Amidst all this adulation the father would walk on, mopping his brow, with his broad three-cornered hat on the back of his head like an aureole, looking about him complacently at the large courts planted with orange-trees, the blue roofs on which turned new weather-cocks, and, in the dazzlingly white cloister, between the elegant, florid columns, the canons clad in new robes, filing two and two with tranquil mien.

"It is to me that they owe it all!" the reverend father would tell himself; and each time this thought would bring a rush of pride.

The poor man was well punished for it. You will see how.

Just fancy that one evening, during service, he arrived at the church in a state of extraordinary excitement,—red, out of breath, with his cowl awry, and so agitated that in taking holy-water he wet his sleeve to the elbow. They thought at first that it was embarrassment at arriving late; but when they saw him make low obeisances to the organ and the pulpit instead of to the high altar, cross the church like a whirlwind, and wander about the choir for five minutes in search of his stall, and then, when seated, bow right and left with a maudlin smile, a murmur of astonishment ran through the three naves. They whispered from breviary to breviary,—

"What is the matter with our Père Gaucher? What is the matter with our Père Gaucher?"

Twice did the prior impatiently beat upon the pavement with his crosier to command silence. Above, in the choir, the Psalms still went on, but the responses lacked enthusiasm.

Suddenly, in the very midst of the *Ave Verum*, our Père Gaucher suddenly sits back in his stall, and sings in a mighty voice,—

Dans Paris il y a un Père blanc,
Patatin, patatan, tarabin, taraban.

There is general consternation. Every one rises. They cry,—

"Take him out! He is possessed!"

The canons cross themselves. The abbot's crosier keeps up a terrible clatter. But Père Gaucher neither sees nor hears anything; and two lusty monks are obliged to drag him out by the small choir door, struggling like one exorcised, and continuing his patatins and his tarabans louder than ever.

The next morning at daybreak the unhappy father was on his knees in the prior's oratory, saying his *mea culpa* with a torrent of tears.

"It is the elixir, Reverend Father, it is the elixir which took me by surprise," said he, beating his breast; and seeing him so wretched and repentant, the good prior was quite moved himself.

"Come, come, Père Gaucher, calm yourself; this will all dry up like dew in the sunshine. After all, the scandal was not so serious as you think. It is true that the song was rather—hum! hum! Well we must hope that the novices did not hear it. And now tell me how it happened. It was in trying the elixir, was it not? Your hand was a little too heavy. Yes, yes, I understand. You are like Brother Schwartz, who invented gunpowder,—the victim of your own invention. Tell me, my good friend, is it absolutely necessary for you to try this terrible elixir upon yourself?"

"Unfortunately, yes, Monseigneur, the test gives me the strength and degree of the alcohol; but for the finish, the velvet, I can trust only to my tongue."

"Ah! very well. But one thing more; when you taste the elixir in this way, by necessity, does it seem to you good? Do you enjoy it?"

"Alas! yes," said the unfortunate father, growing very red. "For the last two evenings it has seemed to have such a flavour, such an aroma! It is certainly the devil who has played me this trick; and therefore I am firmly resolved henceforth to use only the test. So much the worse if the liqueur is not fine enough, if it does not pearl—"

"Oh, Heaven forbid!" interrupted the prior hastily. "We must not risk displeasing our customers. All that you have to do, now that you are warned, is to be on your guard. Come, how much do you need to make sure? Fifteen or twenty drops, eh? Let us say twenty drops. The devil will be very sharp if he catches you with twenty drops. Besides, in order to prevent accidents, I will excuse you from coming to chapel hereafter. You can read the evening service in the distillery. And now, go in peace, Reverend Father, and above all, count your drops."

Alas! it was in vain that the poor father counted his drops; the devil had hold of him and never let go.

They were singular services that the distillery witnessed!

During the day all went well. The father was calm enough; he prepared his retorts and alembics, carefully selected his herbs,—all the herbs of Provence, fine, gray, serrated, saturated with perfume and sunshine. But in the evenings, when the simples were infused, and the elixir was cooling in great pans of red copper, then the poor man's martyrdom would begin.

"Seventeen — eighteen — nineteen — twenty!"

The drops would fall from the graduator into the silver goblet. The father would swallow these twenty at a gulp, almost without pleasure. It was only for the twenty-first that he longed. Oh, that one-and-twentieth drop! Then, to escape from the temptation, he would go and kneel at the other end of the laboratory and plunge into his prayers. But from the still warm liqueur there would rise a little mist laden with aromatic odours which came and played about him, and in spite of himself drew him back to the pans. The liqueur was of a fine golden green. Bending over it, with open nostrils, the father would stir it gently, and in the little flashes which shone against the emerald background he seemed to see Aunt Bégon's eyes, laughing and sparkling as they looked at him.

"Come, one drop more!"

And, from drop to drop, the unfortunate man would end by having his goblet filled to the brim. Then, at the end of his strength, he would sink into a large easy-chair and with half-closed eyes lazily sip his sin, murmuring to himself with delicious remorse,—

"Ah! I am damning myself, I am damning myself!"

The most terrible part of it was that in the depths of this diabolical elixir he would find, by some strange witchcraft, all Aunt Bégon's dreadful songs: *Ce sont trois petites commères qui parlent de faire un banquet;* or, *Bergerette de Maître André s'en va-t-au bois seulette;* and invariably the famous one about the White Fathers,—*Patatin, patatan.*

Fancy his embarrassment the next morning when those who occupied the neighbouring cells would say to him,—

"Ah, ha! Père Gaucher, so you had cicadæ in your head last night when you went to sleep?"

Then there would be tears, despair, fasting, the hair shirt, and the scourge. But nothing could prevail against the demon of the elixir; and every evening, at the same hour, the poor father would be again possessed.

During this time orders were fairly showered upon the abbey like a benediction. They came from Nîmes, from Aix, from Avignon, from Marseilles. Day by day the convent took on more the air of a manufactory. There were packing brothers and labelling brothers, brothers for writing and brothers for carting. The service of God may have lost the tolling of a bell here and there; but the poor of the neighbourhood lost nothing by it, I warrant you.

Well, one fine Sunday morning, while the treasurer was reading to the assembled chapter his inventory for the close of the year, and the good canons were listening with glittering eyes and smiling lips, Père Gaucher suddenly rushed into the midst of the conference, crying,—

"That ends it! I will make no more. Give me back my cows—"

"What is the matter, Père Gaucher?" asked the prior, who suspected what was in the wind.

"What is the matter, Reverend Father? The matter is that I am preparing for myself a nice eternity of flames and pitchforks. The matter is

that I am drinking,—that I am drinking like a fish."

"But I told you to count your drops."

"Ah, yes, count my drops! It is by goblets that I should have to count now. Yes, Reverend Father, I have reached that point; three flasks an evening. You can understand that this cannot go on. Therefore let who you like make your elixir. May the fire of God burn me if I will have anything more to do with it!"

As you can fancy, the chapter was not smiling now.

"But you will ruin us, wretched man!" cried the treasurer, brandishing his ledger.

"Do you prefer to see me damned?" Then the prior rose.

"Reverend Fathers," said he, stretching forth his white hand on which glistened the pastoral ring, "there is a way of arranging everything. It is in the evening, is it not, my dear son, that the demon tempts you?"

"Yes, regularly every evening. Consequently, now when I see evening approach, I sweat, saving your presence, from head to foot, like Capitou's ass when he saw the saddle coming."

"Well, take heart! Every evening hereafter, at service, we will recite for you the orison of Saint Augustine, to which plenary indulgence is attached. With that, no matter what happens, you are safe. It is absolution during the sin."

"Oh! very well then; thank you, Reverend Father!"

And without asking for anything more, Père Gaucher went back to his alembics as light as a swallow.

And in fact, from that time on, every evening after complines the officiating priest never failed to say,—

"Let us pray for poor Père Gaucher, who is sacrificing his soul to the interest of the community. *Oremus Domine.*"

And while over all these white cowls, prostrate in the shadow of the nave, the orison ran quivering like a little breeze over snow, at the other end of the convent, behind, the flaming windows of the distillery Père Gaucher could be heard, singing at the top of his voice,—

> *Dans Paris il y a un Père Blanc,*
> *Patatin, patatan, taraban, tarabin;*
> *Dans Paris il y a un Père Blanc,*
> *Qui fait danser des moinettes,*
> *Trin, trin, trin, dans un jardin;*
> *Qui fait danser, etc.*

Here the good curé stopped, filled with terror.

"Good heavens! Suppose my parishioners should hear me!"

The Camargue

CHAPTER I

THE DEPARTURE

THERE is great excitement in the château. The m e s s e n g e r has just brought word from the gamekeeper, half in French and half in Provençal, announcing that there had already been two or three good flights of *galéjons* and *charlottines,* and that *oiseaux de prime* were not scarce, either.

"You will join us," my amiable neighbours had written; and this morning, when day broke at five o'clock, their large break, laden with guns, dogs, and provisions, came to pick me up at the foot of the hill. Then we were off on the road to Arles, which was somewhat dry and bare on this December morning when the pale green of the olive-trees is hardly visible, and the raw green of the kermes-oaks is a little too wintry and unnatural. The barns were astir. Some farmers, awake before day, showed lights in the windows of their *mas;* and in the stone tracery of the Abbey of Montmajour, ospreys, still heavy with sleep, were flapping their wings among the ruins. Yet we were already passing old peasant-women trotting to market on their donkeys. They came from Ville-des-Baux. Six long leagues to sit down for an hour on the steps of Saint-Trophyme, and sell little parcels of simples gathered on the mountains!

And now here are the ramparts of Arles,—low and battlemented ramparts, such as one sees in old engravings, where the warriors, armed with lances, appear on top of a wall less high than themselves. We pass at a g a l l o p through this marvellous little town, one of the most picturesque in France, with its round, carved balconies projecting into the middle of the narrow streets, with its old black houses with little, low, Moorish, arched doors, which carry one back to the time of William Court-Nez and the Saracens. At this hour no one is yet out of doors. The quay on the Rhone alone is animated. The steamboat which serves the Camargue is lying at the foot of the steps, ready to start. Housewives in red serge jackets and girls from La Roquette on their way to hire themselves out for farm-work go on board with us, chatting and laughing together. Beneath the long brown hoods, thrown forward because of the sharp morning air, the high Arlesian head-dress makes the head small and elegant, with a spice of boldness, a wish to toss itself back in order to throw a laugh or a jest the farther. The bell rings; we start. With the triple speed of the Rhone, the screw, and the Mistral the banks fly swiftly by. On one side is the Crau, an arid, stony plain; on the other, the Camargue, somewhat greener, which stretches to the sea with its short grass and its swamps full of reeds.

From time to time the boat stops beside a pontoon moored to right or left,—in Empire or in Kingdom, as they used to say in the Middle Ages, in the time of the Kingdom of Arles, and as old Rhone sailors still say. At each pontoon there is a white farm and a grove of trees. The workmen laden with tools, the women with their baskets on their arms, disembark upon the footbridge. The boat empties itself by degrees into Empire or Kingdom; and when it arrives at the pontoon of Mas-de-Giraud, where we land, there is almost no one on board.

Mas-de-Giraud is an old farm belonging to the Lords of Barbentane, into which we go to await the gamekeeper, who is to come for us. In the lofty kitchen all the men of the farm,— labourers, vine-dressers, shepherds, and herdsmen,—are at table, grave, silent, eating slowly, and served by the women, who will not eat until afterward. Soon the gamekeeper appears with the wagon. A true Fenimore Cooper type, a trapper by land and by water, guarding the fishing as well as the shooting, the people of the neighbourhood call him *lou Roudeïroù* (the prowler), because they always see him in the mists of dawn or evening, watching hidden among the reeds, or in his little boat, tending his nets on the ponds or the irrigating canals. It is perhaps this eternal watching which makes him so silent and thoughtful. Still, while the little wagon laden with guns and baskets precedes us, he gives us news of the shooting, the number of flights, and the spots where the migrating birds have lighted; and as we talk we penetrate deeper into the country.

When we have passed the cultivated fields, we find ourselves fairly in the wild Camargue. As far as the eye can reach, marshes and canals glisten among the samphires. Clumps of tamarisk and reeds make islands as if upon a calm sea. There are no high trees. The flat, immense aspect of the plain is not disturbed. At long distances apart sheds for cattle display their low roofs almost on a level with the ground. Scattered flocks, lying in the salt grass, or pressing about the red cloak of the shepherd, do not interrupt the great uniform line, belittled as they are by this infinite space of blue horizon and open sky. As from the sea, level in spite of its waves, there arises from this plain a sentiment of solitude, of immensity, further increased by the Mistral which blows without cessation or obstacle, and which seems, by its mighty breath, to level and broaden the landscape. Everything bends before it

The smallest shrubs preserve the imprint of its passage by remaining twisted and inclined toward the south, in the attitude of a perpetual flight.

CHAPTER II

THE CABIN

A ROOF of reeds and walls of reeds, yellow and dry,—that is the cabin. It is thus that our hunting-headquarters is called. A typical Camargue house, the cabin is composed of a single room, lofty, large, windowless, lighted by a glass door which is closed at night with shutters. All along the rough, whitewashed walls racks await the guns, the gamebags, and the wading-boots. At the end, five or six bunks are arranged about a real mast, planted in the earth and rising to the roof, which it supports. At night, when the Mistral blows and the house creaks in every part, with the distant sea and the wind, which brings it nearer and carries and swells its sound, one would fancy himself lying in the cabin of a boat.

But it is in the afternoon, above all, that the cabin is charming. On the lovely days of our Southern winter I like to remain alone near the tall fireplace, in which a few tamarisk-roots are smoking. Beneath the blows of the Mistral or the Tramontana, the door rattles, the reeds crack; and all these shocks are a very faint echo of the great disturbance of Nature about me. Great shadows chase one another beneath a sky of exquisite blue. The light comes fitfully, as do the sounds; and the bells of the flocks, suddenly heard and then forgotten, drowned by the wind, return to sing beneath the shaking door with the charm of a refrain. The

exquisite hour is twilight, a little before the hunters arrive. Then the wind is calmed. I go out for a moment. The great red sun is setting, blazing, without heat. Night falls and brushes against you with its moist black wing. In the distance, on the level of the ground, the flash of a gunshot passes with the brilliancy of a red star, enhanced by the surrounding shadow.

Life makes haste in what remains of the day. A long triangle of ducks is flying very low, as though it wished to settle; but suddenly the cabin, in which the lamp is lighted, drives them off. The one which leads the column raises his neck and flies up, and all the others behind him follow with wild cries.

Soon an immense trampling draws near, resembling the sound of rain. Thousands of sheep whose confused gallop and panting breath, as they are led by the shepherds and driven by the dogs, one can hear, press toward the sheds, timid and undisciplined. I am surrounded, jostled, lost in this whirlwind of curly fleeces and bleating, —a surge in which the shepherds seem borne with their shadows by bounding billows. Behind the flocks come familiar footsteps and cheery voices. The cabin is full, animated, noisy. The dried vine-branches blaze. The more tired the hunters are, the more they laugh. It is an intoxication of happy fatigue, with the guns in a corner, the heavy boots thrown in a heap, the gamebags emptied, and beside them russet, golden, green, and silvery plumage, stained with blood. The table is set, and before the steam of a good eelsoup silence falls,—the complete silence of hearty appetites, interrupted only by the fierce growling of the dogs, which are licking their bowls in the dark outside the door.

No one sits up long. Already the gamekeeper and I alone are left by the fire, which is itself blinking. We talk; that is to say, from time to time we drop each other half words, after the fashion of peasants,—those almost Indian interjections, which are short and quickly extinguished, like the last sparks of the burned vine-branches. Finally, the keeper rises, lights his lantern, and I hear his heavy step dying away in the night.

CHAPTER III

THE ESPERE

THE *espère!* What a pretty name by which to designate the waiting of the ambushed hunter, and those uncertain hours when everything waits,—*espère,* hope, hesitates between day and night. There is the *espère* of the morning, a little before sunrise, and that of the evening, in the twilight. It is the latter which I prefer, especially in these marshy districts, when the water of the ponds holds the light so long.

Sometimes the *espère* is in the *negochin,*—a narrow, keelless little boat, which rolls at the slightest motion. Sheltered by the reeds, the hunter watches for the duck from the bottom of his boat, above which appear only the visor of a cap, the barrel of a gun, and the head of the dog, which sniffs the wind, snaps at mosquitoes, or, with his large paws outstretched, leans to one side of the boat and half fills it with water. That *espère* is too complicated for me, and consequently I usually go on foot, wading through the swamps with enormous boots cut the

whole length of the leather. I walk slowly and prudently, for fear of being mired. I push through the reeds, full of briny odours and leaping bullfrogs.

Finally, I come to an insland of tamarisk, a bit of dry ground, where I stop. The gamekeeper, to do me honour, has left his dog with me,—an enormous Pyrenean dog, with a heavy white fleece, a hunter and fisher of the first rank, and whose presence does not fail to intimidate me a little. When a moor-hen passes within shot, he has a certain ironical way of looking at me as he throws back, with a toss of the head like an artist's, two long flapping ears which hang over his eyes; then he points, his tail quivers, and he displays an impatience which seems to say to me,—

"Fire! Why don't you fire?"

I fire, and miss; then, lying at full length, he yawns and stretches with a wearied, discouraged, and insolent air.

Well, yes, I confess that I am a poor hunter. For me the *espère* is the nightfall, the diminishing light taking refuge in the water, the glistening ponds which polish to the shade of fine silver the gray tint of the darkening sky. I love the smell of the water, the mysterious rustling of the insects in the reeds, the little murmur of the long, quivering leaves. From time to time a sad note passes and rolls athwart the sky like the roaring of a conch-shell. It is the bittern, plunging his long beak into the water and blowing— rrr-ou-ou-ou! Flights of crane pass over my head. I hear the rustling of their feathers, and then nothing more. It is night, dark night, with a little day remaining on the water.

Suddenly I feel a thrill,—a sort of

nervous discomfort, as though I had
some one behind me. I turn about
and see the companion of my clear
nights, the moon,—a large round moon,
which rises gently, with a motion which
is very perceptible at first, but which
grows slower as it gets above the horizon.

A first ray is already distinct close
to me, then another a little farther off.
Soon the whole swamp is illuminated.
The smallest bunch of grass has its
shadow. The *espère* is over; the birds
see us, and we must go in. We walk
in the midst of a blue, dusty light;
and each of our steps in the ponds or
canals stirs up there a quantity of
fallen stars and rays of moonlight
which penetrate the water to the
bottom.

CHAPTER IV

RED AND WHITE

QUITE near us, a gunshot away from
our cabin, is another which resembles
it, but is more rustic. It is there that
our gamekeeper lives with his wife and
his two eldest children,—his daughter,
who prepares the men's meals and
mends the nets, and his son, who helps
his father in taking up the hoop-nets
and in watching the sluices of the
ponds. The two youngest children are
at Arles, with their grandmother; and
they will remain there until they have
learned to read and have taken their
first communion,—for here they are
too far from church and school, and,
besides, the Camargue air would not
be good for them. The fact is that in
summer, when the marshes are dry and
the white mud cracks in the great heat,
the island is really not habitable.

I saw that once in the month of
August, when I came to shoot teal, and
I shall never forget the dreary and
forbidding aspect of this burned-up
country. Here and there ponds
steamed in the sunlight like immense
kettles, preserving at the bottom a remnant of life which kept astir,—salaman-
ders and spiders crawling, water-beetles
seeking the moist corners. The air was
the atmosphere of a pestilence, a heavily floating mist of miasma, which was
still thicker because of the innumerable clouds of mosquitoes. At the
gamekeeper's house every one was
shaking with the fever, and it was pitiful to see the yellow, drawn faces and
haggard eyes of these poor wretches
who are condemned to drag themselves
about for three months beneath this
pitiless sun, which burns those who
have the fever without warming them.
It is a dreary and hard life, that of a
gamekeeper in the Camargue. Yet this
one has his wife and children; while
two leagues farther on, in the swamps,
is a horse-keeper who lives absolutely
alone from year's end to year's end,
and leads the life of a Crusoe. In his
reed cabin, which he built himself,
there is not a utensil which is not of
his own workmanship,—from the ham-
mock of plaited osier, the three stones
which constitute his fireplace, and the
tamarind stumps carved into stools, to
the lock and key of white-wood which
close this singular dwelling.

The man is at least as strange as his
house. He is a sort of silent philosopher, like the solitaries, sheltering his
peasant mistrust under thick bushy
eyebrows. When he is not in the pas-
ture-grounds he is to be found seated
before his door, spelling out slowly,

with childish and touching application, one of those little pink, blue, or yellow pamphlets which are wrapped around the medicine bottles which he uses for his horses. The poor devil has no diversion but reading, and no book but these. Although they are neighbours, our gamekeeper and he never see each other. They even avoid meeting. One day, when I asked the reason for this antipathy, he replied gravely,—

"It is because of our opinions. He is red, and I am white."

And so even in this desert, whose solitude should have brought them together, these two savages, as ignorant and simple the one as the other,—these two oxherds of Theocritus, who go to the city hardly once a year, and whom the little cafés of Arles, with their gilding and their mirrors, dazzle as though they were the palace of the Ptolemies, have found a way to hate each other in the name of their political convictions!

CHAPTER V

LAKE VACCARES

The most beautiful thing in the Camargue is Vaccarès. Often abandoning the chase, I come and sit down on the bank of this salt lake,—a little sea which seems a bit of the large one, imprisoned in the land, and grown familiar from its very captivity. Instead of the barrenness and aridity which usually give a dreary appearance to a shore, Vaccarès displays upon its bold, green, grassy banks an original and charming flora,—centauries, marsh-trefoils, gentians, and those pretty saladelles, blue in winter and red in summer, which conform by their colours to the changing temperature, and in their uninter-

rupted blooming mark the seasons by their varying shades.

Toward five o'clock in the afternoon, the hour when the sun begins to set, these three leagues of water, without a boat or a sail to limit or transform their extent, are admirably beautiful. Vaccarès has not the sociable charm of the ponds and canals which appear here and there between the folds of a marly soil, beneath which one feels that water is filtering everywhere, ready to show itself at the slighest dip of the surface. Here the impression is broad and strong. The glittering of the waves attracts from afar flocks of herons and widgeon, of bittern and of flamingoes, white of belly and red of wing, which form in line along the shore to fish, so that their colours are distributed in a long equal band. Then there is the ibis, the true Egyptian ibis, thoroughly at home in this splendid sunshine and silent landscape. Indeed, from where I sit I can hear nothing but the lapping of the water and the voice of the keeper calling his scattered horses. They all have sonorous names,—Cifer (Lucifer), L'Estello, L'Estournello. Each horse as he hears his name runs up with streaming mane to eat his oats out of the keeper's hands.

Farther on, but still upon the same bank, is a large herd of cattle, grazing at liberty like the horses. Now and again I can see above the tamarisks their bent backs and little curved horns. The greater part of these Camargue cattle are brought up to run in the *ferrades*,—the village fêtes; some of them bear names already f a m o u s through all Provence and Languedoc. It is in this way that the neighbouring herd counts among others a terrible fighter called Le Romain, which has gored I do not know how many men and horses in the bull-fights of Arles, Nîmes, and Tarascon. His companions have chosen him for their chief, for in these strange herds the cattle govern themselves, grouped about an old bull which they adopt as leader. When a tempest falls upon the Camargue, terrible in this great plain where there is nothing to turn it aside or break its force, it is a sight to see the herd form close together behind its chief, all with lowered heads, and turning toward the wind those broad brows in which the strength of cattle is concentrated. Our Provençal herdsmen call this manœuvre *vira la bano au giscle*,—"turning the horn to the wind." And woe to the herd if it does not adopt it! Blinded by the rain and driven by the hurricane, it is routed and scattered in disorder; and the terrified cattle, running straight ahead to escape from the tempest, plunge into the Rhone, Vaccarès, or the sea.